WORLDS IN CHAOS

✺ ✺ ✺

Books by James P. Hogan

THE GIANTS SERIES
The Two Moons
The Two Worlds
Mission to Minerva

Code of the Lifemaker
The Immortality Option

The Cradle of Saturn
The Anguished Dawn

Bug Park
Echoes of an Alien Sky
Endgame Enigma
The Genesis Machine
Inherit the Stars
The Legend That Was Earth
Migration
Moon Flower
The Multiplex Man
Paths to Otherwhere
The Proteus Operation
Realtime Interrupt
Thrice Upon a Time
The Two Faces of Tomorrow
Voyage from Yesteryear

Worlds in Chaos (omnibus)
Cyber Rogues (omnibus, forthcoming)

COLLECTIONS
Catastrophes, Chaos and Convulsions
Kicking the Sacred Cow
Martian Knightlife
Minds, Machines and Evolution
Rockets, Redheads & Revolution

WORLDS IN CHAOS

✵ ✵ ✵

JAMES P. HOGAN

WORLDS IN CHAOS

A Baen Books Original

Baen Publishing Enterprises
P.O. Box 1403
Riverdale, NY 10471
www.baen.com

ISBN: 978-1-4767-3694-5

Cover art by Kurt Miller

First Baen paperback printing, December 2014

Distributed by Simon & Schuster
1230 Avenue of the Americas
New York, NY 10020

Library of Congress Cataloging-in-Publication Data

Hogan, James P.
 [Novels. Selections]
 Worlds in chaos / James P Hogan.
    pages ; cm
 "A Baen Books Original."
  ISBN 978-1-4767-3694-5 (softcover)
1. Life on other planets--Fiction. 2. Human-alien encounters--Fiction. I.
Hogan, James P. Cradle of Saturn II. Hogan, James P. The legend that was
Earth. III. Title.
 PR6058.O348A6 2014
 823'.914--dc23

                              2014034547

Printed in the United States of America

10 9 8 7 6 5 4 3 2 1

❂ CONTENTS ❂

CRADLE OF SATURN

Dedication

❈ ❈ ❈

To the work of Immanuel Velikovsky
and the untiring efforts of Charles Ginenthal.

Acknowledgments

❧ ❧ ❧

The help and advice of the following people is
gratefully appreciated:

Doug Beason, USAF; Jim Dorris; Steve Fairchild;
Andrew Fraknoi, Astronomical Society of the Pacific;
Charles Ginenthal; Jackie Hogan; Les Johnson, NASA,
Marshall Spaceflight Center, Huntsville, AL;
Frank Luxem; Melinda Murdock; Jeffrey Slostad;
Brent Warner, NASA, Goddard Spaceflight Center,
Greenbelt, MD; Betsy Wilcox, USAF

❁ PROLOGUE ❁

Times had always been plentiful. Since the beginning of the age when their ancestors first walked in the world, the People had lived in harmony with the spirits and the elements. Their language had no words for *war* or *want, famine* or *drought*. The forests were vast, the plains fertile. Fair winds brought rain from warm oceans. All of life flourished in abundance.

No memory had been handed down of where the People came from.

Some taught that they were born of Neveya, who ruled the skies during the times of lesser light when the smaller but brighter Sun was absent, and at the end of mortal life they would return to her across the Golden Sea in which the world floated. They learned to farm the lands and tame animals; to study the ways of wood, and stone, and metals; to admire and create music, likenesses, and things of beauty. Their sages pondered over the mysteries of mind and the senses, life and motion, of number and the nature of things. Communities grew under social imperatives and marketplaces for ideas, and became centers of government and commerce.

Iryon stood near the mouth of a broad river, between arms of green hills rising to distant mountains. It was not the largest of cities, but its buildings had been shaped and ornamented with a care that made the whole as much an expression of art as the carved gates and gilded window traceries, or the marble reliefs surrounding the central square. At the summit of one of the five hills on which Iryon was built stood the Astral Temple, where priests of Neveya charted the cycles of the heavens.

Each day began with the world looking out across the immensity of the celestial Ocean that extended away to Neveya's orb, dividing it equally like the plane of a blade halving a water-fruit so that only the upper hemisphere of Neveya was visible. Then the Ocean would rise, tilting and narrowing as it did so until it became an edge crossing past the world to reveal briefly all of Neveya's countenance; from there, now above, it broadened again to expand its underside, at the same time obscuring Neveya's upper part to reach its half-day low, after which it would fall and cross back again. This cycle repeated 5,623 times in the year that the stars took to turn through their constellations.

The proportions of light and dark making up the days changed according to whether the Sun was visible as well as Neveya, and in what situation—which varied with the seasons. The "blue hours" came when the Sun shone from the far side of Neveya, transforming its normally orange glow into a black shadow cast across the Golden Ocean. At certain times in the course of the year, as the Ocean crossed past the world during the blue hours, the Sun would vanish behind Neveya completely, turning day abruptly into darkest night. These were the times when the other worlds that moved about Neveya revealed themselves in their full glories of form and color. They were known as the days of "Dark Crossings." Multitudes would come from afar to Iryon to attend the rites and ceremonies that took place on these occasions.

The pyramid was built such that, from the Eye Stone at the center of the semicircle of astronomers and priests where the Speaker of Neveya stood, the orb was seen as if supported on its apex like a cloud grazing a mountain. Since Neveya never changed her position in the sky, the disk remained balanced in that manner always, varying only from yellow jewel through shrinking face to waning crescent as the Sun rode its distant course about both her and the world, and the celestial Ocean rose and dipped through its daily cycle. As the moment of the Dark Crossing approached, she glowered at the world with full face, black and featureless, fading into the glare as the Sun touched her shoulder.

The crowds assembled on the slopes were hushed as the Speaker intoned the Verses of Passage. Around the temple and across the city below, torches had been lit in readiness for the Darkness. At the top of the pyramid, Neveya reappeared suddenly out of the glare as a black arc sliding across the Sun, her shadow lying now like a black ray cut out of the Ocean, moment by moment advancing closer. When it fell across the world, connecting it to Neveya like a bridge spanning the Ocean, then, it was taught, the souls whose time had come to return would depart on their journey.

A murmuring of awe and wonder, more a wind than a sound, stirred through the crowd as the sky darkened. The astronomers readied their instruments and recording tablets, while the Speaker turned, opening his robed arms wide to greet the spectacle. For an instant Neveya's outline flared into a thin curve of light as if the extinguishing Sun were trying to claw its way back around the edge. . . .

And then all the light went from the sky, and the stars appeared. Above and to one side of Neveya, the pink globe of Jenas became visible, while beyond it Sephelgo's white-veined features shone as crescents of crystal. Lower was Aniar, graying and mottled, swimming to the side of Neveya, transfixed by the spear of the celestial sea seen edgewise, with the white speck of Delem farther out still along the same line. As the astronomers peered and recited their measures, scribes marked the stone that would later be cut for incorporation into the records.

The picture showed a disk pierced by a shallowly sloping line, standing on an arrowhead. Smaller circles showed the other visible worlds and their dispositions, with major stars represented by their symbols. A table incised beneath the design gave precise directions and elevations.

PART ONE

JUPITER:
CREATOR OF WORLDS

❊ 1 ❊

Almost twenty years before, as a nineteen-year-old engineering student at college, Landen Keene had astounded drivers on the interstate near the campus by overtaking them with ease in a 1959 Nash Rambler body fixed to a reinforced chassis on racing suspension, mounting an L88 Corvette engine. He had also more than impressed the two state troopers who handed him a ticket, but they were unable to cite his handiwork on a single safety violation. One of them had even indicated interest if Keene ever found himself of a mind to sell. "Keep at it, kid," he had told Keene. "One day you'll make a damned good engineer—supposin' you live long enough, of course, that is."

These days, it seemed, things worked the other way around. Outdated engineering camouflaged in futuristic-looking shells was hyped as a wonder of the age, the best that taxpayers' money could buy. Keene sat in the cramped crew compartment of the NIFTV— pronounced "Nifteev," standing for Nuclear Indigenously Fueled Test Vehicle—wedged comfortably into the seat at the Engineer's station by the mild quarter-g of sustained thrust cutting the craft across freefall orbits, and stared at the image on the main screen. It showed the elongated body, flaring into a delta tail-wing with tip-fins, of the spaceplane riding twenty-five miles ahead off the port

13

lower bow, closing slowly as the NIFTV overhauled it. Officially, it was designated an "Advanced Propulsion Unit." Its white lines were illuminated in direct light from the Sun showing above the silhouette of Earth, revealing the insignia of both the U.S. Air Force Space Command and United Nations Global Defense Force. (Exactly what the entire globe was to be defended from had never been spelled out.) The NIFTV, by contrast, with its framework of struts and ties holding together an assemblage of test engine and auxiliary motors, external tanks, and crew module, was ungainly and ugly. The APU looked sleek on the covers of glossy promotional government brochures and was pleasing to bureaucrats. The NIFTV was a creature of engineers— a space workhorse, born of pragmatism and utility.

Ricardo's voice came over the circuit from the Ccom station— Communications and Computing. "We've got a beam from them now. I'm windowing onto the main screen, copying you, Warren."

"*Gotcha.*" Warren Fassner, research project leader at Amspace Corporation's Propulsion Division and coordinator of the current mission, acknowledged from the control room at Space Dock, at that moment orbiting twelve thousand miles away above the far side of Earth. "*It looks like you guys are on stage. Make it a good one. We're getting the hookups.*" To avoid giving somebody officious somewhere an opportunity to interfere, Keene had persuaded the public relations people at Amspace to hold until the last moment before slipping word of the mission to the networks. Since it was something new and sounded exciting, the networks were interested.

A helmeted head and shoulders showing a gray flight suit with Space Command insignia appeared in a one-eighth window at the top right of the screen. "*This is Commander Voaks from USAFSC APU to approaching craft U-ASC-16R. You are entering a restricted zone posted as reserved for official Space Command operations. Identify yourself and announce your intentions.*"

Joe answered from the Pilot station, squeezed centrally behind the other two, which were angled inward to face the bulkhead carrying the screens. "Captain Elms from U-ASC-16R acknowledging APU. We are a private research vehicle owned and operated by the Amspace Corporation."

"*We are about to commence a high-acceleration test. For your own safety, my orders are to warn you off-limits.*"

"We're paralleling you outside the posted limit. Just taking a ringside seat. Don't mind us. Let's get on with the show."

Ricardo cut in again: "We've got another incoming—military priority band prefix."

"*This is General Burgess, Space Command Ground Control Center, and I demand to speak to—*"

Joe shook his head in the background behind Keene's console. "We're gonna be too busy here for this. I'm throwing this one to you, Warren."

"*Sure, switch him through. We'll handle it,*" Fassner said from the Space Dock. It had been expected. Ricardo clicked entries in a table on one of his auxiliary screens, and the irate general was consigned off to a string of comsat links around the planet.

"*APU to Amspace 16R. You have been warned in accordance with regulatory requirements. Be advised that your continued proximity to this operation will not be taken as indicative of a desirably cooperative attitude. Negative consequences may result. This is APU, out.*" The window vanished.

"Negative consequences, guys," Keene repeated. "That's it—it's all over for us. They'll find some bug in our parking lot that needs to be protected now. Close down the head office."

"Where do they get those guys?" Ricardo asked as he scanned his displays and made adjustments. "I mean, do they have to be programmed to talk like that? . . ." His voice trailed off, and he leaned forward. "Okay, this is it. We're registering their exhaust plume on thermal: preboost profile." As Ricardo spoke, the APU's image sprouted a tail of white heat, growing rapidly to extend several times the length of the vessel.

"Full burn," Joe's voice confirmed. "We're looking at about, aw . . . two gee initial. Downrange radar is tracking." The Air Force spaceplane was accelerating away, commencing its test. While Joe continued reading off time checks and numbers, Keene rechecked his own panel to make sure all the NIFTV's systems were ready, then turned his eyes again to the image shrinking and foreshortening on the main screen. *Advanced propulsion*, he thought to himself scornfully. Pure hydrogen and whatever they called the latest oxidizer, it was still chemicals. NASA, circa 1960s, repackaged in an Air Force suit, its adequacy a giveaway of what it was intended for: a high-altitude police cruiser to patrol the envisaged one-world state. NIFTV had the potential to bring the Solar System into Earth's backyard, but the powers that Earth's destiny depended on weren't interested. If the day ever arrived when their one-world order looked like becoming a reality, that, Keene vowed, would be when he'd leave it all and go out to join the Kronians. But with enterprises like Amspace still able to find backers, there was hope yet.

Fassner, having evidently passed the general on to someone else, reappeared on the beam from Space Dock. "*Okay, that's looking good now. Let's go after 'em.*"

"On standby at Fire-Ready," Keene confirmed.

"Go, engine. Take it up to eighty," Joe ordered.

Keene initiated the start-up and felt himself being squashed back in his seat as he increased reactant flow to bring the NIFTV quickly up to eighty percent power. Lead gloves encased his hands. He felt his cheeks and lips weighed back over his facial bones, baring his teeth. Smaller screens on the bulkhead in front of him showed deformed parodies of the faces of Ricardo and Joe.

"Lateral thrusters on. Pulsing to commence roll now," Joe grated, his mouth barely moving.

"APU ahead low, declination twenty-seven degrees and increasing," Ricardo reported. "We're twelve-point-two miles off the axis and holding. Course projection is clear."

It was a stunt to get the world's attention. The news channels had publicized that the Defense Department would be testing a new propulsion system designed for low-orbit maneuvering and announced it as a breakthrough. While the spaceplane was now in its maximum acceleration phase, the NIFTV was not only overtaking it but tracing a spiral twenty-plus miles in diameter about its course—literally running rings around it. A comm beam latched on again to deliver another tirade. Ricardo looked questioningly at Joe; Joe made a tossing-away motion with his head;

Ricardo grinned and switched the call over the detour link to Control.

"*Yeaaah!*" Keene whooped, smacking the armrests of his seat. "Was that a bird? Was it a plane? No, it was us, guys. Hey, look at that thing. It's like a dead duck in the water out there."

"Eat our dust, General," Ricardo sang.

The APU went into a slow curve. Joe altered thrust parameters and stayed with it easily. He ran an eye over the monitors and gave a satisfied nod. "Okay," he said to the others. "Take her up to full burn. Now let's show them what we can really do."

As the NIFTV accelerated along its continuing spiral course, a white haze of more distant light appeared along the top edge of the screen, moving slowly down to blot out the starfield background. It grew until it became part of a vast band extending off the screen on both sides, losing the APU spaceplane in its brilliance as it became a background to it.

☸ **2** ☸

The planetoid had come out of Jupiter. It was christened Athena.

For more than half a century, there had been astronomers dissenting from the mainstream view of planetary origins, trying to make themselves heard. The generally accepted nebular theory, in which the Sun, its planets, and their satellites all condensed together from a contracting cloud of primordial gas and dust, they maintained, was not tenable. The observed distribution of angular momentum did not fit the model, and tidal disruption by Jupiter would have prevented the accretion of compact objects inside its orbit. Some proposed an alternative mechanism for the formation of the inner planets based upon analysis of the fluid dynamics of Jupiter's core. According to this theory, the giant planet's rapid rotation and rate of material acquisition would result in periodic instabilities leading to eventual fission and the ejection of surplus mass. The bulk of the shed matter would most likely be thrown out of the Solar System, but lesser drops torn off in the process could go into solar-capture orbits.

In the main, the reaction of the scientific orthodoxy was to dismiss the suggestion as too much at odds with established notions and find arguments to show why it couldn't happen. Then, after the onset of sudden irregularities in Jupiter's rotation followed by several weeks of progressive deformation in shape beneath the gas envelope, it did.

Rivaling the Earth itself in size, white-hot from the energy that had attended its birth, and blazing a fiery tail tens of millions of miles long, Athena had been plunging sunward for ten months, all the time gaining in speed and brightness. Spectral analysis showed it to be composed of a mix of core and crustal materials trailing an envelope of ionized Jovian atmospheric gases. Currently crossing the Earth's orbit sixty million miles ahead of the Earth, it was visible to the naked eye across a quarter of the sky before dawn and after sundown. During the next month it would accelerate into a tight turn around the Sun, bringing it to within a quarter of a million miles at perihelion, covering more than a million miles in an hour and practically reversing direction to pass little more than fifteen million miles ahead of the approaching Earth on its way back to the outer Solar System. It was predicted that the spectacle would dim into insignificance any comet ever before seen in history.

❂ 3 ❂

Space Dock was built in the form of a short, fat dumbbell passing radially through a cylindrical hub. Cramped and dirty, noisy and oily, it normally accommodated between twenty and thirty people. It had been built several years previously as a joint venture by a consortium of private interests, of which Amspace was one of the principals, to provide an orbiting test base for space vehicles and technologies at a time when depending on government to provide facilities had been too fraught with delay and political uncertainties to be reliable.

A stubby-winged surface lifter lay docked at the far end of the hub when Joe attached the NIFTV at one of Space Dock's ports. A minishuttle bearing the Amspace logo was standing a short distance off. It was forty minutes since the NIFTV parted company from the Air Force spaceplane, by which time it had pulled fully a hundred miles ahead despite having traced its circular pattern continuously. The three crew were jubilant as they hauled themselves through the lock into the cluttered surroundings of pipes and machinery to the welcoming shouts and back-slaps of their waiting colleagues. Keene, coming first, waved and grinned in acknowledgment. Behind him came Ricardo, his mouth frozen wide, setting his teeth off white against his Mediterranean-olive skin, with Joe making a double thumbs-up sign as he floated out last. They were making the best of the enthusiasm around them while they had the chance. It was not exactly representative of the reaction they expected from the world in general, which for the most part would no doubt be shocked rather than appreciative. But that, after all, had been the whole idea.

Warren Fassner, in track pants and a red T-shirt, was waiting in the suiting chamber past the lock, where a technician began helping Keene out of his flight garb. Fassner had red hair with a matching, ragged mustache, and a large frame with an ample fleshy covering that gave the impression of sagging slightly when in gravity. Here, it was more evenly distributed, making him appear sprightlier, if maybe a little bloated, compared to normal.

"Great show, Lan!" he greeted. "That should make the high slots this evening. Looks like the baby performed just fine."

"Just as much your show. It's your baby." Keene pushed himself forward to make room as Ricardo and Joe crowded in at the end of the chamber behind. "And how goes it with our friends?" He meant the branches of officialdom connected with the APU test.

Fassner pulled a face, grinning simultaneously. "Mad as hell. Corpus Christi has got lawyers from Washington on the line now."

"Already?"

"Probably being aimed by wrathful agency heads. Marvin says they're trying to come up with some kind of permission or approval that we should have obtained first."

It had been expected, even though nothing had violated any explicit prohibition. Thanks mainly to the reticence of the Russians, Southeast Asians, and the Chinese, the world had not actually banned the launching of nuclear technology into orbit. It was just that nobody had thought that any organization outside government would contemplate doing it, while everyone on the inside was too vulnerable to pressure groups and public opinion to want to get involved. Now the regulatory agencies would be vying with each other to placate the eco lobbies by showing who had the most teeth.

"Anyhow, you've done your part," Fassner said. "The Corpus Christi office can deal with Washington. That's what it's got a legal department for." He clapped Keene lightly on the shoulder and used a handrail to haul himself past to say a few words to the other two.

"Hey, Ric, can't you do something about that grin? You're dazzling my eyes here."

Ricardo's smile only widened further. "Didn't we make a meal out of those turkeys, eh?"

"Joe, you were right on, all the way. So how did the modified RTs handle? Pretty good, I guess."

"Like a dream, Warren, like a dream. . . ."

Keene stowed the last of his gear in an end locker and signed that the technician had retrieved the diagnostic recording chip from his suit. Feeling less restricted now in shirtsleeves and fatigue pants, he exited through a pressure door and transverse shaft outside Number Two Pump Compartment to enter the "Yellow" end of the Hub Main Longitudinal Corridor—the walls in different sections of Space Dock were color coded to help newcomers orientate. More well-wishers, some in workshirts and jeans, others in coveralls, one in a pressure suit, were waiting to add their congratulations as he passed through. He came to "Broadway"—a confusion of shafts and split levels leading away seemingly in all directions, where the hub and the booms connecting the two ends of the dumbbell intersected—and wove his way through openings and between guide rails to the "Blue" well. Several more figures were anchored or floating in various attitudes.

"You guys made the day, Lan," one called out.

"Great stuff, man!"

"Still ain't stopped laughin'. Even if it gets the firm shut down, it was worth it."

Keene reversed to glide into the transverse shaft feet-first. He pushed himself off, using one of the hand hoops along the vertical rail, and felt the wall to one side nudge against him gently. As he progressed farther, the motion imparted by the rail grew stronger, causing him to move faster with a distinct, growing sensation of heading "down." By the time he reached the three-level wheel forming the Blue end of the dumbbell, he was using the hoops to retard himself. He began using his feet to climb down ladder-fashion as he passed through the upper deck, and stepped off at the mid-deck to find Joyce and Stevie waiting for him outside Ccoms.

"Damned good show," Stevie offered. He was thirtyish, British, and sometimes talked like an old movie. Keene nodded and returned a strained smile. He knew they all meant well, but this was getting a bit tiring.

Joyce was the senior comtech. She was one of those who did their best to look clean and professional, but her white shirt and sky blue pants, although no doubt clean that day, were showing grime, and there were flecks of grit in her black, close-trimmed hair. That was one of the facts of life that came with the territory. Dirt in zero-g didn't fall obligingly to the floor and accumulate in out-of-the-way places to be removed when convenient. Despite all the ducts and filters and fans, space habitats tended to be smelly, too.

She smiled, managing to convey the suggestion of freshness in spite of it all. "Even better than you promised," she complimented.

"Always make your surprises pleasant ones," Keene said, yawning in the close air. "People forget bad predictions that were wrong. But tell them one time that things will be okay and be wrong, and they'll never forgive you."

"Getting philosophical? Is this a new postflight syndrome or something?"

"I don't know. But I could sure use a postflight coffee."

"I'll get one," Stevie said, and moved away along one of the passages.

Joyce nodded to indicate the doorway through to the Ccoms room. "We've got PCN on now, asking to talk to one of the crew. You want to take it?"

"Sure. Who is it?"

"Somebody called John Feld from their Los Angeles office. He's linked through via Corpus Christi."

"Uh-huh." Keene followed Joyce between the communications equipment racks and control panels. "Have we a friendly native?"

"It's difficult to say," Joyce answered as they came to a live screen on one of the consoles. The face showing on it was of a man in his forties with clear blue eyes and straight, yellow hair brushed to the side. He turned to look out full-face as Keene moved within the viewing angle of the console pickup.

"Hello. I'm Landen Keene—NIFTV's flight engineer; also one of the principal design engineers involved with the project."

"John Feld, Pacific Coast Network news."

"Hi."

"You are with the Amspace Corporation, Dr. Keene?"

"In a way. I run a private engineering consultancy that Amspace contracts design work and theoretical studies to."

Feld looked mildly surprised. "And does this relationship result in your going into space often?" he asked.

"Oh, Amspace and Protonix—that's the name of my company— have known each other for a long time. I go wherever the job demands. A desk has more leg room, but this way we get to have more fun."

"As we saw," Feld agreed. "That was a spectacular performance you people gave up there earlier."

"And it was in spite of everything this country has done in the last forty years, not thanks to any of it," Keene replied.

"So what were you demonstrating? Obviously you were doing more than having fun. Is it another version of the message we hear from time to time about private enterprise being able to do things better than government?"

Keene shook his head. "Hell no. What we were telling you has to do with the whole future of humanity, not somebody's political or economic ideology. The world is still burying its head in the sand and refusing to face what Athena is telling us: the universe isn't a safe place. For our own good, we need a commitment on a massive scale to broadening what the Kronians have pioneered and spreading ourselves around more of space. What we showed today is that we can start doing it right now, without needing to negotiate any deals with the Kronians—although if you want my opinion, we should avail ourselves of any help they offer. We already have the technology and the industries. The vehicle that we demonstrated today was a test bed for a Nuclear Indigenously Fueled engine. That means it uses a nuclear thermal reactor to heat an indigenous propellant gas as a reaction mass. 'Indigenous': native to a particular place."

Feld seemed to understand the term but looked puzzled. "Okay. . . . But where are we talking about, exactly, in this instance?"

Keene spread his hands. "That's the whole point: anywhere that you're operating. You see, it works with a whole range of substances that occur naturally just about wherever you might happen to be. Venus is rich in carbon dioxide; the asteroids and ice moons of the gas-giants give unlimited water; others, such as Saturn's Titan and Neptune's Triton have methane; you can also use nitrogen, carbon monoxide, hydrogen, argon. In other words, it opens up the entire Solar System by affording ready refueling sources wherever you go. Today we were using water, and you saw the results. Methane would perform about fifty percent better still."

"So was today's effort to get publicity for a new technology that you've developed? If so, it certainly seems to have been successful."

"New? No way. It was being talked about back in the 1960s. But antinuclear phobia took over, and we've been at a standstill. What we're trying to do is more wake the country up again."

"Ah, but weren't there good reasons?" Feld seemed on more familiar ground, suddenly. "Surely there are hazards associated with taking such devices into orbit that haven't been resolved yet. Isn't it true that if the radioactive material from just one reactor were spread evenly through the atmosphere—"

"It isn't going to get spread evenly around the planet. There's enough gasoline in every city to—" Keene broke off as he saw that Feld was glancing aside, as if taking directions from somewhere off-screen. He looked back.

"Thank you, Dr. Keene. Apparently Captain Elms is standing by up there in the Amspace satellite now, and we would like to hear a few words from him too while we've got the connection. That was very interesting. Let's hope you have a safe trip back down."

"My pleasure," Keene grunted. The screen blanked to a test mode.

Joyce, who had moved away to talk to the duty supervisor on the far side of the room and then come back, stepped forward from where she had been watching. "See, you've scared them off again, Lan. You always have to start getting political."

"Hell, the problem's political," Keene grumbled. "How is it supposed to get solved if we can't mention it?"

Stevie reappeared carrying a plastic mug of black coffee and handed it to him. Keene nodded, sipped to test the heat, then took a longer drink gratefully. "But you're right," he told Joyce. "I should know better by now. It's gotten to be something of a reflex, I guess."

"Falling into patterns of habit is normal with advancing age," she assured him cheerfully.

"Thanks. Just what I needed."

The supervisor called over to them. "They're on hold now, Joyce. Do you want it through there again?"

"Yes, we're done with Pacific," Joyce called back over the consoles. "You've got another call waiting," she told Keene. He drank from his coffee mug again, as if fortifying himself. "Oh, I think you'll like this one," Joyce said. She gazed expectantly at the test pattern on the screen. It changed suddenly to present a face once again, this time a woman's.

Keene blinked in surprise. "It's Sariena!" he exclaimed.

She was in her early thirties, perhaps, with the finely formed features combining just the right amount of firmness with a softening of feminine roundness that fashion modeling agencies and cosmetics advertisers will scour a continent for. Her hair was shoulder-length, richly dark with a hint of wave at the tips, and her skin a clear dusky brown, setting off a pair of light gray, curiously opalescent eyes which at first sight jarred with such a complexion, but produced a strangely fascinating effect as one adjusted to them. Keene could have pictured her as an Arabian princess of fairy tale, or a rajah's daughter. And that was just from electronic images; they had never actually met. For Sariena was not of Earth at all but from Kronia, the collective name for the oasis of human habitation established among the moons of Saturn. The name came from Kronos, the Ancient Greek name for Saturn, who had ruled the heavens during Earth's Golden Age.

"Hello, Lan," she greeted. "And is that Joyce with you there?"

"I'm here," Joyce put in, coming closer.

"Ah yes, it is." Sariena's smile was restrained enough to preserve dignity, wide enough not to appear cold. "I just wanted to let you know that the shuttles are in orbit with us now, and we'll be on our way down to the surface later today, arriving in Washington this evening."

"Sorry if I've been out of touch," Keene said. "I've been a bit busy lately, as you've probably gathered."

Sariena was aboard the Kronian long-range transporter vessel *Osiris*, now parked in Earth orbit after a three-month voyage from the Saturnian system. In that time, the communications turnaround delay had decreased steadily from over two hours when the ship set out. With preparations for the NIFTV demonstration taking up all his time, Keene hadn't talked with the Kronians at all during the past week. Now, suddenly, it was a pleasant change to find himself able to interact with them normally.

"Yes. We all thought that show of yours today was terrific," Sariena said. "The timing was perfect. It'll give us a good opening theme for the talks. Gallian asked me to say thanks, and that he's looking forward to meeting you in person at last too." Gallian was the head of the Kronian mission.

"You should thank the Air Force Space Command more than us," Keene replied. "They picked today for their test. We just went along with it."

"So do you have any idea yet when we'll be able to meet you?" Sariena asked.

"Well, you're probably going to be tied up with formal receptions and so forth for a while," Keene said. "I try not to get involved in things like that. But I've made time to be in Washington for a few days, starting Monday. We could probably work something in then."

"I'll let Gallian know," Sariena said.

Besides being a consultant to Amspace in Texas, Keene also acted as an advisor on space-related nuclear issues to various government offices, and maintained a Washington office for the purpose. He evaluated official reports and proposals, prepared recommendations, and testified before committees. A lot of congresspeople and other denizens of the Hill also consulted him privately for off-the-record views and background details. Most of them were better informed on issues that concerned them than the required public posturing sometimes allowed them to admit.

He looked at the face that he knew only from screens, outwardly so composed, yet what kind of agitation and uncertainties—fear even—had to be churning inside? In all her adult life, she had never seen an ocean, breathed a planet's air, or walked under an open sky. She had been taken to Kronia as a child in the early days when the original base, named Kropotkin, was constructed on the moon Dione. Now she was returning for the first time as one of the deputation that the Saturn colony had sent to Earth following the Athena event to press the same case that Keene had summarized to Feld.

Keene raised his coffee mug. "And before any of those guys in tuxedos have a chance to get started with their toasts and speeches, let us be the first to say, Welcome to Earth, finally. The main thing you have to remember is that leaving the outside door open is okay. But don't try walking on the blue stuff."

Sariena laughed. "Will you be able to make it to Washington too, Joyce?"

"Sorry. Not for a while, anyhow. I'm stuck up in this grimy can for another three weeks."

"Is that all?"

"Yeah, right, okay—you've got me. I was forgetting. What's three weeks in space to you guys?"

"But their accommodation is probably a bit more roomy," Keene said to Joyce.

"When are you going back down, Lan?" Sariena asked.

"In a couple of hours, probably. The firm's bus is up here waiting already." He gave Joyce a sideways look. "Then it'll be a shower and a swim, clean clothes . . ." He watched the look forming on her face. "And maybe a good steak and some wine out somewhere nice tonight."

"Pig," Joyce muttered hatefully.

The Amspace minishuttle detached from Space Dock a little under three hours later. As the craft fell away, Keene was able to catch a glimpse of the *Osiris* passing above as an elongated bead of light in its higher orbit. Low to one side, partly eclipsed by the curve of Earth's dark side, stretched the awesome spectacle of Athena's braided tail streaming in the solar wind as the supercomet fell toward the Sun.

❀ 4 ❀

Amspace's headquarters offices were located in Corpus Christi, southeast Texas, on North Water Street, a couple of blocks inland from the marinas on Corpus Christi Bay, at the fashionable, downtown end of Shoreline Boulevard. The company's main manufacturing, engineering, and research center was twenty miles south of the city at Kingsville, with a launch facility thirty miles farther south at a place called San Saucillo, on the plain of sandy flats and sage brush between Laredo and the Gulf. It was Oil Country, and much of the company's founding impetus had derived from the tradition of independence rooted in private capital and sympathetic local politics. All the same, taking an initiative toward developing the longer-term potential of space was a contentious and uncertain issue, and as insurance the corporation was constructing a second launch complex over the border in Mexico, on a highland plateau known as Montemorelos. Besides affording backup capability, Montemorelos would provide a means of continuing operations in the event that San Saucillo was shut down by politics.

It was late morning when the minishuttle carrying Keene and the other two NIFTV crew, along with several others from Space Dock who had been involved in the test mission, landed at the Saucillo site under a sun beating down through a dust haze that tinted the plain blue with distance. A bus carried the arrivals from the pad area to the assembly and administration complex at the far end of the landing field, where there was an interview session with waiting TV reporters. From there, a company helicopter flew them to the main plant at Kingsville for a post-mission debriefing over a burgers-and-fries lunch with senior technical staff in the office of the Technical Vice President, Harry Halloran. A lot of numbers and preliminary flight data were bandied about, and the NIFTV's performance analyzed. The consensus was that the demonstration had comfortably exceeded expectations.

By rights, that ought to have been good news. But such were the circumstances of the times that negative reactions could be expected as a virtual certainty too. And, indeed, by afternoon the protest had already started, ranging from diplomatic notes being delivered in Washington to poster-waving in the street outside Amspace's Corpus Christi offices. All the news channels were airing comments or polling views, and the company's switchboard and electronic mail servers were overloading. So if it was true that there really is no such thing as bad publicity, and since the whole object had been to get attention, then there could be no serious grounds for complaint.

As it turned out, many of the incoming messages were supportive. The British government expressed the hope that the demonstration might mark the beginning of a turnaround in world opinion that was long overdue. A Russian corporation revealed that it was working along similar lines to the NIFTV and would be flying a test engine of its own within six months. By three o'clock, Amspace had received twenty-six inquiries from hopeful would-be pilots. The meeting ended with the hope that the coming weekend might afford a forced cooling-off period. After that, the case the Kronians had come to argue for Earth expanding its space effort would endorse Amspace's position strongly. So all in all, events seemed to have worked themselves in quite a timely fashion.

While people were still collecting papers together and shutting down laptops, Wallace Lomack, the company's Chief Design Engineer, came over to where Keene was sitting with Joe Elms and Ricardo. "It was the Rambler all over again, Lan," he said jovially. "Right?"

Keene looked up, momentarily nonplussed. "Hi, Wally. What?"

"A long time ago, you told us that story about the Nash Rambler that you souped up and wiped out everything on the highway with back when you were a student. The stunt today was the same thing all over again, right? That was what gave you the idea."

Finally, the penny dropped. "Oh, you still remember that story, eh?" Keene said.

"I never heard that one," Joe murmured, tidying up his notes.

"Lan's history of dreaming up crazy schemes and getting everyone to go along with them goes all the way back," Wally replied. Then, to Keene, "I bet you never thought it would come to anything like this, though, eh?"

"You're right. I never thought it would. . . ." Keene shrugged. "So what are you up to over the weekend, Wally? Anything wild and exciting?"

Lomack left his tie loosened and slipped on his jacket, not bothering trying to fasten it over his ample midriff. "Oh, bit of boating, bit of fishing—something to amuse the grandkids, you know. How about you, Lan?"

"We're the mission crew. We don't have no weekend," Ricardo put in, next to Keene.

"They've given you the whole of tomorrow morning to rest up," Keene pointed out.

"Oh, yeah. How could I forget that?"

"Then Les has got a press conference organized in town that we have to be at," Keene replied to Wally. He was referring to Les Urkin, head of Amspace's public relations. "Then I arranged to be in Washington next week. Things are no doubt about to start flapping there."

"When are you flying up there?" Wally inquired.

"Probably Sunday night."

Joe raised his eyebrows and made an *O* in the air with a thumb and forefinger. "Aha! And planning to meet the delectable Saturnian, I'll bet. Can't say I blame you, though, Lan."

"Sure, if the schedules work out," Keene agreed. "Why not? We've been talking to them long enough."

"Is a romance between the planets about to happen?" Ricardo asked, grinning.

Keene shook his head. "Not me. I've been there already. Burned, bitten, and shy. You know how it is."

Wally thought about that, then made a face. "Well, the first two, I might buy. Anyhow, have fun, young feller."

"You too, Wally," Keene said. "And don't let those grandkids tip over your boat. You're needed back here for the profile evaluations next week."

Lomack moved away, while Keene finished stuffing his papers into a document case. As a matter of fact, he had forgotten all about his student escapade with the Nash Rambler. What had given him the idea for showing off the NIFTV when the Air Force was testing its APU was something he'd read about Charles Parsons, the English inventor of the steam turbine, who had used the celebration of the Queen's Jubilee in 1897 to arouse the interest of the British Admiralty. On that occasion, the Royal Navy had assembled 173 warships to be reviewed by the Royal Yacht and a grand flotilla of craft containing the Lords of the Admiralty, various colonial premiers, the Diplomatic Corps, and members from both Houses of Parliament; but Parsons stole the show by roaring around the fleet in his 2,000 horsepower turbine-driven yacht *Turbinia* at thirty-four knots, which was faster than anything the Navy could send in chase. In fact, it was the fastest boat in the world at the time. Such was the spirit of the age, that the British Admiralty had responded by promptly ordering two turbine-powered ships. As he zipped up the document case and rose from his chair, Keene wondered if they could expect a similar display of magnanimity and perspicacity from the Defense Department.

After leaving Amspace, Keene stopped by his own company to show his face and check on how things had gone during his absence. Protonix occupied a five-room suite in an office park on the south side of Corpus Christi, near the interchange between the Crosstown Expressway and South Padre Island Drive. Besides himself as president, it had four other staff, all female. Vicki was Keene's associate and second-in-command; Celia acted as her assistant; Judith had a math Ph.D. and looked after the computers, while Karen was the receptionist, secretary, and general errand-runner. The engineers at Amspace referred to the firm enviously as Keene's Harem. In fact, as a point of professionalism and out of the sheer practical consideration of getting things done in an environment that was complicated enough already, Keene kept business strictly separate from anything personal. As with marriage, he had suffered the consequences of those kinds of involvements in earlier years. Sometimes he thought that the first half of his adult life had served partly as a rehearsal for the second, in which he was finally managing to get a few things right.

He was greeted with laughter and applause, a bottle of Bushmills Black Bush Irish whiskey, and an old astronaut-style cap from the souvenir shop at the Johnson Space Center in Houston. The girls had watched the demo that morning and said it was terrific. Karen thought that Keene looked great on TV—that unshaven, mildly haggard look was exactly what movie producers were hunting for. He ought to apply for a part, she told him. Keene assured her that there had been nothing mild about it.

Although Protonix hadn't been named in any of the coverage, the political and media insiders who knew Keene were already clamoring to get ahold of him, and Shirley, who ran the office that he used in Washington, had called with a tentative list of meetings scheduled for Monday. But the *big* news was that Naomi had presented Celia with five kittens: two tabby, one black, one gray, and one "kind of stripey something," Celia said. . . . Oh, and yes, apart from that, Judith had left early to attend the computer show in Dallas tomorrow; there were problems with machining some of the parts for the reactor Westinghouse was fabricating in San Diego, that Vicki needed to talk to him about next week; the guy in Japan who had done the thermal studies had downloaded the reports that Keene was interested in; and the parking lot would be closed next Friday and over the weekend for resurfacing. When a few more minor items were disposed of, Vicki followed Keene into his office with a list of things to check for Monday, leaving Karen and Celia clearing desks, organizing purses, and exchanging plans for the weekend.

Vicki had light brown, almost orange hair that contracted itself into wiry curls no matter how she tried to comb or wave it, and a freckled, angular face accentuated by a pointy nose, sharp chin, and straight mouth. Her body was petite and lean-limbed, shaped by that chemistry that can eat anything all day and metabolize energy without an ounce of gain. She lived for her work, and she was good. Originally a radiation physicist at Harvard, she had met Keene when he moved there to become a theoretician from conducting plasma physics research at General Atomic in San Diego. She had grown disillusioned with the academic scientific community at about the same rate as he, and rejoined him back in the real world soon after he quit, moved south to Texas, and set up the business that later became Protonix. She had a fourteen-year-old son called Robin, whom she had raised from toddlerhood by herself, and Keene had become something of a father figure as well as a business colleague.

"So . . ." Vicki stared across the office from one of the two visitor chairs below a wall of framed pictures of launch vehicles and satellites, including a spectacular shot of the Kronian *Osiris*.

"So," Keene echoed. They were both flopped loosely, unwinding, happy to forget the week's routine events for the time being.

"You get to go again. I told you, the others can take care of the office. Why do I get this impression that male animals are fickle?" One of their standing jokes was that Keene would get Vicki up on a mission too one day. It had long been a dream of hers to go into space.

Keene put on a mock pained look. "If I didn't know you better, I might think you didn't believe me."

"How can you say that? You know I have undying trust."

"And I have an image of mystique to keep up. You know how the guru thing works: always promise nirvana tomorrow."

Vicki turned her eyes resignedly toward the ceiling and changed the subject. "Did I hear you say they're actually giving you tomorrow morning off to rest up?"

"The galley slaves have to get some air sometime," Keene replied. "Les has got a press conference fixed for the afternoon."

"You want to stop by for a late breakfast at the house on your way in? Robin has been asking after you. I think he wants to show you some of the latest that he's been getting into."

Keene rubbed his chin. "Sure, why not? . . . So how is Robin?"

"Just fine."

"What's he been getting into this time?"

"Dinosaurs. Apparently they couldn't have existed."

"Oh, really? A mass hallucination, then. . . . So how come?"

"It gets involved. Why not ask him tomorrow?"

"Okay."

Vicki searched her mind for anything else. "Did you talk to Sariena? I was at Kingsville when they redirected the call from the *Osiris*. That was just after your spot with John Feld ended."

"Yes, I got it," Keene replied. "She just wanted to let us know that Gallian was happy with the way things went; also, that they'd be on their way down to the surface pretty soon."

"They're down," Vicki said. "It was on the news this afternoon—while you were at the debriefing. Big reception dinner at the White House tonight. Everybody who thinks they're somebody is going to have to be there." She tossed a hand out in a motion indicating both of them. "So how come we didn't get invitations?"

"We left the rarified academic heights, don't you remember? People would probably worry that we might show up in coveralls, carrying wrenches." Keene rubbed his chin. "We could stop for a quick one while it's still happy hour at the Bandana," he offered. "Not exactly black tie, but do you think it would do instead?"

Vicki smiled and gave a snort. "The company might be an improvement, though—I'll say that." She stretched, held the position for a few seconds, then relaxed. "So never mind the pageantry over the weekend. How will things go when they get down to the real talking? Any guesses? . . . I know we've got a lot of the world's attention, but is it really going to take any notice? I mean, okay, Athena's there. But most people are treating it like a spectator sport, not something that actually connects to their lives. Are the Kronians going to be able to change that?"

"They must think they stand a chance, otherwise they'd hardly have come this far." Keene showed his palms briefly. "All they have to do is get the powers that shape science in this world to see the obvious."

"Wow," Vicki said dryly. "Now I really feel better."

Kronia's scientists had reached the conclusion that the conventional picture of a stable and orderly Solar System repeating its motions like clockwork since the time of its formation, was—simply put—wrong. Cataclysmic encounters between planetary and other bodies had, they maintained, occurred through into recent historic times, and there was no reason to suppose that such events would not continue. The Kronian leaders accepted this view and for years had been exhorting Earth to put a greater investment of effort and resources into spreading a significant human presence across the Solar System. For as long as the human race remained concentrated in one place, they insisted, it was vulnerable, literally, to extinction. In fact, they claimed it had almost happened in the not very distant past.

But Earth's institutions remained wedded to their dogma of gradualism, which maintained that only the processes observed today had operated in the past, and, apart from temporary local fluctuations, had done so at the same rates. Extrapolating backward the currently measured rates of such processes as sedimentation and erosion had yielded the immense ages assigned to geological formations, which had come to be regarded as unquestionable.

In the main, Earth's policymakers had rejected the Kronian urgings in preference for the orthodox view. With the military no longer able to press as compelling a case as in the days of superpower rivalry, and other lobbies jostling for a share of largesse at the federal trough, expansion of the space sciences and industries had not been a high government priority. For the private sector, ventures much beyond the Moon were too massively demanding in outlay and too risky to interest the major institutional investors, who looked to areas of secure returns such as launch systems for satellites and limited scientific payloads—which conventional technologies served adequately. Comfort and security had become the world's foremost concerns. Only fringe outfits like Amspace, and a few visionaries who were prepared to back them, had continued pushing for a general commitment to broadening what the Kronians had pioneered, and were calling for the enterprise that advanced, long-range, spacegoing capability would open up: *colonization*. Hence, organizations like Amspace had found themselves natural allies of the Kronians, communicating and cooperating for the same end: the Kronians to impart a cultural imperative; the Keenes of the world—and the Joyces, spending weeks on end in a cramped, orbiting boiler room; the Wallys, hoping to create a better world for their grandchildren—pursuing lifelong dreams.

Then Athena happened—and surely, they had all believed, that would change everything. But astoundingly, it had changed things hardly at all. Of course, the early months had seen a media orgy of sensational pictures of the planetoid and a deformed Jupiter gradually regaining its shape; hurried explanations by scientists; and endless lurid articles and documentaries that the public eventually grew weary of. Sales of amateur telescopes, astronomy books, and videos soared; related college classes reported record enrollments; catastrophism saw a dramatic revival. And yes, the scientific community conceded, with some hemming and hawing and smoothing of ruffled plumage, that their theories needed revising—and then clamored for more funding to support the new research that needed to be done. But the kind of research they had in mind involved bigger and more lavishly equipped departments, computers that even the particle physicists would envy, more chairmanships and committees, and appointments to oversee unmanned missions to various parts of the Solar System. The mainline contractors got in their bids where they saw opportunity, but practically without exception the equipment and techniques envisaged were all safe, proven, and more of the same. Nothing they talked about anticipated any meaningful move toward getting *people* in significant numbers *out there* anytime soon. Finally, in desperation, the Kronians dispatched a political-scientific delegation to present their case firsthand in an attempt to shake Earth out of its complacency.

There was a tap on the door, and Celia stuck her face in. "We're off now," she said to Keene and Vicki. "Have a good weekend."

" 'Bye," Karen's voice called from the outer office beyond.

"Take care with those cowboys out there," Keene called back. One of the ongoing news topics of the office was Karen's latest boyfriend. He nodded a goodnight to Celia. She disappeared, closing the door. Keene looked back at Vicki. "We'll just have to wait and see what the next few weeks bring," he told her.

As he saw things, it was the last chance. If this didn't bring about a change in Earth's outlook and policies, nothing would. Then he and Vicki might well end up applying for jobs at the Bandana instead of just stopping by for happy-hour drinks.

❁ 5 ❁

Thirty years earlier, the world had scoffed and said it was impossible when two extraordinary personalities got together and announced an intention to establish a human settlement among the moons of Saturn. After the parade of mediocrity that had marked the closing decades of the twentieth century, it seemed that leader figures with the charisma to inspire followings had conceded the stage to rock stars and sports idols. Then, one day, a disenchanted California trial attorney with the unremarkable name of Thomas Mondel gave up a promising career to denounce the world's economic system with the contention that humans were made—created, evolved, or "just there"; whatever one chose to believe—for better things. There was something wrong with a society that spent millions trying to make computers and robots imitate humans while at the same time raising humans to behave like robots. California had seen more than a smattering of fads and cults before, of course. But this was different in several ways that mattered. Mondel was not another beard with sandals and beads, reaching out to lost sheep and adolescents of all ages desperate to find escape from the hopeless corners of life that they had painted themselves into. He was professional, articulate, wise to the ways of the world, and he knew how to get attention. His appeal was to the slowly atrophying cost accountant stuck in traffic twice a day, two-hundred-fifty days every year, with the IRS waiting to mop up whatever of his year's income survived Christmas; to the marketing wage slave sitting out a four-hour layover at O'Hare, looking forward to a microwaved TV meal in a solitary apartment and wondering what happened to the glamorous, high-powered executive that she'd created out of movie images in the years she was at college; to the frustrated who had worked to be scientists or teachers or ministers or healers, but found themselves turned into full-time form-fillers and fundraisers instead. In short, to all those people to whom it didn't make sense to have to labor year-in, year-out in dismally unfulfilling ways in order to be allowed a modest share of the produce in a world whose biggest preoccupation seemed to be with moving overproduced merchandise that nobody really needed. And it was amazing how many people like that there turned out to be.

It was hardly the first time that somebody had denounced money value as the sole measure of worth of all things. In the past, Mondel claimed, some such indicator to keep track of who owed what to whom had always been necessitated by scarcity. But knowledge and the limitless capacity that it equated to in today's world made that no longer true. In terms of ability, humanity's material problems were solved. What hadn't been solved was finding the right incentive to induce people to realize that ability. Trying to mesh twenty-first-century technology with nineteenth-century notions of economics produced the constant clashing of gears that the world had been hearing. When the wants of those with the means to pay determined the demand that was supplied, and not what the rest of the people needed, eventually the ones with the needs would resort to force to satisfy them, which was why war, unrest, and rebellion refused to go away.

"Mondelism" caught the mood of the times and spread, attracting followers from all stations in life committed to creating a mutual support network based on principles of obligation and trust, service and duty, instead of buying and selling. But it also attracted a lot of free riders too, as the skeptics had said it would, giving rise to hostility within and ridicule without, and in general the movement wasn't a success. But neither was Mondel a quitter. The problems didn't reflect on the soundness of the idea, he insisted, but resulted from its having to be sown in fields already choked by weeds. The followers continued to believe, and sustained by a core of tireless disciples and some quite influential backers, tottered on through intermittent triumphs and crises for several years. And then Tom Mondel met a geneticist-entrepreneur by the name of Clement Waltz.

Waltz had started a biological engineering company called Genenco that hit on a method for detecting and correcting a number of common genetic birth defects. Health-care systems worldwide rushed to license the process, since the cost of screening was significantly lower than that of the treatment programs avoided later. The result was that Waltz became a multibillionaire before he was thirty, upon which he grew bored with it all and cast around for something more meaningful to occupy himself with than continuing to make money, which he had come to despise. Some scientific and business colleagues introduced him to Mondel, and Waltz was immediately captivated. Mondel, by this time, had reached the conclusion that what his system needed was a clean start in an untainted environment removed from Earth. Accepting the irony that in a money-dominated world, money was necessary to gain freedom from the contamination of money, Waltz assembled sufficient assets from his own resources and sympathetic backers to solicit the Guatemalan government's cooperation in constructing an assembly and launch center at a place called Tapapeque. He imported scientists from Japan, manufacturing know-how from China, disgruntled rocketry experts from NASA and the former Soviet military, and announced that he was going to establish a Mondelist colony elsewhere. The world chortled and jeered—until test shots from Tapapeque circled the Earth, and three months later a four-man lander touched down fifty miles from the UN experimental base at Tycho in a single-stage jump from an Earth-orbiting platform. Here was an illustration of what dedication and human creativity untrammeled by power-lust and greed could achieve, Mondel and Waltz told the astonished world. In the isolated Central American microcommunity, Mondelism worked. They then announced that the promised extraterrestrial colony would be founded not on Mars, as most commentators had assumed, and where a tiny international scientific reconnaissance group lived a hardy life with visitations twice a year; not among the Asteroids, which would be bypassed and exploited later; not even above Jupiter, whose high-radiation environment posed uncertainties; but all the way out at the remoteness of Saturn. This time the world didn't jeer, although there was no disguising that its credulity was strained. . . . And, by God, they made it!

Thereafter, despite the distance and the infrequency of return voyages by the first ship, and—later—more departures by others, the colony grew at a surprising rate. The stories that came back of science free to function as an instrument of pure inquiry, unconstrained by establishment dogmas or the political agendas of funding agencies, attracted a particular kind of mind—not just physicists and engineers but builders, inventors, philosophers, explorers: the curious, the restless, the innovators of every kind. They were drawn by the accounts they heard of a society-in-miniature that seemed to function without budgets or accounting, where value was reflected in what an individual contributed to the common enterprise. Some gave the closest description they could find for the social order there as "monastic." The measure of worth—"wealth"—was knowledge and competence. It couldn't be stolen, hoarded, taxed, or counterfeited. If left to lie unused it effectively didn't exist.

Invariably, there were those who couldn't fit in and came back. And the vast majority on Earth, even if they ever thought about such matters and could relate to them, were unable to comprehend how anyone would choose living amid ice deserts and breathing machine-dispensed air to taking in a movie after a day's shopping at the mall, lying on the beach, or harvesting corn in Iowa in October. But just a few here and a couple there from places scattered the world over proved sufficient to fill the transports lifting out from orbit and establish further bases on Tethys, Rhea, Titan, and Iapetus in a time period that confounded all the experts. Nevertheless, it was still widely regarded as a crazy venture destined eventually to peter out or come to an abrupt end. Earth's commercial and political institutions made no rush to follow, since for them there was nothing to be gained. It was only in the surreal system of economics that Mondelism had created, where a huge infusion from altruistic benefactors had put up the stake money and some of the best talent that Earth had produced was prepared literally to work for nothing, that any significant investment in operations over such a distance could be contemplated.

There had been times when Keene too had thought about going in one of those ships—not during the early days, for he had been too young, but later, when he would have had something to offer out there. The period following the breakdown of his marriage had been one such time. Others were when he despaired that no Earth-based initiative would ever follow to build on the unique combination of circumstances that had founded Kronia—at least not while he was still a young man. But he had stayed, knowing those moods would pass—and they always had.

It would have felt too much like giving up. Big changes were never easy, and always they depended on the rare kind of people who seemed capable of believing in anything except the impossible. And besides, he liked to watch sunsets too—and to scuffle through autumn leaves, eat out at a good waterside restaurant, and lie on beaches. Why should he have to leave all that to people he disagreed with when he could fight them for it? And right now, the prospects for finally getting official recognition that expansion outward was imperative to the security of Earth's culture looked better than ever. He wasn't prepared to become an exile just yet.

The colony's original intent had been to maintain a cooperative relationship with Earth based on some kind of exchange of Kronian technological innovations in return for products and materials that Earth could supply more conveniently. But when Kronia went on to realize in twenty years advanced propulsion systems that Earth had put on hold, attitudes on Earth became more wary, causing the Kronians to withdraw and manage their own affairs. Mondel and Waltz both died together in a craft that broke up on reentry over Titan eight years previously, making them instant martyrs of the movement. But by that time Kronia was established and virtually self-sufficient. The Tapapeque complex was handed over to the Guatemalan government, who maintained shuttle operations to ferry up departing emigrants when a Kronian ship was in orbit, and at other times leased surplus capacity to various national and private interests, providing a welcome supplement to the country's income.

Did Keene really believe that a bunch of mavericks and misfits that most of the world dismissed as deranged or incomprehensible could reroute human destiny? "Sure," he told innumerable reporters and interviewers who called him throughout the rest of the evening. "Just the same as we can run rings around the Air Force."

Southeast of Corpus Christi, a bridge connected across an inlet to a peninsula called Flour Bluff, at the end of which lay the Naval Air Station. Beyond the peninsula, a causeway continued to Padre Island, one of the chain of sandy offshore islands fringing the Gulf shore from west Florida to Mexico. That was where Vicki lived, in an aging but well-kept and homey single-family house that she had acquired when she moved from the northeast to join Keene after he set up Protonix. Robin's father, a Navy man, had been killed some years before in a political bombing incident in the Middle East. Keene's slipping into the role of family friend and father substitute filled a vacant space in both their lives, as well as making a big difference for Robin.

He arrived shortly before ten, after a twenty-minute drive from his townhouse on Ocean Drive, facing the Bay on the southern side of the city, clad in a sport shirt with slacks that he could throw a jacket over for the press conference later. Vicki greeted him in a weekend casual top and shorts. Robin joined them, and they sat down to breakfast in the glass-enclosed summer room that had been added as an extension of the kitchen. Keene had always thought Robin a great kid with a natural ability to get along with anybody, who deserved to have known a natural father. He was fair like his mother, although his hair was more yellow, and his skin, unlike hers, kept a year-round tan. His features seemed to alternate between deep frowns when he was intent on something, to wide-eyed vistas of distant blankness when he was off into the realms of . . . wherever he went. Keene sometimes wished he had kept a notebook to list the questions Robin had come up with in the time they had known each other. For a while, someone at Robin's school had formed the opinion that he had an attention-deficiency problem, but Vicki thought it was more the result of a communications failing somewhere; any kind of communications channel has two ends. It hadn't been Keene's place to interfere, but in his own mind he had agreed with her. He knew from his own experience that Robin was capable of fearsome and sustained concentration on things that interested him.

Besides her job with Protonix, Vicki had a sideline creating advertising graphics at home. When she wasn't breadwinning or single-parenting, she managed to find time for a mix of interests that never ceased to amaze Keene, ranging from biology and medieval history to pen-and-ink drawing and decorating, in between which she desk-published the newsletter for a local church group, made sure that Robin fed and looked after his menagerie, and amassed books on seemingly every subject imaginable. She believed nothing on TV or in newspapers that was of interest, and had no interest in the things she did believe. When she seriously wanted to know something, she dug and pestered until she found sources that were reliable, or she went to someone who knew. She had first entered Keene's world of awareness through tracking him down when they were both at Harvard, to answer questions she had about the electromagnetic properties of space after finding the theories of dark matter to account for anomalous motions of galaxies unconvincing.

"The hounds are baying," she told Keene, referring to reactions that had been building up to Amspace's stunt the day before. "But we knew that would happen. Have you caught much of it?"

Keene shook his head. "I've been screening those out. That's what Amspace has a PR department for. No doubt I'll get my share this afternoon. Who's saying what?"

"The EA secretary was bilious," Vicki said—the name of the

former EPA had been shortened, after some thought the original form sounded too alarmist. "He called it criminally irresponsible and wants a formal ban on space nukes to be declared internationally."

"He's got an image to keep up for the faithful," Keene replied. "It'll never happen. The Defense people need to keep an option open to match the Chinese if they have to, and the Chinese will never buy it."

Robin attended to his eggs and bacon, his mind roaming in whatever realms it turned to when grown-ups got into politics. Keene watched Vicki refilling the coffee cups and then let his gaze wander over the kitchen, searching for a change of subject. Sam, the household dog, lay in the doorway watching him with one eye open, still unable, quite, to figure out whether or not Keene belonged. Labrador and collie contributions were discernible, with various other ingredients stirred into the mix. Vicki had originally christened him "Samurai," but he just didn't have the image. The parakeets squawked noisily in their cage from the kitchen beyond.

There were a few more pictures and drawings adorning the wall. A model of a tyrannosaurus had appeared on top of the refrigerator. "Oh, what's this?" Keene murmured. He remembered what Vicki had said at the office the previous evening. "Is Robin going through his dinosaur phase? I guess he's at just about the right age." Robin returned immediately from wherever, registering interest.

Vicki nodded with a sigh. "His room is practically papered with prints that he's downloaded. It's like one of those science-fiction-movie theme parks. I think he must have checked out every book on them in the local library."

"I hope that won't mean more additions to the private zoo, CR," Keene said, looking at Robin. Keene had dubbed him Christopher Robin, after the character from the British children's books.

Robin appeared to mull over the possibility, then shook his head. "Too much cleaning up after. And they'd probably bother the neighbors."

"What's this I hear about them not being real?" Keene asked. "Has everyone been imagining things all these years?"

"Oh, did Mom tell you about that?"

"Right."

"Theoretically they ought to be impossible," Robin agreed. "They couldn't exist." Keene waited, then showed an open palm invitingly. Robin went on, "Well, you're an engineer, Lan. It follows from the basic scaling laws. The weight of an animal or anything increases as the cube of its size, right?"

Keene nodded. "Okay."

Robin shrugged. "But strength depends on the cross-section of muscles, which only increases as the square. So as animals get bigger, their strength-to-weight ratio decreases. All this stuff you read about insects carrying x times their own body weight around isn't really any big deal. At their size you'd be able to walk around holding a piano over your head with one hand."

Keene glanced at Vicki with raised eyebrows. "Robin's been doing his homework." Keene was familiar with the principle but had never had reason to dwell on its implications regarding dinosaurs.

"That's Robin," Vicki said.

Keene looked back at Robin. "Go on," he said.

"As you get bigger, it works the other way. Do you know who the strongest humans in the world are?"

"Hmm. . . . Oh, how about an Olympic power lifter?" Keene guessed.

"Right on. Now, take one, say, doing dead-lift or a squat. The most you'd be talking about would be what—around thirteen hundred pounds including body weight?"

Keene shrugged. "If you say so. It sounds as if you've checked it out."

"Oh, he has," Vicki threw in.

"Now scale him up to brontosaurus size, and his maximum lifting capability works out at under fifty thousand pounds," Robin said. "But the brontosaurus weighed in at seventy thousand; the supersaur even more than that, and the ultrasaur at—would you believe this—three hundred sixty thousand pounds!"

"My God." Keene sat back in his chair, staring hard as the implication finally hit him. "Are you sure they were as heavy as that?"

Robin nodded. "I got those estimates from a guy called Young, who's Curator of Vertebrate Paleontology at the museum in Toronto. And I checked it with somebody else at the Smithsonian, too." It sounded as if Robin had been picking up tips from Vicki. His expression remained serious. "But the point is, the strongest man in the world wouldn't have been able to stand under his own weight, let alone move—and that's when you're talking about practically being made of muscle. These other things were all digestive system. So how did they do it? See what I mean—they couldn't exist."

Keene looked across at Vicki quizzically. It was a challenge for any engineer. Vicki tossed out her free hand and shook her head. "Maybe they had better muscles," Keene offered as a starter, looking back at Robin.

Robin was clearly prepared for it. "No, that doesn't work. The maximum force that a muscle can produce is set by the size of the thick and thin filaments and the number of cross-bridges between them," he replied. "It turns out they're about the same for a mouse as for an elephant—and it holds true across all the vertebrates. That means the only gain you get from larger size is what comes from the bigger cross section."

"There's no increase in efficiency," Keene checked.

Robin shook his head. "In fact, it goes the other way. Gets worse."

"Okay. . . ." Keene searched for another way to play devil's advocate. "They were aquatic. I saw a picture in a book once that showed them snorkeling around in lakes and swamps."

"Nobody believes that anymore," Robin countered. "They don't show any aquatic adaptations. Their teeth were worn down from eating hard land vegetation, not soggy watery stuff. They left tracks and footprints. That doesn't happen under water."

"Did he find all this out by himself?" Keene asked, turning back to Vicki.

"I helped him with some of it," she told him—which Keene had guessed. "But it does seem to be a real mystery—a big one. You just don't hear about it." She made a vague gesture. "On top of the things Robin's mentioned, you've also got the problem with the circulatory system of the sauropods—those were the ones that were all neck and tail. How did they get the blood up to their brains? A giraffe's head might be twenty feet up, and it needs pressure that would rupture the vascular system of any other animal. Giraffes do it by having thick arterial walls and a tight skin that works like a pressure suit. But a sauropod's brain was at fifty or sixty feet. The pressure would have needed to be three or four times that of a giraffe. The people who've studied it just can't see it as credible."

"Hmm. Maybe they didn't hold their necks upright, then," Keene tried. "What if they walked around with them horizontal? . . . No." He shook his head, not even believing it himself. What would have been the point of having them? And in any case, even without knowing the exact numbers, his instinct told him that the stress generated at the base would be more than any biological tissue could take.

Robin concluded, "And then you've got things like the pterosaurs that somehow flew with body weights of three hundred fifty pounds, and predatory birds of up to two hundred. The most you get today is about twenty-five, with the Siberian Berkut hunting eagle. Breeders have been trying to improve on that for centuries, but that's as far as you can go and still get a viable flier."

Keene looked at Vicki. "Any bigger, and you end up with a klutz," she said. "The big gliding birds like albatrosses aren't good flyers. They often need repeat attempts to take off, and they can be real clowns on landing."

Robin nodded. "That's why they're called gooney birds."

Vicki sat back and finished her coffee while Keene thought about what she and Robin had said. There didn't seem any further line to pursue. "And the people in the business know these things?" he said finally. Of course they did. It was more for something to say.

"Well, we sure didn't make them up," Vicki replied. "I guess they put it out of their minds and get on with cleaning up the bones and fitting them together or whatever. So what's new?"

It was Athena all over again—the reason Keene had quit physics to return to engineering. Most workers just got on with the day-to-day job that brought in the grants and kept the paychecks coming, without worrying too much about what it all meant. It was safer to write papers and textbooks about things that everyone agreed they knew than go dragging up awkward questions whose answers might contradict what people in other departments were saying *they* knew. Before long the whole edifice would be threatened, and the result would be trouble from all directions.

"There must have been something vastly different about the whole reality that existed then," Vicki said distantly. "I don't mean just with the dinosaurs, but about everything: the plants, the insects, the marine life. Walk around the museums and look at the reconstructions. It was all on a different scale of engineering. You can't relate it to the world we know today. Something universal has altered since then. And the only thing that makes sense is gravity. Earth's gravity must have been a lot less back in those times than it is now."

Keene looked at her, coming back from his own line of thought. His brow creased. "How?"

"I don't know. But if it wasn't, dinosaurs couldn't have existed. Yet they did. So what other explanation is there?"

Robin massaged the hair at the front of his head in the way he did when he had some way-out suggestion to offer. "I can think of one. Maybe it wasn't Earth's gravity that was different," he said.

"Huh?" Keene frowned. "What else's, then? I mean, where else are we talking about?"

"You know how what wiped the dinosaurs out was supposed to be an asteroid or something. . . ."

"Uh-huh."

"Well, suppose they weren't on Earth at all before it hit, the way everyone assumes. Suppose they came here with it."

"Came with what? You mean with the asteroid?"

"Yes—or whatever it was." Robin made an appealing gesture. "If Earth's gravity was too big for them to have existed, then they must have existed on something else. That's logic, right? Well, suppose the something else was whatever Earth got hit by. It doesn't have to be an asteroid like we think of them—you know, just a chunk of rock. It could have been, maybe, like something that had an atmosphere they could live in."

"Wouldn't it need to have been pretty huge, though, to have an atmosphere?" Keene queried.

"Not necessarily, if it was cold with dense gases. Titan has an atmosphere. . . . And in any case, the whole thing didn't have to hit the Earth. Maybe it got close enough to break up, and only part of it did."

Keene's first impulse was to scoff, but he checked himself. Wasn't that just the kind of automatic reaction that he was having so much trouble with from the regular scientific establishment? He could see reasons for not buying the suggestion, but simply the fact that it conflicted with prior beliefs wasn't good enough to be one of them. Robin was trying. Keene paused long enough not to be dismissive.

"What about the impact?" he asked. "These things explode when they enter the atmosphere, like that big one over Siberia, oh . . . whenever it was. Or imagine what must have happened when that hole in Arizona was dug. You're talking about bones being preserved intact enough to be put together again. Eggs. . . . And we've even got footprints. Would they really be likely to survive something like that?"

"That was what I wondered when Robin put it to me," Vicki commented.

"Maybe, if they were encased inside chunks of rock that were large enough—say that came down across a whole area like a blanket," Robin persisted. "The air might act as a cushion."

"So you're saying they might not actually have *lived* here at all," Keene said, finally getting the point.

"Exactly. They lived on . . . whatever." Robin looked from him back to Vicki as if to say, *well, you asked for suggestions.*

Keene sat back and snorted wonderingly. Ingenious, he had to grant. But being ingenious didn't automatically mean being right. There was still that other small factor known as "evidence" to be considered.

"I don't know, but I'll tell you what I'll do," he said. "I'll put it to a couple of the planetary scientists that I know. We'll see what they say." Robin deserved that much.

"Really?" Robin looked pleased. "Hey, that would be great!"

"Sure. Why not?"

After breakfast they watched a replay of the Kronian landing and motorcade into Washington from the day before. Seeing the Kronians alongside native Terrans for the first time brought home something that Keene had never really registered before: they were *tall*. Sariena was a natural for the cameras to single out for close-ups, and she came over well when taking her turn to respond to the welcoming address by the President. Keene noted that the Kronians remained seated, and all of them wore sunglasses outside.

Keene and Robin spent an hour experimenting with a new electronic paint board that Robin had just added to his computer. Playing father figure was good for Keene's self-image in enabling him to claim the capacity to be socially responsible if he chose. All in all, it was a relaxed, easygoing morning—the perfect way to recharge after the past week and prepare for the equally demanding one ahead. And then, just as Keene was getting ready to leave to go back over to the city for the press conference, Leo Cavan called from Washington, rerouted from Keene's private number, with some news he said he'd rather not go into just now, but which had to do with the Kronians. Was Keene still planning on coming up to D.C. first thing the coming week? Keene confirmed that he was—probably flying up tomorrow night. Fine, Cavan said. Could he make it earlier in the day so that they could meet for dinner? Sure, Keene agreed. It sounded important. Cavan said yes, he thought it was. And Cavan wasn't the kind of person who did things without good reason.

◎ 7 ◎

The press conference was held in the boardroom of Amspace's headquarters building in downtown Corpus Christi. Ricardo Juarez and Joe Elms, the NIFTV's other two crew members, were present with Keene. Wally Lomack joined them at the table facing the cameras as the official corporate spokesperson. Les Urkin, who headed public relations, and Harry Halloran, the technical VP, were present also in off-screen capacities. The assembly they faced was a fairly even mix of print and electronic news journalists, some hostile, some supportive, most simply following to see where the story led. With the tensions of the previous day's test now over and preliminary evaluations of its results exceeding expectations, the Amspace team was in high spirits.

As had been expected, the initial questions involved the political furore being kicked up over the unannounced testing of a nuclear propulsion system in space by a U.S.-based company. Liberal and environmental groups were committed to protest on principle, and much of media opinion was sympathetic. Joe Elms and Ricardo ducked that issue on the grounds that their line was flight operations, happy to leave Keene the brunt of responding—which made sense, since it was a case he was used to presenting. For a while, he reiterated the line he had begun with John Feld the day before: the risks that had been propagandized for decades were exaggerated and trivial compared to others that the world accepted routinely; energy *density*, not just the amount, was what mattered if you wanted to do better things more efficiently; the densities involved with state-transitions of the atomic nucleus were of the scale necessary to get out into space in a meaningful way, whereas those associated with the so-called "alternatives" were not. None of this was particularly new. But Keene's main hope while they had the world's attention was to emphasize again that a commitment to such propulsion methods would be essential for the expansion across the Solar System that the Kronians were calling for, which was crucial to the security of the human race. The opportunity came when one of the network reporters asked for a response to allegations that Amspace was using the Kronian cause to promote its own commercial interests. Not being on the company's staff, Keene couldn't comment. Wally Lomack took it with a show of shortness.

"Obviously, it would be hypocritical to deny that we'd hope to benefit. But I'm getting tired of these people who seem to think that we're incapable of looking beyond the bottom line of the current quarter's balance sheet. If a serious space development program becomes our official policy, every contractor will be looking for a share of the action, and sure, we'd expect to take our place in line with everyone else who has something to offer. But the issue that should concern all of us is the safety and future of humanity. Look at the western sky tonight just after sundown if you've forgotten what I'm talking about. It's happened before, and now we've just come too close for comfort to seeing it happen again. Saying that you and I won't be around next time isn't an answer."

"The *Kronians* say it happened before," somebody at the back of the room called out. "But they're the ones on a limb out there who need Earth to bail them out. Is it just a coincidence that the line of business you're in happens to be what they're telling us we have to do?"

Ricardo shook his head violently, looking along the table for support. "They're not out on any limb. Hell, man, they've got drive systems that could run rings around what *we* put up."

"But Kronia is economically nonviable," somebody else threw out. "Admit it, their system's shot. They have to get Earth's support somehow or go under."

"That's just a line that the politicians take," Joe Elms retorted, sitting next to Keene on his other side from Lomack. "They don't want to think about what it might do to their budgets."

"Me neither. Would *you* want to pay the taxes?"

"It doesn't have to be a tax-funded thing," Joe answered. "Taken as a whole, this planet has enormous resources. We spend more on cosmetics, alcohol, entertainment, and pet food than—"

"Corporate interests again," another voice chimed in. "That's the whole point that some people are questioning."

Keene didn't want this to degenerate into an airing of suspicions they had all heard before. There were vaster issues to be focusing on. "Look," he said, raising both his hands. "Can we just put all this aside in our minds for a minute? These things are trivial compared to what we should be talking about. What we should be talking about concerns all of us. . . ." He gave the mood a second or two to shift. "It isn't just the Kronians who are saying that Earth has undergone major cataclysms in its past from encounters with other astronomical objects. Scars and upheavals written all over the surface of this planet and its moon say it. Abundant records of violent mass extinctions say it. Evidence of sudden climatic changes and polar shifts say it. And records preserved from cultures all over the world say that it has happened within recorded human history. Traditionally, they've been dismissed as myths and legends, but they show too much corroboration to be coincidental. The facts have been there for centuries, but for the most part we've remained collectively blind to what they've been telling us. Athena is telling us that we can't risk that kind of blindness any longer."

"Exactly," Lomack pronounced, nodding vigorously.

A dark-haired man who was sitting near the front raised a hand, then pitched in. "Phil Onslow, *Houston Chronicle*. Do we take it, then, that you endorse this idea that the Kronians have been pushing about Venus being a new planet?"

For a moment, Keene was surprised. He had assumed it was

obvious. "Well . . . sure. It's intimately connected with what we're trying to say, and what yesterday's demonstration was all about. Three and a half thousand years ago, the human race came close to being wiped out."

"And if we buy that, you're asking us to spend trillions of dollars," Onslow persisted. "But isn't it true that scientists have been refuting that claim for years?"

"Yeah, right," Ricardo scoffed. "The same scientists who said that comets couldn't be ejected by Jupiter, let alone a planet-size body. Then look what happened ten months ago. And they're *still* saying it!"

"Not quite. They're saying there's no proof that it happened before," someone pointed out.

"Then they're still in as much a state of denial as they have been for years. That's all you can say," Keene answered.

What the Kronians had been trying to get accepted since before Athena's appearance was that around the middle of the second millennium B.C., Earth experienced a close encounter with a giant comet. Its axis was shifted and its orbit changed, causing seas to empty and flow over continents, the crust to buckle into mountains, and opening rifts that spilled lavas as much as a mile deep across vast areas of the surface. Climates changed abruptly, bringing ice down upon grasslands and turning forests into desert; civilizations collapsed; animals perished in millions; entire species were exterminated. These, the Kronians maintained, were the events glimpsed by the Hebrew scriptures in their descriptions of the "plagues" inflicted on Egypt, along with the events recorded subsequently.

The "blood" that turned the lands and the rivers red, followed by rains of ash and burning rock and fire, were consistent with the proposition of Earth moving into the comet's tail to be assailed by iron-bearing dust, then torrents of gravel and meteorites, and finally infusions of hydrocarbon gases that would ignite in an oxygen-laden atmosphere. Then came the enveloping darkness as the smoke and dust from a burning world blanketed out the sun. The same succession of events was described not only in writings from across the entire Middle East, but in legends handed down by the peoples of Iceland, Greenland, and India; from the islands of Polynesia to the steppes of Siberia; and places as far apart as Japan and Mexico, China and Peru. The accounts of shrieking hurricanes scouring the Earth and tides piling into mountains read the same in the Persian *Avesta*, the Indian *Vedas*, and the Mayan *Troano* as in *Exodus*, and were similarly narrated by the Maori, the Indonesian, the Laplander, and the Choctaw. And finally, the titanic electrical discharges between the comet's head and parts of its deformed, writhing tail became clashes of celestial deities depicted virtually identically whether as the Biblical Lord battling Rahab, Zeus and Typhon of the Greeks, Isis and Seth of the Egyptians, the Babylonian Marduk and Tiamat, or the Hindu Shiva or Vishnu putting down the serpent.

"I don't think you're being fair," Onslow objected. "A lot of scientists now agree that something extraordinary occurred around that time. A close flyby by a large comet is proposed in a number of models. But Venus is much bigger than any comet."

"Any comet seen in recent times, anyway," Joe said.

"It's a lot like Athena could look three and a half thousand years from now if it lost its tail," Lomack suggested.

The mood of the room pivoted on an edge. The three just back from space were heroes for the day, and the journalists' professional instincts were not to put them down. Onslow was still frowning but seemed disinclined to press his negative sentiments further. On the other hand, they had been heavily influenced by the official line heard over the years. Keene sensed a chance to bring them closer and perhaps win one or two of them around if the case could be put persuasively. He studied his clasped hands for a moment and looked up.

"You're all media people. How do you refer to that thing out there in the sky that's not the same as anything we've seen before? One of the most frequent descriptions I've seen over the past few months is 'giant comet.' Well, people in ancient times were no different, except they thought of celestial objects as gods. In the languages of race after race and culture after culture, the names of the gods they associated with these events turn out to be not only interchangeable with or identical to their word for 'comet,' but also the name that they applied to Venus." Keene looked around. The room was noticeably stiller, eyes fixed on him.

"I hadn't realized that," a new voice said. "This is interesting." Onslow busied himself noting something in his pad and didn't comment.

Keene answered, "It is, isn't it. And I'll tell you something more that's interesting. Old astronomic tables from places as far apart as Egypt, Sumeria, India, China, Mexico—and the accuracy of some of those tables wasn't equaled until the nineteenth century—all show *four* visible planets, not five. And in each case, the missing planet is Venus." He waited a few seconds for that to sink in. Here and there, heads were turning to glance at each other. He concluded, "They all added Venus at about the same time. They all showed it appearing as a comet. And they all described it losing its tail to evolve into a planet. So come on, guys. How much more do you want?"

Afterward, they all agreed that it had gone well. In the chat session that followed over refreshments, most of the questions conveyed genuine curiosity and interest to learn more. Keene felt more than satisfied with the way things had gone, and Harry Halloran was looking pleased. As the session was breaking up, Les Urkin returned from taking a call outside and drew Keene to one side.

"You're still going up to D.C. tomorrow night, Lan, is that right?"

"I switched to an earlier flight," Keene replied. "I'm meeting someone for dinner."

"Good. The Kronians are having an informal reception at their suite in the Engleton on Monday evening. Gallian heard you'd be in town, and he wants you to know you're invited. Want me to confirm? Or I can give you their number."

"Sure, I'll be there," Keene said. "Let me call them, Les. I get a kick out of talking to them without any turnaround delay now. So now we get to meet them finally, eh?"

Things were looking better and better.

❂ 8 ❂

The next day, Sunday, Keene arrived at Washington's Reagan National Airport around mid-afternoon, and caught a cab to a Sheraton hotel that he often used when in the area, overlooking the Potomac outside the city on the far side of Georgetown. After checking in, he called Cavan to confirm that everything was on schedule. That gave him a couple of hours to shower, change, and catch up on some of his backlogged work via the room terminal before Cavan was due to arrive.

Leo Cavan worked as an "investigator" in what was effectively an internal affairs department of a bureaucratic monstrosity called the Scientific and Industrial Coordination Agency, or SICA, charged with planning and overseeing the implementation of a national scientific research policy. Keene had gotten to know him when Keene was at General Atomic. Cavan had started out in the Air Force hoping for a life of travel and excitement, and ended up instead preparing quality control reports and cost analyses in an accounting office. When he put in for a transfer to Space Command to get a chance to go into orbit before he was too old, he was drafted to Washington to review regulations and procedures instead. He had never fit the role well in Keene's experience, being too technically knowledgeable to project the ineptness normally expected from officialdom, and too ready to overlook transgressions of no consequence when his judgment so directed. The result was that the two of them had gotten along splendidly and remained friends after Keene's exasperation with the politics of government-directed science returned him to the world of engineering to develop nuclear drives for Amspace.

Cavan had taken to him, Keene suspected, somewhat in the manner of a father figure seeking to live through a surrogate son the life he would have wished himself. He led a strange kind of double existence. Outwardly a diligent creature of the system, he apparently found a pernicious satisfaction in subverting that same system by leaking inside knowledge that might help its opponents and compensate its victims. It seemed to be his private way of getting even with the forces that throughout his own life had deceived and then entrapped him. He also had one of the oddest senses of humor that Keene had ever encountered.

The restaurant was at the rear of the hotel, looking out over lawns sloping down to the tree-shaded riverbank. Keene had found a window table and was sipping a Bushmills while watching a flotilla of ducks on inshore maneuvers, when Cavan appeared through the entrance from the lobby. He spotted Keene and came over. Keene stood to shake hands, and they sat down. A waiter came to the table to inquire if Cavan would like a drink, and Cavan settled for a glass of the house Chablis. "I assume you wouldn't risk your reputation by fobbing us off with a bad one," he told the waiter. "Or have the accountants taken over writing the wine lists these days, like everything else?"

Cavan couldn't have been far away from retirement. Everything about him suggested having been fashioned for economy, as if over the years the idealizations of his profession had infused themselves and ultimately found physical expression in his being in the way that was supposed to be true of owners and dogs. He had thinning hair and a sparse frame, on which his plain, gray suit hung loosely, a thin nose and sharp chin formed from budgeted materials, and a bony, birdlike face that achieved its covering with a minimal outlay of skin.

Even his tie was knotted with a tightness and precision that seemed to abhor extravagance of any kind. But the pale steely eyes gave the game away, alive and alert, all the time scanning for new mischief to wreak upon the world. Of his private life Keene knew practically nothing. He lived somewhere in the city with a Polish girlfriend called Alicia whom he described as crazy without ever having said why, although sounding as if they had been together for years.

Cavan had followed Friday's event, of course, and added his own congratulations. He pressed for details that hadn't appeared in the news coverage, enjoying immensely Keene's descriptions of the spaceplane's robotlike commander and the splutterings of the Air Force brass, and expressing approval that the media reactions were not all hostile. The wine arrived and was pronounced acceptable. For the dinner order, Keene had worked up enough appetite after traveling to try the prime rib and a half carafe of Sauvignon to go with it. Cavan settled for Dover sole. "And I see they've been keeping you busy since," Cavan resumed when the waiter had left. "I saw that clip that Feld did with you while you were still up on the satellite, and then the press coverage of all of you together yesterday. You came over well there, Landen. That should give a lot of people something to think about."

"I got the feeling that for once we were getting through," Keene said. "You can say the same thing to reporters for months, spell out all the facts, and nothing will prise them away from the official line they've been given. But this time we got them listening." Cavan nodded, but without seeming as gratified as Keene would have expected. Keene could only conclude that what Cavan had wanted to talk about offset the good news.

"And are you still finding time in all this for the ladyfriend?" Cavan inquired, evidently choosing not to go into it just at that moment. His eyes were twinkling.

"You mean Vicki?"

"Of course."

Keene sighed. "Leo, you know very well we're just business partners. And sure, over the years we've become good friends as well. Why do you keep trying to make something more out of it?"

"Well, it's none of my business, I suppose, but a fellow at your stage of life could do worse than consider stabilizing things a little." Cavan sipped his wine. "She has the young son, and does ad work, yes?" Probably through habit, Cavan always sought confirmations and cross-references of information, Keene had noticed. In another life Keene could picture him as a tax auditor.

Keene nodded. "But I've got too much going on right now. In any case, I need my own space."

Cavan indicated the upward direction with a motion of his head. "You mean there isn't enough for you out there?" He studied Keene for a few seconds, swirling his glass. "Are you sure you're not keeping your options open until you see how the land lies with that other lady you've had hovering on the fringes of your life for a while?" Keene frowned at him, perplexed. "The one who'd be a natural for the lead in a Queen-of-Sheba movie," Cavan hinted.

Keene stared. "My God! Are you talking about Sariena?"

"I am, of course. Why act surprised?"

"What on earth makes you think that?"

"Excitement. Something different. The allure of the alien and unknown." Cavan's talonlike hands broke apart a bread roll and commenced buttering one of the pieces. "A perfectly understandable reaction, Landen—especially for somebody of your adventurous disposition. I mean, you've been in communication since before the *Osiris* left Saturn." He paused, glanced up as if to be sure Keene was listening, and then went on, making his voice casual. "I could see your point, after all. She really is stunning. Everyone I talked to thought so when we were with the Kronians last night."

"*What?*" It hit Keene only then that this was Cavan's strange way of leading around to the subject he had wanted to discuss. And it had worked. Keene couldn't deny that his first reaction was a twinge of resentment. "You've met her already?"

The meals arrived then, and Keene was able to let his surprise abate while plates and dishes were positioned, covers removed, and the glasses refilled. Having had his fun, Cavan became more serious. "I was at another dinner on Friday: the official White House reception for the Kronians—to be introduced to my 'marks,' for want of a better word." He eyed Keene suggestively for a moment, as if inviting a response. Keene waited. Cavan explained, "The department has come up with a new angle on what an investigator does. Now, it appears, I'm supposed to cultivate the confidence of our guests of state, the purpose being to spy on them. It's getting to be a tacky world that we live in, isn't it, Landen?"

Unable to make anything of this so far, Keene merely motioned for him to continue.

"I'm one of several persons who have been assigned positions as official host representatives—tour guides, if you will—who will have constant contact with the Kronians. Our brief is to get close to them in order to get as much advance information as we can to help our own negotiators shoot them down." Keene's hand stopped with his fork halfway to his mouth. Cavan nodded somberly. "It's a nonstarter, Landen. A policy ruling has already been made that Earth isn't buying the Kronian line. Our side's only interest is to discredit the whole business and get it out of the public limelight as quickly as possible." For the moment, Keene was too stunned to do more than stare. He looked down at his plate and found that suddenly he didn't feel so hungry anymore. Cavan added after a few seconds, "Sorry if I've spoiled your dinner. The tab's on me, if that helps."

There was a silence. Finally, Keene said, "What's going on, Leo? Are they all blind or something?"

"It's not so much a case of being blind as of not wanting to see," Cavan replied over his soup. "You know the way things work in this business. The academic establishment sees the Kronians as invaders of its turf and a huge potential threat to traditional funding—which has been thinned down in recent years in any case. Government science sold out long ago to become an instrument for justifying government policy, and nobody on the Hill wants to talk about the expense. For the private sector the investment would be colossal, and the return on it just isn't there. That's why the space program was shifted to a lower gear in the first place."

Keene shook his head disbelievingly. "One day, none of that's going to matter. This is something we can't afford *not* to do. I mean, we're not talking about selling laundry detergent here, Leo. Maybe we have to learn something from the Kronians. The know-how and the ability is there, and it's something that *needs* to be done. So you forget all the shopkeeper economics, and you just *do* it."

"Logical enough, and eminently sensible," Cavan agreed. "But the powers who run things here can't think like that."

It didn't need to be spelled out further. Keene stared at his glass and sighed. "So what's the line going to be? The one we've been hearing for a while: The whole Kronian venture was ill-conceived from the start; imagining that a society could function viably at that kind of distance was ridiculous all along . . . ?"

Cavan was already nodding. "And now they're waking up to reality and finding themselves overextended," he completed. "This story about supercomets and the end of the world is a concoction dreamed up to exploit the Athena event and milk support from Earth's governments. That's our line. And naturally the establishment's scientific big guns will have their act coordinated to back it. We wouldn't want to let down the people who ladle out the honors and write the checks, after all, now, would we?" Cavan spooned the last of his soup into his mouth—thin and straight, sparing on the lips—and watched, seemingly until Keene was just recovering sufficiently to tackle his food again. Then he added, "One of the big guns they'll be wheeling up is a certain professor of astron-omy and faculty head at Yale, recently nominated for the presidency of the International Astronomical Union. I wouldn't imagine he needs any introduction."

"You don't mean Voler?"

"I do, of course."

Keene's fork dropped slowly back to his plate. For Herbert Voler was the paragon of perfection that his own former wife, Fey, had fled to and later married when Keene confounded her social ambitions by abandoning the prospect of scholastic accolades to return to the grubby world of engineering.

"I'm not quite sure how that might be relevant at this stage," Cavan confessed. "But conceivably the situation could take a turn whereby the social connection offers possibilities unavailable in the purely formal context. In any case, it was an option that would apply to nobody else, so my first thought was to approach you."

Keene made an inviting motion with his free hand. "Approach me for what, Leo? You still haven't told me what this is all about."

"Let me first give you an idea of how they intend playing it," Cavan suggested. "Then it will be clearer. The softening-up program to condition the public has already been going on for a while. Did you see your friend Voler on TV yesterday?"

"No, I have been kind of busy, as you pointed out. What was this?"

"He gave a talk at Columbia, ridiculing the claims about all those ancient records. . . . But it was planned months ago to coincide with the Kronians' arrival." Cavan produced a compad from his jacket pocket. "Let's watch him." He activated the unit, fiddled with commands to retrieve a stored playback from the net, then turned it the right way around for Keene to see and passed it across. Keene's features remained neutral as he gazed at the familiar figure.

Voler was fortyish, maybe—on the young side for the titles and credentials that he was able to brandish. He had a full head of black hair styled collar-length like a media celebrity, and a tanned complexion which with his pugnacious jaw emphasized a strong set of white teeth that his mobile features put to good effect, constantly splitting into broad smiles and grimaces. To Keene, he had always come across as a little too smooth and slick for a figurehead of academic excellence—but then, perhaps such qualities helped the political image equally necessary to attaining the rarified heights. Keene could have seen him as a pushy prosecution counsel, maybe, or a hustler on Wall Street. Behind him on the screen was a chart carrying names of planets and ancient deities, presumably referred to earlier. Keene turned the volume up just enough to avoid being an annoyance to nearby tables.

" . . . four ways in which the same legend could come to be found among widely separated cultures. One, Common Observation: all of the cultures witnessed a common event and interpreted it in a similar way. Two, Diffusion: the legend originated in one place but traveled to others with the wanderings of humankind. Three, Commonality of Psychology: Humans everywhere are so alike that their brains create similar legends reflecting common hopes and fears. And Four,

Coincidence." Voler paused, grasping the podium, and surveyed his audience. "I think everyone would agree with me that we can reasonably discard the last. And we simply don't know enough to propose number three, Common Psychology, with any confidence—although in my view it seems unlikely." Due court having been paid to reasonableness and modesty, the focus narrowed to the brass tacks. Voler's confident smile broadened, stopping just short of open derisiveness. "The Kronians, of course, are saying that we are therefore forced to accept the Common Observation hypothesis, as if it were the only alternative. But in this they are surely dismissing far too casually—one hopes in their impetuousness—the second possibility, namely that as various peoples dispersed across the globe, they took their myths and legends with them, just as they did their languages, their religions, and their technical skills. . . ."

"You can see what the game plan is," Cavan broke in from across the table. "The Kronians will be projected into roles of sincere but misguided children. After a few days of recuperation from the voyage, they'll be taken on a whistle-stop tour of some selected spots around Earth. None of them can remember much of Earth, and some were never here at all. So we'll see pictures of them gaping at the Grand Canyon and the Amazon, or gawking like tourists in London and Paris, with chaperones like myself pointing out this and explaining that. Earth will have been magnanimous; Earth will have been accommodating. But you see what it will do for their image. They arrive here naive, and we have to acquaint them with reality. The same image will carry over to what the world will perceive as the science, and their case won't have a prayer."

By now, Voler was expounding on details of various human migrations. Keene had heard enough and snapped the unit off. "And what about the evidence written all over the surface of this planet?" he demanded. "None of that counts?" He meant the anomalies in the geological, fossil, and climatic records—all independent of anything that any humans of long ago had to say. There were such things as marks of sudden sea level changes, in some cases measuring hundreds of feet, found the world over; agricultural terraces close to sea level when they were cultivated, now disappearing under the snow line eighteen thousand feet up in the Andes; the remains of millions of animals and trees, torn to pieces and broken, found piled in caves and rock fissures from Europe to China and across the Arctic, in some places forming practically the entirety of islands off northern Siberia; huge herds of mammoths, buffalo, horse, camel, hippopotamus, and other beasts wiped out abruptly a thousand miles or more from any vegetation growing today that could support them. And all in the middle of that same mysterious millennium that the writings of old had chronicled. Was all that to be ignored?

"They'll stay away from all that if they can," Cavan said. "The Kronians make some good points, and many scientists outside the political-academic orthodoxy are siding with them. Nobody argues much anymore that terrestrial catastrophes have happened. Where they'll try and draw the line is with *planetary* catastrophes—that Venus could have been an earlier Athena. If that's allowed, then the whole foundation of the economic power structure as we know it would have to change, which in effect is what the Kronians are saying. But of course that would be unacceptable. So the line will be to discredit the Kronian arguments by any means until Athena has disappeared out of the Solar System and been forgotten—apart from as an anomaly that will generate Ph.D. theses for years—and then we'll all be able to get back to the safe, comfortable lives that we know."

Finally, Cavan took back the compad. He went on, "The reason I wanted to talk to you before you meet them tomorrow, Landen, is that the Kronians need to be made aware of this. But I can hardly bring it up in my position. You, on the other hand, are not saddled with having to wear an official hat. And being in touch with the Kronians already . . ." He left the obvious unsaid.

"Sure, I'll handle it," Keene agreed. There really wasn't anything to have to think about. He picked up his knife but sat toying with it.

"I was sure you would," Cavan said. He paused and refilled Keene's glass. "Oh, do stop staring and try some dinner, Landen. You've come all the way from Texas for it, and it looks so delicious."

For a desk and a base to work from in the Washington area, Keene rented space at an agency called Information and Office Services. Shirley, who ran the facility and acted for him when he was away, had arranged several Monday appointments from the calls that had begun coming in on Friday. The first was not until 10:00, and Keene spent the first part of the morning returning other calls that Shirley had listed. One was to a David Salio, who described himself as a planetary scientist at the Aerospace Sciences Institute in Houston, which Keene had visited on occasion. The Kronians had been getting attention in the Web news groups and independent media of many like Salio who were not among the circle of academic and government scientists fearful of money being diverted into the space corporations. Salio had favored the young-planet theory of Venus for some time and possesed a sizable collection of facts and data supporting it from modern-day space and scientific researches, independent of what ancient writings said. Athena was a clear warning that action had to be taken along the lines that the Kronians were calling for, and he wanted to know what he could do to help. Keene was immediately interested to hear more and suggested stopping by on his way back to Corpus Christi, which would be via Houston in any case. He would let Salio know when he had a firm return date.

Next was somebody called Barney from one of the Washington-based news services, who had tracked Keene down through his connection with Amspace. "What, you're in Washington now!" he exclaimed when Keene called. "Hey, never mind taping an interview over the phone. We'll send a couple of guys over to the hotel. It works for a better atmosphere. How would four o'clock suit? It'll still be going out by this evening. Don't worry, we do it all the time. No problem."

Keene checked with his schedule and agreed. A couple of other concerns were happy to tape from the hotel, and a science magazine with a local office arranged to send a feature writer over that evening, after the TV taping. Keene spent some time confirming and fixing more appointments for the next two days that he would be in town, then left for his first meeting that day, which was with one of the senators for Texas in an office in the Senate Building.

In a TV interview over the weekend, the senator had told the reporter of the need to bring companies like Amspace to heel and enforce a greater compliance with "social responsibility." He explained to Keene that he had to talk that way in order to preserve an acceptable public image. "But I want the people at Amspace to know that they can count on me to be realistic too." Which could be taken as a warning or a wink and a nod, but either way translated into: "Keep the contributions coming and pray." Keene tried to broach issues that went beyond appeasing activist groups while at the same time keeping the corporations sweet, but made little impression. The senator lived in his own world.

Lunch was with a documentary producer called Charles McLaren, whom Keene had known amiably for about two years. McLaren wondered if Friday's event might resurrect the general nuclear-antinuclear controversy for a while and was thinking of putting together a fast tie-in for the public-affairs channels and newsnets. Would Keene be willing to act as a consultant again on short-call if they went ahead? Sure, Keene agreed. McLaren put accuracy before sensationalism and was meticulous in trying to get his facts right; Keene knew he could be sure of getting fair representation. But it was with weary assent. The discussion was pitched at helping a good technician do a job relating to a topic that was expected to be transient. There was no suggestion of a documentary to tell the world that it had come close to seeing the end of its civilization.

By early afternoon, he was in the cocktail lounge of a hotel off Pennsylvania Avenue to meet one of the technical aides to President Hayer. He wanted Keene to convey unofficially back to the management of Amspace, and through them to other allied interests, that as a sop to domestic outcries and world opinion it might be necessary to pass a bill banning the launching of nuclear devices from U.S. territory by private corporations. But the message was to keep up the development effort because provision could be engineered for a repeal in circumstances deemed vital to national security—but not until after the presidential election next year. In fact, the defense agencies were stressing the Chinese threat and could probably be induced to channel in some discreet funding to compensate for the shorter-term inconveniences. The aide paused to assess Keene's reaction, then asked, lowering his voice to impart a note of confidentiality, "Out of curiosity, what would be the chances of matching the kind of propulsion the Kronians have, say within five years—given a suitable financial incentive? The Air Force already has an eye on extending its activities to trans-lunar distances. I can tell you that they for one are particularly interested."

"Give me the top ten names in contained plasma dynamics, superconducting cryogenics, spontaneous vortex computational theory, and nuclear transition phases, get rid of all the political obstructionism, and you can have it in three," was Keene's answer.

The aide looked intrigued. "Really? And you know who these people are?"

"Sure I do. It's my field."

"Just suppose, for argument's sake, that we decided to try and get them to come over to work for us here, in the States. What do you think it would take? Is it something you might be able to help us organize?" The aide paused as if pondering a point of some delicacy. "I'm sure we could see fit to being . . . extremely generous."

"I'm not sure it's something that we have options on anymore," Keene replied. "They all moved to Saturn."

※   ※   ※

Keene grabbed a half hour to stop by at the agency and check on things with Shirley, then returned to the Sheraton to freshen up and change before the Kronian reception at seven. By that time he had consolidated his thoughts sufficiently to call Marvin Curtiss, Amspace's president and CEO, to update him on the situation that Cavan had described the evening before, and Keene's further impressions after his day in Washington. It was all pretty much in line with what Curtiss had been finding out independently.

"It doesn't look as if we're going to be able to count on much support from the main contractors," he told Keene from the hotel room's terminal screen. "They're taking the line that it isn't the business of corporations to decide what's scientifically true or not. That's what we've got universities and national laboratories for." He didn't have to add that it also meant they could look forward to a continuation of low-risk contracts that referees from those same universities and laboratories would feel comfortable with and approve, and which wouldn't frighten investors.

"I don't know, Marvin," Keene sighed, tired after a long day. "How do you deal with it?"

"Just keep saying what we've always said: that we believe the claims the Kronians are making deserve serious consideration, and everyone should forget their vested interests and try to be open-minded to what appear to be the facts." That was what Keene had expected. If Curtiss weren't a fighter, he would hardly have been running an operation like Amspace to begin with. Curtiss went on, "One thing we might try is getting Les working on organizing more voice and visibility for the scientists out there who have been taking a more independent stand—like this character Salio that you talked to. We need people like him."

"I've arranged to meet him on my way back," Keene said.

"Good. Find out what his story is and who else he talks to. Maybe we don't have to let the establishment have a monopoly on the media."

"What about the political side?" Keene asked. "How much do you trust this talk about a defense loophole and Air Force money coming through the back door if that bill goes through?" That news hadn't come as a total surprise to Curtiss, who had apparently heard something similar from another source.

"If it happens, then fine, but I've always believed in insurance," Curtiss answered. "I've been talking to the people here about bringing forward the schedule for getting Montemorelos operational." He meant the backup launch and landing facility being constructed in the highlands not far south of the border—outside U.S. jurisdiction. "Not marginally, but making it our top priority."

"That makes sense," Keene agreed. "But it might only tide us over for a while. The Mexicans are still vulnerable to pressure from our side."

Curtiss nodded. "I know. Beyond that, we're reviewing the options we've negotiated on possible sites farther from home."

"I think there's some for lease at the original Tapapeque complex in Guatemala," Keene said.

"There is?"

"So I heard around a month or two ago."

"We'll look into it." There was a blur in the foreground on the screen as Curtiss checked his watch. "I'm due for another appointment, Lan. It should be interesting meeting the Kronians tonight. Call me tomorrow and let me know how it went."

"I will," Keene said. "Take care, Marvin."

Keene still had some time before the TV reporters were due. Out of curiosity, he scanned the news searcher for items relating to the Kronians and selected one of the current leaders, which turned out to be an NBC panel hookup to debate whether ancient sources constituted a valid basis for formulating scientific beliefs.

"Absolutely not!" was the opinion of a speaker, captioned as Dr. William Ledden, an astronomer at the University of California. "Repeatable observations and measurements determine what is properly termed science. What writers of old manuscripts say happened, or think happened, or think ought to have happened simply has no place . . ." He waved a hand agitatedly, as if too exasperated to be capable of further coherent thought.

A gray-haired woman, president of an archaeological society in Vancouver, agreed. "It has taken centuries to establish reliable methods and standards for disentangling fact from fancy. I agree with Dr. Ledden. This kind of thing will probably sell some Sunday supplements, and we're going to be hearing a lot about it in the news, but it has no place in science."

"So you're saying we should be good hosts and neighbors, but not get carried away by this," the moderator checked sagely.

"Exactly."

That line seemed to be the consensus of the others. The converse view—rather timidly put, Keene thought—came from a historian and author somewhere in England. "I hesitate to cast the dissenting vote here, but is it unthinkable that peoples of ancient times might have described events that they actually witnessed, and maybe have something important to tell us?"

"It's scandalous that we should even be discussing this!" Ledden fumed. "Why are people who call themselves scientists concerning themselves with Biblical quotations? Are we going to be talking about walking on water and dead bodies coming back to life next? The Kronian phenomenon grew from a quasi-religious cult. This whole business is an attempt to give credibility to scriptures by means of concocted pseudoscience. Very possibly there's fundamentalist money behind it. They've got to be supporting themselves out there somehow."

Keene grew more perplexed as he listened. The Kronians had never made any appeal to scriptural beliefs. They used Biblical references purely as accounts of historical events, and then only where corroborated by other sources. The Englishman tried to make that point but was ineffective.

Barney's TV crew showed up on time, but the interview, conducted on the grassy riverbank at the back of the hotel, was aimed too much at trying to provoke Keene into admissions of the dangers of nuclear devices in space. The journalist who arrived afterward had a more balanced approach, but they got deeper into technicalities than Keene had anticipated and ran out of time, arranging to continue over breakfast the next morning. Finally, Keene boarded the cab that had arrived to take him to the Engleton.

"So how was your day?" the cabbie asked over his shoulder as they pulled out from under the lobby canopy.

"Never a dull moment," Keene told him with feeling. "How about you?"

"Aw, not so bad. You know how it is. Just a couple of years more of this to bring a bit more money in, and then it's retirement. Just me and the wife now. We figure we'll move to Colorado. Got some grandkids there. Mountains, scenery. Nice place to take it easy."

"Sounds great," Keene said from the back seat. Sometimes he had to remind himself that most people—probably the vast majority on the planet—didn't think too much about Athena, or care—one way or the other.

❂ 10 ❂

The Kronian mission, along with the security and administrative staff attending them, were on the top two floors of the Engleton, which had restricted access from the general part of the hotel and was one of the regular accommodations for official visitors to the city. In all, there were twelve delegates and eight crew members, the numbers having been kept low to leave capacity for the *Osiris* to carry emigrants back on the return trip. Some of the crew, however, had been left to maintain a skeleton presence on the ship and would get their chance to come down to the surface later.

On arriving, Keene went straight up to the eighth floor as he had been directed and checked with the security people in room 809. A personable young man in a dark suit verified that he was expected and escorted him to one of the larger suites on the floor above, where two more security men in suits admitted them through the doors. From the hubbub of voices, the party was evidently already in progress. Keene recognized the white-haired figure of Gallian, the leader of the Kronian delegation, seated a short distance inside, talking to an Oriental couple who looked as if they had also just arrived—apparently he was greeting everyone personally. Gallian spotted Keene and waved him over, introducing the couple as a Japanese space-technology administrator and his wife. He apologized for the unusual way of receiving guests. "It's the gravity, of course—and then two days of functions and presentations on top of it. Your people are working us hard already. But anyway, why am I making excuses? At my age one doesn't need any excuses." Keene grinned, told Gallian that he didn't know how many times this had been said already but " . . . welcome to Earth," and shook hands heartily. The Japanese couple exchanged pleasantries and were then ushered on to meet others in the room by another Kronian, who Gallian said was Thorel, from the *Osiris*'s regular crew, and who must have stood at around seven feet.

Gallian turned back to regard Keene. He had a crusty, puckish-nosed face with eyes that were clear and mischievous. From their few long-delay message exchanges, Keene had formed an impression of bustling energy and a person who could never be content doing one thing at a time. Already, everything he saw was starting to confirm it. "Well, Lan, hello," Gallian said. "So here we are. You see, we made it. And so did you. Les Urkin obviously got the message through. I'm glad."

"I heard they're taking you off on a tour," Keene said.

"Yes, New York City to start with, then Niagara Falls . . ." Gallian waved a hand. "I'm not sure where after that."

"When will this start?"

"Well, it was supposed to be first thing tomorrow . . ."

"So soon? You're kidding."

" . . . but that may have to be postponed."

"Oh?"

"Allergic reactions," Gallian said.

"Yes, of course. I'd forgotten about that." It was a known risk for Kronian-born making a first-time visit to Earth. Keene shrugged sympathetically. "There's nothing anyone can do?"

"Not much, apparently. Immigrants like me don't have a problem. We prepared the first-timers with the recommended drugs, but several of them are affected all the same. Two are in bed, knocked off their feet. We'll know in the morning what the situation is."

There was a tap on the doors; one of the security men opened them, and two men and a woman were shown in. Gallian extended an arm. "Anyway, I must press on with my hostly duties. Go on in and meet the others. Sariena's around somewhere. We're informal tonight. There's a buffet in the suite. All of us agree, by the way, that whatever its other problems, Earth food is exquisite. And I'm finding that I'm particularly partial to wines. Vineyards are a luxury that we haven't graced Kronia with yet. Our synthetic efforts really don't compare. I'll definitely try to get that changed when we return." Gallian caught the attention of another Kronian, brown skinned and distinguishable by her tall build and casual, brightly colored trouser suit—distinctly not customary Washington dinner wear. "Polli, this is Landen Keene, an old friend of ours. Look after him and introduce him around, would you?" He looked back at Keene as the three arrivals approached. "I'll seek you out and pin you down with more serious questions to spoil the party with later, I promise."

The buffet was set up in the center of the suite, dispensed by hotel staff—a salad bar selection, cold cuts and cheeses, several hot dishes, dessert trolley, and a beverage bar. There were between one and two dozen people so far, Keene estimated, although the far end of the suite had an L-bend so there could have been more out of sight. Sariena was with a group on the far side by the windows, perched on an arm of a couch. And on the far side of the bar, to Keene's mild surprise—although it shouldn't have been, given the kind of job he had described—talking with two men, was Leo Cavan.

Polli was also an *Osiris* crew member, she told Keene as he selected a plate of cold assortments and took a glass of wine from the bar. Four of the ship's eight-person complement had come down with the delegation. The four who had stayed aboard included the captain, whose name was Idorf. Polli was astonished and delighted to learn that Keene was one of the three who had been in the news the previous Friday, and called Thorel over as he passed near after depositing some used plates on a side table. "You know who we have here, Thorel? Landen is one of the Terrans that we saw, who raced with the spaceplane the day we arrived."

Thorel was perhaps thirtyish, curly-headed, sallow-faced yet hefty, with an open and amiable manner. His field area was engineering too, and for several minutes he and Keene talked technicalities about the NIFTV and its performance. "So how is it you have all this trouble trying to convince your governments of things that should be obvious?" he asked in conclusion. "It seems such a waste of energies. And here you need all the energy you can get, just for standing up."

Keene had noticed that nearly all the Kronians around the room were sitting. "Is that how you're finding it?" he asked Polli.

"Also, it is bewildering," she told him. "Already I have seen more human beings than in all the rest of my life put together. And I still get attacks of . . . What is it when you fear going outside?"

"Agoraphobia?"

"Yes, that is right. We trained for the gravity, but it doesn't really prepare you for it. But the brilliance of the daylight is the most astounding. Nothing on screens can come close. But then, at night you have hardly any stars."

Thorel went to collect some more arrivals from Gallian, and Polli took Keene around to meet more of the guests. Besides other Americans, he was introduced to more Japanese, two Russians, and one each German, Chinese, Brazilian, and Australian. Sariena saw him from across the room and acknowledged with a wave. While still tall by Earth standards, she was smaller than average for the Kronian group. Keene remembered her as saying that she had gone to Saturn as a child, with most of her rapid-growth and developmental years completed. The younger ones, born to the environments of Saturn's moons or the low-*g* orbiting habitats, were uniformly one to two feet taller.

The word went around that one of the space crew from "that thing last Friday" was present, "The one who was on the news this evening—didn't you see it? That's him over there," and Keene found himself much in demand.

"Do you really think it has a future—foreseeably, in the practical sense?" one of the Americans asked dubiously. He was a director of Chase Manhattan, it turned out. "Where's the payoff? What can you bring from out there that we don't have already, and cheaper?"

"It iss interesting zat your ship can connect viss der UN shuttle zat brings you down," Keene overheard the German saying to one of the Kronians, who had a blotchy face and was sneezing intermittently.

"Do you build to der same mechanical mating specifications zat you exchange maybe, ja?"

Everything inside Keene wanted to lean in and murmur, *Ve haff vayss of making it dock*. But he behaved himself, bit his tongue, and refrained.

Gallian appeared again and sought him out, accompanied by a man called Druche from an office of the Defense Department that dealt with space matters, whom Keene had met before on one or two occasions. "This is the man you should have building spaceships for you," Gallian told him. "Landen understands how long-range systems have to work. Lan, you would appreciate a real spaceship. Before we go back to Saturn, we must show you the *Osiris*."

Keene blinked at him, surprised. "Are you serious?"

"I don't play jokes on my friends. We'll sort out something for you, don't worry. Make sure you talk to me later about it," Gallian told him.

Gallian and Druche moved on, and Keene was promptly buttonholed by three more Japanese who seemed to be together. "Who are the other companies partnering Amspace?" the one who appeared to be the senior asked when they had been talking for a few minutes. "We could be interested in discussing further funding. How can we get in touch with the correct people?"

Keene mentioned Marvin Curtiss and offered to arrange an introduction. The Japanese seemed pleased. As Keene detached himself, Cavan drifted by, nursing a glass. "Just doing my job, you see," he murmured. " 'Pump them when they don't suspect it,' is what I was told. A tacky world we live in, Landen. Tacky world." And then he was gone again.

Before anyone else could pounce on him, Keene made his way over to Sariena. They had managed to exchange barely a few words so far. She was sitting on the arm of one of the couches, still managing to do justice to the unpretentious but stylish dress that she was wearing—black and sleeveless, with a high, oriental-style neck and just the right touch of trim—but closer he could see that weariness was beginning to show. A slim woman in a light green dress, with graying hair tied high, was standing talking to her. Keene remembered her being introduced earlier as with the Smithsonian but couldn't recall her name. Sariena smiled as he approached.

"Lan, do join us. Have you two met yet?"

"Oh, we all know who he is," the woman said.

Keene smiled uneasily for a moment. "Smithsonian," he managed.

"Catherine Zetl," the woman said, getting him off the hook. "I'm the historian."

"Oh, right."

"Ancient—the history, not me. Well, I hope not too much, anyway."

"Catherine has been telling me some fascinating things," Sariena said. "She's just back from Arabia—involved with the Joktanian discoveries there."

Keene searched his memory. There had been a stir in the news a couple of years back, and occasional mentions since in the scientific literature. "Some civilization they found from way back, isn't it? Caused some surprises for the specialists." Which about exhausted his knowledge of the subject.

"That's putting it mildly," Zetl said. "It's turned all our ideas upside down. The Sumerians and Babylonians were supposed to have been the earliest to settle and build, but these people date from much earlier. Yet some of their architecture and workmanship appears more sophisticated. And there's no obvious relationship to the cultures that came later. It's as if they represent some lost age that flourished long before it should have been possible. For some reason it ended abruptly, and then what we've always thought was the beginning of civilization was a second start that came much later."

"Isn't it fascinating, Lan?" Sariena said again.

"So do we know what ended it?" Keene asked, getting more interested. "Was it your Kronian supercomet again?"

"Oh, I'm impressed by the Kronians' arguments, but I refuse to be dragged into any of that tonight," Zetl said, holding up a hand. "In any case, it couldn't have been the comet, Venus, or whatever. This race existed long before the Egyptian Middle Kingdom and the

Exodus. And I use the word 'race' deliberately. They were large—comparable to the Kronians around here."

"The name Joktanian comes from Noah's grandson," Sariena informed Keene. "I didn't know that."

"That's who the ancient Arabic legends say the first people of the southwest peninsula were descended from," Zetl said, nodding. "Their word is Qahtan." She glanced away. "Oh, there's somebody about to leave that I must catch. Excuse me." She laid a hand briefly on Sariena's arm. "Sariena, we do have to talk more about all this. Do call me when they give you a moment—if they ever do."

"I certainly will."

Zetl excused herself again and hurried away.

Sariena looked at Keene, sighed, and rotated her face slowly to stretch her neck. "Oh my. Is this what it's like to be what you call a celebrity? You do it all the time? Where do you get the stamina? What's the secret?"

"Not really," Keene said. "Most of the time I deal with reactors and engines. This is just temporary, since Friday. Attention spans on this world tend to be short." He looked at the glass that Sariena was holding. "Want me to get you another? Save your feet."

"Oh, please. Any kind of fruit juice with a touch of vodka. . . ." She handed him the glass. "Do I look unladylike up here on the arm like a bird on a perch? If I sit down in this couch I can't get up again. It digests you."

"I don't think you could look unladylike in a boiler suit," Keene replied. "Something more to eat?"

"Thanks, but I've had enough."

He went over to the bar and got a refill, along with a straight Scotch for himself. He wasn't driving tonight. Might as well make the most of it, he figured. "Anything else for you, sir?" the cocktail waiter tending the bar asked. He peered at Keene more closely. "Say, aren't you one of those three guys who—"

"You've got it," Keene murmured, covering his mouth and slipping a ten into the glass set aside for tips. "But don't spread it around."

He went back, handed Sariena her drink, and looked at her while he sipped his own. There had been so many things he'd listed in his mind that he wanted to ask her when they finally met. He wanted to know about her world and what it was like to live out there; how it felt to be without a planet that automatically self-renewed and replenished everything necessary for life; to be totally dependent for survival itself, every moment, on machines. He wanted to know how a moneyless system could function and still sustain—evidently—all the complexities of a technological society. What motivated people to provide for each other in place of the penalties and rewards that just about every authority on Earth insisted were indispensable? . . . So many things. And now here they were, and suddenly none of it felt appropriate.

"Well, you've certainly created some attention," Sariena said. "Let's hope it's a good omen for the talks."

"We can but try," Keene said.

"So what brought you to Washington so soon? Was the President so impressed that he wants you to put together a real space program for them at last?"

"I wish." Keene sipped his Scotch and saw that Cavan was watching them inconspicuously from across the room. "As a matter of fact, somebody wanted me to talk to you while I was here. Not the President, but it was to do with your mission." Sariena waited, curious. Keene looked around. The suite was in the penthouse, with an exterior balcony all the way around. "Let's go outside," he suggested. "Gallian says you need to get used to the air."

Sariena rose and moved toward one of the sliding glass panels that had been opened. Keene picked up a chair and followed her along the balcony to a corner, away from the others who were outside talking. Keene placed the chair by the wall and leaned an elbow on the rail while Sariena sat down. He began: "The person that I mentioned is on the inside here. And I've seen something myself today of what reactions are going to be." He shook his head. "Earth isn't going to buy this line about Venus being an earlier Athena. Yes, Athena happened and the standard theories were wrong. Nobody can deny that. But they're going to fight any suggestion that the two have anything in common. As far as they're concerned Venus is a planet and moves like a planet. Athena is a one-time anomaly that will be a spectacle for a year until it leaves the Solar System. . . ." Keene paused, thinking for a second that Sariena wasn't listening. She was sitting back against the window glass, staring up at the sky with a faraway, almost rapturous expression.

"I love stars," she said.

Keene looked away and turned his head upward. "Polli told me we don't have any," he replied. It was a clear night, not bad by Washington standards. The angle of the walls faced roughly north, making just a wisp of Athena's tail visible behind the building to their left. It only occurred to Keene then that until the last couple of days, Sariena's only recollections of seeing a sky had probably been from inside some kind of enclosure or a helmet.

"Paltry," she agreed. "But you know that, Lan. You've been out there too. . . . But what you've never seen is Saturn from one of its moons. This sky has nothing to compare with it. Pictures don't come close—any more than they can show sunshine. It's like . . ." She turned her face up again. "All the rainbows you've ever seen stirred together into a glowing ball ten times as big as the Moon. And you're looking at it across the rings seen edge-on. It seems to be floating in a golden ocean that extends away into the sky. If you're on one of the moons that has a tilted orbit, the ocean seems to be rising and falling." Sariena looked back at him. "Did you know that there are many legends from the distant past—before the beginnings of our literate age, like those people that Catherine was talking about—that make Saturn the greatest god in the sky and describe it as rising out of an ocean? Isn't that strange? It's almost as if they'd seen it too." Keene frowned at the city lights, searching for a way of turning the subject back to more immediate matters. "Can you pick out Saturn in the sky?" Sariena asked him.

"Er, no. . . . I guess not. It isn't really one of my things."

"Not many people can—nor any of the other planets. And isn't that strange too? They're such insignificant pinpoints that most people can't even find them. And yet in just about every system of religion and myth from times gone by, they filled people with awe and terror and were associated with gods fighting titanic battles in the sky—mightier even than the Sun and Moon. Why would that be?"

Sariena went on before Keene could respond, "Because the planets moved in different orbits then, that brought them much closer."

She hadn't strayed off the subject, he realized. It was just a roundabout way of addressing the issue he had raised.

She went on, "They *saw* Venus being ejected by Jupiter. To the Greeks it was Pallas Athene springing from the brow of Zeus. The Hindus have Vishnu being born of Shiva. The Egyptians, Horus. All names for the same planets, associated with events in the sky that are described the same way everywhere, over and over. Now tell me that Athena isn't the same thing happening again."

"You don't have to convince me," Keene said. "I'm already on your side, remember? But the scientists who'll determine what our governments decide aren't interested in old myths and legends. They're going to want to see facts and evidence and numbers before they'll budge, and none of them wants to budge because they're happy with the ideas they've got and things the way they are."

Sariena looked at Keene dubiously. "Is that really all that matters here?" she asked. "Comfortable livings and safe jobs? Prestige and promotions? Don't things like where we're all heading in the longer term, and wanting to know the truth count?"

"Maybe they did once—I don't know; you hear these things. But people have always thought things were better in the past. Today, the creed is 'Make what you can now and grab as much as you can get.' There might not be a tomorrow."

"One day, that could turn out to be a gruesome self-fulfilling prophesy," Sariena observed. "I don't understand how a system can function that seems to be based on nothing but antagonism."

Keene smiled humorlessly. "Most people here can't understand how your system can, that isn't."

"We couldn't afford anything else out there," Sariena said. "Everyone's survival is at stake. We have to work together. And look what it's achieving." She paused, waiting, but Keene had nothing to add just then. After a short silence, she said, "Of course we have more than just ancient myths and records. They're just the beginning. We have as much fact and evidence as anyone could reasonably need. Otherwise we wouldn't be here."

"I know about the mass-extinctions and geological upheavals," Keene agreed. "But there are plenty of other theories going around as to what could have caused all that. How do you positively connect it all with Venus?"

"Venus is a young planet," Sariena answered. "It hasn't been there for billions of years. The evidence has been piling up for decades. A lot of scientists on Earth that we know of are aware of it."

"I'll be meeting one of them on my way back," Keene said. "But even if you're right, that doesn't mean it nearly sideswiped Earth. That's the biggest single problem you're going to have to deal with: how an orbit that could take it from Jupiter to an Earth-encounter could circularize to what we see today. All of conventional theory says it couldn't happen. That's why people here are saying that Athena is something different. No mechanism known to science could reduce its eccentricity to almost zero in under four thousand years. That's what they're going to tell you. How are you planning on answering it?"

Sariena studied him for a moment. "Do you know about the electromagnetic changes that have been occurring all over the Solar System since Athena was ejected?" she asked curiously.

Keene looked at her uncertainly. "Electromagnetic changes to what?"

"The space environment itself. Its properties are being altered."

Keene was still frowning, but with a new interest. "No . . ." He told her. "I don't think I do. Suppose you tell me."

"I don't think it's something that most scientists here are informed about," Sariena answered. "Earth hasn't been putting enough deep-space probes out to get the picture. We have. We must be getting a better perspective."

"What's been happening?" Keene asked.

Sariena motioned upward with an arm to indicate the night sky. "This white-hot mass, hurtling in from Jupiter for the last ten months, pouring out a tail of highly ionized particles that extends for millions of miles, orders of magnitude denser than that of any comet ever known . . . It's turning space in the inner Solar System into an electrically active medium—at least, temporarily. Now move an incandescent body in a plasma state through that medium at high velocity. . . ." She left the suggestion unfinished.

The expression on Keene's face told her there was no need to say any more. A charged body moving through an electrically active medium would be subject to forces that in those conditions could conceivably rival or even exceed gravity. Forces that conventional astronomy theory, based on the assumption of a pre-Athena, electrically quiescent Solar System, had never taken into account.

Sariena nodded, seeing that Keene had made the connection. "Our scientists in Kronia have been running some calculations. The preliminary results came in to the *Osiris* just before we came down to the surface. They're being rechecked before we present anything here officially. But perhaps you could arrange for them to be duplicated independently here on Earth as well—the more confirmation we get, the better. We'll give you the codes to access the files of original data from our probes. I think you'll find the results interesting."

Next morning, the over-breakfast continuation of the interview with the science journalist went well, and Keene was happy that the treatment would be accurate. Afterward, he went back up to his room and called Marvin Curtiss as promised. Although Texas was an hour behind Eastern Time, he found Curtiss already in his office. Apparently, Halloran, Lomack, and most of the other engineering and project managers were at work already over in the Kingsville plant too, working out figures for a proposal that Harry Halloran had come up with for getting the Montemorelos site operational sooner, as Curtiss had wanted.

Instead of the conventional above-ground pads as used at San Saucillo, where final testing and any last-minute servicing had to be conducted out in the elements, the Montemorelos facility used an experimental design of silo in which all preparations and launch would be effected in one blastproofed location. Equipment installation was virtually complete, and the next phase called for a live test of the launch systems. A live test meant actually launching something. For something to be launched, it would first have to be there. The existing plan called for a regular (chemical powered) vehicle to be moved in sections by road from Kingsville and assembled in one of the silos. However, a separate surface-to-orbit trial was also due to be conducted in the near future from Saucillo, involving a minishuttle fitted with a modified hybrid engine using solid propellant and a liquid oxidizer. Halloran had proposed combining the two programs by landing the minishuttle at Montemorelos after its orbital trials, where it would then be available for the launch test without anything needing to be shipped by road. The planning committee would be meeting that morning to consider it.

Keene agreed the suggestion made sense, but it was an internal Amspace affair and not something that concerned him directly. He went on to summarize his impressions after meeting the Kronians. The most important thing to come out of it was Sariena's disclosure of the changes the Kronian scientists had detected in the solar environment and the need to verify their calculations of what it implied. "I was hoping Jerry could set it up somewhere on one of the big computers you've got access to," Keene concluded. Jerry Allender was the head of research at Amspace. "If he needs some help from a specialist in celestial mechanics, I could probably put him in touch with a couple of people I know."

"How soon do we need this?" Curtiss asked, not looking enthralled. "We're going to be swamped here with this Montemorelos business as things are."

"I think it's absolutely crucial to have the results confirmed or otherwise by the time the Kronians get back from their tour," Keene pressed. "That means we ought to get moving now. I could get Vicki to take care of liaising with the Kronians and getting the files and material together. Judith could even help with running it and tackling a specialist—she's pretty hot. All Jerry would need to do would be to set things up."

"What results did the Kronians get?" Curtiss asked. "Do we know?"

"No, they've just offered to let us have their raw data. That's the way it should be done. Sariena just said she thought we'd find them interesting."

Curtiss drew a long breath, then nodded. "Okay, we'll see what we can do," he promised. "Talk to Harry. I'll tell him to expect to hear from you. Now I have to rush. We've obviously got one of those days ahead of us, and I've a commitment in the city tonight."

"What's on?" Keene asked. "Business dinner? Press Club? Some kind of civic function?"

"My stepdaughter Anna is playing the cello. It's her first appearance in public, and it would be more than my life's worth not to be there." Curtiss looked pleased that Keene had asked. He seemed quite proud. Keene liked it when tycoons showed a human touch. It meant there was hope for the race yet.

He called Vicki immediately afterward and caught her at the house just as she was about to leave for the office. "Something came up at the Kronian party last night that could be important," he told her. "Can you pull Judith off that Japanese project and ask her to take a look at it—maybe give her a hand. I want you to access the Kronian research files and find some data they've been collecting on changes in the electromagnetic properties of the space environment during the past ten months. You can get it from the databank in the *Osiris*—no need for all the delays in dealing with Saturn. I'll send details and access codes to you at the office."

"Changes?" Vicki repeated, looking surprised.

"Yes. It seems that all that stuff that Athena's spewing out has been altering the inner-system free-space permeability and permittivity—for a while, anyway, until the solar wind blows it away. But in the meantime we're in a more electrically active neighborhood. I want to compute the forces that would act on a hot, massively charged body and how they would affect its orbital characteristics."

"You want *us* to do this . . . ?"

"No, no—not all on your own, there, anyway. I've just talked to Marvin. He's going to have Jerry Allender set it up in his department over there. But they're all in a panic this morning over something else that's going on. I just want us to do the go-betweening with the Kronians for them. You might need to involve a specialist too. I can think of a couple of names you could try. I'll send them with the other stuff."

Vicki stared at him for a few seconds, thinking rapidly. "Are we talking about Venus?" she asked at last.

"Could be," Keene answered noncommittally.

"Are you saying that our scientists here don't know about this already?"

Keene shrugged. "All too busy writing begging letters to Congress or getting themselves into the Washington black-tie cocktail-party circuit."

The significance was slowly sinking in. Vicki shook her head, looking disbelieving. "Lan . . . do you realize that what you're talking about could upset half of astronomy all the way back to Newton? I mean, you just call on the phone when I'm leaving for work and mention it as casually as if it were a bookshelf you want ordered. . . ."

"Yes, I know, but I haven't got time to go into raptures over the philosophy of it right now. There's probably a cab waiting for me downstairs already."

Just then, a blurred voice called something in the background behind Vicki. She looked away. "I said on the table in the kitchen," she directed to somewhere off-screen.

"Robin getting ready for school?" Keene said.

Vicki turned back again. "You guessed. How do you do it, Lan?"

"And how is he? Anything new with the dinosaurs?"

"It's led into mammoths. But don't ask me right now; I'll mail you a note if you're interested."

"Sure, I'm interested."

"You want to say hi to him?"

"Sure."

"Robin, it's Landen on the line. Like to say hello for a second?"

A few seconds went by, and then Robin moved into the view alongside the image of Vicki. "Hi, Lan. How's Washington? Did you get to meet the Kronians?"

"Sure did. I'll tell you all about them next time I stop by."

"Is that it?" Vicki asked Robin, gesturing at a blue folder that he was holding.

"Yes. I was sure it was upstairs."

"What's in it?" Keene inquired.

"Oh, a project we're doing at school, in the science class. We have to write an essay on the Joktanians and the kinds of things that have been turning up in the places they're digging at."

"That's the old civilization from around Arabia and Ethiopia that was only discovered in the last few years," Vicki supplied for Keene's benefit. "So give the school system some credit—they're keeping up to date."

"Ah yes," Keene was able to reply airily. "Named after Noah's grandson. Legend says the earliest peoples of southern Arabia were descended from him. The Arab word is Qahtan."

Vicki stared hard and blinked. "I didn't think you'd know that."

Keene managed to keep a straight face and replied nonchalantly, while inside enjoying every moment of it. "Why not? I thought everyone did."

She shook her head. "Lan, you never cease to amaze me."

"Just call it talented. Got to go. Check your mail when you get in. I'll probably stay in town tomorrow too. See you Thursday."

The final thing Keene did before leaving the hotel to begin his schedule for that day was call David Salio. Salio was surprised to hear back from him so soon, but pleased. Yes, it turned out that he was flexible that week and could be available. Keene arranged to see him on Thursday and changed his flight arrangements to stop off in Houston on his way back to Corpus Christi. Things seemed to be moving along.

❂ 12 ❂

The Aerospace Sciences Institute was both a research and educational establishment, set up jointly by a consortium of contractors and allied interests. It was funded privately and made no appeals to the public purse, the goal being to ensure an adequate supply of competent specialists in the fields essential to the industry, without complications arising from any yielding of standards to political agendas. NASA layoffs and the ensuing contraction of the Johnson Center had provided much of the initial recruitment and been one of the reasons for choosing Houston as the location.

Keene was no stranger there, although he had not dealt previously with the Planetary Studies section, which was where David Salio worked. The principal interests of the founder corporations were commercial and defense-related, leading them to focus essentially on launch and Earth-orbit activities, with some involvement in lunar pilot schemes and the scientific endeavor on Mars, the latter of which was a small-scale operation in any case. But putting some effort into theoretical studies of longer-term possibilities bolstered the image of exploration and adventure that excited the public, gratified stockholders, and worked wonders for recruiting ads. And besides, despite their stereotype to the contrary, many of the executives responsible for policy were genuinely curious.

The Institute was run in a spirit that conformed to the open-door tradition of regular universities, more sensitive and secretive work being conducted elsewhere. Accordingly, a little over ten minutes ahead of the appointed time, Keene sauntered in from where the airport cab had dropped him in front of the Glenn Building, verified from the lobby directory that Salio's office was on the fifth floor, and went on up without need of signature, badge, or security check. The elevator delivered him to a carpeted area with plants, padded leather seating arranged around a glass-topped table, and a wall of picture windows looking out over one of the Houston freeway interchanges. A sign directed him past a vending area into a corridor of similar-looking numbered doors and occasional bulletin boards, where eventually he arrived at 521, with a nameplate alongside indicating it to be the office of DAVID R. SALIO. Keene tapped, waited for a moment, and then eased the door open. A voice from inside called out, "Dr. Keene? Yes, do come on in. I won't be a second."

The office was the familiar combination of overflowing desk, computer work station, raggedly packed bookshelves, and wall board that seemed to characterize the natural habitat of *Homo sapiens technicus* the world over. Salio was at the computer, clicking through a series of data-contour images on the screen, pausing to flag a point here and there or add a comment to the caption. "Must get this off to somebody at JPL right away. It won't take a minute. Could you use a coffee or soda or something?"

"I'm fine, thanks. I had plane-food on the way."

Keene judged Salio to be in his mid-twenties to maybe thirty. He had straight black hair, a shadowy chin, and heavy-rimmed glasses, giving him a studentish look that seemed mildly incongruous in combination with the plaid shirt, blue jeans, and pointy cowboy boots. There was an intense, birdlike nervousness about the way he peered at the screen, pecking at icons and hammering quick staccatos on the keys. The desk to one side bore a framed family print showing an attractive woman and two young, happy-looking children. On the wall behind was a poster showing climbing routes up the face of El Capitan in Yosemite, and beside it a cork board with departmental notes, postcards from various places, and a cartoon collection.

Finally, a mail screen appeared and Salio sent the package off to its destination with a flourish. Then he stood and extended a hand. "Sorry about that. One of those things that couldn't wait. Let's see . . . . we need to make some room for you." He lifted a pile of books and papers from a chair by the wall and cleared some space for them on top of a file cabinet. Keene sat down, and Salio moved around to pull up his own chair on the far side of the desk. He looked across and pushed his hair up from his eyes. "Well, I admit I was flattered when you got back to me so quickly. I never expected to see you here in person. We don't exactly get a lot of celebrities stopping by in this office."

"Oh, I wouldn't attach too much significance to that," Keene said. "You know how it is. They'll all have found someone else by the end of the week."

"What's your title with Amspace, if you don't mind my asking?"

"I'm not exactly with Amspace. I run a technical consultancy on nuclear dynamics that's been working with them for a number of years: Protonix—also based in Corpus Christi."

"Ah . . ."

"That's what I really do. The stunt and commercial last Friday were coincidental."

"It's stirring up a lot of hostility out there," Salio said. "But you knew that had to happen."

"If you hope to do anything, you have to be visible," Keene answered. "As I said when we talked, Amspace, myself, and various other interests that we're associated with are trying to help promote the Kronian case because we believe it's too important an issue to let politics and scientific dogmatism get in the way of the truth—which is what's happening. You said you'd like to help. We're interested enough that I'm here."

"This is all very gratifying, Dr. Keene. It's something I've been battling over for years."

" 'Landen' is fine. So can we talk about the kind of work that you and the other scientists that you said you're in touch with have been doing? Particularly about Venus being a young planet. You said a lot of evidence points to it."

"I can't say whether or not it had anything to do with Moses," Salio cautioned. "Things like that aren't written in thermal signatures or atmospheric compositions. But what I can show you is that practically everything we know about Venus is consistent with the notion of a young, recently very hot body." Salio tilted his chair back and clasped his hands behind his head. "The first thing every schoolkid knows is that what the first American and Russian probes found back in the nineteen sixties came as a big surprise—at least it did to the orthodox theory. The expectation had been that since Venus was about Earth's size and had clouds, it would be pretty similar—maybe a little warmer through being nearer to the Sun. What they found was virtually a volcanic cauldron: surface temperature seven-hundred-fifty degrees K and more—enough to melt lead—and an atmosphere of acids and hydrocarbon gases at ninety times the pressure of Earth's. Not the kind of place to put on your list of vacation spots."

"Supposedly a runaway greenhouse effect," Keene supplied. It was what all the texts said, and not something he had ever had much reason to doubt or look into.

Salio pulled a face. "Yes, 'supposedly'—a good choice of word, Mr. . . . Landen. That theory was contrived as an attempt to square the facts with the established assumption of an ancient planet. But it really doesn't stand up. The main weakness is quite simple: a real greenhouse has a roof that stops the hot air inside from convecting upward and being replaced by cooler air circulating down from above. A planet doesn't have such a lid, and so there's nothing to stop the hot surface gases from mixing with the freezing upper layers. A greenhouse process might raise the temperature some, but maintaining a difference of over seven hundred degrees just isn't credible. You'd reach thermal equilibrium through convection and radiation back into space long before it got anywhere near that. The only way such a difference could be maintained is if the heat source is the planet itself, not the Sun."

"A young, recently very hot body," Keene repeated.

"Exactly. And enough heat doesn't get down to the surface in any case. In fact, hardly any does. For a start, most of the sunlight is reflected off the cloud tops thirty miles up—which is why Venus is so bright. And what does penetrate diminishes rapidly with depth in an atmosphere that thick, so that any solar heating you do get occurs at the top. Thermally it's more like shallow seas on Earth, where sunlight is absorbed primarily in the upper three hundred feet. Venus's surface pressure is about equivalent to that three thousand feet down in the ocean. Even at the equator, the temperature at that depth is only about eight degrees above freezing. You see, the greenhouse effect can't simply be magnified without limit. Increasing the insulation also reduces the amount of sunshine that's transmitted. Taking things beyond a certain point becomes self-defeating: The loss in transmission is no longer compensated for by the extra insulation, and the temperature begins to drop. None of the heat from the bottom of the ocean can escape into space, but it isn't boiling hot."

Keene thought it through but couldn't fault it. He nodded for Salio to continue.

"This all fits with other things that have been known since the earliest U.S. and Russian space shots," Salio said. "The planet isn't in thermal equilibrium as the greenhouse explanation would require. It radiates twenty percent more energy out than falls on it from the Sun. Its dark side isn't cooler, even though night lasts fifty-eight days. In fact, it's slightly warmer. We're talking about a planet with a lot of residual heat."

"Has a cooling-curve model been worked out that's consistent with this kind of temperature from an internal source?" Keene queried.

"Oh yes—and it's quite interesting. If you start out with the assumption of an incandescent state three and a half thousand years ago, which is what the Kronians are saying, the calculated temperature today works out at seven-fifty degrees K—precisely what's observed."

"Why not radioactivity in the rocks?" Keene queried. "It warms us up here. Why not there too?"

"Generating ten thousand times more heat than Earth does?" Salio shook his head. "No way."

Keene frowned as he thought back over what had been said. "And this has been known for years? . . . So why do we keep hearing the same story?"

Salio shrugged. "Once people are trained in a particular theory, they become emotionally wedded to it. They can be literally incapable of seeing anything that contradicts it, and will invent the most amazing rationalizations. That's why you have to wait for a generation to die off before you can move on."

"But how can that be?" Keene invited. "Science is objective, impartial, and self-correcting. All the textbooks say so."

Salio returned a thin, humorless smile. It was clear that they spoke the same language. Keene sensed the way to real communication opening between them. It occurred to him what a lonely professional life Salio must lead. Salio went on, "And then you have the anomalies in atmospheric composition. For example, as most people know there's the sulfuric acid in the upper clouds—probably formed out of sulfur trioxide from the hydrocarbon gases binding with what little water ever existed. But sulfuric acid in the cloud tops ought to have a short life due to decomposition by solar UV. If Venus were over four billion years old, there shouldn't be any sulfuric acid left. But there is.

"The middle atmosphere is rich in carbon dioxide. That should have been dissociated in a few thousand years into carbon monoxide and oxygen, which don't recombine again easily and ought to be abundant. They're not.

"And where are Venus's oceans? In billions of years it ought to have outgassed enormous volumes of water. The conventional explanation is that it was dissociated into oxygen, which combined with the rocks, and hydrogen, which escaped. But a lot of us can't buy that. For one thing, the depth of surface you'd need to 'garden' to absorb the amount of oxygen indicated just isn't credible. And for another, if dissociation produced oxygen, the oxygen should recombine into upper-atmosphere ozone the way it does on Earth, shutting out that UV band and terminating the process. How can you postulate one mechanism and ignore the other?"

Keene could tell there was more. "Go on," he said, staring wonderingly.

Salio tossed out a hand idly, as if inviting Keene to take his pick. "Ratios of argon isotopes. Argon-40 is a decay product of potassium-40 and should increase over time—to a level comparable with Earth's, you'd think, if Venus were as old as the Earth. But in fact it's around fifteen times less. On the other hand, argon-36 is primordial and should have decayed to a level like Earth's. It turns out to be hundreds of times more. Both figures are about what you would expect in a young planet's original atmosphere. . . . And if you want, we could talk about the lack of erosion that you'd expect from dense, corrosive winds, and the absence of a regolith; the flatness of the surface; and the enormous lava flows with huge numbers of collapsed volcanic formations. The books say Olympus Mons on Mars is the biggest known volcano. I think they're wrong. Venus is. The whole planet's a cooling volcano."

Keene had already accepted Salio as the kind of person who took his work seriously and would get his facts right. He sat back and massaged his brow. After a few seconds he looked back up. "I assume you can point me to sources for all this?" he said.

"Oh, sure," Salio replied. "And I'll include some on the Moon as well. Obviously, if something came close enough to the Earth to cause polar shifts and all kinds of devastation, the Moon should show signs of it as well."

"And it does?"

"Yes—all the signs of something passing close by and subjecting it to intense tidal stress and heating on one side. The formation of the maria lava sheets is consistent with melting by tidal forces. If they were extrusions of molten material from billions of years ago, they ought to be covered by a deep layer of regolith. It's practically nonexistent."

Keene nodded slowly. He remembered reading somewhere that some of the scientists who planned the original Apollo missions had been worried that the landers might sink in the dust.

"The maria extend across one side in a huge great-circle swathe, which is what you'd expect from a passing encounter," Salio went on. "And moonquakes are concentrated along two matching belts, six to eight hundred kilometers down. If the Moon has been dead for billions of years, there shouldn't *be* any moonquakes. What it says is that something deformed the structure recently, and it's still recovering. That would account for the bulge on the maria side too, which has been a puzzle for centuries. If it were primeval, it should have sunk under gravity long ago." Salio spread his hands in a gesture of finality. "You've got volcanic activity that shouldn't be there today. And the maria lavas have a coherent magnetism that means they cooled in the presence of a field far too strong to have been either terrestrial or solar. So where did it come from? . . . Do you want me to go on?"

"It's okay, David. I'm getting the picture. I can check the rest out myself from your references." Keene stood up and flexed his arms, as if it would help him digest all this information better. There was a chart on one of the walls showing a depiction of the Milky Way Galaxy. Somebody had added an arrow with the caption: *You are here . . . or maybe somewhere near here—Werner Heisenberg.* Salio sorted some of the papers on his desk, allowing Keene time to think.

At length, Keene turned. "So why hasn't *your* thinking been channeled along the standard lines that we keep hearing?" he asked. "You seem pretty free to follow where your inclination leads. How come the difference?"

Salio's intense look softened for the first time into something approaching a grin. "Well, it's really what you might call a hobby interest, so nobody around here cares that much. We're not part of the establishment. The concerns that run this institute are interested in technology as opposed to what you and I think of as science. Ruffling academic feathers isn't something we have to worry about." Salio licked his lips and indicated the door. "Are you sure you wouldn't like a drink of some kind? I'm going for one. But then I've been doing all the talking."

"Okay, maybe a cup of coffee," Keene conceded.

"Splendid." Salio rose from his chair. "We can go to the visitors' area by the elevators where you came in, or if you don't mind muck and squalor, there's our own cubbyhole which is closer—but the coffee's better."

"I'll take that. Probably feel more at home anyhow," Keene said.

He looked at the poster of El Capitan while Salio was coming around the desk. "Is that something you do—climb?"

"I used to. These days, though, other things tend to take up more of life . . ." Salio looked back at the photo on his desk. "Or maybe I'm just getting older."

"Nice family," Keene complimented as he waited for Salio to lead the way out the door. "What's your wife's name?"

"Jean. She's Canadian—also an emergency-room nurse at one of the hospitals here. I've been offered a sabbatical at a university in England, which will mean moving there for two years. She's very excited about it—well, I suppose we both are. It will be her first time in Europe."

"Sounds terrific."

They followed the corridor and came to a double door. Salio stopped, opened one side, and ushered Keene through into laboratory surroundings. "Now I'll show you what I really do," he said.

The centerpiece of the room was a complex assembly of machined parts housing an array of electronic units, wiring forms, lenses, and mechanisms. The whole stood about the size of a kitchen table and was supported in a wheeled cradle. Two technicians in lab coats, one male, one female, were working over it. A youth who looked like a student was sitting at a console by the far wall.

"Looks like satellite instrumentation," Keene remarked.

"Exactly right. This is a package that we're putting together to go into low orbit over Saturn," Salio said. "There will be some descent probes too."

"Is it part of some deal to do with the Kronians?" Keene asked. A number of concerns on Earth had worked out cooperative ventures with the colony where they could be of mutual service.

Salio nodded. "They'll transport the modules there for us and deploy them. Don't ask me what the reciprocal arrangement is. I'm only interested in the scientific side."

A discussion of technical details followed. Keene commented that walking in off the street to find himself looking at a sophisticated piece of equipment like this seemed, somehow . . . "casual."

"Oh, this is just a prototype that we're testing design ideas on," Salio told him. "The one that'll actually be going is being assembled in California. And you're right. There, it's clean rooms, gowns, filtered air—the works."

Salio led the way through to a workshop area at the rear, where a bench below the windows ran the length of one wall. There were racks for tools and materials, and shelves bearing an assortment of containers, boxes, and pieces of unidentifiable gadgetry. Several tubular steel chairs standing loosely around a scratched plastic-topped table, and a small refrigerator supporting a coffee maker denoted the lunch area. Salio filled a mug for Keene, waved a hand at the milk and sugar containers for him to help himself, and got himself a can of lemon soda from below.

"So, do I take it you're with the Kronians about Venus being an earlier Athena?" Keene asked, getting back to the subject as they sat down.

"Well, it fits with the heat, the hydrocarbon gases—all the other things we talked about," Salio replied. "Also, its whole atmosphere is in a state of super-rotation in an east-west direction at about a hundred times the speed of the surface, which is consistent with the idea of a dense tail wrapping itself around the planet and still dissipating angular momentum." He peeled open his drink. "And then you've got the comets. The shower of new comets that accompanied the ejection of Athena is forcing a revision of the idea that comets come from outside the Solar System—which, personally, I never had much time for anyway. I mean how else are you going to get material compressed to the density of rock out in space?

"But it goes further. The whole question of how the Solar System was formed might have to be rethought. There's work going back to the last century that no one has ever refuted, saying that neither of the traditional tidal or accretion models can be right. Because of its disrupting effects, none of the inner planets could have formed inside the orbit of Jupiter. If so, then where did they come from? An obvious thought is that if Venus and Athena originated by fission from Jupiter, then maybe the others did too, which makes Jupiter not just a comet factory but a planet factory too. And that's exactly where the

Kronian line of thinking is taking us." Salio took a drink at last and paused again to think for a moment. "The biggest problem is to account for the circularization of orbits. Conventional theory doesn't do it, and that's where the Church of Astronomy is going to be digging its heels in."

Keene sat back and looked at him, amazed. They had converged totally. "Would you believe I was talking to the Kronians about just that very thing last Monday night?" he said.

"You've actually met them?"

"That was one of the reasons why I was in Washington."

Salio looked impressed "And do they have any ideas?" he asked.

"Yes," Keene answered. "I think they might." He paused, waiting for a reaction. Salio waved for him to continue. "Well, go on. Now I'm the one doing the listening."

"What would you say to the suggestion that the orbits aren't always determined purely gravitationally?" Keene replied. "Suppose an event like Athena could alter the electrical environment to create a temporary regime in which charge-induced forces became significant. Mightn't that make a difference?"

Salio didn't answer at once but stared at him long and fixedly. "Is there some reason to suppose that's true?" he asked finally.

"I think the Kronians might have some good reasons, yes," Keene replied. He went on to summarize what Sariena had said about the Kronian findings and the arrangements being made in Corpus Christi to compute the implications. Naturally, Salio was intrigued. Keene promised to keep him posted on the outcome.

Back in Salio's office, Keen finally got around to asking the question that had been his prime reason for coming to see Salio. "If Amspace were to arrange media coverage and so forth, would you be willing to go public with the kinds of things you've been telling me this morning?"

"I'd be happy to," was Salio's reply. "Wasn't that why I got in touch with you in the first place?"

"It wouldn't create problems with the people you work for here?" Keene checked.

"No. As I said before, as far as they're concerned it's just a hobby.

As long as it doesn't affect their budgets, contracts, or completion dates, no one here is going to worry too much."

Salio offered lunch, but Keene's flight departure time didn't allow for it. He called for a cab to take Keene to the airport, and, to stretch his legs and get some air, said he'd accompany Keene down to the front entrance.

"So what's your version of why so many astronomers don't want to think about it?" Keene asked as they stood waiting. He was curious to see how Salio's view compared with Cavan's. "I mean, you and I don't have a problem. If you tell the ordinary guy in the street that we nearly got wiped out by Venus once, he says 'Say, that's interesting. Tell me more.' Why the difference?"

Salio stared into the distance. Having to ponder the psychology of such things seemed to be something he was not used to. "Maybe if your whole world is built on certainty and prestige, the thought of losing it is something you can't face," he offered finally. "Ordinary people accept uncertainty and insecurity every day."

"Maybe," Keene said. It was a thought, anyway.

Salio went on, "And in any case, it's not true of all astronomers. There's a lot of politics that I try not to get mixed up in. The astronomers I know out on the West Coast would like to see all this debated more openly. But the International Astronomical Union, headquartered at the Harvard-Smithsonian center in Cambridge, sets the official line. That's where the lines and Web links from around the world come in to report observations, coordinate announcements, and so on. Its ties are to Washington investment capital and the defense establishment, both of whose horizons are conservative and Earth-centered."

Keene nodded slowly. Cavan had mentioned Voler's recently being nominated for presidency of the IAU. "So what happens on the West Coast?" he asked.

"There's a kind of parallel information clearinghouse at JPL in Pasadena," Salio said. "The IAU is primarily NSF-supported. JPL is operated for NASA by Cal Tech, which, being a private institution, gives it more autonomy. Certainly, a lot of scientists there would love to start launching stuff all over the Solar System again the way the

Kronians want us to, but the catch is being tied to government money."

"Who'd be the person to talk to out there?" Keene inquired curiously.

"The best I can think of would be a guy called Charlie Hu at JPL. He runs their communications center and big number-crunching operations. I wouldn't be surprised if he talks to the Kronians on a direct line the same as you do, but doesn't publicize it much. Anyhow, sure, I can put you in touch with him."

There was only one more thing. As the cab appeared in the gateway to the parking lot, Keene remembered Robin's theory of dinosaurs arriving with impacting bodies and asked Salio what he thought. At the time Robin mentioned it, Keene had thought it outlandish; now it seemed rather tame.

"Well, it's different," Salio said—with an effort to be tactful, Keene thought. "Is it your idea?"

"No. The son of a friend of mine. He's fourteen."

Salio looked surprised and at the same time impressed. "Well, as I say, it's different—but I can see a few problems. Let me think about it. Can you give me his e-mail code? It would probably make him feel good if he got a response from the Institute directly, don't you think?"

The TV had been left on in the passenger compartment of the cab. Keene was about to turn it off, but paused when he realized that the item that had just come on featured a senator from New York giving his views on the Kronians.

"They're overextended with no credit in the bank. If you ask me, this whole line they're pushing is a ploy to sucker us here on Earth into bailing them out of a foolhardy venture that should never have been attempted in the first place. Well, I'm sorry but my answer is, we have problems of our own to take care of. No, sir, I will not be voting my support."

❂ 13 ❂

Judith was spending a year at Protonix to gain commercial experience before going back to university to continue her postdoctoral work. She confounded all the jokes and stereotypes by being blond, pretty, busty, and leggy, and modeled for girly magazines when she wasn't computing reactor thermal dynamics or charge distributions in ionized gas flows. Her fiancé was from a family that owned a chain of Texas automobile dealerships, but he had passed on his share of the fortune to study and compose music. Keene had never found life to be short on incongruities.

"We need to modify some orbital mechanics programs that Jerry's people downloaded," she told Keene when he stuck his head in her office to ask about progress on his return to Corpus Christi. "I talked to Neuzender at Princeton and he said he'll help out, but can't until something he's working on is done. He asked me to say hi, by the way."

"Okay."

"I'd say, maybe a week or two."

"Um." Keene pulled a face. "I was hoping we'd have it before the Kronians get down to serious business. Is that the best we can do?"

"I'll keep pushing. Maybe we can shave it down a bit."

"Whatever you can do. How was the computer thing in Dallas on Saturday?"

106

"Not bad. I found the perfect replacement for this machine. It's just what we need: image-tank driver, voice directable, and with math-pro conditioning."

"Sounds great, but I'm up to my ears saving the world right now."

"Vicki has the brochures, specs, and prices."

"Okay, I'll take a look. How's everything else?"

"Celia's moving along with the Karisaki thing. We should get the draft done by tomorrow."

"Great stuff. Catch you later."

Back in his own office, he reviewed his messages. A note from Karen confirmed a meeting the next morning with Curtiss and other senior Amspace management to update them after his talk with Salio. Wally had called to say that Harry Halloran's proposal was now officially accepted, and the tentative date set for the hybrid shuttle trial out of San Saucillo, followed by a landing at Montemorelos, was in two weeks. Pretty quick. Keene nodded in silent approval. Then a header lower down caught his eye, saying that a recording from Gallian had been filed around midday. Keene activated it, and a moment later the familiar white-haired features were addressing him from the screen.

"Hello, Landen Keene. You're probably busy, so I'll just leave this for when you get back and not chase you around on your personal number. We're leaving Washington for the tour, finally, and looking forward to it—surely the whole planet can't be as hectic as this city. But I just wanted to let you know that I haven't forgotten my promise on Monday to arrange for you to see the *Osiris*. In fact, I have talked to Captain Idorf and asked him to get in touch with you. It is his ship, after all, and he should be the one issuing invitations." Gallian looked away for a moment. "Well, they're hounding me again. Got to go. Be our guest, as we are yours. Sariena sends regards. More when we've a moment. Bye."

And, indeed, the message from Idorf up in the *Osiris*, inviting Keene to visit the ship, was four items farther down. Idorf regretted that he would have to leave it to Keene to get himself up there, however. Any others that Keene might wish to bring too would also be welcome, since right now there was plenty of space aboard. Keene killed the screen, leaned back, and thought it over. No doubt there would be official vessels shuttling up and down between the ship and the surface for one reason or another that he could probably get a place on, but if his experience was anything to go by it would be a tedious and officious business. The Amspace trial that Wally had said was scheduled to take place in two weeks offered an obvious alternative possibility. Keene warmed to the idea as he mulled over it. If they could kill two birds with one stone, then why not three? He wasn't listed to go on the trial as things stood, since it involved simply a conventional type of engine that didn't involved him, but that could be changed. They were using a minishuttle; there would be plenty of spare room. . . .

He sat forward to the screen again and called Wally Lomack at Kingsville.

"Lan, say, what's up? How'd it all go in Washington?"

"Pretty good, Wally. There's been more since, too. I'll be over at Kingsville tomorrow after I talk to Marvin and his people in town in the morning, so I'll fill you in then. Right now, I wanted to talk about the hybrid and Montemorelos mission."

"It's going ahead—targeted for two weeks from now. I sent you a note."

"I know. I've seen it. I don't suppose you were planning on flying yourself, right?"

Lomack looked surprised. "Why, no. It's just a regular trial. Why would I want to go? I've done enough of all that in my time. That's what we have crew for."

"But you're CDE. You could change the flight roster if you had a good reason."

"Lan, quit playing games. What's this about?"

"How would you like to see the inside of the Kronians' ship?"

"The *Osiris*?"

"Right. I've got us an invitation. The fee is that you provide the transport up there."

It took Lomack several seconds to satisfy himself that Keene was serious. He shook his head in amazement. "Hell, you were only with them one evening. What did you do, offer them some free consulting?"

Keene grinned. "As if they needed any. . . . Oh, come on, you know me, Wally. Smooth operator when the occasion calls. So what do you think? Can do?"

Lomack thought, inclined his head, and pursed his lips. "It's a tempting thought, all right. . . ."

"We can offer other places too," Keene said. "Any number up to what a minishuttle can carry. That should help make it more popular."

"That's true enough." Lomack chewed his lip for a moment longer, and then nodded. "Okay, I'll see what I can do. No promises, mind, but I'll put it to Harry. Good enough?"

"Good enough. Take care, Wally."

"You too."

Keene cleared down and sat staring at the blank screen, savoring for a few moments the rare feeling of everything in life going right for a change. Murphy's Law also operated on itself, which meant that it didn't always work . . . which meant that it did work. He'd never quite been able to figure out the logic. He got up and sauntered into Vicki's office, where she was busy over pages of program code that she had been working on with Judith. "How's life on the lower decks?" he inquired, scanning casually over the sheets.

"It's going to be tight, but with Neuzender's input from Princeton I think we'll make it."

"Good." Keene let it hang for a second. "Maybe we've a cause for celebration, then. Never say that the firm doesn't appreciate the galley slaves."

Vicki glanced up. "What does that mean, Lan? Another happy hour at the Bandana?"

"Well, it would give you a chance to tell me about Robin's mammoths, which you were going to send and never did," Keene said.

"That's right, I never got around to it. Well, we have had this little thing to work on while you've been seeing the sights around Washington, you know."

Keene grinned and studied her curiously for a few seconds. "Suppose I said I can fix that trip into space for you that you've been waiting for? Would that beat a beer at the Bandana?"

Vicki stopped and looked at him as if she couldn't have heard him right. Her eyes interrogated him silently. They had worked together long enough that Keene had the feeling she could bypass sensory intermediaries and verify directly what was going through his mind. "You're serious, aren't you," she pronounced finally.

Keene made a gesture that was at the same time both nonchalant and expansive. "Even better. How about seeing the *Osiris* as well?" This time Vicki did come close to looking as if she thought this might be a sick joke after all.

Keene nodded, his face splitting into a wide grin. "It's real. So do you feel like celebrating? . . . Oh, and one more thing to add to your list. I want us to order a mixed crate of the best Californian wines to take up as a present to Gallian for organizing it. Did you know he's partial to wines? They don't make any of the real stuff on Kronia yet."

❁ 14 ❁

Accelerating ever faster, Athena crossed Mercury's orbit and vanished into the glare of the Sun. After attaining a million miles per hour at perihelion on the far side, it would reemerge and become visible again in just over two weeks. While Judith continued working with Jerry Allender and the Princeton advisers on the computations that it was hoped would throw new light on Venus's early behavior, Halloran put Lomack's proposition to Marvin Curtiss, and approval came down for extending the San Saucillo–Montemorelos operation to include a rendezvous with the *Osiris* in the way Keene had suggested. Keene's and Vicki's places were confirmed, and after some debate within the company, a draw between members of senior management and technical staff was announced for the remaining seats.

With that side of things going so smoothly, there had to be some negative news too. The opposition groups who had been stirred up by the NIFTV demonstration were still seething, and the forthcoming trial offered a timely opportunity to register their protest. That the vessel involved this time was not nuclear didn't matter. The target for attack was the company name.

A couple of days before liftoff was due, Cavan called Keene at home in his townhouse on Ocean Drive. It was mid-evening. Keene had just been sharing a couple of beers by the pool out back with a neighbor from across the street.

"Hello, Landen. I'm returned at last to the land of the comparatively sane. Are you in the middle of anything? I have something that I'd like to show you."

"No, I was taking it easy for once. So, welcome back. How were Hawaii and Japan? Did the Kronians survive it all intact?"

Cavan had been one of those accompanying the Kronian party. The strategy he had outlined for manipulating the public's image of the Kronians had begun to reveal itself. Instead of the independent, free-thinking scientists that Keene had seen personally, they were typically shown as naive, trusting tourists.

"Most of them are bearing up well, a few feeling the strain," Cavan replied. "They'll be going back up to their ship in relays to take a break from the gravity before the negotiations start."

"Sounds like a good idea," Keene agreed. "How's Gallian? He has to be the oldest."

Cavan snorted. "He's got more energy in him than a football team. That's one that you don't have to worry about."

"Now why doesn't that surprise me?" Keene made an empty-handed gesture. "Anyway, what have you got?"

"I've been picking through what's been going on. The name of your friend David Salio at the Aerospace Sciences Institute has been turning up a lot in the department here. The media seem to be showing an interest in him all of a sudden. It's upsetting a lot of people."

"The Amspace PR people have been busy," Keene said. "I put them on to that guy Charlie Hu on the West Coast that Salio mentioned, too, and he's proved a big asset. *Science* magazine might be running a friendly article, and *New Frontiers* is interested in putting together a documentary. It's really moving along."

"Did you know that Coast-to-Coast wants to get Salio on the *Russ Litherland Show*?" Cavan asked.

"We've got this launch coming up. I haven't been following all the details."

"He received a call recently to confirm that he was interested in participating. But the call didn't come from anyone at Coast-to-Coast. It was from a woman called Maria Hutchill, who had gotten wind of their intention. Does that name mean anything to you, Landen?"

Keene felt unease and let it show. "Leo, this makes me nervous. I thought SICA's business was supposed to be national science policy. But it seems we can't mail a letter without you knowing about it. It makes me feel really glad that you're on my side. . . . At least, I hope you are."

"I told you, Landen, we're all spies now. It's a tacky world. Science has been taken over by the mentalities that run everything else. The only way to feel secure is to know everyone else's secrets and think they don't know yours."

"I get by okay just managing my own business," Keene said.

"But you're not neurotic. You had the sense to get out."

"If you say so. Anyhow who's this Maria . . ."

"Hutchill. She's effectively Herbert Voler's second in command at Yale." Keene's eyebrows lifted at the mention again of his former wife's present husband. Now he was all attention. Cavan went on, "Voler has emerged as the coordinator of the campaign to discredit the Kronians. The verdict is political and has already been decided, but the case for the jury needs to be made to look scientific."

Keene stared hard at the image on the screen. "Did you guess that this would happen, Leo? Was that why you came to me?"

"It seemed fairly certain early on that Voler would be involved, yes," Cavan admitted. "The job dovetails well with his own personal agenda."

Keene nodded without needing to be told what Cavan meant. Voler's credentials and professional ambitions had made him the ideal for Fey to turn to when Keene committed the great betrayal of turning his back on the prospects of social eminence and distinction in academia. Keene had suspected a certain bedazzlement on Fey's part in that direction before he announced his decision, but he hadn't made an issue of it since his guess had been that she wouldn't be around for too much longer after that in any case. Voler's sights at that time had been set on becoming Director of Observational Astronomy at NASA, which meant running all their ground-based, orbiting, and lunar observatories. The position was coveted by several notable figures in the academic world, and success in the current task of defeating the Kronian mission would significantly improve his chances.

"Have you been keeping track of him over the years since your paths crossed?" Cavan inquired.

"Oh, come on, Leo," Keene snorted. "Why should I have? You know I got out of all that. I've got better things to do than play the jealous, stalking ex. In any case, I wasn't jealous."

"His pet scheme that he's been trying to get Congressional action on is for a new federal overseeing agency to coordinate all major research in government, the academic centers, and major industrial labs," Cavan said. "With himself chairing the supervisory board, of course."

"Of course," Keene agreed sarcastically. "We really need another one."

"Ah, yes. But the line he's pushing is that science has been getting sloppy, letting in New Age and Mother-Earth mystics, and what's needed is an office with clout that can clean up the faith and reinstate proper discipline. He's got the ear of a lot of people with problems they can blame on deteriorating scientific standards. So you can see what an opportunity this Kronian situation is for him to show everyone he's the man for the job. And it would be particularly valuable to him at the present time, in view of his bid to become NASA's astronomy supremo. He has the support of the academics, but there are other rivals that many of the scientists within NASA itself would prefer—in JPL, for example."

Keene nodded. "I heard something about that from Salio. So where does this call to him from Maria . . . Hutchill come into it?" he asked again.

"She's a disciple in the cause," Cavan replied. "If Herbert makes it big-time, she flies high too. I just happen to have a recording of the call. . . ." Keene shook his head but said nothing.

The screen split vertically to show Salio on one side, and a woman speaking in front of a background of bookshelves and part of a window on the other. Showing just his mop of black hair and heavy-rimmed spectacles, with no jeans or cowboy boots to offset the image, Salio looked even more the student than when Keene had met him. Hutchill was probably in her thirties, a little on the plump side with rounded features, and short, unpretentiously cut hair. Her eyes had a sharp look, however, and her voice was firmer than her appearance would have suggested. Keene sensed a potential antagonism being consciously kept under restraint.

"Dr. Salio?"

"Yes."

"I hope I'm not calling at a bad time. Do you have a few minutes?"

"Not if it's insurance, siding, or you want to lend me money."

Hutchill forced a smile. "No, I'm not selling anything. My name is Dr. Hutchill, from the Department of Astronomy at Yale. It's in connection with the plan to put you on the show with Coast-to-Coast."

Salio looked more interested. "Well, it's not exactly firm yet."

"Yes, I understand that. What I'm concerned with is getting an idea of the probable content to assess its suitability."

"Oh . . . okay. What would you like to know?"

"Note how she's giving the impression of being connected with the show as if she's some kind of official advisor," Cavan put in from his side of the screen.

"Yes, I did pick that up," Keene replied.

The conversation opened with a trading of views on theories of the formation and stability of the Solar System. Salio was candid in the way he had been with Keene, maintaining a humorous note and declining to be unduly deferential. Eventually, they closed over the matter of comets originating from Jupiter. Hutchill's manner became more penetrating. The issue, basically, was whether the shower of new comets that had been born with Athena provided adequate evidence that the previously existing short-period comets—the ones with aphelia showing a statistical clustering at the distance of Jupiter's orbit—had originated in a similar episode involving Venus. Salio's answer was, sure they did. You didn't need the other mechanisms that been speculated about over the years and could throw them away. Hutchill was determined to see them as exceptions.

"There simply aren't grounds for making such a sweeping generalization on the basis of an event that has been observed only once," she insisted. "You're ignoring the transfer of long-period comets to short-period trajectories by perturbation, which is still the dominant process on any significant time scale."

Salio grinned, evidently having expected it. "That's what the textbooks say," he agreed. "But when has it been observed even once? I can point you to a string of papers going back to before 1900 which show that such a mechanism isn't viable. It's a myth that has been exposed now for well over a hundred years."

Displeasure showed through Hutchill's demeanor for the first time. "I think I'd advise caution before dismissing something that's so widely accepted," she said.

"But if acceptance were the thing to go by, then a popular but wrong theory could never be changed," Salio pointed out. "Let's try plausibility instead. All the estimates that I've seen agree that the probability of Jupiter deflecting incoming comets from vast distances on parabolic orbits to an elliptical one is about one in a hundred thousand. So that's the ratio of short-period to long-period that you ought to get. In fact what you have is close to sixteen percent. The number of long-periods is far too small. How many comets are there in the Jupiter family—about seventy? And the typical lifetime would be what . . . four thousand years?"

"Hmm. . . . Maybe."

"Let's take that figure, then, and suppose that Jupiter has to replenish them by capturing long-period arrivals at the rate of one in a hundred thousand. To give seventy in four thousand years would require seven million long-period arrivals, which works out at seventeen-hundred-fifty a year, or five every day. Allowing for the transit time in and out of the Solar System would give us about nine thousand present in the sky by my calculations, of which let's say half would be brighter than average. A pretty spectacular sky." He shrugged and waved a hand, seemingly enjoying himself. "So where are they? And then you've got the problem that all of the short-periods orbit the Sun in the same direction as the planets, as they should if they came from Jupiter. But by capture, some should be retrograde—in theory half of them. You see, the numbers just don't work out."

"Sufficient long-term comets can be produced by periodic disturbances of the Oort Cloud, as I'm sure you're aware," Hutchill said.

Cavan interjected, "It's the same as what I'm supposed to be doing with the Kronians. She's leading him on to sound out his arguments. The idea is to have one of their own people on the show as well, ready to take him on in a debate."

"She looks like she might be getting more of a debate than she expected," Keene commented. "This guy's good."

On the screen, Salio's grin had broadened. "What Oort Cloud?" he challenged. "It's never been actually observed, has it? And it's supposed to extend maybe halfway to Centauri. Comets from interstellar distances would arrive on wide hyperbolic orbits. The short-period comets that they're supposed to turn into don't exhibit the distribution of orbits and inclinations you'd expect from an all-sky parent population."

"I wasn't referring to short-period," Hutchill said shortly. "They are postulated as coming from the Kuiper Belt, near the planetary plane."

"Postulated," Salio echoed. "You've still got the problem of velocity mismatch, which tells against capture. Whatever way you look at it, the number of short-periods is still far too high."

"Dark matter in the galactic disk would put more of them onto an injection trajectory," Hutchill said.

Salio's face registered delight. "So now we have an unobserved Oort Cloud and a postulated Kuiper Belt that's influenced by invisible dark matter. And even if all of them existed, they wouldn't produce the distribution and prograde consistency that we see. Yet what the Kronians are proposing fits all the facts without any inventions. All you have to do is throw out some ideas you've grown up with. So isn't it time we changed the textbooks?"

The rest of the exchange went into more details that didn't change the essentials. Hutchill ended by thanking Salio for his time and hanging up visibly disturbed.

"Interesting," Keene pronounced when Cavan had expanded back to fill the screen. "It's going to be quite a show. Are they just going to let it go, do you think? She obviously wasn't happy. What can they do?"

"All I'm going to say at this point is, don't underestimate anything," Cavan replied. "And that was really why I called. Your man is bright and knows his stuff, Landen, but he's too trusting. Maybe it's just his way of telling the world that he has nothing to hide, but it's giving the opposition a lot of free information. The Kronians make the same mistake consistently."

"You want me to talk to him?" Keene asked.

"Precisely. I can't intervene—you know my situation. But someone should wise him up a little on the ways of the world. In particular, caution him on who he talks to and how much he says to people he doesn't know. If he's going to take on the big guys in front of a couple of hundred million people, he needs to learn something about the rules."

But then Keene became embroiled in last-minute details connected with the impending space shot, and somehow he never did get around to calling Salio before the day arrived for the launch.

❂ 15 ❂

The coverage that the San Saucillo launch received, and the distances over which throngs came to join in the protest, suggested coordination on a national scale. By early morning, the site was already besieged by crowds disgorged from cars, trucks, and campers that had been arriving all night. Tents and sunshades had been set up, several bands were in action, and the atmosphere would have approached that of a rock festival were it not for the angry undertones and the cordon of state and county police and vehicles maintaining a perimeter. Amspace security reported that the approach by road was problematical, and the sheriff was calling on the company to act with minimum provocation. Accordingly, Keene and Vicki were directed to the Kingsville plant to join the rest of the flight complement who were not already at the launch site, and lifted out by helicopter.

Keene looked down somber-faced as the administration and assembly buildings of the San Saucillo site came into view ahead. The launch area itself was situated two miles farther west, at the far end of the landing field with its two vehicle transporter tracks running along one side. Although some problems had been reported with groups trying to breach the security fence marking the two-mile safety zone south, west, and north of the pad area, the crowds were mainly concentrated around the east end of the complex and its approach road. As the helicopter descended, a ripple of hand-waving and gesturing followed it among the upturned faces below. In some places, signs that were being displayed were turned to point upward, although it was impossible to make out what they said. The pilot commenced a pattern of evasive weaving.

"What's happening?" Vicki asked tensely from her seat next to Keene.

"Just a routine precaution. It isn't always like this, you know. You just picked a bad day for your first space hop."

"The story of my life. It never fails."

They landed among an assortment of helicopters and small aircraft on the concrete apron in front of the control building at the end of the landing field. A raucous cadence of several thousand voices chanting in unison reached them from the far side of the main gate and the perimeter fence as they boarded the bus waiting to take them to the assembly and flight preparation area. There was a little under three hours to go before the scheduled launch time.

In one of the admin buildings they met the others who would be going. There were twelve in all: the regular test crew of three, expanded to include Wally Lomack and another engineer from the design team named Tim; Keene and Vicki; and the five winners of the Amspace lottery. They were: Milton Clowes, the financial vice president; Alice Myers from one of the secretarial offices, already uncontrollably jittery—she said the only reason she was doing it was to keep face with her three teenage children; Les Urkin's assistant, Jenny Grewe—much to the chagrin of Les, who had missed by one number; Phil Forely from marketing; and a new hire to the Navigation Systems Group, Sid Vance, who was barely out of college and had been with the firm less than a month. All of the five, like Vicki, would be making their first trip into space.

After changing from regular clothes into flight suits and taking time for a snack, they met with representatives from the mission management team for a final briefing and update. Weather conditions were good at the downrange emergency abort sites in Florida and Algeria, and a "Go" was expected. Demonstrators on the north side of the pads had attempted to compromise the launch by crossing the boundary river in boats, but were being contained by police landed from choppers. The group went back out to the bus and left the main complex to be driven along the edge of the airfield, beside the tracks that carried the heavy vehicle-transporter platforms to the pad area.

For the most part they were quiet as the spires of silver and white ahead loomed closer and taller. By the time they arrived and climbed out from the bus, service trucks and other vehicles were beginning to pick up and withdraw. Ground crew conducted them to the access elevator and across the entry bridge when they emerged a hundred feet above the ground. Minutes later, they were securing themselves into harnesses to settle down for what Keene knew from previous experiences could be the Long Wait—although the latest update was that they were still on schedule. The ground crew who had come aboard to make final checks left the cabin, and the lock was closed. TV shots from outside showed the last vehicles filling up and departing.

In the forward stations, the captain and flight engineer exchanged prelaunch jargon and offhand remarks with ground control. Farther back and below, in the passenger section of the cabin, the first-timers cracked nervous inanities to show they weren't nervous. Beside Keene, Vicki looked around the cramped surroundings of bulkheads, control panels, equipment racks, and cabling. A whirr of machinery sounded through the structure, followed by the clunk of a hatch closing somewhere. "We need your seven-dee markoff," a voice said from a speaker up front.

"Roger," the captain replied. "We have, ah, seven-oh-ten, nineteen-zero-four, and . . . four-six showing on two and five-one on ten."

"Okay, gotcha."

"And how's it going with the Oilers and the Bears? Any news?"

"Let's see . . . last we had was Oilers ahead by six points."

"Yeah, right-on!"

"*Guys!*" Vicki breathed.

Keene grinned. "Life's great once you weaken."

"I think some of it must be rubbing off. I mean, what am I doing here, Lan? You let them strap you to the top of a ten-story bomb that nobody who knows what's going on will stay within two miles of. . . . Is that the kind of behavior that would normally qualify as sane?"

"*Women!*" Keene threw back. He made an appealing gesture to Wally, strapped in farther across, who had heard and was smiling. "For years she gives me a hard time about wanting to come on a mission. Now I'm getting one for bringing her. What does a guy do?"

The captain's voice came over the internal address speaker. "Attention, folks. We've had a slight hold because of the trouble on the north perimeter, but things seem to be under control there now. We're looking at a little over fifteen minutes. The skies are pretty clear across most of North Africa and Asia. We should get some good views."

Places halfway around the world, Keene reflected as he lay back in the harness, waiting. He had expected he might get used to the thought, but he never had. It hadn't been so long ago when people had spent years of their lives traveling distances like that; now they were talking as nonchalantly as if it were a bus ride. In a way it would be little more than just that. The boost into orbit would be measured in minutes; then there would follow nine circuits around Earth for testing the hybrid engine and putting the shuttle through its paces; a day's visit to the *Osiris*; and then back down in time for dinner tomorrow. The Kronians were already talking about going anywhere in the Solar System in ninety days.

Vicki seemed to be thinking along similar lines. "You know, we've worked together all this time," she said to Keene. "I think I'm only starting to realize how frustrating it must be to believe in something as much as you do and have so much of the world not understanding it. Especially when they all stand to gain in the long run."

"Hm. . . . Yes, I think Christ and Giordano Bruno probably knew the feeling," Keene said.

"When I was at Harvard, we had the same kind of thing. It was practically impossible to convince people that low radiation levels are not only harmless but essential for health. We used to call it Vitamin R."

"Should I look for it in the health food store?" Clowes asked from the far side behind Wally.

Anxieties rose as the countdown entered its final phase, and the cabin fell silent. The crew recited their final check dialogue with control. And then the voice from the speaker up front was sounding off the final seconds.

Liftoff came with an all-enveloping roar and sudden force squashing the occupants back in the seat moldings. Vicki's hand groped over the armrest instinctively to find Keene's, and squeezed. A screen in front showed the craft sliding up past the gantry amid clouds of red and white smoke, while another gave a more distant view of it emerging on top of a column of light, with demonstrators on their feet, waving and gesticulating in the foreground. The force intensified, stretching flesh back over face bones. Ground fell away and was replaced by ocean. And already—Keene never ceased to be amazed at how rapidly the perspective changed—the outline of the Gulf was taking shape, glimpsed in parts below an immense whirl of banded cloud. Up front, the exchange between dispassionate voices and ground control continued. The boosters detached and fell away to deploy extendable wings for remote-piloting down to a recovery field in Cuba, while the orbiter engine continued driving the main vessel faster and higher. Florida and the Caribbean passed by below, followed by the huge, unfolding, speckled expanse of the Atlantic. . . .

Suddenly, the sound inside the cabin cut and was replaced by stillness and quiet. It was if they had been transported from the world of humans and machines to some different, ethereal realm. The shuttle was no longer a creature of violence fighting its way free from gravity, but floated serenely now—content, seemingly; at ease in the element it was meant for. The pressure that had pinned everyone immobile was no more. Gradually, the hum of unseen machinery and the subdued hiss of air being drawn into the extraction filters impressed themselves as the only sound breaking the silence. Then the captain's voice came again over the internal circuit:

"That's it, folks. Welcome to orbit."

The faces in the passenger compartment looked about them

wonderingly. Milton Clowes let his arms hang weightless in the air in front of him. "Well, I'll be darned," he told the others. "Look at that."

Alice finally let go of her armrests, which she had gripped, white-faced throughout the launch. "I don't believe we're still here," was all she could manage.

"How many times is this for you, Wally?" Tim, the engineer who was with Lomack, asked.

"I don't know. I've lost count. I thought I'd retired from any more of this kind of nonsense."

The captain spoke again: "Yes, I know the first thing you're all dying to try is the zero-*g*. Anyone who feels inclined to experiment now, go right ahead. Take it easy, though. It works better than you think. People who turn into missiles inside here don't make themselves too popular." It was just a reminder. They had been through it all in the preflight briefings.

The passengers exchanged glances. None of them really wanted to be the first to risk being a spectacle. Finally, Vicki felt for the buckle securing her harness, then hesitated and gave Keene a questioning look. He nodded encouragingly. "Nobody here's gonna laugh," he told her.

She released the catch and eased herself cautiously out of the harness to float above the gee-couch, turning slowly. A touch on the cabin wall stopped her and sent her turning the other way; a push on the wall made her drift toward Wally. Clowes gave her some handclaps by way of applause, and a couple of the others followed.

"This is fantastic!" Vicki told them as she started to get the feel of it. "It's like being a whale with a whole ocean to frolic in. I want to leap and dive."

"Doesn't it make all that business back at the complex seem kind of unimportant now?" Jenny Grewe mused distantly. Vicki drifted down the center of the cabin, turning in a slow cartwheel.

"Hey, that looks cool," Phil Forely said. "I have to try it too."

One of the flight crew had unhitched and was moving back. "Okay, but let me give you a few tips first," he told them. "Just a couple of you at a time, guys. You'll all get a turn, don't worry."

Keene had seen it enough times to leave them to it for a while. He turned his eyes back toward the screen in front and watched the image of the deserts of northeast Africa and the Middle East passing by below. So much had been written about the proliferation of life on Earth. But the planet's real potential for life had never been really grasped because in recent times there had been nothing to give a measure of it. Earth was still only recovering from its devastation.

He remembered how, years ago, when he first started making regular airline flights eastward from the West Coast, it had amazed him that after leaving the oases of human habitation around San Diego, Los Angeles, or the San Francisco Bay Area, there would be nothing for a thousand miles to the Mississippi valley—just parched mountains, deserts, and canyons; everywhere, the dryness. It was only later, when he began grasping the true scale of the planet by seeing it from orbit, that he realized that had been just a small part of the picture. The vastness of the wildernesses extending from Mauritania on the Atlantic side of Africa to Afghanistan, then onward through Mongolia, and in the southern hemisphere, those of southwestern Africa and virtually all of Australia, staggered the imagination.

It hadn't always been that way. There had been times when the Sahara was green, Arabia and Iran fertile; what were now the deserts of northwest India and Afghanistan had supported flourishing civilizations. The Sphinx was older than the great pyramids and showed water damage and erosion that couldn't be accounted for by the conditions that had existed through recorded history.

What it all pointed to was that Earth's climatic bands had been different then, with narrower tropics and broader temperate zones that had brought rain where there are now deserts and caused grasslands and forests to extend into what is today the Arctic. Such conditions were consistent with the Earth's axis being more perpendicular to its orbital plane around the Sun. Something, then, had caused it to shift and increased the planet's tilt, creating the northern and southern desert belts and extending the polar regions.

The flight crew got busy commencing the engine trials that had been the original purpose of the mission. Wally and Tim spent much of the time forward, following events, and Keene got involved in the technical proceeding, too. Vicki made the best of the opportunity to get to know more Amspace people. She seemed to get along especially well with Jenny, Les Urkin's assistant in public relations, Alice, and Phil from Marketing. Sid, the new hire straight out of college, was still too mesmerized by the torrent of events that had overtaken him to be capable of much coherent thought.

"Are things always like this here?" he asked when the group was struggling to master their first peel-wrappered, squeeze-bottle lunch. "I mean, after the way things were at Berkeley, I expected life in the commercial world to be kind of dull. They haven't found me a permanent desk yet, and I'm in orbit already."

Later, he got to talking with Vicki, and then her and Keene, about the Kronian theories and Keene's work with Amspace. Sid was enthusiastic about space development, which was why he had sought a position with Amspace in the first place, but he'd had no inkling of the deeper implications of what was at stake. It all came as a revelation, which he devoured avidly. A solid recruit to the cause, Keene decided.

However, as hours passed by and the novelty wore thinner, weariness akin to that of a long airline flight set in. While at the forward end of the compartment the voice exchanges with ground control at San Saucillo and other stations monitoring the flight continued against a background of electronic beeps and bursts of static, conversation in the rear section lapsed. Some of the passengers dozed or tried to read. About halfway through the mission the *Osiris* made contact to get confirmation that the Amspace vessel would be on schedule; also, there was a message for Keene from Sariena letting him know that she would be one of the Kronians up resting from terrestrial gravity while his party was visiting. Soon after, he found himself with Vicki and Sid, watching yet another turn of the globe sliding by on the cabin screen.

"Did I tell you that Robin got an e-mail from Salio?" Vicki asked. "My eternally curious fourteen-year-old son," she added for Sid's benefit. They had told Sid about Salio briefly when talking about the Kronians' planetary theories.

"I don't think so. He said he would," Keene said.

"Robin was thrilled to bits. Salio knocked a few holes in his

dinosaur theory, but it was nice of him to find the time to respond."
She explained to Sid, "Robin came up with this idea that the
dinosaurs were on the body that impacted Earth, since he doesn't
think they could have existed in Earth's gravity."

Sid pulled a face. "A bit farfetched, isn't it?"

"Give him a break. He's fourteen."

"David Salio's an okay guy," Keene said. "He's going to be
dynamite on the shows . . . which reminds me, I was supposed to call
him." He thought for a moment about calling Salio right there, from
orbit, but then decided that the topic wasn't appropriate for an
audience. "You never did tell me this business about Robin and the
mammoths, either," he told Vicki instead.

"Oh, that's right. I never did, did I?"

"He's not saying that they came from someplace else too, surely?"
Sid said.

Vicki shook her head. "Oh no. It's just that in following his
inquisitiveness, he stumbled on a lot of controversy that's been going
on for years—that even I didn't know about—about when they died
out."

Keene made an inviting gesture. "Well, we're listening. I always
thought it was supposed to have had something to do with over-
hunting."

"Somewhere around ten or eleven thousand years ago, wasn't it?"
Sid said.

"That's the conventional line," Vicki agreed. "That date was
thought to have been soon after the arrival of people. But now it
seems pretty certain that humans were in the Americas much earlier.
So they and the mammoths had coexisted for a long time. That theory
doesn't really hold up."

"I never thought it made much sense, anyway," Keene said.
"Elephants are notoriously dangerous and difficult to bring down
even by hunters equipped with iron and horses. But they were never
hunted to extinction. Yet a sparse population armed with stone-
tipped spears was supposed to have done it? All those millions of
mammoths, mastodons, giant deer, you name it . . . piled up in
thousands in some places? They'd have needed nuclear weapons."

Vicki looked at him dubiously. "So why are you asking me about them? It sounds like you pretty much know the problem already."

"It was something I came across when I got interested in evidence for catastrophes," Keene said. "I was curious to hear Robin's take on it. What else did he come up with?"

"Do you know about varves?"

"No. What are varves?"

"Layers of sediment that are deposited in lakes and so on, which change color from summer to winter and can be counted like tree rings. They contain pollen grains, which tell you what vegetation grew in the area over the years. And in the Arctic during the Ice Age, which is when standard thinking says the mammoths and all those other animals were supposed to have been around, there simply wasn't anything growing there that they could have lived on. It was all just frozen desert."

Keene nodded, at the same time looking puzzled. "Well . . . okay. What else would anyone expect to find in the Arctic in an Ice Age? Am I missing something?"

"I sometimes wonder if I am," Vicki said. "Do they really make people professors for coming up with ideas that it could have been different?"

Sid looked from one of them to the other. "So what it sounds like you're saying is, when the mammoths and all those other animals did live there, it couldn't have been an Ice Age."

Vicki nodded. "Exactly.

"So when was that? Do we know?"

"It has to have been during a much warmer period that came later," Vicki said. "They couldn't have been buried eleven thousand years ago under Arctic conditions. The soil below a few feet down is permanently frozen. So how could all those bodies and bones and trunks of trees have been buried under it? A few might have been caught by things like slides and collapsing crevasses, maybe, but nothing on the scale that's found. And even if they did, nonfossilized bones and body tissue would never have survived degradation through thousands of years when the warming occurred. So they must have been wiped out and quick-frozen much more recently, in some event that marked the end of that warm period."

Keene and Sid looked as if each was waiting for the other to fault it. It seemed that neither of them readily could. "What about carbon-14 dating?" Sid asked finally. "I thought that supports the Ice-Age extinction theory."

"The data that have been published over the years do," Vicki conceded. "But now it's beginning to look as if maybe the indicated dates were too high."

"How's that?" Keene asked.

"The Arctic has huge natural carbon reservoirs—permafrost soil, peat deposits, methane hydrate in the oceans—that would release lots of carbon dioxide into the atmosphere if a mild warming occurred for any reason. We're talking about billions of tons a year. . . . And that 'old' carbon would be breathed and ingested and find its way into plant and animal tissues, making all the dates too high if today's levels with a cooler climate are assumed as the reference."

"How do you know the climate's cooler today?" Keene challenged.

"We don't have big herds of large animals inhabiting the Arctic today."

Keene stared at her. There it was again. If the conventionally accepted dates were high by a significant factor, then once again they were led to the conclusion of tremendous and destructive happenings worldwide around that same mysterious time, several thousand years ago.

Sid drifted away across the cabin to listen to Clowes telling Alice and Jenny some anecdotes from Amspace's history. Keene and Vicki remained buckled into the restraint harnesses in one of the corners, watching the screen. They talked about the time when she had left Harvard after he and Fey split up, and the support they'd found in each other that had led her to follow him south when he set up the consulting deal that had grown into Protonix. They talked about Karen's succession of cowboy boyfriends, Judith's odd mix of talents and even odder-seeming engagement, about David Salio and his case for Venus, and Celia's cat. Keene was glad to have a chance for once to ramble on with Vicki about whatever took their fancy, free from the pressures that never seemed to let up when they were in or anywhere near the firm. The loyalty that she had always shown to everything he did and the things he believed in had played a big part in enabling him to keep going through the rough parts, but he had never found a way of expressing adequately how much it had meant. Hence, it was gratifying that he had been able to keep his word to get her up on one of the missions one day, even if whenever he mentioned it he had made it sound like a joke. Flippancy came naturally as part of his armor for dealing with the world, and sometimes, he feared, brought the risk of having things like promises not taken seriously. It was nice, even if over so small a thing, to be able to feel that it wasn't so.

❂ 16 ❂

The UN shuttle that had brought the Kronians up from the surface was in the process of detaching from the *Osiris* when the Amspace vessel arrived, climbing from a lower orbit. The captain waited several miles off in a matching orbit while the maneuver was completed.

As well as being larger than the types of craft that Keene was used to, the *Osiris* had a unique variable geometry design that combined linear and rotational accelerations to provide a normal internal gravity simulation whether the vessel was in freefall or under drive. Its basic form was of a wheel attached to one end of an axle. The axle formed the main body of the vessel and was shaped like an old-fashioned potato masher, with a handle projecting from one end of a thicker cylinder. The "handle" consisted of the reactant tanks and propulsion system, while forward of it, the "masher" section contained other heavy equipment, cargo bays, and the docking port. Four booms projecting radially from the masher carried the accommodation modules at their ends and were interconnected by a circular communication tube to complete the wheel. The booms pivoted freely to trail back like the spokes of an umbrella when the craft was under acceleration, the angle automatically finding a value such that, whatever the combined motion, the resultant of the forces generated by rotation and forward thrust was always perpendicular to the decks. Telescopic sections in the connecting ring compensated for changes in the wheel's circumference when the trailing angle of the booms altered. The engineers among those studying the details on the screen aboard the minishuttle were impressed. "It makes you wonder if those guys out there are still taking applications," Tim commented to Keene.

Eventually, the UN craft cleared the vicinity and fired a retro burn to begin falling back toward Earth, and the Amspace minishuttle was cleared to approach. Its lock connected with a coupling extended from the *Osiris*'s front-end docking port, and minutes later the occupants were hauling themselves along guide rails into the Kronian ship.

Two Kronians who introduced themselves as Baur and Semad were waiting for them. The first item on the agenda would be an introductory tour of the hub and propulsion section while they were in the central body of the ship, they informed the visitors; after that, they would ascend one of the boom elevators to meet Captain Idorf and the other Kronians in the Command Module, which was the only module being occupied while the *Osiris* was parked in Earth orbit. Refreshments would be available there, in the crew messroom.

In many ways the maze of galleries, shafts, and machinery compartments was reminiscent of Space Dock. But in the unity of expression that he saw in its design—perhaps fitting for a vessel that could cross the Solar System as opposed to a service platform constructed in Earth orbit—Keene sensed a work of inspiration that had found form, rather than a collection of compromises of the kind he had seen too often, hammered out by committees working in semi-isolation to imposed deadlines. It was the difference between a chateau and a shantyville, a patchwork of trailer lots and a landscaped park. If this was an example of what a tiny colony of misfits and dissidents could do, given simply the freedom to become what they were capable of, then what, he asked himself, might the potentials of all the peoples of Earth be capable of achieving?

He and Wally had been curious about two housings on the outside of the wide end of the axle that they had noticed as the shuttle closed in. They were perhaps the size of an average automobile, located diametrically opposite each other at the rear end of the wider hub section, overlooking the projecting spindle forming the tail. They didn't seem to be communications mountings or external tanks, and seemed unrelated to the propulsion system. The locations seemed unlikely places to put machinery associated with the spoke elevators, and they seemed too small to accommodate independent vehicles of some kind, say for external maintenance.

Keene had more or less forgotten about them and was lagging behind the others to study the layout of an instrumentation bay that they were passing through, when a low voice sounded from a short distance behind him. "*Hey, Lan.*" Keene turned and looked back. Wally had drifted off the route and gone through a steel door to one side that he had apparently tried and found open. Now he had come back to the opening and was beckoning. "What do you make of this?"

Keene aimed himself in a slow bound through the microgravity and peered inside. Most of the chamber was taken up by what looked like some kind of hoist mechanism connecting from an enclosed structure below, visible through a stairwell beneath ducting and floor plates. There was more machinery above, crammed into the base of something extending upward. Keene looked back the way they had come, reconstructing in his mind the route they had taken and estimating distances. Unless he was mistaken, they had to be right under one of the strange housings.

Wally indicated the walls of the structure they could see part of below. "Look at the thickness of those sections there and all over there . . . and those panels under the walkway. We're in a hub location here—built for permanent virtual zero-g, right?" He looked at Keene oddly. "This isn't for structural strength, Lan. It's containment. But what's it doing here?"

Keene was a nuclear engineer too, and recognized radiation shielding when he saw it. As Wally had said, the layout didn't add up. They were in the wrong part of the ship for it to have any connection with the propulsion reactors or fuel and waste storage. He looked around, trying to make sense of it. There were signs reading LAUNCH COOLANT, EMERGENCY FLOOD VALVE, and AUTO EJECT. A panel at what appeared to be a local control station carried the legends: *Door Sequence, Inner/Outer, Destruct Override, Acquisition/Director*. Before he had a chance to voice any thought, however, Baur came hurrying back, obviously looking for them.

"That door should be secured. . . . You shouldn't be in there." His voice was short. He seemed agitated.

"Oh . . . sorry." Wally came out, smiling. "I wasn't sure which way you'd gone."

Baur closed and fastened the door, entering a code into its electronic lock. "There's nothing to see in there anyway," he said, ushering them to follow the rest of the party. "Just auxiliary power plant."

Not saying anything, Keene and Wally exchanged glances as they moved on. Each read the same in the other's eye. The *Osiris* was armed. And whatever the weaponry was that it was carrying, it had been devised with a lot more in mind than turkey shoots.

Idorf, not long back from visiting the surface himself, was waiting on the Control Deck with a female officer called Dayda, the remaining member of the skeleton crew, to welcome the visitors. He was characteristically tall, with a lean build bordering on scrawny, a mop of unruly reddish hair, and one of the few beards, short and ragged, that Keene recalled seeing on a Kronian. His face was hollow-cheeked and hawklike, but was saved from an appearance of gauntness by the unwavering eyes and a ruddy, weathered-looking complexion that was perplexing considering the environment he was from. Keene could have pictured him as the captain of a Louisiana shrimp boat, or maybe an old-time frontier-era itinerant preacher. "I'm not yet recovered from being in a place that counts its people in billions," he told the arrivals as Baur and Semad conducted them through from the spoke elevator. "This kind of number, I think I might be able to handle."

With Idorf and Dayda, still wearing orange flight suits, were Sariena and the two other Kronians who had just transferred from the UN shuttle. One of them was called Vashen—a planetary scientist with the delegation, whom Keene had spoken to briefly at Gallian's reception. The other was Thorel, the crew member that Keene had also met on that occasion. Thorel waved an arm to indicate the surroundings. "So you come to see some quality engineering at last, eh, Dr. Keene?" he joked. "Here we can move. Not like those doll-house spaceships you make us squeeze into." Keene couldn't argue with that. Designed for people of Kronian proportions, the *Osiris* was spacious compared to Terran-built craft.

There was a round of introductions for those who had not already met, and then Idorf showed the way to the messroom where the food and drink had been laid out. A lot of it looked familiar, presumably shipped up. It seemed that Earth food was a hit with the Kronians. Rather than make speeches and have his guests paraded around like tourists, Idorf left them to mingle and wander off to be shown other parts of the ship as suited their interests. Wally and Tim stayed with the Amspace crew to learn more from Idorf and Dayda about the *Osiris*'s control and communications systems. The other five Amspace people, with Baur, Semad, and Thorel, drifted off in smaller groups, which left Keene and Vicki with Sariena. The two women knew each other from video exchanges while the *Osiris* was in transit, and for a while they swapped small talk while getting better acquainted. Keene thought that Sariena looked surprisingly fresh for having just been through the rigmarole of launch and the flight up. He said so, wondering if it was due to her being out of surface gravity or escaping from the demands of the official schedule. "Just being back in familiar surroundings after so much strangeness," she told him. "The *Osiris* got to feel like a second home during the voyage out. It probably seems like metal boxes full of pipes to you, but we lived here for almost three months."

"Was Earth really so much stranger than you expected?" Vicki asked curiously.

"I'm still awed by the sheer numbers of people wherever you go," Sariena replied. "We all are. Nothing in Kronia prepares you for that. You see the pictures, yes, but there's a . . . a *mood* created by so many being present all together in the same place, that you *feel* only from being there. . . . And the ocean! Hour after hour of it. I never imagined so much water existed in the universe. The waves at the beach in Hawaii were terrifying."

"Was the gravity very tiring?" Keene asked her.

"Well, I won't pretend it isn't nice to be back up in the ship. But I've had an easier time than some of us. I think that having been born on Earth must make a difference."

"Do you find you've remembered much?" Vicki asked.

"Not as much as I thought I had. A lot of what I thought I remembered must have been imagination." Sariena moved a few paces away and turned, flexing her arms and stretching her head back as if exhilarated by not being weighed down anymore. "I also have feelings that the talks with your governments will go well. The people we've met had a lot of questions. The preliminary tour was a good idea, even if a bit exhausting."

Keene frowned as he listened. No doubt the people asking the questions had been informants placed close to the Kronians in the way Cavan had described. The Kronians didn't seem to be picking up on the negative rumblings sounding in the media, or else they were being shielded from them. He couldn't see them dealing adeptly with Earth-style politics. It wasn't that they were incapable, so much as never having needed to learn how. Their politics back home—or whatever word better described the managing of Kronian social affairs—presumably worked differently.

"How are those orbital calculations going?" Sariena asked.

"What's the latest from Judith?" Keene asked Vicki.

"There were a few delays, but the last I heard was that we could be seeing some of the results anytime," she replied.

Sariena looked around. "We don't have to stay here among things that you see every day. Come on. Let me show you more of the Command Module . . . and something spectacular."

They left the messroom to reenter the Control Deck and walked along one side, past a row of empty crew stations. Sariena described the functions briefly, giving Keene and Vicki an idea of the *Osiris*'s operating procedures. At the far end was a cross-passage with metal stairwells leading to levels above and below. Beyond, they descended some steps into a recess containing low tables with padded seats set around and against the wall, where the low lighting contrasted abruptly with the brightness they had just left. It seemed to be a kind of viewing gallery, perhaps a rest area, with one wall of glass looking out at the slowly wheeling stars. The window was on the module's forward side, with no other part of the *Osiris*'s structure in sight.

"I don't know how much you got to see from the shuttle," Sariena said. "But this has only become visible in the last few hours. Wait . . ." The sky turned for about a quarter of a minute. Then, the shadows inside the gallery sharpened as the Sun came into view low on the right. The window material darkened to suppress the glare as the light intensified, revealing the sharp edge of the solar disk. One side of it had what appeared to be a bump, from which a finger of whiteness streamed away fully half the width of the window, pointing almost horizontally left. "Athena, just emerging," Sariena said. "The tail is over thirty million miles long now."

Keene and Vicki stared, spellbound. After the close pass at perihelion the tail would be at its longest. They were seeing it virtually from the side as it pointed away from the Sun. In the following month its tip would sweep past Earth like a searchlight as Athena swung into its return path, growing even more spectacular as it crossed Earth's orbit fifteen million miles ahead.

"We saw a shot of it on the screen but it was nothing like this," Vicki murmured, not taking her eyes of the scene. "And you're right. That was a few hours back, and it's grown even in that time."

"How does this compare to when we were looking at the stars in Washington, Lan?" Sariena asked. She studied the sky as the Sun and Athena disappeared from view at the top of the window and the glass lightened again. "I don't think we'll be able to see Saturn this time, though—not from this side of Earth, anyway. You know, it's strange. I still haven't gotten used to seeing it looking so small."

"Tell me something about life there," Vicki said. "I've never quite followed it. You have all those talented people moving out. What is it they're looking for? Do they find it?"

"People have always sought something bigger than themselves," Sariena replied. "Something that will give their lives meaning that makes sense, that will still be there after they're gone. Why else did medieval masons pass their skills down through sons to grandsons who would complete the cathedrals that they began?"

Keene turned his face away from the window. "Is that really true? I don't know. It sounds too idealistic, somehow. . . . I thought ideas like that pretty much went out of style two hundred years ago."

"True, for the most part," Sariena agreed. "And look at the disaster that followed. The civilization that could have enlightened the world degenerated into conflicts of squabbling fanatics. Humanity should have become a vigorous, spacegoing culture by now, expanding across the Solar System and gathering itself for the move out to the stars. Instead, it has turned back within itself. We represent what could have been, and we're considered misfits. But there are some from Earth who will never succumb to whatever the disease is. And so they come to us."

"Maybe you're in too much of a hurry," Keene suggested. "Earth is tired. It's played its part. Maybe the culture you're talking about will have to grow from Kronia. But that won't be for a while."

"Maybe."

There was a silence. Keene got the feeling that Sariena didn't entirely agree but was not of a mind to press the subject just at the moment.

"So how does it work?" Vicki asked. "You all have this shared vision, and that somehow provides an alternative reward system to what we have? Is it something like that?"

Sariena's brow creased. "I'm not sure I know how to explain it. I have no experience of your money systems, so it's difficult to find the right terms. I don't expect any overt reward for what I do. I do the things that need to be done."

"But how do you know what's needed?" Keene asked. He was curious himself. "Money's only a common way of measuring obligations. What do you have instead? How do you know who owes what?"

"Owes? . . ." Sariena shook her head. "Owes to whom?"

"To each other, to society in general. . . ." Keene searched for an example. "Look, you told me you're a planetary geologist. That involves a lot of study and ability, knowledge, hard work. Why do you do it?"

"Why? . . . It's, simply . . . I told you. It's what needs to be done."

"But *why*?" Vicki pressed. "What's in it for you? What do *you* get in return?"

Sariena looked at them uncertainly, as if hesitant to state the obvious. "In return, I am alive. I experience life. It was not *I* who designed and built this ship that we are talking in. Others did. Others made the clothes that I wear and produced the food that sustains me. And when we return to Kronia, the same will apply to everything there that keeps me alive: the habitats we live in, the machines that provide our needs. All those things exist because of the work and skills of thousands of people. And you ask me what I get in return?" Sariena shook her head again, this time with an expression of amazement. "You want me to measure *how much* I owe in return? The only answer can be, the best that I am capable of. That is my worth."

Keene had the uncomfortable feeling that it was something she would have expected a child to understand but was being too polite to say so. But they were too close now to so many things that he too had wondered about for a long time for him to feel offended. "But wouldn't you still have all those things if you didn't put in the effort?" he said. "I mean, what are they going to do—throw you out on the ice?"

"Of course not—no more than they would an invalid or a mental incompetent." Sariena shook her head again. "But why would anyone do that deliberately—deprive themselves of the fulfillment of being needed? That's surely what the essence of being human is all about. Has Earth really forgotten?"

Keene stared at her. The message was finally getting through.

"Kropotkin," Vicki murmured distantly. "The first base that they established on Dione was called Kropotkin, wasn't it?"

"Some Russian, oh . . . way back, wasn't he?" Keene said. He was still digesting what he had heard from Sariena.

"Peter Kropotkin," Sariena confirmed, nodding. "Mondel adopted a lot of his ideas. He was a revolutionary who tried to change the face of revolution by arguing that people need each other. The necessity of mutual aid should be sufficient to guide human affairs. On Earth, he failed. But . . ." She waved a hand resignedly and let the sentence hang. Maybe it had just needed the different environment, the gesture seemed to say.

A system that measured success by giving, not taking; where "wealth" was assessed not by possessions but by what one was able to contribute. Perhaps such a scheme came naturally in an environment where the survival of all depended on the competence of each. Keene tried to visualize what it would feel like to be part of such an order, to be motivated by its values. But he was unable. He didn't have the conditioning. Inwardly, he was also skeptical. Such utopian-sounding ideas had been tried through the ages—often with some success in the early phases—but always, invariably, as numbers grew, the ideals of the founders became diluted, and the realities of human nature asserted themselves, such experiments had ended in eventual strife and disintegration. Maybe, as Sariena said, in a new environment removed from Earth and its legacies from the past, the social dynamics could evolve differently. Time would tell.

Vicki seemed fascinated. Perhaps being away from Earth for the first time and seeing it in a new perspective against the vastness of everything else was affecting her. "Is it just a social structure?" she asked Sariena. "Or is there some deeper belief system involved too?"

"Why do you ask?"

"Oh . . . it sounds pretty close to what all the great religions tried to teach for thousands of years—originally, I mean; not the political counterfeits that always end up taking over."

"Kronia doesn't have anything like a formal church," Sariena replied. "It's more of an internal, personal thing." She waved an arm at the panorama outside. "But most of our scientists believe that all of that and our being here talking and wondering about it suggests design for a purpose more than the meaningless, impossible accident that your systems teach. It means that our sciences operate within a different intellectual climate. If you insist that 'science' only deals with the mechanical and material by definition, you might turn out to be excluding it from the only questions that really matter."

Sariena's answer surprised Keene and touched a skeptical note. "So is this intelligence behind it all the same God that armies hacked each other to pieces for, and people used to get burned at stakes over?" he asked dryly.

Sariena shook her head—a trifle impatiently. "Of course not. Those are results of the political counterfeits that Vicki mentioned, when the heirs of a religious tradition sell out to the power structure and give them a means of social control. I doubt if the intelligence I'm talking about has any concern with the day-to-day affairs that we imagine are so important."

Keene fell silent with a nod. It was close to what had been happening with the heirs of the scientific tradition on Earth, too.

"But you think it has a purpose?" Vicki said to Sariena, before Keene could pick up on the political aspect again.

Sariena's expression became distant, highlighted by the glow from the turning pattern of stars outside. "I believe so. It all seems too directed to be otherwise: stars manufacturing elements, fine-tuned to eject them at the end of the production run; planets as assembly stations for complex organisms programmed to evolve toward the expression of consciousness; consciousness, the instrument for accumulating experiences. And if we accept whatever our role happens to be as contributing a stone to the cathedral of eventually bringing the universe to life, then maybe yes, I suppose you could say that Kronians have their religion."

All very fine idealistic stuff; but it caused Keene's misgivings to return. He just couldn't see these people negotiating effectively, Earth-style with hostilely disposed Terrans. The very concept of starting with maximum demands in return for the minimum they thought they could get away with would be alien to them. Instead, they would offer the best they could afford and expect reciprocation. It was by willingness to give, not the power to take, that they valued each other.

"Is Gallian a visionary like that too?" he asked Sariena. "You know, the people that you're going to be dealing with when you go back down there aren't going to be exactly falling over themselves to find reasons for diverting resources out to Saturn. They've got too many other concerns that are closer to home. I'd just like to be sure that Gallian is mindful of things like that."

"You sound as if you might be trying to warn me of something," Sariena said.

"It's just . . . What I'm trying to say is, attitudes here won't be the way you're used to. Hiding one's hand is considered a mark of shrewdness on Earth. You can't take everything you're told at face value."

"We have studied Terran history and ways," Sariena said.

"And that's good," Keene agreed. "But I'm not sure it can be the same as living them."

Sariena gave him a long, thoughtful look, as if she were weighing up something. Then she said, "There is something more, that we haven't made public yet or brought up with your people so far—but nobody has specifically forbidden us from talking about it. We didn't come here expecting to outdo Terrans at Terran political games. Our objective is a scientific one: to gain acceptance for our beliefs on the basis of the evidence, not through debating tricks."

Keene smiled, but with an effort not to appear condescending. "That's a nice sentiment. Maybe you manage to keep science and politics in separate compartments out at Saturn, somehow. But life here is more messy. They have this tendency to get mixed up."

"We're aware of that," Sariena said. "And that was why we chose to bring our case formally to Earth now, when we did. It wasn't just to take advantage of the Athena event—although that was certainly timely. It was to present what we think is our strongest item of proof."

Keene frowned. This was an unexpected turn. "Proof? . . . You mean about Venus being the comet of the Exodus?"

Sariena shook her head. "Much more radical than that. I'm talking about the stability of the entire Solar System, not just a single event in Earth's history. We've believed for a long time that the planets had different configurations in previous ages. Now we're certain of it." She shifted her eyes to look at Vicki, who was waiting just as intently. "Let's go back. I'll show you what I mean."

Keene and Vicki followed Sariena back the way they had come, into the deserted part of the Command Deck. She led the way to one of the consoles and activated it. The layout was unfamiliar, but a standard communications format appeared on one of the screens. "I just want to get Gallian's okay first," Sariena murmured by way of explanation. Moments later, Gallian was looking out at them.

"Sariena!" he exclaimed. "I presume you're back up in the ship by now. No problems, I trust? Have Landen and his friends arrived yet?"

"Yes. He's here with me right now, and so is Vicki."

"Ah, good. You have my unmitigated envy at being up off the surface, if only temporarily. Walking down here still makes me feel as if I am carrying a dead horse. Is that the correct figure of speech? Never mind. I only have a moment and must be brief. What can I do for you?"

"I'd like to show them the Rhea finds," Sariena said. "They're relevant to something we've been talking about. I just wanted to check first that you have no objection."

"The Rhea finds," Gallian repeated. His eyebrows rose. "I didn't want any announcement until we've had the reactions next week."

"This will be strictly unofficial. You know how Lan and his associates have supported us. I don't think we need have any fear that the information will go further."

Were Gallian leading a political deputation on Earth, it would probably have been pointless even to have asked the question in such circumstances. The Kronian, however, thought for no more than a few seconds, then nodded. "Very well. If you think it desirable, Sariena, I bow to your discretion." He remained on the line long enough to greet Keene and Vicki, asked them what they thought of the *Osiris*, and then excused himself and was gone.

Sariena shut down the console and moved toward a doorway leading from the main floor area. "This way," she said over her shoulder. Keene and Vicki exchanged curious looks and followed her again, this time into a small room filled with electronic equipment, screens, and panels, with a worktop extending along one wall. Sariena sat down in the chair at a station in front of a glass enclosure looking somewhat like a small fish tank and began touching buttons and entering commands. A misty glow appeared in the space, which was obviously a holo-viewer. "The articles themselves are in freeze storage in one of the *Osiris*'s other modules," Sariena said as the glow brightened. "We'll be taking them down to the surface with us when we return. For now I can just show you the images. We sent the same images ahead some time ago for evaluation by your experts. As Gallian said, we're hoping for some kind of public announcement next week."

She manipulated a control on an adjacent screen, and a form materialized behind the glass. It looked like a tablet of dark stone with fine white veins, shaped into a semicircle at the top and with a corner missing below. Sariena rotated the image slowly, bringing into view a design etched into the surface. It suggested a disk standing symmetrically on an arrowhead, pierced by a shallowly sloping line. Smaller circles and other shapes appeared to the sides, while below was what looked like the top part of a tabular array of strange symbols.

Keene shot a mystified look at Vicki, frowned, and peered closer over Sariena's shoulder. What they were looking at was clearly a product of an artistic culture. "Did you say Rhea?" he asked her, baffled. Rhea was one of Saturn's moons. Vicki said nothing at once, but stared at the image with an odd expression on her face.

Sariena nodded, keeping her eyes ahead. "A number of items and fragments like this were discovered in the ice fields there. Obviously they are artifacts. We have no idea what the markings mean. There is no life there today, nor even the conditions to permit the emergence of any, let alone an advanced race. So what are these objects doing there?" She turned her head finally to regard the two visitors. "You see what this means. The Solar System *hasn't* been the same for billions of years as your scientists believe. Some things about its past were very different from what we see today. And if that's true, they could become very different again."

◈ 17 ◈

After eight hours of sleep aboard the *Osiris*, the visitors breakfasted with the Kronians before departing. The descent back to the surface and landing at the new Montemorelos facility went smoothly, and an Amspace plane flew the passengers and crew back to the San Saucillo site in Texas. After the postflight debriefings and changing back into their own clothes, Keene and Vicki were among the group that left by helicopter to return to Kingsville, where they had left Keene's car on the way out. The demonstrators were gone by then, since the mission had terminated elsewhere, and work crews were busy around the site and along the sides of the approach road, clearing up the trash left behind.

"Courtesy of our friends of the environment," Keene quipped to Vicki, who was staring fixedly out as the helicopter rose and headed north. She didn't seem to hear. He moved a hand up and down in front of her face. "Hello. Earth to Vicki. You can come back now. The rest of you is already here." She blinked and smiled faintly. "Where were you—still up in the *Osiris*?" Keene asked.

Vicki didn't answer at once. "In a way. . . . I was thinking about those markings on the things Sariena showed us from Rhea. I know this sounds crazy, Lan, but I'm sure I've seen them before . . . or something close. I just can't put my finger on where."

That *was* crazy. How could she have seen markings from objects

145

only discovered within the last year that hadn't even arrived at Earth yet? "Maybe they got into some transmission from Kronia somehow, that you saw," was the only thing he could think of to suggest.

Vicki shook her head. "No, I'm sure it wasn't anything like that. It was in a book or something. I've been dabbling in so many different things lately: Venus and Mars, dinosaurs and mammoths, Biblical history, ancient legends. . . ."

"Yes, but it couldn't possibly have been—" The phone in Keene's pocket beeped and cut him off. "It's started already," he sighed, taking it out and activating it. "Hello, Landen Keene here."

"Lan, it's Judith. You should be down by now. Are you anywhere near getting away yet?"

"We're on our way to Kingsville in a chopper right now."

"Vicki's there?"

"Of course, sitting right next to me."

"How'd it all go?"

"Just great. But that obviously isn't whatever couldn't wait. What's up?"

"I just heard from Jerry. He's finished the preliminary run and sent me the figures. They're dynamite. I'm on my way over to Kingsville right now to see the complete outputs. So I guess I'll see you there."

"All *right!*" Keene pocketed the phone and clapped Vicki's shoulder. "That was Judith. Jerry's finished the first run. She's leaving the office now and coming up to Kingsville. It sounds as if there might be some interesting news."

After clearing more formalities at Kingsville, Keene and Vicki went straight to Jerry Allender's section. Judith still hadn't arrived from Corpus Christi, but Allender took them into his office and showed them the preliminary results. Essentially, tidal pumping induced through combined electrical and gravitational forces in a hot plastic body of the kind Venus was theorized to have been would drive an initially eccentric orbit toward a minimum-energy state, circularizing it much more rapidly than anything in conventional theory permitted. It didn't prove that Venus had originated that way; but it showed that it was possible.

Keene was jubilant. Added to what he and Vicki had seen aboard the *Osiris*, this was a powerful argument for taking the Kronians seriously. Judith arrived and joined them while Allender was still expounding on the details. Keene, however, had already seen enough. Leaving the others still poring over the printouts and putting more images up on the screens, he went into an empty office and called Les Urkin at the downtown building.

"Hey, Les. First, I just wanted to let you know that we brought Jenny back okay. We're at Kingsville now, in case you haven't heard from her already. It went well. She did real good."

"Yes, she called me about half an hour ago. . . ."

"The other thing, Les: I've just talked to Jerry, who's got the results of those computations. It really puts the whole thing on a solid foundation. Jerry says the buzz is going around among the astronomers already. I think we should try for some good general coverage at the same time to tie in with the start of the Kronian talks. Let's get some exposure for Salio, Charlie Hu at JPL, all the other guys we've been talking to who don't buy the party line, and . . ." Only then did Keene register the solemn expression on Urkin's face, and that he wasn't reacting to Keene's enthusiasm. Keene's expression changed. "What is it, Les?"

On the screen, Urkin shook his head and looked bleak. "It's all changed, Lan. Things have been going on that I don't understand. We've lost Salio. He's not going to be in it anywhere. And I don't think he'll be the only one either. I—"

"*Lost* him? What do you mean, lost him? How can we . . . ?"

"He—" Somebody interrupted Urkin from one side. He looked away and muttered something. More voices sounded indistinctly in the background. "Lan, look, I'm sorry but we're right in the middle of something right now. Why don't you give him a call, and I'll talk to you about it later—say, thirty minutes to an hour. Can we do that?"

"Why, sure, Les. . . . Shall I call you back?"

"Sure. . . . Or we could grab a sandwich. I still haven't had lunch."

"Okay. Want me to come into town?"

"If you wouldn't mind. My treat."

"See you then, Les."

Keene got the number from the directory in his pocket phone and called Salio right there via the office unit he was using. Salio was at once awkward, as if he had been expecting the call and not looking forward to it. There was no point in beating around the bush. "I'm just down from orbit and talked to Les," Keene said. "He tells me there's some kind of trouble."

"There isn't going to be any appearance on Coast-to-Coast, Dr. Keene," Salio said heavily.

"Why not? What's happened? Are you saying you were dropped?"

Salio shook his head. "It was me. I canceled out. . . . I got a letter from the university in England raising questions about my legitimacy to conduct what they termed 'serious scientific investigation,' and hinting not very subtly that the invitation for the two-year sabbatical might be subject to reconsideration." He looked embarrassed. "It's more than just a job. Jean's got her heart set on going there, and it would be so valuable for the children. . . . I know it's important to you, but . . ." Salio shook his head. "I'm sorry, Dr. Keene. I don't think I can help you. I'm sure you won't have too much trouble finding someone else."

Vicki looked up from studying a plot of field intensity contours when Keene came back out into the main computing lab. "This is astounding, Lan. If we'd had probes out there too, our scientists would have known about this too, months ago."

"Uh-huh."

"Oh. And Judith says that Karen is probably going to be leaving us. It seems the current boyfriend is from Dallas and can get a job for her, so she'll be moving there. Just when she was beginning to fit in and get the hang of things, too. It's a pity. She's been doing a good job. I guess we have to start going through the replacement routine again."

"Um. How long have we got?"

"About two months, apparently, so it could be worse. . . ." Vicki saw that Keene was only half listening. "Lan, what is it, Lan?"

"I'll tell you later. Look, can you get a ride back with Judith? I've changed my plans. I have to dash into town to see Les."

✳ ✳ ✳

"It's not just with Salio," Urkin said tiredly across the table of the booth. They had walked a block from the headquarters building to a coffee and sandwich shop that a lot of the downtown Amspace staff used. "There's a campaign being orchestrated from somewhere to kill our side of the story. And it's not just your neighborhood eco club saving bugs or weeds. Look how high they went to persuade Salio to back off—and were able to get attention."

Keene had a pretty good idea where from. He nodded grimly. "Okay. So what else have we got?"

Urkin tossed up a hand while he stirred his coffee. "Two talk-show appearances mysteriously canceled at the last minute in the last few days. You remember that guy Herrenberg that I told you about—the astronomer from Hawaii that we were putting on last Saturday night?"

"The one Charlie Hu organized. Yes, sure."

"We'd flown him into LA. He was actually waiting in the green room when the interview was scratched."

Keene was incredulous. "You're kidding!"

"Herrenberg was just as much in the dark too. He was just told that there had been a schedule change, and he was paid off. Obviously, somebody got leaned on by somebody somewhere with a lot of weight. I couldn't get anything out of them that made any sense when I called, although the producer's assistant let something slip about one of the science agencies in Washington. . . . Oh yes, and you know the book that we were waiting for to appear this month?"

"Seymour's book?" Keene said. Entitled *Gods, Myth, and Cataclysm*, it was a popular-level treatment supporting the Kronian cause, which had been scheduled months before to hit the stores when the subject was topical.

"Right. Well, now it looks as if it's being put on hold because scientific buyers are threatening to boycott the publisher's textbook division, which is a big line with them. They're also being subjected to a letter and e-mail campaign protesting about the book. . . . And listen to this. I got the name of one of the scientists who sent in the letters—a geologist in Minnesota, called Quine—and I called him out of curiosity to ask what it was, specifically, in the book that he objected to. Want to know what he said, Lan? He admitted he didn't know too much about it. He never got an advance copy, so he'd never actually read it."

"*What?* Then how . . ."

"He said he tried to tell them that, but they said that was all right. They'd write the letter; all he had to do was sign it.

" '*They*'? Who's 'they'?" Keene demanded.

"He wouldn't tell me. He just said they included someone who sits on the review committee of just about everything Quine gets published. You see what he was being told, Lan: his career could be on the line."

Urkin sat back in his seat and toyed indifferently with his salad, while Keene munched silently on a sandwich. Les was normally upbeat and buoyant, managing to keep up an image that went with his PR function, but today all that had gone out of him. He stared morosely through the window by the booth at the early-afternoon mix of people out on the street, and then looked back at Keene. They had been pals socially for a number of years, mutually available for helping out with the fixing of cars and other new-improved-model gadgets, downing a few beers in the Bandana every now and again, and getting in the occasional game of golf. Also, when the pressures built up, Les sometimes used Keene's male preserve across town as a temporary refuge from marital domestic bliss.

"I don't know, Lan," he sighed. "Sometimes you wonder what it's all about. You think you're getting somewhere, actually making a difference to something that matters, and then one day you wake up and look around, and you realize that all you've really been doing is hanging in there while most of what you made ends up in other pockets, and that's about the way it's always gonna be." He took a gulp of coffee and shrugged. "And that's it. That's what it's all about. And you find that some dumb ball game is the high point that you look forward to in your week. It doesn't feel right. Does it to you? Don't you get this feeling inside that we were meant for bigger things, better things? . . . What kinds of things could we be doing if we weren't wiping ourselves out just trying to make ends meet all the time?"

Starting cathedrals to be completed two generations later, Keene thought to himself. Bringing a universe to life. He drank from his own mug and looked around. Three young children at a nearby table were laughing and giggling, having stopped in for an afternoon ice cream with their mother. Workers from a power-company truck parked along the street outside were closing off one of the traffic lanes with orange cones. "I guess if you leave things even a little bit better than you found them, it means it was worthwhile," he said, looking back and trying to inject something positive. "Philosophers ask the wrong question. They spend years wanting to know if humanity is perfectible. Then, when they finally arrive at the conclusion that the answer is no—which should have been obvious in the first place— they get depressed and commit suicide or something."

"So what should the question be?" Les asked.

"Whether humanity is improvable. And since the answer will always be yes, there's always something worthwhile to be doing."

Urkin stared hard as if trying to fault it, apparently couldn't, and settled for a snort. "All right. So how do we improve this situation we've been talking about?" he asked. "Have you figured out what's going on? It isn't science."

"Now you want me to play psychologist. That's not my line, Les. I build nuclear drives for spaceships."

"I'd still like to hear your take, anyhow."

"Well . . ." Keene drew a long breath while he thought about it. "I guess it's the old story of the in-club being threatened by a heresy that's getting attention. You could lose your standing as the official church and all the gravy that comes with it, and then your disciples will desert to the other side. So you fight it with everything you've got."

"Everything?" Urkin objected. "You mean scruples don't matter? I thought there were supposed to be civilized rules of discourse and conduct."

"Oh, those only apply between gentlemen who are in the club," Keene explained. "They don't count if you're on the outside."

"But we've got flagrant censorship going on. Suppression of facts. What happened to all this I heard about impartial weighing of evidence; seeking objective truth?"

Keene waved a hand. "Like with all religions: it was a nice thought in the early days. Then different people move in and take over, and in the end it's the power dynamics that matter. The rest makes good reading for indoctrinating the initiates."

Urkin looked across curiously. "But that's not true with everyone, is it?" he said. "I mean, how about you? You still seem to care about those things."

"Sure. And that's why I run a five-person office that works with a maverick outfit somewhere in the south of Texas instead of handing out the contracts in Washington. But at least that gives me a reason. What's yours?"

Urkin just shook his head in a way that gave up trying to understand it.

Keene knew he was drifting into being flippant again. It was his reflex defense mechanism while he absorbed the impact of what had happened to Salio and the other things he had heard. But underneath it, now, he could feel his anger rising, like the slow building up of wind before a storm. And he wasn't going to accomplish anything to alleviate it here, or with people like Salio, or by talking to the Kronians, or flying stunts around the planet. The only place to take it was where the source of the problem lay.

Could Cavan have really seen this coming all along?

◉ 18 ◉

Keene arrived at Protonix the next morning with a mood that hung over the office like a temperature inversion. The girls got on with their tasks and stayed out of the way.

He was in the kind of situation that irked him the most: of not being in control of the things that affected him the most profoundly. His professional future was tied to the fortunes of Amspace, which hinged on decisions that would eventually come out of Washington, and he had done all he could do to influence the process that would determine those decisions. And the premonitions he was getting weren't good. To make matters worse, the focus of priorities at Amspace had shifted for the time being from engineering matters that involved him to internal administrative details of getting Montemorelos ready to relaunch the shuttle that had landed there, giving him no ready outlet for his energies.

His approach to life had always been to suspect himself as the first candidate for blame when things went wrong—which put the capacity for learning something and doing whatever needed to be done squarely in his own hands. That was the first prerequisite to being in control of one's life as opposed to a helpless victim of it. The Kronian affair was as far as he was prepared to go in knocking himself out, he decided. If this didn't work out, then to hell with it. He would chuck it all in and go back with them when the *Osiris* departed.

He was still mulling over the thought when Vicki came into his office holding a blue folder and set it down open in front of him. One of the pages showed a contour map of rugged terrain with various locations marked by crosses, squares, and other shapes. The facing sheet had reproductions of what looked like a piece of pottery, a slab that could have been from the base of a statue, and a section of mural relief carving, all with lines of peculiar symbols inscribed, fragmented and obliterated in some parts, others tolerably clear.

"There," she announced, indicating the symbols. Keene stared at them. He knew what she was getting at but acted dumb and looked at her questioningly. "That's where I saw them," she said. "Robin's science project on the Joktanians. I'm sure they're like that script that Sariena showed us on the *Osiris*. I can still picture some of them. The similarities can't be coincidental. They have to be related."

Keene could only point out the obvious. "I'm sure you mean it, Vicki, but I don't have to tell you it's preposterous. How are artifacts from Arabia supposed to have gotten to Saturn? Ancient sea-going cultures making accurate maps of Antarctica before the Ice Age, I can buy. But are they supposed to have built—"

Vicki raised a hand for him to stop. "I know, Lan. I know it's crazy. All I'm telling you is what I saw. I do ad graphics. I've got an eye for things like that."

He made a conciliatory gesture, indicating that he wasn't going to argue about it. "So, what do you want me to do?" he asked, leaning back from the desk.

"I'm not really asking you to do anything. But I saw the way you looked at me when I mentioned it in the chopper yesterday, and I just wanted you to know that I hadn't been having hallucinations or something."

Keene nodded obligingly. "Okay. . . . So you weren't being daffy-headed after twenty-four hours in orbit. But I never thought that anyway." He waited for her to nod, having made her point, pick up the folder, and leave. She didn't.

"Although . . ." She looked at him as if something had just occurred to her, which Keene didn't believe for a moment.

"What?"

"Well, it's got me curious. You said you met this woman from the Smithsonian when you were in Washington, who's involved in the excavations and so on. . . ."

"Catherine Zetl?"

"Right. Couldn't we get those images sent through for her to have a look at? Surely that would settle it. If I'm wrong, then that's the end of it. But if not . . ." Vicki didn't have to complete it. It would add a whole new dimension of impossibility to something already complex enough.

Keene was not enthusiastic. "I'm not sure it's our place to go showing that material around," he said. "Even Sariena checked with Gallian first, remember. And I don't really know Zetl well enough to go involving her in something like that. We exchanged a few words at a cocktail party. I can see your point, all right, but . . ." He finished with another wave.

Vicki straightened up, looked at him reluctantly for a few seconds, then sighed. "You're right. We're not even involved officially, I guess. It's just . . . Well, it's so darned bewildering!"

"Yes, I know, I know." Keene drummed his fingers on the desk. "Tell you what I'll do. Sariena said those images had been sent ahead, so people here will already be going over them. If there really are similarities to the Joktanian script, surely you can't have been the only one to spot it. Let's wait and see what's said next week when the Kronians bring the artifacts up at the talks. Once their existence has been made public knowledge anyway, I'd feel better about bringing it to Zetl's attention if nothing else is mentioned—because then it would seem very strange. Asking questions would be legitimate. How would that sound?"

"You mean I have to wait a whole week?"

"Think you can stand it? Come on—I fix you a visit to a spaceship from Saturn and all I get is a hard time? What is this?"

"Well, if you put it like that, I suppose—" The call tone from Keene's desk screen interrupted.

"Excuse me," he said, sitting forward to accept. "Hello?"

"Catch you later, Lan." Vicki picked up the folder and left, closing the door.

The caller was Jerry Allender from Kingsville. He was red-faced and shaking his head, and had to wave a hand in the air several times before he could speak. "Lan, do you know what's happened? They're throwing them out . . . just tossing them out as inadmissible! It'll be like they never happened. They won't even be a factor to take into consideration—not even worth a can of beans."

"Jerry, calm down. What are you talking about? Who are throwing what out?"

Allender paused to collect his breath. "I just got word from an astronomer called Tyndam, who's on the scientific committee that'll be meeting with the Kronians next week—chaired by somebody called Voler."

Keene nodded tersely. "And?"

"The orbital calculations that we ran. They aren't accepting them."

"*What?*"

"Voler has ruled that until corroboration can be provided by properly organized studies and review, they're not material to the case. And you know how long that could take for anyone with a mind to stretch things out. But in any case it means that as far as next week is concerned, forget it."

Keene felt himself trembling in outrage. "The Kronians ran them. *We* already corroborated them! There's no reason not to accept them tentatively. Every precedent demands it. Is he trying to say that we and the Kronians are both incompetent? . . . Or worse: that we faked it?"

Allender mouthed awkwardly for a second or two, as if choking on something, and then nodded. "I think so, Lan. That was how it came across to me—and what they're maybe putting around. I think they *are* insinuating just that."

Minutes later, Keene exploded into the reception area, startling Karen, who was sifting through the morning's mail at her terminal. "Yale University, Connecticut," he barked. "I want to talk to Professor Herbert Voler, who runs their astronomy faculty. Either get me through to him or a number that's close to wherever he is. I don't care if he's at his grandmother's funeral. Find him."

Vicki appeared, framed in the doorway of her own office behind him. "Lan, don't you think it might be an idea to let it cool for half an hour before—"

"It's gone far enough. First we get shoddy science. Then the kind of dirty tricks you'd expect in some tin-pot dictatorship somewhere. Now this. *We* are being accused of incompetence or dishonesty . . ." He shook his head, left the sentence unfinished, and stalked back into his own office, slamming the door. A moment later, he opened it again long enough to throw out, "*By them!*"

He still hadn't begun cooling when Karen announced, "His department says he won't be there for probably two weeks. The woman I talked to isn't at liberty to give out his personal code. She did give me a Washington number, but he won't be accessible through it until tomorrow or the day after. I have got a home number for him in New Haven, though."

Of course, Keene thought to himself. Voler would be getting ready for the circus in Washington. "That'll do," he growled. "Maybe someone there might know where he is. . . . And thanks, Karen." Moments later, he found himself staring at the features of his one-time wife, Fey.

She looked cool, sophisticated, her hair shorter than he had known it, more composed and organized—altered in the same direction as her life, no doubt. She was wearing a powder blue blouse with a sparkling brooch that looked both stylish and expensive, and what looked like a loose, black cardigan. Glimpses of subdued wallpaper and wooden paneling in the background completed the image of polish and refinement—a fitting setting for a senior academician who was going places.

Surprise flickered barely long enough to be visible before being brought under control. The eyes scanned and recorded, extracting in a matter of moments all the information to be had from the screen confronting her. In the way that happens with people who have spent years together, his mood had communicated itself already.

"Well," she said. "The face from a former life. I had a premonition it might only be a matter of time. You've been in the news a lot lately. But I see it hasn't done anything to sweeten your temper. What do you want, Lan?"

Keene drew a long breath in an effort to steady himself. "Hello, Fey. You're right. . . ." As she always was; it infuriated him. "I wish I had some pleasantries to swap, but I'm not in the mood. I need to talk to him. Is he there?"

"By 'him,' I presume you mean my husband. His name's Herbert."

Keene nodded curtly. She was right again. Whatever the grievance, incivility wasn't called for. In any case, it would only be giving away free ammunition. "Yes. Your husband, Professor Voler. If he's there, I need to speak to him . . . please."

"I'm afraid he's not. He's in Washington, preparing for the talks next week with your . . . friends. I'll be joining him tomorrow morning. Didn't they tell you that at his office? You must have tried there first."

"Do you have a number that will get me through to him?" Keene said. "I presume I don't need to spell out that it is extremely important."

Fey eyed him critically for a few seconds. Finally she shook her head. "I don't think so. You're clearly spoiling for a fight over something. I'm not going to be the one to expose him to such disruptive influences with this business next week coming up."

"Dammit, isn't it obvious that the business next week is what I want to talk to him about?" Keene said shortly.

A hint of mockery played on Fey's lips, just for an instant. "I really don't think Herbert would be concerned with engineering details." She made it sound like the chauffeur's job.

Keene felt his blood rush, knew his buttons were being pressed, but was powerless to stop it. "Look, some work that's crucial to those talks has been recently completed here in Texas," he fumed. "I've just heard that the committee has been instructed to disregard it, and that the instruction came from him. This isn't a trivial matter, Fey. It's a travesty of science and deliberate sabotage of affairs vital to the interests of every person in this country. He won't be allowed to get away with it. If he tries, the effects could be very damaging to that precious career of his. Do you understand that?"

"Oh, how pompous. And now I do believe you're making threats.

Please tell me you are, because dealing with them is very simple and straightforward. Make my day, as they say."

"Take it any way you want," Keene retorted. "But if you won't let me tell him myself, then convey this to him: That deliberately misrepresenting scientific evidence by someone in his position is bad enough; but we have a truckload of evidence that goes beyond that to organized disinformation and manipulation of the media on a scale that for my money qualifies as criminal conspiracy. I'm talking about things like denial and suppression of dissenting views; intimidation of hostile witnesses; organized censorship. Those things would be criminal if the subject of a court case. Well, how is the public going to judge it when they find out? Because that's what's going to happen if he's not willing to reconsider. I'm talking about full exposure of the whole shit heap. And I'm serious. So you just tell Herbert that."

Fey's expression had frosted over while Keene was speaking. The eyes had turned to steel encased in ice. "I think you've made yourself clear," was her response. "If you have any more to say, I suggest you direct it through your attorney." And with that she cut the connection.

Keene was still simmering late that afternoon when Karen put a call through from Sariena. She was still aboard the *Osiris,* due to come back down in two days' time. Gallian, in Washington, had told her the news about the Terran scientific committee's ruling, and she was distressed. The whole Kronian delegation was in disarray. They had been trying to get some guidance from their scientists back at Saturn, who had worked feverishly to have the probe data available in time, but the two-hour communications delay was making things impossible. So Gallian was trying to organize some defense locally. Neuzender at Princeton had declined to speak at the conference on the grounds that his part had been purely to advise on the mathematics, but Gallian was pushing to have Charlie Hu and a couple of his people from JPL attend. Keene had arranged the corroboration run at Amspace, and Allender had performed it. Would he and Jerry be willing to come to Washington next week and testify on the nature and validity of the work they had done?

"Of course I'll be there," was Keene's immediate response.

He called Allender while Sariena was still connected from the *Osiris*, and Allender's answer was equally unhesitating and affirmative. So at least it seemed they were back in with a chance. But it was going to be a nasty fight.

Leo Cavan confirmed as much when he called Keene at home late that night. He'd heard that Keene had been recruited to help the Kronian cause. "I don't know what else you've been saying, Landen, but you've certainly stirred up a hornet's nest," was the further piece of information he had to proffer. "I've been hearing your name all over the place today, and not with the friendliest of connotations. I have a bit of advice: Tread very carefully, Landen. Check that none of your library books are overdue, make sure not to roll through any stop signs, and don't even look in the direction of a female who's under age. There are departments in the bureaucratic netherworld of this fair capital of ours that specialize in dredging up sleaze, and some of the things they come up with would astound you. You are targeted for anything they can get on you. It doesn't have to have anything to do with the scientific case. If I can find anything specific that they're onto, I'll let you know, but it's hardly the kind of information they leave lying around. In any case, don't underestimate these people, Landen. They can be frighteningly effective."

◉ 19 ◉

Keene found himself constructing visions of gleaming metal cities and icy landscapes under star-filled skies; of strange habitats orbiting above distant moons; the hugeness of Saturn seen from outside its ring system. He tried to imagine life where science was not dominated by preconceptions, and to grasp the puzzling yet alluring culture with its different concept of value.

All he was trying to do was get Earth's institutions to acknowledge the possibility that they could be wrong about something vitally important to the entire future of the human race. Yet the response was to be ridiculed, shouted down, and now, it seemed, viewed like some kind of political threat to the nation's security. He analyzed his own feelings to ask himself if he was serious about giving Earth up as a lost cause if this attempt failed, and leaving to start anew in Kronia.

He didn't try to deny that his thoughts about a new world and a new life included an element of intrigue for Sariena. Talking to Fey had brought home how fully he had immersed himself in his work at the expense of any meaningful personal life since they split up—not that it had been remarkably great before. So perhaps new challenge and adventure in a different direction was just what his life needed. It surely wouldn't be before time. He thought back over his conversations with Sariena, looking to see if there was anything that, with a bit of wishful thinking, he could read as hints or leaders that might have failed to permeate his pragmatic engineer's filter of awareness. With someone from a culture that had to be described as alien, it was difficult to tell. At other times he grew impatient with himself, asking what reason she might have for harboring any interest in him that went beyond the professional. . . . But on the other hand, why should that have to be a prerequisite to anything? These things had to start somewhere. Sometimes he caught himself half hoping that the talks would come to nothing and give him a reason for making the break.

Yet, for all that, another part of him deeper down was uncomfortable, and the only honest admission was that he didn't know why. He wanted to rationalize that it would be quitting and he wasn't a quitter, but he knew there was more to it. Because it would be "abandoning" Vicki and Robin, somehow? There was no reason, really, why that should be. He had never let a relationship develop with Vicki in a way that might have implied some kind of commitment, and certainly she had never indicated that she felt he owed her any. And yet it was true that he had drifted into something of a role with them, he supposed, especially where Robin was concerned, even if as little more than an emotional anchor and a psychological prop over the years. But reason and emotion communicate on different wires that don't cross. Had he anticipated this situation a long time ago and avoided any involvement with Vicki precisely to give himself a moral escape hatch now? If so, then had the entire part he'd been acting out for months about caring what Earth did been a charade manufactured to prop up his self-respect, while all along he waited for the time to come when he would follow the course that he had already chosen?

He didn't know. But the effort of thinking about it gradually brought the realization that even if a mental switch were to flip and reveal that going to Kronia was a decision he had already unconsciously taken, suffering defeat here first wasn't necessary as a pretext for a motive. If going there was what he wanted, then that was good enough. In other words, there was no reason why he shouldn't win the battle here first, and still go anyway—and with Earth committed to full cooperation, the prospective future out at Kronia would be immeasurably more promising.

He liked that way of looking at things, he decided. Thereafter, his demeanor brightened considerably. His optimism regarding the forthcoming Washington conference climbed again, and the atmosphere in the offices of Protonix returned to its normal level of productive geniality.

❂ 20 ❂

The Kronian hearings had been in progress for two days, staged in the conference theater of the American Association for the Advancement of Science's new building on New York Avenue. The active participants fell into three broad categories: the Kronian delegation and Terran scientists from various places and disciplines who supported their position; specialized committees representing the prevalent scientific opinions on Earth in such areas as Solar System astronomy, recent geology, Ice Age chronology, climatology, cultural mythology, and the other subjects under debate; and an assortment of political advisors and delegates concerned with the policies that would come out of it all—potentially international in scope, although it seemed agreed that the lead set by the United States would be generally followed. The move to have two of Hu's scientists from JPL added to the astronomy committee had been contested on the grounds that it would produce internal divisiveness. The committee chairman—Herbert Voler—had concurred and upheld the previously agreed arrangement.

These groups occupied three sections in the front part of the auditorium. The dais facing the room had been furnished with a panel table to accommodate the group concerned with the current topic, and a podium for a principal speaker. Some seats and tables in

164

the center at the front were reserved for the current AAAS president, Irwin Schatz, a physics Nobel Laureate, who was nominally hosting and chairing the event, along with several officials from major scientific agencies and their administrative assistants. The rows across the middle were taken up by journalists, science correspondents, and reporters. The remainder of the hall was by invitation only for anyone with the right connections who had managed to get a pass. Since the event had as much to do with world policymaking and public opinion as with science, there were lots of cameras and microphones around.

Although the work that Keene and Jerry Allender had been involved in was not scheduled for discussion until the third day, they had been present from the beginning. Keene recognized a number of familiar faces from his dealings over the years and was able to catch up on events with some of them in the chat room between formal sessions. Also, he noticed Leo Cavan putting in an intermittent presence, usually in a seat to the side of the hall or standing near one of the doors.

So far, the floor had largely been ceded to the Kronians to recapitulate the work that had led them to their conclusions. Practically all of the material they cited had been available before, but—apart from the more sensational items that the media had been popularizing since Athena appeared—fragmented among specialized journals and for the most part obscure. Gallian had wanted it all consolidated for the record, and there were really no grounds on which that could be denied. They went over the parallels between ancient accounts of terrestrial disruptions and violent celestial events, and the implied connection with cataclysms written into the geological and biological records. They pointed to the evidence for major disturbances to both the Moon and Mars in recent times as showing that the upheavals on Earth had been caused by some external agency, and hence the cherished notion of a stable and orderly Solar System was in error. Finally, they recounted the reasons for supposing that agency to have been an earlier Athena-like object ejected from Jupiter, which had since evolved into the planet Venus.

Reactions had grown more animated and vociferous as the two days went by. The Kronian appeals to ancient records and mythologies had elicited mainly pointed silences as the establishment scientists' way of registering their disapproval. They didn't think that this had any place in a scientific debate of the twenty-first century, but courtesy required that the Kronians be permitted a hearing if that was the way they insisted on playing it. The review of recent geological and biological catastrophes initiated more lively responses, not so much of denial that the evidence existed—for that much was generally accepted—but more of resistance to the suggestion that it testified to something universal and global rather than the unconnected, localized events that the mainstream theories still clung to. There was louder protest at revisions the Kronians wanted made to accepted historical chronology—for example, bringing forward the date for the ending of the last ice age, and doing away with the Greek 1200 to 700 B.C. "Dark Age" conventionally held to have separated the Helladic from the Hellenic periods. This, the Kronians asserted, had never happened but resulted from a misalignment of Greek and Egyptian chronologies stemming from faulty nineteenth-century research. The points of dispute were tabled to be covered during the specialized sessions later.

The real objections and choruses of "No!" "Never!" "Rubbish!" began when Gallian, Sariena, and several of the other Kronian delegates began challenging traditional notions of the origin, age, stability, and recent history of the Solar System. This, of course, was the Terran party line orchestrated by Voler finally emerging. The reality of Athena couldn't be denied, but it was acceptable only as a freak event that would never occur again in the timespan of humankind. To suppose that it could be the latest instance of what in fact was the normal scheme of things, meaning that just about everything that had been believed for centuries would have to be torn up and discarded, was inconceivable. Again, according to the rules, points of dispute and contention were supposed to be deferred until later sessions; but this time the mood of the room had reached the point where frayed tempers and wounded egos wouldn't wait, and matters boiled over. The media had a bonanza, capturing red-faced, spluttering professors hurling pejoratives from the floor, the AAAS president pulping a file folder on the edge of his table as he shouted for order, and Sariena at the podium, quiet and dignified, waiting while one mêlée after another erupted and subsided. In all this, it seemed to Keene that Voler played more a role of egging things along and loudly adding to the controversy rather than acting as any kind of moderating influence. It was in keeping with the significance of the Kronian affair to the career ambitions that Cavan had described. Seldom did anything become a focus of the political-scientific community's attention like the current issue, and Voler was making sure to keep himself at center stage.

Eventually, matters spiraled to the inevitable clash over the origin of Venus. Gallian began summarizing ancient astronomical and mythological accounts again but was interrupted by astronomers protesting that this material was irrelevant and demanding that the proceedings be confined to science. Gallian handed over to Vashen, who presented evidence for a young planet along the lines Salio had described to Keene. Despite Schatz's pleas for them to defer until later, several attendees rose to insist that the hypothesis was unnecessary since the accepted theory explained everything adequately. This led to the Kronians making comparisons with Athena, which was countered by reassertions that Athena was a totally different kind of object, moving in a class of orbit that Venus could never have possessed. Sariena contradicted this, stating that data collected over the past ten months by Kronian space probes showed a change in the electrical properties of the space medium sufficient to invalidate conventional models, and that calculations based on the revised model showed that orbits could indeed be circularized in the way postulated, within the requisite time frame. This caused something of a stir until Tyndam, the deputy chairman of the astronomy committee, no doubt following directions, called for the subject to be ruled inadmissible. At this point, Gallian jumped to his feet to protest that nothing pertinent could be excluded from a scientific debate and challenging the other side for a justification. Tyndam's reply was that the claim was unverified—the equivalent of hearsay in a court of law—and had no standing as scientific evidence until either confirmed or contradicted by independent studies. The intransigence of this ruling caused some surprised mutterings.

Sariena rose again and retorted hotly that the results had been verified, and the people who had conducted the corroborative study were right here—she indicated where Keene and Allender were sitting. Gallian demanded to the chair that they be heard. With curiosity mounting all round, and feeling himself under mounting moral pressure, Schatz, clearly with some reluctance, agreed.

Voler's position was most vulnerable here, and he took it upon himself to defend it personally, assuming more the role of a trial lawyer, it seemed, than a delegate at a scientific conference, by coming out from his seat to address the dais from the floor immediately in front of the chairman's table. Keene was at the podium at this point, having just finished describing his part in organizing the computations conducted at Amspace. Allender, Sariena, Gallian, Vashen, and Chelassey, a mathematician with the Kronian group, were at the table to his left, looking out over the hall.

Voler began, "So this wasn't part of any research protocol agreed with the Kronian scientists from the outset. It was decided at a cocktail party after the *Osiris* arrived here. Have I got that right?"

"That's correct," Keene confirmed. He was getting irritated. Maybe that was the idea. It *couldn't* have been agreed any earlier; the first results had only just come in from Saturn. Voler knew that.

"The data files were in the *Osiris*'s computers. You passed on the codes for accessing them so that the calculations could be repeated at Amspace."

"Yes—at least, it was arranged by my business partner and a mathematical physicist employed by our company. Just the original raw data. We had no prior knowledge of what the Kronians' results had been. The solutions computed at Amspace are in full agreement with them. My colleague, Dr. Allender, has complete details of the protocols and procedures." Keene couldn't keep himself from adding, "If you're questioning the competence of Dr. Allender and his staff, their method and setup were worked out in conjunction with Professor Neuzender at Princeton, a specialist in celestial dynamics whose name I have no doubt is familiar to you."

Voler stared for a few seconds and then nodded distantly, his mind seemingly on a different track. "Oh, I have no doubt as to the abilities of the people involved, and I'm sure that their computations were done validly. I've known Gary Neuzender for years, and if he's given his approval I'll grant the results provisional status." He paused again and turned away briefly before resuming—clearly for effect, and succeeding in getting the room's attention. "But it isn't the quality of the computations that concerns me, Dr. Keene. After all, the outcome of a computation can be no more valid than the data that it's based on; isn't that so? And in this case, you've just told us that all of the alleged data came from one source only, and a source, moreover, that has a significant—to put it mildly—stake in the outcome. Isn't *that* so?"

Exclamations of astonishment greeted the statement. Keene couldn't believe his ears. Voler had as good as directly questioned the Kronians' honesty. He shook his head, momentarily befuddled. "What are you trying to suggest, that the data weren't real . . . ? That they'd been faked or something?" he asked incredulously.

Voler raised both arms in an empty-handed gesture. "I'm simply pointing out that these results which we are being asked to accept depend wholly on data that we have no way of verifying, supplied from a single source at the last moment; and that source hardly qualifies as a disinterested party. One cannot but be struck by how conveniently these results accord with the case that's being argued, yet are incompatible with just about everything hitherto believed. An extraordinary coincidence, wouldn't you agree? Extraordinary claims requiring extraordinary proof. And you're saying it should be accepted purely on assurances."

Farther along the table to the side of the podium, Gallian was on his feet again, his face livid. "What kind of suggestion is this? We came here in good faith, believing this would be a debate of evidence, not an examination of our motives. Are we being called criminals now? Exactly what is Professor Voler insinuating?"

Keene had already seen Fey, sitting with a mixed group of people a couple of rows back from the front. She had a satisfied look, as if this whole thing had a personal dimension to it somehow and was settling some old scores. Keene had recovered sufficiently to think coherently again, perhaps, if not quite coolly. The audacity of the double standard being applied was staggering. After all the things that had been going on presumably with Voler's approval, if not actually under his direct instigation, *he* was now questioning the integrity of the Kronians? Keene couldn't swallow it. He had warned Fey that he was in a position and of a mood to expose what had been going on, and he had asked her to convey the message. Either she had ignored him, or Voler had. Well, Keene told himself, there would never be another opportunity like this.

He raised his head to address the whole floor. "This has gone far enough. If there were sound scientific reasons for questioning the claims that the Kronians are making, then of course this conference would be the place to hear them. But instead, it appears it's being turned into a forum for making accusations that can only be described as scandalous." Cries of "Hear, hear!" came from a few scattered places. Encouraged, Keene gripped the edges of the podium and looked around. "Very well. If that is the way it's to be, then let's have the full picture of things that *have* been happening, not unsupported insinuations or speculations about what might have happened. I would have preferred it if these matters had been referred to a more appropriate quarter." Around the room, heads were shaking; others exchanged mystified looks. "However, since we have been turned in this direction, let's talk about scientists I can name who have been intimidated by threats to their careers from voicing convictions to which years of intensive work have brought them; or about suppression of opposing views from the mass media by direct intervention to cancel already scheduled events at the last moment. Let's talk about actual censorship of publishing conducted through organized boycotts and letter campaigns. . . . And I remind you all again, I'm referring to things that *have taken place*, not exercises in fancy about what might have." Finally, Keene brought his eyes back down to where Voler was still regarding him from the floor, and pointed a finger. "And now the *same person* whose influence I can show as central to all the things I've just listed can stand here and make these kinds of allegations? . . ." Keene raised his hands in a brief appeal.

"I take it we're referring to this wealth of evidence that would prove conclusive if the scientific community and the world at large were permitted to share it without prejudice. Is that it?" Voler fired up at him.

"Thank you. I couldn't have put it better," Keene acknowledged.

Voler seemed unfazed by Keene's remarks but stood with his arms folded confidently. " 'Censorship.' 'Suppression,' " he repeated. "Our colleague, Dr. Keene, is quick in his use of strong words. We are accused of intervening in the activities of the media. But since when have the mass media constituted the proper channel for scientific discourse? It seems to me that what we've been seeing is more a case of the other side attempting to shortcut the regular process in order to create a jury of public opinion. When that happens, it's inevitably because the case is incapable of withstanding rigorous scrutiny. Seen in that light, our actions would be more accurately described as moving to prevent the public from being stampeded into graphically and emotionally portrayed beliefs on the basis of suspect claims and half-baked evidence. Well, isn't that what we have scientific institutions for? We've been reminded ceaselessly over recent months of the importance of the decisions that will be made as a result of these hearings. Very well, I'll reiterate it. Let us be mindful of them."

Approving murmurings came from the floor this time. Keene felt the foothold that had seemed so solid starting to slip. Gallian, still standing, was looking confused. Voler couldn't be turning this around. "No!" Keene threw out over the hubbub. "This is not something out of the tabloids. We turned to a public forum precisely *because* the institutions that Professor Voler puts such trust in have refused to see the facts in front of them." He extended an arm sideways. "The Kronians are scientists as competent as any in this room. The evidence they're asking us to look at is as solid and verifiable as anything in your own laboratories."

"Yes, we've just looked at an example of it," Voler remarked derisively.

"*You didn't! You're refusing to look at it!*" Keene shouted.

"Based on data that no one this side of Saturn has seen; allegedly obtained from probes whose very existence we have to accept on faith. You call that verifiable?" Voler taunted.

"What you are insinuating is inexcusable!" Gallian protested again, recovering his voice and rallying with Keene.

"We brought you a lot more than just the data from the probes," Sariena said from beside Gallian. Her face seemed flushed, even with her dark complexion. It was the first time that Keene had seen her registering anger. "Tangible evidence that you can hold in your hand. Was that supposed to be 'alleged'? Did we imagine it? Is that not verifiable enough for you, Professor Voler? Tell us. What else would it take to convince you?"

Voler raised his head sharply and swung to face the hall in a way that said they had just heard something important, so that by the time he turned back toward the dais the room had fallen quiet. There was something triumphant in his manner, as if he had been leading up to this moment all along. Keene sensed that some unexpected turn was about to take place.

"Ah yes, the tangible evidence," Voler repeated. He surveyed the room again, and then walked back to where he had been sitting, while the Kronians exchanged questioning frowns. Voler stooped to lift into view a large cardboard box about two feet along a side and set it down on the table. From it he produced an object wrapped in black cloth, which he uncovered and held aloft to reveal as what appeared to be a broken flake of brown rock, perhaps an inch thick and roughly the size of a dinner plate but with one straight side terminating at a distinct corner. "I assume we're talking about these." The Kronians looked horrified. Gallian started to protest, but Voler waved his other hand. "Oh, don't worry. This is just a plastic replica. The originals are in safekeeping, naturally." He moved back below the dais and turned to face the hall again. Sariena caught Keene's eye but Keene could only shake his head.

"Some of you know about these already," Voler said. "A public announcement was due to be made this week, so I don't think I'll be giving anything away if I bring the essence of it forward a little. Briefly, this is one of a number of objects that, we are told . . ." he paused and turned his head to look up at Keene pointedly for a moment " . . . were discovered in the ice of Saturn's moon, Rhea, around six months ago. They are clearly artifacts from an intelligent culture, and several of them carry samples of a distinct written script and other symbolic markings...." Astonished gasps began breaking out immediately, but Voler raised his voice and concluded, "Holographic images were sent ahead for experts here on Earth to examine, and the actual articles were delivered a matter of days ago. They are offered as proof that the configuration of the Solar System was once very different from what we know today—once again apparently corroborating in a striking fashion the claims that the Kronians have come here to put to us."

This time the flurry of voices took some time to die down. Voler moved back and rested casually against the edge of the dais while he waited. When he had the room's attention again, he half-turned to look up at the podium. "Would you describe your relationship with our Kronian guests as cordial, Dr. Keene?" he inquired. Once again, he seemed to have projected himself into the role of a lawyer conducting a trial.

"Well, yes, I suppose you'd say so," Keene agreed. He had no idea where this was going.

"Friendly, perhaps? You were in communication for many months. You and certain members of their scientific group got to know each other quite well, I understand."

"I guess so. That's natural enough for people who share professional interests. What of it?"

"Ah yes, sharing professional interests. Your interests are tied pretty tightly to whether or not the case that the Kronians are arguing is accepted, isn't it? And the interests of Amspace Corporation, with whom your company does the bulk of its work. If Earth were to initiate a large program of long-range space development in the way we are being urged, then not only would the future of the Kronian colony be assured but the prospects for success and fortune of both yourself and Amspace would be permanently guaranteed. Isn't that so?"

"Kronia's future doesn't need any assurance from Earth," Gallian fumed from behind the table, where he had finally been induced to sit down. "That's a pernicious myth that—"

"Please let Dr. Keene answer the question," Voler requested.

Keene's patience was getting close to its limit. "Yes, it's true," he replied curtly. "So what? Exactly what are you suggesting?"

Voler straightened up and moved forward so that while still addressing Keene, he was facing the auditorium. He raised the piece of imitation tablet aloft again. "Why was the specimen only delivered two days ago? The *Osiris* has been here for almost four weeks. Did somebody somewhere imagine that thorough physical tests wouldn't be possible in that time? If so, they must be getting desperate. Or was it more a case of simple naiveté and inexperience in terrestrial geology?"

By now, Keene was totally flummoxed. "Look, I don't . . . What is this? Will you just tell us what—"

Voler's voice resounded suddenly, cutting him off. "By every test of composition, chemistry, isotope ratios, spectral, neutron activation, and thermoluminescent analysis to which it has been subjected, the original specimen corresponding to this replica that I am holding in my hand is indistinguishable from Lower Cretaceous sandstone laid down here, on our own planet, approximately one hundred and thirty million years ago. Yet we're told it was found eight hundred million miles from Earth on a moon of Saturn. Now, how could that possibly be?"

"I . . . I . . . That's not possible." Keene shook his head.

The Kronians were in consternation. "But we brought them here ourselves," Gallian insisted. "Your analyses can't be as specific as you believe them to be."

Voler nodded and looked pleased. "Yes, I was waiting for that. Of course, the Solar System is just awash with oceans that could have laid down sandstone. Or are our experts supposed to be so inept that they mistake igneous lavas for sandstone? But fortunately, we don't have to rely solely on the word of our geologists. The script that I alluded to has been identified. It turns out to be a version of late Joktanian angular, clearly related to that found in the region of southwest Arabia and the African Horn in recent years, which is yet to be deciphered. In short, there can be no doubt that it came from the same planet that we are standing on, and the people who carved these symbols were of a culture that existed here and not out at

Saturn." Voler turned to face the dais again, finally. "And how, Dr. Keene, do you explain *that*?"

Keene couldn't. Snippets of what Vicki had said flew disjointedly through his mind, but he was unable to assemble them into anything coherent. His thought processes had seized up. Farther along at the table, Gallian was looking dazed. "But how could it have?" he asked. "We brought them here ourselves, from Saturn."

"From the same place as the probe data, maybe?" Voler suggested, stopping short of openly jeering but evidently enjoying himself.

"Are you trying to suggest that we faked that too now?" Gallian gasped. By now, the whole floor was listening in disbelief. The reporters at the back were having a field day, some already muttering into phones. At the central table, Schatz was shaking his head despairingly. This was unprecedented.

"I'm simply asking how objects from Earth could turn up on a moon of Saturn," Voler replied. He walked back to the center table and set the tablet down on the wrapping that he had removed. Then he looked up again. "But then, of course, we don't actually have *independent, verifiable* evidence that they ever were at Saturn, do we?" He turned to look back at the Kronians, as if half expecting an outburst. "The only indisputable fact is that they were brought down from the *Osiris* two days ago by the shuttle that returned a group of Kronians to the surface after spending a rest period up there. Everything else that we are told rests totally on assurances—just as with the data from the probes." Gallian started to rise again, his face crimson beneath his white hair. Vashen and Sariena pulled him back down, but then Voler turned away abruptly, picked up some papers from the table, and moved back to the front of the floor to look once more up at Keene. "And for that one, simple, indisputable fact, I think maybe we do have a simple possible explanation. Do you not think so, Dr. Keene?"

Keene was still trying to collect his wits. He shook his head impatiently. "I wasn't involved in any of this. I don't know what you're talking about."

"Oh, really? Then allow me to refresh your memory of a few things." Voler consulted one of the pieces of paper that he was holding. "The *Osiris* arrived in Earth orbit on Friday, May 6. On the evening of the following Monday, the Kronians held an informal reception at their suite in the Engleton Hotel, which I believe you attended. Is that so?"

"Yes, I did. What about it?"

"You weren't on the officially prepared list of guests, I see," Voler commented.

"I was invited by the Kronians directly," Keene retorted.

"Oh yes, of course. You'd been good friends for a while, hadn't you? . . . And tell me, Dr. Keene, is it true that on that occasion, you were introduced to a certain Catherine Zetl, a paleoanthropologist with the Smithsonian Institution, who has been involved in the Joktanian excavations that have been in progress for some time now?"

"We met, yes," Keene confirmed. What did this have to do with anything?

"And how would you describe Ms. Zetl's attitude toward the Kronians and the case they are arguing?"

"I don't recall that we talked much about it."

"Oh, you didn't. Well, I have it on record that she is extremely supportive of them and critical of what she likes to call 'official stodginess.' "

"Very well, if you say so. Am I being accused of something, or can we get back to what was supposed to be the business of this conference?"

Voler summarized: "So, you have been friends with the Kronians for a long time, in part because your professional interests coincide with their agenda. They arrange for you to attend a social gathering at which you meet another scientist sympathetic to their position, whose work happens to have included studying, cataloguing, and storing the very objects we have been talking about. And now let's move forward almost three weeks to May 24. On that date, isn't it true that you took part in another space mission conducted by Amspace—your long-term business associate who shares the same interests?"

It hit Keene then where Voler was going with this. Sudden dismay jolted him and must have showed. "*No,*" he protested.

"What? Are you saying that you didn't go on the mission launched on May 24?"

"I'm saying that what you're suggesting is ridiculous."

"I haven't suggested anything, Dr. Keene. What was the purpose of the mission?"

"*I tell you this is ridiculous!*" Keene said again, his voice rising.

"Please answer the question."

"What is this circus supposed to be? I came up here to describe our work in repeating the Kronian orbital calculations. Am I supposed to be on trial for something?"

The room had become solemn. "I think you should answer Professor Voler's questions," Schatz said from behind Voler, voicing the general mood.

Keene drew a long breath to calm himself. "It was to test a design of a hybrid engine," he replied.

"A chemical hybrid," Voler supplied. "This was a test of a conventional propulsion system?"

"Yes."

"But you are a specialist in nuclear propulsion, are you not, Dr. Keene? What was your role in the mission?"

"I wasn't involved in that part of it."

"Oh?" Voler feigned surprise. "There was another part? And what was that?"

"You obviously know damn well."

"Yes I do. And allow me to inform the rest of the people present here what it was." Voler turned to address the hall in general. "At the last moment, the mission was extended to include an additional phase: After completion of the hybrid trials, the Amspace craft made rendezvous and docked with the *Osiris*, where it remained for over twelve hours." Voler peeled off the last of the sheets of paper he was holding and held it high. "I have here a copy of the loading manifest of personal baggage items carried by the Amspace craft on that mission. It lists as an item forwarded for Doctor Landen Keene, one carton of weight fifteen point five kilos, described as containing twelve bottles of assorted wines." Keene looked across at the center table, where Voler had left the box that he had taken the replica from.

"Well, let's see," Voler went on, "in my estimation that would be about the size of the box over there. So, a couple of weeks after meeting Zetl, you took a box similar to that one up to the *Osiris*, and lo and behold, two days later the specimens that we are told came from Rhea are shipped down, just in time for this conference. Another amazingly convenient coincidence." Voler wheeled to face Keene fully. Finally, he dropped the playfulness that he had been affecting, and his expression darkened. "Seriously, Dr. Keene, are you really expecting us to . . ."

But the rest was drowned in the rising pandemonium coming from all sides. Keene had no answer to offer anyway. Anything he tried to say would have sounded lame. The Kronians, too, were sitting in silence, stunned. Keene was vaguely aware of figures coming forward into the space below, jabbering, shouting, and gesticulating. Somehow, Cavan's face materialized out of it all. "It isn't true, Leo," Keene said, still feeling this had to be some kind of dream. "You know it didn't happen that way. I can't explain it. Where do we start with something like this?"

"I don't know either," Cavan told him. "But I think that for the time being you need to forget any more arguing with scientists. What you're going to need is a firm of lawyers."

❀ 21 ❀

Until Voler's allegations were either proved or refuted there could be no continuance under the guise of a scientific debate, and the conference was suspended until further notice. Marvin Curtiss was as bewildered by it all as Keene. It was bad enough that public attention should be so completely diverted from the original issue at this crucial juncture; but even worse was Amspace's being implicated, calling into question the credibility and integrity of all the interests that the company was associated with. "Everything's turned into a political show trial," he groaned over the phone when Keene was finally able to talk to him. "It will take twenty years for this to wear off."

Carlton Murray, the head of Amspace's legal department, left on an afternoon flight from Texas with two of the firm's lawyers. They would meet with Keene that evening, and the following day make arrangements for representation by the company's Washington law firm. An outraged Catherine Zetl issued a public denial and announced her intention to sue, which raised the possibility of acting jointly. After a brief conference in a private room at the AAAS building, Gallian, for once noncommittal and subdued, told Keene to let him know what the lawyers wanted the Kronians to do after Keene met with them that evening. Gallian and the rest of the Kronians then retired to the Engleton for the remainder of the day. Keene told Vicki to expect to be effectively in charge of Protonix for a while, and then stopped by Information and Office Services in D.C. to have Shirley take care of everything there. For the sake of privacy and sanity he changed his hotel to the one that the Amspace lawyers would be checking into and forbade Shirley from revealing to anyone where he had gone. Jerry Allender offered to stick around, but Keene told him the whole business had moved way out of his field and there was little further that he would be able to do. Allender left, accordingly, on the last flight that night connecting to Corpus Christi.

The two lawyers accompanying Murray turned out to be Sally Panchard, an old hand who had been with Amspace for years, and Cliff Yeaks, a relatively new recruit from law school but bright, personable, and enthusiastic. Only when he was able to sit down with them in his room, finally removed from the frenzy that had followed him all day, was Keene able to give any real thought to what it all meant.

And what it meant was shattering. The accusations against himself, damaging as they would probably be to the public perception of the Kronians and which constituted Curtiss's main concern, were not what bothered him. Murray was confident that Voler had carried his theatrics too far, and if the true story were as Keene maintained, systematic investigation of the facts would eventually establish it. That didn't mean that somebody else hadn't taken the artifacts up to the *Osiris*, of course. It was hard to imagine any of the others on the minishuttle being involved, but Curtiss had authorized discreet background checks of all of them as a precaution. But all kinds of official craft had been shuttling up and down between the surface and the *Osiris* since its arrival, so there was plenty of room for the culprit to be elsewhere.

So did Voler really believe the line he had strung together about Keene? Or had he simply seized an opportunity to derail the Kronians when a convenient set of coincidences presented themselves, knowing that he would be able to admit hastiness and extract himself later? At this stage, it didn't really matter. What remained—unless some of the world's foremost experts were unable to tell terrestrial rocks and the work of an ancient human culture from things that had originated in another realm entirely—was that regardless of who had taken or sent them up to the *Osiris*, the artifacts *had* come from Earth, which could only mean that the story of their being found on Rhea was a fabrication. And if that were so, then what reliance could be placed on the probe data also? That, of course, had been Voler's real point. The rest, as likely as not, had been staged to grab some limelight for himself and embarrass Keene and Amspace at the same time.

In all his dealings with them, it had never crossed Keene's mind to question the integrity of the Kronians. Was it possible that he could have judged so wrongly? And if so, what else might he be wrong about? Maybe the Kronian colony *was* as stretched to its limit as the politicians and advisors on Earth had been saying all along, and desperation to the point of perpetrating a deception such as this was the result. Whatever their reasons or their situation, the fantasy Keene had toyed with of going back with them had exploded. His only desire now, after transferring all dealings to the lawyers, was to leave things in their hands from here on, get away from everything for a while, and then do some serious thinking about what he wanted to do with the rest of his life. First, however, it would be necessary for him to introduce the lawyers to the Kronians.

Although he had the direct personal calling codes that the Kronians had been assigned for the duration of their visit, matters were more formal now and he called the general number for the suite. A security man answered, and after verifying Keene's authentication put him through to the floor above. Vashen took the call, and when he saw that it was Keene, passed it over to Sariena. She was sleepy and not very communicative, which was hardly surprising. After checking with Gallian, she confirmed that tomorrow morning would be fine for a meeting with the lawyers. Since everything on their schedule had been canceled, there was little else for the Kronians to do anyway.

The next morning after breakfast, Keene was waiting in the hotel lobby, where he had arranged to meet the lawyers, when three men detoured by him while on their way toward the main doors.

"Aren't you the guy who was all over the news yesterday—the one who took the fake tablets up to the space ship?" one of them said.

Keene was momentarily taken aback. "Excuse me? . . . Oh. No, what they said wasn't true. There's a lot to be uncovered. Don't believe anything you hear at this stage."

"Oh yeah? Well, you tell those kook friends of yours that if they want to go back where they came from and freeze, that's okay. But don't come here expecting us to make it work for them, because it can't work. Especially when they have to lie about it. Okay?"

The three walked away before Keene could respond further. Just a month ago, he'd been a space hero taking on the Air Force. Already, he'd turned into a lackey of alien interests. Celebrity, it seemed, could be a short-lived thing.

The mood in the Kronians' suite at the Engleton was very different from what Keene remembered of the last time he was there. Instead of a party atmosphere and optimistic talk of exciting changes to come, the tone was set by somber-suited lawyers with laptops, heavy briefcases, and legal pads. No longer did the Kronians joke about the strange sights and experiences of Earth. Instead, they were listless and reticent, volunteering little beyond what they were asked, giving the impression of going along with something they had no choice in but being already resigned to the futility of it.

Keene didn't have a large part to play after making the introductions, having given his own story the evening before. Murray opened with general preliminaries, explaining Amspace's relationship with the Washington law firm, and since Amspace and the Kronians were implicated together, outlining the advantages of arranging comprehensive representation for all of them. However, that would depend on the outcome of talking with partners of the Washington firm, which he hoped to do later that day or tomorrow. The Kronians had no real questions, and Murray got down to the business of going over the reports and transcripts of the previous days' conference item by item to get the Kronians' version and their verification where quotes were attributed to them. All the time, Sariena kept giving Keene curious looks, while he did his best to avoid her gaze. Gallian's answers to the lawyers' questions became shorter and more strained. He seemed to be containing himself only with difficulty against rising impatience.

Finally, Murray leaned back in his chair, his pen held lengthwise between his fingertips, and contemplated Gallian for several seconds as if weighing how to make a delicate point. Gallian scowled back unhelpfully. "Look, I appreciate that ways of going about things might be different where you're from, and I've tried to allow for that," Murray said. "But I have to say, the answers you've been giving aren't exactly going to serve your best interests. You don't seem to understand how the system here works. We are not your adversaries in this. We're on your side. Our job is to put together a strategy that will get us through with the minimum of damage. But to do that, we need complete cooperation."

Gallian's jaw tightened. "I'm sorry. I thought we were cooperating," he replied.

Sally Panchard put in, "I think what Carlton's trying to say is that whatever else is admitted publicly, *we* need to know where those artifacts came from. But as far as the case itself is concerned, our position will depend on what we think the other side is able to prove. In other words, we give nothing away. Without proof, how can anyone know for sure if the artifacts were ever up in the *Osiris* at all? If they were given to you by someone here on Earth after you landed, who *said* they'd come out of the container that was shipped down, then Lan Keene, you, and everyone in your mission would be exonerated."

"Yes, yes. Those are just the lines I was thinking along," Murray interjected.

Sally went on, "There would still be the images that were beamed from Kronia to account for, but they could have originated here and been turned around. So the whole thing could have been engineered between a group of unknown parties here and in Kronia, and you were all used unwittingly."

Vashen was shaking his head, trying to follow. "But that wouldn't change what Voler was trying to say yesterday. You'd just be making others guilty instead of us."

"That's our job," Cliff Yeaks said. "You and Dr. Keene are our clients. The other guys are not. If Voler can't prove who did it, that's his problem. The thing that matters is, you guys will be off the hook."

Gallian emitted a loud sigh suddenly, got up from his seat, and stamped over to the window to stare out at the Washington rooftops. " '*The thing that matters,*' " he repeated. "All this posturing and antagonism, obsessions over who will win and who will lose. When will the people of this world ever learn to stop fighting each other and do things together? Doesn't it occur to anybody that the thing that matters might be *truth*?" He turned back to face the room. "Which side are you people on? All I'm hearing is nonsense about legal contortions and antics that don't interest me that can be dragged out to divert attention from the real issue forever. Is that what you want? I thought this was supposed to be a scientific matter. When are we going to get back to that? The only one among you who speaks that language is Landen, and he has said practically nothing. So why don't we stop talking about what stories we can invent and try concentrating on asking what really did happen?"

Keene answered, since Gallian was still staring at him. "I think that's what Carlton is trying to do. As he said, he needs to know exactly at what point those objects—the actual objects, not some kind of container that they were supposed to be in—came into your hands." Keene paused, then added as the thought struck him, "Come to that, *did* you ever actually see them outside of a container?"

"A good point," Sally said, nodding.

Gallian frowned from one to another of them. "I don't understand. I was quite familiar with them before they were crated. I was involved in some of the studies of them." He waited, inviting some explanation.

"Gallian," Keene said despairingly. "Now you're starting to sound as if they really did come from Saturn. Carlton just told you: he and his people are on your side, yet you're still giving them a hard time. I'm beginning to see his point."

"We're trying to get you out of a mess. This isn't helping." Yeaks groaned.

Total silence hit the room. Gallian stared at the Terrans first in noncomprehension, then with slowly growing incredulity. The rest of the Kronians were exchanging shocked looks or just sitting with dazed expressions. Involuntarily, Keene turned in Sariena's direction with a what-did-I-say? look.

"Oh my God," Sariena whispered. "Even you don't believe it, Lan." She faltered, looking at him in disbelief. "These fairy stories that you're talking about; they're not just for Terran melodramatics. You really imagine that some kind of alternative explanation has to be manufactured somehow."

Keene almost started to laugh. "You're not trying to tell us they're genuine, that they really were found on—"

"*Of course they're genuine!*" Sariena shouted. Keene blinked, feeling as if she had slapped his face. She raised a hand to her brow, started to say something, then rose, shaking her head. "I can't believe . . . Lan, how long have you known us? How long have we communicated, worked together? You know something about our values, our commitment to truth. Could you really imagine we'd be capable of such a thing?" Gallian moved to a chair and sank down onto it.

Keene didn't know how to respond. The two older lawyers saw that they were out of their depth and shut up. Yeaks looked at Sariena and showed his hands. "But how could that be possible? We've heard the evidence from yesterday. Nobody has even hinted of any doubts about it. We can hardly argue that those things didn't come from Earth."

"Oh yes, I'm sure you're right. They came from Earth," Sariena agreed tiredly.

Yeaks glanced at his colleagues as if checking that he hadn't missed something, then looked back at Sariena. "Then how can anyone believe they were found on Rhea? You can't go back out there and keep saying that. Nobody on Earth is going to believe it."

"It's as we said," Gallian declared, speaking to the Kronians. "Getting involved in the complications here will just be a waste of time and achieve nothing. I say we pack up and go back. We'll sort it out ourselves with our own scientists back in Kronia."

"Leave now, just like that?" Vashen said. "What about the emigrants we were due to take back?"

"Get the word out for them to bring their plans forward. Speed things up at Tapapeque. We'll wait for them in orbit," Gallian replied curtly.

Now Keene was confused. "What is there to sort out?" he demanded. "Cliff's point seemed pretty clear to me. You're admitting that the artifacts came from Earth, but at the same time you want to stick to the story that they were found on Rhea. You can't have it both ways, for heaven's sake. It doesn't make any sense. We're here. Saturn is eight hundred million miles away. Are you telling us that the Joktanians are supposed to have had space travel now?"

Sariena came over to sit down across from Keene and looked at him. There was no aggravation in her eyes now but something deeper, sadder—for a moment, it seemed, almost pitying. "Oh, Lan," she sighed. "You've tried so much to think like us, but you're still a Terran underneath, locked into your preconceptions. You really can't turn it around the other way, can you?"

"What do you mean?" Keene said. "Turn what around what other way?"

"We've been discussing it most of the night. Just believe the facts and accept their implication. Don't try to force anything to fit with what you think you already know. And you end up with only one answer." Keene looked to the lawyers for help. They shook their heads helplessly. He looked back at the Kronians.

Vashen raised a hand to enumerate on his fingers. "Fact one: those objects originated on Earth. Fact two: they were found on a moon of Saturn. Fact three: no interplanetary transportation existed at the time of creation."

"In other words, they couldn't have gone from here to there," Sariena said.

Silence fell again. "Now turn it around the other way, as Sariena said," Gallian told him from across the room.

Keene still couldn't figure what they were driving at. He looked at Sariena and shook his head.

"Therefore, they must have been created there, not here," she completed. "They were ejected off Earth in some kind of impact event, and later fell on Rhea."

It took Keene a further three or four seconds to grasp the only way in which that could have been so. Then his eyes widened slowly. "Surely not," was all he could manage.

Sariena nodded. "Their journey across space wasn't from here to there, but from there to here. And since there wasn't the technology to transport them, they must have come with the Earth itself. *Earth was once a satellite of Saturn!*"

Was it genuine? Or was it a face-saving ploy to let the Kronians extricate themselves from the affairs of Earth and depart? Keene didn't know. His confidence was not bolstered when Gallian refused to throw the matter open for debate on the grounds that after seeing the reaction of Earth's scientists to the Venus proposal, he wasn't even going to try getting them to listen to something like this. The Kronians would go back and pursue the matter themselves, with their own scientists. They abandoned plans for any further serious discussion on Earth, and began making departure preparations accordingly.

So, what were they: true visionaries impelled by an ethic that would never be understood on Earth; or failures who had fooled even Keene for a year, pulling out under a contrived pretext when it became clear that their bid to enlist help from Earth had failed? And the *Osiris*: Was it really the exemplar of what freed science could accomplish, as he had believed, or just a one-time showpiece achieved by hurling everything into a single-purpose project? Had the Kronians known all along that their position was precarious, and that they could well end up with enraged authorities on Earth opposing their departure if things went wrong, and was that why the *Osiris* was armed? Keene still didn't know what he believed when, a day later, with nothing more to be accomplished in Washington, he and the three lawyers boarded a plane at Reagan National Airport to head back to Texas.

◎ **22** ◎

The question nagged at Keene for days, allowing him to get little else done. Either the Kronians were guilty as charged and he had made one of the biggest misjudgments of his life, or one of the most stupefying scientific conjectures of all time was being missed because of politics and petty vanities. If the first, he was on the wrong side and it was time to redirect his life toward staking some claims in everything he had been missing out on. If the latter, then human-kind's way ahead lay with the different ethic of the Kronians, in which case Keene belonged out there and not here, and if they were already getting ready to leave he needed to make his mind up soon if he intended doing something about it.

It all hinged on the proposition that Earth had once been a moon of Saturn. If that were credible, then so were the Kronians. So how believable was it? Keene decided that he needed somebody suitably knowledgeable to help him untangle the questions clogging up his head. Most of the astronomers he knew—especially after the recent happenings in Washington—wouldn't want to get within a mile of something like this. In the end, he called David Salio. At first, Salio was still embarrassed after what he felt had been a betrayal, but his manner eased when it became clear that Keene was calling about something entirely different. Keene's opening sentences were enough to get him hooked, and they arranged a meeting for that same afternoon. Keene flew up to Houston on the midday flight and spent the afternoon and evening with Salio. Salio couldn't guarantee to Keene that the latest Kronian proposition was not a line they had fabricated to extricate themselves; but neither did he dismiss it as impossible. Certainly, the suggestion that the motions of other planets too, not just Venus, might have been different in times gone by didn't offend him in the way it had other astronomers Keene had talked to.

"There's good reason for supposing that Mars moves differently from the way it used to," he told Keene. "The Kronians think that after Venus's close pass with Earth, it went into an orbit that brought it close again periodically—though never with anything like the devastation of the first encounter, of course. That was why just about every ancient culture watched it so closely, keeping charts to track its every movement and viewing its approaches in trepidation as a portent of destruction. Finally, somewhere around 700 B.C., it came close to Mars in an event once again recorded everywhere as a celestial combat of gods, altering Mars's orbit and afterward settling down to the circularized orbit we see today."

"Cooled down from the plasma state, with the electrical effects dissipated," Keene remarked.

Salio shrugged. "We don't know enough about that yet to say. But if something as recent as that is at least plausible, who's to say what the situation might have been in this more distant era that the Kronians are talking about? Without knowing the truth about those artifacts, I can't tell you that the Kronians didn't make it up. That's for your lawyers to figure out. But it's certainly not grounds for writing them off, either."

Keene caught the last flight back to Corpus Christi, where Vicki met him at the airport—he had lent her his car that day since hers was in the shop. She looked trim and classy in a cool summer dress and greeted him with a hug that felt nice after a long, hectic day. "We could redeem one of the outstanding rain checks at the Bandana," she said as they walked out past Baggage Claim. "Robin's overnighting with a friend, and I can live it up—the life I've always dreamed about."

"You must read minds too," Keene said. "Sure, I could use a beer. Planes and peanuts always make me dry."

"So how did it go with Salio?" she asked as they began crossing the parking lot. "What did he have to say?"

"He was fascinated. Said it was the most exciting thing he'd heard for years. He even came up with some thoughts of his own about it that could answer a number of puzzles that have been going around for a long time. For example, Saturn could have provided a more benign environment for life to have gotten started in than here, close to the Sun. No fierce ultraviolet to break up early, fragile molecules before there was ozone."

"He didn't think it would be too cold out at that distance? That was one of the things that bothered me."

"Not necessarily. If Saturn was a protostar at one time that didn't make it to fusion ignition, it might still have radiated enough to warm its satellites."

"What about when Earth escaped?"

Keene shrugged. "Maybe there's your Ice Age. . . . In any case, with all the other things going on that we've been talking about, Saturn might not have been at the same distance then. I can see why Gallian thinks there's enough new science to keep them busy for fifty years."

Vicki glanced at him silently as they walked. Her expression still held a touch of skepticism. "Could it really have been that recently?" she queried. "Enough for humans to have seen it?"

"Well, it's beginning to look as if things could change a lot quicker than has always been thought. Salio thinks the whole geological and astronomic time frame is screwed up."

"Don't tell me 4,004 B.C. is true after all."

"No. But he's pretty certain that the conventional figures are going to have to be drastically revised downward, all the same."

"So does he buy the idea of a one-time satellite of Saturn?" Vicki asked.

"Until we know for sure one way or the other about the artifacts, he can't say," Keefe replied. "It could be a scam; it could be straight. That's where Murray and the lawyers ought to have been pitching in. Where we go next, I'm not sure."

Vicki handed him the keys. He opened the passenger door for her and saw her in, then walked around and got in the driver's side.

"I'm surprised they didn't stay on in Washington longer," Vicki said as they moved out. "I can see why you and Jerry would be out of it now. But doesn't the legal mess up there need attention?"

"There wouldn't be any point," Keene said. "The Kronians aren't interested. They're going back—either to work on their theory or figure out how else they're going to save their colony. I don't know which. It depends on whether they're genuine or not. The last I heard, Idorf was bringing the *Osiris* up to flight readiness."

"Ouch. I didn't realize it was so soon. It's really that hopeless?"

Keene sighed. "Well, if you and I have trouble buying it, the establishment isn't even going to want to hear. If they really are genuine, then Gallian is probably right in thinking that getting tangled up in legalities would just be a waste of time. He told Murray that no law firm would take Kronians on anyway. After Voler's act, they'd be too worried about the bill being paid in faked money."

Vicki smiled and snorted, but remained serious, staring out into the night in silence for a while. Then she said, "You know, there's a lot more at stake here than I realized before. If the whole thing is a scam, the only thing that makes sense as to why the Kronians should have gone to such lengths is to get a share of the real power structure instead of being just an outpost on the fringes. Because if they'd gotten Earth behind them in this program they came here to sell, that's what it would have meant. It does makes a crazy kind of sense."

Keene shook his head. "It's not crazy at all. That's the jackpot question, Vicki. If it was a scam, and we bought it but the people we thought we were so much smarter than didn't, Kronia is finished. But if it's straight . . ." he sought for a phrase, "then they could be the next leap in the social evolution of the human species."

Vicki fell silent again while she thought about it. "You don't really believe them, though, do you, Lan?" she said finally. "The Kronians. Deep down, you're not convinced."

Keene looked across at her, surprised. "I said I don't know what to believe. What makes you say that?"

Vicki shrugged lightly. "You're here, back in Texas. You didn't stay around to see them off. What does that tell you?"

They pulled into the parking lot in front of the Bandana and parked next to a pickup, where a group of a half dozen to a dozen youths and girls were standing around talking in the flickering glow from the neon signs. The sound of heavy-beat country music from inside greeted them as they climbed out of the car. The air was warm and close after Washington, but with a fresher scent coming in with the breeze off the coastal plain. Keene stretched his arms and looked up at the sky. All that could be seen of Athena now was a pale glow over the western horizon. Even though the time was approaching midnight, a matter of days ago it would have been a bright column climbing halfway up the sky. It meant that the tail was foreshortening as Athena came around from perihelion, swinging around like a lighthouse beam to sweep past Earth before Athena crossed Earth's orbit in just a few weeks time. Between now and then it would become the most spectacular object to fill the sky ever in human history—unless, of course, the Kronians were right about the Venus encounter.

"How ya doin'?" one of the youths inquired genially as Keene walked around the car to join Vicki. He was tall and lean, wearing jeans with a plain shirt and vest, and had a white ten-gallon tipped to the back of his head.

"Doing okay," Keene replied. "How about you guys?"

"Oh, just fine. It's busy in there tonight, I'm tellin' ya."

"We'll risk it."

"Take care, now."

Keene followed Vicki up a few steps up to the entry porch. "I think I'll get a hat and some boots," he said as he stepped ahead to hold the door. "The prettiest girls always seem to hang around with the cowboys."

"Those could be your granddaughters," Vicki told him. The noise intensified suddenly as they went through.

"Even better. . . . Which reminds me, have we heard anything more about what Karen's doing?"

"Yes, she's definitely moving to Dallas. It might be a bit sooner than she thought, though."

"Um." Keene stood looking around. The dance floor was filled, and a mostly male crowd was clustered in the vicinity of the bar. It wasn't going to be easy to get a booth or a table in the front lounge. Keene looked across to the far side. "Maybe we could go through into the restaurant," he said. "They look as if they've got more room in there. I never thought to ask, have you eaten?"

"I did earlier—but I could use something with a drink, sure."

They made their way through the bar and dance area to the restaurant and grabbed a corner table just as another couple were vacating it. A waitress came to clear the dishes and give them menus, announced that she was Julie, and took an order for drinks. Keene decided he wasn't up to a full meal or in the mood for a burger. The steak sandwich sounded good. Or maybe something lighter, like a salad. . . . "I suppose we get the recitation about the specials when she gets back," he said, scanning the Mexican section. "Have you ever noticed? They don't listen. 'I'm Julie, your server. How are you today?' And if you say, 'Suicidal,' it's, 'That's nice. Our specials are . . .' I'll show you when she gets back. . . . But I guess it's not really surprising when they have to say it probably a hundred times a day." There was no response. He looked up and realized that Vicki wasn't listening either, but was staring past him with a strange, fixated look on her face. "Hello?" he said. "Anyone home?"

Vicki answered after several seconds, seemingly from a million miles away. "Dinosaurs. . . ."

"What?" Keene waited, but that was all he got. He turned to see what she was staring at. On the wall behind him was an old movie poster from the nineties or thereabouts advertising something called *Jurassic Park*. It showed a tyrannosaurus, various characters and a truck, and a pack of smaller dinosaurs bounding across a grassy landscape. "What about them?" he asked, turning back.

Vicki remained distant, speaking almost to herself. "They couldn't have existed unless conditions then were very different. Gravity had to have been smaller. The whole scale of the engineering was wrong. . . ." She focused back on Keene slowly. "Lan, how easy is it to figure an estimate of this in your head. Suppose Earth were orbiting a giant primary like Saturn just outside its Roche limit, with one side phase-locked toward it. How far out would that be? And at that distance, how much would the primary's gravity reduce Earth's surface gravity by on that side? Could it be enough to allow things like that to live and move around? And if Earth escaped, the gravity would increase. Could that explain why all of the giant forms died out, and the things that replaced them were smaller?"

Keene looked at the poster again, turned slowly back toward Vicki, but already he wasn't seeing her. In his mind he was picturing a world of gigantic beasts, with enormous plants and trees, and a huge, mysterious globe ever-present in the sky. Gradually, he became aware of a voice saying, " . . . with our own, homemade, Bandana peppercorn sauce. . . . Gee, I don't know why I bother. Nobody listens. Would you like me to give you another couple of minutes?"

"Er, yes . . . please, Julie. Sorry, we were away on something else." Keene picked up his beer, which had arrived unnoticed. "My God," he breathed when Julie had gone.

"They *were* right!" Vicki said in an awed voice. "Earth was out there when those artifacts were made. The Kronians were right. . . . It means they're genuine, Lan. Oh, my God, and look how they've been treated here. Even you didn't believe them in the end, and came back. And they're right. . . . I'd be going back too. Their science might get to the bottom of this. Here, it wouldn't even get a hearing."

Keene pushed himself back from the table, all thoughts of eating suddenly gone. "We have to talk to them about this," he said. "I can't do any figuring or call them with this noise. We need to go back to the office."

"You're going to call them now? It'll be nearly one A.M. in Washington."

"This can't wait. They could be shipping out in the morning for all I know. Come on, we have to leave."

Vicki nodded and rose without protest. Keene took a ten from his billfold and put it on the table. They met a confused Julie coming the other way when they were halfway back across the bar area. "Oh, you're leaving? Was there something wrong?" she asked them.

"No, nothing to do with you. We've taken care of you," Keene told her. "We'll be back another time. Just a rain check."

"It's the story of my life," Vicki murmured to Julie as she followed Keene toward the door.

❂ 23 ❂

Keene didn't want to wake up the entire Kronian mission at this hour by calling the general number. So, reversing his earlier decision of keeping to a more formal level of dealings, he called the direct personal code that Sariena had given him. She answered sleepily in voice-only mode, obviously having already retired. Her first reaction was surprise. She clearly hadn't been expecting to hear from Keene again—at least, not for a while.

"I'll be honest," Keene told her. He was in his office in the darkened Protonix building. Vicki sat listening in a chair pulled up to one end of the desk, which was littered with scrawled diagrams and calculations. "I left because I didn't know what to believe. I had doubts; I admit it. It's embarrassing to look back at, but it's the way it was. What else can I say?"

"Well . . . I'm glad that you seem to be having second thoughts about us," Sariena said. "And I don't want to sound ungrateful that you called, or disinterested. But couldn't it have waited until morning?"

"That could," Keene agreed. "But there's more that couldn't. I'm with Vicki in the office in Corpus Christi."

"In the *office*! At this time? . . ."

"I think she might have hit on something that clinches your case. It's something she and I have talked about before, but there was never any reason to connect it with Saturn. The whole age of gigantism with the dinosaurs and everything—I don't know if you've ever gone into the scaling implications, but nothing of those sizes could function in the conditions that exist on Earth today. The gravity is too strong. But suppose those conditions didn't always exist. Suppose Earth were a phase-locked satellite, close-in to a giant primary. The primary's attraction would reduce the value on the facing side. Combine that with what you've told us about Rhea. . . . It all fits."

There was a long silence. Finally, Sariena said, "Let me put something on and get to a real phone. Stay on the line. I'll be about a minute."

"Seems like it got her attention," Vicki murmured.

Keene looked across at her. "Boy, isn't Robin going to be pleased."

They waited. Then the screen of the desk unit brightened, and Sariena appeared against a hotel-room background, wearing a dark wraparound robe. She had evidently been doing some hurried thinking. "It appears to make so much sense," she said, then mustered an awkward smile. "It's *I* who ought to be apologizing, Lan. You *can* think like Kronians."

"Thank Vicki," Keene grunted. "Or, maybe we should all thank Robin."

"Who's Robin?"

"Vicki's son. He's fourteen. He's the one who's been telling us that dinosaurs couldn't have existed."

"Are you there, Vicki? Robin sounds like quite a person. Life must be interesting at your house."

"Tell me about it," Vicki called from where she was sitting. "I'm sorry things in Washington went the way they did."

"Well, no doubt we shall survive it. What it tells us is that Kronian and Terran science can't work together. And maybe that was something that needed to be seen and understood plainly. So perhaps, if for no other reason than that, the mission served its purpose. In the long run, it might be for the better in any case. These things that we're still only touching on will lead to a whole rewriting of just about everything we thought we knew. We're probably better off being free to pursue it in our own way."

"You sound as if you could buy this idea of Vicki's, then," Keene said.

"I could in principle," Sariena replied. "It would be nice to see something quantitative that at least fits the picture."

"I did some rough calculations here before we called," Keene said. "To be frank, they don't look too promising. Even with the most extreme assumptions that I can justify, the answers I get aren't anywhere near big enough. . . . But I could be missing something. You're the planetary scientist. I'll leave it with you."

"Well, all we can do is pass all of this new material back to the scientists in Kronia," Sariena said. "They know more about the dynamics of the Saturnian system than anyone. I don't know where it will go from here. We might have to wait years before anything can be answered with confidence."

Even after dealing with Kronians for a year, Keene was astonished at the ease with which Sariena was able to adjust her horizons to accommodate these new possibilities. Already he could sense an entire new program of research about to take shape out at Saturn after the *Osiris* returned. Now that his fears were allayed, all doubts had fled that he should have been going too. But the moment was gone. He had wavered at the crucial juncture, and the effect couldn't be undone. Doubtless, there would be another ship, another time— but not this time. All the same, it was nice to think that until that time, whatever transpired out there now, in a way he would still be part of it.

"Well, I guess that for a while we'll have to leave it with you people," he said. "Do I take it you'll continue staying in touch and keep us posted on developments?"

"But of course." Sariena sounded surprised that he should have thought it necessary to ask.

Keene was relieved. "Do you know when you'll be leaving yet?" he asked.

"No. There's some kind of administrative complication. The arrangements are on hold right now. I'm not sure of the details."

"Maybe if it's going to be a day or two, we could come back up and say so long to all of you properly," Keene offered.

Sariena smiled. "I appreciate the thought, but it isn't really necessary. I'll convey it to Gallian."

"I guess you've got something more to throw at him when you see him in the morning," Keene said. "How's he bearing up under all this?"

"Oh, he's not asleep. He and Vashen are away at some meeting somewhere. They've been gone for several hours."

"*At this time?* What kind of a meeting, for heaven's sake? Who with?"

"I really don't know. Some people came here earlier this evening and talked to him in private, and then he and Vashen left with them. I don't know what it's about. Whatever it was, Gallian was looking very serious."

Mystified, Keene looked across at Vicki as if for suggestions. "Maybe they're billing him for the rooms and just wanted to make sure nobody got away first," she suggested dryly. Sariena didn't quite seem to follow the remark.

"It doesn't look as if you'll be leaving anytime soon, then," Keene said, looking back at the screen showing Sariena. "We thought it might be tomorrow morning. That was why I didn't want to put off calling you."

"Well, I don't think you need worry about that," Sariena answered. "As I said, I really don't know what's going on. But if it's something important, I'll let you know. I'm sure Gallian would want to talk to you again before we leave, anyway."

"Yes, do. I'd like that. Well . . ." Keene made a casting away gesture. "There we are. In case we don't get another chance to say so before you go back, it was an experience meeting you and the others face-to-face finally. Working with you even for this short time has been a revelation. I'm only sorry that your mission here didn't produce a more positive result. But maybe we all realize now that perhaps that could never have been. I get the feeling there's going to be lots going on that we'll be talking about. It's just a pity that it'll be from so far away again."

"And it has been an experience for us," Sariena replied. "This is truly an amazing world. Our whole race is amazing. And it will continue to expand and grow despite these setbacks. That's what we should all remember, and work toward making happen. . . ." She hesitated for a moment. "I'm glad that we didn't part on a note of misunderstanding and bitterness, Lan. Take good care of him, Vicki."

"I just run a business with him." Vicki smiled, got up and moved around the desk so that she was in the viewing angle with Keene. "But I like the things you say, Sariena. And I'm sure you'll be proved right one day. Have a safe voyage."

"Make sure you take care of Robin, then. Perhaps we'll even see him at Saturn one day—at least for a visit. It sounds as if he has the makings of a Kronian already." There was a drawn-out moment of silence. Then Sariena raised a hand. "Good-bye, Lan . . . Vicki, for the time being, anyway. And thanks for all you've done. It won't be in vain. You'll see."

The screen blanked out.

❂ 24 ❂

Keene slept late and arrived back at Protonix around mid morning. He had already talked to Marvin Curtiss, Les Urkin, Carlton Murray, Harry Halloran, Wally Lomack, Shirley in Washington, and everyone else who had been looking for him during his absence the previous day, so there were relatively few surprises waiting to pounce. Neither, to his mild disconsolation, was there any message from Gallian or Sariena. He waited until noon and then decided to call them, using the general number. The manner of the security man who answered was cool and detached.

"I'm sorry, Dr. Keene, but I can't connect you. You're name isn't on the cleared list."

Keene was flabbergasted. "What? But that's ridiculous. I was one of their guests. . . . I mean, I've *been* there. You put me through yesterday."

"A restricted policy is in force now. I'm not authorized to give you access."

"But, but . . . they're personal friends of mine. This is insane. I demand to speak with Gallian, head of the Kronian delegation there."

"I'm sorry, Dr. Keene, but I have strict orders. I can give you the number of my superior if you wish."

Keene noted the number but sat staring at it for several minutes after he hung up. Deciding he had better things to do than get involved in arguments with layers of officialdom he tried Sariena's personal number, only to get a recording: *We're sorry, but the number you have called, 202-555-3325, is not currently in service. If this appears to be in error, please check with the directory or press 611 for assistance.*

His apprehension rising, he clicked to his own directory and retrieved the off-surface code to connect with the *Osiris*. A jarring tone told him the channel was unavailable. Now certain that something was wrong, he punched in the digits for the long-distance operator.

"I'm sorry, sir, but that service is temporarily discontinued," she advised.

"What do you mean, discontinued? It's the trunk beam up to the Kronian spaceship that's in orbit. I'm a personal acquaintance of the captain."

The robotlike voice repeated, "I'm sorry, sir, but all I can tell you is that the service has been temporarily—"

Keene cut the connection with a snarl, pounded the arm of his chair, and sat staring exasperatedly at the screen for several seconds. Then he rose to his feet, paced over to the door and back, glowered at the screen some more, finally turning for the door and storming through into the corridor just as Vicki was coming out of her own office on the other side. "Oh, not again," she groaned, stepping back a pace to stay out of the way.

Keene strode through into the reception area, where Karen was helping Celia check some figures. "Karen, look up the numbers for Leo Cavan of SICA and track him down, wherever he is, would you? I need to talk to him now, right away, *maintenant, jetzt, ahora, adesso.* If you can't find him, find Herbert Voler."

"Lan, what are you doing now?" Vicki asked despairingly as he turned to head back to his office.

"There's something strange going on," he told her. "I don't like the feel of it. I can't get through to the Kronians or their ship. There are two kinds of people that they won't let you talk to: ones who don't want publicity, and prisoners. The Kronians came eight hundred million miles to try and get publicity. So what does it tell you?"

Karen got through to Cavan ten minutes later on a permanently open personal code that he had given Keene, only to be used in emergencies. He was on his way to a meeting in the SICA offices and had to keep things brief. "I'm not sure what's going on, Lan," he said. "Something's in the wind here, but nobody's talking. I do know it goes all the way to the top. There's an information blackout in force, which obviously includes the Kronians. Even I haven't been able to get access to Gallian this morning. Somebody doesn't want the world talking to them. It was ordered by a security official in the middle of the night. But what seems significant to me is that it's still being applied. It hasn't been rescinded."

"It's more than just an attempt to stop them leaving in such a hurry, then," Keene concluded, which had been his first thought.

"It would be a pretty drastic way of going about it," Cavan agreed. "Any guesses?"

"I'm afraid not. For once in your life, you have me at a loss, Landen."

Keene drummed his fingers on the desk and hesitated. "The other thing might be to try Idorf," he said, finally. "If it involves their plans or something to do with Saturn, he'd know about it, surely."

"You won't get through. The *Osiris* is restricted to an official channel only," Cavan said.

"I know, I already tried calling. But Amspace can bypass the regular net and get it on a direct beam when it's above the horizon. We've still got the access protocols they gave us to get into their file system. It might be possible to create a message link from there."

There was short silence. Then, "Give it a try, Landen. Keep me posted. And if I learn anything more at this end, I'll do likewise. Must go now. Why does life happen in tidal waves?" Cavan hung up.

Keene went through into Judith's office and found Vicki there. He waited in the doorway for them to finish speaking.

"Oh, is the beast fed?" Vicki checked warily.

"Yes, it's safe. . . . Judy, do something for me when you're through, would you? Lines to the *Osiris* are being blocked. I want to bypass the public system and try getting through direct. Would it be possible to create a connection via a beam from Amspace, using the access codes we've got for the file system?"

Judith thought for a few seconds. "It should be. . . . But with just a skeleton crew up there, it mightn't be set up to get attention at their end."

"Okay, well, get onto Amspace and find out when the ship's due overhead, and give it a try. If it works, I want to talk to Idorf."

"What are you getting us into now, Lan?" Vicki asked suspiciously.

"I'm not getting us into anything. I'm just trying to find out what's going on."

Vicki gave a resigned nod. "That's how it always starts."

Cavan called back around mid afternoon to say that Voler and a number of other leading astronomers had been called to a meeting at the White House, as well as top officials from the Federal Emergency Management Agency, the Departments of State and Defense, NASA, and the principal security agencies. It was being given a low profile to avoid media attention, but a lot of encrypted communications traffic was passing between departments involved in orbital and lunar operations and space agencies overseas, and all kinds of routine business was being canceled. There was a lot of strain and tension in the air. That was about as much as Cavan knew.

An hour later, Judith called Keene in his office to say she had Idorf on a link through Amspace. "You did it!" Keene got up to close the door with a foot and then resumed his place before the screen. "Good girl. I knew you'd hack it."

"It wasn't me," Judith told him. "I was still working on it. This is incoming. He's calling you." Moments later, Keene found himself looking at the lean, hawkish features with the reddish hair and raggedy beard. Idorf didn't look in the friendliest of moods; neither did he have time for social pleasantries.

"Dr. Keene, I'm sorry if this is inappropriate, but I don't pretend to understand how things work in your world. I'm contacting you because you are a person who gets attention and can convey a message to the proper people; also, I respect you as someone whose word can be relied upon. I cannot say the same for many of the others that I've been hearing recently. My impression is that they are likely to say anything they think I want to hear if they believe it might get them what they want. I'm told this is what you call politics."

Play this ree-al easy, Keene told himself. He tried to look composed. "I appreciate the compliment, Captain Idorf. How can I help?"

"Are you aware that the departure of our delegation is being obstructed?"

"No, I wasn't. I knew there was a block on communications, and in fact was trying to get through to you via Amspace to find out more. I'm back in Texas now, away from it all. What's happening?"

"The transportation that was supposed to be made available to bring them back up to the *Osiris* is not forthcoming. I am also informed that the emigrants who have been booking earlier flights to the Tapapeque base in Guatemala have been put on hold." Keene started to inject that he knew something strange was going on in Washington, but Idorf went on, "Today, I announced that if your government was not going to provide a shuttle to bring our delegation up, I would send one of our own surface landers down to get them. I was *warned off* by Terran defenses, Dr. Keene! They advised me that any such unauthorized landing would be treated as a hostile act, and the craft seized. So, are we at war now, eh? Does Earth jump to the only kind of solution it has ever been able to conceive for any problem?"

Keene was aghast. "My God! Look . . . I know something's been—"

"Ah, but that's not the end of it. Two hours ago, I was advised of an intention to send a military boarding party up to this ship and asked to cooperate peacefully 'for our own security and protection,' whatever that is supposed to mean. . . ."

"*Jesus Christ!* I—"

Idorf's hand appeared in the foreground on the screen, pointing a finger. "Very well, they have made their rules clear. Now this is what I would like you to convey, if you would, to whoever down there should hear it. Years ago, when relations between our two societies were more strained than in recent times, there seemed a real possibility that Earth might send an expedition to take over Kronia forcibly. We devoted considerable effort of the kind that produced vessels such as this one to the development of advanced defense systems, and it has been our policy ever since to build all new ships with a dual-role capability. The *Osiris* is armed, Dr. Keene. The weapons that it carries are of extreme potency. We will fire upon any craft, manned or otherwise, that attempts approaching closer than one hundred miles without authorization, whether or not it acknowledges further warnings. I trust you will have gathered by now that I am not of a mood to make jokes. I'm hesitant to put this to the people I've listened to today, because I fear they might attribute the same slipperiness to my words as appears to apply to their own. But as I said, you strike me as someone who will put it in the right way, to the right persons. Have I been clear enough? And if so, will you do as I ask?"

Keene eased himself back in the chair and exhaled a long, silent whistle. "Yes. Perfectly clear, Captain. . . ." He thought furiously about how much it might be wise to divulge. Finally, he decided that the way to respond to candor was with candor. "I already knew that the ship was armed," he said. "When we visited you, a colleague and I strayed off the path we were supposed to be on, and saw inside one of the hub cupolas. The machinery looked like an ejector, and whatever it launches is obviously nuclear. What is it? At a guess— some kind of fission-pumped, multipointing beam device? X-ray laser, maybe?"

Idorf's eyebrows arched. "I respect your frankness, Dr. Keene. And you are remarkably well informed. Each capsule deploys a gigajoule charge and generates multiple, independently targetable beams at a ten-thousandth of an Angstrom. I don't think I have to spell out what that would do to a target at a hundred miles."

Or a thousand, Keene thought to himself. "I am a nuclear engineer," he said. "And I worked in plasma physics research for a while. In fact I've been involved in studies of that kind of system. How much of the specification are you prepared to release?"

Idorf shrugged. "As much as it takes to convince them."

"I think I can do that for you," Keene said dryly. "Okay, let me ask you for some numbers." He paused and looked at the screen quizzically. "But first . . ."

Idorf waited. "Yes?"

"What's going on? Do you know any more than I do? . . . What is this all about?"

"Nobody's told you yet, eh?"

Keene showed his palms. "I've been trying to find out all day. It's almost like you said. The whole of the Washington's acting as if there is a war about to break out."

Idorf regarded him fixedly for a few seconds; then, he seemed to make up his mind and nodded. His expression was grim. "Yesterday evening, I passed some news down to Gallian that had just come in from Saturn. Our observatories there have been able to make measurements that won't be possible here for a few more days until Athena moves farther out from the glare of the Sun. It seems we can forget further speculating about whether the electrical environment can be altered, Dr. Keene. Athena has come out from perihelion on a changed orbit. It isn't going to cross fifteen million miles ahead of Earth as was previously thought. *It's coming straight at us!*"

Keene called Cavan on a secure channel to inform him as he had promised he would. Cavan seemed too stunned to make much by way of reply just for the moment. However, he wouldn't be the person to send Idorf's message through, since doing so would invite questions about his and Keene's previous dealings. Instead, on Cavan's recommendation, Keene contacted a presidential defense advisor called Roy Sloane and passed on Idorf's warning. To back it up, he quoted the figures that Idorf had revealed, adding a few pertinent observations that he and Wally Lomack had made during their visit. He kept strictly to the script that Idorf had indicated, making no mention of Athena. Sloane was familiar with Keene's name, took the warning seriously, and asked Keene to leave it with him. Thirty minutes later, he called back.

"You say that you and your colleague Wallace Lomack actually saw these weapons with your own eyes, Dr. Keene?" he checked.

"Yes, that's right."

"You can describe the construction and layout, detail the main assemblies, give performance estimates?"

"Not of the actual pods, which were in shielded storage. But of the hoist and ejection systems, yes. And some idea of functions from the local backup controls."

"We need both of you here, Dr. Keene. Can you contact Mr. Lomack down there and tell him he needs to get ready to travel tonight? Or would you rather we have one of our people call him?"

"*Tonight?* I don't know if we can get a flight at that notice," Keene said.

"Oh, we'll take care of that. When you're coming to meet the President, it's on Uncle Sam's tab."

Keene called an astonished Wally Lomack and told him the minimum that was necessary at that point. He debated with himself about telling Vicki everything but decided that until he knew more than he did, there was little purpose to be served. So, giving her just the Idorf's-warning part of the story, he entrusted the office into her charge once again and drove home. He just had time to pack his bag once again before a staff car with a lieutenant and a WAVE driver arrived from the Corpus Christi Naval Air Station at the end of Flour Bluff to collect him. From Keene's place they went on to Lomack's house to pick up Wally, and from there to the airfield, where an executive jet with Navy markings was warmed up and waiting. They flew to Andrews Air Force Base, Washington, and were met there by a car from the White House vehicle pool. The radio was running a program about vacation spots in South America for the rest of summer and fall. Athena was due to intercept Earth in less than three weeks.

❂ PART TWO ❂

SATURN: NURTURER OF LIFE

✵ 25 ✵

The meeting was clearly destined to run through into the early hours. It was being held in what Keene had been told was the Yellow Room in the South Wing, furnished in Queen Anne period against a background of satin hangings, ochre carpeting, redwood panels, and landscape paintings. Twenty or so people were present, including President Samuel Hayer, David Novek, head of the National Security Council, William Born, Deputy Secretary of Defense, and General Patrick Kilburn of Air Force Space Command. Voler was there also, with his astronomer colleague Tyndam, so far acting as if Keene didn't exist. He spent a lot of time conversing with a man called Vincent Queal, apparently from one of the intelligence agencies. Most notably absent was the Vice President, Donald Beckerson, who was conferring with defense officials at the Pentagon.

A large wall screen uncovered by sliding panels showed several views of the *Osiris* and a chart of its internal layout that the Kronians had released some years previously. On it, the weapon-launch housings were left unidentified and the armory serving them conveniently obscured by other details of the structure. Keene had described his and Lomack's impressions close-up, and outlined the nature of the weapons. After being launched a safe distance from the vessel, each pod would detonate a moderate nuclear charge at the

211

center of an array of heavy-element lasing rods, probably in the order of six feet long, that could be aimed independently at a mix of near and distant targets. In the billionths of a second before the rods and the ellipsoid-walled focusing cavity surrounding them were vaporized, the energy from the bomb would be concentrated into intense beams of X rays aligned along the rod axes, which could be aimed with precision. From the scale of the hoist machinery between the shielded armory where the weapons were stored and the launch housings, Keene guessed that the pods carried a propulsion unit, indicating that they needed to get a long way from the ship before activating. This gave a minimum estimate for their power, which fitted with the numbers that Idorf had supplied. Keene explained from beside a table near the screen, where he had placed his notes.

"A medium hydrogen bomb produces around ten to the power fifteen joules of energy in a millionth of a second, which works out at ten to the twenty-one watts, or a one followed by twenty-one zeros. That's equivalent to the output of a trillion large power plants. That power radiated equally in all directions would be distributed over a sphere, which is divided into four pi units of solid angle called steradians. That gives you a density of around ten to the twenty— twenty zeros—watts per steradian." He paused to let that sink in and invite questions. Solemn silence persisted.

"As a conservative estimate, assuming figures I was using ten years ago, the divergence of a beam generated by this kind of device might be five feet over a distance of a thousand miles, or in other words a millionth of a steradian. That means that anything within the cone defined by that beam will be hit by a bolt of energy a trillion times brighter than a hydrogen bomb. Putting that in practical terms, you could easily destroy an ICBM booster at launch from lunar distance. Or you could take out a harder target, such as a reentry warhead, say, from ten thousand miles." Low whistles and some ominous glances greeted his remarks.

General Kilburn shook his head. "I don't know. . . . You said you were working on this? We could have *had* it years ago. What happened to it all?"

Keene shrugged. "It was talked about. But a lot of people said it was impossible, and they were the ones who were listened to. The same ones who said planes could never fly, satellites were impossible inside a hundred years, and the Moon landing would never happen, I guess."

"So what happened to the other people who were working on it?" Kilburn asked.

"One of the top ones I used to know was Robert Sterman at Los Alamos," Keene said. "He and his family moved out to Kronia. It wouldn't surprise me if he had a hand in what we're talking about now."

Novek from the NSC sat forward on one of the couches to reach for the last of some salmon sandwiches that had been brought in earlier. "So at the hundred-mile limit that Idorf has stipulated . . ."

"Don't even think about it," Lomack said from a chair near where Keene was standing. "Any material absorbing energy at that rate will turn into a piece of the Sun."

Seemingly, Novek had ordered the block on communications with the Kronians as a precaution immediately after he learned of what was still being referred to as the "situation"—which Keene wasn't supposed to know about and Lomack still didn't. Nobody had criticized the decision, and President Hayer had expressed approval that Novek had done no more than his job. The hold on providing a shuttle to take the Kronians up to the *Osiris* was simply an extension of the same policy until the official line was decided.

More serious was the demand that had been put to Idorf to allow the *Osiris* to be boarded, which Keene obviously knew about since it had been the last straw that prompted Idorf to contact him. The explanation given was that the President had authorized the signal after satellites observed launch preparations at Chinese and European military bases, and intelligence analysts voiced fears that a foreign move to seize the *Osiris* might be imminent. These reports had been exaggerated, and Born had given a contorted account blaming the confusion on a mixup in communications between Defense and State. Keene had no way of knowing whether the story was accurate or just for his and Wally's benefit. He had a feeling of some wriggling and shoe-shuffling going on, and from Hayer's reaction got the impression that the President had suspicions too—but it was hardly Keene's place to comment. Why foreign powers should want to seize the *Osiris* had not been explained.

Hayer's immediate concern was to smooth things with the Kronians before Idorf took it into his head to start broadcasting his grievances to the whole world. "Let's make sure we manage our own public affairs," Hayer said to the room. "That Idorf chose to communicate privately with Dr. Keene tells us he'd still prefer to straighten things out with us than compound the problem, so let's use that chance while it's there. Then we can do something about relaxing these restrictions."

A silence followed. Keene waited for any further technical questions but everyone had evidently gotten the message. Eventually, Voler spoke. "It sounds as if we're talking about just restoring our relationship with the Kronians to the point where we feel we can trust in their discretion, and then sending them on their way."

Hayer nodded. "Yes, that's pretty much the way I meant it, Professor. Their mission here is over, and we're going to have other things to worry about. Did you have something else to propose?"

"I think that the possible seriousness of the situation forces us to be realistic about considering all our options," Voler replied. He looked pointedly in the direction of Keene and Lomack. "However, before continuing, I should point out that there are still people present here who do not possess the necessary clearance for the subject to be discussed. Could I suggest that we remedy that situation before proceeding?"

Hayer eyed Voler pensively for what dragged into several seconds, then shifted his gaze to regard first Keene, then Lomack, with curious looks. Hayer had straight yellow hair parted conventionally, and a somewhat florid face. It was his second term, and while Keene had always regarded him as basically honest in his dealings and well-meaning, he had never been what could be described as a strong leader determined to leave his mark. Although competent and solid enough, he was not a great innovator of change, tending to opt for the easier life that came from preserving the safer, proven ways that the established corporations and institutes thrived on. He kept them happy, while they had kept the campaign funding healthy, and stability and order reigned. It really was no surprise that the Kronian endeavor should have run aground as it had, against such an administration. Keene wasn't sure if the blandness was in Hayer's nature or due simply to the absence of any occasion to rise to. If the latter, then the next couple of weeks should certainly put that right.

"Under normal circumstance you'd be right," Hayer agreed. "But what we're facing is hardly normal. We're going to need more people like these, but we can't use them if they don't know what's going on. In a matter of days, a week at the most, maybe, it's going to be common knowledge anyway."

"I protest," Voler said, tossing his papers down on a table by his chair. "What I have to say is of an extremely sensitive nature."

"I have to agree," Queal chimed in. He was heavy-jowled and stocky, with a shadowy chin and close-cropped black hair. Keene had mentally dubbed him "Bluebeard the Black Belt" when they came in, before he knew anyone's name. "It's a breach of procedure. Unnecessary risk."

"Noted and understood, but I'm pulling rank," Hayer replied. He looked back at Keene and Lomack. "Out of curiosity, have either of you formed any theories concerning what this is all about?' he inquired.

"Something pretty big to keep all you people up at this time of night," Lomack said.

Keene decided he could do a little image polishing without arousing suspicions about Idorf's discretion. Why act dumber than one needs to? "As a matter of fact, yes I have," he replied.

"Namely?" Hayer nodded for him to continue.

Keene glanced around. "Well, we all know what happened at the recent conference at the AAAS. I see that Professor Voler is here. And suddenly the Kronians are being held incommunicado—from what I've heard, because of the risk of them broadcasting something that the public isn't ready for yet. Could it be something they learned from their people at Saturn, which is in a different observational position? My guess is they have been proved right, and what supposedly couldn't have happened with Venus has happened again to Athena: its trajectory has altered, and maybe we're in trouble." He looked around the room as if for confirmation and nodded in a way that said there was no need for anyone to answer. Keene was glad now that he hadn't given Lomack the whole story. The shock on Lomack's face couldn't have been faked. Keene couldn't resist a lordly look in Voler's direction. Voler turned his head away ferociously.

"I'm impressed," Hayer said, addressing everybody. "I said we need people like these two with us. You're absolutely correct, Dr. Keene. Currently we're waiting for indications to come in of just how much trouble. Our own observatories have the matter on top priority, obviously, and we're getting the Kronian readings transmitted from Saturn. . . . And now, Professor Voler, you had a point to make."

Voler sat up tersely, still looking ruffled. "Very well. As I said, in view of the possible seriousness of the situation, I'll be perfectly blunt. If the first estimates I've been hearing are close, we could be talking about major disruption, conceivably comparable to all-out war. In times of war, one does not settle for half measures, gentlemen. Until we know more, we cannot exclude the possibility that it may prove necessary to evacuate key personnel from the surface for a period in order to ensure a smooth reintroduction of order and social controls after the worst of the disturbances have abated." Voler raised a hand to point directly overhead. "In orbit right now over our heads is the most advanced and dependable means of affording such capability that we're going to see. In my opinion, it would be the crassest irresponsibility not to take full advantage—for the nation's benefit—of the unique opportunity that it represents."

"In plain English, you mean keep the ship here as a lifeboat in case things get rough," someone said.

"In war, you requisition whatever is needed," Tyndam, the other astronomer, replied.

"I second it," Queal informed the room. "Are we supposed to just sit here and let it go back to Saturn when we could end up needing every cubic foot of ship capacity we can get?" He made an appealing gesture that took in everyone. "We're already looking into what we can mobilize from the lunar bases and remote stations. What's the sense in talking about bringing that back while at the same time we're letting go what's already here?"

"So the first overt act of war is to be on our part?" the President queried. "We steal it or impound it by force—supposing we could find a way. That's what you're saying?"

"Not really," one of the defense advisors pointed out. "The *Osiris* only came here with a complement of, what was it—twenty or something?"

"Twelve on the delegation and eight crew," Keene confirmed.

"But it's built to carry a hell of a lot more than that. We'd only be asking them to stay on and help their own kind in an emergency. Is that so unreasonable?"

"And what about the emigrants it was supposed to take back?" Novek asked. "Some of them have already started arriving in Guatemala. More are on the way. They've had places booked for months that they've given up homes, everything for. What do we do? Just throw them out and say sorry?"

Voler emitted a long sigh and extended his hands in a gesture of regret. "Oh, I admit, I admit . . . It's a harsh decision. But sometimes harshness is forced." He looked up. "I said I would be blunt. The emigrants are a mixed selection typical of the seven billion persons on this planet. Nothing exceptional or extraordinary. The space aboard that ship should be kept for individuals who *are* exceptional and extraordinary—the kind of individuals who will be needed if leadership and rebuilding on a large scale has to be undertaken."

"What kind of individuals do you think go to Kronia?" Keene couldn't help asking. Voler ignored him.

"I repeat, to let misplaced sentiments take priority at a time like this would be foolish and irresponsible. The knowledge that enabled that ship to be built originated on Earth. The wealth that went into founding the Kronian colony was created on Earth. The ship belongs to Earth."

"How are you proposing we take it, then?" someone invited. "You heard what Landen Keene said. It could melt a battleship from a hundred miles away."

Voler bunched his mouth for a moment, then replied, "We are

already holding passports onto it. The Kronian delegation is still down here. We keep them here until the situation becomes clearer. Then, should it be necessary, we return them on the condition that the remaining places are filled with people of our choice. It's as simple as that."

Hayer stared hard at him. "Blackmail now? They come here as guests and you want to make them hostages. Is that it?"

Having gone so far, Voler could hardly back down. "I would have preferred a less indelicate word, but if we must use such terms, then yes. I urge us to be realistic, Mr. President. It is a time when pure pragmatism must decide."

Hayer held his gaze for a few seconds longer, then shook his head. "No, Professor. If the situation turns out not to be so bad, we would have disgraced ourselves for no purpose. If it does turn out bad, then the goodwill of Kronia might not be something we'd want to throw away lightly. This isn't a problem to be worked out by calculus. Proposition noted and considered. Overruled."

From there, the meeting went on to consider practicalities closer to home. Keene was surprised that he and Lomack were involved, but Hayer seemed to want them present. National governments and UN organizations were being alerted to prepare for collaborative action, and instructions were already quietly going out to military, police, and public services to be ready to suspend leave and vacation schedules and mobilize reserves. Obviously, just about every professional and amateur astronomer on the planet was watching Athena, and it could only be a matter of time before alarms began sounding from other quarters at home and overseas. Nothing could be done about that. Assuming the news didn't first break from elsewhere, no general announcement would be made to the media for a further twenty-four hours, by which time more information would be available from the scientific community.

The most obvious fear was of intense meteorite and dust showers from the cloud of ejection debris that had been accompanying Athena since its fission from Jupiter. The effects could be expected to be comparable to heavy, widespread air attack, with some impacts on nuclear-equivalent scale, with a small but not negligible probability of these occurring on dense population centers. Coastal inundation from ocean and offshore impacts was a virtual certainty, with hurricane-force seas likely in all areas and a distinct risk of tidal waves maybe a hundred feet high—worse if a big one hit, say, fifty miles off Miami. FEMA was cleared to activate standing evacuation plans and emergency measures at the state and city level. Military and civic command and coordination centers intended for use in national emergencies were to be readied, lists drawn up of public and private buildings with basements or parking garages, subway stations, natural caverns, and other structures capable of serving as shelters, and stocks of food, fuel, and medical supplies set aside in strategic locations. Police and auxiliary units would be briefed and equipped for dealing with looters and rioting, and the military should be prepared to take over the direction of essential services. The President's final words before leaving were, "From what we've been hearing over the past year, it seems that the place to look for more hints of the kinds of things to expect might be certain parts of your Bibles. For anyone with time left over, I'd recommend reading the rest of it too."

Keene and Lomack were asked to wait after the meeting ended. For about forty minutes they talked intermittently and drank coffee with others who were still around, and then were called into a side room where Hayer wanted to see them privately. "I kept you back because I want you two on the team," he informed them. He looked at them searchingly. "Give me your opinion on something. This argument of Voler's about needing the Kronian ship. What do you make of it?"

Keene and Lomack looked at each other. Keene took it. "I can't see that it's justified. Sure, from the guesses we've just listened to, the world is in for a bad time, all right. . . . But enough to warrant getting the leadership off the surface? Either he's overreacting, which I find hard to believe. Or he knows more than he's letting on."

Hayer nodded and looked satisfied, as if that was all he had been waiting to hear. "And I suspect that this move to send a boarding party was not unconnected. There was more to that than we were told." He paused. "The AAAS thing and everything before it are history, but the fact remains that you were right and the experts I'd relied on were either wrong, or they deceived me. Either way, how can I put any trust in what they tell me now? I need somebody whose word I can depend on to talk with those who are in a position to assess the situation, and report back to me independently of the people you just heard in there. That's you, Dr. Keene. Transportation, authorization, access to anywhere you need to go—name it and you've got it. Mr. Lomack, you've been up to the *Osiris* too and met Captain Idorf. I want you to help us defuse the situation with the Kronians before he starts sending the world messages from the ship. Do I have your cooperation, gentlemen?"

What else was there for them to do but agree? It was past 3:00 A.M., and Hayer was weary. He still hadn't adjusted fully to the responsibilities he found himself with suddenly, and there was no denying the edge of fear that Keene detected in his voice. But Keene also noticed something else. Though he might feel fear as much as any human, Hayer was able to control it. And there was a resoluteness in his face that Keene had never seen before in all the public images that had filled the telescreens and news magazines in the last six years.

Voler and Tyndam had left by the time Keene and Lomack came out from their interview with the President. So had Vincent Queal, the intelligence-agency official, and several others who had sided with them. Keene remembered Cavan saying something about the East Coast academic interests that Voler represented having ties to the defense and investment sectors, but what it might signify he wasn't sure. Neither was he in a condition to think too much about it. The time was after dawn, and Keene dragged himself away to one of the White House guest rooms to grab a few hours of sleep that could no longer be put off. It was afternoon when he awoke. After showering and shaving, he emerged to join others who had also stayed over and more arrivals who were being introduced to the situation. The President was elsewhere, reportedly at the Pentagon. Lomack had left with a group who had gone to the Engleton to repair relationships with the Kronians and prepare the way for more cooperation between Terran and Kronian scientists.

The world was still unsuspecting. While emergency and mobilization orders had begun going out as agreed the previous night, and similar measures were being initiated in other nations whose leaders had been informed, few people were as yet discerning the wider pattern and starting to talk in ways that would arouse the media. At the same time, high-level contacts in the news organizations had been notified to be ready for announcements of national importance, probably within the next twenty-four hours.

Meanwhile, reports were being logged worldwide of increasing radio disturbance and unusually bright auroras at higher latitudes due to high incoming fluxes of the particles that cause ionization in the upper atmosphere. The first whispers of Athena's approach were already reaching Earth.

❀ 2b ❀

The two primary focal points into which observational data poured from astronomers worldwide were the IAU center in Cambridge, where Voler's associate Tyndam was based and seemed to command a lot of influence, and the parallel operation at JPL in Pasadena, both of which Salio had mentioned. The dependability and possible motives of the authorities responsible for the official reporting from those centers was precisely what Hayer was uneasy about, and Keene's task, basically, was to carry out some checks by going back to the main locations where the inputs to such collecting points originated. He was given office space at the White House and assigned two secretarial staff, Barbara and Gordon, as helpers. The eventual list that they came up with in the limited time available included NASA's Laboratory of Astrophysics at the nearby Goddard Space Flight Center, where data came in for processing from the orbiting and lunar laboratories; the Palomar, McDonald, Kitt Peak, Lick, and USN observatories in the U.S., the NASA, UCLA, and Caltech observatories on Mauna Kea in the Hawaiian Islands; the British Herschel Observatory, located in the Canary Islands; the European Astronomical Center in Geneva; and the Russian network centered on the Pastukhov Institute. Keene also called David Salio for suggestions as to possible sources in the private sector.

Salio stared somberly from the screen after giving Keene some names for him to follow up, including one at the Aerospace Sciences Institute where Salio worked. "It's Athena, isn't it?" he said finally, keeping his voice low.

Keene answered guardedly. "Why do you say that?"

Salio gave one of his humorless smiles, only this time coming closer to a grimace. "I know what kind of an object it is, and I saw how your case was being undermined from the beginning in that charade in Washington. Jean was telling me over dinner tonight about rumors she's been hearing at the hospital of emergency measures being activated on a major scale. Its orbit has shifted, hasn't it? It's going to come closer than they thought."

Keene nodded mutely. Laughter from one of Salio's children sounded somewhere in the background and was answered by a female voice calling something about it being way past time for bed. It was eleven-thirty in Washington, an hour earlier in Houston.

"How bad is it going to be?" Salio asked.

"Nobody's sure yet. That's why I need to talk to these people. I've been asked to report independently of the official channels . . . as a check." There wasn't much else Keene could say.

Salio nodded that he understood, then hesitated. "Look . . . this may sound pathetic after what happened before, but if there's any way I can help . . . Well . . ."

"It's okay," Keene said. "It wasn't just you. That was part of something much bigger. . . ." He bit his lip and hesitated. "But if they start talking about evacuation, don't wait for the panic and congestion. Get inland, away from the coast. In the meantime, if I need more help, sure, I'll give you a call. Okay?"

The Goddard Space Flight Center was located twelve miles northeast of Washington center in Greenbelt, on a sprawling site of office and experimental facilities interspersed with grassy open spaces and woodlands occupying approximately two square miles. The shapes of the buildings outlined in pools of light and patterns of orange lamps marking the roadways and parking lots expanded out of the night as the helicopter bringing Keene descended beneath an overcast of cloud. Goddard had been the planning and management center for NASA's Earth-orbiting missions and space-based observatories since its inception, and later assumed the coordinating role for all the agency's astronomical work.

A security guard was waiting to drive Keene and the pilot from the grassy landing area to Number Two Building, a long, three-story, edifice of brick walls and a white frontage with black tinted windows, where much of the work on extraterrestrial science was concentrated. They left the pilot with the supervisor in the night office and went up to a part of the top floor which, unlike the rest of the building, was brightly lit and full of people working at screens or poring over printouts and images strewn across desktops. Waiting in his office to receive Keene was Dr. Jeffrey Hixson, who headed the Interplanetary Physics branch.

Hixson was a big, fleshily built man with a flabby neck and second chin, red-eyed and unshaven. He spoke while eating a mixed plate from a batch of hamburger meals and breakfasts that someone brought in from McDonalds just as Keene arrived. There was a hollowness in his voice, and he seemed to have a haunted look. "It's going to come close—maybe even inside the Earth–Moon system. Never mind what they talked about yesterday night at the White House. Those were just guesses based on what they know about comets. This animal is in a different league from comets—I mean, totally. What we're in for is going to be *big*."

"You mean more than just meteorite storms and big dust infusions?" Keene said.

"That's a piece of Jupiter coming at us. We've never known what's really down under the gaseous envelope, but the core material that was ejected took part of what appears to be a rocky crust with it that has broken up and elongated into a stream of debris moving ahead of and trailing the main body. When that gets funneled down into Earth's gravity well, it'll be enough to obliterate whole regions."

For the first time, a measure of the panic that Hixson was struggling to control communicated itself. Perhaps the clamminess on his brow wasn't due just to his being overweight. "What kind of regions?" Keene asked.

"Let's put it this way. A month from now, countries the size of England and Japan might not be here." Hixson snatched another bite of hamburger and went on, "And it's not just the impacts that you have to worry about. Athena carried away parts of Jupiter's atmosphere, which make up a large part of the tail—heavy in hydrocarbon gases. Vaporized crude oil, Dr. Keene. If that penetrates and mixes with our oxidizing atmosphere, you've got fuel-air munitions on a continent-wide scale. They can burn at a temperature that will melt stone. With hot incoming and exploding meteorites to ignite it, a cloud like that could incinerate everything from here to the Rockies."

Keene had in fact been prepared for something like this. The Kronians and their supporters had been reconstructing this kind of scenario for years from interpretations of ancient records and geophysical evidence written all over the planet, and they had been ridiculed or ignored. Now Keene was hearing it as if it had all been discovered the previous night. What he needed now was actual figures for how close the encounter would be, magnitudes and intensities, estimates of what they would mean on the scale of events. Hixson walked him around the other offices and lab areas to meet the scientists and analysts, some with computers on-line to the tracking stations, who summarized the latest findings and provided printouts. One of them produced a series of telescopic images of Athena moving clear from the disk of the Sun. The body of the planetoid itself was obscured by the enormous tail now pointing Earthward, twisting and contorting into fantastic plumes and braids. It brought to mind, uncannily, ancient depictions of the grotesque, multi-armed goddess, Kali, advancing across the heavens to wreak destruction upon the world. More images taken at radio wavelengths revealed structures of magnetic fields and particle streams extending across half the sky and already engulfing Earth.

They went back to Hixson's office to discuss the implications and for Keene to complete his notes. Hixson's last words as Keene was about to leave were to ask when a public announcement would be made. "I don't know," Keene replied. "That's what this information is wanted for. I just report back."

"What are your own plans?" Hixson asked him. He made it sound as if he was hoping to hear of something official that he might be included in.

"Plans?" Keene could only return a blank look.

It was only when he was in the elevator on his way back down to the lobby that the full realization finally sank home that this was real. It was going to happen, and he was going to be here when it did. And for the last thirty-six hours he had been too busy and too tired to give any thought to what he intended to be doing about it.

People had begun arriving to start the day when he emerged into the entrance lobby. The sky outside had cleared, but to Keene the morning still had a cold, bleak feel about it. His pilot was in the reception office, on the far side of a glass partition wall, leaning on the counter and talking to a woman who had taken off her coat but not yet hung it. The pilot said something as Keene came into view, and the woman looked in his direction. It seemed she had been waiting for him. Keene entered. A sign on the counter carried the name Christie Jones.

"Hi. Are you Dr. Landen Keene?" she greeted as he entered.

"I am he."

"What's going on? Anything exciting? From what I'm hearing, it sounds as if half the place has been up all night."

"It'll have to keep for now, I'm afraid. What can I do for you?"

Christie consulted a scribbled note. "I've got a strict instruction not to let you go. Somebody wants to talk to you."

"Who?'

"It doesn't say. Not someone who works here. He's waiting in Room 108. I'll show you the way."

"I'll try and keep it brief," Keene told the pilot.

"No hurry, Doctor. The coffee's pretty good here. So's the company."

Christie led Keene back out across the lobby floor, past the elevators, and along one of the ground-floor corridors. There was a display featuring models of orbiting space observatories and placards showing samples of images and other data obtained from them.

"Your face looks familiar," she said as they walked. "I've seen it on TV recently, haven't I?"

"Sometimes I lecture on the College Channel," Keene said.

"Yes, that must have been it. Wow, a real celebrity."

"Hardly."

They came to Room 108 and stopped. Christie tapped a couple of times. "Come in, please," a voice called from inside. She opened the door, stood aside while Keene entered, and closed it behind him. A figure was standing by the window, wearing brown cords and a shapeless green sweater that looked as if they could have been for working in the yard. He was obviously tense, which perhaps explained why he hadn't availed himself of one of the chairs while he waited. Keene's jaw tightened. It was Herbert Voler.

The room had the basic furnishings of an office but was bare and devoid of the personal effects that denoted permanent occupancy. It looked like a room set aside for use by visitors, chosen for privacy. What was Voler, dressed this casually, doing here at such an hour, looking as if he too had been up all night? Keene waited.

"So now you know," Voler said.

"I'd phrase it the other way around," Keene replied. "It's what we've been telling you for years happened once before. Now *you* know."

Voler held up a hand as if to stay an attack. "Very well. Before we waste time getting into accusations, I admit to them. We refused to see what might threaten the things we had come to regard as the whole point of existence. Since losing them was unthinkable, we were unable to think it. Does that satisfy you? The collective psychology would doubtless make a fascinating study, but it will be a long time before this world will enjoy the luxury of being able to embark on serious psychological studies again."

"Maybe so. I don't have much time to think about it just now," Keene said.

"Of course you don't. So what are you going to do?"

"It's funny, I was just asked the same thing upstairs. I don't know."

"It should be obvious to you by now that the President has no understanding of the scale of what's going to happen," Voler said. "None of them do. Oh yes, they're counting their candles and checking the first-aid boxes like good Boy Scouts, but none of it is going to make a nickel's worth of difference one way or another. It's over, Dr. Keene—the works, the whole ball of wax. Before long, the surface of this planet may not be habitable for anything much bigger than cockroaches. Is that how you want to die—choking on smoke while you grub under rocks or fight over roots for something to eat?"

Keene answered woodenly, "I said, I haven't had time to think much about it. You do what you can do, and that's it. What's your solution—find a friend in Congress who'll cut you a better deal? That won't work this time, Herbert."

"There is one place where at least the semblance of civilized life will be able to continue," Voler said. "I tried to be realistic about it the other night, but the minds involved weren't capable of grasping what is necessitated. You're not like them, Keene. You understand reality too, even if we have seen it from different sides in the past."

Even now, Voler could consider himself among the rare few able to perceive reality—after he had been blocking it out for years? Again, Keene found himself listening to a distortion that he couldn't quite believe. The psychology at work was indeed fascinating. "Are you talking about Kronia?" he asked.

"Of course I am. Look, the only people who are going to survive this with any chance of a life worthy of the word, and perhaps raise a generation with a hope for any kind of future, will be the ones who can make it there. And the only means of getting there is the one that's in orbit over our heads right now." Keene was already staring incredulously. Voler raised a hand before he could say anything. "I admit that the suggestion of using coercive measures to gain the cooperation of the Kronians was imprudent and hasty. There's no need for anything so drastic. We can make a bargain with them that would be in their own best interests. Their ship has space available. We can offer knowledge and abilities invaluable to their colony, as well as other material resources that they'll probably never get the chance to see again. All it would need is a competent mediator whom the Kronians know and trust. Someone such as yourself, for example. . . . You see my point."

Keene did, quite clearly. Voler was unable to conceive of a situation that was beyond his ability to manipulate. He actually believed he could induce Keene to bargain a passage on the *Osiris* for himself and his friends. Keene remembered the military and intelligence people who had seemed close to Voler at the White House meeting. He was beginning to see now where the idea of sending a boarding party up to the *Osiris* had come from.

Keene looked as if he were experiencing a bad taste. "Even supposing that they offered me a place, what makes you think I'd want to take you along?" he asked.

Voler licked his lips. "Let's not allow past personal animosities to affect things at a time like this," he said. "I don't have to remind you that I possess powerful connections who would be permanently in your debt as a consequence. The future position that you could expect to enjoy in the new setting could be, shall we say, very advantageous."

New setting?

So that was it. Voler had given himself away. Already, he was talking about not merely getting to Kronia as a refugee but aspiring to running things there. Keene could guess the nature of some of the friends who would be on the list. He shook his head and smiled, managing to enjoy the moment despite the circumstances.

"No deal, Herbert. You don't seem to understand. Your kind of influence doesn't count anymore. Kronia doesn't need friends like yours. They don't have anything to offer that's wanted there. I guess you'd better go home and start boarding up the windows of that mansion of yours."

With that, he turned and left the room.

Ten minutes later, Keene was staring down at the morning commuter traffic filling the Beltway. News announcers were describing widespread radio interference and attributing it to Athena's tail fanning out wider than had been expected. There was some risk of meteorite showers, and emergency services were being ordered to take precautionary measures accordingly.

❀ 27 ❀

The first matter, as opposed to accelerated charged particles, to begin arriving was in the form of molecular clouds and microscopic dust swept ahead of Athena by the solar wind, recorded by satellite-borne instruments and measuring stations on the lunar surface. On Earth, the effect was seen in spectacular sunsets worldwide, followed, as the grain size increased, by brilliant displays of burnup trails in the upper atmosphere. From California to Calcutta, people threw barbecue parties or just ate outside to relax in the cool while watching the shooting "stars" and electrical displays. Others took the warnings of meteorite showers more seriously by putting a fire extinguisher or two in the attics and making sure to park the car in the garage.

Not all reactions were that complacent, however. Astronomers around the world were comparing results and beginning to realize that something was amiss. While some were cautious and unsure what to make of the new factors affecting orbital calculations that had been claimed at the Washington conference, others were quick to take their fears to the media. Observational data were shared over the Web as a matter of routine, and there were thousands of amateurs and enthusiasts with the software to determine that what had been predicted wasn't happening. Some were already connecting the rumors with visions of Athena being a repeat of Venus, and news stories appeared in Germany, Taiwan, and Australia asking if something was being covered up. Very soon it would be noticed that public and emergency services everywhere were shifting into higher gear, and then the stampede to get information would begin. In fact, more than a few news reporters, journalists, commentators, activists, and others who made a business of sensing things in the wind were already asking questions. President Hayer's policy, in which he had asked the other world leaders' cooperation, was still to avoid risking a premature panic by deferring an official statement until the scientific community could at least present a consensus as to the scale and extent of what should be expected.

The problem was that the stories Hayer was getting were contradictory. Hixson at Goddard, for example, was now giving figures less daunting than the ones he had supplied to Keene and had backpeddled to a position of saying that perhaps his initial fears had been exaggerated. Reports from the IAU's Cambridge center, where Tyndam was based, were confusing and seemed to vary between Hixson-like hopes for things perhaps being not be so bad, to violent disagreement, depending whom one asked. This contrasted with the input from JPL, which was consistent and bad—worse, in fact, than the predictions that Keene had heard from Hixson to begin with. And in this, the JPL line agreed with the picture Keene was getting from the other sources that he was in contact with directly.

The Russians in particular were taking the Kronian probe measurements and revisions of the electrical properties of free space in the inner Solar System very seriously, and had calculated that Earth and Athena would come close enough for their magnetospheres to intersect. This would result in titanic electrical discharges from a white-hot body that had just picked up additional charge in its grazing course around the Sun. Nobody knew what the effects on Earth's atmosphere or surface might be. The JPL scientists had reached similar conclusions. In one of Keene's conversations with Pasadena, Charlie Hu said it would be like "sitting on one of the electrodes of a carbon arc." Beyond that, the gravitational upheaval of a pass at that range would cause tides that would make the earlier estimates based on large offshore impacts seem puny. According to some European and Japanese estimates, it was not beyond the bounds of possibility that the Earth's orbital and rotational motions could be affected, in which case entire seas could slop across continents.

All a terrifying and appalling prospect. But was it true? JPL said it was, and the collective view emerging from the sources that Keene had been polling directly seemed to agree. But Hixson disagreed, and the main center that was supposed to be the official source kept vacillating. When Voler was sought for an explanation of what was going on in Cambridge, no one could find him. Hayer's predominant fear remained that of precipitating a wild overreaction needlessly. But with the media now converging on the scent and starting to bay, he only had so much time. Many of his advisors were amazed that a general panic hadn't broken out already.

"This is what we're going to do," Hayer told a progress meeting late in the evening of the day Keene returned from Goddard. He looked spent, having been up, as far as Keene knew, since the last time they'd spoken and probably taking something to stay awake. He had stated that this would be his last function today.

The First Lady, Celia Hayer, was also showing a presence now. Tall, stately, with shoulder-length dark hair, she had always maintained a role that was strong and supportive but low-key, seeking little prominence herself in the public limelight. She had been constantly in the background throughout the day, unobtrusively filtering communications and organizing the White House staff to deal with the flood of visitors that had continued since Keene first arrived.

The President continued, "Something strange is happening with the Eastern reporting system. Some of the people we ask say one thing, others say another, and now nobody knows where Voler is. . . ." He turned to an aide as an afterthought occurred. "Did you track down his wife, George?"

"Yes, we did. She said she doesn't know where he is. I don't believe her."

Hayer appealed to the room. "You see. . . . What's going on? We don't know, and we haven't got time to make a deal of finding out. So from now on JPL in Pasadena becomes our official source. They seem to have their act together out there, and Charlie Hu has been pushing for the right side in all this from the beginning." Nods and murmurs of agreement greeted the announcement. "Lan Keene has been doing a great job getting a consistent story together out of the mess. So what I want is for Lan to go there and get this set up with Hu, and for them to go through this whole thing one more time and give us a final opinion before we make a statement to the nation. I'm going to try and hold it for another day." He looked at the harassed White House press secretary. "Can we fix it for six P.M. tomorrow, say? Have everybody here—the works."

"That means I'll need to leave tonight," Keene put in. "Sleep on the plane, which will give me all morning tomorrow with Hu—plus the three-hour time-shift bonus."

Hayer nodded and looked around. "And that brings me to the second thing. You've been hearing all day what we could be in for. Since we're going to find ourselves very short of time if it's all true, I'm setting AMANDA in motion now. What's the status of the advance team?"

"Standing by on three hours' notice," one of the staff secretaries said. "The governor of California has notified the appropriate people there."

Hayer caught the questioning look on Keene's face. "That's a standing plan for providing a second seat of government on the West Coast, headed by the Vice President, in the event of emergency," he said. Keene nodded. Hayer looked away and went on, "Then let's get them out there and begin the initial preparations tonight. Dr. Keene can go on the same plane. I'll expect to hear from you and Dr. Hu by five o'clock Eastern Time tomorrow at the latest, Dr. Keene. Is that acceptable?"

"We'll have an answer by then," Keene promised.

"Any other questions?"

"No questions."

The First Lady, who had moved to the front of the group while Hayer was speaking, came forward. "Then before anyone thinks of any, I'm going to get you out of here. It's time to give it a break, Sam. You have to save something for later."

Hayer looked around at the company. "Then, if you'll excuse me, people, your President is about to hit the hay. By this time tomorrow we should all know for sure. It's going to be a long day."

The party would travel in an Air Force jet scheduled to leave Andrews for March AFB, southeast of Los Angeles, at midnight. The AMANDA group would proceed to an undisclosed location where a West Coast headquarters had been prepared years previously as a precaution in the event of a major war—Keene guessed it was under the mountains somewhere east of the city. Donald Beckerson, the Vice President, was expected to follow with his staff in the next day or two, after the local preparations were completed. Barbara and Gordon would accompany Keene to JPL, along with one of Sloane's scientific aides, Colby Greene, who had been working with them.

Relationships were again on an even keel with the Kronians who, it was no longer questioned, would leave Earth's governments to inform their respective peoples in their own way—in fact, it had never occurred to the Kronians to do otherwise. Accordingly, their plans for departure were moving again, the launch schedule for the emigrants due to leave from Guatemala had been reactivated, and in the meantime the communications block was lifted. They had not taken lightly the allegations made at the conference, all the same. In normal circumstances, a period of strained diplomatic exchanges would no doubt have resulted, probably commencing with a demand for a public retraction. But this was hardly a time to be making an issue of such things.

A staff car had been put at Keene's disposal, and he decided there would be time to stop by the Engleton that night on his way to Andrews Air Force Base. It would be his last chance to see the Kronians on this visit to Earth—and while nobody cared to say so openly, quite possibly his last chance ever.

The setting could have been better for what would have been one of those touching farewell scenes, had it been in a movie. While the Kronians collected together not only the belongings and material they had brought with them, but in addition all their gifts, mementos, and other acquisitions, Terran officials and administrative personnel came and went and buzzed around, including Cavan, who still had duties involved with the departure preparations. Wally Lomack had gone for the night but would be staying on in Washington to see the Kronians off. At least this time Keene's absence would have been forced.

Keene found Sariena wearing a dark jumpsuitlike garment and drew her aside for a few minutes in the suite where the reception had been given the night they first met, which now seemed so long ago—like part of another world, which in a way it was. Even now, there was no peace or solitude. Hotel staff were using the room to pack and crate an assortment of objects, and a waiter was collecting dishes from a meal brought in earlier and loading them onto a cart. Keene had said all there really was to say when he and Vicki called Sariena from Texas, and Sariena had made the appropriate responses. There was no point in repeating all that now. And besides, it would have detracted, somehow, from the understanding they had shared then—as if it needed to be reaffirmed or reinforced.

She sighed and made a gesture that could have meant many things. "How totally and unexpectedly things can change. Just when we had glimpsed what will surely be one of the most astounding discoveries in human history: the birthplace of the Earth itself; the cradle of the human race. How much more will it lead to what's still waiting to be uncovered? The work ahead will last for generations—like those cathedrals that you talked about once."

For the past few days, Keene had forgotten all about such things. For a moment, inside, he was surprised and troubled. Sariena was neither thoughtless nor insensitive; yet here she was talking about faraway futures when for all he knew his world might end in weeks. He tried to put it down to just not knowing how to react in a situation that was as unprecedented as it was painful. Maybe the cultural differences were greater than he realized, even now.

"Whatever follows, it seems it'll more likely happen out there than here," he said gruffly. "Maybe that's the way it should be . . . if that's where it all began."

Sariena looked at him and shook her head. "Oh Lan, this all feels so wrong. It's as if we're walking out somehow . . . abandoning you to this."

"There's nothing you can do," Keene said. "We had our chance long ago to be more ready. And we'll bounce back again, eventually, the same as we did before. But it won't have to be right back to the beginning again. Everything doesn't have to be lost this time. We'll be depending on you for that. It's your turn to run with the ball now, for a while. Just don't drop it."

They looked at each other silently. Sariena took a step toward him, it seemed involuntarily, and hesitated. . . . Then they extended their arms and pulled each other into a hug, both at the same time. It was the first time they had touched in any way intimately. Keene felt the fullness of Sariena's body through the suit and drew her close, oblivious to the others around them; her arms found his neck and tightened to bring the sides of their faces together. In a few timeless seconds, all the things they had left unsaid communicated themselves between them.

"I have a plane to catch," Keene murmured, finally loosening his hold. He felt her nod and draw back.

"Be sure to see Gallian before you go," Sariena whispered. "I think he wants to talk to you."

"Of course I wouldn't leave without seeing him," Keene told her. He turned one last time to the door and sent a wave back at her.

He met Gallian in the corridor, talking simultaneously to an assistant manager from the hotel on one side and a woman with a clipboard on the other, apparently on two different subjects. At the same time, Keene's driver, who had been waiting by the elevator, stepped forward. "Excuse me, Dr. Keene, but I have to remind you. We need to be leaving soon."

"Just a couple of minutes," Keene said. "Go and find Leo Cavan for me, would you? I think he's in one of the rooms that way."

Gallian excused himself from the two people he was with and steered Keene into one of the bedrooms—from the look of the clothes scattered around, quite possibly his own.

"Just to say good-bye," Keene said. "More hurried than I'd have wished, but there we are. It's been a busy couple of days."

"Things don't look good," Gallian said gravely.

"It's not your concern. Kronia did what it could."

Gallian moved closer to grip Keene's shoulder. Although the door was closed, he lowered his voice instinctively. "Landen, you don't have to go through with this, you know. Not only Kronia; *you* did all that you could too. Why not leave it now for those who wouldn't listen? With the departure schedule changed, not all of the emigrants who have places are going to make it to Tapapeque. There will be room to spare on the *Osiris*. We can take a few more in any case. Just a few days from now. . . . You can still see Saturn, Landen."

Now Keene realized why Sariena had spoken the way she had. She had been trying to put visions in his mind of what could be. It had been her way of asking him to come back with them. And while every facet of reason and rationality within him said yes, take it, nothing else made sense, something underneath it all held him back. Gallian either saw it or sensed it before Keene made any response, and released his hold.

"Sariena said she felt as if she were running out," Keene said. "Yet this isn't even her world or your world. How do you think I'd feel?" He forced a tired smile and shook his head. "Of course I appreciate the thought. But I belong here, to do what I can. Don't ask me to explain it or make sense of it."

Gallian sighed heavily, nodded, and didn't argue. "I'd kind of guessed, but I promised Sariena I would try. It's a part of your culture that I don't pretend to understand. And yet . . ." he stepped back, shaking his head, "I have to admit there is something strangely magnificent about it. Is it the same quality that makes those like Mondel—a refusal to see the obvious odds? But without it our world wouldn't exist at all. You're wrong about where you belong, though, Landen. You belong out there. But, of course, you'd have to experience it before you could know that."

Keene held his eye for a moment, then checked his watch. "Maybe one day," he said. "But not in the next couple of days. A safe voyage. And thanks for trying." A tap sounded on the door. They shook hands firmly. Gallian opened the door to reveal Keene's driver with Cavan standing behind.

"I'm sorry, Dr. Keene, but we really have to—"

"It's okay. I'm done. Let's go." As he came out of the room, he turned Cavan around to stay with him as they walked toward the elevators. "Leo, I need a word with you and there isn't time here. Ride with me to Andrews and we can talk on the way. The driver will bring you back afterward."

The elevator arrived, and they stepped in. Keene saw Sariena watching from the entrance to the suite as the doors closed in front of him. He still wasn't sure what had held him back.

The staff car moved briskly through the night streets of the capital, preceded by a police escort flashing red and blue lights. On the way out of the Engleton and for the first couple of miles in the car, Keene summarized the events of the past two days. Cavan, alongside him in the backseat, listened grimly but without interrupting.

"Something strange is going on in the reporting setup, and I'm pretty sure Voler's at the center of it," Keene concluded. "I want you to put these espionage skills that you've been developing to work, and see if you can follow up on a few things."

"My word, you are moving up in the world, Landen," Cavan said. "At this rate I'll be working for you officially before much longer. Very well, what do you need?"

"The Cambridge IAU Center, Interplanetary Physics at Goddard, and a couple of other places on the East Coast are the ones causing the confusion," Keene replied. "And they're all places that Voler has connections with. I don't think it's a coincidence. It's as if they're trying to delay a clear picture coming out of it all for a few days. Now why would they want to do something like that? Or more specifically, why would Voler?"

"I don't know. You've obviously done a lot more thinking about this than I have, Landen. So for once, why don't you tell me?"

"All right, how does this grab you? If JPL is right and it's going to be bad, Voler already knows. The moment it becomes official, all kinds of controls are going to be slapped on everyone's freedom of action. The longer he can stall that, the more time he'll have to move on whatever he's cooking up. Because that's what I think it is, Leo. A day like today, and he's not around? He's up to something."

"Hmm. It sounds likely. How much do we know?"

"When I went to see David Salio, he said something about commonalities of interests between the academic establishment and the financial-defense sector. That could give some leads as to who Voler is working with—obviously he's not on his own. I noticed at the meeting with Hayer that he seemed to be part of a group that voted together. It's no secret that Tyndam up at Cambridge and he are old cronies. And Hixson at Goddard has to be part of it from the way he changed his tune so suddenly—I mean, what else was Voler doing there at that time? But most of all, I'd be interested to know more about this guy, Vincent Queal, that Voler seems to have a connection with. All I can tell you right now is that he's with one of the intelligence agencies, which could mean that some part of the military is involved. Let me know whatever you can find out. As far as I know I'll be with Charlie Hu at JPL, or I'll make sure that somebody there knows how to find me. They've got a direct landline, so I'll be accessible whatever happens with the communications."

They arrived at the main gate of the air base. A sentry checked them through and directed them to the terminal building, where the rest of the party due to leave for Los Angeles was assembling. As the car drew to a halt, Keene turned and extended a hand. "Let's hope it doesn't turn out as bad as some people are saying. But just in case . . ."

Cavan clasped it solemnly. "It's been an interesting few years, Landen. You know, it's a pity you didn't go to Kronia long ago. That's where you should be."

"And take care of Alicia. I never did get to meet her."

"Ah, she's crazy."

"You never told me why."

"Look at the company she keeps, for heaven's sake."

Keene paused and looked up as he climbed out of the car. There was a distinct reddish tint to the Moon. The sky everywhere was lit up continuously by brief flashes crossing an eerie background of violet, pink, orange, and green traceries.

◎ **28** ◎

Maybe because of West Coast connotations and constant mentions of the observatories in Hawaii, Keene had been half expecting somebody chubby and jovial in sandals and a beach shirt. Charlie Hu turned out to be of Oriental origins, sure enough, but lean and soberly attired in a light gray suit with necktie, even at an unearthly hour of the morning. He was in his fifties, Keene judged, with streaky graying hair and a neatly trimmed beard. He greeted Keene and his companions formally but warmly, standing as they were shown into his office and bowing slightly when they shook hands. "What in God's name are they doing in Washington?" were his first words after the introductions. "Everyone else in the world knows what they're supposed to be announcing, yet they have to send you here to ask me?"

The news media, abuzz by now that something big was about to break, were pressing the scientists, and many of the scientists were getting impatient and starting to talk. Rumors of the wealthy and famous quietly commencing arrangements to board up and vacate waterfront properties in Argentina and Brazil, the African Cape, Hong Kong, and to move themselves and their valuables to higher, inland retreats didn't help to assuage the rising anxieties of average people without such options. Religious groups of every persuasion were thumbing through their tracts and finding the fulfillment of a score of prophecies, all different. Several cities in India were seeing unrest and demonstrations demanding more positive action from the government—although precisely what action was left unspecified. Several places reported mob unrest, and a number of states were preparing to proclaim martial law.

But not everyone was overreacting. Holiday package-tour operators and cruise lines reassured customers that they would get full refunds for any schedules that had to be canceled, or a discount if they let them carry over to next year. The British Prime Minister, after returning from his Scottish estate for an emergency session in Parliament, had urged his cabinet to enjoy the fireworks display, put off for a month any plans they might have to go sailing, and returned to continue his vacation.

The mood among the workers at JPL, when Hu took the arrivals from Washington out to meet them, was very different, ranging from numbed shock through restless nervousness to open fear barely being kept under control. They hadn't had the distraction of the activity going on in Washington, and they were under no illusions as a result of contradictory accounts. After spending the night in consultation with Russian astronomers at the Pastukhov observatory, they *knew*. And although a direct collision with Athena was not indicated, some of the further consequences of the close pass that was expected exceeded even the horror stories that Keene had heard before leaving the East Coast. A white-haired astrophysicist whom Hu introduced as Margaret Ikels explained in a room where about a dozen somber-faced scientists and assistants were gathered:

"What they told you before about the electrical effects might be only part of the story. You see, the plasma tail streaming ahead of Athena generates an intense magnetic field. Earth's iron core passing through it at the distance that's predicted will become a gigantic induction generator of huge circulating electrical currents. According to our estimates, the heat generated could open up fault lines in the mantle and melt through to the crust." Ikels nodded her head to indicate a lanky, yellow-haired young man in shorts and a sweatshirt, sprawled across one of the chairs, his arm draped along the back of another, one foot resting on a third. "John has some interesting thoughts on plate tectonics that you might like to hear." Keene merely jerked his chin inquiringly. This latest revelation had left him momentarily incapable of saying anything.

"The conventional picture might be wrong by orders of magnitude," John said. "The ocean floors didn't take millions of years to spread from the rifts. That's just the answer you get when you extrapolate back the cooled-down rate of spreading that we measure today. If the Kronians are right about Venus—which is what a lot of us here have thought for a long time—it happened only thousands of years ago, maybe in days or weeks."

For several seconds, Keene stared, aghast. If the upswelling of the sea-floor ridges and sideways spreading that created the ocean floors had taken place on the kind of timescale that John was talking about, the rates of lava flow had to have been immensely greater than anything previously imagined. So, therefore, would the amount of heat necessary to produce it—which was what Margaret Ikels was saying.

"You're talking about boiling oceans, here," someone threw in from the side, as if confirming Keene's thoughts.

"So . . . in that case, what wrote the stripes?" Keene asked, finding his voice at last. He meant the parallel lines of alternately directed magnetism found across seabeds the world over. The generally accepted theory was that they had been produced by unexplained reversals of the Earth's field, occurring at intervals of thousands of years or more.

John shrugged. "The Russians think they're also tied in with all the electrical activity somehow. I guess we're about to get some interesting lessons in planetary physics. Too bad nobody will be taking notes."

A silence fell over the room. Keene saw hopelessness written on every face. Charlie Hu looked uncomfortable, as if aware on the one hand that the morale of the group was his responsibility, yet at the same time unable to insult their intelligence by trying to tell anyone that things mightn't be as bad as everyone knew they were.

"Maybe these guys should get some rest," Keene suggested,

looking at Hu. In case they hadn't been informed, he added, "The President is due to make a national statement at three o'clock Pacific Time today. The main input regarding what's to be expected will come from here. Maybe we could get together at, say, around ten to compare notes and check numbers? That would give us about four hours to get a final line together."

John straightened up suddenly, his feelings now venting themselves as anger. "What's the point?" he demanded. "Do you think there's anything they can do that's going to make a difference? Look, if they want to make speeches and play survival games, that's okay by me—but don't drag me into it. I might decide I wanna spend my time getting drunk, getting high, or getting laid, but I'm not gonna pretend anything." Charlie Hu looked at his shoes. He knew that John was out of line but apparently couldn't argue.

"It's over," a girl sitting near Keene told him. "It's taken me all night to face it, but it's real. Nobody's going to survive this, Doctor."

Keene turned away and paced across the room to a wall board covered in scrawled diagrams and calculations rendered in assorted colors. Maybe she'd had all night to get around to facing it, but he had not. There were people in Washington still of a will to do what they could and who were depending on him. He couldn't let this come apart now.

"*No!*" he said sharply, turning to confront them. "I won't accept that." His tone surprised everyone. He looked around at them. "What is this? It's easy to pretend things about yourselves when everything is going your way. It's when things are at their worst that you find out who you really are. Did any of you imagine that it was going to last forever? Life is the chance to show that you're up to doing what needs to be done, when it needs to be, the best that you can. That's still as true if the time you've got to do it in is weeks, or thirty more years, or a thousand. Everybody can be someone special tomorrow, when everything will be just right. But it's what you can be *today* that matters, when it's not." He extended an arm to point at the window, although it was still dark outside and he had no idea whether it faced eastward or not. "That's what the President and the First Lady of this country are doing. The last time I saw them they hadn't slept for two days either. They're doing what needs to be done, as best they can, because it's their job. . . . Well, I have a job too. And so do you."

He looked around. Some of the eyes met his for a moment, then shifted away. Others remained staring back at him. He was getting through to them. He went on, "I know what some of you are thinking. That might be fine when it's all for a better future. But what's the use when there isn't any future? You all heard it a moment ago: 'Nobody's going to survive this.' Well, I don't buy that either, and I'll tell you why. John said that a lot of you here believe the Kronians were right about Venus. Very well, I do too. And that means it happened before—three and a half thousand years ago. And some of those people back then *did* survive! And they didn't have what we've got today. They didn't have underground shelters, nonperishable foods and medical supplies, generators, water pumps, communications equipment, and transportation to get away from the bad spots, or our knowledge and education. And they didn't have the Kronians out there, able to preserve that knowledge and help with the rebuilding when the time came. But some of them made it. Maybe it was just a couple here and there, or the remnants of a tribe on a mountain, but some of them had what it took to rise to something more than just getting drunk and waiting to go down in the mud. It was because of them that we were here to have a second chance. And some are going to make it this time too—and because of them there will be another chance one day to get it right." He studied the faces searchingly for a second. "Who knows? Some of them could be you."

Keene moved across to a table where he had placed the papers he had been given and collected them together. "If anyone here is planning on going over the hill because there's no hope, I'd appreciate it if you leave whatever notes and figures you have available. A final, considered report *will* be sent from here to Washington this afternoon. When the President goes on camera to face the nation, I'll have done my job. Who else here will be able to say the same thing?"

There was a long silence. John's anger had subsided. He exhaled, closed his eyes, and nodded. It wasn't necessary to say anything. Finally, Charlie Hu took it. His manner was still grave, but with a new decisiveness. "Dr. Keene is right. We all need to get some rest," he said quietly. "Can I take it that we will all convene back here at ten?" There were no dissenters.

With all the rushing around in Washington, Keene hadn't learned much about the three who had traveled with him until they got a chance to talk on the plane. Barbara was built on the heavy side and moved slowly, but she was systematic and methodical in her work. Her White House job was to tide her through while she looked after an invalid mother. After that, she had planned to go abroad, maybe to take up political journalism. Gordon was the opposite: lively, impulsive, constantly on the move or on the phone with some new angle. He had intended making some kind of a career in Washington and was due to be married in August. Clearly, they were both rational, realistic people, and yet each had talked as if those plans still meant something. Keene wondered if it was because letting go of the things which at present filled those spaces in their minds would leave no way of dealing with having nothing to replace them with. Whatever the explanation, he had tried to avoid saying things that would dispel their illusions.

Colby Greene was in his thirties, slightly built with prematurely thinning hair and large, rimless spectacles that dominated his face. Originally a mathematical chemist before joining Sloane's staff via a stint in one of the regulatory agencies—which he had despised—he was knowledgeable and quick witted, with a weirdly cynical humor that pervaded everything he did. He was under no illusions about what Athena meant, but seemed almost to regard it as not especially surprising—as if some kind of disaster or other had been the inevitable destiny toward which the absurd theater of human existence had been directing itself from the beginning. "Life is a plane you never wanted to get on, which you know is going to crash," he'd explained to Keene in the bus that had brought them from March Air Force Base to JPL. "So what's the big deal if you get shot down a little bit sooner?"

It all answered a question that Keene had sometimes pondered, of how people had coped and somehow managed to get through such things as genocidal war, mass bombing, political terror, earthquake, plague, and other situations of devastation and terror, and in particular how he himself would behave if ever faced by the kind of inevitability they were seeing now. The short answer seemed to be that you pretty much carried on as normal as best you could, for the simple reason that there wasn't a lot else that you could do.

Since they had also grabbed some sleep on the plane, they spent the small hours going over the work done so far and preparing a general form for the report to be sent that afternoon, details to be filled in when the scientists returned later. Charlie Hu stayed up to guide them through and offer what other help he could. It made horrendous reading. When dawn came, Keene found himself by the window, watching the line of the San Gabriel Mountains slowly taking form in the first pink hint of day. The night had been hazy, and the now constant display of meteorite trails flashing across the sky, which had been awesome seen from the plane on the way from Andrews and was apparently all the talk among jet travelers, was obscured. He stared at the lights of the still sleeping city below, and for a moment the picture came into his mind of foaming walls of water brimming up behind the peaks and bursting through the gaps between to roll over the towns in the valley like breakers sweeping away footprints on a beach. Then he put it firmly out of his mind and turned to Hu, who was explaining some calculations to Colby.

"Charlie, is there a phone with a screen somewhere that I can use?" It would be a reasonable hour of the morning back east, even if on the early side.

"Sure." Hu showed him into one of the empty offices and left, closing the door. A minute or so later, Keene was talking to a sleepy-eyed Marvin Curtiss. With all the things that had been going on, they hadn't talked for two days.

"Lan, finally. I was going to call you priority today if I didn't hear anything. Where are you?"

"At JPL in California."

"Good God. What do you know about the confusing stories we're hearing from everywhere? No two sources seem to be saying the same thing."

"That's what I'm here to straighten out. It seems there's politics involved, even at a time like this. Don't ask me to go into it."

"I won't. But is it as bad as some people are telling us?"

"Worse. I don't know if it's general knowledge yet, but the President will be making a statement at six tonight, Eastern Time."

"Yes, they announced it last night."

"It probably won't go into everything. . . . Look, Marvin, major evacuation and emergency measures are going to be set into motion very soon. When it starts, the public authorities are going to be swamped. I think Amspace should start putting a plan together now to get its own people out to somewhere safer and then take care of them for a while. There isn't going to be much for them to do at Kingsville."

Curtiss compressed his mouth and nodded. "We might really lose some of the coastal areas, then?"

"Marvin, we might be losing all of the Central Plains. This is what I'm urging you to do. Collect all the transportation you can muster—the firm's trucks and buses and whatever people have got that's sturdy and rugged, and also anything that can fly. If things deteriorate rapidly, it may be a question of use it before you lose it. Try to keep the people together before they start scattering, and have them sort out things they're going to need from stuff that can be left, and have it packed and ready. The rule is, travel light. Begin now on stocking food, fuel, and so on before the restrictions. Stake a claim on any piece of real estate you can get them to that's high. I'd like to include my people over at Protonix in it too."

Curtiss nodded his head and swallowed. "Yes . . . yes, of course." His eyes had a glazed look. "I'll start on it today. . . . When will you be back?"

"I don't really know yet. But here's a priority code that will get me if they start restricting the public system. I'll talk to you again tonight, after we hear what Hayer has to say."

"Very well, Lan. And thanks. . . ." Curtiss took in a long breath and shook his head. "Phew! . . . I don't know. All of a sudden you find you have to rethink everything. I'm not really sure what's the thing to say."

"Don't worry about it," Keene replied. "I've been seeing it a lot lately."

Next, he called Vicki, who had also been wondering what had become of him. He summarized his call to Curtiss and asked her to let the girls at the office know to begin their own preparations accordingly. Apparently Karen hadn't shown up the day before. Vicki thought she might have changed her plans and gone to Dallas already.

Uncharacteristically, Vicki seemed to be looking for something further to say when there really wasn't a lot more, as if she wanted to keep him there just a little longer. Keene realized with a start that, for the first time in the years he had known her, he was seeing her close to tears. "Oh . . . it's not so much me, it's Robin," she told him. "You give your whole life and do everything you can for them, and it comes to this. . . . What did he ever do?"

What was Keene supposed to say? "What do any of the kids ever do?" he grunted. "Or most of any of the people, come to that? There was never any contract that said it has to be fair. This is the way the deal came out." He wanted to be consoling, but to his own ears it came out gruff and callous. Maybe he was weary of the subject already; or just tired. It seemed to help, nevertheless.

Vicki nodded and brushed her cheek quickly with a knuckle. "Sorry, Lan. I'm being silly."

"Not a bit of it. We're all going to be getting a lot sillier before very much longer," he told her.

◉ 29 ◉

While it was still morning in California, a train of meteorite impacts stitched its way like a gigantic bombing run over the tip of South America and across the southern Atlantic to beyond the Falkland Islands. Shortly afterward, a similar fall peppered the South Island of New Zealand, and satellites reported another shower in the North Pacific. The areas affected were thinly populated in all cases, but unconfirmed reports spoke of damage and some casualties in a couple of townships on the Chilean coast. An airliner on a scheduled flight from Wellington to Dunedin had disappeared, and a NASA observation satellite was no longer transmitting. On the Moon, seismometers were picking up steady impact activity; outside excursions were being limited to crews using earth-moving machinery to cover exposed parts of the bases with protective layers of regolith. Space transporters and personnel carriers were being readied to be brought back to Earth. It was evidently dawning on people in various places that life at the bottom of a deep gravity well could soon become distinctly hazardous.

"Have you ever heard of the Carolina Bays?" John asked Keene across a paper-strewn table in the lab after they had watched the latest news update on one of the terminal screens. All of the scientists had returned on time. There had been little talk among them.

"Sounds like a foxhunt somewhere," Colby Greene murmured without looking up from what he was doing.

"No. What are they?" Keene asked.

"A lot of elliptical depressions in the ground and offshore all the way from New Jersey to Florida but mainly in the Carolinas—thousands of them; over a million by some counts if you include all the smaller ones. They're all aligned in parallel from northwest to southeast, with a raised rim at the southern end. You get similar things in other places around the world too. They have to be from bombardments by huge meteorite swarms. And they're recent—a few thousand years."

Keene tossed down his pen and looked back sourly. "Well, that's just great to know now. Where were you guys a couple of weeks ago and in the years before that when the Kronians needed some support?"

"That's not really fair, Lan," Charlie Hu said, turning from the wall board. "John was one of the people trying to get us into the Washington thing. We were cut out."

Keene nodded tiredly. "You're right. I take it back. Sorry, John. I guess we're all a bit edgier than we think."

"Forget it," John told him.

Cavan called around lunchtime to report what he had, using the landline connection from Washington and a personal encryption code for security, since regular communications channels were getting erratic. Keene talked to him in an empty office.

"This character Queal that Voler seems to know is with Air Force Intelligence, so I was able to get a couple of things from nameless friends at my former employer that I remember so fondly," Cavan said. "He's involved with high-level security at Space Command, which gives him connections. A look at message traffic over the past forty-eight hours turns up a hive of activity between Queal's office and a section of the Pentagon that handles FAST operations, headed by a Colonel Winter. And Winter turns out to be the person that Beckerson was visiting at the Pentagon the night before last, when you were at the White House meeting. In fact, it seems that Beckerson was instrumental in getting Winter the position."

"Interesting," Keene pronounced. The Facilities Security Teams were the Air Force's assault and infiltration units, trained for the penetration of air bases, launch sites, and other installations in the event of seizure by terrorists or other such situations. Not only did Keene's suspicion of something being planned that involved Voler appear to be well founded, but now it was beginning to look as if the Vice President might be part of it too.

"It gets more interesting," Cavan said. "As of this morning, your man Hixson at Goddard has gone missing too. Now that strikes me as strange, seeing as how he's supposed to be near the center of a crisis situation. So what do you make of that?"

"Something extreme, and sometime soon," Keene replied. "Any ideas?"

"Not really," Cavan confessed. "One thought I had was that they could be fixing to grab themselves a ready-equipped bolt-hole somewhere deep and safe, but it didn't add up. Voler would have no trouble getting onto the official lists anyway."

"Maybe they've glimpsed what's coming and prefer to control their own private guns," Keene suggested.

"Will it really be as bad as that, Landen?"

"Afraid so. Worse than anything you'll hear tonight. If you get a chance to get on a list for one of those deep shelters yourself, go for it."

Cavan nodded slowly and somberly. "And what about yourself?"

"I'm not sure where I go after the job's done here, Leo. Maybe back to Texas to help Marvin with whatever can be done there."

"The Kronians lift off tomorrow morning. You should have gone with them. They would have found you a place, I'm sure."

"Gallian offered me one. There were things to be done that I couldn't leave."

Cavan shook his head. "You are aware that you're crazy, I hope, Landen?"

Keene snorted. "First Alicia, now me? It must be you, Leo. You just attract crazies. That's what it is."

Something exploded in the upper atmosphere above Mali,

showering debris over the western Sahara and heard from Upper Volta to customs posts on the southern Algerian border. Another breakup occurred over the Sinkiang province in Central Asia, where a hysterical surveyor on a road-building project described in a phoned interview cabins and trucks at a construction camp being set ablaze, and fleeing workers cut down in a rain of red-hot fragments. In Western Australia and parts of Indonesia, red, ferruginous dust was coming down out of the sky and turning rivers and lakes the color of blood. Herd animals from Africa's veldts to the Canadian tundra were seen moving in huge, restless, undirected surges, and swarms of birds everywhere, numbering millions, fluttered agitatedly in the trees long into the night.

Not just America but practically the entire world was watching or listening when President Hayer at last went on the air from the White House to acknowledge officially what most people by now were sensing. Grave-faced leaders of Congress flanked him on either side, along with defense chiefs and scientific advisors. Celia Hayer stood a little back and to one side with their two young children, a son and a daughter.

He did not deny any of the rumors and predictions that were circulating; neither did he go out of his way to dwell on any of them unduly in a way that would make anxieties even worse. His line was in essence a more professional and resounding version of what Keene had said to the scientists at JPL that morning. In fact, as he listened, Keene got the feeling that his own effort had perhaps been unconsciously inspired by what he had known instinctively, after meeting him, the President was going to say.

Hayer called upon everyone, individuals and organizations of every kind, to forget all the things that weren't important anymore, and perhaps never had been: paychecks and promotions, prices and profits, prestige and pretenses. All that mattered now was helping each other get through. And he was insistent on making the point that some, maybe a lot more than the world was being told from some quarters, *would* get through—and, again as Keene in his own words had anticipated—that anyone listening might be among them. It appeared that humanity had faced a comparable crisis in its earlier history and pulled through. And that had been without modern technical resources and knowledge. Surely their descendants could do at least as well. They owed that much to the descendants who would follow. He concluded by quoting a paraphrasing of Winston Churchill's words from 1940, in Britain's darkest days of World War II:

"Death and sorrow will be the companions of our journey; hardship our garment; constancy and valor our only shield. We must be united, we must be undaunted, we must be inflexible. . . . Let us, then, brace ourselves to our duties, and so bear ourselves that those descendants and their descendants a thousand years from now will say of us, 'This was their finest hour.' "

It was hardly a moment for applause. But the nation, as it listened, had never before stood so solidly as one. But why, the question came to Keene's mind, should it have taken something like this to do it?

Afterward, while Hayer was exchanging words with the diplomatic representatives who had attended, a TV reporter managed to get a moment with the First Lady and asked her if there was any truth to a rumor that a shuttle was being prepared specifically to evacuate children of the privileged off the surface when the danger reached its worst. She seemed taken by surprise at having to make a public comment, but recovered herself rapidly.

"Well, speaking only for my own, I can hardly do better than follow my husband's example and give you the British Queen Mother's response when she was asked the same thing about moving her children out of London to escape the German bombing. And what she said was, 'They won't go unless I go. I won't go unless the King goes. And the King won't go under any circumstances whatsoever.' "

By late afternoon California time, the country was already responding. Airlines, railroads, bus and trucking companies placed their equipment and services at the disposal of the evacuation authorities. Hotels, schools, malls, and office buildings inland began working on plans to accommodate influxes from the coasts and the lowlands. The mayor of Denver virtually opened the entire city as a refugee camp. Switchboards were swamped with calls from householders offering accommodation. Late in the evening, a White House aide called to ask Keene if he would stay on in California to assist Beckerson's staff in briefing state administrators on the nature and scale of what was to be expected. Keene could hardly refuse. For the time being anyway, it seemed that much of the world was finally preparing to pull together. How much good would come of it in the long run was something he wasn't prepared to brood about. The last thing anyone needed was discouragement. John was detailed to drive Keene and his companions to the hotel they had been booked into on the outskirts of Pasadena a few miles away. On reaching the parking lot, they found his car and all the others covered with a sooty ash that stuck to the windshield and needed wiping with a wet cloth to clear. The air was muggy and smarting to the eyes, and Barbara had to hold a handkerchief to her face. Colby found a dent in the roof and another in the hood. The parking lot had a grainy feeling underfoot. "Don't hold your breath waiting if you decide to claim on the insurance," he told John laconically. John said something about topping up with gas as soon as he got a chance.

Although it was late by the time they reached the city, the streets were restless with people emerging from their isolation to seek security in numbers. There was a lot of hurrying this way and that, groups standing and talking, others carrying things out of houses and loading up cars. At one corner, some people were trying to restrain a struggling man shouting obscenities at a woman with a bloody face, who was screaming hysterically. Farther on, a line of cars was backed up into the street from the pumps at a convenience store, where three big men carrying baseball bats were positioned conspicuously, watching the forecourt. John tried calling the hotel to confirm the rooms but was unable to get through.

The situation when they arrived in the lobby was chaotic, with a frantic manager trying to deal with guests unable to get credit card verification, as well as a swarm of unexpected arrivals who seemed to be under the impression that rooms should be available to anyone on demand. Having reservations from JPL helped, and Keene and the others obtained two connecting rooms. For safety, they decided to have Gordon take one of the beds in the double room allocated to Barbara, and keep the connecting door open. When he showered before turning in, Keene found that he had to scrub thoroughly to shift the sticky orange dust from his skin and hair. People he'd heard in the lobby had been talking about rivers and reservoirs from Arizona to Illinois turning red.

Despite his fatigue, he slept sporadically and uneasily. He was awakened before dawn by Charlie Hu hammering on the door. Keene's personal phone was dead like everyone else's, and the hotel switchboard hadn't answered. Roy Sloane had called from Washington and needed to talk to Keene immediately. Leaving Colby Greene in charge at the hotel, Keene drove back with Hu beneath a luridly flaming sky along roads already beginning to fill with loaded-down vehicles. He found Sloane in a highly agitated state. The entire Kronian delegation had vanished from the Engleton. It appeared they had been kidnapped.

❂ 30 ❂

It had been done smoothly, quietly, and without fuss; so smoothly that it was almost an hour later before anyone realized the Kronians were missing. Transportation to take them to Andrews had been expected, although without an exact time being specified since the shuttle arrangements were uncertain. Not trusting Terran arrangements, Idorf had stated that he would send down a surface lander from the *Osiris* for them; but with the increasing meteorite influx he was also taking the ship out to a more distant orbit. According to the security officer in charge at the Engleton, an Air Force major with escort had arrived and presented papers that appeared in order, the authorizing officer at the Pentagon had confirmed, and the party departed fifteen minutes later in an official bus. That was the last that had been seen of them.

Keene, using the same office that he had talked with Cavan from the day before, asked Sloane if the Pentagon contact given to confirm the order had by any chance been a Colonel Winter. Sloane had to ask Keene to hold while he checked, and then came back astonished a couple of minutes later to announce that yes, it was. How in hell had Keene known? Keene hesitated. He didn't want to compromise Cavan's position; on the other hand, this could be the moment for getting Cavan some official help, which would probably be the biggest favor that Keene could do for him right now. In the end, he summarized the parts of the story that he was reasonably sure of, making it sound like an offshoot of his own scientific investigating and mentioning Cavan as an old friend that he'd involved to check some references. His biggest dilemma was over the Vice President, Beckerson, whose connection so far was purely circumstantial. If Beckerson was a part of whatever was going on, as Cavan suspected, then obviously it should be said; but if the suspicion was wrong, then the whole operation to set up a shadow government on the West Coast could be impaired. As a feeler, Keene slipped in a casual question as to whether Beckerson and his party were still due to follow on to California as planned. Sloane replied that they were and should be leaving late that day. So Beckerson hadn't vanished; nothing had changed. Keene decided to hold off on that issue until there was more to go on.

"It's starting to make sense now," Keene said. "Voler and his group knew early on how bad this could get. The confusion was to gain them some time before controls really start tightening up. Their aim all along has been to get themselves out, and safely to Kronia with the *Osiris*. That's what it's all been about."

Sloane stared, silently assessing the pattern for himself. "They've grabbed the Kronians as bargaining chips," he said finally.

"That was the line he tried to push at the White House meeting," Keene said. "You were there, Roy. You heard him. But Hayer shot him down. Then, when it was clear that he wasn't going to get any help officially, he tried selling me on the idea at Goddard the next morning, hoping I'd be willing to bargain with the Kronians to take them. That didn't work, so now they've taken matters into their own hands and seized the delegation as hostages. . . ."

Sloane had followed it through and nodded slowly. "To force their way aboard the lander that Idorf is sending down to Andrews," he completed.

A brief silence ensued while they thought over the various angles and options.

"Correct. And we *have* to let it land, just as Idorf has to send it, even though we know," Keene said. "There's no way we can afford to hold off."

"How come?" Sloane asked.

"Because we don't know how much time there is. Put yourself in Idorf's place. Those are your people down there, and conditions are worsening. Even if they've got guys holding guns to their heads, you have to bring them up because if you don't do it now you might never get to bring them up at all. If you refuse, who would be holding them hostage then? And the same applies to us. That's what Voler and his people are banking on. Idorf has to provide the lander, and unless we can separate Voler's group from the Kronians, we have to let it go. It's out-and-out blackmail, Roy, I know, but we're stuck."

Sloane glowered from the screen, but there could be no serious argument. Keene was right. "Well, at least we know they're still in the area somewhere," he said tightly. "Probably they'll be gearing toward all the action happening around the pad. If we can locate them it might be possible to go in with a CT team sooner, when they're not expecting it."

"Be careful. They've got Air Force FAST guys there," Keene cautioned.

"I'm aware of that," Sloane said. "At least we have foreknowledge now of where they'll show up and when. One thing you can be sure of, Lan, is that from now on they won't be able to afford one false move. We'll have our best people in on this. Andrews will be covered tighter than a presidential parade."

"Well, I'm not going to pretend to be an expert in that department," Keene said. "You've got them all there. I'll go with whatever you and they come up with." He left Sloane still frowning and looking thoughtful, glad it wasn't a decision he was going to have to make.

Further news since the previous night was that, with the failure of several more satellites and increasingly capricious atmospheric conditions, the world's communications were beginning to falter. Domestic broadcasting cut back to reserve capacity for official traffic. Although the communications difficulties made it impossible to know the exact number and doubtless caused exaggerations, more aircraft had been lost, with the result that some airlines had grounded while others were attempting to maintain a reduced level of lower-altitude services for vital needs—in some instances against the opposition of rebellious crews. On the other hand, many among the public had taken the message of the U.S. President and other leaders who had spoken in similar vein to mean that airlines were now public property and descended on the already beleaguered airports in droves. Amsterdam, a vital European hub, was closed after a panicking crowd numbering thousands, who had been arriving throughout the night, started a rampage that led to riot police being called in with water cannon and tear gas. In JPL's vicinity, police checkpoints had been set up to control access to both John Wayne and Burbank airports, while LAX reported traffic at a standstill on all approaches. Despite the appeals for dedication and nobility of spirit in the common cause, marauding and looting mobs had taken to the streets in several cities. Violent incidents were occurring already. People had been shot.

When people are afraid, they stop talking about individual rights and freedoms, and draw together under authorities that promise protection. The JPL employees turned spontaneously to its administration for organization and guidance, and to Charlie Hu's admitted surprise, began showing up more or less on time, many of them bringing children that they were unwilling or unable to entrust to any other care, or simply too fearful to let out of their sight. Obviously, there was little thought of carrying on business as usual—most of which had ceased to mean very much, anyway. The Medical Department was busy treating cases of skin and eye irritation from the falling dust. A bulletin was circulated around the departments advising people to stay inside as much as possible, cover up when outside, bathe the eyes every hour in a weak alkaline solution, and avoid drinking any water tainted red. Keene was only able to catch Hu sporadically, hurrying between offices and phone calls as the Laboratory's directors tried to formulate some kind of plan and coordinate with institutions such as UCLA. A Pasadena police guard had been added to the regular security force at the main gate after a gang tried forcing its way in the previous night—nobody knew why.

Police were trying to keep the populations static in places farther inland like Pasadena so that the evacuation of areas closest to the ocean could be got under way first, but not everyone was heeding. The National Guard was already deploying in the LA basin districts, where hoarding had been declared illegal and food stocks beyond a stated limit per person or family were being requisitioned for official redistribution. There were rumors that an incoming widebody, damaged in flight, had crashed on approach somewhere in Inglewood.

Hu sent a technician with two security guards to collect the other three from the hotel. They arrived with their belongings packed, including Keene's. It seemed there was no manager, and the few staff that had shown up were letting friends from the neighborhood help themselves to bedding, linen, and the contents of vending machines, and selling off the kitchen stores. With credit cards already as good as useless, cash was becoming suspect. Preferred currencies were nonperishable foods, any kind of drink, drugs, and gasoline. After Keene left the hotel, there had been trouble with people siphoning gas from cars in the parking lot, and somebody had been shot. Gordon, still incredulous, described the scene to Keene. "The cops were there, but then they got called away on some higher priority. Can you believe that? There's a guy lying dead in the parking lot, and they have to leave! I mean, I know this is LA, but I thought it was only like that in the movies."

Gordon was concerned for his folks and his fiancée back in Washington. Barbara was worried about the help who was supposed to be taking care of her mother. Keene agreed that their work here was done and asked Colby Greene to talk to the local command about getting them back before things got any worse. Colby himself offered to stay on and help Keene with the task of briefing Beckerson's West Coast administration. "It might be safer here," he remarked, eyeing Keene indecipherably through his huge spectacles. "From what we've been hearing, everything the other side of the fault might just as likely fall into the Atlantic. I always wanted a beachfront pad."

Wally Lomack got through to Keene on the Washington line around lunchtime. He was still at the White House but due to leave that evening on an official plane going to Houston. His job with the Kronians was done, and whatever happened when they reappeared would no longer involve him. The lander from the *Osiris* was on the ground at Andrews; the next move was up to Voler's group. It was time for Lomack to get back to Emma and his family in Texas.

"I don't know that there's much a fellow of my age can do, but what else is there?" he said from the screen. Keene couldn't help thinking that he seemed to have aged another ten years. "At least whatever happens, we'll all be together. I just wanted to say so long and all that while there's still the chance. It's been great working with a guy like you, Lan. It's a pity we won't be doing too much more of it for a while. What about you?"

"I don't know. There's more to be doing here for a while," Keene said.

"Will you be heading back afterward?"

"Right now, Wally, it's impossible to say. In case that turns out not to be practicable, I talked to Marvin about including my people there in whatever plans the firm works out—you know, Vicki and the others."

Lomack nodded. "I talked to Marvin too. Look, there's something you ought to know about. He's arranging for that minishuttle that's at Montemorelos to be fueled and kept at launch readiness. There's no hard and fast plan as to how it's to be used or when. Just a precaution. It seems like everybody in the world with access to launch capability is trying to take insurance. Everything that will move is coming back from the Moon. There's fighting going on for possession of some of the European bases. Apparently there have been some unscheduled launchings from Eastern Siberia and China."

Keene's eyebrows rose in surprise. "Already?"

Lomack nodded wearily. "Nobody's sure exactly why. But then, a lot of people aren't reacting exactly rationally, anyway."

There wasn't a lot else to say. Keene showed his hands and sighed. "Well, Wally, what can I tell you? It was good, as you say. We sure ran some rings around those guys, didn't we? I guess the Kronians have the ball for a while now. . . ."

Lomack looked away as a voice shouted something from the

background. "Yes, it's him now," he called offscreen. Then, turning back to Keene, "Roy Sloane says he wants a word. Sounds urgent."

"Okay. Try and take care, Wally."

"Good-bye, Lan."

Sloane's features replaced Lomack's on the screen. "Lan," he said without preliminaries. "They picked up Hixson. He was shacked up in a motel twenty miles outside the city with another Goddard name who must have been on the list."

"You *got* the son of a bitch!" Keene exclaimed.

"Damn right. The FBI are interrogating them now."

"Are they getting anywhere?"

"It looks like it. Hixson's cooperating and agreed to carry on normally so as not to give away that he's blown—I guess, trying to work a deal that'll get him out. Seems we're talking about an H-hour just before dawn tomorrow. We know the times, their movement plan, how they'll be coming in. With that information, our CT guys can have their units right there—plus the surprise. They say they've got all the odds."

Keene frowned as he thought about it.

"You don't look too pleased," Sloane commented.

"The intention must be for Hixson and this other guy to be collected sometime. Obviously you're going to have to let them go. They have to be there."

"That's true," Sloane agreed. "But for my money we can trust him. He's got no future with Voler now, and he's desperate. I can smell the sweat from here. With us he might have an out. That'll be enough to turn him. I know the type."

"Let's hope you're right," Keene said. He was still uneasy. Why wait that long if the lander from the *Osiris* was already down? Maybe they had a larger party to collect together than had been realized. "Are Beckerson and his party still coming as planned?" he asked curiously.

"Leaving tonight on schedule," Sloane answered. "No changes. Why?"

"Oh, just checking. I've got my own plans to think about too," Keene said vaguely. So Cavan's suspicions in that regard seemed to have been misplaced. Keene was glad that he had held back before making insinuations. He just hoped that when the showdown came at Andrews, nobody would lose their head or start overreacting in the ways that get people killed. Too many people would be there that he cared about.

An hour after Keene talked to Sloane, reports started coming in over the channels that JPL was linked into that a meteorite carpet had unrolled in a thousand-mile hail, which was falling from Minneapolis to Ottawa. Aerial shots showed parts of Detroit on fire and miles of suburbs with houses demolished, roads blocked by stricken vehicles, and in low passes, people frantically waving at the camera aircraft to send help. Footage from the ground in Chicago looked like the aftermath of an air raid: fire trucks and ambulances in smoke-filled streets littered with rubble; mangled cars; rescuers digging into piles of glass and debris fallen from shattered high-rises. A dazed woman talked incoherently about "a river of stones that came down out of the sky. They just kept falling and falling. . . ." Nobody knew the extent of the damage among the smaller townships and rural dwellings spread across such a huge area. The police commissioner in Toronto was filmed as saying, "There have to be thousands dead out there. . . . We've no way of telling. Communications are out. Everything's out. Jesus, and this is only the beginning!"

And then Charlie Hu told Keene that he was wanted at the Tracking Center in one of the other buildings, which was still managing to maintain a link to the *Osiris* by juggling with the surviving relay satellites. Idorf was asking for him, and the President in Washington was also on the circuit. Four craft that had failed to identify themselves were approaching the *Osiris* and had ignored attempts to communicate. Idorf wanted to remind whoever had dispatched them that one of the *Osiris*'s laser bombs was armed and ready to launch. Until the Kronian delegation was returned safely to the ship, the hundred-mile limit that he had declared previously still stood.

✺ 31 ✺

Keene, Colby, and Charlie Hu stood in a semicircle of tense-faced controllers and technicians, facing an array of consoles. The screens showed Idorf on the Control Deck of the *Osiris*, President Hayer with several aides and service chiefs in Washington, and various data plots. All that could be ascertained of the approaching vessels were their positions, courses, and estimates of their likely sizes from radar echoes. They still hadn't responded to signals. Nobody knew where they were from, or even if they were crewed or being remotely operated. The only observation satellite in a position to make a visual identification had been malfunctioning for several hours and couldn't be oriented in the right direction. Suspicion was that they were the launches detected earlier in eastern Asia, but attempts to contact the authorities in those regions had so far elicited either no response or denials. Colby Greene's guess was that Voler and Company—hardly surprisingly—had not been the only ones to think of escaping to Kronia by commandeering the *Osiris*. While Keene and the others had been on their way across from the other building, the *Osiris* had launched its bomb. The weapon was now sitting in a parallel orbit a little over fifty miles off, ready to fire.

"I want it witnessed that I have made every attempt to reaffirm my warning to whoever ordered this," Idorf said. "The only contacts that we have been able to make from up here all claim to know nothing. It seems that your attempts have fared no better. I am left with no choice."

"Communications everywhere are in shambles," Hayer said.

"Then it would behoove those responsible, all the more, to make their intentions plain," Idorf replied. "Consider my position. Our delegation has been kidnapped, almost certainly to be used as hostages. So we already have evidence of designs in some quarters to seize this ship. In such circumstances I have no option but to treat these vessels as hostile. As captain, I must place the safety of the *Osiris* before all else."

Hayer closed his eyes, and nodded. Several of those with him exchanged solemn looks but none spoke.

"The lead object is approaching the fire line," one of the operators handling the radar data announced from his console. Attention turned to a holo display that was copying the situation report relayed from the *Osiris*. It showed part of a translucent red sphere centered on a white, three-way cross representing the *Osiris*, with the four vessels shown as blue dots moving in from outside. Idorf had stated that he would have no part in any verbal melodramatics. The weapon would detonate automatically if the boundary was breached. Since the *Osiris* did not carry an unlimited supply of them, it was set with lasing rods registering on all four targets.

"We are transmitting at them continuously on all of your recognized international bands. . . ." Idorf reminded everyone.

Keene watched with a strangely detached fascination, having to force himself to be mindful that these slowly moving patterns of light were not part of some simulation or one of Robin's computer games, but a depiction of real events taking place some hundreds of miles above their heads at that very moment. Beside him, Colby Greene stared unblinkingly through his spectacles and licked his lips dryly.

"Lead object at the limit now," the radar tech announced.

Moments later, a different voice reported, "Detonation has been detected."

And after several more seconds: "Target echoes getting weaker, starting to break up."

On the screen showing the *Osiris*'s Control Deck, Idorf turned and left without another word. And that was all there was to it. Impersonalized, soundless warfare, automated and sanitized modern style.

While the link was still open, one of the Kronian crew patched in the current views from high orbit. Fires were spreading across what looked like half the grasslands of southern Africa, with burning patches of oil lighting up the western Indian Ocean from Madagascar to Somalia. The world was turning into a ball of dirty smoke. A view away from Earth showed Athena like an immense, glowing octopus, its incandescent tentacles reaching ahead as it drew nearer.

Late in the afternoon, Keene managed to get a connection to Corpus Christi through a JPL hookup into Amspace's spacecraft tracking net and talked to Harry Halloran, the technical vice president. Curtiss had gone ahead and put together an evacuation scheme since there was still no clear direction from the city and county authorities. The intention was to move inland to Lubbock, where the state was preparing reception centers, and which put them on the way to still higher country if a further move became necessary. There had been scattered meteorite falls all over southern Texas. Les Urkin's bedroom and the family room beneath it were demolished five minutes after he went down to join his wife for breakfast. The family had packed their things and moved to Kingsville, where everyone was assembling. The downtown office was already closed. Harry couldn't say if any of the girls from Protonix had arrived, and as far as he knew there was no sign yet of Wally Lomack back from Washington. The weather over the Gulf was doing strange things, and fears were rising of hurricane and tornado conditions developing. The sea out there was like black, moving mountains. Keene told him that the JPL scientists had talked about immense amounts of heat being dumped in the upper atmosphere. Nobody was sure what the effects of the resultant instabilities might be. Harry said that cattle inland were going crazy from corrosive air and thirst. Water supplies were already the big concern.

❊ ❊ ❊

After Barbara and Gordon left in a JPL shuttle bus to catch an overnight military flight heading east out of March AFB, Keene and Colby Greene sat in one of the labs, wearily contemplating the updates still coming in via JPL's various connections to the world. The full magnitude of what was happening was at last becoming plain, leaving them numbed to the degree that they didn't want to hear any more. There was no point.

"So what's it with you, Colby?" Keene asked. "Don't you have anyone there to rush back to as well? Never got married, eh?"

Greene pulled a face and regarded the papers lying around the desk in front of him indifferently. "Oh, I thought about it once or twice. I looked at the way it usually seems to go, and figured I'd do it the easy way—you know, without wasting all that time that most guys seem to go through."

"Oh? And what's the easy way?" Keene asked.

"Just pick a woman you don't like very much and buy her a house—then you can forget about it and get on with your life. But I never could find the right one, somehow. I always ended up liking them. . . . How about you?"

"Aw, did it once. Crashed and burned. You won't believe who she was."

"Try me."

"Her name's Fey. She's Herbert Voler's wife now."

"I don't believe it. What happened? . . . If it's any of my business."

Keene really wasn't in a mood to go into explanations. "If I just say that she found her perfect match at last, would that tell you?" he offered.

Greene nodded. "Pretty much." He rubbed his nose with a knuckle. "So will she be involved in this showdown at Andrews?"

Keene hadn't really given it much thought. "Yes, I guess she will," he said. So much for the social set and the mansion in Connecticut.

Keene's disquiet over the situation in Washington was increasing. It would be late into the evening there now, yet the latest news was that Hixson and the other man with him were still at the motel. The FBI had reported only a note delivered by messenger telling them to sit tight. If communications were a problem, it would be all the more reason to move them out sooner. Something felt wrong.

The door opened, and Charlie Hu stuck his head in. "I just wanted to let you guys know: Don't be surprised to see Guard patrols with guns in the area if you go out. There's been some trouble with looting. All kinds are coming through from the city, and we've got some pricey real estate just west of here around La Canada."

"As if that's going to matter for much longer," Keene snorted.

Hu shrugged. "I guess the same people will be giving the orders for a while yet. But anyhow, be warned. The police chief advises that if you possess weapons it would be a good idea to carry them." Colby said nothing but opened his jacket to reveal the butt of an automatic sitting in a shoulder holster. "How about you?" Hu asked Keene.

"I went to Washington to attend a meeting with the President, remember?"

"I'll see if we can get you fixed up."

Cavan called a little over thirty minutes later. There had still been no move to collect Hixson and his companion from the motel.

"It's too quiet, Leo," Keene said. "Things should be happening by now. Either they're onto us, or there's more going on than we think."

"Exactly the sentiments I've been having," Cavan informed him. "So I thought I'd try using some of these official resources that I find I have access to now. It's really quite amazing. It occurred to me that whatever Voler is really up to, his charming wife won't be far behind. Perhaps we could get a pointer to his movements and possible plans if we knew something of hers."

"Fey? We were just talking about her here. So did you get anywhere?"

"Yes, as a matter of fact. After I'd drawn several blanks elsewhere, I tried checking the airline reservation computers. And there she was, booked to LA. The original flight has been canceled, but she got transferred to an emergency service that left Boston earlier this evening. That must have taken a fair amount of string-pulling on the part of somebody, somewhere."

"To *LA*?" Keene could only stare bemusedly.

"Intriguing, isn't it?" Cavan agreed. "And it gets more so. Who do you think is on the same flight also? Our friend Tyndam from Cambridge. I doubt very much if they're eloping together. I doubt if he'd be her type. I can only assume that they're joining the rest of the party." Cavan waited, expressionless, for Keene to figure the rest out.

Fey and Tyndam were flying to California that night. And, interestingly, Beckerson was also flying to California, practically at the same time, nominally on official duties. Perhaps Cavan's suspicion had been correct after all, and Beckerson *was* part of it! . . . But if that were so, then the whole business at Andrews had to be a diversion. Nothing was going to happen there.

"Hixson and this guy with him have been set up," Keene murmured. "They're not going to be collected at all. They're sacrificial—to keep us busy watching."

"You're getting there, Landen," Cavan said. "So the real action will be in California. The question is where. There's only one place I can think of. And with Queal and his connections through Air Force Intelligence, it all fits."

Keene stared back at the sparse frame and features watching patiently from the screen. The aim, surely, was still to get aboard and probably seize control of the *Osiris*. They already had the hostages to get them past the defenses. The only other thing needed was a vessel to get them up there. As Cavan had said, if they were on their way to southern California, there was only one answer.

"*My God!*" Keene breathed. "It's got to be Vandenberg. While everyone's waiting for something to happen at Andrews, they've been quietly getting a shuttle organized there. Queal would have the contacts to arrange it."

"Full marks," Cavan said.

"Have you talked to Hayer?"

"Yes, but he's not sure how to deal with it. If somebody like Beckerson is involved, how do we know who can be trusted? If the commander there is in on it too and we tip him off so that he warns the others away, the Kronians will never leave at all because Idorf is on limited time. The only way we'll get those people back is by letting the thing go through as if we know nothing and grabbing them when they appear. And there's only one person anywhere close who can move soon enough without drawing the wrong kind of attention. And that's you, Landen."

❁ 32 ❁

Red sulfurous dust and blinding vapors, mixed into a choking haze with the exhausts from thousands of vehicles, swirled through the headlight beams of the traffic groping its way along Interstate 5 North out of Glendale. Sheila, the technician driving the JPL shuttle bus, craned forward in her seat to keep sight, through the arc smeared by the laboring windshield wiper, of the flashing red and blue lights of the police escort leading them on the inside lane that was supposed to be reserved for official use. Outside in the murk, police, military, and volunteers in hooded capes and chemical warfare garb yelled, cursed, and waved flashlamps to direct the lines, hauled breakdowns clear, and kept interlopers out of the official lane, while fifteen million people tried to squeeze through the four main routes inland from the Los Angeles basin.

Keene, clad like the others in a military combat jacket, woollen comforter cap, and hooded smock that some JPL high-up's talking to the local National Guard commander had procured, and packing underneath it a hip-holstered .45 automatic, sat behind the Guard captain occupying the front passenger seat. Charlie, Colby Greene, and John were wedged in the other seats, along with an armed trooper, and two more troopers were at the back, inside the rear door. The bus itself looked as if it was equipped for a safari, with boxes of

271

supplies, extra weapons, jerrycans of gasoline and water piled inside, and a layer of sandbags lashed to the roof as a protection against falling rocks. It had been decided earlier in the day to have all the Lab's trucks and buses preequipped for evacuation at short notice. Keene, Charlie, and Colby would be flying on to Vandenberg, 160 miles north on the coast, with a hastily organized Marine Corps detachment that they were to meet. John had come along to keep Sheila company and would return to JPL with the bus and its Guard escort afterward.

The plan was as simple as it was audacious—and in the time available, about as much as could have been contemplated. The first point agreed was that with no way of knowing where anyone stood, no approach could be made to the Space Command hierarchy at Vandenberg, which was headed by a two-star general called Ullman, commander of the Fourteenth Air Force, who lived on the base. However, Charlie Hu had, in connection with missions staged over several years involving both the Air Force and JPL, dealt with others there that he was willing to guess would be reliable. Admittedly, that meant relying totally on Charlie's personal experiences and gut feeling, but it was the best there was. The air-base section of the Vandenberg facility was commanded by a Colonel Lacey, who, everyone was agreed to gamble, would probably not be a part of Voler and Queal's scheme. The plan, then, was to get a small group into the Vandenberg air base, recruit Colonel Lacey's help in making contact with names in the space-launch facility that Charlie had vouched for, and figure the rest out from there. Communications problems and other pressures had defeated attempts to contact Lacey ahead of time, and they had decided they could wait no longer. Sloane in Washington was continuing to try, but failing that they would place their hope in being able to convince Lacey after they were in. That, of course, left the question of how to get an unauthorized group of people into a top-security military facility without advance clearance. Colby Greene had come up with the obvious way after they had debated several impractical alternatives: "It's an Air Force base. The sky's unloading and causing emergencies everywhere. You fly in posing as a plane in trouble that needs to get down. Then play it by ear."

One of the JPL directors had talked with the area National Guard commander, who, after being satisfied that this was coming from the President's office, had gone back through the local military chain to acquire the means. The outcome was that a Cessna Caravan with support squad was being rushed in from the Twentynine Palms Marine base and would meet them at Burbank. JPL had essentially ceased functioning as a national laboratory and was being adapted as a transit center and shelter for public-sector workers and their kin en route inland. The last Keene and the others had seen of it had been bulldozers working under floodlights in the fog to bank earth against the walls of suitable buildings, while crews sandbagged the roofs and lower floors. South of the Laboratory, the Army was taking over the Rose Bowl golf course as a transportation depot and supply dump.

Sheila muttered something and braked as the escort car in front slowed. Tail lights beyond showed vehicles ahead of it. The sound of the police cruiser's siren floated back above the traffic noise, but the lane to the left was solid. Finally, risking unlit vehicles pulled over, the cruiser swung onto the shoulder and began overhauling the obstructions leapfrog fashion on the inside, with the shuttle bus clinging yards behind. Lights ahead as they pulled back into the regular lane showed a group of military vehicles parked on the shoulder. Two of them moved off and swung in behind the shuttle bus as it passed, and then dropped back to head off the encroachers. A smoky halo of light in front of a stopped car revealed a knot of windblown figures struggling to change a wheel on a jacked-up camper. More lights ahead marked the tail of a military convoy. The police escort and bus closed up and stayed with it to the Burbank exit, where the tailback from the exit ramp extended for at least a quarter mile along the shoulder. The escort led them past, and they were waved through by police in capes and motorcycle visors directing airport traffic at the top.

The airport approach was a confusion of cars parked haphazardly in the roadways and others jostling for whatever space became available. Checkpoints had been set up across the road leading into the departures drop-off area. The cruiser led the bus to a gate bearing the sign AUTHORIZED ACCESS ONLY and halted. A dust-covered shape, looking in the glare from the lamps like a yeti of the desert, materialized outside Sheila's window. He had a hood with an enormous, fur-trimmed rim, in the shadows of which could vaguely be discerned a transparent visor and mask covering the lower face. Colby squeezed forward alongside Sheila, brandishing a plastic wallet showing his White House ID and a pass from the Pasadena regional military command.

"There's supposed to be a Marine Corps flight coming in to collect us," he shouted out the window. "It's top priority—White House directive. What do we do?" The yeti gave the papers a perfunctory glance, as if acknowledging that they belonged to a world already passing. "Wait," a voice instructed from somewhere inside the hood, and the figure disappeared inside the gatehouse. Keene was impressed by the amount of organization that was managing to persist. Power was flowing; planes were flying. People were still at their jobs. But as he had said himself the previous day, what else was there for anyone to do?

Lights appeared in the roadway behind the bus, and a horn began blaring.

"All we needed was an asshole," Sheila sighed, resting her arms on the wheel and staring at her mirror dully. More figures came out of the shadows and went back to deal with it. The desert yeti reemerged. "I can't get ahold of anyone who knows anything. Look, there's a traffic information center set up somewhere off the Departure Hall. They've got a line through to the tower, so they'll know about as much as anybody."

"What's the name of the room it's in?" Greene yelled back out.

"You'll have to find somebody in there to tell you."

"Where do I park?" Sheila asked.

One side of the cape rose as the gesture of a shaggy forelimb. "What are they gonna do, give you a ticket?" Sheila drove around into a service yard and found space among a jumble of vehicles and baggage carts around a side entrance. The captain detailed two of the Guardsmen to stay with the bus while he and the other accompanied the rest of the party inside.

The scene inside the airport building resembled a refugee

station—which in effect it was. People sat among piles of bags or huddled on blankets and sleeping bags laid out on the floor, some trying to calm cranky, overtired children, some managing to doze, others just staring blankly. There were lines at a number of the check-in desks, where hand-lettered signs identified parties being assembled and destinations. Regular schedules had been abandoned, and it seemed that which airline owned or was operating any particular flight no longer meant very much. The public address system endlessly paged names to call various numbers or meet other parties at stated places. As Keene watched, a woman with a clipboard waited while a group whose names she had called collected their belongings, and then led them away in the direction of the gates. Along the far wall, several dozen young children in wheelchairs, many of them cuddling toys, waited while a procession of nurses brought more in from a line of ambulances and buses drawn up under the canopy outside the main entrance. Keene swallowed a lump in his throat and looked away.

Colby came back from the throng of people around the Information Desk, followed by a couple of uniformed police. "We follow these guys," he told the others. Sheila and John fell in on either side of him, Keene and Charlie behind, the Guardsman and captain bringing up the rear. They passed a restaurant area where soup, sandwiches, and beverages were being handed out at a long table; a knot of people were sitting on the floor playing cards; a young man was playing a violin to a bar where there was no TV. Many of the faces had looked bloody, but closer up Keene realized that the streaks and blotches were red dust lodged in creases or mixed with perspiration, and skin sores angry from rubbing and scratching. There was little show of belligerence. The prevailing mood was tiredness, resignation, waiting.

The Traffic Information Center turned out to be a large room off one of the side corridors, where a score or so of people were working at tables covered with papers piled among constantly ringing phones. An improvised wall board with information entered by hand showed traffic situations and projections, and an Army field telephone exchange had been installed at the rear with cables trailing out through a far door. In one corner was a coffee pot with a tray of plates containing remnants of bagels, muffins, and vending snacks. A line of tables across the near end of the room formed a counter barring off the rest of the area. Clerks at the front were trying to deal with a press of people jostling for attention, while others updated the board.

"I always wondered what they'd do when all the computers went down at once," Colby remarked, surveying the scene.

One of the policeman called over a man in shirtsleeves and a headset and beckoned Colby forward. Colby identified himself and explained the situation. The man in the headset went away to consult with one of the others, who referred to a screen that evidently was able to report something, then called somewhere on a phone. He returned to the counter.

"We have that flight logged, but it doesn't look as if it's here yet. The tower has instructions to clear it in, priority. I don't know yet where it will be directed. We'll put a call out when we know something more."

"You are aware that we're on a presidential directive here," Greene said, appearing irritated by what he seemed to take as perfunctory treatment.

"Sir, if you were here under a directive from Jesus Christ, there's nothing more I could do. When it shows up, we'll let you know. A lot of flights aren't making it."

"Ease up, Colby. They can't wave wands. We're just taking up space here," Keene murmured. Mollified, Greene let himself be ushered out to the corridor. They walked back to a part of the main ticketing concourse, where more people with children and baggage were sitting along the walls. A sad-faced black woman was dispensing coffee and hot dogs from a snack bar that seemed to have run out of all else.

"Are you people gonna need us for anything else?" one of the policemen asked.

"I'd prefer it if you stick around," Colby told them. "We may need directions where to go when the plane shows up."

"Could you guys use some coffee?" Sheila asked them.

"Sure, why not?"

"Better make it all of us while we've got the chance," Keene said.

Sheila went to the counter and picked up a tray, John following to lend a hand. "How do we pay for this?" Sheila asked the black woman.

"You might as well just take 'em. I don't know what else to do with it."

They stood around, like everyone else—waiting. Sheila and John found a couple of vacated chairs. Colby stood to one side, talking with the Guard captain. Charlie Hu leaned back against the wall and sipped his coffee. Keene moved over to the policemen. "How bad is it getting to be out there?" he asked them in a low voice.

"It's a mess, but still pretty orderly," one of them answered. "Most people are trying to do the right thing. They're not panicking yet."

"You figure it'll get worse, eh?"

"Oh, while there's somebody to tell them what to do, and they've still got food and gas and electricity, to a lot of them it's still just an adventure. When stuff starts running out and they realize it isn't a game anymore, that's when it'll get ugly."

"We've been lucky down here so far," the other cop said. "There were some big falls north of San Francisco and farther on up the state. They've got blocked freeways up there. Lotta cars hit right out there on the road."

Two middle-aged ladies came over and drew the policemen away to ask them about something. Keene moved over to join Charlie. "You know, we only just met, and you're already beginning to amaze me. You're actually managing to look serene. What's the secret?"

Charlie smiled distantly. "Well, you know how it is. Inscrutable Orientals and that kind of thing."

Keene drank from his coffee cup. "So which particular brand of inscrutability are you from? Chinese?"

"Taiwanese, actually. But I was born in Carson City, Nevada."

"So . . ." Keene frowned, wondering how best to put it. "This business up the coast. You know things are going to get worse. Traveling might soon get really problematical. You don't have someone somewhere that you should . . . You know what I'm trying to say."

Charlie smiled again, this time cynically. "Well, yes, there is a Mrs.

Hu. However, relationships are not exactly, shall we say . . . exemplary. She disappeared off to LA a week ago, I think to see the boyfriend. Anyway, I haven't heard from her since. Which is all a long way of saying, you don't have to worry about it."

"Oh, I'm sorry. Look, I—"

"No, it's okay. Thanks, I appreciate the consideration."

Sheila got up and left them—out of sensible anticipation, she said—after noticing that the line from the ladies' room was backed up into the concourse. Colby wandered away along the side of the concourse, stood looking around for a minute or two, then came back. "If LAX is anything like this, they could easily miss them," he said to Keene. Keene could only shrug.

Cavan had told them that Washington was arranging for Fey and Tyndam to be watched when they arrived at Los Angeles, but not apprehended. Beckerson's flight was routed to Edwards AFB, situated in the high desert above Palmdale—reinforcing Keene's belief that the regional command center was somewhere under the mountains in that direction. However, the plan could be to divert the flight to join up with Voler's group, wherever it was, perhaps collecting Fey and Tyndam from Los Angeles on the way. Alternatively, another aircraft could be waiting at Edwards. Various possibilities existed as to how they might all get together. The hope was that observing how Fey and Tyndam were met and in which direction they were taken might provide further clues as to what might be expected at Vandenberg.

One of the cops left to make a circuit of the concourse. Sheila came back.

Charlie Hu returned from a newsstand with a week-old copy of *Time*, which he proceeded to thumb through sitting on the floor with his back to a wall. The front cover showed a picture of Athena rounding the Sun with the caption: WHY THE DOOMSAYERS ARE WRONG.

And then public address announced: "Colby Greene, contact Traffic Information Center. Mr. Colby Greene from Washington. We have flight information for you."

Everyone hastened back to the room with the phones and the wall board. The same clerk that Colby had talked to before told them, "It should be landing now—a Cessna Caravan, flight code MU87. Board out on the tarmac. They're bringing it right up to the door. Go to Gate 3 and wait at the top of the stairs leading down to the outside access door. Somebody will meet you there." He handed Greene a pass. "Gate-area access is being controlled. You'll need to show this."

Preceded by the two policemen, the party hurried through the departure concourse and through the check to the gates. There was a flight boarding at Gate 3 when they arrived. A girl with dusty, windblown hair and wearing a crumpled Delta uniform under a red-streaked raincoat led them past the slowly shuffling line and unlocked a door next to the jetway entrance. They went down two flights of steel-railed stairs to a lower space and across to a door, where the girl stopped to peer through a narrow window. "Your plane is just taxiing up now. We'll give it a minute to make its turn."

Keene and the two leaving with him turned to face the others. There was a moment of awkward silence. Then John extended a hand and shook it with each of them. "Well . . . I guess this is it. Let's hope it works out. Maybe we'll . . ." He seemed to think better of whatever he had been about to say and left it unfinished.

Sheila followed suit, shaking hands first with Keene and Colby; then, on impulse, she threw her arms around Charlie in a hug. Suddenly, she was crying. "Oh shit. . . . I can't believe you won't be there in your office tomorrow, Charlie, with everything back the way it was. Are we even going to see you again?"

"They're here. The door's open," the Delta girl informed them.

Charlie released Sheila gently, and managed a smile. "All good things, you know. . . . It's like Lan said yesterday, you do what you have to. Take care of her for us, John."

"You guys take care too," the Guard captain said.

The Delta girl opened the door, and immediately swirls of wind-driven dust spattered through. A boxy, single-engined craft, its airscrew still turning, was waiting in the shadow of the huge widebody loading from the regular jetway above. Colby wrapped his parka tightly about himself, held onto his hood, and ducked out into the swirling orange fog. Charlie followed, then Keene. "Good luck, whatever it is," one of the cops called after them.

Acrid fumes stung Keene's nose as he followed the two hunched figures across to the plane. It had a fixed tricycle undercarriage. Military camouflage markings showed dimly in the lights from the terminal building. A shadowy figure was holding the door open below the high wing. Colby and Charlie climbed in, and Keene followed, assisted by a strong pull from above. "Lieutenant Penalski, Marines," the figure informed them as the door closed. There were empty seats in the forward part of the cabin. Farther back, more figures in combat dress sat outlined vaguely in the semidarkness. "Which of you is Dr. Keene?" the lieutenant asked as the Cessna revved its engine and began moving again.

"I am."

"Can we bring you up front, next to the pilot? They didn't tell us much about the mission. You're going to have to start filling us in right now. But there is some good news. We can forget the plan for going in flapping like a lame duck. It won't be necessary. Somebody must have gotten through from Washington finally. We got cleared for Vandenberg just before we left."

"I warn you guys, it's still gonna be a rough ride," the pilot shouted above the engine noise. He flipped his mike switch. "MU87. Burbank, we're ready for clearance, departing Burbank to Vandenberg, IFR, military priority."

"MU87, Burbank. ATC clears MU87 as file, SID departure runway one six. After takeoff, contact SoCal Control on three-ninety-seven point nine, or if unable, contact SoCal on one-twenty-five point four. We've been having trouble with higher frequencies. Contact Vandenberg approach on tower frequency one twenty-four point nine five. If contact lost, proceed with pilot's discretion flight procedures. Vandenberg and flight service stations are notified via ground lines and will be listening."

"Roger, clearance."

"You guys sure you want to do this? It's bad along them hills out there."

"Not a lot of choice here. Thanks again."

"Normally, I'd say have a good one."

The Cessna rolled forward a short distance and stopped while a dark, humpy shape, looking like a whale in the mists and the dark, passed across in front of them. Then the pilot got an okay from the tower to move out. Wind hit the tiny plane like a water wave as it emerged from the shadow of the terminal building, causing it to rock crazily. Keene hadn't realized how much the wind had been rising. He had the feeling of being inside a kite that was likely to be snatched away at any moment. As they turned onto the taxiway, lights outside revealed at least three wrecked aircraft pushed off to the side. Two of them looked as if they had collided while maneuvering on the ground, their wings entangled.

"There's worse moving in behind this," the pilot told him, keeping his eyes on the shapes moving in the murk ahead. "Lotta boats in trouble out there. When it hits, everything's gonna be shut down."

"How long have we got?" Keene asked him.

"Hours . . . maybe."

◎ 33 ◎

"Santa Barbara tower. Flight MU87 en route from Burbank to Vandenberg at three hundred feet south east, three miles. We're going to fly right through your airspace just off the coast." A burst of static punctuated with voice fragments filled the cabin. The pilot tried again.

"Roger MU87. We were looking for you. What the hell are you doing up in this stuff? Over."

"We just can't resist a challenge."

The cloud canopy above the Cessna was solid. Below, fingers of dark, coiling vapors blotted out and then revealed briefly the lights of the traffic on coast Highway 101 off to the right, beyond a line of breakers and beaches dimly discernible in the flickering of electrical light above the cloud. Sticky buildups on the wings, control surfaces, and windshield had made it impossible to clear the 3,000-foot hills inland, forcing the plane to head southwest along the Santa Clara Valley to Ventura, turning right to follow the coast from there. There had been several ominous *thunks* of hard objects hitting the structure, but nothing so far had penetrated the cabin.

"Okay. Watch out for three radio towers along the water's edge, two just as you pass us, one farther up. Altitudes are three fifty feet, and the position lights are out. What are you planning up ahead?"

"Follow the highway on into Vandenberg."

"*I wouldn't advise it. In about twenty miles, the highway turns right and climbs through some twenty-eight hundred foot hills. Try following the railroad bed along the coast, around Point Conception to Point Arguello, where there's a navigation light. From there, you should be able to contact Vandenberg. That would put you about seven miles south, in position for approach to runway one-six. The big launch complexes should stand out. We think they still have lights there.*"

"Thanks, Santa Barbara. Wilco."

"*Caution, traffic climbing out of Santa Barbara airport. Heavy to severe turbulence at all altitudes in this region. We're getting pilot reports of intermittent meteor strikes. Set your Vandenberg security transponder settings. Over.*"

"We've been dinged by a couple of those rocks too. No serious damage. But we'll be glad to get this thing on the ground."

"*You must have some hot dates waiting up there.*"

At least, something appeared to be going right. Not only was the stricken-aircraft ruse unnecessary, but they would no longer be faced with the task of having to convince Lacey from a cold start. Of course, there still remained the possibility that Lacey could be part of the plot and was simply allowing them to fly on into the parlor, but it seemed remote.

The dark mass of one of the drilling platforms off Point Conception loomed to the left. It was showing no lights or sign of life, and was being battered by heavy seas. The pilot was having to alternate left and right turns to try and gain some forward visibility.

"I see it!" Keene said suddenly, peering through the right-hand window and gesturing as the yellow smear of Point Arguello's beacon emerged from the unfolding muddiness ahead.

"Vandenberg, MU87 is five south at three hundred feet en route Vandenberg, following railroad tracks."

Incredibly, a voice answered. "*Roger, MU87. You're expected. Barometer is twenty-nine point five-five and falling, visibility three hundred feet to occasionally zero, ceiling indefinite at around two hundred, gusting winds quartering from twenty-five to forty knots. If able, continue along tracks until you have visual. I don't think you're going to like this. Over.*"

"Not many options here. What aids do we have?"

"ILS is out, and GPS is crazy. We're having trouble with the VASI lights and runway lights. You should be able to see the launch complex towers; they're still lighted. When they're to your right, fly three-forty degrees for one minute, then start a right standard-rate turn to heading one-sixty-two. When you cross the railroad tracks, the runway is a half mile farther. Report abeam the launch complex. Over."

"Roger that."

The thought came to Keene out of nowhere that the spontaneous urge to help others just because they were also humans was what Sariena had been trying to explain all along. To the Kronians it was simply a natural expression of what being human meant. Why, here, did it always seem to have wait for a war or some kind of disaster? A pool of lights curdled together oozed through the darkness on Keene's side of the plane; then another.

"Vandenberg, we're abeam the complex, turning three-forty degrees."

"Roger. We don't have you yet. Turn your landing lights on."

"Roger, lights. No joy on the runway. We should be on final."

"Keep the complex on your right and watch for the tracks."

"We just crossed the tracks. It splits, and both tracks go south on my left. Still no runway."

"MU87, the tracks should be on your right—ON YOUR RIGHT! BANK LEFT, BANK LEFT!"

The left side of the world fell away, and the haze racing through the landing light beams streamed sideways as the pilot threw the plane into a turn that seemed to bring it head-on into a succession of buffeting humps in the air; then the pattern reversed itself as they quickly rolled level again. The end of a strip marked by a few dim lights slid into view in Keene's window. "Runway to the right!" he shouted, pointing frantically. The plane banked in the opposite direction, held for a few agonizing seconds while the airscrew clawed and the overloaded control surfaces hauled it around, and then leveled out again just as the wheels thudded against solid ground. The center line was off to the left, but the Cessna had sufficient room and slowed to taxiing speed without mishap. Charlie Hu emitted an audible, shaky sigh somewhere in the shadows behind. Keene found that his palms were sweaty and he had been unconsciously rubbing them on his knees.

"Okay, we're down. Still can't see much, though. . . . Oh, wait a sec. We have headlights ahead."

That's a follow-me truck. Follow it to parking and remain on this frequency. And welcome to Vandenberg."

The truck led them off via a connecting ramp to a taxiway. A large military transport silhouetted in the gloom began rolling forward to takeoff position. As the Cessna moved on by, two more transports became visible, waiting behind. Everything that could move, it seemed, was being got out before the wind front moved in.

Colonel Lacey was a big man with wide, pale eyes set in a florid, fleshy face, lank ginger hair, and a matching toothbrush mustache. Or maybe his hair just appeared lank from his running his fingers through it countless times, as seemed to be his habit when considering a decision, through who-knew-how-many hours of the night and probably the day before. He looked haggard, with dark scores underneath the pale eyes and perspiration stains showing through the shirt of his crumpled uniform. Frequently, when a moment presented itself, he would close his eyes and draw in a long breath, as if to gain a few seconds of respite. He was also, Keene could tell—though doing a commendable job of containing it—very scared.

"Okay, I've listened, and I hear what you're telling me, and the bottom line is: I don't care," he told Keene, Colby, and Charlie Hu as they came out from a glass-walled office space where they had gone to talk privately. Lacey had received the visitors up in the tower since he couldn't spare time to be away. Lt. Penalski was with them also, having left a sergeant in charge of the other five Marines, who had been given coffee in a room on the floor below. The pilot, who they now knew to be Sergeant Erse, was with the Cessna, checking for damage and getting the aircraft fueled and cleaned. Sloane had gotten through to Lacey from Washington about two hours previously to advise that the mission would be arriving, but not trusting communications security he had not elaborated on what it was about. Around them, staff sifted reports and passed on orders, while harassed controllers tried to make sense of the fragmented information coming in and grappled with the chaotic traffic conditions. The Cessna had been one of a few landings that night. Inside the launch complex, a minimum work force was readying the few craft that could be sent up at short notice to provide additional hardware in orbit for contingencies. A large "Samson" military transport was being held back in one of the hangars to evacuate them and the tower crew after the launches were effected. Otherwise, everything was moving out.

Lacey gestured at the windows commanding views out over the field. Water was running down one of the glass panels on the far side of the floor, where a crew outside was sluicing off the encrustation of dust with a fire hose. "We have a permanent population of three and a half thousand people on this base. Ten thousand contractors' employees live in the surrounding areas, most of them with families. I've got a couple of hours to do what good I can with the planes I've got. After that, they're just junk. That's my first responsibility, Doctor. I don't care about who's going out in a shuttle. If they've got somewhere to go, good luck to them."

An adjutant with a red-streaked face, wearing a tarmac jacket, interrupted. "Excuse me, sir."

"Yes?"

"296 isn't going to fly. The valve isn't responding, and it's a strip-down to replace."

Lacey grimaced, running a hand through his hair. "Has that C-80 started loading?"

"Not yet. It's just rolling up now."

"Divert it out alongside 296. Get some stairs out there and transfer the passengers straight across. Don't bring it back to the gate."

"Sir." The adjutant turned away to another officer who was waiting.

"But we don't know what they've got planned," Keene persisted. "If they show up with a FAST team and take over the runway area, it could halt your whole operation."

"I'll take that chance when we come to it. In the meantime, my operation is best served by moving out what I can."

"Secure the approaches to the launch complexes at least. The APs aren't moving aircraft."

"What APs? Do you think we've been expecting an invasion? They're on the other side of the base, getting everyone out onto Highway One."

"Colonel." Colby Greene was visibly exasperated, managing only with difficulty to refrain from shouting in the middle of the control tower floor. "As an officer of the armed services of this country, may I remind you that you took an oath of loyalty to—"

"A week from now there isn't going to be any country," Lacey said. "You know that. I know that. And the only reason we're not getting open murder and rape on the streets right now is because most people haven't realized it yet. My first loyalty is to the people I've worked with on this base. It's a family thing now. I never took any oath that talked about protecting aliens from some other planet who didn't think our system here was good enough for them." Lacey paused to check an indicator screen above the floor showing the current departures, where the data had just been updated. "Besides, if what you're telling me is correct, I'd be doing them a favor by not interfering. That way, they'll be on their way home." From the conversation earlier, it was plain that Lacey had no particular fondness for Kronians. In a way reminiscent of the ancient practice of venting wrath upon bringers of bad news, it had almost seemed that through some devious process deep in his mind he held them responsible for Athena's having happened at all.

Keene and Colby looked at each other helplessly. Then Charlie Hu raised his hands in a placatory gesture. "Look . . ." he pleaded. "This isn't going to help. We're all under stress here. Let's recognize it. Maybe the problem doesn't need to be addressed out here at all. The important thing is what happens inside the launch complex. If we can get the right people in there alerted, they might be able to close off access to the shuttles before Voler's people get here. . . . They know what the options are in there better than any of us do. I've got some names right here of people I believe are reliable. One or two have to be in there somewhere, right on the other side of the security fence. All we have to do is call. Colonel Lacey has gotten us in this far. That's as much as we might need. Let me make some calls, and let him get on with his job."

"How can they deny access to the shuttles?" Colby demanded. "Voler and his people still have the hostages."

Charlie shook his head. "I don't know.... If it becomes obvious that they're not going anywhere, they might throw it in. Whoever they've got helping on the inside might turn around if they realize they're on their own. Anything that complicates the issue opens up more chances for their plan to go wrong. What else do you want in the kind of time we've got? They could land out there at any minute."

"I can deploy my men to cover the access gate from the landing area," Lieutenant Penalski offered. "In these conditions, we could have them in prepared positions right up there on the edge of the runway—even after daybreak. It's just a question of knowing where the plane will head after it lands. Maybe the tower could cooperate by directing it to us."

Keene looked at him: young, eager, as if it was going to affect his record for a promotion next year. Seven Marines against a planeload of Air Force FAST specialists. The spirit of Balaclava was not quite dead yet. It seemed to affect Lacey too. He stared at the Marine, then at Charlie Hu silently pleading for reason, Colby fighting back his anger, and finally at Keene. "I might be able to rustle together a few APs to help," he said gruffly, and strode away to a desk by the far wall to pick up a phone.

They stood watching anxiously behind Charlie as he tapped in the first code at a console in a corner of the control tower observation floor. Penalski had left to collect his Marines and scout the ground while waiting for the Air Police reinforcements to show up.

It turned out that Major Sorven, who headed one of the communications sections and had been Charlie's first hope, had moved from Vandenberg several months previously. His successor was a Major Myran, but nobody knew where he was. "Can we try a guy called Crowe Thompson, then?" Charlie asked. Thompson was a civilian technician who had worked under Sorven.

The MP operating the phones sounded as if he was beginning to think that perhaps Charlie was a little crazy. "There isn't anybody in the labs. Didn't anyone tell you, it's not exactly a normal working day today?" Keene and Colby exchanged glances. Colonel Lacey, standing with them, turned away for a second to catch the dialogue of one of the controllers behind, who was getting a distress call from something coming in over the Pacific.

Charlie licked his lips. "This is important," he told the MP.

"Everything's important."

"Just hold a second, will you?" Charlie consulted his notes again hurriedly. "How about the launch complexes themselves? There are things going on in there. We can see the lights. Is there anyone answering in OLC-6 East?"

"Yeah, they're busy over in there, all right."

"The Boxcar Flight Checkout Area. Try and find an Andy Lintz. Like I said, it's important. I wasn't kidding."

"Gimme a sec. I'll check around."

Orbiter Launch Complex-6 East was a refurbished version of the old SLC-6 facility built for the primal NASA shuttle and virtually dismantled following the cutback in operations after the *Challenger* accident back in the eighties. Now it handled the newer design of one-stage "Boxcar" orbiters that were simpler, easier to assemble, and had the convenience of being prepared and loaded horizontally and under cover, to be elevated vertically only for launch. Charlie had worked for a week with Lintz on a NASA-supplied image-processing computer that had been found faulty after it was delivered to the assembly area for installation.

Across the floor, an officer who had been hunched with two operators in front of one of the consoles straightened up and turned to call to Lacey. "Sir, we've got something coming in low and fast from the east, not responding to calls. Strong radar emissions. ATC has no information."

"The lame duck's signaling that it's coming straight in," the former operator reported from another part of the floor. "They're on one engine, and it's intermittent."

"Clear the main runway," Lacey ordered. "Dispatch crash tenders and ambulance, and hold further movements till it's down." He started to turn back to the officer and the other two operators, but then looked back at the screen in front of Charlie Hu as movement caught his eye. A woman in a green coverall and yellow hard hat had appeared; but she seemed to be distracted and was looking away.

"My name is Hu. Is Andy Lintz there? It's vitally urgent that I speak to him. . . . Hello? Ma'am? . . . I said, is Andy Lintz there, anywhere?" The woman moved aside without replying, gesturing vaguely to somebody else and keeping her eyes on something distant that seemed to be happening behind the viewer. After a few seconds, a chubby, bespectacled man in a white smock showing grease stains appeared.

"Say, Charlie. . . ." He spoke in a low voice, as if not wanting to be overheard.

Hu tossed a quick, relieved grin back over his shoulder at the others and made a thumb's-up. "Yeah, right, Andy. How's it been going? Look, I need some help, and it's really important. I'm with some people across in the Vandenberg tower right now. We think something serious is scheduled to happen in there fairly soon, and I need access to somebody reliable who can organize security."

Lintz seemed only to be half hearing, and was watching something beyond the screen in the same inexplicable way that the woman in the yellow hard hat had. The sound of voices shouting indistinctly came through in the background, and then the louder echoing of something being said over a bullhorn.

"Yeah . . . well, it might not be a good time right now, Charlie. It seems we've got what you might call a 'situation' developing here. There are guys in combat gear waving guns, and somebody just yanked the Launch Supervisor out of his office. Could be you're a little late, Charlie."

A roar from outside the tower, rising rapidly and then falling again, signaled the unknown intruder making a low pass over the base. Charlie turned in his seat to confront the stunned expressions on the faces of Keene and Colby. Lacey, his face paling, stepped forward behind them. "We're too late," Charlie repeated, his voice barely above a whisper. "All this time we've been trying to figure out how to stop them getting in. And they're in there already!"

❀ 34 ❀

Most of the others around the floor were too busy with their tasks to realize what was happening. Lacey's adjutant, however, had been following from a short distance and came across. "It was the C-130," he breathed.

Numbed, Keene merely jutted his jaw at Lacey inquiringly. "We had an old C-130 come in earlier," Lacey said. "With everything that's been going on I'd forgotten about it. It had all the proper clearances from Launch Operations. We sent it up by Security Gate Three, which leads straight through to the Boxcar launch area. That has to be how they got in."

"Queal fixed for it to be opened from the inside," Colby groaned.

"The Distress Call is on final, looking okay," the operator tracking the approaching plane from the west announced.

On the screen showing the inside of OLC-6 East, Andy Lintz looked up, sending what looked as if it was meant to be an apologetic grin to someone behind the viewing angle, and backed away with his hands raised. A moment later, the screen blanked out.

"What's that intruder doing?" Lacey shot across at the other operators.

"Going into a tight turn about five miles out, climbing slightly. Looks as if it's going to circle."

"Maybe they're not all in yet," Colby said suddenly. "The C-130 might just have been the door-opener for Queal's FAST team to make contact with the inside group." He pointed to the console where the intruder was being tracked. "*That* has to be Voler and the rest of them showing up now. They were supposed to land as soon as the move was made inside, but the runway's obstructed by that S.O.S. that's coming in."

It made sense. "Maybe . . ." Keene nodded slowly. But what could they do about it? An AP officer was trying to pull together a security contingent, but he hadn't reported back. In any case it was all too late now. All they could do was watch impotently and wait for events to unfold. To have gotten this close . . . As the realization slowly soaked in, Keene found himself feeling sick somewhere deep in his stomach.

And then the adjutant officer took a call from the tower switchboard downstairs. "Somebody in OLC-6 is asking to talk to the tower supervisor," he announced.

"Tell them to put it through here," Lacey said. Moments later, a swarthy-faced figure wearing an Air Force parka and colonel's insignia appeared on an auxiliary screen of the console that Charlie was sitting at. "This is Colonel Lacey, base commander, at present supervising tower operations. Who is this?"

"It doesn't matter who I am. All you need to know is that we have control of the OLC complex and access to it from the runway area, and we are currently holding General Ullman and his immediate staff. Just cooperate, and nobody need get hurt."

"His name's Delmaro," the adjutant murmured, moving alongside Lacey. "One of General Ullman's staff officers."

Keene started and caught Colby's look as his eyes widened. Ullman *hadn't* been part of it! Queal's inside man was one of Ullman's subordinate commanders. They *could* have gone to the top, all along. Keene's feeling of nausea increased.

"What do you want?" Lacey asked tightly.

"Good." Delmaro nodded. "The aircraft that is about to land on the main runway now is carrying the visitors from Kronia, who are under armed supervision. Their well-being, I don't have to remind you, is a matter of considerable importance to the government of this nation. It will therefore be in your own best interests to cooperate. We require safe passage for them to Security Gate Three, where they will be received by a force from inside this complex. Is that clear and understood?"

The screen split to show a view looking out into the night, showing hooded figures with rifles moving away from the camera through a chain-link gate, perhaps taken from a vehicle parked in the vicinity. The message was that the people Delmaro represented had the gate and its approach already secured.

"Quite clear," Lacey replied.

"Then you will give the order."

Lacey hesitated, glancing at Keene. Keene could do nothing but nod. Lacey turned his head to address the controller and inhaled a long breath. "Turn the approaching aircraft around at the north end, and have a truck in position to lead it through to Security Gate Three," he instructed. "Hold all other movement."

"Very sensible, Colonel," Delmaro approved from the screen.

Now Keene was confused. If the aircraft currently landing was the one bringing the hostages and their captors—ironically, employing the same ruse that Keene and his group had intended using—then who was in the military jet performing low, screaming turns around the base? The situation promptly got even more confusing.

"The lame duck is down," the operator reported. His voice held a puzzled note. "But it's not alone. We have a second contact following it, heading in on approach."

So now there were three out there?

"Get a view of the first from one of the crash trucks," Lacey instructed.

"Tender Two. Do you read?"

"Two here, Roger. Proceeding."

"We're with you back here. What do you see?"

"Difficult to make it out. . . . Some kind of turboprop, high-wing." A view on another screen showed landing lights approaching through curtains of smoky gloom. "No sign of engine trouble. It's running straight and true."

"Stay out there, Two. There's another one coming in behind it."

"*Another one?* What's going on?"

"We're not sure."

The lights swept by, accompanied by a passing roar of healthy engines, and the shape disappeared, heading for the remote, northwest end of the main runway, where it would turn and taxi back to pick up the guide truck. Meanwhile, the view alongside Delmaro's image showed the armed figures moving out into a dim pool of light from a lamp over the gate approach area.

All of a sudden, the other operator called out in an alarmed voice, "The intruder is descending from the southwest, lined up on Number Two runway. It looks as if it's going to land right across them!"

"*Warn it off! Warn it off!*" Lacey snapped.

"It isn't responding to anything, sir. . . . Man, it's coming down *steep!*"

"Get those crash tenders up the other end. Move 'em!"

"What in hell's going on there?" Delmaro demanded, looking suspicious.

"We don't know," Lacey answered. "Except that everyone in those planes could be about to get killed."

"The duck is at the far end, turning now," one operator sang out.

"What about that intruder?"

"It's down! I don't know how he did it. Blind radar approach. It has to be a VTOL."

"We're getting a shot of him from the crash truck now," the adjutant said. The bellow of powerful jet engines reversing thrust came from the screen showing the view from the tender racing back toward the north end of the main runway; then landing light beams appeared to the left, coming from a low, sleek shape sliding out of the night, closing until it seemed it was about to collide with the tender. The tender veered right as the driver started to evade, but then the intruder slewed around in a reckless turn that brought it ahead of the tender, going the same way.

"My God! It's heading straight at the turboprop that just landed!" Colby cried out, horrified. "They're going to hit head-on!"

And so, for an eternity of drawn-out seconds, it seemed, as the jet pulled away ahead of the tender, its tail silhouetted against the glare of the other aircraft's lights approaching from the opposite direction. But the jet was braking hard, its shape growing larger again as the tender caught up with it. The lights of the turboprop beyond grew in brilliance until everyone watching was tensed, waiting for the impact that seemed inevitable . . . and then, at the last instant, the lights slewed sideways and then canted as the turboprop was forced off the runway. The crash tender pulled up seconds later, the view from its cab showing the two aircraft stopped with just yards separating them. Figures brandishing weapons were already pouring from doors on both sides of the intruder to take up positions around the plane it had headed off.

"How far away is that other plane that was following?" Lacey called out. "Can it get down in front of that mess? How much distance does it have?"

"It's leveling out, sir. Looks like it's changed its mind."

"See, he already knows. That means they're in contact. They must be together," Charlie Hu said, trying to take it all in. Keene could only shake his head. Crazier and crazier.

"What was that other plane that just landed?" Delmaro demanded, looking worried now. "Where are the Kronians?"

"If they were in that first one, then they're stranded at the top end of the runway," Lacey said. "I can't get there, neither can you, and I'm just as much in the dark as to what's going on, whatever you think." Delmaro's composure was falling apart. He seemed about to say something, when the screen showing the scene at Gate Three suddenly brightened. He must have had a copy of the same view also, for he looked aside abruptly.

A ring of floodlights had come on, throwing the figures moving out from the gate—now revealed clearly to be FAST troopers—into sharp contrast against the darkness. There were maybe two dozen of them. Then an amplified voice boomed. *"Do not make any move! You are covered from all sides. Throw your weapons in front of you and step back three paces with your hands on your heads."* The figures came to a confused halt, some raising arms to shield their eyes against the glare, others looking at each other questioningly. *"You have three seconds before we fire,"* the voice warned.

Keene, Colby, and Charlie Hu gasped in unison as they recognized the voice. "Jesus! . . . That's Penalski," Colby breathed. "He's doing that with just si—" Keene signed to him frantically to shut up and nodded his head at the screen showing Delmaro. Colby put a hand to his mouth and turned away.

But it was true. Confident of having full surprise on their side, the FAST squad had not deployed into what they had presumed to be deserted surroundings, but just waited before the gate for the turboprop to roll up and deliver the hostages. Penalski had just six men with him out there in the darkness. Crazy Marines!

Delmaro hadn't heard Colby, however, but was gaping on his screen, seemingly at a loss. Then the sound of a brief burst of automatic fire came from the screen showing the gate, and several of the figures ducked, presumably from bullets passing over their heads. Then, one by one, they began tossing down their guns.

Seizing the initiative, Lacey stepped forward to face the screen squarely. "You are Colonel Delmaro, I believe, right? Well, it's over. You're on your own, isolated from your hostages, and your men out here are disarmed. What are you going to do now? Shoot General Ullman? And what do you think that will achieve?"

Delmaro's eyes shifted desperately. "There are still enough of us in here to take the Boxcar up," he replied.

"Where to?" Lacey scoffed. "The *Osiris*? Do you know what happened to the last bunch that tried?" He shook his head. "Give it up, Colonel. Try and carry this through, and you're definitely finished. Quit now, and you might work out a place for yourself in whatever comes next. But none of you is going to Kronia."

Delmaro licked his lips and looked away. He seemed to be listening to others off-screen. Then he asked for a fifteen-minute hold. Lacey looked at Keene.

"Give it to them," Keene murmured. Anything that calmed things down could only help.

"Fifteen minutes," Lacey agreed.

The wind was causing sand and dust to rattle against the windows of the control tower as Keene and the others watched several vehicles carrying Air Police arrive to provide backup behind the cordon around the stranded turboprop transport. The turboprop's doors opened, and figures began emerging to surrender in the light from the headlamps of the circle of vehicles. After them, the rescuers began leading out a procession of tall forms who could only be the Kronians. They were difficult to distinguish in the heavy outer garments they were wearing, until Gallian threw back the hood of his flapping parka to reveal his white hair as he shook hands with a helmeted figure toting a submachine gun, who seemed to be in charge of the rescue troops. Keene thought he glimpsed Sariena in the background, but it was impossible to be certain. And then the figure with Gallian turned to say something to one of the soldiers, at the same time removing the sand visor he was wearing and tilting back the helmet to scratch the front of a scrawny head. Keene's knees almost buckled right there in the middle of the control tower floor. The figure who had arrived in the nick of time with his cavalry from the sky was—Leo Cavan!

Outside Gate Three, a truck filled with Air Police arrived to join the seven Marines in rounding up the incredulous FAST soldiers just as Delmaro reappeared on the screen, his face registering defeat. "Very well," he agreed. "We have released General Ullman and are turning over our weapons."

The other plane that had been following—a jet, from the sound— had been circling without making any further attempt to land. It broke off, finally, and flew away toward the south.

❀ **35** ❀

While the tower controllers got back to their business of dispatching the remaining transports, and ground crews towed the two recently landed aircraft into hangars for protection against the incoming storm, Keene, Colby, and Charlie Hu drove out with Lacey to meet the convoy from the north end at Gate Three, where others were appearing from inside the launch complex. The first feeble light of a restless, orange dawn was filtering through. Figures came tumbling out of vehicles laughing and back-slapping with relief after the tension, oblivious of the rising wind carrying needles of ocean spray mixed with the stinging dust. Colby went around shaking hands with the rescue team, who turned out to be a Special Forces unit that Cavan had "borrowed" from a friend in the Pentagon. Lacey poured congratulations on Lt. Penalski, who seemed slightly bewildered and not quite sure what he was supposed to have done that was exceptional. Keene sought out Gallian and Sariena to make sure they were all right, as well as others among his Kronian friends. And finally, he confronted Cavan.

"You've always had this habit of dropping surprises, Leo, but this time you've surpassed yourself," he shouted above the wind. "Okay. How, for God's sake?"

"Do you really want to stand out here discussing it, Landen, or shall we go inside first? I don't know about you, but I could use a cup of strong coffee. We've been flying supersonic for over two hours. I don't know how that aircraft held together. An incredible machine, Landen. Enough electronics to fly itself to China. It's a long-range bomber airframe fitted with a modified power plant for Short and Vertical Take-Off and Landing—intended for getting Rapid Deployment units to odd corners of the world fast. Called the 'Rustler.' Just what we needed."

"Where the hell did you get it?"

"Come on, Landen. I was in the Air Force for long enough as you well know. I still have friends there. Most of them have been at their wits' end for something useful to do in all this. They were only too willing to help. I've been telling you for years: I wasn't cut out for shuffling pieces of paper around."

A broad figure wearing a beret under the hood of a combat smock and wearing a pistol as well as carrying what looked like an Uzi came out of the background. His insignia showed him to be a major. "Seems it's all buttoned up," he said to Cavan. Cavan gestured toward Keene.

"This is the man in the middle of it all, Mitch. Lan, meet Major Harvey Mitchell." They shook hands.

Following Mitch was a woman wearing some kind of cap under a fur-trimmed hood, with blond hair showing on either side of her face, tucked down into her jacket. She moved over to stand close to Cavan as they came up, and smiled. Even with the outlandish garb and the spray and the wind, the first impression that Keene registered was that she was stunningly beautiful. "Hello. You are Dr. Keene. I recognize you from the television," she said. Despite everything, her voice was managing to laugh. Keene came close to falling instantly in love.

"Ah, yes. It's about time that you met Alicia too," Cavan told him.

Keene blinked. "*This* is Alicia? But how on earth did you find the time to collect her as well?"

"I could hardly leave her behind, Landen. There's no telling how, or when, or even if we'll be going back."

They moved with the others through the gate into the launch

complex. Wind whistled through the fifteen-foot-high, razor-wire-topped fence. Engines opening up for takeoff roared from somewhere behind them.

The turboprop, it turned out, had been carrying just the Kronian hostages and their escorting force. Voler and the other names involved in the plot had all been in the plane following, which had flown away. Evidently, the idea had been for the inside force to seize one of the Boxcar orbiters being readied for flight and secure the launch facility, then board the hostages and their guards, with the elite arriving last, when everything was in place.

General Ullman, none the worse for his experience, met them in the Transit Lounge of the OLC-6 East complex, which was where outgoing personnel were assembled prior to launch and incomers awaited transportation. Nobody had any idea where the jet might be heading now, but with the hostages freed that had become a secondary issue. The first priority was to get the Kronians out before conditions got any worse, and the means to do it was right there, in the form of the Boxcar orbiter that Delmaro's force was supposed to have seized. The Launch Supervisor was summoned and asked to initiate preparations accordingly, while the communications section tried to get a connection through to the *Osiris* to update Idorf on what was happening.

Communications with the East Coast administration were erratic and confused. When Cavan and his Special Forces contingent left, preparations had been in hand to relocate the entire executive arm of government to the FEMA Southern Region command center in Atlanta, using one of the special aircraft originally equipped to provide a mobile headquarters in the event of nuclear war. An AWACS flying command post that was to provide communications while the Washington facilities were being moved had gone off the air suddenly, it was suspected from a meteorite hit. The Washington area had suffered heavy bombardment, with a lot of fires started. Cavan didn't know how much of the East Coast was affected, but when they took off there had been huge detonations lighting up to the north. On the flight over, they had seen large fires in the vicinity of Indianapolis.

Then it was discovered that one of the launch technicians, acting on his own initiative when Delmaro's soldiers appeared, had disabled the hydraulic systems that elevated the Boxcar orbiters to the launch position. The damage wasn't fatal, but it could take several hours to fix. And that meant that the Kronians were not going to get out before the storm.

Personnel not involved in fixing the Boxcar elevation hydraulics or trying to establish communications with the *Osiris* had been moved into the sturdier, safer structures. Grid power had gone, and the facility was running on its own gas-turbine-driven generators. Outside, the air was filled with pieces of sheeting torn from roofs, metal covers and cowls, and other windborne missiles. Fifty-foot waves had demolished the boat dock and were washing over the beaches and dunes on the north side of the base. The launch complex and runway were situated on the three-hundred-foot-high Burton Mesa dominating the area, and had escaped inundation so far, but the winds had torn loose and wrecked several launch vehicles at the exposed gantries and carried away parts of the buildings and other structures. The Boxcar orbiters were protected beneath the doors roofing their enclosed servicing bays, but there could be no question of launching them until conditions eased. In the general base area, those who had not yet left on Highway One had no choice but to sit tight. Perhaps they were better off than those who had gone.

Sitting scattered around the Transit Lounge were Keene, with Charlie Hu and Colby, most of the Kronians, including Sariena but not Gallian, a mixture of Mitch's Special Forces and Penalski's Marines, and some staff from the complex. The walls carried posters and cutaway drawings of various spacecraft, engineering charts and procedure guides, a map of the base and another showing the surrounding area, and a bulletin board covered with notices concerning things that didn't matter anymore. All the windows were sandbagged, and those not already blown in or smashed by flying objects had been taped. Cavan answered the remaining questions from a worn easy chair by one of the tables, sipping black coffee from a plastic mug. Alicia sat by him, her parka thrown over the back of an adjacent chair to reveal golden hair that fell to her shoulders in sinuous waves, and an equally sinuous body that drew glances from every male in the room.

"Landen and I had already agreed that it had to be Vandenberg. We figured the rest out from what happened at LAX. Beckerson and a small group who were with him on the flight from Washington announced a change of plan and transferred to a T-43 that was waiting for them when they got to Edwards. It took off within minutes, before anyone there knew what was going on. A half hour later, the same T-43 landed at LAX and collected your good woman, Fey, and her traveling companion, along with a couple of others that had also arrived there. Now, a T-43 is a biggish aircraft to be using for such a small number, but all the same we didn't think the Kronians were on board it. You wouldn't bring your hostages into a place like LAX. Too much risk of something going wrong. You'd keep them out of the way until the time came to produce them. But it would either lead us to them or rendezvous with them somewhere, depending on the plan."

"Now, just a minute. Let's get this straight," Colby Greene said, sitting forward. "You weren't still in Washington when this happened. You couldn't have been. I don't care how fast that Rustler is, you couldn't have got all this organized and crossed the country in the kind of time we're talking about here."

Cavan shook his head. "We were already on our way by that time—just about over Nevada?" He looked inquiringly at Mitch, who was tilting his chair back with his feet on the table on the far side of the room.

"We were close to Vegas when we got the report from LAX," the major confirmed.

Keene looked at Cavan, even more perplexed. "So what are you telling us, Leo? You'd left Washington two hours or whatever before? Without knowing where they were or when they were going to show up? You help yourself to a plane and a bunch of guys, and just decide to go joyriding west with the end of the world going on, just in case something turns up. Is that what you're telling us?"

The others around the room could do little more than shake their heads at each other, too much out of it all to really follow what was being said.

"Ah, well, it wasn't really like that, now," Cavan said.

Alicia raised her eyebrows at Keene, then looked at Cavan. "Maybe you don't know him so well, even after all these years, Lan," she said. "You're being too modest, Leo. I'd say it was pretty much like that, yes."

"Not at all, not at all. We knew they were heading for LAX. And something had to happen pretty soon after they got there. All we needed was to be in the vicinity and equipped to react quickly." Cavan looked around the room and appealed as if to a jury. "All right, I took the law into my hands and cut a few corners. So I'll take the reprimand when it comes, right? But if I'd stopped to try it the proper way, we'd still be in Washington waiting for the right rubber stamps even now. There's an old piece of Irish philosophy that says contrition is easier than permission. The service doesn't agree, of course. But I don't think they'll be doing too much worrying for a while. As I said, I'll take the reprimand when it comes."

Keene leaned back in his seat, managing a thin smile and shaking his head. "Okay, Leo, go on. Then what?"

Cavan was about to reply, when the crashing sound of something large striking the building came from above. The lights flickered, then stabilized again. Several people started or raised their arms protectively. Others exchanged strained looks. Everyone was getting jumpy. Several seconds went by, but apart from the ongoing background of wind gusts thudding and the rattle of sand scouring the walls, nothing further happened. Cavan went on, "We got them on radar as they climbed out from LAX—another nice thing about that machine I borrowed. They headed north, and seemed to rendezvous with another plane that appeared from somewhere inland."

"Which had to be carrying the Kronians," Colby completed, nodding in a way that said he could see it all now.

"Exactly. Both of them headed out to sea for a while, and then went into a wide turn that brought them back lined up on Vandenberg. The one carrying the hostages was in the lead, obviously intending to land first. And there was our chance. If we could get in ahead of the second plane and grab the Kronians while they were separated from the Society of Friends, there would be nothing for anybody to bargain over. And the rest you know. . . . We weren't aware at the time that an orbiter had already been seized, of course. But it worked out all right. Without the hostages to get them a safe passage aboard the *Osiris*, what could Delmaro and his force inside do with it? I must say, our young lieutenant friend from the Marines couldn't have timed things better. His move at the gate clinched it. Where is he?" Cavan looked around, but Penalski was not in the room.

"I think he's with General Ullman," one of the technicians said.

The Launch Supervisor came in through the doorway. All the heads turned, waiting. "It looks as if we might be able to get two Boxcars off if this mess ever eases up," he announced. "Forget the rest. Nothing else is getting off the ground. We've got forty-eight places in each one. There are thirteen Kronians. The Kronians have nominated six individuals for places on the *Osiris*. We have two children separated from their families, who get to go. There are eight more children with mothers only—six mothers—and they get to go. We have one expectant mother; she gets to go. That means there's room for sixty more, assuming the *Osiris* confirms that it can take them. We think it's likely that it will, since not much is going to be going up from Guatemala—but we haven't made contact yet. In the meantime, we're taking names now in the office outside of all those who want to be on the list. The places will be decided by drawing lots. Immediate family groups—that's parents with children—get one chance, but if it comes up they all go. I've got my name down. Anyone else who wants to leave the planet, step along. It's open to all. General Ullman and his family are there, just the same as the rest. Nobody's playing God over this. For once, that job's being left where it belongs."

◎ 36 ◎

Keene stood with Sariena on one side of a concrete-walled space full of motor housings, cables, huge pipes, and color coded valves in the lower levels of the complex serving the Boxcar launch bays. People were camped around and under the machinery, and children were having fun climbing about on the pipes. Those who could, kept themselves busy preparing soup, sandwiches, and hamburgers, or bringing pieces of furniture or other comforts from the offices and labs higher up; others played chess or cards, read, or tried to entertain the children. An area had been set aside for treating the growing number of casualties, from people venturing outside and being hit by flying debris to lacerations from imploding windows.

Not being as big as most of the Kronians, Sariena had managed to find some Air Force fatigues to change into from the clothes she'd been wearing since the abduction in Washington, and so looked a little fresher, if obviously tired. She had told Keene their side of the story, not that there was a lot to it. They had been collected from the Engleton by what everyone assumed to be the official bus to take them to Andrews AFB, but the escorts turned out to be captors who took them to another airfield somewhere. From there they flew several hours to a landing strip in a desert location, where the plane was covered under an awning until departing an hour or so before its arrival at Vandenberg. Their escorts were all military, following instructions, and couldn't or wouldn't disclose anything beyond what the Kronians could see for themselves. The Kronians had been held in a couple of trailers under guard. All in all they had been treated well and courteously, if firmly.

"Why not try and get some rest?" Keene said. "Even when they get the repairs finished, nobody's going anywhere until the weather lets up."

"Oh, I'll try and hold out until we get back to the ship. Then I'll sleep for a week. I'm sure all of us will." Sariena's eyes flickered over him briefly. "At least we were just sitting around most of yesterday and last night, waiting for something to happen. You should be just about ready to collapse when we get up there."

Keene grunted and shuffled restlessly, looking away. He knew that Sariena had made the remark deliberately to sound out the discontentment that she sensed in him. Keene wasn't sure himself why he felt it.

Following the example of their commanders, none of the Marine contingent or the Special Forces rescue team had put themselves on the list for the draw. Keene had been one of the six named by the Kronians for guaranteed places, but he had declined to be privileged and opted to go into the draw along with everyone else. Nevertheless, his name had come up anyway. It didn't sit well with him. The other five had been Charlie Hu, who had accepted; Cavan and Alicia, who had accepted only because Cavan had insisted on Alicia's accepting, and she had refused flatly to do so without him—but he didn't seem happy with it; the engineer who had foregone a place on the last evacuation plane in order to supervise the hydraulics repairs; and Colby Greene, who, like Keene, had opted for the draw instead but been unlucky. Gallian admitted that perhaps it had been a mistake to offer any nominated places, but it was done now and couldn't be changed.

"It's not a time to feel ignoble," Sariena told him. "Sending the women and children first might have some point on a sinking ship, where there's an intact civilization for them to go back to, but in this situation we're going to have to rebuild civilization. It's going to need people like you every bit as much as new blood. You're an engineer and a scientist, Lan. What will you do here when it's over? Charlie can see the logic of it. He's only being realistic."

Keene was reacting to an instinct that he was unable to articulate and so took the opportunity to steer the talk onto a different tack. "I used to be a scientist," he said. "But that was only until I saw what it was turning into."

"What Earth turned it into," Sariena replied. "What's at Kronia is different—the way you've always said science should be. We've talked enough about it. Don't you want to be a part of that?"

Keene leaned his elbows on a guardrail beside an access pit leading down under some machinery and sighed, giving her a tired smile. She was still selling hard—and doing a good job. "The beginnings of a whole new science," he said. "It was just starting to get interesting too, wasn't it? Did you ever think any more about the dinosaurs? When did Vicki and I call in the middle of the night? Five days ago, was it? I've lost all track."

"We had some exchanges with the Kronian scientists while we were in Washington," Sariena said. "Basically, they're intrigued by the idea. They've got a possible theory about why that estimate of yours didn't work." She meant the rough calculation that Keene had made of how much Earth's surface gravity would be reduced in a phase-locked orbit close to Saturn.

"What?" Keene asked.

"They think Earth may have gone through not one phase of gravity increase, but two. You only covered one of them."

"Two?" Keene repeated, looking puzzled.

"Somebody there came up with the thought that maybe the account of an impacting body wiping out the dinosaurs, is only half the story. If it was high in density, say, five to ten times that of the crust, and large enough, then absorbing it into the Earth's core would cause a significant increase in surface gravity. So before the impact, *two* factors were operating: the mass was smaller, *and* you had the effect of being close to the giant primary. When the gravity increased due to the extra mass being added, none of the giant life-forms that had existed previously could survive."

Keene stared at her, trying to visualize what she was saying. It did make a strange kind of sense. A planet like Earth was molten inside a sticky bag of mantle, topped by a crumbly crust—not solid all the way through in a way that would shatter. A small, dense object penetrating and being absorbed would certainly have been possible. "But we're still a satellite of Saturn," he checked.

"Right. Maybe knocked out to a looser orbit."

"So life is reduced in size, but still bigger than what we've got today."

Sariena nodded again. "And how's this for a coincidence? Taking the figures I used a moment ago, with the impacting body a fifth of Earth's initial volume, the amount you'd have to shrink a dinosaur by to get back to the same strength-weight ratio that you had under the lower-gravity conditions, works out at about forty percent. That gets you just about down to the size of the *titanoheres*—the giant mammals that lived until the end of the Pliocene."

The implication was clear. Keene scanned her face, as if looking for a hint that he wasn't jumping ahead prematurely. "So are you saying that was when Earth detached from Saturn—and gravity increased a second time to become what we've got now?" He nodded slowly to himself as he thought about it. And by that time, humans could have existed to witness it—the Joktanians and very likely others, long predating what had been thought to be the earliest civilizations. Huge, too. The giant humans had existed along with giant mammals.

"We don't know what caused it to detach," Sariena said. "Maybe another impact event—enough to have ejected the artifacts that were found on Rhea. That's just a guess, of course, but it fits. . . . In fact, it fits with a lot of things." Keene stared at her again. And so the temporarily orphaned Earth would have begun falling toward the Sun, away from the cradle that had seen its life begin, and warmed it benignly and nurtured it. For how long would it have fallen inward?

"The ice age," he murmured.

"Yes. And when Earth found a stable orbit the ice melted, and Earth entered an age where grasslands and forests flourished where there are now nothing but deserts, temperate belts extended up into what today is the Arctic, and animals of every kind flourished in millions. The axis was more perpendicular to the orbital plane. We think those times lasted about five or six thousand years, through to three and a half thousand years ago."

"And then Venus happened," Keene said. The axis was tilted more. The climatic bands shifted and became narrower.

"Well, maybe. Some of our scientists have suggested that it could have been the Venus encounter that detached Earth from Saturn— which might explain why astronomy didn't reemerge as a science for nearly two thousand years. All kinds of things become possible once you free yourself from the insistence on gradualism that has been stifling science here for two centuries." Sariena moved forward to grip his arm. "These are the things we will be working on through the years ahead, Lan. A new science of Earth, written around a new history of humankind and its origins. Who knows what more it may turn up? The old, sterile ideas are dead. They were the products of a world that's over. A new world is being born out there. And one day Kronia will rebuild Earth, but that might be generations away. It first has to build itself. There's nothing for you to do here in the meantime. The place where you can do something that will matter is with us."

Keene looked across at the children playing among the piping. He still didn't feel at ease and wasn't sure why. "I don't know. . . . Somehow it feels like running out. A lot of people are going to need help," was the best he could manage.

Sariena stopped short of scoffing. "From doctors and priests. And maybe later, anyone who can catch a fish, grow a potato, or throw together a shack that will stand up. But it's going to be a long time before they need nuclear engineers again."

Cliff, the Rustler's young Flight Electronics Officer, who along with the pilot, Dan, made up its two-man crew, appeared at the top of a metal stairway nearby. He looked down over the machinery bays, spotted Keene and Sariena, and waved to get their attention. "You're wanted upstairs," he called to them. "They've just got a connection to the *Osiris*. There's no telling how long it might last."

The global satellite system had suffered appalling attrition, causing havoc with the official networks. A connection had eventually been established via the ground line to NORAD and Space Command's underground city at Cheyenne Mountain near Colorado Springs, and a still-operational AWACS flight, to Amspace's tracking facility, which was still managing to get through when the *Osiris* was above the horizon.

Idorf was on a screen in a local control room in the OLC complex, patched through from the main communications center. Colby and Charlie Hu were there with a group of comtechs and engineers, watching infrared views, taken from orbit during a temporary thinning of the haze, of the devastation farther down the coast from Los Angeles to San Diego and beyond. Marina Del Rey, Venice, and Long Beach no longer existed. Whole waterfront districts had been washed away, with street after street of wind-flattened houses farther inland looking as if they had been carpet bombed. LAX looked like an aircraft breaker's yard, and JPL was a mess of collapsed buildings, upended and scattered vehicles, and demolished communications hardware—which explained why there had been no success in getting a link in that direction.

By the time Keene and Sariena arrived, Idorf had been updated on the freeing of the hostages and had confirmed that the *Osiris* would be able to accept the the two Boxcar loads of additional evacuees. "But you should begin boarding them now," he advised. The wind you are getting is part of a general pattern that's developing across the northeastern Pacific, but a calmer center is moving south toward you right now. As soon as it gets there, you should be ready to go. We'll transmit a beacon for you to home on."

"What's happening in other places?" Colby asked. "We weren't prepared for the whole global system going down at once. Since Washington went off the air, we don't know what's been going on."

"Visibility in most places is too bad to for me to say much," Idorf replied. "There have been large bolide explosions over Eastern Europe and much of Asia. Our radar shows more to be expected in the next few days. Big waves caused by offshore impacts in the western Mediterranean have done a lot of damage along the French and Spanish coasts. Barcelona has been practically wiped out by a direct strike.

The room listened grimly. Nobody asked further questions. Keene licked his lips. "You're coming in via Amspace?" he queried.

"Yes."

"Is there anyone available on the circuit there? Can I see how they're doing while we've got the connection?"

Idorf looked away and seemed to be asking somebody something about how long they'd got. "Yes, we have someone there," he replied. "They're putting him on. But keep it brief. We're getting near the edge of our range."

The screen faded for a moment, then stabilized again to show a begrimed figure with a bandaged head, wearing a forage cap and dust-streaked shirt. It took Keene a moment to recognize him as Harry Halloran. "Harry?" he said, just to be sure.

"Lan Keene. Since we're linking the Kronians to their ship, I take it you've got them back."

"Yes, but don't ask me to tell you the story. Listen, Harry, we may not have much time. I just wanted to know how it's going there. Did Marvin get the evacuation started?"

Halloran shook his head. "Everyone's still here at Kingsville. When we began assembling them here, rumors started going around that Amspace was buying up food and gas and hoarding it, and we got invaded."

"Invaded? Who by?"

"People coming in from the coast. Some of them just seemed to go crazy—tearing the fences down and taking whatever they could grab. It's still ugly, Lan. We've had to fight to hang on to what's ours. There's been shooting. I don't know what we'd have done without our own security guys. The police are too stretched to deal with it."

"Shooting? Anybody hurt?" Keene asked.

"Sure. Some dead on both sides. The plant was like a battleground this morning. It's calmed down now, but for how long, I don't know. We're still trying to organize the move to Lubbock but a lot of people here are quitting and just going with the general flow."

Keene put a hand to his head. It had to come. But so soon? And it was going to get worse. "Harry, do you know anything about the people from my outfit—Vicki and the girls there? They were supposed to have come into Kingsville too. Have you seen them anywhere? Do you know where they are?"

Halloran shook his head. "I did see them here last night. But now? Who knows? They could be anywhere in this, if they're still around. There are people showing up and leaving all the time."

Keene stared at the screen. Sariena was watching him. Suddenly, he knew what it was that had held him back. It had been there all the time, for years, and he just hadn't let himself see it. He needed to get back there. But once he did—if he did—there would be only one way out.

"Harry, do one thing for me," he said. "Find Vicki and tell her to get to San Saucillo with whoever of the girls can make it there. And tell her to *stay* there. Whatever happens."

"Lan, we've got about—"

"*Just do it, Harry. Find her, and tell her!* This one thing. Okay?"

Halloran gulped and nodded. "I'll try."

"Not good enough, Harry."

Halloran nodded rapidly. "Okay. If she's here I'll find her and I'll tell her. What are you going to do?"

"Did Wally ever get back from Washington?" Keene asked.

"We heard he was on a plane that had to put down in St. Louis. I don't know where he is now."

"He told me that Marvin was getting the shuttle down at Montemorelos checked out. You have to know about it."

Halloran nodded. "But we never figured it into anything."

"Well, that's where we're going," Keene said.

"We?"

"Don't you want to get out of this, Harry? You've seen how bad it's getting already. You think that's the end?"

"But where is there to go in it?"

"A new world. To Saturn. Get us a pilot. I don't know about who else you want to bring. You know how many the shuttle will take. Just get to San Saucillo. I'll be there."

"But how do we know the *Osiris* will still be there?"

"Let me worry about that."

Halloran started to reply, but Idorf interrupted to warn that the

Osiris was losing contact. Moments later, the connection was broken.

Keene turned to confront the astounded faces around him. He felt light inside, suddenly, the feeling that comes of knowing that one has finally done what some instinct that knew best wanted all along. "Well, there it is," he told them. "Scratch me off that list and let somebody else have the place. I'll see you in orbit later."

Nobody tried to argue, not even Sariena. Keene could have sworn that he saw a tear in her eyes when he looked at her, half expecting an objection. But at the same time there was a look that knew him finally, and accepted that it couldn't have been any other way.

❀ 37 ❀

When the winds eased, it was found that a fallen gantry had fouled the overhead doors of one of the Boxcar launch bays. A crew went out to haul the obstruction clear with a tow tractor. The shower of rocks and gravel had slackened, but the hazard had not gone away completely. Within fifteen minutes one of the crew was killed outright. A dozen others stepped forward to fill the place. Getting the two Boxcars away had become a point of pride for all of the launch staff and workforce.

Meanwhile, loading went ahead of the first Boxcar, which would be taking the Kronians, the balance being made up of family groups and mothers with children, the children who had become separated, the expectant mother, and after them, the names heading the draw. The second Boxcar would be launched as soon as its covering doors could be opened. After that, the facility would be shut down and the remaining personnel, including General Ullman with his wife and two daughters, flown out in the Samson transport that had been held back. They would head for Peterson Air Force Base at Colorado Springs, where accommodation had been promised in the underground complex at Cheyenne Mountain. The only problem with that was that more people who had missed the evacuation by road for one reason or another were beginning to appear from among the shattered base-area buildings, many of them injured or in shock, and there was only so much room in the Samson. A search was being made for more ground vehicles, but many had been damaged and it was still far from clear how the situation would be resolved. Lieutenant Penalski with his six Marines and their pilot, Sergeant Erse, would wait for the launches, then endeavor to return in the Cessna to their unit at Twentynine Palms. Keene talked to Mitch, who agreed to detour via Texas and Montemorelos before attempting to rejoin the Eastern administration in Atlanta. Colby said he might as well go too. "I can't think of anywhere else that appeals to me right now," he explained. "Besides, I always wanted to see Mexico."

Sariena and Gallian stood outside the tunnel leading through the bunkerlike concrete walls to the boarding ramp in the Boxcar launch bay, while behind them the other Kronians waved farewells and disappeared into the entranceway. General Ullman, who had come to see them off with a short, official message, watched with some of his aides. Keene stood with Colby, Mitch, Penalski, the Launch Supervisor, and others from the launch crew. He shook Gallian's hand solidly, then took both of Sariena's. "Well, I guess this is it again. . . . How many times have we done this? Saying good-bye to you is getting to be a habit."

She nodded, unable to do more than whisper a low "Good-bye, Lan" in reply. Her expression and her manner conveyed as clearly as any words could have that she expected this to be the last time. Keene didn't want to dwell on it.

The technicians directing the boarding ushered through a mixed group, among them Charlie Hu, carrying a canvas bag slung over one shoulder. He stopped in front of Keene and regarded him evenly.

"Well, Lan. . . ."

"I guess it's time, Charlie."

Hu looked past Keene, and his brow knotted. Cavan and Alicia were standing watching, but with Colby and the military officers, not with the line that was moving forward to board.

"I changed my mind," Alicia said in answer to the question written across Hu's face. "I'm too much the romantic. . . . Lan going off all the way to Texas to find this woman. I have to see what happens."

Hu looked at Cavan. "I can't do anything. She's crazy," was all that Cavan had to offer. Hu frowned; then his eyes moved to Keene. Keene said nothing. Theirs, along with Keene's, meant three extra places available.

"We do have a couple with two young sons," the Launch Supervisor said, keeping his tone neutral. "They're next on the draw, but we had to put them down for the second launch."

Sariena and Gallian had gone. The remaining passengers were moving through quickly. Charlie looked from Keene to the others, and then around. The family was standing anxiously a short distance away, where they had been told to wait in case something changed. "*Shit!*" He unslung his bag, and stepped aside to join the others. Without further ado, the Supervisor waved the family forward, and a technician followed them into the access tunnel. Keene and the others began making their way up to the control room where they had talked to Idorf earlier, from where the launch would be initiated.

Thirty minutes later, the first Boxcar roared skyward trailing a plume of flame and quickly vanished into the turbulent overcast. There would be no guidance from the ground, or even knowledge that it had reached the *Osiris* unless a contact was reestablished through Amspace or via some other means. Piloting would be entirely manual and rely on the homing signal that Idorf had promised. It would take about an hour for the Boxcar to climb to the distance that Idorf had pulled the *Osiris* back to and match its orbit.

With the first launch completed, the crew that had been working to free the doors of the second launch bay was able to go back outside and resume. Until they were through, there was little for anyone else to do. Charlie Hu and Colby remained in the control room with the engineers keeping the communications vigil. Alicia, who was a trained nurse, was helping with the casualties. Keene and Cavan, the leaders of the two military squads and their aircrews, accompanied by six of Mitch's twenty-two Special Forces troopers, went out to the hangars by the runway area to check their aircraft.

※　　※　　※

Most of the buildings had sections of roof or wall torn away, and all were missing windows. The spaces and roadways between were covered with rubble and broken glass. One office block had been cleaved through the middle by a steel-frame tower which now lay twisted amid piles of desks, file cabinets, wall sections and other wreckage that had spilled from the sagging floors. A number of cars, some turned over on their sides, were buried under wreckage, two more thrown against the chain-link fence separating the runways from the launch complex. Medics wearing helmets with red crosses were tending a blood-covered figure on the ground, while APs and others struggled to extricate another. Three more forms laid out nearby were not moving.

The runways beyond were littered with fallen gravel and wind-blown debris. An earthmover with a blade would be needed to clear the way before any takeoffs could be attempted. True, the Rustler could get off vertically or from a football field if it had to, but it gulped fuel doing so. The control tower was a splintered shell open to the winds and looked out of commission, although figures were moving around inside. The other base buildings were all damaged, and a fire had started in one of them. The group from the launch complex walked on, saying little, their boots crunching on the grit and gravel. Keene stooped and picked up a piece curiously. It was still warm, not especially dense, like a bit of sinter from a furnace. A year before, it had been part of Jupiter.

People were clustered inside the open doors of the large, concrete-roofed hangar housing the Samson. As Keene and the others drew closer, they saw that a group of maybe two dozen was confronting several Air Force officers backed by a knot of APs carrying rifles unslung. The smaller hangar beyond, where the Cessna and the Rustler were parked, was still closed and seemed to have escaped attention. A big man, wearing a leather jacket, red hair hanging to his shoulders, was berating the officers loudly.

"Who was in the shuttle they launched? How many more shuttles are they getting ready in there?"

"There aren't any more. That was it," the officer at the fore told him.

"Then what about this plane you've been saving here? It's big enough for everybody. There are people hurt back there."

"It's reserved for the launch personnel and their dependants. All the space has been allocated."

"Well, nobody asked *us* about any allocating. What right does anyone have? We say the allocation needs to be gone through again, with fair chances for everybody."

"You should have availed yourselves of the road evacuation. Why weren't you there when you were supposed to be? We're trying to find more vehicles now. That's the best I can tell you."

"What good's that? There's people coming back in off the highway. They were murdered out there. . . ."

The rest was lost as Keene's party moved to the farther hangar. They let themselves in through a small door that gave access to the main area inside via offices. The floor was covered with glass from shattered windows above, and wind blowing through had left a coating of fine dust over everything. The roof had been breached at the end where the Cessna was parked, and the plane had been hit and punctured in several places. A check over the Rustler showed it to be unmarked. Sergeant Erse would have to stay on and assess the degree of damage to the Cessna. Dan, the Rustler pilot, said he'd give him a hand. Mitch assigned two of his troopers to stay behind with them.

As they came back out onto the tarmac, the radio on Keene's belt squawked. He fished it from its pouch and acknowledged. It was Charlie Hu, calling from the control room inside the launch complex, where they had found a NASA cable route to the tracking station on Hawaii, which had opened up again, giving another connection to the *Osiris*. "Hello, Lan. The Boxcar is about five hundred miles out and starting to close," Charlie said. "We thought you'd want to follow it."

"We're on our way," Keene acknowledged. "The Boxcar's going in to dock with the *Osiris* now," he told Cavan.

Cavan nodded but seemed more concerned about what was going on at the larger hangar. "Leave your other four men here as well to secure those two planes," he said to Mitch. "When we get back, draw up a roster with the others to relieve them. I want a permanent guard mounted here until we're ready to leave."

As Keene, Cavan, and the two commanders passed the large hangar, a jeep carrying Colonel Lacey and an AP escort drew up in front of the doors and became the focus of attention. Leaving him to it, they continued tramping back in the direction of the gate to the launch complex. When they were about halfway, the gloom around them brightened, making them look up. The light was from above, too high to be the setting sun. Through a brief thinning of the blanket of dust and cloud, they glimpsed Athena, looming ever more huge, glowering redly behind the folds and twisting pillars of its tail. Far above, a hollow boom rolled down from something exploding high in the atmosphere. The air had a smell of crude-oil vapors, like the areas around the refineries on the Texas coast.

◉ **38** ◉

The bay doors had been freed when Keene and the others got back to the OLC complex. Boarding of the second Boxcar was about to commence. Mitch and Penalski disappeared to organize the guarding and resupply of the two planes, while Cliff, the Rustler's second officer, left with an airframe mechanic to help the two pilots working on the Cessna. Cavan went with Keene up to the control room.

Colby and Charlie were with a group around the console handling the Hawaii link, which was showing Idorf on one of the screens. He was looking suspicious. The atmosphere seemed confused. Idorf spoke before Keene or Cavan could ask anything.

"I was told that you were having trouble with one of the shuttles, that only one had been launched. How is it we have two craft approaching? I hope this isn't some kind of trick, I've seen enough of them already."

The Launch Supervisor, who was standing immediately in front of the screen, shook his head. "The other Boxcar *is* still here. . . . We're as baffled as you are."

"Did our delegation leave in the one that was launched?"

"Yes, of course they did."

"How do I know that? Something strange is going on here." Idorf moistened his lips. "I'm deploying an X-laser as a precaution. It can be recovered later if this is a false alarm." He proceeded to issue orders to others off screen.

"*What is it?*" Keene hissed at Charlie.

Hu indicated a display showing the projection of a hemispherical radar plot being generated by the *Osiris*'s radars. "There are two ships closing up there. One's leading the other by about a hundred miles. Nobody can figure it."

"Which one is the Boxcar?"

"We don't know."

The Supervisor turned around, saw that Keene and Cavan had joined them, and shook his head. "We don't have any ground-station or satellite data to go on anymore. What can I tell him?"

"Maybe there was something up there already that latched onto the *Osiris*'s beacon," Cavan mused.

"Maybe."

Idorf looked back. "So far we have had no identification response," he said. "Why are there two if you only launched one? How can we even be sure that either of them is the one that you launched? Once again, I have to take precautionary action." As he spoke, a blip detached itself from the *Osiris* symbol on the radar plot and began moving away toward a standoff position. Keene felt his stomach tightening. He had seen this before. Visions raced through his mind of a ghastly mistake about to unfold.

"We think one of them might just be something that picked up your beacon," the Supervisor said. "Don't do anything hasty, for God's sake."

Idorf's brow creased. "What are you implying? I can assure you that I don't relish being in this position. But need I remind you that one attempt has been made already to take this ship by armed force?"

"*What?*"

"It happened yesterday," Colby said from the back of the group. "Four of them. We're not sure where they were from."

The Supervisor glanced back, read the confirmation on Keene's and Hu's faces, and looked again at the screen. "I . . . didn't know about that," he told Idorf.

Idorf looked away, off-screen, suddenly. "Just one moment. . . ."

"What happened?" one of the techs next to Hu murmured.

"They didn't get even close," Colby answered. Idorf looked back. "Apparently we have just begun receiving an identification transmission . . . BZ650 . . ." He glanced away again. "Which is as we were given to expect."

"That's it! That's the Boxcar!" the Supervisor confirmed. Exhalations of relief came from around the room. Keene's muscles untightened. He moved forward into the viewing angle of the screen where Idorf would see him.

"Hello, Captain. It's no trick. Who the other ship is, I don't know, but I can vouch for these guys."

Idorf's expression relaxed. "Ah, Landen Keene! You, I know I can trust. Why didn't you tell me sooner that you were there?"

"I only just arrived. We've been kind of . . . busy down here."

Idorf nodded. "I can imagine. . . . A moment, Lan. . . . Yes, okay, we're getting a beam from them too, now." Again, he looked away to follow something that was going on nearby. Then, tension around the control room rose again as his face took on an ominous frown. Evidently, all was not so well after all. "They're saying they have an emergency," Idorf reported. "They're being pursued by an armed vessel that's attempting to use them as cover to get to the *Osiris*. They have weapons trained on them. They're asking us to fire on it."

Keene and Cavan exchanged looks. Neither had anything to offer. There could be craft up there from just about anyone with launch capability, in who-knew-what state of desperation. This wasn't exactly a time to be expecting everyone to be displaying rational behavior.

"The beam is definitely coming from the lead ship?" Charlie Hu queried.

"We can't tell. . . . And apparently it's not clear that they are receiving our signal. They're not acknowledging, just transmitting."

"Who is sending to you? Who do you have on your screen?" the Supervisor asked.

Idorf paused to check off-screen once more. "Dr. Stacey."

The Supervisor looked around, puzzled. "Stacey? Who in hell's he? . . . That's not right. Who's commanding the Boxcar?"

"Corlaster," somebody said.

"That's what I thought."

"He says he's the senior person aboard, and in control," Idorf informed them.

Somebody had produced the passenger list and was scanning it frantically, but nobody had heard of the name.

"Can you copy us here with your incoming channel?" Keene said after a few more mystifying seconds. Idorf nodded and made a signal mutely to somebody. One of the technicians seated at a console near Keene read a code and entered a command. . . . And moments later, Keene found himself looking in astonishment at the features of Herbert Voler. Colby gasped somewhere behind him. Cavan was staring in disbelief. Nobody else in the room knew Voler or recognized him. Fey was to one side of him, Queal slightly to the rear on the other with the shoulder of somebody else showing next to him.

"Well, is this your man or is it not?" Idorf snapped. "Be quick. The range is closing."

Meanwhile, Voler was imploring, "*Please*, if anyone there is receiving us, our situation is critical. This is Doctor Stacey, in command of Boxcar BZ650 from Vandenberg, calling *Osiris*. Repeat, we are being pursued by unknown craft that is armed. Suspect intention is to use us as cover to board and seize your ship. Imperative that you intervene and destroy. Your delegation is aboard with us, and their lives are in jeopardy."

Then Voler moved to reveal the view along a cabin extending behind him. Soldiers in combat jackets were in the nearer seats. And behind them, farther toward the rear were . . . the Kronians! All of them. Keene could make out Sariena's black tresses distinctly and, beside her, Gallian's white crown. Clearly, the image was being faked. As much would be evident to the others in the room as well. Besides the obvious fact that Voler's people had not been aboard the Boxcar, Sariena was wearing a green tunic, as were the others. When she went aboard the Boxcar, she had changed into freshly supplied light blue Air Force fatigues.

"This is Captain Idorf of the *Osiris*. We are receiving you, BZ650. Can you hear me?"

But either Voler couldn't or was pretending not to. "This is urgent. Boxcar BZ650 from Vandenberg calling the *Osiris*. We are closing to dock with you. . . ." Everyone in the room was looking bewildered. The Supervisor threw his hands up helplessly. "What in hell's going on?" he pleaded. "Who are those other people?"

"What do I do?" Idorf demanded.

Keene thought frantically. There was no reason for Voler's group to think anyone might be monitoring this latest stunt, let alone anyone who knew them. They had banked on being able to get away with faking the image because they had presumed this encounter would involve only the *Osiris*. On the screen, a figure behind Voler moved aside, showing itself to be Beckerson, at the same time uncovering more of the cabin beyond. Several of the soldiers had rifles propped between their knees. The Kronians had been wearing green tunics when Mitch's force got them out of the turboprop just after it had landed early that morning—the tunics they had been wearing since they were hijacked in Washington. The picture was a superposition of Voler and the others with him, which was genuine— they were up there now, inside one of the ships—and a background taken aboard the aircraft in which the Kronians had been flown to California the day before. The two had been combined to give the impression that the transmission Idorf was receiving was coming from the Boxcar just sent up from Vandenberg. But the ship was transmitting the Boxcar's correct identification code. The Boxcar with the Kronians aboard was up there in orbit somewhere. It had to be the radar blip that was *following*.

"Charlie," Keene shot across. "Would it be feasible for the ship in front to intercept the ID code from the ship following, retransmit it, and use some kind of ECM to blot out anything else from the ship behind?" he asked.

Hu looked at him strangely for a moment, then nodded. "Sure . . . if you had somebody who knew what they were doing. Just about any ship would carry the equipment you'd need."

Keene moistened his lips. He looked back at Idorf. "That view of the Kronians is a fake," he said. "They're not there at all. The background is being manufactured."

Idorf's face hardened. "Target both objects," he instructed off-screen.

Keene felt perspiration on his forehead. Everyone else was leaving it to him now, with no idea of how his mind was working. There was no time to debate with them.

Voler and his party had left at first light in a T-43 jet transport, heading south and climbing. Keene did a quick mental calculation, then added several hours for storming a launch pad, taking up a shuttle that had been readied in hope of arriving emigrants, making orbit, and maneuvering into position. "Guatemala," he muttered aloud. "That's where they went. They seized a shuttle at Tapapeque. That's what the lead ship is." Colby looked emptily at Cavan. Cavan shook his head and shrugged. Keene followed his reasoning through, visualizing in his mind what would happen if the seized shuttle were allowed to dock with the *Osiris* by an unsuspecting crew expecting other Kronians. A FAST team, armed and waiting to go, would take the ship in minutes. And then, the full extent of what was intended unrolled itself in all its ghastliness. The Boxcar and everyone in it were sacrificial. Idorf was being urged to fire on it—with his own people aboard—to provide a diversion and maximize the surprise when the shuttle carrying Voler and his force docked.

And with extra room aboard the *Osiris* thus created, and its defenses neutralized, how many more of Voler's "elite" would be brought up afterward? With all but a skeleton crew to fly the ship eliminated, how many of their kind would go to Kronia, and with what intentions? And so it would start, all over again.

"Captain Idorf," Keene said. Despite himself, the words came out shakily. "Ignore what he's saying. There is no Doctor Stacey. Target the lead vessel only and fire. The one following is BZ650, and your people are aboard it."

If Keene's reconstruction of events was correct. . . .

The room around him had frozen into statues, all staring at him. From the screen, Idorf's eyes interrogated him silently. Both of them understood that there could be no discussion or inviting of second opinions. "You are certain of this?" was all he said.

How could Keene be? His shirt was sticking to his back, his throat dry. He closed his eyes and nodded mutely. Idorf gave the order.

And somewhere high above the Pacific, a spacecraft and several score human beings flashed briefly and turned into vapor that dispersed into the swirling gas clouds of Athena's tail.

Hawaii lost contact before Idorf was able to identify the vessel that remained.

The second Boxcar was launched a little over an hour later, into the night. By then, everyone remaining was too exhausted to contemplate evacuating before morning. There were several incidents that night involving bands from outside coming into the base, presumably looking for supplies and weapons, some involving sporadic shooting. Mitch and Penalski posted extra guards on an extended perimeter around the hangar, with the reserves sleeping under the wings of the Rustler.

PART THREE

ATHENA:
BRINGER OF
DEATH

❀ 39 ❀

Next morning, two of the Special Forces troopers had disappeared. So had two girls from the base that they had been seen spending a considerable amount of time talking with. It could only be concluded that they had unilaterally deemed their military careers to be over.

The showers in the changing rooms at the rear of the hangars still worked and delivered hot water, and for fifteen minutes Keene abandoned himself to the luxury of washing away the feeling of two days and two nights spent in the same clothes, and of getting rid of the all-pervasive red dust. It got in the eyes, in the ears, and in the nostrils, and lodged in the creases of collars, hoods, and seams until it found a chink to get inside. It itched and it burned, and when rubbing and scratching broke the skin it caused sores that inflamed. "The plague of boils," Keene thought to himself as he applied a soothing cream to painful areas on the sides of his neck and the backs of his hands, then covered them with adhesive dressings. Then, wonder of wonders, he put on a clean change of underwear, shirt, and pants from the bag he hadn't opened since before leaving the hotel in Pasadena.

Penalski and his Marines had not changed their minds about rejoining their unit at Twentynine Palms. The Cessna had taken minor damage but was up to making the short return trip, for which its fuel was ample. They also had enough space aboard to take four casualties who would otherwise have had to be moved by road. Dan and Cliff drove with a couple of Air Force ground crew and two Marines riding shotgun to refill a bowser at the fueling point on the far side of the airfield for the Rustler. While volunteers from among those who were due to leave in the Samson—now pushed up beyond 400 people—risked intermittently falling gravel to clear debris from the main runway, the remainder of Keene and Cavan's groups held an impromptu conference inside the smaller hangar.

There was some dissent among Mitch's force. General Ullman had offered them a clearance into the Cheyenne Mountain refuge, and Mitch's second-in-command, a Captain Furle, felt they should take it. Since there were no fixed orders to return East, and it was far from certain that there was anywhere organized for them to return to even if they made it, their first priority should be to get the men to safety while the opportunity was there. Although Mitch hadn't gone into details with the men as to why they were talking about going to Texas and Mexico, Furle gathered it was some private business of Keene's and didn't think it should be their affair—certainly not something to be risking lives over. They should put down first at Peterson Base near Colorado Springs where the Samson was heading, Furle argued, and anyone who wanted to do Keene a favor could carry on from there.

"The problem with that is that we might not get past Peterson," Mitch replied. "We didn't exactly come by this piece of equipment in a way that you'd call official. Some brass there might just take it into his head to decide that it's government property with better things it could be doing, and impound it."

"And he might have a point there, right enough, too," Furle agreed, not giving an inch. And maybe Furle had a point too, Keene had to admit as he stood listening. Normally, he would have been surprised at such discord within an elite fighting unit of this kind. But Cavan had mentioned that not all of these men had trained together in the way that creates trust and cohesion. It was a scratch force, thrown together at a moment's notice from whoever had been available.

Mitch stepped to the center of the group, his hands raised for attention. He was tall and broad, with solid, square-jawed, handsome features topped by a mane of black, wavy hair. Keene saw him as confident and capable, but with something of a flamboyant streak that put him in his element before a crowd. Good leader material and a natural as a showman, easily pictured as a performer or media personality if he had applied himself to it. But there was a lot of the adventurer there too, which perhaps went some way to explaining how he had ended up in an irregular military unit—and perhaps why he had agreed to go along with the Texas escapade.

"Guys, strictly, Terry is correct," he began. "What we did the other night was without official orders. A matter of pure initiative. But as a force, we've always taken pride in our ability to act independently when the need is there, right? That's what we've all trained for, what our reputation is built on. And there's no question that what we accomplished was fully in accord with top national priority. The President—your commander-in-chief—was personally concerned that the Kronians were returned safely to their ship, and that was what we helped him do."

He turned, appealing to all of them. "One, maybe a couple of hours longer than we'd take anyway. That's all that's being asked, guys. How long did it take us to make it here to Vandenberg from Washington? This time we're talking about four states, that's all. Half the distance we did the other night. We drop down into Texas, pick up a few people, shuttle them across the border—and then it's on up to Atlanta for dinner. Only the difference is that you'll be able to enjoy your dinners better from knowing that we finished the job."

Mitch put his fists on his hips and looked around. From the looks and the glances being exchanged, Keene could see he was carrying them. Even Furle was looking less militant. "What do you say, guys?' Mitch invited, looking at the Rustler's two crew.

"Sure—one, maybe two hours extra should do it," Dan agreed, nodding.

Cliff seconded by nodding. He was curly haired and boyish, said little but was widely liked. He seemed to have touched a mothering reflex in Alicia.

It was enough. The majority responded with nods and assenting murmurs. Furle accepted the verdict without further protest.

The bowser returned, and while the Rustler's tanks were being filled, Keene went with Cavan, Penalski, Mitch, and a squad of Mitch's troopers to the larger hangar to present compliments to General Ullman and mount rearguard while the final boarding of the Samson was completed. The Cessna, already loaded, taxied up to collect Penalski and then took off first, banking into a turn out to sea and disappearing southward at low altitude, following the coast. The huge Samson went next, rolling almost the length of the runway before lifting, fading quickly, and then vanishing into the overcast— a slightly higher ceiling than before after the previous day's winds, but still agitated and muddy. Lightning flashed distantly among the heaps of cloud, which were beginning to disgorge spots of rain. The raindrops were black and oily with soot.

Keene stood for a minute, looking at the derelict control tower and the savaged buildings around it, and across to the wrecked launch complex with its fallen gantries while the sound of the Samson's engines grew muffled and more distant. Only days before, it had all been vibrant and thrusting, a symbol of endeavor and industriousness; now . . . a preview of what was to come everywhere. Silence took over as the engine noise faded, broken only by the cawing of gulls wheeling in from over the point. A feeling of stillness and desolation overwhelmed him suddenly. He turned away to catch up with the others.

A small procession of vehicles, presumably drawn by the sounds of the planes taking off, approached from the direction of the base as a trooper driving a tow tractor pulled the Rustler out onto the tarmac. There were several cars and trucks, a Dodge van with boxes and baggage piled under netting on the roof, and a four-wheel-drive pulling a U-Haul trailer. They were way overloaded, all their occupants disheveled, many of them bandaged, most seeming dazed. Several badly injured cases were laid on makeshift beds or blankets in the trucks and the trailer. Three men got out from the front of the car leading. Three more people were crammed in the back, along with some small children. The man in front had a gray mustache and face disfigured by angry-looking, open sores. He half raised an arm feebly.

"We don't know what to do with 'em. . . . They'll never make the trip, but we can't stay here." There was nothing demanding or even expecting in his voice. Just a plea for help.

"This is a military mission," Mitch replied. "We're not going anywhere you'd want to be—probably as bad as this. Worse." An ashen-faced woman stared from the window of the car following, mechanically rocking a baby that was crying.

Alicia looked at them, then Mitch. "We can't just leave them. The plane wasn't full on our way over. We can take the worst, yes? What did you say yourself—a few hours to Atlanta? I'll look after them. That way the others will have a chance."

Keene could see the resistance in Mitch's face, the beginnings of the double standard that demands loyalty to one's own group but hostility to outsiders when survival becomes the issue. But it hadn't asserted itself strongly enough yet to prevail. Mitch turned his head toward Dan in an unvoiced question.

"How many stretcher cases?" the pilot queried.

The men looked at each other and muttered between themselves. "Eight that are bad," one said finally.

Dan did a quick mental estimate. Besides its passengers, the Rustler was carrying a generous reserve of supplies, fresh water, weapons and ammunition, various types of tools and equipment. "Those, then, plus four more," he announced. "But let's be sensible about this. If somebody's obviously not going to make it, don't waste the space." Mitch looked at the man with the mustache and nodded curtly. Keene and Cavan caught each other's eye, then looked away. Although there was nothing more to be said for the moment, each had read the same in the other's look: They were going to have to learn to harden themselves to leaving a lot of people to their fate before this was over.

The Rustler carried four folding stretchers, which were brought out. The troopers helped people from the vehicles load them aboard the plane, along with four more of the injured on improvised pallets. The worst seemed to be a woman who was moaning deliriously, both her legs crushed in a traffic accident out on the highway. After another brief conference, the men who appeared to be speaking for the group selected two couples to accompany the eight. Keene was relieved to see that all the children would remain. This was already getting complicated enough.

Keene watched the hapless group through one of the forward windows as the Rustler turned to begin taxiing out, standing expressionlessly before their vehicles. They were still there when the plane roared back along the runway and lifted off, as if not knowing where to go next.

The sea seemed amazingly calm, Keene thought as the strip of dunes and beaches came into view. Then he realized that what he was looking at was mud. The tide was out to a distance that must have been close to a mile.

At the back of the plane, the woman with the crushed legs was starting to scream.

Cliff scanned through frequency bands as the Rustler climbed. "Santa Barbara's out. LAX is out. Seems the West Coast is about out of business," he reported. Charlie Hu was behind him in the jump seat, following the procedures. "Military Sector Control is operating at San Bernardino. They're routing us over Phoenix. Come around onto zero-nine-eight degrees and make for thirty thousand to try and get over the turbulence. Two transports and a high-altitude reconnaissance flight in the area. I've got 'em on radar. Otherwise free of traffic. Still a lot of clutter. Reports of heavy rock falls in the Midwest, all flights grounded there."

"Gotcha," Dan drawled from the captain's seat.

When they leveled out, Alicia and the medic in Mitch's team, whom the others called Dash, opened up the Rustler's medical locker and went back to see what they could do for the injured who had been brought aboard. With some sedation, the woman with the hurt legs quieted down. There were two more women, both hit by falling rocks, one with a shattered arm and shoulder, the other comatose from a head wound. A man had a leg almost severed at the thigh by a piece of flying metal. Two more were head injuries, both with concussion. One had lacerations and probably fractures from being in a truck hit by a mast that was blown down. The last was a youth of about seventeen who had been blinded by flying glass. Dash confided quietly to Mitch that he didn't think the kid's sight could be saved.

Between washing and dabbing with pads, and helping to place dressings and tie bandages, the two couples—Denise and Al, Cynthia and Tom; it was funny how they had suddenly become people now that they had names—who had accompanied the injured recovered their faculties sufficiently to tell the gist of their story. They had been among somewhere around fifty or sixty friends, neighbors, and relatives from nearby Vandenberg village, many of them employees of the base, who had decided to travel inland to Arizona as a group. Less than twenty miles along the highway, they had been caught in the the gravel storm of the previous day. Seven of the party were dead, including the husband and sister of the woman with the crushed legs, who was called Joan and worked as a teller in one of the banks on the base. A group of them had brought the worst cases back into the base believing they would find help, while the rest had arranged to meet farther up the highway. There were a lot like that out there. Police, paramedics, and volunteers had set up emergency dressing stations along the way, but they were swamped.

As the Rustler with its forty-two souls aboard climbed above the denser blanket of cloud, the surroundings transformed into a shimmering panorama of surreal yellow and orange sculptures twisting and unfolding upward toward a sky woven from streamers of electric violets and pink. Beneath them, foaming curtains of vapor descended, raining amber and ochre into the cauldron that the world had become. Above it all, blurred through the watery opacity of the cloud and the plasma filaments, glowed the light of two suns.

Cavan and Mitch were up front, immediately behind the flight deck, conferring in low voices. One of the NCOs handed out breakfasts, which today consisted of reconstituted egg, sausage and hash browns, rolls with butter and jelly, apple juice and coffee. Colby sat next to Keene, staring past the seats in front and for a while lost in thoughts of his own. Then, suddenly, he said, "Those people back there. Just imagine, a week ago they were anyone you might have sat next to at a movie or met in a restaurant. Last night we mounted armed guards against them as if they were enemies. The veneer's about to come peeling off, Lan. We're all about to go back to being jungle tribes again."

Those that survive, Keene thought. He had been thinking similar things too. For what they'd just heard described had to have been typical of events that had been happening on other highways too, leading inland from San Diego and Anaheim, San Luis Obispo and San Jose, Napa and Kelso; and not just in California but every other state and all the provinces he'd never heard of in every other country too. If the rate worldwide was even a tenth as great as the sample figures he had heard, Keene estimated that the number killed would already be about equal to the total battle and civilian dead of both world wars put together.

❀ 40 ❀

The hit came with a bang like a bomb exploding in the forward part of the cabin. Keene had a fleeting impression of a flash and Charlie being hurled back from the flight deck like a rag doll; and then came a roar with an invisible, freezing fist that snapped him back in his seat. Mitch, Cavan, and a couple of others who had been near the front were swept back along the aisle in a tangle of arms and legs. Shouts of alarm came from all round, terrified screams from the back. Next to Keene, Colby had gone into an emergency crouch, head down, arms crossed and braced against the seat in front. Keene hauled himself up against the pressure and peered forward with streaming eyes. A hole the size of a door had appeared where Cliff and the electronics officer's station had been. Around the sides, torn edges of metal and a section of switch panel still attached to a finger of ribbing flapped crazily in the airstream. The plane was dipping to starboard. On the still-intact left side of the cockpit, Dan pulled a yellow oxygen mask over his face, at the same time fighting to keep control as violent judderings shook the plane from end to end. One of the smashed consoles began smoking, and moments later choking fumes poured back into the cabin.

"*Jesus! Jesus!*" one of the women at the rear was shrieking.

"What is it? What's happened?" Jed, the blinded kid, yelled from his pallet.

The pressure drop following the blast pulled air the other way, carrying bodies and loose objects toward the breach. Dan banked and throttled back, shedding speed, and the press of bodies trying to untangle themselves in the aisle fell forward and went down again. Mitch dragged himself out and braced himself half-standing between the front seats and bulkhead, where he was able to tear a fire extinguisher from its mount and smother the burning. Then he folded over and sank to his knees. Keene tried to stand up further and leaned over the seatback to find Charlie . . .

A report sounded somewhere distantly, like a bucket being struck by a hammer, and a shock jolted him. Then came two more, sharper. Keene found himself slumped over an arm of the seat; he realized muzzily after a few moments that he had passed out. He straightened up stiffly. Dan's voice shouting into his microphone came from up front over the roaring of the wind.

"Still taking multiple impacts. What's your range, what's your range? I need a vector. I have no radar and controls are jamming. Visibility nil up here." Keene looked around. Some of the others were moving groggily, others slumped unconscious in their seats or lay still on the floor. At the back, Alicia was standing, clinging to the side netting with one hand while she tried to revive Dash, the medic, with the other. Dan's voice came again, louder this time, switched into the cabin address. "Attention all. We're near an evacuation reception area, but going down. This wagon is shot. Get everyone into seats or buckled down. Use whatever you can for padding and brace hard. This may not be the softest landing I ever made. . . . And thanks for choosing U.S. Government Air."

Keene turned and lifted Colby up in his seat. He was out cold, his face ashen, lips blue. Keene took his glasses, which were hanging from one ear, and slapped his cheeks alternately, then shook him by the shoulders.

"Uh? . . . Wha . . ."

"Colby, snap out of it. We're going down. We need you here, fella."

Colby leaned his head back and gulped in a series of long breaths. "God I'm cold. . . . The job description never said anything about this."

"You need to move. There's guys the other side of you that we have to get up off the floor."

Still wobbly, Colby moved into the aisle, and Keene followed. Mitch was up again, and several others were moving to assist, including Cavan, who seemed to be okay. They maneuvered the still-inert forms into seats or positions against the bulkheads, wedging their limbs with seat cushions, packs, and clothing. Keene went around the front seat to see to Charlie, who was crumpled across three seats and motionless. Colby helped Keene buckle him into one of the seats and pile up as much protection as they could. Then the floor tilted back, and the roar came of the engines diverting to reverse and vertical thrust. "This is it!" Dan's voice yelled. "Maybe ten seconds. Hang on!" Keene wedged a pack on his lap and hugged it to his chest, arms gripping the seatback in front.

The impact was fierce but not as bad as Keene had feared—Dan was using what power he had as a brake. They were thrown sideways, and then the starboard side of the cabin imploded amidships as the broken main spar of the wing plowed into the ground and was driven inward. The plane pivoted around the wing, grating over rocks, and slewed to a standstill with its fuselage broken into two parts lying joined at an angle. Cries of pain and fear came from all sides as the last movements and shrieks of rending metal died away. Keene raised his head gingerly. It was as dark as night, dust everywhere. Shadowy figures were moving, cursing, fumbling with flashlamps. Somebody farther back was calling for help. Keene spat blood from his mouth. He had bitten his tongue. His knee burned and his neck felt as if it had been wrung, but nothing seemed broken. Releasing his seat harness shakily, he rose to follow Colby, who was feeling his way into the aisle. A thudding concussion like an artillery shell landing came from somewhere outside.

In front, Dan was clambering back from the flight deck over a crazily leaning floor panel. "*Move, move! Get 'em out!*" Mitch's voice came through the gloom and the dust. "This whole thing could blow. Furle, are you there? You okay?"

"I . . . think so."

"Good. Go check the tail section. The rest of you who can move, give a hand with the ones that can't." One of the soldiers rose and just stood, staring dazedly. Mitch jabbed him several times in the chest and shoved a shoulder. "Behind you. Out that way. Move it!"

Ignoring the doors, the ones who were able began passing the injured and unconscious out through the break in the ruptured fuselage. Slowly, the rest came to their senses and lent help. Colby already had Charlie by the shoulders; one of the troopers took his legs. Several who had been sitting where the wing root had broken through were past any help. From the rear section, Al was helping Denise out, blood streaming down her face, while Alicia and Dash directed others lifting out the pallets and stretchers. A corporal called Legermount—strong, black-haired, always silently competent— became a human conveyor line, effortlessly carrying out one limp form after another and returning for the next.

They were on a slope of rock and sand that could have been a valley side or part of a mountain, vanishing into the dusty air. A hundred yards or so away was a ravine flanked by mounds of boulders. Mitch waved everyone toward it, then, while they were making their way across, he ducked back inside the front section of the fuselage to check that no one had been left. Keene and Dan hung back in case he should need help. Mitch reappeared briefly to go into the tail, and reappeared finally, hauling two packs of provisions and a medical chest. He threw them down and jumped after. "Let's get out of here!" he yelled. Keene grabbed one of the food packs, Dan, the other, and Mitch picked up the medical box. They got to the ravine, which was dry, and passed the items down to the others, who were spreading along the sides and finding places. And then, suddenly, the murk in the direction away from the plane lit up as if aflame, and for several seconds a ridge above them, rising to a rocky peak at one end, was silhouetted through the haze against a blaze of light from somewhere behind. Darkness closed again. Five seconds or so went by, and then the foot-jolting shock wave arrived through the ground, causing everyone standing to stagger. Cynthia and one or two others were knocked over. They all looked at each other bemusedly. And then, as if responding to the same cue, everyone not already down there threw themselves into the ravine. "*Cover!*"

Mitch shouted one way, then again the other. *"Get down! Take cover!"*

Keene had landed near Tom, who was holding a blood-drenched handkerchief to Denise's head. Together they leaned over to shelter her. Keene pressed his face down into the coarse sand of the ravine bed, pulled his hood close over his cap, and covered his head with his arms. The boom came maybe twenty seconds later, like something solid hitting his head, jarring his teeth and numbing his ears. How many miles away did that put it? He couldn't think. *"Stay down!"* Mitch's voice called from a thousand miles away through the ringing in his ears. They waited, unmoving. Denise was twitching and moaning. And then earth and rocks rained down out of the sky in a torrent. Keene felt it peppering his arms and landing in drumming waves along his back. It was like being in a grave with the dirt being shoveled in. He convulsed suddenly, slapping at his leg as something hot seared through the calf of his trousers. From beyond the ravine the sound of rocks hitting the plane came like hail on a tin roof.

The rain eased gradually to become just a waning spatter of lighter particles. Keene waited, then moved to look up, feeling rivers of sand running off his neck and shoulders. The other mounds of dust around him were stirring, shaking themselves, starting to sit up. . . .

And the next impact came five seconds later.

He lost all track of how long they lay there, clawing and scraping as if trying to burrow into the earth, while detonation after detonation shook the ground and pounded at their senses. The large bolides came over with a noise that sounded like freight trains crossing the sky; others made sighing moans mixed with jet-engine-like whines. The concussions grew so frequent that it was impossible to say which blast wave was associated with which flash, and the rain of ejected debris became continuous. In a temporary lull, four of the soldiers ran to the plane to get folding entrenching spades, hard helmets, and flak jackets. One was hit on the way back and had to be dragged by the others. Keene's mind went into a numbed, suspended state, rejecting the sensory overload, ceasing to register the passage of time.

Somewhere in the middle of it all, the fuel from the Rustler's punctured tanks ignited.

It was another hour, maybe two, before the infall eased and the dazed survivors finally began emerging.

Thirty-four were left. Charlie Hu had come around at last, and was miraculously okay except for head-to-toe bruising down one side of his body that would keep him wincing for weeks—assuming they lasted that long. Cavan was bearing up well, and Colby and Alicia had nothing worse than bruises and cuts. Three soldiers had died in the crash, two more in the impact storm, and six were hurt badly enough to be nonfunctional. Of the party taken on at Vandenberg, Denise had scalp cuts, not as bad as had at first been feared; the man with the severed thigh had died from blood loss, which was probably merciful; the woman in a coma had succumbed; one of the two men with head injuries had been thrown loose in the landing, breaking several bones, and was not looking good. Joan was rallying and showing astonishing strength. Most remarkable of all was Jed, the blinded youth, who seemed the most resilient of all and was trying bravely to crack jokes. Maybe it was delirium. Keene saw tears on Alicia's face as she changed his dressing.

It was mid afternoon, although the sky was too dark to give any hint. They had flown for a little under an hour after leaving Vandenberg early in the morning, which put them just short of Phoenix. The broken starboard wing and nose of the plane had burned out, but the fractured center section and tail were not completely gutted. Some usable items, including most of the food packs and water containers, were retrieved. The port wing, remarkably, while looking as if it had been shotgunned, was still in one piece. All electronics were dead, and the mobile radios unusable with the static.

Twenty-two unscathed or with minor injuries; twelve unable to walk. There were two choices. The twenty-two could divide into two groups, one to stay with the injured while the other went to find help; alternatively, the twenty-two could simply press on together, promising only to send help if they found any. In normal circumstances, the latter would have been unthinkable. But as things were, it had an undeniable element of realism. Keene expected that Mitch, if anyone, would take the lead in stating the unmentionable but obvious: that huge numbers had already died, and more would yet, by far; that leaving the fit behind if there was no help to be found would just be condemning them along with the unfit; that any potential help they might find would be already overwhelmed and unlikely to be swayed much by the thought of a dozen more one way or the other. Alicia was waiting to hear it too; Keene could see the anticipation on her face. Maybe Mitch saw it too, and perhaps that was why he refrained. Or could it have been that even in Mitch's eyes everyone had become "ours" already?

Cavan asked Dan how much he could tell them about where they were and the reception area he had been talking to just before the crash.

"It was an Army mobile unit operating at a local airstrip where they were setting it up," Dan said. "From the fix they gave me, we must have been almost there—maybe just a few miles short. The last bearing they gave me was . . . I think, one-twenty-four degrees." He stood up and looked back, estimating the final course that the Rustler had been following and trying to reconstruct the turns he had made bringing it down. Finally, he pointed to a low pass, barely visible through the dust, a little to the left of the now-invisible ridge behind which the first impact had occurred. "I'd say it has to be that way."

Mitch nodded as if to say that was good enough for him. "I'll take a squad to check it out," he said. "The sooner we leave, the better. Debating will only waste time." Cavan agreed but said he'd stay with Alicia, who insisted on remaining to help Dash; in any case, at his age, he said, he would only slow everyone down. Mitch didn't argue. Charlie Hu had little choice, since he would have been hard put to walk the length of a football pitch. That left Keene and Colby to go with Mitch, which seemed advisable in case their political credentials still carried weight, and Dan as the navigator. Nine fit soldiers remained, including Legermount and Furle. Mitch assigned four who were at least up to marching to stay behind under Furle's command with the injured and the civilians. The other five would accompany Mitch and his party, Legermount acting as second in command.

Keene saw suspicion in Furle's eyes as he watched the departing party sorting out supplies and equipment to take with them. "A couple of hours in Texas, then on to Atlanta," he heard Furle murmur sarcastically to one of the others as they picked up entrenching tools and went back to remove the bodies from the plane for burial along with the others.

When that task was complete, the soldiers began cutting and dragging parts of the plane to bridge a narrow section of the ravine, which they fashioned into a shelter with draped camouflage netting weighted with rocks and sand. Then they got a couple of stoves going, so at least the departing party were able to get a hot meal inside them before setting off.

❀ 41 ❀

If ever there was a preview of Hades, this had to be it. The nine—Mitch and Dan; Keene and Colby; Corporal Legermount and the four troopers—trudged in single file up the slope, their bodies stiff from hours of lying pressed against the rocks, slipping and sliding on sandy gravel that rolled from under their feet, wind-borne grit stinging their faces and eyes. Around them, a desolation of humps and boulders extended away to shadowy forms of hillsides and mesas outlined dimly in the dust-laden, sulfurous air. The knee that Keene had struck in the landing was throbbing, and after about thirty minutes he had to stop to put a dressing over the burn on his calf, which was chafing painfully. He was grateful that they had accepted the Guard-issue kit in Pasadena, including boots. His civilian shoes wouldn't have hung together for a mile in this.

At the top of the rise, Dan halted to check his compass bearing. The men stood waiting, adjusting pack straps and repositioning weapons. Then Legermount pointed; Keene looked with the others, his eyes at first narrowing in puzzlement. . . . They were looking down over what seemed to be an expanse of desert extending away into the pall of dust through which something was glowing dull red. Then, as the pattern resolved itself, his jaw fell incredulously. The size and distance were impossible to estimate, since in the murk there was nothing to provide a reference of size—but a part of the desert seemed to be burning. He felt a nudge on his shoulder and turned. Mitch handed him a pair of field glasses. Keene raised them to his eyes, adjusted the focus, and peered.

The ground itself was glowing.... A vast, smoldering depression extended back into invisibility, looking like a lake of fire behind a darker dam of boulders and earth mixed with embers. He was looking at a crater. The "dam" was part of the wall. As he studied it more, he made out another glow, dimmer and more distant, with no details discernible, that had been invisible without the glasses. They could be just two of thousands scattered for hundreds of miles. Too stupefied to speak, he passed the glasses to Colby. They resumed moving to cross the head of a valley descending away to their left, and followed the far side around a shoulder of mountain, all the time angling down the slope. After about another mile they came to a track heading in roughly their direction, which made the going easier. Following the track, they came across an abandoned pickup with dents in the roof and a shattered windshield. Legermount tried jumping a wire from the battery to the starter in the hope of getting them a ride, but the pickup was out of gas.

Lower down, they heard screams—not human but shrill and whinnying, which sounded even more blood-chilling. They found horses, dozens of them, in a corral behind an obliterated farm. Most of those not already dead were writhing with smashed legs, burns, broken backs. The soldiers stopped long enough to despatch them with bullets. A handful remained, milling around each other aimlessly, their eyes bulging in terror. Legermount looked at Mitch questioningly. Mitch scowled, then shook his head. "Hell, let 'em have what chance they've got." He waved toward the gate. One of the troopers opened it to turn the surviving animals loose.

Below the farm was a graveyard of cattle piled in heaps around a pond of red sludge. Nearby was what was left of a car that looked as if it had been hurled some distance, its wheels in the air. There were bodies inside, and two more thrown clear. What little light there had been had faded, and Mitch and Dan, leading, had to use flashlamps to find the trail. From somewhere ahead came the sound of an aircraft climbing. At least, it seemed Dan's sense of direction had been good.

The valley seemed to be opening onto flatter terrain. The ground still rose to their right, but on the other side fell away more gently and broadened. The track merged with another and became gravel now instead of just dirt, though sometimes disappearing beneath mounds of rubble and sand that looked as if they had been thrown by a giant shovel. Light began appearing below on the left, strung at intervals along a still-invisible road. Dan confirmed that it had to be Interstate 10. There didn't seem to be a lot of movement on it.

Some distance ahead, the lights became more numerous, fading into the darkness along a line veering left as if the road curved suddenly in that direction. But interstates didn't change direction that abruptly. An area beyond was still glowing. They could feel the heat on their faces, even at that distance. It seemed that something sizable had impacted square across the highway. Mitch and Dan conferred briefly. The choice was either to head directly down to the road now and follow it to what appeared to be workings in progress to create a traffic road around the far side of the crater; or alternatively, to stay above the road and head right of the crater, which while more direct could mean having to negotiate the broken rim in the darkness and possibly being driven farther uphill again. Deciding not to risk any further unknowns they went with the first, taking the next track they came to pointing directly down toward the lights. From somewhere in the direction of the highway, the muffled *whop-whop-whop* of a helicopter rotor came distantly through the night.

In the darkness and with all the dust in the air, the road turned out to be closer than they had thought. They passed several houses, some stores, and a gas station, all ruined and partly buried in rocky debris. There were more wrecked vehicles, some thrown topsy turvy, others pinning bodies of people who had apparently tried to shelter under them. And then lights and activity, accompanied by the sounds of voices and motors, were immediately ahead. Approaching, they found there were more vehicles than they had realized; the lights were from just a few with engines running that were being used to illuminate rescue operations in progress among more houses and commercial premises built along a service road paralleling the interstate, now discernible beyond. Workers were shining lamps among collapsed timbers and shoveling away rubble. One building, lit by the headlamps of a couple of trucks in front, had been adapted as an aid station, with casualties being helped and carried in out of the surrounding darkness. A group of hooded and hatted figures approached, presumably having seen the flashlamps coming down the road off the hill. The one leading had a bandage showing below his hat and was wearing a sheriff's deputy's badge with a storm coat.

"Looks like we've got some fit people here. You boys wanna enlist? We need all the help here we can get."

Mitch answered. "We need help ourselves. Bunch of people in a plane crashed back over in the next valley, some of them hurt."

"Are you serious? They're only just starting pulling bodies out of what's left of Phoenix. Right here we've got wrecks backed up into California that nobody's gotten to yet and probably won't for days. There's about a couple of hundred thousand people in line ahead of you already." The voice was weary, not prepared to debate the obvious. Mitch sighed and nodded. It was obvious that they didn't have a case.

"Military mission. We have to try and see it through."

The deputy shrugged. "Well . . . good luck."

"Which way's the reception center?" Mitch nodded in the direction of the crater ahead. "That way, past where the big one hit?"

"Right—about two miles farther on." The deputy's face showed for a moment in the light of a turning car: young, crusted with dust, streaked on one side with congealed blood that had trickled down from the bandage. He wiped his mouth with the back of a gloved hand. "Say . . . would you guys have any spare water? We've been waiting two hours for our truck to get back. Can't take any from these people. The ones that thought to bring some are gonna need it."

Mitch passed his water bottle over. Several of the other troopers did likewise. The deputy took a modest swig, washed it around, swallowed, and nodded gratefully. "Oh boy. You've no idea . . ."

"Is that where the chopper we heard would have come from?" Mitch asked.

"Right."

"Who's operating them?"

"I couldn't tell you. The Army's in charge now, trying to get some organization together. Where are you guys heading?"

"Texas."

"*Texas?* Jeez! I'm not sure there is a Texas anymore. It might be part of the Gulf. Everybody else is coming the other way."

"Like I said, it's an official mission."

"Well, I'm glad something's still functioning. Just follow along where they're leveling a road around the crater—there's no way you can miss it; you've got a mountain blocking the road. You can see the lights they've got set up from here. Then pick up the interstate again on the other side."

It was like a scene out of a war. There were hundreds of wrecked and damaged vehicles there in the darkness, stretching in a gigantic tailback from the crater, they realized as they came out onto the highway. Thousands. Standing amid a litter of glass and debris, roofs and hoods buckled by falling rocks, some apparently unscathed, others flung or pushed off the roadway completely. A number were burning. Twisting lines jammed nose to tail showed where drivers had weaved as far as they could before being brought to a halt. Many were helping each other check among the vehicles with flashlights and in headlamp beams, pulling out the injured and doing what they could for the ones trapped. Others just sat along the verge, in shock and bewildered, waiting for direction. Farther along, a tractor trailer had somehow balanced itself on end. A woman was wandering among the cars, frantically calling someone's name. A headless body hung from the window of a Chevrolet, dripping blood onto the asphalt. A dog whimpered at the door of a stove-in Nissan van full of tangled forms, none of them moving.

Keene walked by it all at the center of the silent column, unable to suppress a feeling of callousness, yet mindful that nothing they could have done would alter anything materially. Millions of people were dying, millions no doubt already had, and many more millions would still, and nothing was going to change it.

Crunch . . . Crunch . . . Crunch . . . Crunch . . . He followed Legermount's tirelessly swinging heels ahead of him and let his mind sink into numbness, shutting out the groans, the cries, the shouts of the rescuers, the bodies laid out in rows under blankets and tarpaulins. Others who were part of their own microworld were depending on them, he told himself, and for now nothing more mattered beyond that. *Crunch . . . Crunch . . . Crunch . . . Crunch . . .* In such a way was life reducing to minor achievements and small things taking on immense significance; that kept you alive and got you through to tomorrow. And that was good enough. Both his legs hurt. The boots were chafing his heels, and he could feel blisters starting to form. He hadn't hiked like this for years. He would have to get used to it again soon. There would be plenty of it in store when gasoline stocks started running out.

Crunch . . . Crunch . . . Crunch . . . Crunch . . . And so it went until the mounds of rocks and debris rose to become a huge rampart of earth and boulders standing fifty to a hundred feet high in the light of arc lamps running from a mobile generator. In places, crushed and partly buried vehicles protruded from the slope. Police, military, and emergency vehicles were clustered along a strip that had been leveled to the left of the crater wall, beyond which more lamps illuminated earth-moving machines and road gangs making an earth-and-gravel road to reconnect the severed portions of the interstate. Mitch led the way along the foot of the crater wall, at the top of which figures were clambering about, taking photographs of the other side and making observations with various instruments. The object that gouged the crater had come in from the east, throwing most of the ejecta westward in the direction that Keene and the others had come from. As they progressed along the edge, the wall gradually became lower until they were walking almost on the rim itself. The ground underfoot was hot, and the heat radiating from inside was intense enough to keep them several yards back from the actual edge, in the shadow of the lip. Even so, every now and again one or a couple of them would venture closer for a few seconds to get a glimpse of the crater floor, glowing eerily red. Red was shining above them, too, reflected down through the dust pall by the cloud blanket. What was left of Phoenix was on fire.

A sound came of distant freight trains in the sky, followed minutes later by the rumbling of explosions somewhere to the north.

❈   ❈   ❈

The reception center was another oasis of light and activity involving trucks and earthmovers, located a short distance from the interstate beside a small airfield littered with wrecked planes. It looked like an original cluster of buildings from a one-time military base of some kind, expanded probably within the last few days to the beginnings of a minicity by the addition of scores of portable huts and cabins, only to be flattened by the meteorite storm. The work going on currently was to clear the devastation and convert as many of the buildings as were salvageable into earth-covered dugouts and sandbagged shelters. Refugee arrivals were already being moved into one part, where food was being dispensed from a field kitchen. In another area, bodies were being carried from where they had been laid out in lines numbering dozens and loaded onto a truck, presumably for burial or disposal elsewhere.

Everything was improvised and chaotic, and Mitch's initial queries yielded mixed answers as to who was in charge. No one seemed to be, exactly, but different individuals were running different things, which they seemed to have taken charge of on their own initiative. Hopes were that it should all get more coordinated tomorrow. Eventually, they found an Army major who had set up with a small staff in a sandbagged trailer equipped with a telephone exchange operating over landlines. Apparently, he was in touch with the regional command center being established at El Paso.

Colby Greene produced his government credentials and explained that people who were involved in a vital official mission were stranded up in the hills about ten miles west where their plane had crashed, and he needed assistance. The major regarded him with much the same look as the sheriff's deputy had given them back along the interstate.

"Well, I'm not sure that kind of authority means too much anymore," he said. "And even if it did, we've got our hands kind of full right now to be worrying about a few more people ten miles up in the hills. And even if we didn't, we don't have any way of getting anyone there."

"You've got choppers," Dan said. "We heard one ourselves, coming in—when we were back the other side of the crater."

"No av-gas," the major told him. "A plane that went out of here earlier took the last we had. Two road tankers were on their way here to fill our tanks, but they didn't make it through Phoenix. We're supposed to be getting an emergency load flown in tomorrow morning, but until it gets here nothing's going out. So why don't you and your boys get something to eat, find a corner to bed down, and rest up for the night? You all look as if you could use it."

◉ **42** ◉

The tanker flight was diverted elsewhere. Back in the trailer the next morning, Keene listened with Mitch, Colby, and Dan while the major talked on the line with somebody in El Paso.

"Look, we've got half of California coming in off the interstate this morning. I need food, I need doctors, and I need medical supplies. But I can't have anything flown in, because until I've got something to refuel them with, nothing that brings any of it can get out again. . . . Base facilities? What are you talking about, base facilities? There aren't any base facilities. They got wiped out yesterday. What planet have you been on? We're having to dig ourselves holes in the ground here."

He listened a while longer, then replaced the receiver and looked at the four who were waiting. "All I can tell you is that this isn't the only area that got pounded. It's still going on in some places. Everywhere's a mess. They said they'll do what they can. We might be able to get a supply through by road from a depot I've located in California. What else do you want me to say?"

It seemed there was nothing more to be done, probably for the rest of that day. The group vacated the space they had been using in one of the previously prepared shelters, and Mitch detailed Legermount and three troopers to begin constructing one of their own. He outlined a plan for a rectangular pit five feet deep, the excavated material being used for sandbags to build up the sides, with a roof of alloy beams and corrugated steel sheet from some wreckage nearby, topped with four feet of sand. With that task under way, he left for a tour of the center, accompanied by Dan and the two other men to see what else was happening and if they could be of help. Thousands of people were beginning to appear now, jammed into their own vehicles or brought in by emergency trucks, many others walking. There simply weren't the facilities or staff to take care of the horrendous numbers of injured; trucks stacked with bodies left regularly for the mass graves that had been bulldozed behind a hill a mile or so from the center.

The entire center had become a maze of workings and diggings along one side of the airfield, made by human moles burrowing into the soil. Keene tried to put in his share of pickaxing and shoveling, but it was hard to match the pace of younger men at the peak of fitness and training, especially since his legs had stiffened since yesterday. The dust choked, even through a wetted handkerchief tied around his mouth. His lips had swollen and dried, and his tongue was painful where he had bitten it in the crash, making speaking and eating difficult. His face felt like one throbbing, open sore, and he could no longer bear the touch of trying to wipe off the perspiration.

Halfway through the morning, meteorites and gravel began falling again. There were no big detonations like the one that had gouged away part of I-10 the day before, but a steady rain continued of missiles thumping into soil or impacting on rocks and metal with bangs like rifle bullets. People were hit, though surprisingly infrequently. But they had no choice but to press on. Those who weren't actually digging or roofing stayed under cover, making whatever excursions they had to as quick dashes from one shelter to another. In a depression a short distance from the main area, a crew in hard hats and Army flak jackets began erecting a derrick to drill for water. Meanwhile, three sandbagged trucks loaded with drums were sent to see what could be recovered from the ruined water tower serving the area.

By the middle of the day, Keene was realizing that more than the years and his sedentary lifestyle were slowing him down. He found himself alternately sweating and shivering, and once or twice almost keeled over from dizzy fits; but he settled to a rhythm and drove himself doggedly, resolved not to become an additional burden to the others. When the roof was completed, a scavenging party went away to see what they could find to make the new abode more habitable. At this, Mitch's men turned out to be quite accomplished, coming back with a forklift pallet and some boards for flooring, assorted pieces of tarp, several sticks of furniture, and even a mechanic's inspection lamp with good batteries. Finally, they were able to flop down and rest. Keene lowered himself gratefully onto a strip of foam rubber laid on the pallet, which had been set aside for him and another of the men who was also feverish, and another hit on the knee by a ricocheting rock. At last, he could just lie back, let his whole body go limp, and abandon himself to the exhaustion that had been building for days. . . .

And then the rain started—not like a spring freshening but hammering and relentless, turning the dugout city into a labyrinth of mud and pools through which rivulets trickled, then poured, joined up and grew into a network of torrenting streams within minutes. Water seeped through the loose-packed roof and flowed down into the entrance; just as they had started to get comfortable and talked about eating, everyone had to get up, put on coats and capes, and go out again to dig drainage trenches. When they finally came back inside, Keene drifted into a series of fitful dozes that really weren't sleep or rest, coming back to semiconsciousness each time to be greeted by the drumming of the rain. At one time he was vaguely aware of Colby holding a dish of soup and urging him to eat, but Keene's mouth was too sore to accept more than a taste of water. Thoughts flitted through his mind of Cavan, Alicia, and the rest still up on the mountain; but in too much of a detached kind of way to for him to feel concern. Enough of his faculties were working to tell him he should feel concern, but the numbed remainder admitted that he didn't. Not just now, anyway. All that registered was the sweating and shivering of his fever, the single, continuous ache that his body seemed to have turned into, and the burning pain of his mouth and face. Maybe tomorrow, he would.

※   ※   ※

Rain was still falling the next morning. But the meteorites had slackened, and, wonder of wonders, Mitch announced that the road tanker from California had arrived! The major was making calls to El Paso. Keene was able to manage a breakfast of hot cereal and coffee, and afterward, finally, felt his body easing sufficiently to rest. He began drifting away, warm and comfortable at last, telling himself that he never wanted to move or have to think again. . . .

And then Colby was shaking him. Keene forced his eyes to open. Then he heard the sound of helicopter rotors getting louder, then settling to a steady roar somewhere not far away. "Lan, move. Mitch has gotten us a ride out," Colby was saying. Keene sat up groggily to find the dugout full of bustling figures collecting kit, closing and strapping packs, snatching up weapons. Colby helped Keene get his things together and pull on his parka and helmet. "They just ferried in a medical team and supplies from El Paso. They're going straight back as soon as it's topped up. Say good-bye to Phoenix. I hope you didn't want to send any postcards."

Keene pulled on his boots and took his pack as Colby thrust it at him. They stumbled out after the others into the rain. Ahead, Legermount and two others were assisting the sick trooper and the one with the hurt leg. Several times, Keene had to take Colby's arm to steady himself over the slippery rocks and gulleys. Mitch was at the edge of the airstrip, waving them in the direction of a large Sikorsky sitting with its rotor idling. Another helicopter farther back was being unloaded. Dan and one of the helicopter's crew were waiting at the door to give them a hand up and inside. Another half dozen or so passengers going back with the chopper for one reason or another were already inside. The pilot, the only other crew member, was turning and looking back from his seat, waiting for the boarding to be completed.

"That's it," the copilot called forward, closing the door while the men found places among the folding side seats and rubber cushioning on the floor. Keene was ushered forward to one of the fixed seats behind the crew stations, along with Colby, Dan, and Mitch. The copilot went up front beside the pilot, and the engine note swelled. The pilot tried a couple of times to contact someone by radio, then shook his head and flipped the set off as useless. He checked his instruments, peered through the rivers of rain running down the windshield, and prepared to lift off.

"We're looking at El Paso in about two hours, maybe a little over," he shouted above the din. "What are you guys up to in all this, as a matter of curiosity?"

"Just an official mission," Dan called back vaguely.

"You mean there are people around who still care about stuff like that?" the copilot threw in.

The Sikorsky rose and began turning. Only now was Keene able to begin collecting his swimming thoughts. . . . And suddenly his mind rebelled as the words that he had just heard replayed themselves. "El Paso in two hours . . ." *No! This was all wrong!* He turned to look at Mitch, but the soldier's face was set impassively, staring ahead at the windshield. Keene looked at Dan. Dan was looking forward between the crew seats, scanning the instruments—as if to distract himself.

Keene remembered the look on Furle's face when they had left him in charge of the group on the mountain. Furle didn't really know Mitch, and he hadn't been sure if he could trust him. Keene didn't know Mitch either, he realized. And what little he had seen cast Mitch as one who confronted brutal realities. Was this his way not only of saying that there was only one realistic option for them to take now, but presenting it as a *fait accompli*? Keene tried to moisten his cracked lips, asking himself if he could accept it. In his weakened condition, he simply wasn't up to a face-off with somebody like Mitch. He glanced at Colby, and from the concerned look on Colby's face could see that he was wrestling with the same problem. Maybe it was time, Keene told himself. Eventually, one way or another, they were all going to have to learn hardness. Was that what Mitch was telling them?

The blank wall of orange-pink outside brightened as the chopper climbed. Takeoff complete, the engine noise settled back to its cruising level.

And then Mitch said, "Oh, there's just one more thing. We have another group to pick up. They're about ten miles back the other way, where our plane came down. Twenty of 'em." At the last count there had actually been twenty-five. But the Sikorski had plenty of room to spare.

The pilot raised a hand and shook his head. "Sorry. We're on a tight schedule. I hate to say it, but twenty isn't any big deal one way or another in all this."

"This twenty happen to be important to us," Mitch told him.

"Everybody's got someone who's important. Like I said, sorry, but this isn't a taxi service. I'm under orders to return directly to El Paso. They don't say anything about going the other way."

Mitch produced his automatic and pointed it. "Now you have orders," he said.

The copilot turned around sharply, his arm reaching out reflexively, but Dan produced another pistol and eased him back. Several of the other passengers started in alarm, but none seemed prepared to risk interfering. It seemed Mitch and Dan had planned it. "Go on, pull it," the pilot challenged, showing his teeth. "Then the only way you're going to get back down is as a piece of jelly."

Mitch turned his head toward Dan. "How long did you fly choppers in the Air Force?" he asked casually.

"Oh, five or six years, probably." That was news. Keene had never heard Dan mention anything about choppers.

"You reckon you could handle this bird?"

"Sure. No problem."

Mitch looked back at the pilot. "Sometimes things work two ways," he said him. "I hate to say it, but one pilot isn't any big deal to me one way or another in all this. It's your call."

There was a long, agonized silence. Finally, the pilot sighed. "Okay, you've got it. Ten miles? Which way do I go?"

"Back along I-10 past the crater, then over a ridge to the left a couple of miles farther along. Stay in sight of the ground, and I'll direct you from there."

❀ 43 ❀

When the rain turned their shelter into a torrent, the group left on the mountain had abandoned the ravine and made a new refuge for themselves underneath the surviving parts of the Rustler. Jed was still cheerful and had been making himself useful cleaning cutlery and pots and talking to the injured. Joan was hanging on but needed surgery urgently. Two of the ones left hadn't pulled through: the man with the head injuries and fractures whose chances hadn't looked good when Keene and the others left, and a soldier with his back broken in the crash. In addition, three more were missing through a tragedy of a different kind.

After two days passed by, Captain Furle had seen himself with no other choice but to assume that no help would materialize and his group was going to have to make its own arrangements. Accordingly, he sent two of the soldiers that he had available to reconnoiter the way down to the Interstate to see if help could be summoned, and failing that to search around for a vehicle, cart, or any other means for moving the nine badly injured that they still had with them. Tom, the civilian, Cynthia's friend, had offered to go too, pointing out that two would be a perilously small number if anything happened to one of them, and he was an experienced mountain hiker. Furle had agreed, and the three departed shortly afterward. They still hadn't returned when the helicopter arrived. By the time loading was complete there was still no sign of them and attempts to contact them by radio had failed. There could be no question of tarrying longer. Mitch ordered supplies, water, and ammunition to be left for them. Furle and a couple of the troopers stacked a selection of items in the space under the Rustler's wing and prepared to clamber aboard as the Sikorsky revved up for takeoff. And then Cynthia, who was still on the ground with them, announced blank-faced that she would stay and wait for Tom. Apparently, they had lived together for eight years.

"Ma'am, you're being crazy," Furle said. "What if they don't come back? You'll die out here."

"What if they do come back . . . and I'd never see him again?"

Mitch glowered down from the helicopter door. "There isn't time for this. Grab her and put her on board," he ordered. The three soldiers closed around her, pinning her arms, and lifted her inside forcibly over her struggling and hysterical protests. Moments later, the Sikorsky lifted off once more into the violent skies.

El Paso was about as far west as it was possible to go and still be in Texas. But at least they had made it to Texas—twenty-nine of the forty-two who had left Vandenberg in the Rustler.

The scene as the helicopter came in was like the reception center at Phoenix, but with everything on a vaster scale. A quarter of the city had been obliterated by a new crater, which had buried the former downtown area under its wall. The pilot, who seemed to have relented after being uncooperative earlier and wouldn't be filing any complaints, said reconnaissance flights had shown an immense crater field extending westward from Phoenix and to the northeast, but he didn't know how far. The ruins of what was left of the city were being reinforced and bombproofed, while for miles around, earthworks, bunkers, and connecting roads looking like extended military fortifications were appearing across the desert slopes and among the mountains. But it still wasn't matching the scale of the problem. The numbers of people pouring in were even vaster, their vehicles visible everywhere in thousands, in some places pulled off the roadways in untidy sprawls stretching for miles, filling the verges and any open ground, in others tossed like the aftermath of an air strike.

They landed at what looked like a regional airport, amidst the kind of scene that was becoming familiar: demolished and damaged buildings, excavations and repairs going on around the runways. One runway appeared to be serviceable. Mangled aircraft of all types were everywhere, and the hangar buildings that had survived reasonably intact were being shored up and earthed over as protective bunkers for any that were salvageable. The air, as they climbed out of the helicopter, was hot, heavy, clammy, and oppressive.

Leaving Furle to supervise the unloading of the injured and find them some kind of temporary accommodation, Cavan and Dan left on what showed signs of being an impossible task of finding them medical attention while Alicia and Dash stayed to do what they could. The best the helicopter pilot could suggest as a lead to whoever was running things was the colonel in charge of flight operations, and Keene went with Colby and Mitch to seek him out. After some asking around they found him in the glassless but functional control tower, following the approach of an incoming aircraft on a screen connected to an Army mobile field radar located somewhere nearby. He was obviously busy, stressed, and listened to them impatiently. When Colby presented his White House papers and Presidential staff ID, the colonel seized the opportunity to have his switchboard call the office of the acting commander of the area to get rid of them. The colonel then returned his attention to the business at hand, and a guard escorted them back downstairs to wait.

Less than half an hour later, an Army sergeant driving a Ford van with netting draping its sides and a layer of sandbags on the roof arrived to collect them. Apparently, everything had happened too quickly and universally to allow martial law to be declared formally in the U.S. Military control had been instituted as an automatic reaction locally, nevertheless—as doubtless had been done in all areas retaining any organizational capability at all. In El Paso an Army general called Weyland had taken charge after just about all of the area's regular command structure and FEMA directorate were wiped out along with the fifty-plus percent of the city that was now craters and rubble.

As the sergeant talked, they negotiated their way around mounds of fallen rock and debris, wrecked vehicles, and mud traps created by the recent rain. Parts were like Boston in January, but with paths being cleared through mud and sand instead of snow. Along whole blocks, rescuers were still hauling the dead and injured from collapsed buildings. Sandbagged bunkers and shelters were being constructed wherever opportunity presented itself, and undamaged stores, homes, and offices adapted into dressing stations. But even with all the bulldozing and shoveling, the medics and nurses working frantically under tents and awnings and in hollows dug amid the debris, the mobile kitchens and relief workers handing out rations from trucks, untended cases and others too shocked or exhausted to help were everywhere: laid out along the roadsides, sitting blankly outside their vehicles, or just wandering aimlessly. The sergeant said that the services had been hard put to cope even before yesterday, which had been a massacre. Today they were overwhelmed.

The route took them west of the city along another piece of Interstate 10, with dry red mountains flanking the road on one side, and slopes leading down to the Rio Grande river marking the Mexican border on the other. They exited on a road that climbed for a short distance through a spread-out residential area that had been fairly evenly battered, and led into a valley with boulder-strewn sides and a scattering of industrial buildings and other facilities strung along the bottom. A gate through a chain-link fence, attended by sentries outside a gatehouse that had been reinforced by sandbags and corrugated steel sheeting, brought them into a parking area in front of a couple of office buildings, some sheds, and several unidentifiable structures standing below a high cliff with a mountain ridge rising beyond. Work crews in helmets, flak vests, and military fatigues were clearing rubble, filling craters, and finishing more dugout constructions. Both office buildings had every window shattered and were showing damage, especially to the upper parts.

The sergeant took Keene and the two others through a side door into one of the sheds, across a floor where stores were being sorted and vehicles unloaded, to the entrance of a tunnel leading into the mountain. He explained that Weyland had located his headquarters in a former mine working that had been converted years before into a repository for banking and financial documents as a precaution in the event of a major war. The tunnel led to a cage elevator which they took to a lower level, emerging into well-lit corridors with white, ribbed-concrete walls. After all the destruction and chaos of the preceding days, the order and normality of the surroundings seemed almost unnatural.

They came to an open area where military personnel at desks were working in front of a situation board occupying most of one wall, the others covered in charts, maps, and an array of aerial photographs. A large map of the surrounding parts of Texas and New Mexico was marked with red circles showing what looked like craters, and various other annotations. Weyland's office was at the far end, consisting simply of a smaller space separated by a partition. It had a desk and side table covered with papers, more wall maps, and several upright chairs along two of the walls. A naked bulb hung from a cord overhead, shaking slightly to the vibrations of machinery somewhere nearby.

Weyland was tall and wirily built, on the young side for his rank, Keene thought, forceful in manner, with straight black hair brushed to one side and dark, intense eyes that refused to be cowed by the situation. His face was dark with stubble, and he wore a flak jacket over a grimy, sweat-stained shirt. The three arrivals were shown in by the sergeant, who then left. They introduced themselves; Weyland invited them to take seats. He draped his elbows over the arms of his chair and looked them over.

"I understand from the phone call that you just got here from Phoenix, and before that you were in a plane crash. You just about look it, too. We've got soup, beans, and coffee going, if you could use some."

Mitch said that sounded great but explained that they had some injured back at the airfield who needed medical attention urgently. Weyland stared at them for several seconds. Then, sparing them a lecture on the obvious, he got up, went to the gap at the end of the partition that served as a doorway, and called over one of his officers. He outlined the situation, and the officer went away to make some calls. Keene and Colby nodded their thanks. Keene didn't feel entirely comfortable about jumping the line. But there are times when one has to look after one's own. "And now can we get you people something to eat?" Weyland asked again. They accepted.

It turned out that the general's readiness to receive them stemmed more from a hope of being told more himself of what was going on than any recognition of a need to inform them. He had assumed from Colby's credentials that they represented, or at least could enlighten him as to the existence of, some administrative authority that had survived of a national or even international nature. He was in landline contact with the military command at Cheyenne Mountain, several regional headquarters, and also a number of FEMA centers. As far as he was aware, Washington had ceased functioning. The President, along with his family and immediate staff, had vanished three days previously with Air Force One when the administration left for the war-survival and command center located near Atlanta. The Secretary of State was supposed to have taken charge in Atlanta provisionally, but Weyland hadn't had any contact from there. A further mystery was the disappearance of the Vice President, who had left to set up a West Coast shadow government a day before the President's departure from Washington. Colby set the record straight on that score, which led to an account of the mission that had taken him and Keene to California. It was the first news Weyland had heard of what had become of the Kronians. Keene presumed that General Ullman would have reported it at Cheyenne Mountain, which seemed by default to have become the nearest that existed to a national coordinating center. Weyland noted the details, clearly with the intention of reporting them independently anyway. His unspoken implication—that there was no guarantee that anyone from Vandenberg had made it to Cheyenne Mountain—didn't hit Keene until a couple of minutes afterward. Maybe he was more tired than he realized, he told himself.

Weyland then moved to local and more immediate matters. Sitting on America's rocky spine, El Paso was the focus of two floods of evacuees converging eastward from southern California, Arizona, and New Mexico, and in the opposite direction from Texas and

Oklahoma. They were arriving hungry, thirsty, exhausted, and traumatized, the survivors of meteorite falls, firestorms, hurricanes, and rain torrents, bringing their sick and their injured by the tens of thousands; by the hundreds of thousands. And there, in the dust, the dryness, and the heat that was setting in after the rain, they would die, as they were already starting to, in numbers almost as large. The emergency measures that it had proved possible to mobilize in the time available were too few and too late. And in any case, all the planning had been a product of the slowly evolving thinking of years gone by. None of it had envisaged anything like this. The worst that had been imagined was nuclear war, in which strikes on worthwhile targets and perhaps population centers would produce intense devastation in relatively localized areas, but with comparatively unscathed regions between, able to provide help and relief. But with *everywhere* smitten equally, there was nowhere to turn to. For every township and community, enclave and locality, anything beyond the preoccupation of staying alive from one hour to the next and securing a refuge to gain some respite vanished from the equation of reality. The result was that the whole infrastructure by which the nation maintained itself as a cohesive social and productive organism was coming apart with a rapidity that in any other circumstance would have been deemed impossible; and the same was no doubt true for every other part of the world also.

"What you've told me confirms what we already guessed," Weyland concluded. "We're going to have to rely on our own resources to get us through this. No supraregional authority is going to emerge and start giving directions. The centers that I mentioned earlier have all got problems of their own as bad as ours here. Nobody has anything to spare. Our immediate concern is providing shelter accommodation and conserving fuel and provisions. The eventual aim is to consolidate communications between key centers along a line running through here, Denver, and up along the Rockies, that will enable mutually supportive logistics, including the restoration of a minimal power grid. With tight management I'm estimating hitting a rock-bottom situation at about three months from now, after which we should be able to start pulling things back together. In the war game scenarios, they used to figure on getting back to normal forty years after an all-out exchange. So maybe if we doubled that, we wouldn't be too far out. What do you think? I wouldn't be around to see it, but at least it would mean leading a useful life. So there's my take. Where are you people going to fit in? What kind of plans do you have next?"

Three months? Start pulling things back together? The words echoed dully in Keene's mind. It seemed that President Hayer had done too good a job in instilling hope and optimism when he addressed the nation. No concept of what the present events were leading to had yet taken root on any significant basis. Probably that was just as well.

Right now, Keene wasn't about to launch into anything that would give Weyland cause to reappraise the prospects. Nothing was going to change them, and there was probably no better way in which he could expend his energies. And besides, Keene could feel his own energy draining, even as he turned the thought over. His eyes were closing involuntarily; he felt himself sway on the chair and checked himself with a start. The surroundings seemed to float out of focus and reverberate with hollow sounds and voices that came and went. He was distantly aware of Colby and Mitch looking at him strangely, and himself murmuring that he didn't have any plans. . . .

And either he passed out then, or simply fell asleep on the spot.

◉ 44 ◉

Keene was out until the next day and awoke to a feeling of having slept solidly for the first time in a week, probably having been given sedation. His sores had been cleaned and treated. He felt stronger. And once again a shower and a shave worked their wonders. He was in a room that Weyland had assigned in the mine vaults, where Cavan, Alicia, and Charlie Hu had also been brought. Cynthia, now resigned to the loss of Tom, had come too rather than remain with the group from Vandenberg. It seemed she wanted to break from everything connected with her old life. Nobody objected. Mitch and Dan, with the uninjured remnant of the Special Forces contingent, had moved into military quarters in the upper levels.

Charlie Hu was mobile again, although stiff, and hobbled in with the others when word went around that Keene was conscious. The news was that Ullman's group in the Samson had made it to Cheyenne Mountain. Meteorite storms east of the Mississippi had been severe. Communications were poor, and nothing had been heard from the national administration supposedly being set up in Atlanta. Huge tides were developing in all coastal areas. Aircraft losses had been horrific; since the surviving equipment would have to serve for an indeterminate time, further flying, except where deemed essential by the highest authorities, was discontinued until conditions eased. In the El Paso area, rock and gravel falls were continuing steadily, with occasional showers of flaming naphtha. There had been armed confrontations over demands for supplies, access to care and shelter, and possession of ownerless goods and vehicles.

Alicia appeared just as Keene was settling down to the first food he had been able to enjoy for days. She had conceded to the inevitable and cut her hair short. Her face, while less red and inflamed than when he had last seen it, was smeared with cream and still a far cry from the cover-model complexion that had emerged from the Rustler at Vandenberg. "You're looking amazingly better already," she told Keene. "Quick recovery means there's a lot of reserve left yet. Eating well, too. Even better."

"I never thought there'd be a day when I'd say Army cooking beats anything I can name," Keene replied. "But there it is." He dug hungrily into the plate of eggs, biscuit, gravy, and sausage. "What about you? How have you been? Have some coffee."

"Apart from the outside, not too bad. My face feels as if it's been sandpapered." Alicia poured coffee into a mug for herself, adding milk from a cardboard carton.

"You've been working nonstop. How do you do it?"

"It must be my virtuous character. And then having Leo around is always an inspiration."

"There's another one who amazes me. How did you get to meet him? You know, in all the years I've known him, he's never told me."

"Oh, really?"

"No. Tell me. I'm curious."

"Oh, it was in a bar in Manhattan. I was young and new here— just took a notion to see the other side of the world. This guy was coming on strong and being a pain—you know, a jerk. Leo saw that I didn't know how to deal with it, so he moved in and gave him a lesson in charm and manners. I think I just wanted to see the look on the guy's face when I walked out to go someplace else with a man twice his age." Alicia chuckled. "Leo knew I would, because he's got the same kind of humor. Anyway, it grew from there. He thinks I'm crazy, you know."

"Does he really?"

"Don't tell me he never told you."

"If he had, I'd probably choose not to remember."

Alicia started to smile, then winced as it stretched the dried skin around her mouth. "Oh, how gallant! I love it. You see, underneath all this outside, you're just a romantic too."

"Maybe."

"You give up your place on the shuttle to go and find Vicki, and even that gorgeous Kronian woman can't make you change your mind? Of course you are! What else is there to call it?"

"Maybe I just didn't like the thought of being privileged," Keene suggested. "Equal opportunity. An old American tradition."

"Pah. I don't believe a word of it. It's just the gruff outside switching itself on again." Alicia helped herself to a spare piece of biscuit. "So tell me about her, Lan."

Keene leaned back in the chair and sighed. "Oh . . . It wasn't anything romantic. Just a kind of closeness that comes from two people who think the same way and share a lot of values and things. You know—she was the kind of person you never had to explain to about what you were thinking or how you felt, because she already knew. I don't think I even realized it myself much until these last few weeks. . . ." Keene broke off when he realized that Alicia was frowning at him. He raised his eyebrows quizzically.

"Why do you say she 'was'?" Alicia asked. "You make her sound like a thing of the past, a piece of history already."

Keene stared at her uncertainly, then jerked his head in agitation. "Well, I mean, it's . . ." He faltered, unable to say the painful but obvious.

"*Lan, what are you saying?*"

"What else is there to say? We tried. . . . That's not an option anymore. All we can do now is stay here and figure out what—"

"*Lan!*" Alicia protested. "You can't! We're not staying anywhere. We're going on to San Saucillo like we said. You can't change your mind now."

"But . . ." Keene shook his head. What other way was there to put it? "Alicia, there isn't any way to get there. All flying is over, finished. They're saving the planes for when things get better. It'll be years before anyone can make any again. The roads are all choked or blocked, and whatever can move on them is going the wrong way."

"We don't need the roads," Alicia said. "I've been talking to some of General Weyland's staff. Stocks of gas and supplies from south and east Texas have been concentrated in San Antonio. A train is leaving here tonight to bring a load back up to El Paso. There will be plenty of room on the outward run."

"And what do we do after San Antonio, walk?" Keene demanded. The words came out sharper and sounding more sarcastic than he had intended. He realized that his nerves were still on edge.

"Snap out of it, Lan. It's not like you," Alicia said. "I don't know what we do from there. Maybe with everyone coming the other way the roads will be easier between there and the coast." Her eyes flamed at him. "But you just said yourself that things are going to get worse. How long will sitting down here do any good? There is only one way out now, and that's off the planet. And the means to do it is down there in Mexico, not here."

Keene felt himself starting to object; then he checked himself, hunched forward to rest his elbows on the table, and stared at her. She was right. Like a soldier who refuses to leave a foxhole under fire, even though the position must ultimately fall, he wanted to put longer-term considerations from his mind and cling to the respite they had found here after the ordeal of the last few days. The security was an illusion that would last only so long. The more they delayed, the worse, at the end of it all, the odds must become. He shook his head, as if to reawaken the sense of realism that normally resided there.

"Have the others said what they think about it yet?" he asked her.

Alicia shook her head. "You are the first one I've told. I assumed they'd think the same way as I did—that there wouldn't be a problem."

Keene finished the last of his coffee and stood up. "Then let's go and find out," he said.

The upshot was that Cavan knew Alicia well enough not to bother arguing. Colby, in his inimitable way, agreed as casually as if they were planning a weekend vacation trip. Charlie Hu, more than any of them, was under no illusions as to what was in store. He expected there to be a lull of several days as Athena and Earth locked gravitationally to gyrate past each other like two passing skaters momentarily linking hands, during which time the bulk of the tail would be directed away. The train of debris following Athena would then wrap around Earth, causing falls more fearsome than anything that had occurred so far. Then, after actually receding for a distance as it swung by, Athena would be drawn back in for a final close pass before being ejected on a trajectory away from Earth. Charlie's vote was to go for any chance of getting out if a chance was there. And Cynthia, having committed herself, had little choice but to go along with the rest of them.

The only unresolved question was whether Mitch and his men could be induced to. With conditions deteriorating and violence breaking out, to press ahead without the protection of an armed force would be folly bordering on recklessness. There was only one way to find out. First, they went to talk to Mitch.

Mitch's initial reaction was surprise that they were still even contemplating Mexico. He had assumed that they'd tried their best, the fates had come out against them, and the only thing left to consider was whether to stay in El Paso and place themselves under Weyland's command or head for Colorado. He changed his opinion somewhat when Charlie explained why the worst was far from over yet, but he still seemed uneasy at the thought of deserting his command and taking useful men away from where they might be needed. Cavan tried to set his doubts at rest.

"This is hardly a normal situation, Mitch. Your sentiments are admirable, but I have to be honest here. The figures Weyland and his staff are estimating are wildly unrealistic. They're doing their best, but they just don't have any concept of what's going on. Don't you understand? A month from now there isn't going to *be* any command worth talking about to have deserted."

Mitch pondered the point, scowling at the wall for a minute or two before turning back to face them. "You're talking about getting to a place that might no longer exist, for a shuttle that mightn't fly, and if it does, taking it up through this mess to find a spaceship that mightn't be there. And I'm supposed to believe that the odds are better than what I'd have if I stay on with this outfit. Is that what you're telling me?"

"Just the latest of Landen's crazy schemes," Cavan said, as if that explained everything. "Only this time he's got Alicia with him too."

"Sure, they're lousy odds, no question," Charlie Hu said, nodding and keeping a serious note. "But better than the alternative. I'll take them."

Mitch looked around at them. He seemed persuaded, and was running over the practicalities in his mind. "It means we have to be up-front with the men too," he said finally. "This isn't something I can order them into blindly—or would be prepared to. They have to make their own choices too."

Everyone looked at everyone else. Nobody dissented.

"So be it," Cavan said.

"The reason we've been talking about getting to Mexico is that there's another shuttle down a silo at a site just south of the border," Mitch told the soldiers a half hour later. Apart from himself and Dan there were Furle, Dash, Legermount, and six troopers: four from the group that had hijacked the chopper and two uninjured from those who had stayed with the crashed Rustler. "Now, we're not talking about huge numbers of people being there like you saw at Vandenberg. There'll be just us here, plus a handful to be picked up in Texas. That means there'll be extra room. After listening to Charlie, I'm willing to go for it. And for anyone else who's prepared to take his chances, that's the bonus at the end of the ride. But I'm not going to hang this on you as an order. It's a volunteer mission. You've all heard the arguments. Each man is free to make his choice."

Captain Furle still remembered the couple-of-hours-extra assurance that he'd heard the last time they talked about going to Mexico. "I can't say I see how it's going to change anything," he objected. "Except for making our chances worse, that is. Whatever hits here, the same thing is gonna hit there just as bad. The only difference is that here we've at least got protection and some backup that's halfway organized. There, we'd have nothing. We did what we could once, and it's over. I'm still for heading north to Cheyenne Mountain. General Ullman promised us at Vandenberg that he'd find us room there."

They showed mixed reactions. Keene could understand why. It hadn't been that long ago when he himself had been looking for excuses to stay with the apparent safety that the military bases represented. Dan decided to attempt returning to the Air Force command in Colorado too and throw his lot in with Earth, come what may. The trooper with the hurt knee and the other who had come down sick were not up to such a further mission, and two more stayed with Furle through choice. That left two—their names were Birden and Reynolds—who would go with Mitch, Legermount, Dash, and the six civilians, including Cynthia.

Keene wondered if he was the only one who understood how much smaller the Amspace minishuttle was than a regular Air Force shuttle or the Boxcars that had gone up from Vandenberg. There was no telling how many people Harry Halloran might have brought with him, assuming he made it to San Saucillo. Keene didn't relish the thought of possibly having to explain the situation to armed and angry men, should it turn out that there were no spare places after all. A likely response in that event might be an insistence at gunpoint that *everyone* submit to a draw. But first, they would have to get there. He would worry about it then, he decided. It was always possible that by that time the problem would have solved itself.

Eleven in all were driven that night to the repaired siding in the railroad yards on the east side of the city, where the train to make the run to San Antonio was being assembled and fitted out. It consisted of six locomotives, three in tandem to the front and rear of a long line of boxcars and tankers with protected tops, with flatcars at intervals mounting sandbagged machine guns and posts for armed guards. Two coach cars in the center carried the command staff and guard reserves. Two flatcars pushed in front of the lead locomotive carried rails and equipment for track repairs. To reconnoiter and clear the route ahead as far as possible, a small scout train comprising a locomotive pushing several cars with engineers and a work crew, more rails and track-laying equipment, lifting gear, a couple of small earthmovers, and an Army escort had left earlier in the afternoon.

The big train rolled out shortly before midnight under the light of floodlamps and the orange glow from a sky of flame dancing among black clouds. Beyond, the diffuse incandescence from Athena showed, moving around to Earth's night side. Above the growl of the diesels and the rumbling of the wheels, distant thunder boomed continually. In the wilderness to the north and the south, patches of orange and red flickering through veils of unseen smoke glowed where the mountains and the desert were on fire.

❂ 45 ❂

The eleven shared space in one of the coaches with guards who were off duty or resting. It had open seats that could be folded down to make beds, rather than being divided into compartments, and a galley and dining space at one end next to the bathrooms. Several layers of corrugated sheeting alternating with sandbags overlaid the roof, and the windows were covered outside by steel mesh. Most of the soldiers were making the best of the chance to rest, and the lighting was kept dim.

Keene and several of the others remained awake, but there was little talk among them. They sat staring out through the windows at the Dantean sky and the intermittent glows shimmering through the dust and smoke-laden air—perhaps, like Keene, able for the first time since the nightmare began to reflect on the meaning of what they were seeing. The world they had known was being destroyed, never to be rebuilt in any of their lifetimes. Having risen to the highest peak in its history of comprehending and harnessing the physical universe, the human race had become distracted from its quest for truth and worthwhile knowledge, and been mesmerized instead by the pursuit of false values based on vanity and petty ambitions. The remnant that was holding together did so on time bought with the salvaged residues of a civilization that had already died. When the machines became still and the bulbs flickered out, the last ruins were ransacked for a surviving stash of cans, ammunition for a useless gun, a cake of soap, a knife, then those left would be reduced to the condition of the tribes that had wandered amidst the devastation in the years following the Exodus. The only hope for recovering in a period that would not extend over millennia now lay with the Kronians—assuming that Kronia itself was able to survive. The biblical accounts had been pretty close to the truth when they said that God periodically destroyed the world and its life, and replaced it with a new world. Now, it seemed, He was displeased with the latest life that had set up its own golden calves. Keene wondered if the next form to arise would meet with better approval as a more faithful rendering of what life and its expression were supposed to be. Did the Kronian model hint at a possible way? A light flaring suddenly, close enough to be visible through the murk, then followed several seconds later by a *whoosh* ending in a sharp report like a thunderclap, reminded them that the bombardment had just eased for a while, not ceased.

About three hours out from El Paso, the train halted. The lights were turned up, and the NCO in charge ordered the guards down with their weapons to stand to outside. A few minutes later, an officer from the staff coach in front came through to say that they had picked up a detail left by the scout train ahead to warn them to slow down over a risky stretch of patched track. Searchlights played over the area revealed just broken cliffs, rocky slopes, and clumps of scrub. The guard contingents manning the flatcars were changed, and the train got under way again. Everyone began settling down except Mitch and Legermount, who sat around the dining counter at the end with the troops who had just been relieved, talking, drinking coffee, and eating. Cynthia, who had been tending Charlie's bruises and lacerations, was now huddled up with him. Tiredness overcame Keene too, finally. He stretched out, using his folded parka as a pillow, pulled his blanket close around him, and slept.

It was a little after eight the next morning when they caught up with the scout train in the rugged country between the Davis Mountains and the Tierra Vieja Mountains. They were roughly a hundred fifty miles from El Paso, having left the Rio Grande valley to cut across the large southward bend in the river, which they would rejoin two hundred miles farther on at Langtry. The scout train had halted on the approach into a shattered township, where the engineering crew were still fixing torn track and improvising repairs to an embankment. The activity had drawn out the survivors, now clustered along both sides of the tracks with the same shock-widened eyes staring from dazed, blackened faces, holding up unfed babies and injured children in the desperate appeals for help that Keene had seen a hundred times already and was sickened by because he knew there was no help, would never be help for them. But there was a lot of anger out there too. An officer came back to tell everyone other than the guards deployed outside to remain on the train.

The second in command got down from the staff coach to talk to what seemed to be the representatives—it was virtually the scene outside the hangars at Vandenberg repeating itself. The train had ample room, and the people wanted to be taken aboard. The officer tried to explain that there was nothing for them in San Antonio, where the train was going. Their hope lay in the other direction. They didn't care. After days of exposure, all that mattered was the chance of respite and to come inside anywhere that offered an escape from the terror. The problem was that the space was needed to bring supplies back. If these people were taken aboard they would never be induced to leave again, and forcing them off at San Antonio would only leave them in a worse predicament still. The officer was adamant. The best he could offer was to leave them supplies and water and pick up as many as could be fitted in on the return trip. Moreover, there was always the possibility that another train could come through before then.

With the repairs complete, the equipment was loaded and the guards climbed back aboard. Slowly, the train began moving to howls of anguish and rage from outside. Several seconds later, a window farther along the car shattered. "*Incoming!*" a voice yelled. Everyone threw themselves away from the windows and down behind the seats and the sills. But there were just a few scattered shots. It was impossible to tell where they were coming from. The guards didn't return any fire.

When the train was clear, Cavan moved over and sat down opposite as Keene regained his seat.

"It's a sad world we live in, Landen," he observed somberly. "A sad world."

Birden and Reynolds, the two Special Forces troopers who had thrown their lot in with Mitch, were both from his own unit and not part of the scratch force that Cavan had thrown together in Washington. Birden had dark wavy hair and an easy smile, and was from New York City. Raised in an orphanage, he had not done well in foster homes and joined the military as soon as he was old enough. This was the first time he could say he was honestly glad to have no immediate family or anyone close anywhere.

Reynolds was from Texas originally—not that far from San Antonio, as it turned out—but had moved with his family to South Carolina as a child. He was tall, with olive skin and straight black hair that suggested an Indian or Hispanic element, and was from a solid Baptist upbringing. For him, serving in the military was a way of answering a calling to serve the nation. He tried not to think too much about his folks back East, but his staunch belief enabled him to accept that whatever happened was for a reason. Keene almost envied him for that. As far as Reynolds was concerned, they would make it to Montemorelos and get away if the Lord needed them for other things, otherwise not, and that was all there was to it.

"But you're not saying we should just sit back and wait for things to work out by themselves," Alicia said as they talked while the miles rolled by. "I couldn't accept a philosophy like that. I have to do what I can."

"That was what got Charlie and the rest of us this far," Keene agreed.

Reynolds thought about it. "No, ma'am, I wouldn't say that," he conceded finally. "The Lord is never ungrateful for a helping hand from those who are disposed to lend it." He added, after a moment more of reflection, "Unlike some people."

Legermount had grown up partly in Europe, where the family had been expanding its sporting goods business, and come back to

Pennsylvania to complete high school and two college years. He had fled to the military from a tyrannical father bent on molding him into a management executive and fitting heir. "I just don't have a head for it," he told the others. "Never could get the hang of double entry bookkeeping. Every way I figured it, I always ended up wanting to make the entry on the wrong side. So I tried putting it on the opposite side from what I thought, instead. And that was always wrong too. So that was when I gave up."

"Maybe too hastily," Colby mused, cleaning his spectacles, which had still, somehow, miraculously survived. "I'm sure you'd have qualified for a high position in government accounting somewhere."

Dash had an unassuming but intense personality. He was from a small town in Ohio, had wanted to be a doctor but been deterred by the demands of med school and joined the service to acquire practical medical skills a different way. He remembered seeing Keene on TV in the weeks before the conference in Washington. "You were one of the guys trying to get scientists to take the Kronians seriously about Venus," he said. "And now everything's happening again just the way you said. I was with you. It made a lot of sense to me. I mean, the evidence was right there all the time. They're supposed to be logical people. How come you couldn't get through to them?"

"I asked that question a lot too," Keene replied. "I guess once people are indoctrinated into a system, they're unable to see things in any other way than from that worldview. What you get is experts trained to know every detail and argument of the subject, but only within the system. They can't question its premises. The notion that the whole system itself might be wrong is literally inconceivable. To do that, you almost always need somebody from outside—like you. Most of the big scientific revolutions happened in that kind of way."

Cynthia, who was doing a wonderful job of putting the past behind, looked at Charlie Hu questioningly. "Hear what he's saying about scientists, Charlie? Are you going to let him get away with that?"

"Oh, that's not us. He means those guys at Yale and Cambridge," Charlie replied.

Keene turned his head toward the window and thought back to it all. It all seemed an eternity ago, not just weeks—as if belonging to another world. Outside, the clouds of dust, smoke, and ash writhed in wind that was beginning to rise again. They passed a creek bed choked with rotting corpses of cattle underneath a strangely swaying black cloud that it took Keene a moment to realize, when they swarmed outside the window, was composed of flies. Fortunately, the window hit by the bullet had been covered with a plastic sheet. Close by, a bus had gone down the side of a ravine, spilling bodies that still lay where they had fallen or crawled to. There were more clouds of flies. Cynthia gripped Charlie's arm as she stared out tight-mouthed, her face white and strained.

What had he been thinking? Keene asked himself. There was no "as if" about it. It *had* all been part of another world.

Progress was slower now that they were following behind the scout train. For long stretches the railroad ran close to the main east-west highway—still Interstate 10, running from the Atlantic coast of Florida to Los Angeles. The masses flocking into El Paso had been just the beginning. For mile after mile, the train rolled past the same scenes repeating themselves: of packed vehicles winding their way cautiously forward through the rock debris and wrecks; survivors from abandoned ones huddled in makeshift shelters, others continuing doggedly on foot; crowds pressed around emergency service vehicles; relief camps trying desperately to cope; and everywhere were the black clouds of flies signaling their gruesome message.

Keene found that he was registering it merely as a record of events having happened. The sights no longer had the ability to evoke any feelings. Twice in the course of the day, the train had to stop for major track repairs, each time being besieged by supplicants who had to be turned away. On the second occasion, a group of them tried to rush the train and were stopped by the machine guns.

Nightfall found them past the halfway mark, descending from the southern Texas plateau into the valley of the Pecos. Repair crews had been pushing westward from San Antonio also, and the going actually became easier.

❆   ❆   ❆

"You must be a man uniquely gifted with persuasiveness, Landen," Cavan said. His tone was low, not intended to carry. "Did you ever think of yourself as charismatic? It isn't a quality that I'd normally associate with my image of engineers." It was mid morning of the second day. The country to the north was dotted with fires fanned by fierce winds. Draperies of oily flame still descended from a heaving sky. Cavan was wearing Army pants and a sweater with a scarlet neckerchief knotted at the throat. The incredible thing was that he looked younger and more vibrant than Keene had seen him for years.

"What are you talking about?" Keene asked.

Cavan raised a hand vaguely. "Look at all the people you have following you to help you find this woman of yours."

Keene snorted. "Ah, come on. It's the only chance they've got to get out of this to something better, Leo. That's the reason, and you know it."

"I'm not so sure that Alicia would agree that's the only reason."

"Well, she doesn't count. She's crazy. You've told me enough times."

Cavan lowered his voice further. "But not crazy enough to think you could do it alone, without the military to help. That's why they're here, you know. She can be quite an engineer of things too, in her own way."

"Oh?" Keene knew what Cavan meant but chose to act dumb, letting his frown ask the question.

"She bewitched Mitch into it, and the others followed. He's a compulsive performer in front of any woman that happens to be around. Don't tell me you hadn't noticed, Landen."

Of course Keene had. It just wasn't the kind of thing to go making uninvited comments on. "Well . . . I suppose it's not something I really thought about," he replied. He studied Cavan's face for a moment. "Why? It's not bothering you, is it, Leo? If she did, it's as you say: to get some backup for me. Unless my judgment of people has gone to hell in the last week, there's nothing for you to worry about."

"Oh God, I've been around too many years for that. She could do worse. He's got nerve, he's dependable, and he commands loyalty. If she had any sense, she'd have found herself someone like that years ago."

Keene managed a wisp of a smile. "Well, there you are, Leo. Who's got the charisma now?"

"Charitable of you, I grant, but where would be the future? Back in the days when there was a future, I mean."

Keene looked at him reproachfully. "Don't tell me you've given up hope."

"Seriously, what do you think the chances are?"

Keene stared down at his hands. They were blistered and split from all the digging and shoveling that he wasn't used to. He looked up. "If we'd had a clear run through with the Rustler, I'd have said pretty good. But with the way things have gone instead . . . who knows? Maybe Furle was right. What else can I tell you?"

After a long wait near Uvdale for a damaged bridge to be shored up, they were held in a siding to let a loaded train from San Antonio through the other way, heading for El Paso. They reached San Antonio late that night to find the city in flames. A shrieking wind turned the buildings into torches, lighting up the overcast for miles. Spitting trails of burning naphtha left veils of smoke curling downward between the cloud blanket and the ground. The scout train had stopped a couple of hundred feet ahead. Two of its officers came back to confer with the commander on the wisdom of taking the main train any farther in until the route had been reconnoitered. The decision was to hold it back until more was known. Keene and his party transferred their kit to the lead train to go into San Antonio with it and explore what further options existed from there.

◎ 46 ◎

The railroad yard and its surroundings were an inferno of burning rolling stock and warehouses. There appeared to be no organized effort to fight or contain the conflagration. It was past being containable in any case, and from the look of things any focus of authority capable of organizing anything had ceased to exist; very likely, there wasn't enough water available, anyway.

Many people had headed for the open ground along the tracks and were trying to follow that route out of town. A crowd closed around the train as it slowed to a halt, their eyes wide against streaked, smoke-blackened faces, some wailing uncontrollably, obviously aiming to get aboard and stay there till the train departed. The soldiers accepted the injured, laying them out among the sandbags and what materiel remained on the flatcars, while the officers did their best to control the numbers trying to follow. A woman tore at Keene and Colby's jackets as they climbed down. Her face was a mass of sores and blisters in the light from the fires; her hair looked charred. *"My husband! He's trapped . . . over that way. You have to help me get to him!"* Colby disengaged himself, not wanting to be brutal but needing to keep sight of the officer in charge, who was already striding ahead along the track with two of his aides. A couple of the guards drew the woman away. Keene hastened on after the others, raising an arm to his face to ward off the sparks and cinders being driven in the wind.

An effort was under way to salvage as much as possible of the stockpiled stores. Heavily muffled figures were manhandling crates out of a burning warehouse and stacking them beside the track while others played hoses over them. A forklift following waved directions came out through the doors at the end of the building and deposited a loaded pallet. After being pointed from one place to another, the officers from the train eventually found an Army colonel and a couple of railroad managers who were trying to keep the operation moving. As Keene and the others caught up, the gist of the exchange, shouted above the roaring of the wind and the sounds of cries and screams in the background, was that it would be too risky to bring the main train in until the fires had burned down. If the track was blocked the next morning, they would move what they could out to it by road. There was no shortage of trucks, since they had been bringing loads in to San Antonio for days—although how many of them might survive the fire was another matter. Meanwhile, they could make a start by using the scout train to take back what it could carry while the connection was still there.

Mitch, Keene, and Cavan exchanged glances at the mention of the trucks. While the officers from the train were organizing their men to begin loading, Mitch identified himself to the colonel and asked which way the trucks were. The colonel, who was clad in a water-doused firefighter's smock, pointed farther ahead, beyond the blazing remains of some tank cars that had exploded. "There's a whole bunch around the loading docks that way. A lot of the drivers quit here and went out on the train that left this morning."

"Is there anywhere we can go to for gas?" Mitch asked.

"Like everything else—grab what you can." The colonel shook his head uncomprehendingly. "You don't *want* to go back to El Paso?"

Mitch shook his head. "We're going on through."

"Where to?"

"The coast, Corpus Christi."

"What in the name of Christ for? There's nothing left there."

"Special mission. . . . So there's nothing like any kind of train heading that way?"

"You're out of your mind. I just said, there's nothing left there. Mission? No kind of mission makes sense anymore. Put your men on this job instead, and you might stand a chance. Get sane."

"Sorry. We have to give it a shot."

The colonel shook his head hopelessly. There was nothing more to say. Mitch clapped him on the shoulder and moved on, waving for the others to follow. Dash and Birden stayed close behind him, Keene and Colby next, followed by Cavan and Alicia, Charlie and Cynthia. Legermount and Reynolds brought up the rear to prevent anyone from straggling. Even after everything, Keene was unable to avoid a stab of guilt as he looked back at the colonel and the others returning to their tasks.

The heat from the burning tank cars was too intense for them to pass, forcing them to detour behind a locomotive shed that seemed to have escaped major damage. A roadway flanked on one side by office and commercial buildings in various stages of burning and collapse led in the direction that the colonel had indicated. Survivors were still emerging from the side streets amid overturned autos with motionless forms inside or thrown nearby. More bodies lay scattered along the roadway. The sight no longer attracted attention.

The road ended in a large parking area outside the loading bays of warehouses serving an end of the rail yards that the scout train had been unable to get to. There must have been hundreds of trucks, lined in some semblance of order in some places, scattered haphazardly in others, many smashed or on fire. Not all had been unloaded, and in places groups of figures were braving the heat and the risk of exploding gas tanks to pass cartons and boxes down to others who were loading cars and other vehicles. Who were they? . . . Who could tell?

Mitch stopped beneath one of the high concrete lamp masts that was still standing. "The quickest way to get separated is if we all start running around without a system," he yelled through the wind. "This is the reference point we'll work from and use as base." He looked at Charlie Hu, who was clutching his side and wheezing heavily.

"Charlie, you're not up to any more. Cynthia, stay with him. And Legermount, stay here too to keep an eye on them. The rest of us divide into twos: Lan, you can come with me; Leo, go with Birden; Alicia, stick with Dash; Reynolds, you take Colby. We'll take a quadrant each, and when you find something to report, you head back *here*." He pointed at the base of the mast. "In any case, check back after thirty minutes. We want a vehicle that's intact, all wheels good, preferably with the keys. If you can, check for lights, battery, and gas. Flatbed trailers would be better. If this wind gets any worse, anything higher is gonna get blown off the road. Okay?"

"Assuming we find a road, that is," Colby muttered in Keene's ear as they split up.

Keene went with Mitch toward the west side. They passed the wreckage of several trucks and cars all entangled with another truck that looked as if it had landed on them, scraping them all into a heap. Beyond that were two more trucks almost burned out, several abandoned cars, and a truck that looked reasonably unscathed until walking around the front revealed the cab smashed in by a rock. The next two were in good shape; one had its keys in but wouldn't start. A short distance farther on Mitch tried the cab of another, then reemerged, shaking his head. As they turned away, they saw watching them two men who had been draining fuel from the tank of a tractor unit minus trailer. They looked apprehensively at Mitch and Keene's military garb and the automatic rifle that Mitch was carrying.

"It's okay, ain't it?" one of them said. "Hell, it's not as if there's any law left to be breaking."

Mitch had noticed the several cans that they had with them. "What do you guys have planned?" he asked, ignoring the question.

"Getting the hell out of here." The heftier one gestured over his shoulder with a thumb. "Our rig's shot, but we found another that'll move. No sense staying here to be roasted. Looks to me like you two guys was pretty much figuring on the same thing yourselves, anyhow."

"What have you got?" Mitch asked them. "Another tractor-only, like this, or does it have a trailer too?"

"It's a full rig," the hefty one replied. "We figured on picking up more people along the way. Chances are gonna be better for bunches of folks that stick together."

Keene and Mitch exchanged quick glances. Both nodded at the same time. "Then you've got that already," Mitch said, looking back. "There's eleven of us, including five Army. The others are over that way, not far."

"Which way you intendin' on headin'?" the smaller of the truckers asked.

"South—toward Corpus Christi."

The larger trucker shook his head emphatically. "That's crazy. Everyone's going the other way. You're on your own, soldier. They're collecting everybody around El Paso. That's where they're gonna hold out until it's over."

"We just came on a train from El Paso," Mitch told them. "You're not going to get through by road. It's blocked all the way."

"So what in hell do you think you're gonna do in Corpus Christi that's any better?" the big trucker demanded. "It's all under water. You expecting an ark?"

"Do you guys know the road down that way?" Mitch asked.

"Sure we do. Been driving it for four years."

"Okay. Then this is the deal. We pick up some people south from Alice and then head on into Mexico. Not too far past the border there's a space base that's got a shuttle down a silo, ready to go." Keene marveled at the unqualified uncertainty that allowed Mitch to say this, but he wasn't about to muddy any waters. "We launch and meet up with the Kronian ship that you've been hearing all about, and we go back with them. There it is."

The trucker looked at Mitch warily. "Man, you *are* crazy! Even if it was still up there, you think it's going to hang around for you? What makes you think they'd even have heard of you?"

Mitch fumed impotently for a second, then threw out a hand to indicate Keene. "Do you recognize this guy?" he snapped. The two truckers looked, shrugged, obviously didn't. "On TV all the time just a couple of weeks back," Mitch said. "The guy in that nuclear stunt that made the Air Force look stupid, who'd been trying to tell the world to wake up to what the Kronians had been telling it."

The smaller trucker peered more closely at Keene, squinting his eyes against the wind. "You know, it could be him too," he pronounced. "Tried to take their side in that stuff that went on in Washington."

"Landen Keene. I am," Keene confirmed.

"That's him, Buff. That's the name, all right," the smaller trucker said, nodding. Buff, the larger of the two, looked back at Mitch, uncertain now.

"You see, they know him. He's with them," Mitch said. "That's why they'll wait. Now are you with us? I'm telling you, there won't be anything for you in El Paso, even if you got there. This is gonna get a whole lot worse yet." He looked at Keene. "We could fit a couple more in, right?"

Keene just showed his hands and shook his head. "Why not? Sure." He didn't know. It wasn't a time to be calculating liftoff weights.

The two truckers looked at each other in bewilderment. "What do you think, Luke?" Buff asked, seemingly willing to be sold now.

"I dunno. . . . Goin' off somewhere all that different. Where is it? Saturn out there some place? . . ."

"There isn't going to be anything for you here," Mitch said. He looked from one to the other. "What do you have? Any folks you can get to?"

Buff looked down at the ground. "Mine were in Virginia. . . . I don't want to think about it." Luke just shook his head bleakly. Keene turned his head away, not sure how much more of this he was going to be able to take. Mitch seemed about to say something, then stopped, trying to let the obvious speak for itself.

Finally, Luke said, "Maybe, if it's like they say. . . . We should give it a try, I reckon."

Buff looked back at Mitch, tightened his mouth for a second, then nodded. "I still think you're crazy. But Luke's usually right. We'll do it."

Leaving Keene to give Buff and Luke a hand filling the cans, Mitch went back to the rendezvous point to round up the others. "So who else you got with you in that group back there?" Luke asked Keene as they moved on to check another tank.

"One's from SICA—one of the guys who went with the Kronians on their tour. There's a scientist from the tracking labs in California. And then we have one of President Hayer's aides from the White House."

"Holy shit," Buff breathed, shaking his head.

The others appeared in a gaggle, Mitch in front, Legermount shepherding from the rear. With the soldiers taking some of the cans, Buff and Luke led the way through to the rig they had found. It was an eighteen-wheel Freightliner, aluminum sided full-box, its windows still intact and showing just a few dents in the trailer. "Are you sure this will handle in the wind?" Mitch yelled dubiously to Buff, looking up at it.

"There's only one way to find out. It'll run. That's the main thing. You wanna go looking around the whole of San Antonio for something better, go right ahead."

The two troopers helped Buff and Luke finish filling the tank, while the others loaded whatever they could find that might come in useful. Then everyone climbed aboard except Mitch, who would ride up front in the cab. Buff closed the rear doors. A minute or so later, the truck began moving.

It started rocking violently almost at once. As they went into a turn, Keene sensed it veering erratically, trying to lift. Moments later, there was a crash as they struck something, followed for a few seconds by a rending noise outside. A short distance farther on they halted again.

"Don't tell me this isn't going to work," Cavan muttered, sounding worried.

"I suppose they *are* truckers," Colby mused. "Did anyone think to check their licenses?"

"Colby, you're insane," Cynthia told him.

"That was a prerequisite for anyone wanting to work in the White House," Colby said. The truck remained at a standstill.

"Seems like they're having a conference up front," Keene observed. The troops sat stoically, waiting for what they couldn't change to reveal itself.

Cavan produced his pocket radio, usable at short range, and

buzzed Mitch. "What's the problem?" he said into the mike end. There was a short pause. "He says something about a shopping trip," Cavan told the others. "Don't ask me. I don't understand it either."

At last the truck pulled away again. For what felt like a mile or two it slowed, speeded up again, turning and stopping several times. It didn't feel as if they were on a highway or making discernible progress anywhere. All the time, the trailer heaved and bucked, seeming a couple of times to be on the verge of turning over. Then they stopped again, reversed slowly, and a few seconds later the shock came of the tail hitting something, accompanied by crashing and the sound of breaking glass. The gears shifted, and the truck moved forward again and stopped. Doors slammed up front. Moments later the rear was opened to reveal Mitch and Luke.

They were at a shopping mall and had demolished the side entrance of a Montgomery Ward store. Buff was climbing in over the wreckage of the wall and doors, probing into the darkness with a flashlamp beam. "We need everybody out again," Mitch called inside. "This thing will never take the wind. We're going to have to turn it into a flatbed ourselves."

The store had been broken into already from a different entrance and was well ransacked. However, there were still axes, sledges, and other heavy tools in the hardware and garden sections, which was what they needed. For the next two hours they labored to cut and hammer the side and roof panels from the trailer, leaving the supporting ribs. From the pieces and the doors, and with the help of line and wire from the store, they fashioned a crude, ridged shelter, looking like a shallow tent, standing on the trailer's chassis between what had been left of the sides. For ballast and protection they lashed mattresses from the bedding department over the top, weighed down with bags of fertilizer and lawn food, to be supplemented by sandbags when they came across some.

Finally, Keene stood looking at the result of their handiwork. It looked oddly inappropriate. A moment of doubt assailed him. "I don't know," he said to Cavan, shaking his head. "Are we wasting our time? Is there really any point to any of this, do you think, Leo?"

"Who knows?" Cavan replied. "There's an old Irish saying: 'Now is the time for the futile gesture.' I've always thought it had a wonderful ring of magnificence about it. If anything does, it surely characterizes this obdurate species of ours. . . . Without it, I doubt if we'd even be here at all." Keene was really beginning to believe that Cavan was enjoying it.

The time by now was well into the small hours of the morning. Everyone was exhausted. They rested up until dawn, and then set out for the ring road on the south side of the city. As they negotiated their way around blocked streets and through burning suburbs, sometimes having to bulldoze wrecked or abandoned vehicles aside, a huge fireball came out of the sky and exploded to the north, sending up burning tracers dripping flames. Minutes later, another fell farther away to the west. The frequency increased as the truck made its way onto Interstate 37 South, signposted for Pleasanton.

But at least it handled manageably now.

◎ 47 ◎

Progress was slow but steady. The surroundings became emptier of people, the vehicles fewer, all going the other way. A couple of hours after leaving San Antonio, Mitch voiced the question that perhaps had been forming in many of their minds. He had come back to allow Cavan a spell of riding up front in the cab.

"Look, I know she's important to you, Lan, and it has to be a big thing in your book, but in a situation like this we have to be realistic. ... I mean, how likely is it, really, that anyone is still going to be at this place? If this shuttle that we're betting on is down over the border, wouldn't we be doing everyone here a favor by being honest and heading straight on there direct? I hate having to say this, but . . ." He gestured at the desolation around the roadway unrolling behind them, and left it at that.

"It isn't just Vicki and Robin," Keene replied. "We need a pilot too. I told Halloran to try and find one."

Mitch looked puzzled. "But I thought you could fly it," he said.

Keene shook his head. "What gave you that idea?"

"You were on that ship that all the news was about, the one that outflew the spaceplane, right?"

"Sure, as an observer-engineer. I helped design the propulsion unit, that's all."

394

Mitch stared at him for a few moments of revelation while the universe took on a new perspective suddenly. "Well, shit," he pronounced resignedly. The others exchanged ominous looks but said nothing. Colby took out a handkerchief to wipe his indestructible spectacles. "Isn't it funny how life always has one more thing in store that you hadn't thought of," he remarked to nobody in particular.

Interstate 37 continued all the way into Corpus Christi. The plan, however, was to exit at Highway 281, seventy miles before, which followed a direct route south to San Saucillo, where Keene had told Vicki to wait. Since they were now entering his home territory, he changed places with Cavan to ride up front in the cab.

If anything, the bleakness of the depopulated surroundings was even more unnerving than the scenes they had witnessed from California to San Antonio. The smoke and clouds had mingled into a heaving canopy of orange and brown from which hissing streamers of flame and bursting fireballs continued to lash down over the hapless landscape of deserted townships and abandoned farms. Buff and Luke were silent, staring out in awed, uncomprehending dread. Closer to the coast now, with two circulation systems in collision, the winds alternated between violent spasms and sudden calms. With the windows closed, the cab quickly became unbearable in the heavy, humid heat that had descended. Opening them brought in fumes that produced burning nostrils and smarting eyes. The air had a greasy stickiness that matted the hair, permeated clothing, and lodged in the throat, giving everything an oily taste.

As the miles rolled by from Orange Grove to Alice, recognition of familiar places and old landmarks triggered images of the world that Keene had known. The contrast between his recollections and the things he was seeing at last brought on the dispiritedness that he had been fighting. How far, and for how long, had he been fooling himself? Whatever chance there might once have been of finding anyone had faded long ago. He'd had the chance to escape to the stars. Instead, all he was coming back to was a graveyard. He pushed the thought from his mind, wiped the sticky film from his lips, and waved away the flies.

✖   ✖   ✖

Things went well until twenty miles or so past Alice, when Buff slowed suddenly, craning forward in his seat to peer through the windshield. "What the hell have we got here?" he growled.

"Damn!" Luke groaned on Keene's other side.

Outlined ahead was what looked like a shadowy hump extending across the highway. Closer, it proved to be part of a ridge of impact ejecta and boulders thrown from a crater somewhere to the side, with tangled branches of trees protruded in places. Buff brought the truck to a halt, and they climbed out, pulling hoods over their heads and batting away flies. The others from the rear joined them.

Reynolds climbed to the top of the ridge to reconnoiter, reporting when he came back down that the blockage extended as far ahead as he could make out. Surveys to the right and left revealed no ready way around. A number of other vehicles that had tried finding one had been left bogged down in the sandy soil. A brief conference inside the shelter yielded no alternative to turning around and finding a way through to Highway 77, which ran parallel to 281 twenty-five miles farther east, about halfway to the coast. They would follow 77 southward to below Kingsville, and then cut west to get back onto 281.

They retraced their route accordingly, and turned off Highway 281 at the first opportunity. But the patchwork of minor roads and tracks was constantly blocked or obliterated, forcing them ever farther northward until well into the afternoon, when they finally made Highway 77 just short of Robstown—almost back where they would have been had they stayed on the Interstate from San Antonio. But at last, they could resume heading south again.

For the past few miles, Keene had noticed the landscape taking on a peculiarly flattened appearance, the vegetation lying in one direction as if it had been combed, houses leaning and coming apart. And there was wreckage that seemed not to belong—house contents and belongings; parts of structures; all kinds of trash and debris—not scattered in the patterns that had become familiar but lying in endless carpets. Some of the piles included human and animal bodies, grotesquely bleached and bloated. What it meant didn't hit Keene until he saw the mounds and ribs of sand on the highway, in places holding pools of trapped water, and realized that the dark masses and clumps draped across them were seaweed. "Stop the truck!" he told Buff sharply.

From the map, they were thirty miles inland. Yet already, they had ventured below what was now the level of high tide. From the condition of the sand it appeared to have receded only recently. It would return, Charlie said, in six hours at the most. The roadway they were standing on would then be under the Gulf.

They had two choices: either turn around yet again and go back to Alice, which would mean finding a way to San Saucillo via a long detour inland; or they could make a dash south now, while the highway was above water, and hope for a way inland before it was submerged again. Buff and Luke wanted to turn back. Even Mitch seemed subdued, and for once Alicia couldn't raise the spirit to dispute him. It was Cavan, amazingly still unflagging and indefatigable, who provided the spur.

"Six hours? We could make the Mexican border in half that time," he told them. "There have to be a dozen ways back across to 281 in that distance. You've seen what kind of a mess it is once you get into those back roads. We'd still be blundering around there when it gets dark, and then lose another night." Keene watched him, cutting an almost jaunty figure in Army fatigues and a combat smock, for some unknown reason still carrying his submachine gun slung across a shoulder. Cavan waved an arm to indicate the direction ahead. "Did we come this far from California to be stopped now? The people who are depending on us are that way, and so is our only way out. We don't have time for any more excursions around Texas. In any case, speaking personally, I've seen enough of this bloody state. The more we stand here talking, the more time we're giving the tide to turn. So let's shut up and get on with it."

"Leo is right," Alicia told the others. "I've seen enough of Texas too. We have to give it a try, yes?"

Buff and Luke shook their heads at each other but said nothing. Mitch nodded his assent to the troops. Charlie, Colby, and Cynthia turned away without commenting and went back around to the rear of the truck. They all climbed wearily back aboard. Soon, Keene found himself looking out once again at the stretch of road from Corpus Christi to Kingsville that he had driven so many times. But he had never seen it like this. The road was thick with flotsam and trash as well as fallen rubble, making progress slow. There were upturned cars, downed trees—even wrecked boats carried from the coast. Through the outskirts of Kingsville, the remnants of houses demolished by impacts had been broken up by the water and dispersed. The whole area looked like a shantytown in the wake of a hurricane, extending for miles.

They were ten miles or so past Kingsville, anxiously watching east for the first signs of the wave front, when Keene saw the figures ahead, standing across the roadway. They were holding automatic weapons trained on the cab of the truck. Two standing ahead were waving it down. Farther back in the haze was what looked like a barricade on the road. Keene took the radio from the shelf below the dash panel and buzzed Mitch in the trailer three times. At the same time, he felt for the automatic in the holster at his belt. "Forget all the stuff you've seen in movies," he muttered to Buff. "They could cut this tin box to ribbons in seconds with those things. You'd better pull over."

◎ **48** ◎

Keene counted eight of them, muffled in a variety of coats with hoods or hats, a couple wearing poncholike capes. Their faces were all dark, although whether this was their complexion or due to the effects of smoke, dust, and dirt was impossible to tell. They looked exhausted and desperate.

"Okay, stop it right there," one of the two who had come forward ordered. He had a thick beard and was wearing a torn gray jacket with a hood that revealed tangled hair protruding around the edge. With six rifles trained from fifty feet farther back, there was no question of accelerating through the line. Buff halted the truck and looked down from the window. The leader had a lean, high-cheeked face with narrow, yellow eyes. He motioned with his rifle for them to get out of the cab. "Let's see what we got here. You're going the wrong way, doncha know? Now we've got us a ride going the right way. Come on, everybody out!"

"*Not so fast!*" Mitch's voice barked from the trailer behind. The leader's head jerked sharply to look back past the cab. Keene moved his head to view the nearside mirror and saw three barrels protruding from gaps in the forward end of the shelter. "This is an Army Special Forces fire team. We are in here, behind cover. You are out there, in our sights. Your call."

The leader glanced uncertainly at the other, wearing a purple scarf across his face, who was standing just behind. The others farther back shuffled awkwardly or stood in bewilderment. One of them started to back away cautiously. "*Hold it right there!*" Mitch's voice ordered. The man froze.

Then the leader waved at them to lower their guns, and his face split into a grin of broken teeth with gaps. "Well, sa-ay. It's okay, we don't want no trouble, man. We were, like, just bein' careful, you know. Doesn't do to take chances, the way things are. You never know who you might run into. But you're still goin' the wrong way, man. We've been where you're headin', and there ain't nothin' to go there for. It'd make more sense to just turn around and get us all out o' here."

"That's fine. So you can lay the guns down," Mitch answered. The leader hesitated. In the cab, Keene raised his automatic above the window level where it was visible, leaving no doubt who would be the first to go. The leader nodded to his men and put his own gun on the ground. One by one they hesitantly followed suit. He turned back toward the truck and spread his arms wide, again switching on a broad grin to show he was the most reasonable fellow in the world.

Mitch appeared from the back, accompanied by Cavan, cradling his submachine gun in the crook of an arm. Legermount and Birden got out too, but remained in covering positions by the rear corners of the trailer. Keene climbed down to join them, still holding the automatic. Other rifles were still being aimed from inside the shelter. "Okay, now we've established a talking relationship, what's it all about?" Mitch asked. "Did you people just decide to go out for a walk or something? Look around. Don't you know this is going to be seabed in a matter of hours?"

"Yeah, we know all about that, all right." The leader looked back along the highway. "But whatever your plans are, you people ain't gonna get no farther in any case. There's a bridge down just back there. Nothin' the other way for us to turn around for—'cept wait for the tide to come in like you said." He waved toward the side of the highway. "Then we saw that boat there and figured we'd come across to check it out—think maybe it'd see us through till we found somethin' better, like maybe another truck. Then you showed up."

Keene looked the way the leader was pointing and noticed for the first time the hulk lying on its side against a gravel bank about a hundred feet off the highway. He turned with Mitch and Cavan to peer past the men still cordoning the road. The wind was gusting, but not to the levels that it had reached earlier. Flies attacked in vicious, swirling flurries. Ahead, he could make out, now, the canted surface and bared pilings of what he had taken to be a barricade across the roadway. More figures were standing on the near side of the break.

"Where are you making for?" Mitch asked.

"Corpus Christi, then thirty-two to San Antonio. What other way is there?" The leader shrugged as if it were a pointless question. "Where the hell did you think *you* are going?"

"It's a long story." Mitch squinted into the distance. "So how bad is this bridge?"

"Not even good for walkin', man. Washed out. We just about got ourselves over, an' that's it. Like I said, you ain't takin' that truck nowhere that way."

"Let's have a look." Mitch waved to Buff, who slipped the truck into gear and eased it forward. The leader directed a torrent of Spanish at the others back on the road. They parted sullenly. The leader and his second led Mitch and Cavan through them, the truck following ten yards behind.

There were four more in front of the bridge, three women and a boy, maybe in his mid teens. The leader said something in Spanish as he approached, sounding as if it was meant to be jocular but evoking only a suspicious look from the youth as he saw the strangers carrying guns and his own people without any. Moving to the edge of the break, Keene saw that the bridge spanned a shallow ravine containing a creek. The structure had collapsed on one side, shedding most of the pavement except for the right-hand shoulder, which hung as a succession of tilted slabs and flakes to afford a precarious crossing from the far side. The ravine was littered with trash and debris washed up by the tide and carried down by the creek from farther inland. The wreck of a small coastal freighter lay half buried in mud a short distance below the bridge on the seaward side. Keene guessed that the boat being slammed against the bridge had caused the initial damage, and the flood waters had taken things from there. On the far side of the bridge was an ancient green truck of the kind used for local deliveries, with a miscellany of boxes, bicycles, plastic-wrapped bundles, and suitcases tied to the top. Mitch and Cavan came up to stand alongside him and silently took in the scene. It told its own story.

"You see what happened," the leader said, waving. "We get that far, and that's it. We don't wanna go back anywhere we've seen, man, I'm tellin' you. Then Augusto sees the boat over this side here, and we come over to check it out. Figure maybe we're gonna need it when the water comes in again, you know? So now, what you say? That big truck can easy take all of us. You ain't goin' anywhere this way, in any case. We don't give you guys no trouble. I mean, what else you gonna do, just leave us here? Come on, man. We all gotta stick together in this, you know?"

Mitch swatted flies away from his face and looked at Cavan for guidance. "Looks like there might not be any other way," Keene heard him say above the wind.

"What about my guys back there?" the leader asked. "Is it okay for them to come back now? We're all friends together, right?"

"Over there, where we can see them," Mitch said, waving at the shoulder on one side of the roadway. "Have one of them pick up the guns and leave them by the truck." The leader yelled back to relay the directions in Spanish. Buff and Luke had come down from the cab and were staring at the bridge and the strip of highway disappearing into the swirling vapors beyond. Luke turned and said something; Buff shook his head stolidly. The others were appearing from the back and coming around to inspect the situation. "You guys bring some women too," the leader commented, tugging his beard and grinning approvingly.

"What else are we going to do?" Mitch said. "Shoot them? We don't have any choice but go back toward Corpus Christi. We can't just drive away and leave them here to drown?"

"I suppose we have to take them that far," Cavan agreed. "Then it would depend on what we decided. Are we still talking about finding a long way around, or do we give it up and head back for San Antonio?"

Mitch pulled a face and looked toward the sky. The booms and rolling of distant thunder had intensified in the last few hours. "I don't like the way this is going. It feels like it's building up toward the Big One that Charlie talked about. I don't want to be anywhere near any ocean when it hits." Cavan looked at Keene to invite comment, but in a way that said Mitch was speaking for both of them.

"What's happening?" Charlie asked as he joined them.

Cavan gestured. "See for yourself. The only way now is back. What we do when we get to I-37 is the question."

Alicia was turning her head from side to side, as if searching for a way around. "But . . . San Saucillo?" she said. "What about the shuttle?"

"What do you want us to do, fly the truck over?" Mitch asked her.

"What's the deal? Are we trying for the long way, then?" Colby asked, moving into the circle.

"That's what we're debating," Cavan told him.

"Athena's closing in," Charlie said dubiously. "Every tide is going to be higher than the last."

"How far inland could the next one go?" Cavan asked, looking alarmed.

Charlie showed his hands in what could be the only honest answer. "How can I tell you? Maybe to Saucillo." In which case, he didn't have to add, there would be no point in spending maybe all day tomorrow looking for a long way around. It would achieve only the guarantee of their getting trapped also. Cynthia moved closer to Keene and squeezed his arm as if in a gesture of sympathy for how he must be feeling.

"You people talk much longer, and we're gonna need that boat up there anyway," the leader called over at them.

Mitch looked away, indicating that as far as he was concerned there was nothing more to be said. Cavan stood waiting for Keene to acknowledge the inevitable. Alicia shook her head protestingly but could add no words that would change anything. Even Colby was reduced to an awkward silence. Keene stared across past the bridge; unrealistic, romanticized images poured into his mind of Vicki, Robin, others, waiting somewhere. Everything in him rebelled at the obscenity that was being forced upon him. His gaze came back to the battered green truck, weighed down by its almost comical burden of accoutrements. And finally, the obvious dawned on him.

He stabbed a finger, pointing. "*There's your answer!*" he threw at the rest of them. Their eyes followed, then came back to him disbelievingly.

"What are you talking about?" Mitch asked uncertainly. Keene was past debating; in any case, there was nothing in the way of reason or logic left for him to debate with. He turned and began shouldering his way back between the others.

"What are you asking us to do?" Alicia pleaded as he passed her.

"I'm not asking anyone to do anything. I just know what *I'm* doing." Keene walked to the end of the truck, climbed up into the shelter, and began collecting a share of rations, water, and other oddments to fill his pack. They had brought spare rifles and magazines. He selected a standard Army pattern and a pouch filled with clips. Alicia and Colby arrived as he clambered back down off the tailboard, Cavan not far behind. Alicia gaped at him for a moment, then grabbed his jacket with both hands, pulled him close, and kissed his cheek.

"Have you gone completely mad, Landen?" Cavan called ahead.

"Why me? Wasn't it you who was mad a short while ago?" Keene gestured the way ahead. "You said it yourself. There's people depending on us. You change your mind if you want, Leo. I'm going on."

"But . . . you heard Charlie."

"All the more reason to get moving, then."

Alicia started saying something to Cavan. Keene came back to the leader, who was watching, confused. "How far did you come in that?" Keene asked him.

The leader waved vaguely. "Was a long way from south, a place you never heard of."

"It runs? It's got gas?"

The leader made a face, shrugging. "Well, is like you expect, you know. We take some from a car we find here, a truck there. But is good for a few miles yet, sure."

"Okay. Then I need the keys." The leader seemed to hesitate reflexively. "Hell, come on! It's not going to be any more use to you." Keene said.

The leader stared at Keene for a moment longer as if confirming that he was dealing with someone crazy, then shrugged and looked away. "*Augusto. Come here,*" he called, and followed it with something in Spanish. One of the men came forward and produced a set of keys. He removed a couple carefully and presented them to Keene. God alone knew what he thought he'd need the rest for.

Keene looked quickly around the rest of his party, the troops, Buff and Luke still standing together. More than anything, he was conscious of time relentlessly passing. "I would have wanted a better way to do this, but it's what we've got," he told them. "You're all great people. It's been a privilege. Let's consider the rest all said, eh?" Some of them managed a response; others just stood mutely, as if unable to believe it was happening. Keene glanced back at the leader and indicated the green truck with a wave. "And if you want any of that stuff off there you'd better get your people moving, because I'm dumping it." Slinging the rifle around behind him to leave both hands free, he moved onto the bridge. Behind him, the leader's voice launched into a tirade at the others.

Picking his way over the chunks of broken concrete was trickier than it had looked. The sloping surfaces were slippery, making it necessary to find footholds in the breaks and where possible hold onto the jagged edges higher up. In places he had to move on exposed steel reinforcement, greasy and treacherous, causing his body to tense involuntarily as when sensing insecurity walking on ice. All the time, the wind gusted and raged around him in its attempts to pluck him off. He was perhaps a quarter of the way across when Alicia's voice floated through from behind. "*Lan!*" Holding tightly to the stance he was on, Keene raised his head to look back. She was coming around the truck, lugging a pack in one hand and what looked like a medical kit in the other. Cavan was behind her with another pack and his submachine gun. "*We're coming with you.*" Such was Keene's concentration at that moment, that the message only partly sank in. He kept his head turned for a few seconds, letting the gesture say what his position prevented him from articulating, and then looked back to his task.

Near the midpoint, he came to a section where the group crossing the other way had tied ropes as improvised handrails—the worst part, with all the pavement gone and the creek visible below, from where the smell of decay reached his nostrils. Clutching the ropes and the girders, he had no defense against the flies. The sky to the west lit up with an incoming fireball landing closer than most. Keene braced himself for the boom and the shock wave, waited until they had passed, and carried on.

Then he was once again among flakes of shattered concrete, and by comparison the going seemed easy now. The last few yards, and he was standing on unbroken roadway again, in front of the green truck. At close range it looked even more antique than before. He walked up to it. All the glass was gone from the passenger side of the cab, and what looked like the rear window from a different vehicle had been lashed in place of the truck's absent windshield. The sides were dented everywhere and missing a few panels. Keene picked out a scattering of what looked suspiciously like bullet holes. Grunting to himself, he turned back to look for Alicia and Cavan. They were close together on the bridge, Cavan helping Alicia at the awkward center section.

But that wasn't all. There was another figure some yards behind them . . . and another two farther back still, just moving onto the first stretch. Keene peered, and after a few seconds made them out to be Colby, followed by Charlie and Cynthia. A tall figure that had to be Mitch was walking from the truck, at the same time slinging a large pack over a shoulder; as Keene watched, two more jumped down from the rear of the trailer and followed. *They were all coming!* Keene wiped the grime and perspiration from his face. It felt sticky and stubbly, but all of a sudden none of the discomfort mattered. Something warm and uplifting, brushing a depth of the spirit that in his life had seldom stirred, flooded through him. He rubbed an eye with a knuckle. More than just the fumes, he realized, was causing his vision to blur. He turned away and climbed up into the cab.

He first tried the engine. After a couple of backfires and two unsuccessful attempts at starting with different setting of the choke, which was manual, it finally coughed into life with a celebration of blue smoke from the tailpipe, indicating burning oil. Looking out through the improvised windshield, Keene saw the figure of the leader on the far side, beaming and giving him an enthusiastic thumb's-up as if to say, *See, I wouldn't fool you.* For what it was worth, the gas gauge claimed almost half a tank. Check with a dipstick before setting off, Keene told himself.

By the time the others began arriving off the bridge, he was already tossing out filthy blankets, piles of clothes, and pots of partly eaten food from the back. The inside stank of tobacco and pot, too many unwashed bodies crowded together for too long, and fear. While he was still clearing space, he heard the sounds of the rest of the baggage being cut free from the roof. Legermount and Dash appeared at the doors and began heaving in packs and equipment. Keene climbed out and found Cavan and Mitch poring over a map that they'd brought from the other truck. "Come on, we need you, Lan," Cavan said. "This is your country we're in now."

"Buff and Luke aren't coming?"

"It appears not," Cavan said. "Perhaps they decided that trucks, not spacecraft, were more their line." Keene realized that for some reason he had half expected it.

"Here," Mitch said, handing Keene his radio. "You want to wish them luck?" There was still a set programmed to the same frequency in the cab. Keene took the unit and pressed the call button. Across the bridge, one of the figures near the truck turned around and walked back to the driver's door.

"Yeah?" a voice answered in the radio that Keene was holding. It sounded like Buff.

"Lan Keene here. So you guys aren't coming along after all?"

"Well, you know how it is. . . . I could never really see me up in one o' them spaceships, anyway. And these people aren't so bad. Someone's going to have to get them to San An or wherever they want to go. And then Luke and me figured that if it works out that it's possible, we might try heading back east when the worst is over, and try to find our folks—just the way you're doin'. I reckon like maybe you gave us some inspiration. Anyways, we're set on giving it a try."

Keene swallowed. There wasn't a lot left that he could say—or the time to say it in. "Well, you've been a big help to us. Good luck."

"We'll take whatever comes. Hope it all works out for you."

Keene clicked off the radio. The others were already aboard, Legermount waiting on the driver's side of the bench seat. Keene and Mitch squeezed in with him, while Cavan went around to the rear. Nobody else from across the bridge was coming back to collect any belongings. Evidently, the things they had found in the larger truck would suffice. Legermount fought the shift into reverse with a frightful grinding of gears, backed around onto the shoulder, then engaged forward and turned onto the highway. A series of blasts from the other truck's horn sounded behind.

As they lurched their way among the washed-up debris, broken paving, and fallen rock rubble, Mitch nudged Keene's arm and pointed ominously in the seaward direction to their left. Through the patches of brown haze twisting in convolutions with clearer air drawn in off the sea, a line of fuzzy whiteness had become visible, extending as far as they could see to the south ahead of them and northward behind, paralleling the coast.

❁ 49 ❁

They had to get back across to Highway 281 running parallel with them farther inland, and then south along it to the San Saucillo site. The road they were on ran a little above the flat expanse of land to their left, stretching away twenty-five miles to the coast. Watching the approaching line of foam as it appeared and disappeared in the murk, Keene put it at two miles away at most. If Charlie was right about progressive tides getting higher, and they took 281 as a likely guess for the next high-water mark, the water's average rate of advancement from the former coast would be between six and seven miles per hour. That meant it would reach Highway 77, the one they were on, in around twenty minutes. Timing the truck's odometer with his watch told Keene that they were averaging close to twenty-five miles per hour, and with the state of the road and the obstacles, Legermount wasn't going to push any more. The turnoff that Keene normally took when driving to San Saucillo was fifteen miles farther south, which at this rate would take them thirty-six minutes. They weren't going to make it. It was as simple as that.

He looked up at Mitch after timing another mile and shook his head. "Scratch the plan for taking the exit that I said. It isn't going to work."

"Great. So what do we do?"

"A few miles ahead, the road goes down into a dip where it crosses a valley with a creek—kind of wide and shallow. You come up the other side onto a ridge that extends west. Our only chance is to try and pick up a farm track or something going that way. We'd be running ahead of the tide and should gain on it. Saucillo's on high ground too, so if we can make 281 with time to spare we should be okay."

Mitch turned to Legermount, relaying the proposition unvoiced. Legermount nodded and said nothing as he wound the wheel around and then back, keeping his eyes on the road.

They passed a succession of overturned vehicles, carried off the roadway and containing disheveled, water-sodden corpses, that looked as if they had been caught in a previous tide. As the truck began descending into the dip that Keene had mentioned, a bus filled with people, its roof loaded up the way the truck's had been, appeared going the other way. "We can't stop," Mitch said sharply. Legermount didn't have to be told. He slowed down enough to gesture back with a thumb and wave his hand negatively. After the bus had passed, he took his eyes off the road intermittently to glance at the mirror, finally shaking his head. "They're not turning." Keene sighed, but there was nothing to be done. God knew what those people were doing here in the first place.

Looking to the left as the ground began to slope, Keene could see the approaching front plainly now, still maybe a half mile off but with a tongue surging ahead into the valley that the road descended into. It was not a placid, beachlike rising of the tide accompanied by rolling breakers, but an angry, boiling wall of foam, flailing the land ahead with wreckage, debris, and pieces of uprooted trees as it advanced, while behind, the ocean rose and heaved in impatiently jostling hills of water and wind. Keene felt a coldness at the base of his spine and a sweaty slipperiness in his palms. The tension of the other two in the cab communicated itself palpably. A wheel hit a rock, and the truck bounced sickeningly. Legermount swore under his breath.

As the road leveled, the first fingers of water were streaming across the lowermost point ahead. They were below the level of the oncoming crest, now a churning cliff of water bearing down on them.

A building of some kind on the creek bank came apart as they watched and was swept away in pieces. Parts of the roof reappeared again, bobbing and cartwheeling in a surge of whiteness that engulfed the roadway just yards ahead. Then, momentarily, the surge retreated, but the truck slowed as it hit the resistance of water, throwing the occupants forward.

"*Don't slack off now! Go for it!*" Mitch shouted.

Legermount straightened his leg as if he were trying to push the gas pedal through the floor. Keene felt them sway as a swell caught them on the side, and for a moment he thought they were afloat without traction. Just at that moment, he could have done without being an engineer with the picture in his mind of the probable state of what was under the hood, and what water would do to it. But it was time they were due a small miracle, and somehow the motor shuddered and roared defiantly through to claim a tiny victory of abused technology. The road began rising, and while the land to the left and ahead of them was still being swallowed up, they had gained some margin, however temporary. Keene leaned out and looked back. The water was already far into the valley, cutting off the opposite side like a strait separating an island. He knew that the road dropped again not much farther on. Very possibly, the water would have covered it already. They had to get off the highway before then.

Beyond the ditch, the road was now bounded by a wire fence strung between wooden posts with a plantation of young firs on the far side, mostly flattened or uprooted and thrown together in tangles. The fence was down in places and sagging in others under debris that had been thrown against it, but there could be no crossing the silt-laden ditch between it and the road. Keene scanned the margin ahead anxiously. Just as it seemed that they were going to have to start descending again, he spotted a shoulder ahead where the ditch disappeared into a pipe under a gravel ramp crossing to what looked like a gate. "Slow down," he yelled across the cab. Legermount eased off the gas. Below, to their left, a sheet of ocean extended away where there had been nothing but land an hour before.

There was a gate, but it was intact between concrete posts and appeared locked. Behind it, a fire break led away between the trees, offering just a watery, sandy surface littered with branches and downed trunks. "That's gotta be a way into a trap if I ever saw one," Mitch said.

"That's something we'll have to risk," Keene replied. "It'll be worse farther on."

"How do we get past the gate?" Legermount asked.

Keene took in the situation rapidly. "Forget the gate. We can take out the section of fence next to it."

Legermount steered the truck onto the ramp and brought it nose-up to the section of adjacent fence. Before it had stopped, Keene was out of the door and on his way back, hammering on the side with a fist as he ran. Birden opened the rear door from the inside. "Tool bag!" Keene shouted. "We need cutters . . . maybe claw hammer, pry bar." Colby threw the bag out, then tumbled out himself, along with Birden and Cavan. Keene tore the bag open, took out a large set of cutters, and ran back to begin attacking the fence, snipping the mesh squares vertically down a line by one of the posts. Mitch found a pair of heavy pliers with cutter edges and went to work at the bottom, while the others held the strands back as they parted. Keene looked back across the highway behind the truck. Fountains of white spray were already exploding upward from below the end of the ridge. "*That'll do it!*" he yelled at the others. "Let's get moving." While Birden and Cavan held the cut section of fence aside, Legermount eased the truck through the gap.

"We might need help if anything needs clearing," Mitch told Birden. "You ride shotgun outside Legermount's door."

Keene stepped up into the cab as it passed. Mitch followed him but remained standing, holding the door open. Birden did the same on the other side. The others threw themselves in the rear while Alicia held the door from the inside. Legermount eased the clutch up. For a moment the rear wheels spun and skidded sideways, and then they gripped. They began snaking a way through the fallen trees and heaps of washed-up brush. But the way turned out to be not so bad as they had feared, the fallen branches giving traction in the sandy soil. The soldiers riding the cab only had to get down twice to haul obstructions aside before they came to a dirt service track, following the remnants of a power line, that led in the right direction and it looked as if it might keep to the ridge. They stopped long enough for Birden to return to the back of the truck. Mitch hauled himself in beside Keene, closed the door, and leaned his head back, letting his helmet rest against the cab wall to release in a long, slow gasp the tension he had been accumulating. Legermount reached forward and slapped the dash panel of the truck affectionately.

"Well, I'll be darned," he breathed. "The old gal done did it."

"We still have Mexico to make," Keene reminded him.

Legermount settled down more comfortably behind the wheel. "The way she feels right now, I reckon we could make Argentina," he replied.

The service track brought them to a wider farm road, which they followed south for a mile or so before curving around to follow the contours in a more-or-less westerly direction once again. They emerged onto Highway 281 at a point Keene recognized as being only a couple of miles north of the turnoff to Amspace's San Saucillo launch site. As they turned left onto 281, they could see water northward, away to the right. That would be the valley of the river that bounded the north side of the landing field, Keene informed the others. Past the landing field, the river curved south, marking the perimeter of the two-mile safety zone around the launch pads. Depending on how far upriver the tide had penetrated, and if the water had reached 281 farther south, the San Saucillo facility could have become an island on three sides by now.

❀ 50 ❀

It was like coming back to a place of fond remembrances and finding everything bulldozed away for a new highway intersection or a shopping mall—except the recollections weren't from some idealization of distant growing-up years but a matter of mere weeks ago. The last time Keene saw the grounds bordering the approach road had been from the helicopter taking him and Vicki back to Kingsville after flying from Montemorelos, when cleanup crews had been collecting the trash left after the launch demonstration. There had been stone falls and cratering, and the area to the south was charred and blackened. Disabled vehicles stood along the roadside, all of them dented and holed, several burnt out, most with wheels missing and hoods and trunk lids open, stripped of movable essentials.

Loud concussions sounded from the north. The sky was the eeriest they had seen, causing even Mitch to gaze up wordlessly with an awed expression that probably came as close as he was capable of to dread. With the clearer masses of air coming in from the ocean, the canopy that had remained solid for days with dust and smoke from the conflagrations inland was now a turmoil of fiery clouds rolling down to blot out the landscape at one moment, then a minute later opening into vast vaults of emptiness extending upward like inverted canyons between walls of incandescent colors. All the time, the rumbling of distant thunder and the booms of bodies passing above or exploding in surrounding regions merged in a background of noise punctuated by occasional nearer detonations that were becoming practically continuous.

There was something ironic about the way the familiar sign by the main gate had survived unscathed, still proclaiming it the entrance to AMSPACE INC. ORBITAL LAUNCH & FLIGHT TEST FACILITY. The gatehouse was demolished, and there were gaps torn in the outer security fence. The parking areas beyond had been pulverized, and Legermount had difficulty finding a path through the wrecked vehicles. A mound of recently bulldozed earth near the ruin of what had been the Sports and Social Club perhaps explained the absence of bodies.

Immediately ahead, one end of the main administration building had collapsed, while the remainder presented the familiar scene of a windowless facade with shattered upper levels open to the winds. The second floor was now a reinforced roof, and below, the ground floor had been turned into shelters behind earth banks and walls of sandbags. A number of wrecked military trucks suggested that the site had been used as a relief or evacuation center, probably on account of its large landing field. Behind the front offices, the flight preparation and assembly complex was for the most part a burned ruin, above which the larger vehicle assembly building had split down the middle into two parts that now hung outward in a deformed V against the sky. Legermount brought the truck to a halt. They sat surveying the scene.

"So this is what it all came to, eh?" Mitch said after a silence. "The end of the dream."

Keene was too overcome by images of how he remembered it all to respond. Legermount murmured, "Maybe Reynolds is right. It all needed a new start over again—but with different people."

"Don't tell me he's got you as a convert," Mitch said.

Legermount shrugged. "I dunno. But looking at the way it all happened . . . It makes you think."

They felt the jolt of the rear door being opened. Moments later,

Cavan, still toting his submachine gun, appeared by the passenger-side door. Mitch picked up his rifle and got out to join him. They stood, letting their eyes roam over the desolation. "Well, is there any hope here, Landen?" Cavan asked finally.

"There's always hope," Keene replied, sliding across the seat to get out.

"So where should we begin? Isn't there a pad area too, somewhere?"

"It's two miles away at the other end of the airfield." Keene shook his head. "Anybody who was waiting wouldn't hide back there. The only way out of it is up."

"Look, I hate to sound pessimistic, but shouldn't we agree on a time limit on this before we start?" Mitch said.

Just as Keene eased himself down off the end of the seat and straightened up, an amplified male voice rang from the administration building ahead of them.

"DO NOT MAKE ANY SUDDEN MOVES. YOU ARE BEING COVERED. EITHER LEAVE NOW, OR ONE PERSON ONLY COME FORWARD UNARMED AND STATE YOUR BUSINESS."

Keene looked along the bottom level of barricaded windows and sandbagged openings but could see nobody. Cavan moved a few yards from the truck, presumably to show no hostile intent.

"What's happening?" someone said from behind. Keene glanced back and saw Colby peering around the rear corner of the truck from inside.

"Near the center, just right of the main doors," Mitch said, keeping his gaze ahead.

"Interesting, but at the moment, academic," Cavan observed. "I'd say we have little initiative in this particular matter, Mitch."

"I guess you're right."

Keene moved out from the truck, keeping his hands high to show he wasn't carrying a weapon. "I'll go," he muttered to the other two. "This was supposed to be my party, anyway."

He began moving forward, picking his way through the rubble and glass fallen from the building. As he approached, he caught a movement from the place Mitch had indicated: a sandbagged opening into one of the ground-floor rooms where there had formerly been a door and adjacent window. Closer, and he saw that it was a figure in a woollen cap and combat jacket, covering him with an automatic rifle. "That's far enough," the figure called in his own voice when Keene was about five yards away. Keene halted. The figure straightened up from behind the sandbags to see him more clearly. Keene caught a glimpse of another farther back, also holding a leveled gun. "Okay, who are you, and what do you want here?" the one in front asked. Keene drew a breath to launch into the simplified explanation that he had been composing in his head. . . . And then, instead, his posture relaxed, and his face creased into a grin. "What's so funny?" the figure demanded.

Keene waited a second or two. "Have I really aged that much? Although, I suppose it wouldn't surprise me. Or is it the fancy dress like yours?"

"Look, I'm not in a mood for games."

Keene gave it a moment longer. Then, "Oh, stop it, Joe, you stupid shit. It's Lan Keene, for Christ's sake. I'm sorry we took our time getting here, but the traffic was a bitch. . . ." He broke off and could do no more than shake his head as the flippancy drained from him. It was Joe Elms, who had piloted the NIFTV the day they took on the Air Force spaceplane. He had the same reddened, blistered face as everyone else, with the beginnings of a beard, and looked more like a guerrilla fighter than a spaceship pilot. But it was Joe.

Even now, Elms came out warily, the other behind him still covering. He moved closer and peered disbelievingly. "It *is* you. . . . You look like you've been in a volcano. Jesus, have we all changed that much?" Elms turned to the other and waved for him to lower the gun. "It's okay, Sid. *It's them.* They made it!" Elms looked back at Keene, his expression dazed. The message seemed only now to be sinking in. "We . . ." He gave up and shook his head.

Keene looked past him at the younger man stepping out over the parapet of sandbags. "Sid? I know you. . . . Sid Vance, right? You came with us to the *Osiris.*" It was the Sid who had won the place on the shuttle, the kid from Navigation Systems Group, just out of college, who had been with Amspace a month.

"I never gave up on you," he told Keene. "I kept telling them. You just never seemed the type."

It hadn't fully sunk in yet with Keene either. Only now was he beginning to realize how much, inside, he had been steeling himself for the worst. There was only one more question. He interrogated Joe with a look for a second as if hoping to divine the answer before he dared ask it. "And Vicki?" he managed finally.

Joe nodded. "She's here. Robin's hurt his arm, but he should be okay. Too bad we didn't have a doctor. We had some trouble here a couple of days ago, and he took a bullet. I did what I could . . ."

Keene didn't hear the rest, partly because the relief that swept over him, and the strange, sudden weakness that came with it, almost causing him to collapse. The other reason was that he could see into the room behind the sandbagged opening; another person had appeared framed in the doorway at the far end. Keene was unable to make out the face or expression in the shadows; but without really trying, in some unconscious reading from years of learning her postures and her body language, he knew it was her.

Keene moved away from Joe and Sid and stepped over the low wall of sandbags into the room. It had once been an office but had been turned into a watch post, with an improvised bed, a collection of coats, capes, hats, and weapons hanging along the opposite wall, and the desk serving as a general table. Vicki didn't make any immediate move but stood staring from the doorway as if paralyzed. Keene was distantly aware of Joe's voice outside saying something over the bullhorn. He crossed the room slowly and looked at her. She was wearing jeans with a stained shirt and sweatband around her forehead; her hair was matted, and her face, he could see even in the dim light, was cracked, swollen, and streaked where perspiration had carried away the grime. He didn't think he had ever seen anyone look more wonderful. Her eyes looked him up and down silently. Keene waited for the offbeat remark, the dry understatement. He could see her mind running over the combinations, rejecting one after another as not fitting the moment. And then, instead, she just came a step nearer, hugged him with both her arms, and buried her face against his shoulder. Keene pulled her tight, rubbing his face onto her hair.

He felt her gripping tighter, then starting to shake as everything she had been storing up found release. In that strange way things had always been with them, it was the things they didn't say that said the most. Finally, he drew back enough to speak.

"About Robin. Joe said . . ."

"His arm's broken, but it seems clean. We tried to set it."

"I've got a couple of medics with me. He'll be okay." A hundred questions were tumbling over one another to get out. Keene shook his head, not knowing where to begin. "What about the others?" he asked. "Karen, Judith?"

"Karen left for Dallas with her boyfriend before the evacuation started. Celia came here with me but left with the military. I never heard from Judith. . . ."

Keene could see the tears starting, her fighting to hold them back. "I guess we won't be going back to the Bandana this time," she whispered.

"I never liked the music there, anyway."

Now the stupid talk. It had to come. They were never going to change. And then Vicki abandoned the attempt and hugged him close again, and he kept holding on because he felt his face wet too and didn't want her to see. And all the time he wondered to himself why this was the first time they had ever let each other know their feelings like this.

The noise of the truck pulling up outside and the voices of the others finally parted them. Another figure appeared from the corridor behind the door that Vicki had come through, thirtyish maybe, with sandy hair and stubble, dressed in baggy pants and a red T-shirt. Vicki said his name was Jason, an Amspace prelaunch technician that Joe had brought with him after Vicki relayed Keene's message. Jason had actually worked on some of the equipment installation at Montemorelos and knew the layout there. And that was it: just the four of them, and Robin.

Keene was perplexed. "No others? Harry Halloran? Wally? Ricardo?"

Vicki shook her head tiredly. "Sorry. Harry got here but he didn't make it through. I don't know about any others. It's a long story."

Cavan came in with Joe, who from the shouts and laughs Keene could hear outside had already passed out the news that Vicki was here. "We've been on the move since first thing this morning," Cavan was saying. "Everyone could use a meal. How are you stocked here?"

"Not too badly. Our dining room is across the corridor. The menu's a bit restricted, but there's plenty of room. We've got the whole place to ourselves."

"We'll need to be ready to move out as soon as the water recedes."

"And travel overnight?" Joe sounded skeptical.

"There's no choice," Cavan said. "The next tide will cover this whole place." Joe whistled. It seemed he hadn't realized things were that close.

Alicia and Dash came in with a medical pack. "Where's Robin?" Alicia asked.

"This way," Jason said, turning to lead back the way he had come. Keene followed them to a room across the corridor that was evidently being used for living quarters. Robin had been napping on a couch, from an office suite or reception area somewhere, that had been made into a bed. He had his share of blotches and facial sores like everyone else, but he was clean and looked rested. From his expression as he rubbed his eyes and looked the arrivals up and down, he evidently couldn't say the same about them.

"I never knew you dressed like that," he told Keene. "It's like out of some movie. You look like you should be in a war somewhere."

"Me?" Keene objected. "You're the one who got shot in the arm." Robin conceded the point with a rueful nod. "How does it feel?" Keene asked.

"Oh . . . it could have been worse, I guess."

"We've got a couple of people here who are going to take care of it. Professionals. You'll be okay."

"Mom told me about Earth being a satellite of Saturn, and the gravity being less then, and that's how the dinosaurs existed. Is that the way you think it really was?"

Keene shook his head incredulously. At a time like this, *that* could still bubble to the surface of his mind? "That's only part of it," he answered. "Half of science is going to have to be reconstructed. You're going to be a busy guy when you get older."

Alicia, who had been waiting near the door with Vicki and Dash, moved forward. "We'd better take a look at that arm," she said.

"I get squeamish about these things. I'll leave you to it," Keene said, moving toward the doorway.

"Do you really think I could get to be involved in work like that, Lan?" Robin called after him.

Keene winked back at him. "You'd better believe it."

Robin's upper arm had been hit by a ricochet, but the break was a simple one. Alicia and Dash reset it and announced that it should heal without complications. Over bowls of a spicy beef and vegetable stew that Joe had concocted, accompanied by hunks of crusty buttered bread and, incongruously, a selection of not-bad wines purloined from a cabinet in the Executive Suite, the arrivals told their story and listened to a condensed account of events at San Saucillo.

The trouble at Kingsville, which Harry Halloran had described when Keene called him from Vandenberg, had resulted in different groups deciding to go their own way instead of the concerted early evacuation that Keene and Marvin Curtiss had hoped for. When Vicki began recruiting for a group to go with her to San Saucillo and wait for Keene, others had conceived the idea of organizing a launch from San Saucillo themselves and trying to join the *Osiris*. By that time the military was using the San Saucillo airfield as an adjunct to the vulnerable coastal bases around Corpus Christi to fly essential cargos inland. One shuttle was launched but exploded in the boost phase—it was thought from a meteorite hit. After that, the pad area rapidly became unserviceable and further attempts were abandoned. Most of the others gave up then, and left with the military when they pulled out three days previously. "We might have done too," Vicki concluded. "But some kind of local gang came in—because of the stuff the military had left behind. But that wasn't enough; they wanted what we had too. There was fighting. That was when we lost Harry, along with a couple of others who'd stayed. They got away with the truck that we'd kept, so we were stuck here. So you can see why Joe was jumpy when you showed up in that circus truck. I mean . . . what kind of breaker's yard did you find it in?"

"Don't jest. It's still your only ticket out," Keene reminded her.

There was little more to be done when they had finished eating. Joe had made sure to have everything they needed to take sorted and packed in case a quick getaway was called for. They had also collected a supply of gasoline, which the troops transferred to the truck's tank, with a reserve in the rear in cans. They took an extra half hour to sandbag the truck's roof and fix spotlamps on the cab door pillars for the night drive. Mitch used an ax to cut a hole through the wall at the back of the cab to allow communication with the rear compartment.

As distasteful as it was for Keene to have to admit it to himself, having the numbers reduced did simplify things. The normal load for a minishuttle of the type at Montemorelos was twelve persons—which had been the size of the party that visited the *Osiris*. As things were, they had fifteen adults plus Robin. By throwing out inessential equipment and eliminating fuel for reentry, Joe felt they could accommodate the extra. But he wouldn't have wanted to push things any further than that.

While the others were loading the last items, Keene went out the back of the admin building to stare one last time over the landing field and toward the pad area, where so much of the latter years of his life had been invested. Although night was coming on, the flaming sky was creating enough of a lurid light to see. The scene looked like the aftermath of a battle with the litter of abandoned military equipment, vehicles, and a number of wrecked aircraft, including a cargo plane that had been picked up by the wind and cartwheeled into one of the heavy transporters on the tracks bordering the landing field. As he watched, something burst like a falling bomb somewhere near the far end of the main runway, toward the ruins of the pads. Boots crunched on the concrete behind him. It was Mitch.

"We're ready to go, Lan." He stopped beside Keene and followed his gaze. "End of the dream, eh?"

"Maybe the beginning of another," Keene said.

"You mean out at Kronia?"

"That's where the ball will be for a while now."

Mitch looked at him. "Is the *Osiris* still going to be up there, really?"

Keene sighed. That was something he hadn't wanted to think about. It wasn't on the list of things he could change. "Let's just play things the way that's got us this far, Mitch," he answered. "One crisis at a time."

They walked back through the building to the waiting truck. Keene decided to let Vicki spend some time introducing herself to the others and rode up front again with Legermount and Mitch.

For once, fortune seemed to have worked in their favor, and on regaining Highway 281 they found that the tide had cleared it rather than introducing new obstacles. Although the meteorite bombardment continued to increase, they made the sixty-odd miles to the border in close to two hours and, setting the last of their immediate worries to rest, the bridge across the Rio Grande at Reynosa was still passable. And more, the coastline now to the east of them bulged seaward, taking it farther away, which would give them an additional margin of distance when the tide returned to its next high point.

❂ 51 ❂

They were a few miles into Mexico, when the entire western sky lit up for ten or twenty seconds in a sheet of yellow that illuminated the surroundings like an eerie, off-color dawn coming from the wrong direction. It could only be what the scientists had feared early on: A huge area of hydrocarbon-vapor-saturated atmosphere had ignited. Legermount halted to stare incredulously. Mitch was equally stupefied. Keene felt as if his insides were turning cold. "Get out of here!" he shouted at them. "We can't stay exposed out here. Get under a bridge or something."

Mitch shook himself back to reality. "How long have we got?"

"If that thing is a hundred miles away . . . maybe ten, twelve minutes."

They pressed on, but nothing like a bridge or flyover materialized. When they had left it as long as they dared, Keene directed Legermount to steer off the highway at the bottom of a cutting they were in, and to park as close as he could get against the rock face forming its side. Keene ran around to the back and threw open the door. "*Everybody get out and get down!* Cover your heads and your ears! There's a shock coming in, and it's going to be a big one!"

Bodies tumbled out and scattered to find niches among the rocks and sand gulleys along the verge. Keene waited to help Vicki and

Robin down, and then guided them to a muddy fissure near the base of the cutting face, which Colby and Reynolds were hastily scraping deeper with entrenching tools. They threw themselves in, hands and whatever padding they could find clamped over their ears, Keene using his body to shield Vicki protectively. Even so, the pressure wave when it arrived was excruciating, and he heard Cynthia scream with the pain. In its wake came a howling wind that tore dust off the ground in sheets, blowing branches and whole trees past the end of the cutting and pinning the truck on two wheels against the rock. Out in the open, they wouldn't have stood a chance. As things were, it was two hours before the tempest fell sufficiently for them to risk moving again.

When they emerged from the cutting, the sky to the west had dulled to a red maelstrom boiling along the horizon, shimmering with lightning that was all but continuous. With the wind, they would not be able to maintain the rate they had managed from San Saucillo to the border. It was ninety to a hundred miles to Montemorelos, the last stretch being uphill into the highland beyond Cruillas. They had something like eight hours in which to get away, racing against not only the water on one side now, but a wall of fire advancing from the other.

They did well for the next sixty miles. While the din of bolides passing through the atmosphere, and of airborne and impact detonations, grew to terrifying dimensions, the rising tidal incursions had emptied the coastal region of population, and the road remained free of traffic. And grotesque though the images were that they fashioned from the landscape, the fire to the west and the incendiary skies illuminated the way ahead and gave early warning of obstructions.

But past the San Fernando River, things changed. Emergency evacuation plans had evidently been less advanced south of the border, or less vigorously implemented, and the truck began running into the stragglers still heading for the high ground. Although relatively few in number, they were the slowest and most heavily laden, creating agonizing moving bottlenecks, seemingly at every narrowing of the road or uphill stretch. And crossing over the road to try and pass was invariably frustrated by another driver swinging out ahead and moving only slightly faster than the obstruction, and who once in possession of the passing space, stayed there.

"This isn't looking good," Keene announced over the noise as he checked his watch. "We made pretty good time for a while. Now we're losing it all again."

"What do you want us to do, shoot 'em?" Mitch yelled back.

Stalled vehicles were also an impediment. At one point, a car right in front of the truck lurched to a halt suddenly, hit by a falling rock, and Legermount was only just able to avoid hitting it as figures tumbled from the doors. A mile farther on, a group of people by a stranded van were waving frantically, several of them running out into the traffic lane and trying to grab the doors of anything that slowed close to walking speed.

"How is it back there?" Keene shouted back over his shoulder through the hole Mitch had cut in the cab wall.

"Bumpy, but we're surviving," Cavan's voice answered. "We've felt a couple of hits on the roof. Let's just hope we don't collect a big one. What's it looking like outside?"

"Grim."

A big explosion occurred a mile or more to the left. The shock came, followed by a volley of debris. There was sharp *crack* from somewhere near Legermount's head, and the side window shattered. A truck a hundred yards or so ahead slewed off into the ditch. Legermount gripped the wheel tighter and kept going.

The new site at Montemorelos was up on the plateau away from any major route, and Keene had hoped that they would lose the other traffic when they left the highway. But it didn't work out that way. Word of the likely size of the impending tide must have gotten around, for everyone was turning off to follow any road leading in an upland direction. Congestion built up, and it seemed that everything would come to a standstill. But though it brought greater immediate hazard, the increasing intensity of the bombardment proved to be the saving factor. Few of the other vehicles had protected roofs, and as the hail of stones from above grew heavier, more of them pulled off the road for the occupants to scramble out and seek shelter underneath, enabling the truck to pass through.

The makeshift windshield exploded inward, covering Keene and the others with rivers of shards; Mitch knocked out what was left with the butt of his rifle and yelled at Legermount to keep going. A tracer of flaming naphtha hissed down and draped across the road ahead of them, but they carried on over it, bucking and bouncing to the smell of burning rubber from the scorched tires. To the right a hillside was on fire, showing the forms of trees as blazing silhouettes.

The village of Montemorelos lay among scrubby hills at the top of a long rise from the coastal plain, a few miles before the launch site itself. There was no route farther inland, and by the time the truck arrived, lines of vehicles were jammed around the outlying area. Maybe their intention had been to sit out the high tide here, and then descend again to the highway and get to the main Sierra Madre range during the next period of low tide. Very likely, many of the refugees hadn't thought beyond simply getting to the nearest high ground. But now, with nothing but a wall of flame to the west, they were choked along the lanes and pulled off into the surrounding fields under the increasing downfall, with nowhere to go. Some were trying to improvise shelters out of the vehicles or farm buildings, while others seemed to have lost their heads and were running around aimlessly or just sat immobile as if seized by a stupor. The spotlight that Keene was directing from the cab window picked out people struggling to get others out of a crumpled car, more falling out in the open. Ahead, one side of the village was in flames; even as Keene watched, something landed among the houses, throwing up a shower of debris in the glow.

The main thoroughfare through the center was jammed with vehicles, wreckage, and milling people, and several times Legermount had to stop and back up to find a way around the alleys between the houses. People pressed around constantly, either trying to stop the truck to get help or to gain access to it after losing their own transport. It would have been suicidal to stop. There was no way of telling if any of the cries, angry shouts, and thuds of fists and other objects beating the sides were due to the truck's hitting any of them; there was nothing to be gained from thinking about it.

Keene had worried that some might have taken it into their heads to look for shelter among the launch site constructions, even though there was nothing else beyond the village in that direction and no route inland. However, past the village center the way became clearer, and as they came to the outskirts it began to look as if they might have a clear run for the last few miles. Then, as it rounded a bend in the road, the truck came upon several cars and a van pulled over to the side with a cluster of figures apparently trying to repair something.

At the truck's approach, several of them stepped out in front of it, waving it down with flashlamps, giving Legermount little choice but to brake or run right over them. There was just time for Keene's spotlamp to pick out the stove-in side of the van and the mixture of capes, parkas, and uniforms—whether police or some kind of military, it was impossible to tell—when a harsh voice barked something on the driver's side. A figure outside grabbed for the door, but Legermount had already locked it. An arm came in through the broken window to seek the inside handle; Mitch lunged at it with his rifle butt. At the same time, another figure twisted the lamp from Keene's grasp and opened the passenger door. Whoever they were, they were desperate and panicking. Their van was out of commission, and they wanted the truck. There was more shouting, and Keene felt himself gripped by the jacket and pulled from his seat. He managed to produce his automatic, but a gloved hand swiped it aside. For an instant he was looking at a swarthy, mustached face framed by a parka hood pulled up over a peaked cap, eyes wide, teeth bared; he saw a pistol coming up toward him and knew that moment of slow-motion awareness, like the split-second before a car crash when what's about to happen is clear but a dreamlike paralysis makes it impossible to intervene. . . . And then Legermount fired three times in quick succession across the cab with a handgun, and the figure cried out and recoiled backward.

Shouts were coming from inside the rear of the truck. Looking back through the cutout in the cab wall, Keene saw light flooding in as the doors were torn open and more figures appeared, waving rifles.

Somebody fired a shot from inside but without effect. The ones outside began raising their weapons to aim into the truck.

Mitch yelled "*Down!*" and fired a burst back through the length of the truck from the cutout. Keene slammed the passenger door. A form loomed toward him; he aimed the automatic, and the shape ducked away as Legermount hit the gas pedal.

But as the truck pulled away, a bright lamp from outside illuminated the interior to show Cavan trying to untangle his gun from a pack, Dash reeling off-balance and tumbling from the sudden jolt, with the others frozen in confusion. It would be a slaughter in there. The truck would never pull away fast enough, and Mitch, blinded by the light shining in from outside, couldn't see to protect them.

Legermount hit the brakes, and even while Keene and Mitch were slamming into the dash panel, crashed the shift into reverse and gunned the truck backward. A series of sickening thuds accompanied by screams came from the rear end. The light disappeared abruptly, and Keene felt a wheel lurch over something. Legermount braked and reengaged forward gear. Again, the gruesome lurch, and they picked up speed. Shots followed, a few hitting the bodywork, but the truck was away by now. Keene put his face close to the cutout. "Anybody hurt back there?" he called through.

Cavan appeared outlined against the frame of the still-open door a few seconds later. "No . . . I think we're all okay. Would you believe it, Landen? The first chance I get to actually use this bloody thing, and it gets caught up in the straps. Maybe the desks were more my line after all."

The last stretch of road up to the launch site was clear and deserted. From the final bend at the top of the slope, the view to the side looked down over the direction they had come, visibility being better now as a result of the conflagration to the west, drawing in clearer air from the Gulf. Several new craters glowed below on the plain, while beyond, shining pink in the ghastly light, the line of the inrushing tide was already visible as an immense wall dwarfing the scale of the previous one.

❂ 52 ❂

Finally, they came within sight of the launch facility. Apart from the ubiquitous rock debris and some superficial damage in places, the structures stood intact. The gates were still locked. Jason and Joe ran forward and severed the padlock hasps with bolt cutters. Legermount took the truck through, waited for them to reboard, and Keene pointed the way to the access building serving the silo that had been made operational. Again, Jason and Joe came around with tools to force open the doors. As the last lock gave, they waved the others out from the cover of the truck. Legermount gave it a friendly parting slap before grabbing his kit and hastening away.

While Jason and Joe disappeared inside with Legermount, Keene and Mitch stood by the doorway ushering the others through while Cavan saw them down from the truck: Cynthia and Charlie; Colby with Vicki, helping Robin; Alicia, followed by Dash; Birden and Reynolds. . . .

"There's one more," Keene called. Cavan looked momentarily uncertain. "Where's Sid?" Cavan turned back toward the truck. Keene went over as Cavan shone his flashlamp inside. Sid Vance was still sitting at the far end, his back to the wall, his face blank. Keene threw Cavan an ominous look and climbed in. "Sid?" He nudged Vance's shoulder cautiously. Vance keeled sideways silently, then doubled over. Keene lifted him back up while Cavan played the flashlamp from the door. Sid's head lolled limply to one side. There was a single bullet hole in the front of his jacket, hardly any blood. Keene checked his face and raised an eyelid with a thumb, then turned away, shaking his head.

"I never really found out who he was," Cavan said as Keene got back down.

"Just a kid who always hit lucky—until this time," Keene said. He looked past Cavan and stiffened suddenly. Cavan turned and looked back. Three sets of headlights were coming up the road from the village.

"It seems that our friends back there don't intend letting the score go unsettled, Leo," Keene said. "You might get a chance to use that gun yet."

They went in, found Mitch, and set him about organizing some defense while Keene, Jason, and Joe went on down to the service bays adjoining the silo to check the situation. Only dim emergency lights were on, running off a battery system in the generator room that had also been left driving the refrigeration plant for the liquid oxidizer portion of the hybrid fuel mix. That was the most crucial part. It meant that the oxidizer storage tank was ready to deliver to the shuttle now—the operation had to be done at the immediate prelaunch phase. Had the refrigeration been turned off, liquefying the oxidizer would have taken hours. With a supply ready to flow, transfer could be accomplished in about fifteen minutes. Keene breathed a silent prayer of thanks to whoever the engineer had been who allowed for this kind of situation.

Jason threw switches along a panel and started the standby diesel generator. They had power. Keene heard him go into the control booth, and moments later lights started coming on in the concrete-walled rooms and equipment bays, through the stairwells and corridors, and among the ramps and service platforms around the silo above. Keene went through to the pump room and ran quickly over the valve settings. As he started up the oxidizer transfer process, Jason's voice came from the general address system serving the area. *"Okay, Joe, you should have power. The access hatch should be at green, bridge extended."*

"Right. That's what we've got," Joe's voice shouted down from the access bridge to the shuttle, higher overhead.

"The onboard system's showing live. I'm disconnecting power umbilicals and switching everything to internal. Okay, start getting everyone inside."

The lower gantry through to the silo was down. While Jason went through the blast door into the silo to release locking pins and safety latches, Keene went up to the monitor panel at the access level to begin retracting the service gantries and power up the silo's covering doors. Charlie Hu was at the bridge crossing the gap to the white body of the shuttle. Joe had already gone through to commence flight-deck procedures.

"We're still missing some," Charlie said. "Where are Cavan and the troops?"

"Securing the outside. It looks like trouble followed us up from the village."

"What about Sid?"

"Sid didn't make it." Keene saw Charlie's hesitation, wanting to contribute something more. "Go on inside and make sure the others get strapped down, Charlie. There's nothing you or they can do. We can't have everyone out there." Charlie nodded, turned, and disappeared into the hatch.

Jason appeared, having finished his chores below. "Just the oxidizer to complete," he announced.

"I can take care of that," Keene said. "Where can we get a connection to the flight deck?"

"This way." Jason led him back to a control room outside the blast wall of the silo and activated a screen on one of the panels. It showed the face of Joe, working systematically inside the shuttle.

"Roger," he acknowledged.

"Can we get some remotes from the security cameras outside?" Keene threw as an aside to Jason. "And see if you can pick up Mitch or Cavan on the band they were using." He turned to the screen showing Joe. "All in order here. How are you doing inside?"

"Well, if you never heard of seat-of-the-pants spaceship flying before, this is gonna be it," Joe replied. "I've got a reading on the outside wind. We could never launch in this with a regular sequence. I'm programming the side thrusters to fire as we come up out of the hole and create a horizontal counter thrust. Just hope I've got these numbers right."

Keene had never heard the like of it. "I don't have a lot of confidence in first-time guesses," he answered dryly.

"That's why you need a pilot, not an engineer."

A shudder ran through the structure as something large impacted not far away.

"Lan, look at this," Jason called from another console.

"Keep the line open, Joe," Keene said to the screen, and moved across. Jason had operated one of the external cameras to view the main gate into the compound. The three cars had arrived outside, but somebody had driven the truck back and parked it there, blocking the entrance. As Keene watched, a helmeted figure jumped from the tailboard, ran a few paces, then turned and threw something back inside. Seconds later, the truck flamed into a torch. Keene remembered the spare cans of gasoline they had loaded at San Saucillo. *"Who is that crazy bastard?"* he yelled.

"I think I've got Mitch here," Jason said, passing Keene a mike.

"Mitch, can you hear me?"

"Just," a voice acknowledged distantly through a blur of static.

"This is Lan Keene. That's not you at the gate?"

"I'm on my way up to the roof with Legermount and Dash. Birden and Reynolds are covering the entrances."

That accounted for five. Then it could only be Cavan. "Oh Jesus," Keene groaned. "Head for the front, Mitch," he shouted into the mike. "Leo's gone out there to delay them. He's going to need cover."

"Got it."

On the screen, two cars were bumping their way along the outside of the fence toward a place where something had torn a gap. The third car was still outside the gate and had disgorged a figure who began firing at Cavan through the fence. Cavan turned and dropped to one knee, and for a heart-stopping instant Keene thought he had been hit. But it was just to aim, and Cavan dropped his target with a quick but accurate burst. However, more were appearing from the car.

With one gun against several, and being out in the open, Cavan would have no chance. He rose and began zigzagging back across the compound. But with the distance still to go, there was no way he was going to make it.

"Perimeter lights!" Keene snapped at Jason. Jason reached for a panel beside the console and began flipping switches. White light enveloped the gate area, throwing the burning truck into relief and highlighting the figures clustered against the fence. One of the soldiers from the building—either Birden or Reynolds from what Mitch had said—ran forward into view and began firing at them. They retreated in confusion into the darkness farther back, and Cavan sprinted for the building, followed by whoever had covered him. Meanwhile, Jason had managed to direct a second camera at the two cars making for the gap, which was now also clearly visible in the fence lights. One of the cars stopped suddenly, figures tumbling out and throwing themselves for cover, evidently from fire coming from somewhere, probably the roof. The other veered off into the shadows and doused its lights.

"Is it you doing that, Mitch?" Keene asked into the mike.

"Right. We're on the roof at the front. Good move with the lights. How's Leo?"

"Looking good."

One of the lights over the gate was shot out. Seconds later, the two nearest the gap through the fence went the same way.

"I'm just about done here," Joe's voice called from the screen showing the flight deck in the shuttle. "We need everyone on board."

The third car was coming out of the darkness, heading for the building. Behind it, several dark forms came through the gap and began spreading out. One of them fell. Muzzle flashes were coming from the others and from the car.

Then Keene realized that there was something odd about the background in the scene. Unless his sense of direction was confused, the view from the roof in that direction should have shown the plain below, lighted up by the fires and the glowing meteorite craters. Instead, it was black and featureless except for flecks and patches of white. He stared, puzzled for several seconds; and then, suddenly, a chilling feeling ran through him as he realized it had turned into ocean. And then, even as he watched, the fires of the village they had just passed through, maybe one or two hundred feet below them in his estimation, dissolved under what he could now make out to be an oncoming front of churning foam.

"*Mitch! It's time to pull out!*" he shouted into the mike. "*Look down the hill!*"

"*Christ!*" Mitch's voice exclaimed.

Keene turned to Jason, "I'm going down to wrap up the lox. We need to open the silo doors."

"I can do it locally from the ramp." Jason crossed the room at a run and disappeared out the doorway.

Keene flew down the stairs to the lower level, checked the gauges, and shut off the pumps. As he retracted the umbilical, the sound of firing came from inside the building. He climbed a steel stairway to a platform above the pump area and entered a passage as Birden appeared at the far end, stopping to send a burst of fire back from the cover of the corner, then ducking back around as it was returned. In the other direction was a steel door that led through to the access stairs. "*Birden!*" Keene yelled out. "*This way.*"

Birden looked back and saw him. "Dash is coming through. Hold that door."

Keene ran to the door and pulled it open. Behind was a work area with a tool bench. Birden stepped out and fired again as Dash appeared around the corner and ran past him. Keene held the door while Dash went through. At the far end of the passage Birden fired again and turned to follow. Keene waited, holding the door. But before Dash could cover effectively one of the pursuers appeared and cut the running figure of Birden down with a stream of bullets. Keene found that he was still staring, horrified, when Dash slammed the door.

"*He's gone! Move!*"

They dragged the bench behind the door and tipped it over to form a block, then started away again; but Keene, on a second thought, turned back and took down a heavy sledge from a wall rack while the bench rocked from the pounding against the far side of the door. Turning again, he found that Dash had waited to cover him in case the door gave. They raced for the stairs that would take them up to the access bridge.

They arrived to find Mitch bundling Cavan across the bridge into the shuttle, and Legermount and Reynolds holding off more pursuers at the far end of the boarding antechamber, where one body was already lying on the floor among splashes of blood. Dash followed Cavan and Mitch across the bridge and disappeared inside. Keene stopped just past the blast door to wait for Legermount and Reynolds. Looking up, he saw the silo doors open, revealing a circle of orange-streaked sky. Jason must have already gone through. Legermount detached and ran through with Reynolds covering and took the door. "Where's Birden?" he asked Keene.

"Out of it."

Reynolds backed through, firing from the hip, and went through to the shuttle. Legermount waved for Keene to go after him. Keene shook his head, motioning with the sledge in both hands. Reading his intention, Legermount swung the door shut and stood back while Keene delivered a series of heavy blows to jam the hinge and latch mechanisms. By the time Keene tossed the sledge down and turned away, Legermount was across the bridge and in the shuttle, waiting at the hatch.

Inside, Dash and Reynolds were fastening themselves into harnesses; the others were all secured. While Legermount closed the hatch and settled down, Keene paused to find a grin for Robin, who was hunched between Vicki and Alicia, looking pale. "Bearing up okay?" Keene said to him. "That's the worst over. We're on our way." Robin nodded, managing to keep a brave face. Keene squeezed Vicki's shoulder in a way that said everything would work out okay—it wasn't as if he would ever have to answer for himself if it didn't.

"Okay, I've seen Mexico," Colby said from his seat. "Can we move on?"

Keene went forward to join Joe in the crew section and buckled himself into the flight engineer's seat. He would have to handle the electronics too, since they had no Ccoms operator this time, but that didn't make a lot of difference to anything, since there was nowhere to communicate with. The first thing he made sure of, however, was that the computers still contained the navigation beacon and homing codes that had been used for the rendezvous with the *Osiris*. A quick run through the checks showed engines, fuel, power, hydraulics, environment, and cooling all looking good. He keyed in the command to retract the access bridge, and an auxiliary screen with a vertical view down between the silo wall and the body of the shuttle showed it sliding back cleanly into its recess.

"Tank and pump pressures good, temperatures good, auxiliaries functioning," he told Joe. "Do we want the whole list?"

"With guys out there wanting to shoot this thing full of holes? Hell, no. Let's get outta here!"

"Then you're all set. We have delivery. . . . What's this? *Oh, my God!*" Keene stared at the screen, horrified, as it showed the blast door at the bottom of the silo being opened from the other side. A group of figures in helmets and combat gear ran out, brandishing guns, onto a concrete ledge flanking the duct that directed the exhaust out to a water-cooled pit on the far side of the structure—Keene and Jason hadn't bothered to flood it; what would have been the point?

Joe's finger was already straightening against the button.

The figures came to a confused halt and stood gaping up at the tail and booster nozzles of the spacecraft towering above them. Then, realizing their mistake, they began a frantic scramble to get back through the door.

"Ignition."

◉ **53** ◉

Keene counted seventeen gut-wrenching hits or lightning strikes on the structure as the ship climbed through the winds, the flaming clouds, and the meteorite storm. But it stayed together, and as it emerged from the atmosphere the occupants got their first view of Athena since the last transmissions before the satellites were knocked out, and the shots that had been relayed from the *Osiris*. The nucleus was clearly visible now, appearing six times the size of the Moon, which meant that it was well inside the lunar orbit. It hung as a malevolent, white-hot presence, its tail of dust and incandescent gas engulfing and extending far beyond the Earth, with twisted and braided secondary streamers discharging immense sparks through the plasma envelope to the main body and between each other.

The regular flight-planning programs were unable to compute a stable orbit through the changing gravity now permeating the region. Charlie Hu, Joe, and Keene calculated a burn that would send them coasting out on a long ellipse away from the two bodies as they closed. Although it meant expending an alarming portion of the remaining fuel, their estimates indicated that it would be better in the long run than constantly having to fire to correct a closer-in orbit. And with the ship's vantage point lengthening, its occupants watched the devastation of an entire planet as the encounter between Earth and Athena entered its final, cataclysmic phase.

The seas of fire that they could see engulfing parts of the southwestern and central U.S. were repeated across huge tracts of every other continent also. From the size and sharpness of the spiral chasms carved in the smoke-laden atmosphere, they were generating winds more ferocious than anything seen previously. Watching in horrified yet compulsive fascination, they were able to glimpse through the slowly shifting patterns fragments of what was happening on the surface.

The tides filled the valleys of the Amazon, Mississippi, Congo, Ganges, and Yellow Rivers, rising over the southeastern states all the way to the Appalachians in the U.S., covering the plains of southern India and Argentina, and creating temporary seas that immersed London and Paris, Baghdad, Beijing, and Montreal. When the water receded, a mud bank running from Florida to Venezuela turned the Caribbean into a six-hour lake; Britain reemerged amid a plain of lakes extending from Norway to Spain; Asia became reconnected to Australia except for a narrow channel twisting its way between Borneo and Celebes.

As the magnetospheres of Earth and Athena intersected, colossal electrical bolts began flashing incessantly not just between parts of Athena but directly down upon Earth itself. After two days, Charlie, who had been trying to make measurements from the ship's imaging displays, announced that the tidal extremes were getting less even though Athena was still closing. It confirmed the fears that Keene had heard voiced back at JPL: The motion through Athena's field was making Earth an immense Faraday generator, heating the beds of the oceans and actually inducing boiling in places, causing sea levels to fall by hundreds of feet. The recondensing vapor turned into a pall of cloud miles thick, which the winds stirred with the browns of the hydrocarbon gases and the smoke from the continent-wide fires to draw a curtain over the death throes as Earth and Athena commenced the slow mutual gyration that would mark their closest pass. But the broad story told by the shuttle's infrared scans left no need for every ghastly detail.

Under the close gravitational influence, the crust seemed to slip in its rotation. Softened and melted toward the surface by the induced heating, it buckled and tore into huge north-south running paroxysms of earthquake and upheaval. The great African Rift opened up into a two-thousand-mile-long lake of lava that could be seen widening hour by hour, soon to become a new ocean, while to the east the tip of India extended into a ridge of upthrusting, colliding slabs of seabed snaking its way southward across the equator. The trench system running from Japan via the Phillippines to Indonesia was opening too, and starting to cleave Australia—very possibly, Charlie guessed, presaging a continental uplift somewhere in the western Pacific. They were literally watching the next world being born, even as the old one died.

The shifting of the spin axis caused oceans to slop across continents. Swathes of blue and green cold advancing hour by hour across the previously yellow and orange hot areas on the false-color infrared images told of miles-high cliffs of water bursting over the Appalachian barrier to descend upon Cincinnati and Pittsburgh, surging up into the funnel formed by Siberia and Alaska to spill over into the Arctic basin, and turning the southern Himalayas into an archipelago. With the surface charted simply by its temperature variations, the images quickly lost all resemblance to maps that were recognizable. In any case, it was already clear that those maps would hence be of interest only to future historians, geologists, and archaeologists. "Could *anything* survive that?" Vicki whispered amid the horrified silence that had enveloped the cabin for hours.

"Nothing could survive that," Joe murmured. His voice was numbed.

"It happened before, not all that long ago," Keene reminded them. "And some survived then. It may have been just a handful, scattered across a mountaintop here and there or a few places that the floods didn't reach. But it was enough."

"Go forth and multiply, and repopulate the Earth," Reynolds recited softly.

"But could it really have been this bad?" Vicki persisted.

"They didn't have the technology either," Charlie said. "Some of those down there might pull through, even with all that." Keene didn't know. All he could do was look with the rest of them at the dark ball that Earth had become and know that in the cities disappearing under towering walls of foam in the darkness beneath, the forests and grasslands that had become carpets of ash, the exposed seabeds being consumed under spreading lava plains, the splitting mountains and sinking islands, humans and life of every kind were dying in billions. The things he had seen in the past week had hardened and wearied him to the degree of showing little external sign, even to this. Vivid though the pictures were that he created in his mind, nothing in his experience enabled him to relate to the the calamity he was witnessing. But inside, in his soul, he wept for the tragedies taking place everywhere, a million every minute, on the scale he was capable of grasping. He wept for all the Marvin Curtisses with stepdaughters who would never play their cellos to a public audience now; for the David Salios with pretty wives and young children who would never see Europe; the Wally Lomacks and their grandchildren; the Washington cab drivers and their wives who weren't going to retire to Colorado; the Lieutenant Penalskis, Colonel Laceys, and General Ullmans who had stayed to carry through their duty; the Buffs and Lukes who had gone back to find their kinfolk.

And he mourned the passing of the culture that had emerged from squabbling European tribes to produce the cathedrals of Cologne and Rheims, the paintings of Michelangelo and the music of Bach, the calculus, the steam engine, the Boeing 747, the IBM PC, and yes, even Wall Street. Would visitors from another age return one day to take pictures of New York's steel skeletons standing stark against a sandy desert, or to excavate the ruins of Tokyo and its seaport among some range of inland hills as others had the pyramids or the ziggurats of Nineveh?

The momentum of the two bodies' turning embrace parted them, and Athena at last began withdrawing to find whatever future was destined for it among the other objects of the Solar System. As a macabre finale to its act, it recrossed the lunar orbit close enough to draw the Moon toward itself until the Moon started to break up. It receded with what had been Luna slowly transforming into a trail of debris, curling around to circle Athena like a triumphal garland. The bulk of the material could be seen plunging down in a torrent to be consumed into Athena's incandescent surface. The residue would accompany Athena as a ring system, a trophy from its victory, which it would carry across the heavens as a taunting reminder for thousands of years to come.

◉ **54** ◉

The ellipse carried them out past what had been the Moon's orbit, into regions of space that were cleaner. However, being intended for short missions, the shuttle was not equipped with solar panels or a long-life power source, and use of the sampling instruments and external imagers had to be limited. The craft had evidently sustained some damage during the lift up from the surface, for nothing could be picked up on radar. Neither could a signal be received from any surviving ship or other source that might be out there. This naturally raised the question of how they could be sure that *any* of the communications equipment was functioning properly—in particular, the beacon that was supposed to provide a signal for the *Osiris*. As time continued to drag by, the more sinister but obvious question raised itself of whether the *Osiris*'s failure to materialize might be due not to any malfunction of the shuttle's equipment, but the fact that the *Osiris* was no longer out there at all.

As nerves grew frayed, and fears worked on by the mind acquired the substance of virtual certainties, Keene was the one who had to bear the brunt. It wasn't simply that something that the others, now relieved from the pressures of just staying alive, were beginning to see as a Mad Hatter scheme from the beginning, had been his conception. With the change in circumstances and environment, roles had altered, and he had become the leader that all of them recognized now. Keene had acknowledged Charlie's seniority within JPL. Mitch had accepted Cavan in Washington as the natural commander of the force mobilized to go to Vandenberg, and then assumed the dominant part himself when the situation changed from political intervention to virtual combat. Now they had returned to the world of technology and space engineering; and the natural person to take charge in it was Keene.

He did his best to reassure them, telling them to put themselves in the position of the Kronians aboard the *Osiris*: the only representatives of their culture to be within hundreds of millions of miles of what had happened. "Imagine you're all scientists, like Charlie," he appealed to the others. "You're in a unique position to record close-up and take back records of events that nobody alive will ever see again. Priceless data and information. What are you going to do—just head off home and ignore it? Of course you're not. But you wouldn't exactly want a ringside seat, either. You'd pull back to a safer distance. They're out there somewhere. We're on a long, eccentric orbit. It'll take some time, sure. But they're there."

"But even supposing they are, what's to make *them* think that *we're* still here?" Legermount persisted. Legermount had been restless and brooding now that the action was over. Cool, competent, and given to few words when there were demanding things to be done—the ideal second to someone like Mitch—he was affected the most by the passivity of being shut up, waiting for something that was beyond their control to happen.

Which brought them back to the original point: How did they know the beacon was working?

"It's still a good point," Cavan agreed.

Keene wasn't sure if any of them had the expertise to do very much if it wasn't, and he doubted if the ship carried the full range of parts that might be needed anyway; but it quickly became clear that not even knowing if they had a chance would drive everyone slowly crazy. He and Jason talked about rigging up a simple transmitter-receiver that they could launch on a tether and communicate with by wire to test the ship's receivers and see if a beacon signal was being emitted. But Robin, looking livelier now, his arm strapped comfortably and doing well, reverted to his habit of spotting the obvious that had been missed. "Couldn't somebody be let out and just do it in a suit?"

Of course, that was the way to do it. And with Joe resigning himself to the position of driver and galley steward in this operation, the natural choice of who should go fell upon Keene.

Joe helped Keene put on one of the three EVA suits that the shuttle carried as a normal complement, and Keene squeezed into the narrow entry space inside the main hatch, which was fitted with an inner door to serve the double function of acting as a lock. Joe pressured the chamber down and opened the hatch from the flight deck. Keene rechecked the tether attached to his harness, its mounting, and the straps holding the test set that he would use in addition to the suit radio. Then he shoved himself through, orienting to align the gas thruster on his backpack. Moments later he was coasting away, turning to watch the distance steadily increasing between him and the vessel, apparently motionless in space. It looked a lot more scarred and battle-weary than he had imagined.

"Hello, Joe? This is Lan, testing. Anybody there? . . . Lan Keene to ship. Hello, Joe, are you reading? . . ." Nothing. He flipped on the portable unit that he had brought and tried the first frequency they had set. "Jason, are you reading? . . . Come in, ship. This is Lan, out on the line." Silence. He tried the other frequencies, ship standby, and emergency bands. Still the same. Worried now, Keene raised the forearm carrying the suit controls and switched to the wire circuit. "Joe, can you hear me?"

"Nice and loud, Lan. How are we doing?"

"Not good. I've been trying you and Jason on all the channels. You didn't get anything?"

"Negative. . . ." There was a pause. *"Jason says he was tuned all the while. Not a thing."*

"I don't like this, Joe."

"Me neither. Have you tried the beacon yet?"

"I'm just about to now." Keene looked down and switched the

portable unit to receive mode. He realized then that his chest was pounding. His breathing was shaky in his helmet, the clothes next to his body clammy with perspiration; his mouth and throat had gone dry. In the next few seconds he might find out that they were all destined to die out here. He selected one of the Kronians' homing settings and plugged an audio decode connection into one of the suit circuit's external jacks. . . . And a moment later, he was shouting out aloud in a relief that was almost crushing.

"YEAH! . . . OH, YOU BEAUTIFUL, BEAUTIFUL SHIP! I COULD MARRY YOU, YOU BATTERED PIECE OF BEAT-UP JUNK!"

The tone was coming through clear and strong in his helmet. It was the sweetest music he had ever listened to.

"*Lan? . . . We're okay?*" Joe's voice inquired, sounding a little unsure.

Keene nodded to himself, feeling drops of perspiration run off his head. "We're okay, Joe. The receivers might be out, but the beacon's singing. We're getting out of here, Joe. They're going to be coming for us."

"*Yeah, well, that's great.*" Joe didn't seem fully to have absorbed it yet. "*Lan, don't do that to me again.*"

They reeled him back in, still ecstatic and intoxicated by the sight of the stars, and for a few minutes with the weight of what had befallen Earth actually gone from his mind. It was only when he was almost at the hatch and about to guide himself in that his thoughts went back to the radar display he had watched at Vandenberg of the blip closing in toward the *Osiris*. The connection had been lost before they'd had a chance to be sure that the unharmed craft really *was* the Boxcar as Keene had assumed. If he was wrong, then none of the Kronians would ever have arrived at the *Osiris* to tell their story of Keene's last-moment change of plan; and whether the shuttle was transmitting a signal or not wouldn't make very much difference, since with Idorf and his ship long ago seized, nobody would be looking for it.

The grim set that the thought imparted to Keene's face must still have been in evidence when he emerged through the inner door into the cabin, and Jason helped him off with his helmet.

"What's the matter, Lan?" Vicki asked. "Joe said everything was all right. You look as if there's bad news."

Keene looked around at their apprehensive faces, the silent pleas to be reassured. He couldn't dump this latest doubt on them now, he decided. But neither could he lie to them. There had to be some bad news.

"I didn't realize how much you all stank," he told them instead.

They turned off all the unessential electronics, wound the environmental control and air recirculation down to minimum, and made do with just the dim emergency light in the cabin. Keene surreptitiously increased a little the carbon dioxide level that the monitors would set to. It would relieve the load on the system and make people drowsy, passing the time more easily, lowering their oxygen consumption, and making them less likely to vent their anxiety in querulousness. All the same, Legermount tossed and fidgeted until it seemed he would start dismantling the ship with his hands, just to find something to occupy himself. Reynolds was just the opposite, calm and accepting in his belief that all was in the hands of a higher, wiser power.

Mitch and Cavan talked idly about military affairs and the old days, not realizing how much it sometimes affected the others, and wondered what the future might be for their line of business on Kronia. Dash revealed a literary bent and began composing a detailed account of all he could recall, at first using any scrap of paper that came to hand, later getting Keene's okay to transfer to an on-board laptop whose drain wouldn't make a lot of difference to anything. When Dash wasn't writing, Jason and Joe would take the laptop forward to the flight-deck seats and play chess. Colby went off into long excursions of thought that resulted in few revelations, returning periodically to use the laptop for notes of his own that he was compiling, or to quiz Keene about workings of the ship that aroused his curiosity. He also attempted to entertain Robin with a variety of coin, card, and pocket-item tricks, none of which would work. Colby's explanation was that he'd never realized how much they depended on gravity.

Vicki and Alicia talked about science, history, life in America and in Poland, and personal reminiscences involving Keene and Cavan. Charlie and Cynthia continued getting to know one another, making an effort to forget the lives that were gone and swapping stories about Kronia as if deliberately rejecting any possibility that they might not be on the threshold of new lives about to begin. Charlie was also intrigued by Robin's novel thoughts on such things as planetary evolution and biological origins, and they talked about the Venus encounter, the Joktanian discoveries of humans who had lived beneath a sky dominated by Saturn, and the science that would have to be rewritten.

"I was just starting to get to know a planetary scientist in Houston when . . . you know, it happened," Robin said. "His name was Salio. He said the whole time scale that all the books teach was much too long—that it had been invented that way to justify theories that don't hold up anyway. Everything happens much more quickly. It's all going to have to be rethought. Is that what you think?"

"Well, I never thought about it much at all until the last few days," Charlie answered. "But you saw how it happened: new oceans starting to open up, mountain chains lifting while we watched! And it must have gotten even worse after Athena closed in and we lost track. But the information that we've got will be keeping scientists busy for years. You saw how those lava sheets were pouring up out of the rifts in those last images?"

"Yes." Robin shuddered at having to remember.

"I've been thinking about them ever since. There were huge electrical discharges going on between Athena and Earth all the time the sheets were spreading. I figure *that's* what could have caused the magnetic stripe patterns on the old sea beds. The conventional line is that they were written over millions of years by unexplained reversals in the Earth's field. Well, maybe it didn't take millions of years at all. Maybe it was just days!"

Vicki was listening, looking skeptical. "Could it have cooled quickly enough in that short a time?" she asked dubiously.

"We don't know what was going on down there under all that cloud," Charlie pointed out. "Hundreds of feet of ocean had been boiled into the atmosphere. Suppose that under the smoke cover it precipitated out again as ice. Maybe that could cool a surface skin sufficiently to retain magnetism. I don't know. I haven't analyzed the numbers yet."

Keene clipped to an anchor line on the wall and stretched out to rest, tired of following it all. Or was it the carbon dioxide level? He looked around the cabin and yawned. Most of the others were settling down except Dash, who was busy with his narrative, and Cavan and Alicia up front, talking in low voices. . . . And an irritating clanging that he'd just noticed.

It stopped for a few seconds, then started again.

"Is that you, Legermount?" Keene grumbled irritably. "Stop rattling the cage. We're trying to settle down."

"It's not him this time. He's out of it," Reynolds's voice mumbled.

"Then what?" Keene straightened away from the wall, alert suddenly.

Colby turned and showed his empty palms. "It's not me." Joe looked up from something he had been fiddling with close to one of the lights and shook his head.

It came again: *Clang, clang, clang. . . . Clang, clang, clang. . . .*

Keene's head jerked around sharply. There was nobody in the direction that it was coming from. . . . Just the entry hatch. His and Joe's eyes met for a second.

"*Oh my God!*" Joe whispered. He tore free from his anchor line and hurled himself forward to the flight deck section with Keene following.

"Hallelujah!" Reynolds murmured.

Cavan and Alicia were already moving out of the crew positions to make room. Joe's trembling fingers raced over the touchpad to activate the imagers; Keene powered up the controls for the external cameras. A screen came to life showing a drifting starfield as the shuttle turned. Keene rotated the camera outward to get the view abeam of the ship. And, slowly, the most beautiful sight he had ever seen moved into the frame: one of the *Osiris*'s surface landers riding parallel perhaps half a mile off.

"*It's them! They're here! That's them banging on the door!*" he heard himself shouting. Joe brought up the lights. Within seconds, everyone in the cabin was shouting and hugging, laughing and crying. Keene grabbed one of the rifles, which for some reason they had brought aboard, and hauled himself into the entry space behind the hatch. *Thunk, thunk, thunk.*

Joe had a camera trained along the outside of the shuttle's hull. Two figures in bulky, Kronian-style suits were outside the hatch, one poised to beat the surface again with a metal hand tool, the other holding the end of some kind of tube pressed to the hull. Keene beat against the ribbed inner surface of the door again. *Thunk, thunk, thunk.* On the screen, the figure with the tube started making excited gestures and pointing at the ship. The other leaned forward.

Clang, clang, clang sounded from outside the hatch.

Keene responded deliriously. *Thunk, thunk, thunk . . . thunk, thunk, thunk . . . thunk, thunk, thunk . . .*

The lander moved in to make a docking connection, and the fourteen exhausted survivors from the shuttle were transferred over. The two Kronians who had come across were Sariena and Thorel, the engineer from the *Osiris*'s crew. Sariena had wanted to be one of the first to greet them if they were found.

Kronia was sending all the help that could be mobilized. In the meantime, the *Osiris* had been searching the vicinity for days. A number of other ships from Earth had also managed to get away, and the *Osiris* had collected a full complement to take back. The shuttle that Keene had been hoping to organize when last heard of was the last it could afford to wait for. Idorf had been ready to give up, but Gallian wouldn't hear of it.

Events after the launch of the Boxcar from Vandenberg had been as Keene deduced. A second, mysterious ship had inserted itself ahead of the Boxcar as it closed, transmitting fake signals claiming to be the Boxcar pursued by a would-be attacker attempting to use it as a shield. Keene's on-the-spot guess of which one to fire on had been correct. On a sadder note, after all the heroic effort that had been put in, the second Boxcar sent up from Vandenberg later had never been seen. Just one more tragedy among the billions.

❁   ❁   ❁

Thirty minutes later, the Kronian vessel detached and drew away under a mild nudge from an auxiliary thruster. On a screen inside, Keene looked at the empty, silent hulk turning slowly in the sunlight, presenting on its side the last, scarred rendering he would probably ever see of the Amspace Corporation logo.

The lander's main engine fired, and the craft pulled away into a curve that would take it to the waiting *Osiris*.

◎ FURTHER READING ◎

The scientific ideas in this book are based largely on the work of Immanuel Velikovsky (1895–1979). Many readers of the hardback have asked where they might learn more on this background, or catastrophist views in general. The following sources would provide some good starting material.

(1) Immanuel Velikovsky's three major works:

Worlds in Collision, 1950, ISBN 1199848743.
The book that started the whole controversy, identifying the comet of the Exodus as Venus, originating from Jupiter.

Ages in Chaos, 1952, ISBN 0385048971.
Reexamining ancient history in the light of catastrophic events.

Earth in Upheaval, 1955, ISBN 0385041136.
The evidence written into the Earth's geological and biological records.

(2) Carl Sagan and Immanuel Velikovsky,
by Charles Ginenthal, 1995, ISBN 9781561840755.

Over 400 pages presenting findings from space missions and other sources that are consistent with Velikovsky's claims, while contradicting the experts who vilified him.

(3) Velikovsky and Establishment Science,
by Lewis M. Greenberg and Warner B. Sizemore,
eds. ISBN 0917994035.

A comprehensive rejoinder to the publication *Scientists Confront Velikovsky*, which followed the 1974 AAAS conference. What really went on, earning Velikovsky a standing ovation that the media didn't mention.

(4) The Velikovskian

A journal dedicated to studies of the evidence for global catastrophes in human times, along with such related issues as the ancient historic record, evolution and extinction, the dynamics of the Solar System, methods of chronology and dating. Normally 4 issues per year of typically 100-120 pp. each, with occasional special-topic issues. Editor-in-Chief: Charles Ginenthal.

Some titles include:

"Comparing Magnetic Fields: Neptune and Uranus,"
        by Charles Ginenthal
"Velikovsky's 'The Dark Age of Greece,' " by Clark Whelton
"Puzzles of Prehistory," by Roger W. Wescott

"Revisiting Venus's Heat," by George R. Talbott
"The Emerging Revision of Ancient History: Recent Research,"
        by Martin Sieff
"The Origin of Craters on the Moon and Large Lunar Boulders,"
        by Charles Ginenthal
"Thales: The First Astronomer," by William Mullen
"Ocean Sediments, Circimpolar Muck, Erratics, Buried Forests,
        and Loess as Evidence of Global Floods,"
        by Charles Ginenthal
"Phobos and Deimos," by Lynn R. Rose
"Shattering the Myths of Darwinism," by Richard Milton
"The Relevance of the Velikovsky Scenario to the
        Homeric Question," by Hugo Meynell

Send inquiries to:
Charles Ginenthal
IVY Press Books
65-35 108th St, Suite D-15
Forest Hills, NY 11375
718-897-2403

Web: http://www.velikovskian.com/

(5) *Aeon*

A journal of myth, science, and ancient history, frequently exploring theories of different early Solar System configurations.

Send inquiries to:
Ev Cochrane
PO Box 1092
Ames, IA 50014

Web: http://www.aeonjournal.com/
E-mail: ev@aeonJournal.com

(6) Society for Interdisciplinary Studies

Biannual catastrophist journal providing articles and papers on a wide range of related topics, books sources and reviews, and digest of Internet coverage.

Send inquiries to:
The Membership Secretary
Society for Interdisciplinary Studies
45 Mary's Mead
Hazlemere
High Wycombe
Bucks, HP15 7DS, UK

Web: http://www.sis-group.org.uk/

(7) The Immanuel Velikovsky Archive

Archive of Velikovsky's unpublished works.

Web: http://www.varchive.org/
E-mail: reply@varchive.org

THE LEGEND THAT WAS EARTH

◎ PROLOGUE ◎

Sunday was cloudy but WARM in Washington, D.C. The crowd below the Capitol steps, extending westward along the Mall, numbered over ten thousand and was still growing. Although many were colorfully arrayed in summer garb with a sprinkling of coats and jackets, its mood was ugly. Banners displayed above the forest of raised arms, fists punching skyward in unison, proclaimed contingents from individual states. The most highly represented were those like California, Texas, Illinois, heavily dependent on advanced-technology industries. Other banners being waved in the foreground before the news cameras panning over the scene protested: ALIEN PAYOFFS MEAN EARTH LAYOFFS; another: NO TO FARDEN SELLOUT; and: DEMAND TRADE CONTROL. To one side near the front, a black female agitator in red leather and braids was leading a group chanting militantly: *"Fuck you!/Where's ours too?"* Riot police looked on from the sides, with vehicles and reserves being held back on Canal Street and Louisiana Avenue.

From the podium at the top of the steps, flanked by grim-faced figures in suits and a few military uniforms behind a cordon of police armed with shields and batons, the speaker who had been repeatedly interrupted leaned toward the microphone again.

"Will you people hear me out? . . . Is a little bit of common decency and courtesy too much to ask? . . . What I'm saying is that things are

not the way you think. The contraction of some businesses and industries is natural and inevitable when two diverse cultures come into contact. It spells even greater opportunities opening up in other areas—areas where the things we're better at will be uniquely favored."

Somebody with a bullhorn replied from among the crowd. *"That's bullshit."*

The voice of the police commissioner in charge of crowd control came over loudspeakers set up on pylons: *"THIS IS THE LAST TIME. THERE WILL BE NO FURTHER WARNINGS."*

The speaker resumed. *"To suggest that our economy is being sold off piecemeal is an emotionally motivated misrepresentation of the facts. The facts are—"*

"Tell it to the Bolivians," the bullhorn responded.

Somebody at the front, a TV camera trained directly on him, raised both arms wide to draw attention and shouted, "Why won't Farden come out and speak for himself? We know he's in there. What's he afraid of?"

"Senator Farden is—"

"Selling us out," the bullhorn completed. A roar went up to endorse the judgment. The speaker at the podium looked in the direction of the senior police and Internal Security Service officers watching and shook his head helplessly. The commissioner nodded to an aide, who gave orders into a hand phone. From among the police massed on the lawns bordering Independence Avenue came a helmeted snatch squad in gas masks. Flailing batons and using their shields as battering rams, they plowed through the crowd toward the spot where surveillance cameras had located the bullhorn. Some of the crowd closed protectively around the target, while others assailed the snatch team with bottles and other missiles. Reinforcements moved in; figures began falling, others retreating, and within seconds mêlées were breaking out across the entire scene. An angry surge pressed back the cordon guarding the Capitol steps. Above, the police helicopter that had been circling came in lower. The commissioner signaled, and security agents began herding the speaker and entourage back toward the doors into the building. Armored cars

with mesh-protected windows nosed out from the side streets. Through the rising clamor, the flat *plops* sounded of gas grenades bursting where the clashes were fiercest, followed by figures falling back, coughing and retching amid clouds of white vapor.

Senator Joel Farden from Virginia watched darkly from a window in one of the rooms of the Capitol. He had said there was no point trying to reason with a crowd in that mood. People with no concepts beyond immediate gratification or waiting passively for a better investment to pay off would never be possessors of anything worthwhile to bargain with. Therefore, inevitably, they were the first to lose out in any reshuffle. There was nothing anyone could do; it was the way things were and had always been. The exploitation they complained about was in their genes, just as it was in those of others to come out on top. Trying to deny what everyone had to know deep down was obvious could only result in the denial and rage that they were seeing. Now the mess would take years, probably, to work itself out. Then somebody else with delusions would start demanding fairness for all, and the pattern would go on as it always had. Unless those with the power to do so changed the system. Orderliness and discipline. The Hyadeans had the right idea.

Below the window, knots of demonstrators broke through the police cordon and started scrambling up the steps toward the building. A squad that had been kept in the rear moved forward, equipped with back-mounted devices connected to nozzles. They resembled flame throwers but fired a white stream that turned into an expanding foam engulfing the oncoming rioters. In moments, the foam congealed into an elastic, adhesive mass, inside which the forms of victims could be seen struggling ineffectually. Those immediately behind fell back, while howls of outrage came from farther back. On both sides of the Mall violence intensified as groups trying to flee the area ran into police reserves moving in. An intense, low-pitched drone that seemed to fill the air came from outside, rattling the window, vibrating the structure of the building, and churning Farden's stomach even at that distance, making him feel mildly dizzy and nauseated. Across the Mall, figures were screaming and clutching their ears, others doubling over and vomiting. A hand gripped his shoulder. He turned. It was Purlow, the ISS security agent assigned for Farden's personal protection.

"I'm sorry, Senator, but speeches are over for today. The whole situation's deteriorating. We're getting you and the general out early. The flyer is waiting now. This way please, sir."

Farden hesitated briefly, then nodded. He followed Purlow back through the suite of rooms, across a marbled hall, and down a stairway to one of the entrances on the far side of the building. A secretary was waiting with his briefcase and topcoat among the group of officials, uniformed officers, and several Hyadeans in the vestibule. Farden took them from her just as Lieutenant General Meakes appeared with his own small personal retinue. Meakes was another figure that the agitators had demonized and the mobs loved to hate. Farden had never really seen the connection, since Meakes didn't have a financial angle, stayed out of politics, and had always confined himself to Army matters. But since when had truth or concern about character defamation troubled political terrorists when they saw an opportunity?

Edmund Kovansky, from the White House staff, seemed to be organizing things. "You were right, Joel," he said as Farden approached. "This was ill-conceived from the start. I guess we'll be having a moratorium and plan-of-action meeting out at Overly later." Farden would be going back to Overly Park, the Maryland estate where he was staying while visiting Washington. It was owned by a financier called Eric York, who was part of Farden's social and business circle. There was little gratification in being told that just at this moment. Not bothering to reply, Farden stepped forward in the direction of the doorway, following Meakes and another officer who it seemed would be traveling with him. Kovansky caught him with a gesture indicating two of the Hyadeans. "And there's a last-minute addition," Kovansky said. "These two want to go with you, if that's okay. They have business with Eric."

Farden paused long enough to return a shrug. "Sure. Why not?" It was their flyer, after all.

Surrounded by a security escort, the party left the building and walked briskly across the open area of grass and trees separating the

Capitol from the Supreme Court and Library of Congress, which had been blocked off by police barricades. The Hyadean flyer was waiting among an assortment of official vehicles and several black-painted ISS helicopters. Dull silver, about the size of a typical hotel courtesy bus, it had the form of a flattened ellipsoid blending into stub wings toward the stern, with a tail fin and several streamlined nacelles and bulges. There were no crew stations, operation being fully automatic, and no nozzles or visible propulsion unit. Farden climbed the steps unfolding down over the port wing root and entered behind Meakes and the other officer, with the two Hyadeans following. The interior was typically Hyadean: stark and utilitarian, with seats and decor of uniform gray making some concession to comfort, but beyond that not a hint of pattern, contrast, or ornamentation to relieve the drabness. Hyadean minds just didn't work that way.

The occupants settled themselves in; moments later, the door closed soundlessly, and the vehicle lifted off. One of the Hyadeans said something, and two of the cabin's upper wall panels became transparent to admit a tinted view of the cloud bank enlarging and taking on detail as the flyer climbed; at the same time, a screen at the forward end activated to present a downward-looking view of the turmoil among the crowds along the east end of the Mall and the surrounding streets.

Farden studied the two aliens in a detached kind of way as they peered at the screen—they had been around long enough, and he had seen enough of them by now, not to be unduly curious. They were tall and blockish in build, with square-cut features like the heroes of old-time comic strips, giving their faces a squashed look, and skin color ranging from purple to light blue-gray. Their generally humanoid form had caused consternation among scientific ranks when they first came to Earth, because according to the then prevailing theories such similarity resulting from separate evolutionary processes unfolding in isolation shouldn't have been possible. The matter had been one of indifference to Farden, who had never paid much attention to scientific theories anyway, and as far as he knew it still wasn't settled. Their hair came in all manner of hues, the two present on this occasion having glossy black showing blue highlights in one case, and a dull coppery red in the other, both trimmed in the standard Hyadean manner. And both wore the familiar tunic-like garb, plain in color, one drab green, the other brown, purely functional, devoid of decoration or appeal to aesthetic styling.

They exchanged utterances in their own language. Then the black-haired one spoke down toward his breast pocket. A voice replied in Hyadean, but including recognizably the words "very long." Hyadeans carried a kind of pocket Artificial Intelligence that acted as a secretary and librarian, and could help them with language translation and other matters. Terrans called the device a "veebee," standing for voxbox. The Hyadean explained to the three Terrans:

"My companion is not here, at Earth, for very long. The ways are new and strange. At Chryse, people acting like that would be . . ." He consulted his veebee again. "Unthinkable." Chryse was the Hyadeans' home world, a planet of the hitherto unnamed star Amaris, in the vicinity of the constellations Hyades and the Pleiades, in the sign of Taurus.

"That word tends to suggest disapproval," Meakes commented. "That he doesn't agree."

The Hyadean who had spoken conversed briefly with the red-headed one. "He does not approve. He asks how leaders can function."

"Tell him we agree on that," Farden said, at the same time praying inwardly that this stunted attempt at conversation wouldn't endure all through the flight.

"One reason we are here is that we educate . . ." (the veebee interjected something) "to educate Earth in organizing a system that will avoid such things. That way means wealth and peace for all. As is true for Hyadean worlds."

Meakes nodded. "I'll say amen to that."

"Excuse me. I am not familiar with 'amen' in this context," the veebee's voice said from the black-haired Hyadean's breast pocket.

"It means . . . True? Truly?" Meakes looked at Farden and the other Army officer inquiringly. They returned shrugs. "Anyhow, I agree with that too," he said.

"Thanks. Noted," the veebee acknowledged.

The black-haired Hyadean waved to indicate the interior of the vehicle. "And we will make Terrans into better scientists, so maybe one day you build craft like these too." What most people considered "tact" wasn't exactly the aliens' strongest point. When they felt superior or considered themselves to be at an advantage in some respect, they made sure to let everyone know. Farden nodded noncommittally. The exchange continued bravely for a minute or so more and then died, and the occupants lapsed into talk in lowered tones with their own kind.

Farden leaned back against the rubbery headrest and thought over what his position would be later at the meeting Kovansky had alluded to, in the light of the day's events. At least the seats were of alien proportions, which was an improvement over a lot of traveling accommodations that he had endured. Another reason for preferring to use Hyadean vessels whenever possible was that the on-board defenses were fast and accurate enough to stop any Terran-produced missile before it got closer than ten miles, or a ground-launched shot from immediately below within a second of firing. With political terrorists in the U.S. taking on the regular military now, and acquiring all kinds of weapons, one couldn't take too many precautions. . . .

Unfortunately, the bolt of plasma fired from below when the flyer was twelve miles north of the city came from a weapon that wasn't Terran, and the radars on Hyadean vessels fitted for Earth duty were designed only to look for missiles. It hit the flyer dead center, vaporizing it instantly.

❀ CHAPTER ONE ❀

Roland Cade stood on the boat dock at the rear of his waterfront villa on an inlet at Newport Beach, taking a moment off from the preparations inside the house to enjoy the cool air and admire the embers of a flaming California sunset. Lights were beginning to show from the other homes across the narrow waterway and among the moored boats, reflecting off the barely rippling surface. A mild breeze brought the aroma of steaks being barbecued somewhere. On the inland side, clouds of starlings were rising and wheeling in their last sortie of the day. For some people, life was good.

Warren Edmonds, the skipper of Cade's ninety-foot motor yacht *Sassy Lady*, appeared on the foredeck and came down to join Cade on the dock. He was wirily muscular, with lean features that a shock of black hair receding at the temples seemed to throw into hard-lined relief. Edmonds had managed boats large and small, corporate and private, from Seattle to San Diego. He ran a number of enterprises of his own—some of which were quasi-legal at best—which Cade didn't ask about, hence working for Cade suited him. And Cade's numerous legal contacts and acquaintances who owed him favors could be useful at times.

"Everything set and standing by, if we decide to go," he told Cade. Given the balmy condition of the evening, Cade was considering moving the party out onto the water later if the general mood so inclined.

"Did Henry bring out the extra case of Chardonnay?"

"Yes, it's in the cooler."

"No sudden changes expected in the weather?"

"I checked about fifteen minutes ago. It's gonna be calm like this all night, somewhere in the low sixties. Maybe a little cloud tomorrow. Nothing that'll change your day."

Cade showed his palms. "The gods are smiling, Warren."

"I guess we must have done something right lately." Edmonds sighed in a way that said he couldn't think what, but to make the best of it. "Did their flight get out on time—with all the trouble in Washington earlier?"

"The Web said it did when Luke checked, just before he left to go meet them. I don't think Andrews was affected. Vrel would have let us know by now if there were any changes. . . ." Cade looked back as Henry's voice called from the house to see if he was out there. "Uh-uh. You can't hide anywhere. It sounds as if all's in order out here. Carry on, Chief."

"You bet."

Cade walked back along the short path past shrubbery and flowers losing their colors in the fading light. The white-haired figure of Henry, the house steward, wearing a maroon jacket and tie, was peering from the doorway of the glass-shuttered patio. "Norman Schnyder and his associate are here—Anita Lloyd. Julia and Neville are talking to them now. Also, the catering people have started setting up." That was in case Cade wanted to check anything personally before it got too late to change. Henry had been with Cade long enough to know his ways.

They crossed the patio and passed through a sun lounge with cane furniture and potted plants to the central area of the house, where staff from the catering company handling the buffet were arranging tablecloths and unpacking dishes. While Henry bustled off to attend to something else, Cade ran an eye over the linen, satisfying himself that it was properly pleated and pressed, examined the china and silverware for quality, and looked inside the ice chest containing the marinated crab claws and Oysters Rockefeller to verify that the serving shells were real and not ceramic. Finding nothing amiss, he contented himself with straightening the slightly crooked bow tie of one of the servers, winked at him with a mild "Tch, tch," and went through to the sitting area of paneling and leather upholstery surrounding the bar. Neville Baxter, a businessman from New Zealand, who had arrived early, stopping by at the party to say his farewells before going back in the next few days, was sprawled in one of the easy chairs, a foot crossed over the other knee. He was florid-faced, beefy, and jovial, tonight sporting a lightweight cream jacket and scarlet crimson shirt, open-necked with a riotous silk cravat at the neck. Norman Schnyder and Anita sat nursing drinks on the couch opposite him. Julia must have gone off somewhere to attend to some detail—ever the conscientious hostess.

"Here's the man!" Baxter said, waving across as Cade came in.

Cade helped himself to a Jamesons Irish from the bar and joined them. "Hi, Anita . . . Norman. So how are things? I don't detect any signs of incipient poverty."

"Norman showed up in that new Lamborghini I'm told he's been talking about for a hundred years," Baxter told Cade. "It makes me feel really glad that I don't pay any of that firm's bills."

"Got to be able to catch the ambulances," Schnyder said, sipping his drink. He looked suave and opulent, with hair showing silver at the sides of his tanned face, a dark suit with narrow pinstripe, and expensively glittering tie clip and links. Anita Lloyd, in her early thirties, with auburn hair styled into chic, forward-sweeping points, wearing a sleeveless navy dress with elbow-length satin gloves, had just banked her first million the last time Cade talked to her. They were senior partner and associate respectively of an LA law firm that had been seeing some good years. Henry always got his terms precisely right.

Anita eyed Cade's five-eleven frame in white dinner jacket with black tie. He kept athletically trim at thirty-six, and had wavy brown hair combed back at the sides above an angular face with narrow nose, easy-smiling mouth, and eyes that never quite lost a puckish glint. "You seem to be bearing the burdens of life pretty well yourself, Roland," she remarked.

"Which just goes to show the wisdom of pure thoughts, clean living, and faith in the Lord."

"But be sure to keep a good lawyer in your back pocket all the same," Schnyder said.

"You mean like something to break the glass, in case of an emergency?" Cade quipped, making a toasting gesture.

"Don't joke. You never know. We had a bar in town sued the other week for serving a guy who had a liver condition and *knew* he couldn't take it. Would you believe that? I mean, what are they supposed to do—check everybody's medical records now?"

Julia appeared in the archway to the front part of the house, calling something back to Henry about a rose tree by the front door. She saw Cade, picked up a glass of champagne that she had left on a side table, and came over, perching herself on a couch-arm next to where he was standing and resting her free hand lightly on his shoulder. Julia was Cade's business partner and significant other in life, having moved in to share the house a little over a year before. She was tall, lithe, and red-haired, with a feline elegance of movement that exuded sexuality. Tonight she had enhanced the effect with an ankle-length dress of body-clinging moiré that altered in the light between bottle-green and sage-yellow, set off by an emerald bracelet and earrings. Her former husband ran a couple of night clubs that the right people in southern California frequented, which meant that she knew a lot of names that were worth knowing, making her a natural for Cade to get attached to. Knowing the right people was what Cade's business was all about.

She tasted her drink and ran a questioning eye over the company. "So, what problems of the world are we putting right tonight?"

"Have you seen Norman's new wheels yet?" Anita asked.

"Yes. And I feel sick. Why do you think I'm wearing green?" Julia nudged Cade pointedly. "I want one."

"Sounds like I'd better check with Simon and see what our money's in," Cade replied.

"Well, I hope you don't have too much of it in computers or electronics—or anything high-tech, by the sound of it," Baxter said. "Norman was saying just before you came in that the bottom's falling out across the board. The Hyadeans are going to be flooding the market here with better stuff at prices you can't even think about."

Schnyder was already nodding. "Their production is all run by AIs—totally automatic. Matching what we use here costs them practically nothing. It's like beads. A lot of industries are in trouble."

Cade tried not to let things like that affect him. It was the way life was. Things changed; you couldn't stop them. If you were smart you adapted and let yourself go with the flow. It wasn't his place to protect those who chose to stay in places where they were going to lose out. "There's a lot of opposition out there," he said. "That has to have some moderating effect, surely. The government isn't going to just let it happen."

Schnyder shook his head. "Forget it, Roland. The bills will go through. Too much of Congress is in for a piece of the action. We're talking big bucks here. They're not going to lose out."

Cade and Julia looked at each other, and both made a face. "So what should we be buying into?" Julia asked, looking back.

"You really wanna know?" Schnyder invited.

"Sure. That's why I asked."

"Navajo blankets and sand paintings. Porcelains and sculptures. Hand-built cabinets and carvings—like from that little firm in Santa Monica that they did the show on last week. Did you see it?"

"No, I don't think so."

"Native talents," Anita said. "The Hyadeans don't have anything to compare."

"Is it really the way some people say?" Julia sounded incredulous.

"We've got someone coming here tonight who's been saying the same thing," Cade told the group. "Damien Philps—an export dealer in that kind of thing to Chryse and the other Hyadean worlds for a few years now. Says it's going to grow like crazy."

"Then you should listen to him," Schnyder urged. "It's getting to be a rage with them. You wouldn't believe the prices I've heard for some of the things that went there."

"Want to buy into some totem poles?" Cade asked Julia. He looked away as Henry appeared once more from the depths of the house. "Yes, Henry?"

"Luke just called. He's at LAX now, with Dee. The aircraft has been cleared for landing. With traffic as it is, he says they'll be here in about an hour."

"Tell the caterers to start setting out the food in thirty minutes," Cade instructed. "But let's have a few appetizers out here in the meantime."

❧ CHAPTER TWO ❧

"Side-panel to view mode," Vrel told the veebee, which he had laid on the tray at the front of his seat's armrest along with the screenpad he had been using during the flight. The veebee passed the order on to the control system of the Hyadean staff transport descending over the Terran city of Los Angeles, and the part of the wall alongside became transparent. Vrel rested his chin on a hand and stared out at the carpet of horizon-to-horizon lights. Of the dozen-odd other Hyadeans around him in the cabin, some were talking in murmurs, others wrapped in their own thoughts. Krossig, the anthropologist, was reading. Orzin had dozed through the flight, after a busy schedule in Washington as an official observer assessing Terran reactions to further moves in Hyadean–U.S. cooperation. Hyadean policy was to concentrate on the United States as the focus of Terran political and economic influence.

As with all the cities he had seen here, the conception and layout showed little regard for efficiency or logic, although Terrans were not incapable of such qualities when it suited them. The failure to strike a better balance between building out and building up multiplied travel distances enormously. Trusting to manually controlled vehicles in this kind of traffic density brought appalling problems that the Terrans didn't deny, yet they made no serious attempt to do anything about them. Vrel sometimes thought that the chaotic daily sorties along the Interstates might provide some kind of ritual combat that their adversity-conditioned psyches needed. And they had no concept of segregating north-south traffic flows from east-west on different levels with connecting ramps, with the result that everything was squeezed onto a two-dimensional grid where all movement one way had to be stopped for half the time at every intersection. He wondered what they'd have thought of a computer chip designed that way, with all the wires on one plane, and switches to allow current through a crossover one way or the other at any time only.

But things like electronics and optronics weren't really Vrel's line. A political economist and social commentator, he had first come to Earth almost six (Terran) years ago now, with several trips back and forth to Chryse in the interim. And even after that time, he still found himself more than occasionally bewildered by this intoxicating world with its wild extremes of ecology and climate: plunging chasms and slabs of crust thrown up into snow-topped mountains, and stupefying proliferation of every form of life imaginable to the Hyadean mind—and then some. And to crown all of it, this volatile, quarrelsome race of pinks and yellows and browns and black, short and slender in form, yet curiously appropriate as the culminating expression of the unruliness and vivacity that characterized the whole planet.

At first, Vrel had been bemused by the diversity of governing systems: money-based, land-based, hereditary, military, planned and chaotic, popular choice or authoritarian; by the clashes of ideologies and traditions, spawning creeds and sects of every description, and mixtures of all of them which not even the Terrans seemed to understand. That was the usual Hyadean reaction. It was as if the only discernible universal attribute was the determination not to let anything be universal, leaving such authorities as existed virtually powerless to channel collective energies into achieving the kind of planetary efficiency that could have yielded ten times the productivity with a tenth the effort and spared all the grief and chaos entirely. Weren't the events that had occurred today in Washington illustration enough?

A year ago, Vrel would have thought so unhesitatingly. Now, after spending the last six months at the Hyadean West Coast Trade and Cultural Mission in Los Angeles, he was no longer so sure. Earth was an exotic planet, its surface fresh and young, sculpted only recently by catastrophic forces that affect planetary systems from time to time, and which Terran scientists, for the most part—until the arrival of the Hyadeans—had ignored or failed to understand. This made Earth unlike any of the other worlds to which the Hyadeans had so far spread, including Chryse, whose surfaces were old, shaped over eons by processes of erosion and leveling that rendered them by comparison weary-looking and drab.

The Terrans too were products of those same upheavals which not long ago had reformed, revitalized, and enriched their planet. Vrel was finding that their capacity for seeking fulfillment and finding "meaning" to their existence in ways that went beyond the obvious aim of attaining tangible benefits—which in the early days had been so baffling—now intrigued him. Could their astonishing intuitiveness and creativity, which both enabled them to soar into realms of fancy that no Hyadean mind would conceive, and at the same time wrought havoc with their sciences, represent a state of being that was "closer" to the origins of the forces that drove life, just as they themselves were closer to the creative impetus that triggered the last epoch of their evolution? If so, then maybe there were things the Hyadeans might stand to learn from Earth before they got too zealous about importing their own ideas and social system. Things the Hyadeans themselves had once possessed and forgotten, perhaps?

The veebee beeped to attract attention, then announced, "Incoming call. From Luke, who will be meeting the flight. He says to tell you Dee is with him."

"Put it through." Vrel smiled as he picked up the screenpad. Luke's face appeared: elongated Terran features, black hair, and the tuft of "beard" that some Terrans cultivated—Hyadeans didn't have facial hair. "Hello, Luke," Vrel acknowledged in English. He had been working at it assiduously through his stay and was as proficient as any Hyadean. "And Dee's there?" The image shifted for a moment to show Dee waving, then returned to Luke. Vrel thought of Luke as Roland Cade's second-in-command as well as being a personal friend of Cade and Julia—usually around to make sure things got done, generally a part of the house and business. On Chryse, senior political and military figures relied on somebody like that, who was more than just an assigned administrator, to manage the detailed aspects of their lives and channel the right information to them.

"We're out on the field and will pick you up right off the plane," Luke said. "There's a car from the mission here too. I guess somebody there has decided to pass on the party and made their own arrangements."

The others in the cabin had been alerted by the cabin indicators to prepare for landing and were collecting their belongings together. Krossig would be going back to the house, naturally. So would Erya, the female involved with education, who was on her way back to Chryse and would be joining one of the orbiting Hyadean ships via the spaceport in Brazil. She was the type who could overcome Hyadean reserve sufficiently to enjoy a little unofficial entertainment Earth-style before returning to her familiar world, where everything had to be as stipulated and directed. Shayle, on the other hand, returning to her administrative post in the South American enclave, was always officious and disapproving of the irregular. She would shun any suggestion of letting standards slip and go back to the mission. Orzin, a figure of some authority, maintained an outwardly correct manner, but Vrel had seen hints that it concealed a different self that wasn't above a little off-limits relaxation when the occasion permitted. The rest of the group were either returning from Washington to their posts in South America or going on to Chryse. Vrel didn't know them well enough to guess who would be going where. Given Orzin's lead, most of them might opt for Cade's party, if for no greater reason than curiosity. Three sitting together, upright and proper, would no doubt be going back to the mission with Shayle. Somehow, Vrel couldn't imagine Terrans making such an issue out of an invitation to attend a party. Maybe he was starting to think a little bit like one.

The transport landed, and the Hyadeans disembarked via a covered escalator brought up to the door. Shayle and the three that Vrel had picked out departed at once in a Terran automobile, registering disapproval by declining to say a word. Luke and Dee were standing in front of a limousine-quality minibus. Vrel introduced the remaining Hyadeans except Krossig, whom they already knew because he worked with Vrel in LA. Dee had shoulder-length blond hair, fringed at the front, and was wearing a light wrap over a stretchy orange dress. She slipped an arm through Vrel's as they began walking around the bus. He had to suppress an impulse to flinch at the public display, reminding himself that he was back among Terrans now. A week of conforming to Hyadean protocols had reawakened his social reflexes. One of the arrivals nudged a companion and raised his eyebrows, not a little enviously. Terran women had a reputation among Hyadeans for being sensuous. Vrel pretended not to notice, resisting the conflicting urge to put on a little showiness. Opportunistic exhibitions of good fortune or superiority were considered bad manners here.

"Good flight?" Dee asked him.

"Just fine."

"I was a bit worried . . . with all that trouble on the news this afternoon."

"It was ugly. But we weren't really involved. How's Roland?"

"Oh, he never changes. Going with the flow."

That was a new one. Vrel checked with his veebee. It returned the best it could come up with. "He's on the river?" Vrel repeated, looking puzzled.

Dee laughed. "It means living life as it comes. Not fighting it. Making the best of whatever comes along."

"That sounds like Roland," Vrel agreed.

"One day you'll learn how not to rely on a computer all the time and develop your instincts instead," Dee told him. They climbed into the minibus. There were all-round leather seats, a screen, and a bar. Background music was playing of a kind that Vrel had learned to identify as strings. Classical Terran music had a big following among Hyadeans.

"Who was the composer of this piece?" Vrel asked the veebee in Hyadean.

"Antonio Vivaldi. 1678 to 1741. Born in Venice, Italy."

"And did you get the thing about the river. . . . What was it again?"

"Going with the flow."

"Oh, right. It means . . ." Vrel frowned and thought back. "Not fighting life. Taking things as they come. Is that right?"

"Close enough," the veebee replied.

❀ **CHAPTER THREE** ❀

Other Hyadeans had arrived direct from the Trade and Cultural Mission by the time Luke and Dee returned with the party from the airport. A number of unattached Terran women, all of them attractive, stylish, sophisticated, and sociable, had also begun arriving.

To most Terrans, Hyadeans came across as rather conformist and image-conscious. From what they were told or saw on Hyadean productions carried by Terran media, life on Chryse and its colonized worlds seemed overstructured and regimented. An example was the rigidity of rules governing dealings between the sexes, which by most Terran standards came across as stiff and prudish. Partly in consequence, Hyadeans found Earth a mysterious, exciting place, where sensual indulgence and freedom of expression which at best would have been frowned upon back home were regarded as normal. Biological nature being apparently much the same in at least the nearby regions of the galaxy, it followed that more than a few Hyadeans would develop a taste for, or curiosity to sample, at least, a little of the risqué that Earth's cultural phantasmagoria had to offer.

Of course, it wouldn't do for visiting officials and other prominent individuals to be seen actively pursuing or even expressing interest in such diversions. But if the price was right, most things could be arranged with discretion. That was where people like Roland Cade came in. Cade was a "fixer." He knew the right people. If a Hyadean wanted to send a small package of coffee, spices, perfumes, a selection of alcoholic bracers, perhaps, to impress the folks back home, where such things tended to be illegal or restricted, Cade had a contact who did business with the Hyadean in charge of loading the surface lifters going up from their spaceport at Xuchimbo in western Brazil. Or if one was tempted to get away from routine for an evening to eat a dinner Terran-style with fresh animal meat (practically unheard of) cooked in unimaginable sauces, washed down with delicious fermented plant juices, while listening to the music they composed spontaneously, and afterward maybe get to dance with a Terran girl (body contact!)—Cade could set something up in places from California to New York, or beyond that refer you to somebody in Russia, Algeria, Britain, or Japan. For a particular kind of souvenir of one's stay on Earth, or for importing high-demand Terran creations, or to find an outlet on Earth for spare Hyadean production capacity that could be made profitable, Cade had the contacts. And naturally, everyone paid for the favor. Sometimes Cade thought that it was impossible for a Hyadean and a Terran to meet without money falling out of the sky for him somewhere. Indeed, it seemed that for him the phrase had come true literally.

He stood with Michael Blair on one side of the buffet area in the center of the house, catching strands of conversations. The Hyadeans who were new to this had at first stood together, males and females alike in their plain, tunic-like suits, sipping fruit juices and surreptitiously popping the pills they were told they needed to guard against untamed Terran germs and food prepared by suspect methods—the Hyadean authorities were tyrannical over health care. Now, at last, they were livening up: sampling the seafood dishes, sipping from the glasses that the wine steward had been told to move liberally, and beginning to mingle. There was a hot food table with roasts of beef, pork, and ham for the more daring. Julia was doing her usual great job as hostess, prying the more stodgy out of chairs and corners where they had taken refuge, steering together the right introductions, and igniting conversations with the élan of an arsonist loose in an oil refinery. The two lawyers and a couple of Hyadeans were talking to George Jansing, who was making a fortune contracting Terran software design skills to the Hyadeans—and also taking the opportunity to show off some Hyadean that he had learned. With them was Clara Norburn, tall, lean, raven-haired, from the state governor's office, her sights firmly set on the opportunities for social and professional advancement that political visibility offered. "I'd like to redirect more of California's technical talent in that direction," Cade heard her telling them. "It sounds really profitable."

"Five times what you'd get from the home market," Jansing said.

"It's this human thing that you call flair," one of the Hyadeans explained. "Our machine designs do the job and are solid. But they are never what you'd describe as brilliant. I have examined some of the tricks and shortcuts that Terran programmers come up with. They astound me."

Dee and Vrel's precedent had encouraged several of the other Hyadeans to try nervous lines with the Terran girls—becoming less nervous as the girls and the wine steward assiduously plied their respective trades.

"I have a wife back on Chryse," a Hyadean told a brunette in purple and pink. "But she doesn't really . . ." He questioned a veebee in his pocket. "Understand me."

"Gee," the brunette said to her companion. "Now there's one I haven't heard before."

"You see, Roland—the same genes everywhere," Blair said to Cade. Blair was some kind of scientist involved with behavior and biology, formerly with the University of California. Nowadays, he conducted private research, a lot of it at the Hyadean mission, trying to learn more of the aliens' sciences, since just about everything he had believed before they showed up had turned out to be wrong. He had been explaining to Cade that the reason why human and Hyadean forms were so alike, confounding traditional ideas of evolution, was that the genetic programs that directed the building of life forms didn't originate on planets at all, but arrived there as space-borne microbes. Planets were simply assembly stations where cues provided by the local environments triggered the programs to express themselves differently. So, similar environments would produce similar collections of shapes and forms. Earth's was more diverse, hence richer in diversity, that was all.

"So where do these programs get written in the first place?" Cade asked.

"They don't know."

"Do they have any theories about it?'

"Not really. They've never really thought about it."

Cade turned his head incredulously. "You're kidding!" Although no scientist, he assumed that would be the obvious question.

Blair motioned with his glass. He looked the academic, with graying hair brushed to the side and parted, metal-framed spectacles, and a rubbery, expressive face that made a joke of any attempt to conceal his mood. As a concession to the occasion he had donned a dark jacket with tie and slacks. But he could have added an evening shave while he was at it. "That's the amazing thing. Their minds just aren't like that. They don't make big theories that try to explain everything. They just look at the evidence that's there and stick to that."

"So is that how come they got here, but we didn't get there?" Cade queried.

"Maybe that's what it needs—just accepting the facts and not trying to go beyond them. They don't have religion either. That's another thing about us that fascinates them. Krossig says Hyadeans could never have come up with anything like that. But they see a lot of what we think is science as being not very different. We get wrapped up in our own inventions and then convince ourselves that what we see is really out there."

Neville Baxter sauntered by, telling a joke to a petite blonde in blue who was clinging to his arm and looking appreciative. ". . . and God said, 'It doesn't cost anything. It's free.' So Moses said, 'I'll take ten!' " He nudged Cade in passing, as if to say, *See, even fuddy-duddy, middle-age-spreading New Zealanders can make out okay too.*

The group that included Norman Schnyder had got onto the subject of Terran industries folding because of cheap Hyadean imports, and the increasingly militant political opposition movement. "I've never understood why we need those markets," one of the Hyadeans commented, maybe trying to be diplomatic.

"Oh, I'd have thought it's obvious," Schnyder said. "To earn currency here that can be reinvested in land. That's where the big payoffs are going to be. Industrial trading is just the key to the door."

"Isn't that what the guerrilla war in South America is all about . . . ?" Anita Lloyd began, then faltered as she realized it wasn't a good topic to bring up in polite Terran-Hyadean company. Cade rescued her by stepping closer and moving things along.

"You're bound to have clashes when different kinds of people meet, and there's change. But it always works out better for everyone in the long run. The hotheads will get hurt, but they bring it on themselves. There's nothing you can do." He smiled as Julia came over with a fresh drink for him, and slid an arm around her waist. "The woman I used to be married to was a hothead like that," he told the group. "Not accepting change; thinking she could stop it. Well, she's not here anymore, and all of us are. That should say something." He wasn't quite sure himself what it should say, he realized; but it sounded good.

Damien Philps, the arts and crafts dealer that Cade had mentioned to Schnyder earlier, was listening to Erya, the Hyadean educationist who was on her way back to Chryse, marveling at the powers of human creativity. Vrel and Dee were with them along with Wyvex, a colleague of Vrel's from the mission, who was currently collecting information on Terran art forms to satisfy the interest being generated back home. He was tall, even for a Hyadean, and had dark rust hair with orange streaks, cropped fairly short to a central point. Hair styling was one of the few modes of personal expression that Hyadeans seemed to permit themselves—maybe as a consequence of the wide natural variations of colors and textures. Although attired in the unvarying Hyadean gray tunic, he had made the virtually unheard-of concession of adorning it with a badge sewn on the breast pocket, showing a colorful Navajo design, proclaiming his newfound specialty on Earth. Apparently, it had never occurred to Hyadeans to ornament clothing and other objects for no other reason than pure aesthetics. The practice had begun catching on lately on Chryse, putting research like Wyvex's in great demand.

"Erya has discovered Terran classical composers," Vrel told Cade. "She's started learning the violin and wants to set up a music school on Chryse when she gets back. Do you know any teachers who'd be interested in emigrating?"

"I'm sure I could find a few," Cade answered.

"*Ode* is causing a sensation there," Erya said.

"So I heard." *Ode to Joy* was an exported Warner movie about the life of Beethoven. Cade thought for a moment. "How soon will you be going back?" he asked Erya.

"I'll be in LA for a week. Then flying down to Brazil a day before launch. Why?"

Cade's eyes twinkled, as if he were stretching out something suspenseful. "How would you like one of the actual violins used in the movie as a present to take with you?" he asked. He knew someone in Hollywood who he figured could probably swing it.

Erya stared at him disbelievingly, and then, evidently not knowing what to say, asked her veebee for a suitable expression. "You're kidding!" she told him finally.

Cade shrugged, not letting his amusement show. "I won't stake my life on it, but I'll see what I can do. We might be able to surprise you." Hyadeans found it hard to conceive of a simple favor. Everything they did seemed to be determined by some kind of intricate cost-benefit analysis that computed tangible gain. Their actions tended to be totally pragmatic, directed toward measurable "efficiency" with little feeling for any deeper value system. Maybe that was why they found Earth so incomprehensible and mysterious.

Wyvex spoke, looking at Erya. "There is a Hyadean called Tevlak, down in South America—in Bolivia, I think. He's very much involved in promoting Terran art back on Chryse. You ought to meet him before you go back—or at least talk to him if your schedule doesn't allow it."

"I'd like to," Erya said.

"I'll try to arrange it."

At that moment, Luke appeared with Henry in the archway from the front part of the house and signaled for Cade's attention. Cade excused himself and went over. Luke drew him through, away from all the attention. "We've got police at the door, and a Lieutenant Rossi from the ISS," he murmured.

Cade frowned. "What's it about?"

"Something to do with that aircar that was shot down near Washington this afternoon," Luke said. Cade sighed and went with them to the front door. Two men in suits were waiting, with figures in police uniforms standing behind and in the driveway. The smaller of the two introduced himself as Rossi. He had fair, sleeked-back hair, a thin line of a mustache, and that cold-eyed, dispassionate look that seemed to go with factotums of enforcement bureaucracies everywhere.

"As you probably know, Mr. Cade, four individuals were assassinated in an incident that took place in Washington today, including two Hyadeans. We have reason to believe that the deaths of the Hyadeans were not planned. However, it's still an embarrassment to the administration. As a precaution, it has been decided to keep prominent Hyadeans under extended security protection for the time being. A guard has been placed at their mission building in Lakewood. Our instructions are to escort your Hyadean guests back when they are finished here. I apologize for any inconvenience."

Cade snorted. "We were thinking of maybe moving things out on the water," he commented, mostly to test how serious this was.

Rossi shook his head. "Under the circumstances, we don't think that would be advisable, Mr. Cade."

Cade nodded. Whatever the form of the words, the tone left no doubt. He turned his head to address Henry. "I guess you'd better go and tell Warren he can stand the crew down."

People who were smart didn't mess with these guys. There were too many ways they could make life miserable. And apart from the occasional intrusion like this, life wasn't that bad. So go with the flow, Cade told himself. What else could anyone do?

❀ CHAPTER FOUR ❀

More than twelve years had passed since the first reconnaissance squadron of five Hyadean ships was detected coming in fast from the outer Solar System. In a matter of days they had arrived. There were no claims of mysterious objects seen by questionable people, or allegations of strange happenings in unlikely places as had been depicted in generations of fictional imaginings. These aliens were here, and all the world knew it. A week later, they commenced descents to the surface.

The first landings were in parts of South America, western China and Tibet, and northeast Australia. The selected areas were similar in being sparsely settled, rugged, and having climate that varied with terrain ranging from dense forest to bare mountains. Since the aliens appeared to be shunning population centers, and their motives were obscure, official contacts were initiated by Terrans.

The effect on the nations and peoples of Earth was, understandably, stupefying. Some of the first organized representations to descend on the alien bases after the nervous military withdrew to a watchful distance and governments had presented diplomatic calling cards were by the scientists. Some of their most cherished beliefs were already in ruins, after all, and their questions came in torrents.

How was travel over such distances possible in the time the aliens said, given the limitations imposed by the laws of physics? Well, it turned out, the "laws" were wrong. Getting around inside the galaxy fast wasn't a huge problem. And while distances beyond that were certainly vaster, and the Hyadeans had not as yet contemplated travel between galaxies, the distances to them weren't as immense as Terran astronomers believed. The red shift had been misinterpreted.

Okay, even if the supposed restrictions were wrong, how do you get the power, when even nuclear fusion would be impractical for the superluminal velocities that the Hyadeans said they achieved? Raw fusion only tapped into one percent of the mass equivalent, the Hyadeans replied. Nuclear processes could be catalyzed to be far more efficient, in a way comparable to chemical processes. And there were other forces beyond those, anyway. The phenomena hinting of them were there all the time, but Terran scientists too concerned with protecting their theories had ignored or denied them when they wouldn't fit. For the same kind of reason, the theory that life originated on planets was wrong, that it evolved through natural selection was wrong, and the theory of planets and stars forming out of rotating gaseous nebulas was wrong. What about the theory of the Big Bang and the origin of it all? the Terran scientists asked. The Hyadeans didn't know. They hadn't really thought about it. Looking at the claims the Terrans presented, they couldn't say they were all that convinced.

So much for all of that.

The aliens had little concern for big pictures, grand designs, or greater schemes of things that went beyond advancing their immediate interests. They discovered that humans, often to their own detriment, possessed unique imaginative powers, unlike anything the Hyadean culture had known. At the same time, Earth was fragmented into a patchwork of adversely disposed political units with constantly changing patterns of alliances and rivalries, whose leaders could surely benefit from Hyadean notions of efficiency and order. Hence, a Hyadean market existed for Terran creativity; those who commanded Terran resources had a need. In other words, grounds existed for trade.

In the main, the Hyadeans became natural allies of Western governments and financial interests faced with declining home markets and attracted by the prospect of establishing profitable links to the alien economic system. The supportive nations, including principally the United States, Western Europe, and much of South America, organized formally into a Global Economic Coalition, which became known popularly as the "Globalists." On the other hand, a group of reactionary nations, led by China and the southeastern Asian region, desiring to preserve a position of growing economic strength, and supported by the Arab states and much of central Asia in a tradition of resisting external influences, established themselves as the Alliance of Autonomous Nation States, or AANS. Largely because of their exposed geographic positions, Japan and Australasia maintained positions of uneasy nonalignment. The Hyadeans abandoned their stations in China and Asia to concentrate in an enclave straddling the border regions of western Brazil, Bolivia, and Peru, retaining the Australian base as a scientific field research station and outpost. As the Western regimes became more openly committed to policies that seemed designed to promote the advancement and enrichment of a favored few, opposition movements the world over multiplied.

❀ CHAPTER FIVE ❀

Two days after the reception at Cade's house, Neville Baxter stopped by on his way to LAX airport before returning to New Zealand. He imported agricultural machinery and was experimenting with installing Hyadean AIs for greater autonomy of operation. Cade and Julia ate a salad lunch with him in the sun lounge overlooking the rear of the house. It was a fine day with blue skies, and the glass shutters were open, letting in air from over the water. The boat dock was empty, Warren having taken the *Sassy Lady* out to check some new navigation equipment. Baxter had appeared in a light tan traveling jacket with plaid shirt, and a straw hat crowning his ruddy countenance. As usual, he was in a jovial mood.

". . . so this Maori chief is sitting there while the tourists are taking his picture—old as the hills, wrinkles and white hair—and he says, 'It's going to be a cold winter.' One of the women says, 'It's amazing! How do you people *know* these things?' The chief points across the street. 'White man stacking wood.' "

Cade smiled, leaned back in his chair at the glass-topped cane table they were using, and dabbed his mouth with his napkin before taking a sip of wine. "That's good, Neville. I'll try and remember it. We'll have to find an excuse to come out and visit you some day."

"Do that!" Baxter enthused. "We'll give you a great time. Balance the books for the way you've taken care of me here."

"What time's your flight?" Julia asked.

"Not till three. But I want to stop by the mission and say so long to Vrel and the guys. Dee too, if she's there. If not, say it for me when you see her, will you, Julia?"

"Of course."

Baxter shook his head. "Dee . . . there's one thing. How long has she been going with Vrel now? At least since the last time I was over. It was a pretty rare thing then—with aliens, I mean. She's just . . . you know, does her own thing, and to hell with what anyone thinks."

"That's Dee," Julia agreed.

"My kind of person," Baxter said. "I think it's starting to rub off on Vrel too." He halved an artichoke heart with the side of his fork. "You're doing a great job, stripping the uptightness off these aliens, Roland. Do them good."

Cade held up a hand. "This isn't a social adjustment center. I'm just an opportunist taking what comes, same as you. Same as practically everyone you saw here the other night."

Baxter became more serious. "What drives them? Have you figured it out yet, Roland? It's not just wealth or money. They're all filthy rich by our standards. But they never let up."

"You should have talked more to Mike Blair," Cade answered. "He spends most of his time with them and knows a lot more than I do. . . . But from what I can make out, it isn't so much that what you've got says who you are, as who you are decides what you get. Except 'get' doesn't mean just owning things—as you just said, all of them practically own everything anyway. It involves things like privileges you're entitled to, what positions you qualify for, the recognition you can expect. . . ."

"Sort of like a social rank," Julia put in. "But more complicated. Think of it as a combined credit rating and grade-point average based on just about everything you do. They need computers to figure it out. It translates as 'entitlement.' "

"No wonder they come across like robots off an assembly line," Baxter remarked.

"Oh, be kind, Neville," Julia chided. "You just said yourself that a lot of them are loosening up."

"But not the other way around." Baxter motioned appealingly with his fork. "Does anyone really think they could import their system here? Who'd want it?"

Cade made a face. "I'd say it would suit a lot of people that I can think of just fine," he replied.

Baxter left twenty minutes later. Cade saw him to the front door. As the cab was pulling away, a maroon Chevrolet carrying two people entered the driveway and came up to the house. Even before the driver got out, Cade recognized the fair, sleeked-back hair of Lieutenant Rossi from the Internal Security Service. The passenger was a woman in a blue-gray, two-piece business suit, hair tied high on her head, carrying a black document case. Cade waited at the door as they came up the steps.

"Mr. Cade. I hope I haven't caught you at a bad time," Rossi opened. "This is a colleague of mine, Investigator Wylie. We'd like to ask you a few questions."

"Ms. Wylie," Cade acknowledged, then looked back at Rossi. "What now?" He had a policy of never inviting government into his life, and if they invited themselves, to offer as little encouragement as possible.

Rossi looked past him through the doorway. "Er, could we go inside?"

"Okay." Cade held the door while they entered, closed it, and led the way back through to the sun lounge. Julia was just finishing her meal. Rossi caught Cade's eye pointedly. "Oh, that's okay," Cade said. "We don't have any secrets. Julia, these are Lieutenant Rossi and Investigator Wylie from the ISS. Apparently, they have some questions."

"For *you*, Mr. Cade. I'd rather it were in private, if you don't mind." Rossi's tone left no doubt that whether Cade minded or not had nothing to do with it.

"I was in the middle of something, anyway," Julia said, getting up. "I'll catch you later." She left with a quick nod to the two visitors. Cade indicated a couple chairs, which they accepted. He settled himself in a wicker seat facing them.

"Well?" he invited.

Rossi began, "I assume you're aware of the assassination of Senator Joel Farden from Virginia, General Meakes of the Army, and also two Hyadeans, that happened two days ago in Washington."

"You already asked me that the last time you were here. When you poured ice water on my party."

"I explained then that it was orders, and we regretted the inconvenience," Rossi said. Cade let it go with a nod. Rossi resumed, "Since then, information has come into our possession that establishes a probable connection with the affiliation of political subversives who call themselves 'CounterAction.' You've heard of them, I trust?" Rossi leaned back, waiting for a reaction. Beside him, Wylie had taken some papers from the document case lying opened on her knee.

"Just what you see and hear. It isn't something I make a lot of time for." CounterAction was the illegal militant wing of the protest movement known as "Sovereignty," which had grown in North America over recent years out of various groups opposing what they saw as the Globalist sellout to Hyadean economic imperialism. Sovereignty had organized the rally in Washington the previous Sunday. After other incidents that had been reported over the preceding months, Cade wasn't surprised to learn that CounterAction might be behind this latest act.

"It's pretty widely assumed—and *we* know for *certain*—that the activities of CounterAction in this country are supported clandestinely by the AANS," Rossi said. Cade made a conciliatory gesture which again admitted to knowing nothing beyond what the media said. Rossi gave him a further moment, as if hoping that Cade might help a little more by not making him spell everything out. Cade waited invitingly. Rossi sighed.

"Up until now, AANS support for illegal groups operating in this country has been in the form of money, training, and the infiltration of weapons. We believe that the incident last Sunday might mark a new phase of escalation. You see, as is normal for Hyadean flying vehicles sent here, the aircar carrying the four victims was equipped with an automatic counter-missile system capable of stopping anything produced by the technology of this planet." Rossi showed a hand briefly. "But the assassins didn't use technology from this planet. They used a Hyadean directed-plasma weapon, which the defense system wasn't designed to deal with because up until now only the Hyadeans had it. But one went missing somewhere, and it found its way into this country. We're pretty sure that the people it found its way to were CounterAction. Can you see the implications, Mr. Cade, if the route by which weapons like that can enter this country isn't uncovered and stopped?"

That much was clear enough. But how did it affect Cade? He replied in the only way he could. "Well, yes, I take your point, Lieutenant. So . . . ?"

Rossi took a couple of sheets of paper from the ones Wylie had extracted and glanced at the top one. "You were married at one time, I believe."

"That's right."

"Your wife's name was Marie Ellen, formerly Hedlaw?"

"Yes." Cade had no idea where this could be going.

"Do you still have some means of contacting her, Mr. Cade? Do you know where she is now?"

Cade could only show both palms and shake his head. "No. That was three years ago now. The last I heard she was supposed to have gone to China." He stared from Rossi to Wylie and shook his head again, this time nonplussed. "Look, can I ask what this is about?"

Rossi seemed to hear, but pressed on with his own line. "Can I ask why you split up?" he said.

Cade had half felt this coming. "It was fun in the early days—you know, a wild kind of fling. But when that wore off, really we had nothing in common. She was an idealist with strong politics—serious ideas about what was wrong with the world and how to fix it. . . . I guess I'm just the opposite: I let the world be and ride with the tide."

"So there's no way you might still be in touch with her?" Rossi tried again.

"I already said, no. And even if I could, I'm not sure I'd want to. Life is good and comfortable. Why should I want to get mixed up in whatever you're talking about? I don't know anything about Hyadean weapons." He cocked an eye pointedly. "Anyhow, you still haven't told me what you're talking about."

Rossi stared at him for a few moments longer, as if perhaps giving him a chance to change his mind if there was anything to reconsider. Then he said, "Your ex-wife's views and her going to China were not a coincidence. We think she's back in the U.S. now, with one of the cells that CounterAction is organized into. We think that cell might be the one that the Hyadean plasma weapon found its way to."

Cade sat back slowly, massaging his brow. Now it all made sense. They were following up any lead, and the ex-husband would be an obvious name to put on the list. But still, what they were saying didn't feel right. Yes, he and Marie had had their differences, which at times had erupted into rows of her venting exasperation with what she saw as lack of principle on the one hand, and his protesting the wasting of life on what struck him as futile posturing on the other. And yes, he could see her agitating for what she believed in, or even wielding a gun if need be when passions ran high. But premeditated assassination in cold blood? . . . That didn't sound like her style. Rossi had evidently been prepared and was letting him think it over.

"You said on Sunday that you didn't think the two Hyadeans were planned as part of it," Cade said at last.

"They were hitching a ride at the last moment. The targets were Farden and Meakes."

"So what was so terrible about those two? Why should Counter-Action have singled them out?" Cade wanted to know if they were guilty of anything which by any stretch of the imagination he could see Marie reacting to so drastically. Rossi looked at his colleague and nodded for her to take it. Wylie handed Cade a pamphlet from the document case. It showed a picture of Joel Farden over the caption WHO'S SELLING BOLIVIA? and below, a page of angry denunciation. Large banner type above showed the piece to be a product of SOVEREIGNTY.

"Farden was pushing Congressional bills to open up big sales of Hyadean services and products," she answered. "Their minerals extraction program in Bolivia owes a lot to his pushing." Cade knew a bit about that from his various contacts. The Hyadeans were constructing huge facilities to mine and process minerals from the Bolivian central Altiplano region, which was rich in deposits but underdeveloped due to capital shortage. Their advanced technologies could cut out traditional Terran industries with prices that couldn't be beat.

"A pretty good way to open up resources that it seems no one figured out how to touch before now," Cade commented. "And sure, the people who did figure it will come out okay. Why would they bother if there was nothing in it for them? You have to have movers."

Wylie waved the pamphlet she was holding and nodded. "But you can see how it can be turned into a propaganda piece for stirring up lots of people looking for something to blame their problems on. Some of them get mad enough . . ." She left it unfinished.

Cade nodded. Yes, he could see how somebody like Farden could be made into a hate figure. "How about Meakes?" he asked.

"Even simpler," Wylie replied. "He wanted to revamp our defense capability by incorporating Hyadean weapons and methods. We'd be talking near-invincibility here. You can imagine how the AANS would feel about that. So it was turned around into a story that he was going to put our defense under Hyadean control."

Cade could see how that would work too. But he still couldn't see Marie getting involved in murder over it—simply *because* she had strong principles. Or could she have changed that much in three years? Who knew what she had been exposed to in China? Why get mixed up in it? He showed his hands in a way that said he understood but really couldn't help.

He thought that should have ended it, but the two ISS agents continued to regard him skeptically. Cade could tell when people didn't believe him. They went over some further details, but he still had the same feeling when Rossi and Wylie finally left twenty minutes later.

What they suspected only hit him later. It was that his and Marie's splitting up might have been just a cover, and he was still in contact, acting as an information source for Sovereignty, for which his Hyadean and other contacts would make him uniquely valuable.

And if they believed that she was with the cell of CounterAction responsible for the assassinations, then Cade would be their prime hope for uncovering a lead back to it. There was no way he was going to keep them out of his life this time, he realized bleakly.

❀ CHAPTER SIX ❀

The movie showing at the theater in downtown Baltimore involved an egg-shaped planet whose ends formed immense "mountains" projecting beyond the atmosphere and providing habitats for a range of progressively more bizarre life forms able to exist virtually to the fringes of space. Space adventure had become popular in recent years—the Terran-made varieties, at least. Adaptations of Hyadean imports had been tried in earlier years, but with limited success, mainly due to curiosity which soon passed. The Hyadean themes were invariably exercises in social role modeling more than entertainment, with character stereotypes reflecting approved attitudes and behavior. Terran movies, by contrast, were a sensation back on the alien home worlds.

Reyvek had come here to lose himself in the anonymity for a last hour before committing himself and to reflect one last time on his decision; and also as a precaution. Although there was no particular reason why he should be an object of attention on a routine day off-duty, he had changed seats twice, the second time to put him within a couple of rows of the exit at the rear. Nobody slipped into nearby seats in the minutes following; none of the faces profiled in the flickering light from the screen showed undue interest in him. He checked his watch, waited for a moment when the action quickened to an attention-grabbing high point, then quickly got up and left.

Nobody came after him; nobody was watching from across the foyer. Carrying a red plastic bag as he had been directed, he went out onto the street and turned right. It was already dark. His pocket phone beeped when he was halfway along the block. He drew it out and held it to his face. "Yes?"

"Is everything clear?" The voice, a man's, was electronically disguised and sounded tinny.

"As far as I can tell."

"Cross over the street now and take the next left." Presumably, Reyvek was being observed from somewhere. He passed a couple of run-down stores, the front of a boarded-up office building, and the weed-fringed parking lot of a hotel. When he was opposite the entrance, the voice in the phone said, "Enter the hotel that you're outside now. Go to the desk, and ask for an envelope left for your name." The caller hung up. Reyvek did as instructed, was asked for ID, and received an envelope containing a magnetically coded key for Room 843. He took an elevator to the eighth floor and found the room empty except for a set of clothes laid out on the bed, including shoes, wristwatch, replacement phone, and pocket compad; even a new billfold, key ring, and pen. There was also an envelope containing another coded room key. The voice called again while he was examining the items. "Strip completely, and leave everything that you brought with you there in the room. You can take currency, keys, documents, and other paper items that you wish to keep."

"What about this ring that I carry?" Reyvek queried. His mouth was dry, making him sound scratchy. His nervousness was showing. "It's not cheap, and I'm kind of fond of it."

"How long have you owned it?" the voice asked.

"Fifteen, twenty years, maybe. A gift from times that were better. Kind of sentimental."

"That will be acceptable."

Fifteen minutes later, wearing his new outfit, Reyvek reentered the elevator and got out on the second floor, leaving the building via stairs and a side exit. A taxi was waiting. If the contact really was what he had been given to understand, CounterAction certainly didn't believe in taking chances, Reyvek reflected as they pulled away. Or maybe they knew more about ways of keeping tabs on their people than even he did. The thought reinforced his resolve further.

The room in the second hotel was also deserted. Besides the usual bed, side tables, TV, and wall unit, it had a recliner in one corner. Set up in front of it was a TV camera on a folding stand, connected to a laptop operating via a satellite modem. Reyvek sat down facing the camera and smoothed his clothing while he composed himself. Then the tinny voice spoke again, this time from the laptop speakers. "We regret having to take these measures. The risks associated with this kind of contact are extreme—as someone like you will be all too aware."

"I understand."

"So you are Wayne Reyvek, captain in the uniformed division of the Internal Security Service."

"That's correct."

"And you say you want to change sides: to place your services at the disposal of this organization."

"Right, I want out."

"And how would you describe your motivation, Captain Reyvek?"

"Disillusionment."

"Could you be more specific?"

Reyvek had expected the question, of course. He sighed and raised his hands briefly. "Maybe I'm some kind of old-fashioned idealist that doesn't belong anymore. Remember that phrase they used to teach the kids in school: 'Protect and Serve'? Well, that what I used to think this work would be all about. And for a while, I guess, that's the way it used to be, more or less: defending what was best for this country; for Americans." Reyvek shook his head. "But that's all changing. Americans are the victims of what's going on now. The interests that we're really defending are the aliens'. " He paused to make sure this was the kind of response that was wanted.

"Can you elaborate?" the voice invited.

Again, an open-handed gesture. "The whole Security Service is coming under alien influence—instilled with *their* ideas of what's effective. Those aren't our values, human values. You saw what happened in Washington the other day—people screaming, throwing up in the street like dogs; stuck in goo they have to be dissolved out of. Just ordinary people protesting about losing their jobs, watching their towns fall apart, while a few guys are making millions. They didn't deserve being treated like that. . . . And it's going to get worse. Right now, the training programs are being rewritten to include indoctrination for firing on U.S. citizens. That isn't right. They're gearing up for war here in the cities. It'll get the same as it is down south. I've had combat experience in Brazil. The public isn't being told what's happening in places like that. I've had enough. I'm with you guys, okay?"

A series of probing questions followed. The voice, and the people that Reyvek presumed to be with him, were cautious—wary of this being a plant. Reyvek had anticipated it. Infiltration was one of the classic weapons against subversives. "I have information to give you that will prove I'm genuine," he said.

"What kind of information?" the voice asked.

"Proof that Farden, Meakes, and the two Hyadeans weren't killed by CounterAction, the way the country is being told." That would get their interest, he had decided. If the assassination hadn't been the work of their own organization, the people Reyvek was talking to would presumably be aware of the fact.

There was a pause. Then the voice asked, "Does that mean you know who *was* responsible?"

"It was carried out by an operative of the ISS," Reyvek replied. "The order came from an unofficial source connected to the administration. I have the names. I can document the origin of the weapon that was used. It wasn't smuggled into the country by CounterAction via China—as you or your people know already. I've mailed it all to a box in the city. You can have the address, number, and key."

Again there was a pause, longer this time, as if those at the far end of the link were conferring, or perhaps communicating with others elsewhere. At last the voice spoke again.

"A good move, Captain Reyvek. The matter will have to be conveyed higher within our own command structure before I can give you a response. We had considered asking if you would be willing to remain with the ISS as an internal source for us. But the information you have indicated promises to be of such value as to rule out the risk of letting you go back. We'll move you to a safe house tonight. You'll be comfortable there until word comes back down. From now on you will be referred to as 'Otter.' "

Reyvek felt satisfied that he had achieved enough for this first contact. However, he had another important piece of information to impart. A particular cell within CounterAction's Southeastern Sector was being blamed for the Farden-Meakes incident—operating from Charlotte, North Carolina, which was close enough to Washington to have plausibly been assigned the mission. To make things look authentic, security and police units around the country had been fed details to be checked for the official record. The reason that cell had been chosen was that a captive who belonged to it briefly had revealed a lot under interrogation. The ISS knew the names of some of its other members, its drop boxes, the locations of its supposedly "safe" houses. In short, it was blown and readily targetable. After a delay to give the appearance of leads being uncovered and followed up, the cell would be taken out by a kill team. Retribution for the Farden-Meakes incident would thus have been seen to be dispensed; witnesses who might one day have contested the official version of the story would be silenced permanently; the file would then be closed.

The other message Reyvek had to deliver was for the cell that was referred to within CounterAction as "Scorpion" to disperse fast.

✺ CHAPTER SEVEN ✺

The Hyadean West Coast Trade and Cultural Mission on Carson Street in Lakewood occupied a four-story office block of gray and white panels alternating with glass, and a roof crammed with strange antennas and other structures. Formerly, the building housed an assortment of small businesses. It stood back from the highway behind palm-tree-lined lawns and a visitors' parking area, with access drives on either side and a larger parking area at the rear. The idea had been to establish an informal alien presence without visible barriers isolating it, that would eventually blend in as part of the local scene. Of course, such openness would have been intolerable to the security authorities, had it been genuine. The fences bounding the area were more than they appeared to be, and the building itself had quietly acquired various refinements that the original architects had never contemplated.

It was a week after the reception at Cade's house: the day Erya was due to leave Los Angeles for the Hyadean space port at Xuchimbo in western Brazil. Cade and Luke arrived at the mission around midmorning in the silver-gray BMW, Luke driving. Luke had been with Cade for five years now. He was a rugged-faced forty with a full head of black hair and a beard that he kept meticulously trimmed. He spoke little, was totally dependable, and was not above overlooking a few legal or quasi-moral niceties when the occasion required. Formerly with the Navy, Luke had done Warren Edmonds a favor by introducing him to Cade's employ at a time when Warren's risk-taking with frowned-upon enterprises would otherwise have made his demise only a matter of time.

The security people had relaxed from their tension following the Washington incident, and the temporary police check at the gate had been removed. A number of Hyadean personal flyers and freight lifters were visible to the rear of the building, standing among the regular Terran ground vehicles. A dispensation for operating them had been given when it became clear that the sophisticated Hyadean flight-control AIs presented no hazard to air traffic in the area.

Luke parked in the visitors' area at the front and released the trunk lid using a button below the dash. Cade got out, went back around to retrieve the black, vinyl-finished violin case that they had brought, and rejoined Luke in front of the car. They began walking toward the main entrance of the building.

"I feel like something out of an old gangster movie going in to rob the place," Cade remarked, touting the violin case. "All it needs is the fedoras." Luke grunted.

Inside was a reception counter attended by a Terran woman, with several Hyadeans in an open office area behind. A short passage flanked by display cases of Hyadean gadgetry and pictures showing scenes from Chryse led from the entrance foyer to a door opening to the interior. Two Hyadeans in dark blue garb and gray caps were stationed by the arch framing the near end.

Cade greeted the receptionist with a grin. She had been expecting them. "Hi, Mimi. How's the world been treating you lately?"

"Good morning, Roland. You're looking dapper. You want an update on my life?"

"Just the wicked and exciting parts."

"Yeah, right. . . . Hi, Luke. Still managing to keep him out of trouble?"

"It's tough at times," Luke acknowledged.

Mimi glanced at the violin case that Cade was holding. "What's this? Have you come to give us a recital?"

"A going-away present for Erya."

"Oh, that's right. She's into that, isn't she? How thoughtful!"

"What else did you expect?"

"*Please permit inspection of the article.*" The voice came from a Hyadean AI in the form of a purple, dome-topped cube, dotted with lenses, sitting on the counter by Mimi's elbow. Cade hoisted the case up onto the counter, opened it, and stood back while one of the guards lifted out the instrument to examine it curiously, then poked here and there along the lining of the case and lid. Either he was a new arrival or his English wasn't up to par yet.

"That looks like a quality piece of work," Mimi commented.

"Not exactly special," Cade said. "It was used in that movie about Beethoven that came out a while back—the one with David Quine."

"Yes, I saw it. He was perfect for the part. I loved the bit where he marches through the town waving the cane with the silver knob on the end."

"It's a rage back home there. Erya will get a kick out of it."

The guard replaced the violin and closed the lid of the case. "*Thank you. You are free to proceed,*" the AI announced. "*Hec Vrel has been advised that you are here.*" Cade led the way through, Luke following. There was no call for any ID check. Cade had always thought there was something unnatural about that arch. Probably they had been scanned, sniffed, sensed, and verified before even entering the passage. The door at the end opened automatically and they passed through, into the office section.

The inside had been opened out from the original configuration of suites into larger, interconnecting work areas. Hyadeans tended to shun individual responsibility, Cade had found, making their decisions through committee or relying on the authority of precedent. Perhaps the open layout was preferred for obtaining group consensus and approval. The surroundings were an unimaginatively utilitarian repetition of cream-painted walls and gray or brown furnishings and other equipment, suggesting more the clerical underworld of a low-budget socialist state than the local showcase of a world that could have bought the United States. Screens were everywhere, some showing faces, others graphics mixed with captions in strange scripts and symbols. One type presented its images in relief, looking like windows with solid scenes beyond. Cade remembered Mike Blair telling of his shock at first being confronted by Hyadeans nonchalantly talking to their home worlds with turnaround delay close to instantaneous. The equipment in the mission building communicated electronically with some kind of gravity-wave converters in Earth orbit, which could send signals somewhere around ten billion times faster. The orbiting converters relayed to more powerful devices that the Hyadeans had placed at the edge of the Solar System, which in turn beamed to the home planet. None of this had been especially bothersome to Cade, who had grown up taking instant around-the-world communication for granted; Blair, on the other hand, was a scientist in whose scheme of things it wasn't supposed to have been possible, and he had taken weeks to adjust to it. Sometimes, Cade concluded, there were advantages in not being too scientific.

Cade and Luke threaded their way among the desks and consoles, where Hyadeans sat staring at screens, sometimes murmuring exchanges with them. Just about everything the Hyadeans made was controlled by a built-in AI of greater or lesser capacity, and voice was their normal way of interacting. Another thing that always intrigued Cade were their reconfigurable pages—sheets of flexible plastic, no thicker than regular paper, upon which characters were generated electronically to produce whatever was desired. A stack of them bound like a book could thus become any book or document at all, selected from a library stored in the spine or loaded externally. Mike Blair had calculated that the spine held the equivalent of half the Library of Congress.

Some of the Hyadeans nodded in recognition, though without displays of overt familiarity—as a rule they were more stiff and formal by day. A number of Terrans worked there too in such roles as advisors and translators—the pay the Hyadeans could offer was impossible to turn down. Whether because they had never become comfortable with the practice, or because the Hyadean translation programs couldn't capture the subtleties of natural language sufficiently for fluency, they prefered using conventional touchpad and wireless mouse rather than voice when operating equipment.

The brave attempts at color and decoration that Cade noticed here and there were doubtless due to the Terrans too. A noticeable exception was anything of floral design, which the Hyadeans wouldn't permit, even to the extent of prohibiting it from acceptable office dress. Seemingly, their managerial caste had some hangup about displays of sexual organs, whatever the species.

Vrel was waiting at the far end, his mouth stretched into the faint smile that was the most a Hyadean would allow while on duty. However, he had followed Wyvex's example in relieving the drabness of the standard tunic with a colorful patch on the breast pocket—a fractal pattern this time. Vrel's hair seemed almost to glow in a strange mix of electric blue and violet hues that coordinated well with the paler blue of his skin. He had been among the original group to set up the mission six years previously, and had first met Cade then, already expanding his business circles to make Hyadean acquaintances.

"Hello, Roland . . . Luke," he greeted. "Exactly on time. I'm surprised. The traffic is supposed to be bad this morning."

"Luke has his own routes," Cade answered. Vrel was picking up Terran ways. In some places, conversation opened with the weather or inquiries about one's health. In Los Angeles it was the traffic. Cade gestured at the patch on Vrel's pocket. "What's this riot of abandonment? You'll be showing up in beach shirts next."

"I kind of like it. It amazes me that Hyadeans never thought to put pictures on things. Besides, I couldn't let Wyvex get all the attention."

The complex Hyadean system of social ordering, which Cade had given up trying to understand, exploited competitiveness and was what made them so conscientious about having to conform. By their standards Vrel's gesture would constitute a blaze of individuality bordering on irresponsible. The interesting thing was that Vrel seemed to be enjoying it. "Is Wyvex here?" Cade asked.

"No. Damien Philps took him up to San Francisco to tour some galleries. His friend Tevlak in Bolivia is talking about opening up outlets on Chryse. I was talking to Tevlak about it earlier."

Erya appeared in an entrance behind Vrel and came forward to greet Cade and Luke. "Mr. Cade and Mr. Luke. Mimi said you wanted to see me."

"We couldn't let you go back without saying goodbye," Cade said.

"How thoughtful." Only then did Erya's gaze drift down to the case that Cade was holding. She looked at it uncomprehendingly as Cade, grinning, lifted it onto a nearby worktop and opened the lid. Erya's jaw dropped incredulously.

"From the movie, like I said," Cade told her. "I couldn't get the first violin, as I'd hoped. But this is the next best."

Erya was speechless for several seconds. "You remembered! . . . But I don't understand. I'm just about to go back. There's no possible return. Why would you choose . . ." She consulted her veebee for an appropriate phrase. "Negative payoff."

Even Vrel, who should have known better by now, seemed taken aback. Cade shook his head, doing his best not to let his bemusement show. It was this strange Hyadean calculus of short-term returns again. They couldn't comprehend giving for its own sake. "Don't let worrying about it spoil your trip," he said. "It'll do more good on Chryse than it would have done if it stayed where I found it. You're still on Earth now. Just accept it as a Terran way of saying we're friends. Maybe one day it'll become your way too."

While Erya was making a round of the offices to show Cade's gift before she left for the airport, Michael Blair yawned and stretched in one of the rooms upstairs as he rested his eyes after two hours of concentration at a display screen showing Hyadean text and mathematical representations. Learning the language was part of the program he had set himself for understanding the Hyadean sciences. It no longer awed him to think that some of the sources that he accessed, and individuals that he was growing accustomed to interacting with, were located on strange worlds that existed light-years away.

The ironic conclusion he had come to was that, contrary to everything that anyone raised in the self-congratulatory Terran tradition would have believed, the very unimaginativeness that Terrans found incomprehensible was what had enabled the

Hyadeans to make breakthroughs that left Earth's scientific community dazed and incredulous. Truth was, the insights he had vowed to share were turning out to be not really that exciting after all. It was the flights of imaginative fancy dreamed up by generations of Terran scientists that were exciting; the only problem was, overwhelmingly, they had this tendency to be wrong.

The Hyadeans ploddingly followed wherever the facts led, without subscribing to elaborate theoretical constructs that emotional investment would cause them to defend tenaciously instead of testing impartially. True enough, the textbook accounts and rhetoric bandied around on Earth praised the scientific method as an ideal; and academia could always count on a staunch cadre of apologists to exalt it into reality. But the basic human drives were emotional, not objective, resulting in commitment to protecting ideas that were comfortingly familiar instead of openness to the research that might threaten them. Most of what Earth took such pride in as "science" was as much a product of human inventiveness as its other arts and fables.

By contrast, the Hyadean attempts to understand the universe were closer to what would have been described on Earth as engineering. What didn't work was abandoned without compunction, and what did was accepted at face value without need of credentials to fit with prevailing theory. The resulting scheme of things was messy, incoherent, and to Terran eyes, crying out to be organized under grand unifying principles postulating answers to questions the Hyadeans had never asked. But so what? At the end of it all the fact remained that they were here, while we hadn't gotten there. That had to say something.

Krossig, the Hyadean anthropologist who was here to study humans, came in and began rummaging for something among the shelves on the far wall. As Blair watched him across the desktop, he reflected on the irony that the Hyadean inclination not to question was also what made them so susceptible to their own social conditioning propaganda, and hence ideal subjects for a conformist society. His brow creased at the seeming paradox. Wasn't readiness to question supposed to be the hallmark of what science was all about? If the Hyadeans didn't question, how could they have made such superb scientific accomplishments? He sat back in his chair and mulled over the problem.

Questioning led to good science when what was being questioned was a belief system that had become dogma. Since the Hyadeans didn't create dogmas, they could get by without need to question them. Accepting uncritically worked when the facts were allowed to speak for themselves. It also produced rigidly structured social orders.

❀ CHAPTER EIGHT ❀

Hyadeans had never fallen into the Terran habit of creating false gods that would reveal the ultimate truths of the Universe. One of the most recent creations to be elevated to the status of infallible deity was mathematics. The Hyadeans took advantage of the fortuitous fact that some mathematical procedures approximated real-world processes sufficiently closely over a limited range to be useful, and looking no further than that, found an invaluable servant. Terrans turned things upside down by persuading themselves that their manipulations of formal systems of symbols defined "laws" that reality was somehow obliged to imitate. In doing so they subjected themselves to a tyrannical master.

Relativity theory had pursued mathematical elegance by seeking to extend to electromagnetism the familiar principles of Galilean relativity, whereby the equations describing mechanical motion came out the same regardless of whose moving reference frame measurements were made from. A consistent solution required that the velocity of light be the same for all observers, which became one of the theory's postulates. Peculiar distortions of space and time were necessary to maintain a velocity as constant, and the various relativistic transformations followed. These also enabled the famous experiment by Michelson and Morley in 1886, and its variants repeated to greater accuracies ever since, which failed to find an ether "wind" due to the Earth's motion around the Sun, as demonstrating *that there was no ether—no "preferred" reference frame in which "true" laws of physics operated.*

The Hyadeans went out into space—which required, after all, solid engineering more than esoteric theories—and discovered that the sought-after medium was simply the locally dominant electromagnetic field. Since in the vicinity of Earth this traveled with the Earth around the Sun, the Terran physicists had, in effect, been trying to measure the airspeed of their plane with their instruments anchored solidly inside the cabin.

In the Hyadean scheme of things the Galilean transformations remained valid; yet experiments performed on the surfaces of planets yielded the same results that appeared to support relativity. The reason was that the electric field surrounding a photon experienced an aerodynamic-like distortion when moving through a gravity field, which affected the propagation velocity. Since local gravity varied from place to place, the speed of light changed in different parts of the cosmos, upsetting all manner of long-cherished Terran calculations and models.

This distortion was responsible for the phenomenon measured as inertial mass, which explained why mass increased with velocity. Increase in mass resulted in the slowing down of a moving system's clock rates. Hence, "time" didn't dilate in the way relativity maintained—for example to extend the lifetimes of incoming muons created in the upper atmosphere. The "clocks" of particles moving through the Earth's gravity field ran slower than laboratory clocks at rest in it. Hence, the Twin Paradox didn't arise, and space and time remained what common sense had always said.

The associated energy dynamics restricted velocities in situations where the gravitational field of the body being accelerated was small compared to the field through which the acceleration was taking place. This had been observed in experiments performed on Earth using nuclear particles, and been misread as a universal limit. But that was merely a locally valid approximation. Away from large gravitating masses, hyperlight velocities could be achieved with surprisingly little outlay of energy, and that was why the Hyadeans were able to measure their interstellar journeys in weeks and months.

The gravitational effect itself emerged as a residue of the electrical asymmetry arising from the distortion of hadrons within nuclei by intense internal field stresses. Disturbances superposed on it propagated at close to ten billion times the speed of light, which afforded the basis for Hyadean long-range communications.

Evidence hinting at such possibilities had been available on Earth all along, filed in the reports of unfashionable experiments and cited by critics of the orthodoxy. But the mainstream had always ignored it, or found ways to explain it away.

Because it didn't fit with the theory.

✹ CHAPTER NINE ✹

In New York, the sun was shining from a clear sky, reflecting as a subdued orb from the tinted windows of the skyscraper at the end of Manhattan island housing the offices of the Global-Interplanetary Export-Import Bank. The board room on the floor below the penthouse commanded a clear view over Battery Park, past Governors Island and the upper bay all the way to the Narrows, with the Jersey City docks fading in haze across the mouth of the Hudson to the right, behind the Statue of Liberty.

Casper Toddrel appended his signature on all six copies of the Deed Transfer Agreement, handing each to the financial secretary to be witnessed and dated. These were followed by a ten-page Disclosure Affidavit, Financial Underwriter's Statement, and Supplementary Articles of Contract. The documents were passed along the table to the signatory for the three representatives from the Brazilian Land Commission, and finally to the head of the Hyadean delegation at the far end. These were top-level Hyadeans, the real movers—taking in the U.S. and parts of Western Europe in what came close to a state visit. They sat aloofly in a group, with fans directing scented air streams on the table in front of them—as if not really comfortable at being this close to sweaty, smelly Terrans. Toddrel would have welcomed a greater display of togetherness, but he wasn't troubled all that much. By his estimation, when the various transactions, payments, share allocations, and commissions were completed, his net personal worth would have increased by somewhere in the order of a cool half-billion dollars.

Toddrel was a medium-set man in his midfifties, with black curls of hair fringing a smooth head, and dark, moody eyes adding depth to a face controlled and inexpressive about the mouth and jaw but otherwise untroubled. He believed in being thorough in all that he did, expected the same from the people he paid, and accepted his secure and comfortable existence as no more than the due return for hard work, innate intelligence, and summoning the will to get things right. He was tired of hearing about the self-inflicted problems of people who never had developed a worthwhile thought in their lives, refused to make decisions, did nothing with opportunity when it came, and then complained that they'd never been given a chance. Professionally, if not entirely socially, he had to admit he had a grudging admiration for Hyadeans. They did what was necessary to get the results they wanted.

Murmurs and chattering broke out around the room when the formalities were over. People began rising. Everyone looked pleased. Toddrel returned the pen to the holder on the table in front of him and stood up, pausing to exchange a few words with some of the other directors. He declined an invitation from the Hyadeans to lunch, on the grounds that he was flying to Europe later that day and had matters to attend to, and left before getting involved in anything further. Ibsan, his former SEAL/Secret Service bodyguard, joined him in the anteroom outside, and they walked together to the elevators. Toddrel's limo was drawn up in the basement motor lobby when they emerged. Ibsan opened the door for Toddrel, then got in up front to ride with the chauffeur. Drisson was waiting in the rear compartment as arranged. Toddrel leaned forward in the seat next to him to pour a Scotch and water from the decanters beside the entertainment unit. Overtly, Kurt Drisson was a colonel in the Internal Security Service. Covertly, he coordinated operations related to higher policy, of a kind that it was preferred not to have recorded in official orders.

"So, what have we got?" Toddrel asked as the limo began moving out though armored doors, then up a ramp into the downtown streets.

"Not good," Drisson replied. "Reyvek has vanished without trace.

Given the last two evaluation profiles we have on him, the indicated conclusion is that he's defected. Since he was involved with Echelon logistics, I'd guess he took that information as collateral. We have to assume that we're compromised."

Toddrel exhaled heavily. "Echelon" was the code designation for the operation to eliminate Farden and Meakes. Toddrel had made arrangements for the meeting at Overly Park ensuring that the two of them would fly together. The last-minute addition of the two Hyadeans had been an unexpected complication, with unthinkable repercussions now if the story got out. The ruin of Toddrel and his accomplices would be the least of it, with a good chance of a life sentence as a gesture toward making interplanetary amends.

"If they had the profiles, why was he allowed to continue on-duty?" he fumed. "Why wasn't he suspended? What's the point of having profiles if nobody's going to act on what they say?"

Drisson made a vaguely placatory gesture. "It's like a lot of things. Sometimes it takes hindsight to make the right interpretation." He waited, as if giving Toddrel time to vent further before being more receptive. Toddrel gulped irascibly from his glass, savored the taste for a moment, then looked out the window. They were en route for the Waldorf, where Toddrel was staying. In one of the side streets, police were keeping an eye on a speaker addressing a ragged-looking gathering from a platform.

"So what do we do?" Toddrel asked, turning back.

Drisson rubbed his chin, indicating that there was no obvious easy option. "The plan was to sanitize the situation by putting it on Scorpion's account and then taking them out," he said.

Toddrel nodded impatiently. Scorpion was the compromised CounterAction cell being set up to take the official rap. "I know what we planned, Kurt. I'm asking what we *do*."

"Obviously, we have to eliminate Reyvek. But the only way we'll find him now is through someone on the inside. So the proposal is this. We put a hold on taking out Scorpion. Instead, we infiltrate somebody into it to find Reyvek."

"Is that likely?" Toddrel queried. "Isn't CounterAction supposed to be highly compartmentalized?"

"I think there's a good chance. With Reyvek being involved in the operation Scorpion is supposed to have carried out, there are good reasons why they might end up meeting. The operative takes out Reyvek. When that part's done, we send in the cleaning team as scheduled. End of problem."

"You make it sound like just part of a regular day's work to put somebody inside CounterAction," Toddrel commented.

"Normally it would be a tough thing to do on demand," Drisson agreed. "But in the case of Scorpion, we might have a break. One of the cell members that we've identified is the former wife of a wheeler-dealer on the West Coast who sets up business deals with Hyadeans. Our people visited him a few days ago on a routine check. He says he doesn't have contact with her anymore, but they weren't convinced. This guy knows everybody and has wires into everything." Drisson shrugged. "If we can get him to locate his ex for us, we've got a conduit through to Scorpion."

"And what makes you think he's likely to do that?" Toddrel asked.

Drisson looked across the seat and smiled enigmatically. "Ways and means," he replied.

✵ CHAPTER TEN ✵

North Carolina state troopers had set up a checkpoint on the road out of Greenville, a mile before the junction where Kestrel and Len in the battered farm pickup, and Olsen driving the truck laden with fifty-gallon drums of timber preservative, would go separate ways. Kestrel and Len would trace a route through the minor roads crossing the Great Smoky range; Olsen would keep to the interstates, following I-85 south to skirt Atlanta, then taking I-75 to meet up with them again in Chattanooga that night.

The Scorpion cell in Charlotte had been disbanded suddenly on terse instructions from above. Other members were dispersing to destinations known only to themselves and whoever gave the orders; the names Kestrel had known them by had been retired. On joining the Chattanooga cell, she would no doubt cease being "Kestrel" anymore, too. At first, CounterAction had given her the pseudonym Kay, but she rejected it. Care was needed in making sure that code words bore no accidental similarities or connections to the things they were supposed to disguise. Lives had been lost through such coincidences. "Kay" would have been too suggestive of her real name: Cade. Marie Cade.

A couple of jeeps manned by armed National Guard and mounting machine guns were positioned at the sides of the roadblock, ready to go. A sergeant came up to the driver's window, while two troopers went back to probe among the bales of roofing shingles that the pickup was carrying. Len presented a wallet containing the vehicle documentation and his ID, then followed with Marie's, made out in the name of Jenny Lawson, as she passed it across. The sergeant perused them casually, recited the names aloud into a compad and waited a moment for the screen's response.

"Where are you heading?" he inquired, running an eye over the interior of the cab.

"Up to Hiawasee. Stuff for a cabin being remodeled along by the lake there," Len replied. He looked the part: unshaven for two days, with a crumpled tweed hat, plaid shirt and padded work vest, a carpenter's tool belt over blue jeans. His voice was gruff and neutral.

"That wouldn't seem to me too much like a lady's kind of work," the sergeant commented, looking at Marie.

"What century are you from? I'll hammer 'em as good as anyone," she answered defiantly.

"Would you have such a thing as a bill of sale for this material?" the sergeant asked. Len produced one from Lowes in Spartanburg, where they had loaded the prom guns. The sergeant glanced back toward the rear of the pickup, where the troopers had been scanning the load with a hand-held spectral analyzer, explosives sniffer, and a metal sensor. "On your way," he told them, waving. Len eased the pickup away amid rattles and grinding of gears, taking care not to seem too hasty. Marie kept her eyes ahead until they were a good hundred yards clear, then exhaled shakily. In the side mirror, she could see Olsen's truck standing in line behind a couple of cars.

It had been intended that the load would attract attention. The prom guns were inside the double-walled back of the cab and the hidden compartment beneath the bed at the rear, between the chassis girders—both metal-enclosed, opaque to the regular search instruments. The guns Olsen was carrying were inside the false-bottom drums—although a spot check and sampling would have drawn the wood preservative they were supposed to be filled with from an internal chamber.

Interesting weapons, prom guns. They had disappeared from Hyadean stocks in South America, and the only details Marie knew were that they had come into the U.S. via Morocco and the Caribbean. "Prom" was a contraction of "programmable munitions." The gun was the size of an assault rifle and launched a stream of self-propelled projectiles containing lateral-thrusting charges carried in a counter-spinning ring, which could be fired to alter the trajectory in flight. Quite complex control patterns could be programmed into the launcher, enabling targets dug in under cover, hidden around corners, or concealed by obstacles to be hit. A skilled user could seek out a target blocked by combinations of them. Marie had tested and practiced with them in remote parts of the mountains east of Charlotte.

"I don't believe what this country has turned into," Len growled as the pickup ground and shuddered to gain speed. "Roadblocks; people being pulled out of bed in the middle of the night. Things never used to be that way. Yet the media talk about it as if it's normal. People forget. It's alien ways. They're turning us into a colony in our own country."

"That's what we're fighting," Marie reminded him unnecessarily. The hills back from the highway looked green and peaceful. Water behind the trees reflected patches of sky. Marie felt weary of it all: combat training and sabotage; constantly having to be ready to move; always being haunted by the specter of capture, interrogation, and everything that went with it. Why couldn't she just live a safe and familiar day-to-day life somewhere, enjoying little things like friends stopping by to visit, or being alone with her thoughts on a hill after a walk up through a forest?

All that the people needed to take their country back was solidarity and awareness. Even with all their technology and alien backing, the powers that were robbing them of their livelihoods and turning them into property like some modern version of a feudal order could never prevail against a determined majority. But the majority were uninformed and unorganized. What did it take to wake them up to what was going on? Why did Marie care? She could go back to China, find a niche there, and probably never have to worry about being directly affected to any serious degree again. So why had she come back?

For the same reason she had left the comforts and security of her former life in California, she supposed. The restlessness that compelled her to contribute even a token to putting something right with the world. How anyone could remain complacent when there was so much going wrong with it, she was unable to comprehend. How could she once have dreamed of making a life with Roland? Because he was Roland. She still thought of him, even though all that had been a different universe, a million years ago. That was the stupid thing.

"Do you know there was a time when you could drive from anyplace to anyplace anytime you felt like it?" Len said. "Didn't have sensors under the road reading who was leaving the state. Didn't need no ID with a tax compliance sticker to get gas."

"Anywhere? Like New York to California?"

"Yep, if the fancy took you. Just get up and go."

"It sounds unreal." Marie was distant, still partly lost in her own musings.

"People don't remember," Len said again. "Everything's rules and restrictions. We're being turned into an alien military base, that's what it is."

Marie used to wonder why, if their world was so disciplined and orderly, governed under a single ruling system, the Hyadeans possessed a military establishment at all. Their answer was that they needed to protect themselves against a rival power known as the Querl, who inhabited a group of worlds loosely strung across the same star systems. The Querl were of the same race as the Hyadeans, having split off as a rebellious faction and left to found a culture based on their own political and economic principles. According to the Chryseans—which was the correct name for the Hyadeans of the home planet and its subject worlds—these principles were unsound and illogical, resulting in chaotic rule by ill-defined authorities, with consequent depletion and degradation of the Querl planets. The Chryseans would educate Earth and provide guidance to prevent similar things from happening here. And the institutions that were ultimately in control of things—in the West, anyway—were lending themselves readily to bringing their own houses into line. A compliant media establishment spread the word and the imagery, and for years the people, by and large, had been buying the line and not seeing the regimentation, exploitation, and the slow erosion of what had once been their rights. But now they were feeling the effects, and that was changing. Recruitment for Sovereignty was on the increase, and support was quietly spreading across a wide but largely invisible infrastructure of American life that didn't have access to the interplanetary financial markets and saw little prospect of benefiting significantly from the proceeds. As resistance grew, the classical escalating pattern would develop of what one side saw as protest and suppression being viewed by the powers in control as provocation and response. The times would get ugly before they could improve. CounterAction was preparing.

Marie didn't see herself as a subversive fighting against America. By all the principles she had been told about and grown up believing in, she was fighting *for* what America was once supposed to have stood for.

❁ CHAPTER ELEVEN ❁

The message on Cade's laptop offered a flat introduction fee plus a 2.5 percent commission on net proceeds if Cade could put the sender's brokering agency in touch with a Hyadean concern interested in buying Terran graphical programming services. There was a big demand for Terran software skills on Chryse and its associated worlds. Most programming there was performed by various kinds of AI, with results that were solid, reliable, acceptable . . . and utterly without trace of any insight or creative flare that went an iota beyond meeting the minimum specification. The efforts of Hyadean manual programmers fared about the same: in Mike Blair's phrase, which was his favorite appellation for just about everything they did, "dull and plodding." Terran programmers, by contrast, could come up with ways of doing things that Hyadean minds were incapable of mimicking. More often than not they worked for companies whose existence was threatened by Hyadean competition.

But it wasn't a time to be thinking too much about things like that when Julia was sitting at the vanity in her underwear and a negligee, combing out her hair and attending to the feminine bedtime ritual of removing makeup and applying lotion and perfume. Cade stared at her for a while from the bed, watching the tossing waves of her red hair and the lithe, feline motions of her back. Sometimes, he reflected, it seemed as if life treated him too well.

He initiated shutdown, set the computer aside on the night stand, and stretched back comfortably to rest against the headboard, his hands clasped behind his head. Julia caught the movement in the mirror. "So, are you going to fix them up with the same contact that Vrel gave you last time?" she asked over her shoulder.

"Maybe better than that. I was thinking we could use Sigliari. It might lead to a whole bunch of direct lines in there." Sigliari was a promoter from San Diego who had visited Chryse recently and was actively soliciting business there. Who knew what possibilities a lead like that into the home planet might open up?

"Sounds like a cool idea," Julia agreed.

Cade shrugged. "Who knows? I might even work a trip there myself one of these days."

"Even cooler. Does that mean I'm invited?"

"Just try staying behind. Can you see me having fun running wild and free with nothing but Hyadean women around? You're essential baggage—also wanted on the voyage."

"Women here don't seem to have a problem with Hyadean guys," Julia commented. "You've only got to look at Dee and Vrel."

"Which only goes to show how less discerning women are," Cade replied. He realized that didn't sound very good. "Not that there's anything wrong with Vrel. I mean, he's a great friend. It's just . . ." He threw out a hand helplessly. There was no gracious continuation. He had painted himself into a corner. Julia rose, came over to the bed, and disposed of the few garments she was still wearing. Cade let his gaze wander over her, and in moments all thoughts of his impasse had fled. She slid in beside him, entwining bodies, and drew close.

"Then think about a Terran woman for the time being," she murmured.

They made love skillfully, satisfyingly, with the ease and confidence that come when time has bred a familiarity that goes beyond just good companionship and has banished uncertainties. The physical gratification that they shared at night was the ideal complement to the professional intimacy that they shared during the day. At times, Cade was tempted to bring up the possibility of marrying again; but then, he would ask himself, why risk messing with a good relationship?

Afterward, they lay contentedly, Julia resting her face on his shoulder, her finger tracing idle designs on his chest. "You make me feel like a woman," she told him.

"What did you expect? Orangutan? Wildebeest? Sumatran two-horned rhinoceros?"

"Oh, don't be so unromantic. You know what I mean."

Cade grinned and slid an arm around her shoulder. "Of course I do. Life just gets better, doesn't it?"

A few seconds of silence passed, as if Julia were pondering something. "Wasn't it ever good before?" she asked finally.

"It depends when did you mean? Any time in particular?"

"Oh . . . when you were with Marie, for instance. Was it good like this then?"

"It had its ups and downs, I guess." Cade was surprised. "What made you bring that up?"

"I'm not sure. . . . Maybe when those two ISS people came here, asking about her."

Cade shook his head. "Like I told them, that was all over years ago. The last I heard, she was in China."

"They seemed to think she's come back," Julia reminded him. She seemed to let the subject rest there, then added lightly, "Do you ever hear from her?"

"What? Hell, no. Why should I?" Cade turned his head. "Don't tell me you're getting jealous."

"I was just curious," Julia replied.

The next morning, Mike Blair called to inform Cade that he was going to Australia. Krossig, the Hyadean anthropologist at the LA mission, would be leaving almost at once to join the Hyadean scientific field station still being operated there. He and Blair had gotten to know each other in the course of Blair's long periods of ensconcing himself at the mission, which had resulted in an invitation for Blair to go too as Krossig's Terran scientific understudy and consultant.

"It sounds good, Mike," Cade told him. He had taken the call in the gym behind the garage at the side of the house, where he had been working out with Luke. "So when is this likely to happen?"

"Once these guys make their minds up, they don't fool around. It could be a matter of weeks."

"What's the political situation like there?" Cade asked. He was always curious about backgrounds that could affect business.

"With a pure scientific research station, it's okay. The government's trying to keep the contact but stay out of any main currents. The Hyadeans have had a presence there since the first landings. It's probably good diplomacy to just go along with them."

Cade nodded. "It sounds like we're going to need another party to send you guys off, then."

"Well, I wouldn't say no to that."

Luke came through on his way to the shower room, clad in a blue track suit with a towel tucked around the neck, his face still red and perspiring. "It's Mike," Cade told him, gesturing with the compad. "Krossig's transferring to that place they've got in Australia, and Mike will be going too."

"Great," Luke acknowledged.

Cade thought for a moment. "What do you think Hyadeans might say to a day out fishing, Terran style, instead of another party?" he asked Blair on the screen.

"Vrel would like it for sure. Probably Krossig too. . . . I don't think he's ever tried anything like that. Sounds like a good idea."

Cade looked back up at Luke. "Talk to Warren when we're done, would you? Tell him to get the boat set up for a day out. We'll make it a smaller thing this time, just family—something different for them to talk about when they go back to Chryse."

Julia brought up the subject of Marie again that evening, while she and Cade were driving to a dinner party in San Clemente. It struck Cade as unusual. Julia was of a practical disposition and had always tended to leave what was over in the past, where it belonged. What kind of a person had Marie been? Intense, Cade said. A human perpetual-motion machine. One of those women who would never have a weight problem because she burned everything off with nervous energy, regardless of what or how much she ate. So how would he describe their relationship? Julia wanted to know. Cade took one hand off the wheel to make a side-to-side motion in the air. "Mercurial," he told her.

"How did it end?"

"She could never really get comfortable with being comfortable. Know what I mean? When life took swings for the better, she seemed to get more guilty about it—as if it wasn't right for her life to be coming together while so many other people's were messed up. She always had this idealistic streak about helping to make the world a better place. . . . I guess when it became obvious that I wasn't going to change, she decided to move on to find somewhere she could do something about it." They drove in silence, while Julia either contemplated her next question or digested the information. Cade turned his head to glance at her. "What is this? You've never gone into any of this before, and you never do anything without a reason. So what's the reason?"

Julia remained quiet for an unnaturally long time. Finally, she answered, "An old college friend of mine tracked me down recently— through Dee. Let's say her name's Rebecca. She's in some kind of trouble with the authorities and needs help getting out of the country."

Cade whistled silently. "As bad as that? What kind of trouble are we talking about?"

"I didn't ask. But you know what it's like trying to get through the regular exits. Everywhere's watched. They've got everything about you in the computers."

"Have you decided to start a new line—people smuggling?" Cade asked. Even now he was unable to refrain from a mildly teasing note.

"She was a close friend, the kind you'd like to do something for." Julia paused again, then drew a long breath as if committing herself finally. "Look, I was asking about Marie to see if there was a chance you might still be on speaking terms. If she is back in the country as those ISS people said, what might the possibility be of contacting her? Doesn't that organization that they said she's with have ways of getting people out—to Asia or somewhere maybe? They're supposed to have a whole underground organization for moving contraband and people, right?"

Cade glanced at her in mock apprehension. "What are you trying to get me into here? Look, I sympathize with your friend. But even supposing I wanted to get involved, I don't have any idea where Marie is now. I've only got those two spooks' word that she's even back from China."

Julia, however, was evidently not ready to leave it there. "Come on, you're the Mr. Fixit with connections everywhere, aren't you?" she said. "I know how you work, Roland. Are you really telling me that with all the friends you and she made over the years, you couldn't find a way of getting a message through to her if you really needed to?" She reached out and laid a hand on his knee. "Rebecca *was* a close friend. And it does sound as if she's in a lot of trouble."

Cade took his eyes off the road to look across the car for a second. Julia was serious, he could see. "So where is she right now?" he asked.

"In a hotel downtown. I guess one of those nondescript places where invisible people go. Dee didn't give me any details."

Cade shook his head. "That's no good. You'd better bring her to the house while we figure something out. At least it'll be more comfortable. Can you arrange it with Dee?"

Julia hesitated, as if giving him time to reconsider. "Does that mean we're going to help her?" she asked.

Cade stared at the highway ahead, wondering what options he had let himself in for now. "Let's see what she has to say first," he replied.

After they got back home, Julia went out again and returned a couple of hours later with Rebecca. She was mousy haired and plain, a little on the plump side, not given to talk; or perhaps it was the strain of the last couple of days and whatever experiences had preceded them. Henry took her bags and showed her to one of the guest rooms. Later, she reappeared for a late supper of chicken pieces and fries in the kitchen. Cade and Julia joined her just for coffee, since they had eaten earlier. By then, Rebecca had pulled herself more together.

Her story was that she and another woman had coauthored a hard-hitting piece in an underground political newsletter that circulated in print and on the net, detailing dubious and in some cases flatly unlawful electoral machinations that had accompanied the installation of the current administration in Washington, which if proved would make it illicit, and not the result of a constitutionally correct, democratic process. The governor of California, William Jeye, had picked it up in a speech to the Constitutional Club of San Francisco, and the result had been consternation in the Western media, condemnation from the East, and public outcries everywhere. The other author had been arrested. Another woman, who lived on the next street to Rebecca in a house with the same number, was picked up by the ISS at the same time but released twenty-four hours later with an admission of mistaken identity. Rebecca had packed a bag and gone into hiding; she wouldn't even say where in the country she had arrived from.

"I know I come across like a wimp," she said. "But I can hold my own with anyone when it comes to words. Julia will tell you that. She knew me at college."

"She used to tie us all in knots debating," Julia confirmed.

Rebecca shook her head and drew in a sharp, shaky breath that came close to a shudder. "But I'm not good when it comes to physical things. You know, the things you hear about: interrogation drugs; all the intimidation; worse. . . . I couldn't go out on the street, knowing they might pick me up anytime. Haven't really been able to sleep since it happened. . . . I have to get out of here."

"Out of the country completely?" Cade said. "It's really that bad?"

"She's right," Julia told him. "They won't quit now—not after the fuss that this is causing." The news that evening had brought reports of demonstrations in several cities, with more use of Hyadean sonic disruptors on the crowds, as had been seen in Washington, along with water cannon. In Kentucky, a group armed with shoulder-launched missiles and assault weapons, believed to be Counter Action, had attacked an ISS depot, declaring it to be an arm of the occupational forces of an illegal regime installed to advance alien interests.

"So how did you find Dee?" Cade asked Rebecca. "Did you know her at sometime too?" It seemed an unlikely coincidence. Julia had met Dee only after getting to know Cade and joining his circle of friends.

Rebecca shook her head. "When I started asking around the people we used to know way back, one of them put me on to Brad." She looked at Julia. "He used to be your husband, right? Owns a couple of clubs." Julia nodded. Rebecca went on, "Brad put me on to Dee and said I should try through her."

Julia cupped both hands around her coffee mug and drank from it, then gave Cade a searching look. He stared across the table at Rebecca. Despite what she had said earlier about her verbal skills, her voice tonight had been little more than a whisper. She seemed all done in.

Just one more thing crossed Cade's mind. "Do you still have your phone with you?" he asked. "And in your bags is there a laptop, compad, anything like that?" Virtually all electronic devices of any value, as well as things like automobiles and appliances, contained GPS chips able to fix their location on the Earth's surface to within a few yards. In the case of loss or theft, dialing a specified number would cause them to return details of where they were. Rumor had it that government agencies had special numbers too, that would override the normal enabling functions. Cade had never been able to determine whether it was true or not.

Rebecca shook her head. "I threw the phone away. There isn't anything else." Cade nodded, satisfied.

"Well, there's not a lot else we can do tonight," he said. "Why don't we all get some rest? Tomorrow we've got a boat trip organized with some friends. Why don't you come along? A little bit of sun and ocean might make you feel like a new person."

"Maybe," Rebecca answered. She didn't sound enthralled by the idea.

After Rebecca had left them, Cade and Julia went through to the bar for a nightcap. "If you do manage to pull something, I assume it will cost us," Julia said.

Cade pulled a face. "I'm not sure. Rebecca sounds like a pretty good ally on their side. They might be happy just to get her over there." This didn't seem a time to let something like that get in the way. It wasn't as if they were hard up, just at the moment. He downed a mouthful of his drink. "We can worry about that side of it later."

"I can make the necessary arrangements . . . if that helps," Julia said.

Cade looked at her. He knew Julia had assets of her own that he had never made it his business to pry into. "It's really that important to you?" he said.

Julia nodded. "Yes," she told him. "It is."

Later, after Julia had retired ahead of him, Cade sat brooding in his study for a long time. He checked the clock, made several calls, and sent out a few carefully worded messages into the net.

◎ CHAPTER TWELVE ◎

A few miles north of Catalina Island, the *Sassy Lady* trailed a foamy wake across a placid sea rolling gently under a cloudless sky. Cade, in a straw hat and swim trunks, leaned over from a sun lounge on the boat deck aft of the wheelhouse, helped himself to another beer from the ice chest, and passed one to Blair. Vrel and Krossig declined, nursing their previous ones, still somewhat wary of this dubious Terran habit. Julia and Dee were sunning themselves on the bow, while Luke kept Warren company in the wheelhouse, and others were in the main cabin below. A crewman was preparing rods and tackle on the fishing platform at the stern. Rebecca had stayed behind, preferring to remain within the security of the house. Blair was still enthusing about his forthcoming move to Australia. He had some things to finish up in Los Angeles, and would be following on a month or so after Krossig.

"Just think, they're giving me a position to study Hyadean science officially," he told Cade. "I'll be getting paid for it."

"But don't our own people have jobs like that here?" Cade said. "I thought half of Washington was into it."

Blair shook his head. "I'm talking about understanding the *real* science, the attitude of mind that let them get it right. The government collaborations focus too much on short-term applications—better ways to make weapons and profits. I got offers there a couple of times but it wasn't what I wanted."

Cade really didn't know one way or the other. He nodded, sipped his beer, and left it at that.

"We got a message from Erya, on her way to Chryse," Krossig told Cade. "She says you've shown her a new way of seeing things. She hopes she'll be able to spread it on Chryse."

"Sounds as if the place could do with it," Blair commented.

"I just received a gift too," Vrel told them. He had acquired an outrageously gaudy pair of beach shorts and was sprawled on a blanket spread out over the deck. The Chrysean sun, Amaris, shone more brightly and slightly more toward the violet. Hyadeans had no problem with the solar intensity on Earth and soaked up all they could get. Blair had speculated to Cade that maybe that was why they chose mountainous areas. Vrel made the announcement sound like a special event.

"What was that?" Cade asked him.

"From Neville Baxter—at the party. It's a Maori sculpture, a kind of figurine. Very attractive. I'll show it to you next time you're at the mission. Dee says it's probably worth quite a lot."

"That sounds like Neville," Cade agreed.

"He also says I have to visit him in New Zealand. Apparently, it's important to see that all the world isn't like America. What does he mean by that?"

"A kind of private joke that we have between countries," Cade said. Vrel nodded vaguely but didn't really seem to understand.

"Well, I'm looking forward to seeing the East," Krossig said. "I might even get a chance to visit other areas . . . even the Himalayas, maybe." He leaned back against the sun lounge he was on and tossed out an arm in a sweeping gesture. "Have you any idea how unique this planet of yours is? These huge mountain ranges; chasms like the Yangtze gorges. The whole surface is young, sculpted only yesterday. That's why life here is so colorful and varied. It's life that has been renewed and reinvigorated. The worlds we know are old and tired—endless expanses of monotonous plains and eroded hills, silted rivers, insipid swamplands. Worlds in their old age, awaiting rejuvenation."

"Have those planets been around all that much longer, then?" Cade asked.

"No. They've just been wearing down for longer," Krossig said.

"They haven't had the disruptions that Earth has gone through," Blair put in. "Not anytime lately, anyhow. Our conventional notion of slow, gradual change over huge time-spans got it wrong. Changes happen quickly and violently."

Cade knew that Blair could go on for hours if he was allowed to warm to a theme. He looked over at Vrel. "I don't know about quick and violent changes to planets, but I've seen plenty of them in people. This is starting to sound more like your field." Vrel was the political economist.

Vrel raised the can he was holding, twirled it around and contemplated it for a few seconds, then seemed to change his mind and lowered it again. "Hm. There's something paradoxical here," he said. "Terrans believed in gradualism, but their whole history is violent and catastrophic. Hyadeans accept upheaval as the natural way of change, but we deplore it and try to eliminate it from our affairs. That's what's at the bottom of our problems with the Querl— why we and they are in armed opposition."

"How's that?" Blair asked. The reasons for the standoff and occasional conflict between the Hyadean and the Querl worlds was something that Cade had long wanted to understand better too.

"Well, we are taught that their system reflects values that are incompatible with ours," Vrel said. "They take pride in what we consider to be social ills in need of correction. They could never conform to the system of approvals and entitlements that our social structure is built on."

"So does that make them a threat that you have to defend against?" Cade asked.

"We've always been told that they are," Vrel replied.

Krossig conceded the field to politics and elaborated. "Their system can't work. Our economists have proved it. Because it's based on conflicts and rivalries that consume nonproductive effort, it must devour resources faster than it can replenish them. As the situation becomes more critical, the conflicts will increase, making the imbalance worse. Eventually, the only solution left to them will be to try and take from us—provided we let them. If we make that impossible by maintaining sufficient military strength, the outcome, eventually, must be the Querl's downfall."

Cade drank again and stared at him. It was too pat, like a memorized line that had been drummed in through life. Typically Hyadean. He shifted his gaze to Vrel, whose response had been less automatic. Twice, Vrel had qualified his statements by cautioning that they were what Hyadeans were "taught" or had been "told." Those were surprising words to hear coming from a Hyadean. "I assume the Querl must know the Chrysean position," he said. "So how do they see it?"

"They don't see themselves as disorderly or unruly, but simply as pursuing their ideals of independence and freedom," Vrel replied. He thought for a moment, and then smiled uncomfortably. "And we're supposed to be here to save Earth from going the same way. Yet it seems that those same things are also regarded as ideals by most humans." He looked from one to another of the others helplessly. "Another paradox. There's something wrong somewhere, isn't there? But I can't put my finger on what it is."

Warren came out from the wheelhouse at that point to announce that they had reached the fishing grounds and were slowing down to begin casting, and Vrel's question never did get answered. Later, when Cade and Blair were leaning on the rail together, watching the waves, Blair remarked that it was the first time he had ever heard a Chrysean questioning the home world's system.

"I know," Cade replied. "Interesting, isn't it? Maybe this crazy world of ours is starting to rub off on them more than we think." He lifted his head to follow a group of porpoises as they broke surface to frolic a hundred feet or so from the boat. "And then again . . . maybe it was just the beer."

◉ CHAPTER THIRTEEN ◉

It was strange that the theory Earth's scientific establishment finally put together for shaping the evolution of the cosmos should be based on gravity, when the electromagnetic force was ten thousand billion, billion, billion, billion times stronger, and 99 percent of observable matter existed in the form of electrically charged plasma that responded to it. More so when galaxies, certain binary stars, and other objects were found not to move in the ways that purely gravitational models said they should, and various forms of "dark matter" and other unobservables had to be invented to explain why.

The Hyadean universe, by contrast, was electrical. Matter was fundamentally an electrical phenomenon. The basic force was electrical, and gravity a byproduct. The cosmos, its galaxies, stars, and other constituents, hadn't condensed gravitationally out of gas, dust, and spinning nebulas produced from the debris of some primordial Big Bang. Such an explosion would have resulted simply in permanent dispersion of energy and whatever particles formed out of it. Again, the Terrans' grand theory had gotten things backward. Cosmic objects, from dust clouds and planets to neutron stars and quasars weren't the results of condensation and collapse from rarefied clouds of matter, but of the progressive breaking down from superdense concentrations of it. Electrical interactions operating on a titanic scale spun these objects to instability, causing them to throw off parts of themselves which then repeated the process, engendering a succession of bodies of progressively diminishing mass, rotation, and magnetic energy. Depending on the mass of the original fragmenting singularity, the products could be quasars, which in turn gave rise to radio galaxies, and from them, spiral galaxies; globular halos of younger stars around galaxies; or supernovas evolving into pulsars or white dwarves. Gravity only had any significant effect as a comparatively feeble cleaning-up process in the latter phases.

Fragments that didn't make it as stars cooled to form the gas giants, which when meeting and entering into capture with a star or another gas giant threw off what became minor planets, their satellites, comets, and the other debris that formed planetary systems. These were the times when space became an electrically active medium, transmitting forces that disrupted orbits to bring about the encounters that renewed and revitalized worlds. During the quiescent periods between, the interplanetary plasma would organize into an insulating configuration in which gravity was allowed to predominate. Local observations conducted during a few centuries of such a quiet period had led Earth's astronomers to overgeneralize such conditions as representing the permanent situation.

However, many surface characteristics of bodies in the Solar System were impossible to reconcile with the conventional picture of nothing having essentially changed for billions of years.

Furthermore, the farthest, hence oldest, objects visible in the cosmos—such as quasars—were the most massive and energetic: precisely the opposite of what gradual condensation from initially rarefied matter would predict. And the detection of vast structures of galaxy-cluster "walls" and voids at the largest scales of observation indicated processes having been operating in the universe for far longer than the fifteen billion years that the Big Bang model allowed since its inception.

But things like that didn't fit with the theory.

❀ CHAPTER FOURTEEN ❀

Cade hadn't put a lot of trust in the messages he sent out electronically via the net. They had been worded cryptically, with obscure references that only the recipients would recognize. A friend who worked on communications had told him that most computers these days were required to carry chips that tagged messages with invisible codes enabling senders to be traced. As was his custom, he'd had more faith in word of mouth.

He had no idea how to go about finding a channel to contact Marie directly. People who knew about such things told him if she were indeed back in the U.S. and was working with CounterAction, she would be using a different name and operating in an environment carefully structured such that she *couldn't* be located. However, Cade knew a minister in San Pedro by the name of Udovich, a staunch Republican disapproving of Ellis's Washington regime, who ran a church and a shelter for evicted families by day, and at other times disappeared on long camping and hiking trips up into the Sierra. One of the people that Cade talked to whispered that Udovich was involved with some kind of conduit that routed arms in via Mexico to paramilitary groups up in the mountains. Californian laws would have made this impossible in earlier years. But by this time, even law enforcement agencies were rebelling against the Washington line and turning blind eyes. Many took it as seeds of revolution in the wind.

That suggested Udovich could have connections with Sovereignty, and through them access into the higher levels of their militant arm, CounterAction, somewhere. If so, Cade reasoned, they ought to have a way of getting a message through to Marie, even if it meant going all the way back up the tree and then down again via China. Around noon on the day following the boat trip, he drove up to San Pedro and talked with Udovich over iced teas at a sidewalk table outside a sports bar called O'Reilly's, down by the bay.

After opening small talk, Cade mentioned casually that ministers were traditionally respected for keeping confidences, and therefore often trusted to convey sensitive communications. Smiling out at the ocean, Udovich agreed that this was often so. Cade hazarded the guess that a man of Udovich's convictions probably wouldn't be overenamored by the current policies being enacted in Washington. Dreadful, Udovich agreed. Professional middle-class Americans being sold out like cheap labor. Cade regarded the minister long and hard, stroking his chin as if the thought had just occurred to him for the first time, and remarked that Udovich didn't strike him as the kind of person who would sit back and watch it happen. If there were people organizing in opposition, he'd want to get involved. Well, certainly anyone with principles and a conscience would want to do something, Udovich told the ocean, giving away nothing.

His oblique references not having been rebuffed, Cade interlaced his fingers, leaned closer across the table, and came to the point. "I want to contact somebody who I believe might be with one of the underground political groups in this country. I've reason to think you might have connections who might pass a message in the right direction. Can you help?"

Udovich's pink, moonlike, bespectacled features—surely the most incongruous image for the kind of thing Cade was asking—didn't register surprise. He had clearly been expecting something like this. His manner, however, shed its protective cover of vague geniality and became businesslike. "Who is this person?" he murmured.

"My former wife, who went to China. I've heard that she's back now, with CounterAction. I have someone who needs to leave the country invisibly. CounterAction are supposed to have ways."

"What kind of problem prevents this person from buying a ticket and getting on a plane?" Udovich asked.

"Giving the wrong people a bad press can get you into bad favor these days," Cade answered. "If the people who don't like what you say have the power to take you off the streets, things can get awkward."

"Why should I or anyone else care? Why risk it?"

"Because it's the same cause." Cade shrugged. "And in any case, you run a ministry. Protecting your flock depends on donations. You know a little bit about me. I can arrange generous contributions from the most unlikely quarters. I'm sure it all helps."

Udovich considered the proposition for a while, crunching on an ice cube from his tea. "Supposing I *were* able to pass this request on to where you ask, why wouldn't that be enough?' he queried at last. "Why does it need to find this ex of yours specifically?"

"It wouldn't if whoever makes the decicions were happy to take my word for it," Cade agreed. "But why should they? She and I might have had our differences, but she'd vouch that I can be trusted to play straight. I'm not political. I deal in people. Reputation is my work." He smiled faintly and gestured across the table. "A bit like you, I guess."

Udovich nodded slowly and seemed satisfied. "I'd need her name and a little about when you were together," he said. "And something that would convince her this has come from you."

Cade supplied the minimum details that seemed necessary. Udovich committed them to memory. The second part was tougher. "Tell her . . . there's some red coal," he said finally. Udovich nodded and didn't ask. In their more romantic days, one of the things Cade and Marie had liked doing together was solving cryptic crossword puzzles. It was an anagrammatic play on his name: ROL*and* CADE; take the conjunction out, and the remaining letters rearranged into *red coal*. With a bit of playing around, Marie would get it.

"No guarantees, but we'll see," Udovich pronounced. He finished his tea and stood up. "Well, I must get back to tending my flock." He looked back over his shoulder as he was about to leave. "We must watch out for the wolves, you see." He walked away, leaving Cade to take it whichever way he pleased.

❧ ❧ ❧

Late that afternoon, Dee and Vrel stopped by the house to collect
a share of the previous day's fish catch, which Henry had cleaned,
gutted, and set aside in the refrigerator for them. Julia was in the guest
suite keeping Rebecca company, since she preferred to stay out of
sight of visitors. Cade entertained Vrel and Dee to drinks in the
lounge area around the bar.

"Getting daring these days, aren't we, Vrel?" he quipped as Vrel
mixed himself a gin and tonic—with a generous measure of tonic.
"Taking fish back to eat at the mission, now, and halfway toward
becoming an alcoholic."

"I think I'm just beginning to realize how insipid our food is,"
Vrel said, making a face.

"I hope you're remembering to take those pills they give you.
Wouldn't want you going down with any of these terrible Terran
germs."

"I know you used to take them once," Dee said. "But I don't
remember seeing them for ages."

Vrel made an indifferent shrug. "Maybe, getting to know Earth-
people better has made me start to think that maybe Hyadeans can be
a little . . ." He groped for the word, then muttered something to his
veebee.

"*Neurotic*," it supplied.

"Neurotic," Vrel repeated.

Dee laughed delightedly and squeezed his arm in a way that said
she liked him better like this. Vrel grinned.

"How is he going to fit in again when he goes home?" Cade asked
her.

Dee pouted. "*Roland!* Don't talk about him going home." She
looked at Vrel. "That's not going to be for a long time yet, is it?"

Vrel's face became more serious. "I don't know. I suppose a lot
depends on what happens here. Two Hyadeans from the mission
were harassed and jeered at in a mall near Lakewood yesterday. The
police escorted them back. They've put extra security around the
mission again."

"Oh. . . . That's a shame," Cade said. The outbreaks of protest and violence across the country were causing anti-Hyadean reactions in places. ISS agents landing in a helicopter assault had wiped out what was said to be the base of the group that had mounted the attack in Kentucky, and security units across the nation were cracking down with arrests of suspected CounterAction supporters. Cade had always tried to steer clear of such things. Yet now, he reflected, his action in harboring Rebecca was probably enough to get him on a wanted list already. He hoped Udovich wasn't being affected. If pressures developed that prevented him from following through, Cade could find himself saddled with having a fugitive from the federal government in the house indefinitely.

He sighed and tasted his drink wearily. One mention of Marie, and life was getting complicated again. Even at this distance—whatever distance; he didn't even know where she was—and after so long, it seemed her nature was still that of catastrophic upheaval, disrupting what had started to become his predictable, gravitationally stable universe.

◈ CHAPTER FIFTEEN ◈

Two days passed by. Independent sources on the net circulated critical accounts of "search and intern" sweeps being carried out by airborne security forces landed in remote parts of Appalachia, Colorado, and Utah. The media billed the actions as counterterrorist, directed at the groups who had begun a campaign of political assassination, which the authorities would not tolerate. A number of helicopters were alleged to have been brought down by missiles. An ISS spokesman called for Hyadean defensive equipment to be fitted to government-operated air vehicles as a precaution.

Then, Cade received a phone call one morning when he was with Julia and their accountant, who had stopped by to review some figures. A smoothly articulated masculine voice asked him what the color of coal was. "My kind is red," Cade replied.

"Then I gather I'm speaking to the right person."

Cade asked the accountant to excuse him but this was private and important, and took the phone through to his study. He closed the door and indicated it was okay to go ahead.

"I have a message from Mole Woman. It says you could always be depended on for surprises," the caller informed him.

Despite everything, Cade couldn't contain a smile. This was his proof of validity. "Mole Woman" was one of the names that he used to call Marie in their lighter moments—from the comic-book

Catwoman, a joke at the way Marie had of burrowing into the bedclothes on cold mornings to leave just her nose showing.

"It must be my nature," Cade affirmed. "Okay. What do we have?"

"I understand you have a job applicant seeking an overseas position," the voice informed him.

"Looking for less stress and pressure. An escape from the rat race," Cade confirmed.

"The positions we offer normally pay around twenty thousand. Was that the kind of figure your client has in mind?"

It was double talk, spelling out what the service would *cost*. "We could settle for that, yes," Cade agreed.

"Fine. Of course, we would need to arrange an appropriate interview. Where does the applicant currently reside?"

"I guess you could say on the West Coast."

"Hm. . . . These things are usually managed by our Eastern region. However, if that should be impracticable, it would probably be possible to arrange a preliminary meeting with a local branch representative."

Cade chewed on his lip while he thought about it. The reference to the East probably meant that CounterAction's route for spiriting people out of the country led in that direction, maybe through the Caribbean to Africa, and then Asia via the Middle East. He didn't want to get any more involved here, in his own backyard, he decided. Midnight callers and furtive meetings around the locality would be the last thing he needed. Better to get Rebecca there as quickly as possible. And if something came of it, she would already be partly on her way.

"I'd prefer that the regional office handle it, if they're the proper people," he said.

"You will be contacted in due course." The caller hung up.

That same evening, a fax came through in Cade's study of a promotional brochure from a hotel called the Metro in downtown Atlanta. Typed across the bottom were terse instructions for the "applicant" to be outside the main doors of the ground-level motor lobby at a given date and time, holding an Atlanta city guide book for recognition.

The date stipulated allowed four days, presumably making allowance for a journey by road. Luke advised against it on the grounds that, with all the trouble in the news, spot checks of travelers on major highways, railroads, and public buses were likely to have been intensified. And besides, he didn't think Rebecca was up to the stresses of a protracted trip. But Cade had never contemplated such alternatives in the first place. What was the point of doing favors for wealthy friends, he asked, if you couldn't ask one back now and again for yourself?

There was one Lou Zinner, based most of the time in Las Vegas, who had interests in casinos and the entertainment world, and fingers in various associated sleazy dealings. It was Lou, for example, who provided the available girls for Cade's Hyadean parties and boat trips. He remained at a distance behind Cade's more respectable front and didn't deal with the Hyadeans directly. Lou also happened to own an executive jet, which he used for attending business meetings, visiting "family," and flying a seemingly inexhaustible supply of mistresses, young admirers, and hopeful starlets to be entertained in exotic places. Lou was always happy to hear from Cade because high-ranking Hyadeans taking time off talked in big bucks. Hence, he was a hundred percent receptive when Cade called and said he wanted the loan of Lou's plane and its pilot for a day.

The craggy, balding head guffawed heartily on the screen in Cade's study. "What's going on, Rolie? Don't tell me. You're expanding the operation. The boat's too tame for 'em now. You've got aliens that wanna join the twenty thousand club, right?"

"Wrong. No, nothing like that. I need to make a rush delivery across the country. It'll be back the same night."

"Okay, then I'm not askin'. So what's the cut?"

Cade thought for a second. "Maybe I'll be able to get you some high rollers out there yet. You know how those ones that come across from Washington are loaded."

"I'll settle for that. Okay, Rolie, you've got it. Just try to send it back in one piece, willya? I've got it booked for the weekend after."

That solved the immediate problem. But Luke thought that if they were going to have an entire aircraft at their disposal, they could

make better use of it. "Just to take one person to Atlanta?" he said to
Cade when Cade gave him the news. "Why on her own? What
happens if something screws up—say nobody shows, and she finds
herself stuck there? We couldn't just leave her like that. One of us
ought to go too. I say we keep a good eye on her until we know she's
in the right hands."

Cade agreed. "In that case I'll go," he said. "This isn't really your
affair. I got us into it." Luke shrugged and nodded in a way that said
it was fine by him.

Julia, however, was perturbed when they updated her on their
thoughts. "Why risk getting mixed up with CounterAction people
directly?" she objected. "If you're seen or identified with them, it
could start trouble that will never go away. We've had the ISS here
already. You know what's going on all over the country. We don't
need to get mixed up in all that."

It seemed a strange turn of attitude after the things Cade had
heard. "Because she's an old friend, remember?" he replied. "Look,
I'm not planning on getting mixed up with anybody. All I'm doing is
taking her as far as a hotel lobby. I don't even need to wait there with
her—just close enough to see she gets picked up. That's it. Then I'm
on my way back."

Eventually, Julia relented, but she still didn't seem happy about it.

Accordingly, Cade and Rebecca made their preparations the
evening before the appointed day. Lou Zinner's jet appeared at the
John Wayne/Orange County airport early the next morning as
arranged, and they took off on time. En route, the plane was
challenged by two Air Force jets that radioed for identification and a
mission statement. Fortunately, the pilot had filed a flight plan, stated
as serving the private business needs of a Nevada-registered VIP. The
plane landed at Hartsfield International Airport, Atlanta, a little over
four hours after leaving California.

❀ CHAPTER SIXTEEN ❀

Frank Pacelli had worked night shift stocking supermarket shelves, sold kitchen ware, and part-timed at a gas station to pay his way through college, and emerged with a degree in chemistry and metallurgical engineering. He had worked first with a couple of mining corporations in Minnesota and Colorado, later at a smelting and rolling plant in Korea, done well, and come back to a position as process designer with a company in Minneapolis. Then the Hyadeans began flooding the world markets with bulk minerals extracted from places like Bolivia by methods no Terran industry could compete with; the company folded, and now Frank drove a taxicab. He got pretty mad when he heard about some of the dealings that went on in Washington and the kind of money some people were reputed to make out of them. But with three children of high-school age to think about, he couldn't afford to risk getting directly involved in the more militant protest organizations that everyone pretended not to know about. But sympathizing with them was another thing. Much passed his eyes that he didn't see, came to his ears that he didn't hear, and he helped the cause when he could.

He turned off Peachtree Street into the motor lobby of the Metro hotel at the time he had been given, and slowed to scan the few figures outside the main entrance. The pudgy woman in the light blue coat and yellow hat, holding a city guide prominently in one hand had to be the person he was to meet. She had a suitcase and a large traveling bag beside her and seemed to be waiting, looking around anxiously. Pacelli eased the cab forward, steering in toward the curb in front of her.

Then it struck him that a tallish man in a gray jacket, standing a few yards away by the doors, was watching her. The conviction solidified when the man's head turned to follow the cab as it closed in. An alarm sounding in his head, Pacelli shifted his foot back to the gas pedal and sped up again, passing the woman just as she was beginning to step forward. He caught a glimpse of her mouth dropping open before he turned away to leave again through the lobby's exit way. He stopped in a parking strip halfway around the block and pressed the "redial" button of his phone to call the number already entered.

"Yes?" The voice that had given him his instructions answered.

"This is Collector. The party's there, a woman. But there's a guy there too, who looks like he's watching her. It didn't feel right, so I thought I'd better check."

"Good thinking. Where are you now?"

"Just around the block."

"Wait."

Pacelli drummed his fingers on the wheel nervously. He was just driving a cab, sent to pick someone up from a hotel. They couldn't nail anyone for that, right? He wasn't sure. From the things he heard, who knew what they could do these days?

The city of Chattanooga lay just under a hundred miles north of Atlanta in southeastern Tennessee, on the Tennessee River near the Georgia-Alabama line. Three large mountain masses overlooked it, each one of strategic importance and the scene of a major battle in the Civil War.

Marie and Len had arrived after an erratic tour through the Great Smoky range to find Olsen safely there too, several hours ahead of them. That had been over a week ago now. Their new temporary hideout until they were regrouped consisted of a double-width mobile home situated among trees on hilly ground to the north side of the city, between Signal Mountain and the river. Sharing the quarters with them were two other CounterAction people known only as "Vera" and "Bert," both seemingly proficient, with another man that they referred to as "Otter." Marie could tell that Otter was not from the organization. She got the feeling that he was in transit and temporary hiding, in the process of being moved to somewhere more permanent.

That Otter should in this way meet former members of the Scorpion cell that had been hurriedly disbanded was not accidental. Scorpion had been identified by the authorities, blamed for the assassinations that were partly the cause of the current unrest, and targeted for elimination. Otter apparently knew who *had* been responsible: an officer of the security forces themselves, acting on orders from a source close to the administration. Otter could name the officer and give the source of the Hyadean weapon that was used, which had come from a cache stolen in South America, later recovered but never acknowledged officially. It seemed that Otter was being taken to report his information to higher echelons of CounterAction, but the current disruptions and hasty relocations going on everywhere were slowing things down. Whoever was giving the orders had authorized Olsen to let Otter pass on what he knew in case Otter didn't get to wherever he was being taken, and as a further precaution Olsen had included Marie. It wasn't as if the information was something that Sovereignty would want kept secret.

Otter lay sprawled along a couch in the living area watching a movie. Bert was in a room at the back, sorting and checking through various items of equipment. Vera had kept night watch and was sleeping. The number of beds and amount of kit scattered through the rooms and closets suggested that more people used the place, but at present were elsewhere on undisclosed errands. Marie paced restlessly behind Olsen, who was seated at the table in the room that served as his quarters and office, talking to the taxi driver who had been sent to make the collection. He held the phone away suddenly, and cursed beneath his breath. "What is it?" Marie asked, going over.

"A woman showed, but it could be a setup. He thinks she's being watched."

"*What?*" Marie stared at the phone in his hand, as if it could tell her something. Roland wouldn't be involved in something like that. Not knowingly, anyway. She felt embarrassed and guilty, as if she had led them into this. "I can't believe it," was all she could say.

"Let's see what Len thinks." Olsen used a mouse to click the "Call" box of a communications dialer already displayed on one of the screens in front of him. Moments later, Len's voice answered from a connected speaker.

"Watcher here."

Len was at the Metro in Atlanta, observing from back inside the motor lobby entrance. The situation had demanded that somebody else be on hand in case of problems developing, not just the cabbie. The phone that Len was carrying had a video pickup.

"Collector thinks the subject may have a tail," Olsen said at the mike. "How do you read it?"

"Yes, I've got him too. The subject's a woman. It looks like they know each other. Collector came by and then took off. Subject is making like 'What do I do?' The tail is shaking his head." As Len spoke, the screen in front of Olsen switched to show a crazily angled shot of a woman in a light blue coat, wearing a yellow hat, standing beside two bags. Her face was indistinct in the light under the roof outside the lobby doors. She was looking to her right, then turned away in the other direction. The scene cavorted as the camera swung, then settled on a tall man in a light-colored jacket, keeping farther back in the shadows. The figure became clearer as Len moved out toward the doors, then jumped into closeup. It was a man his midthirties, angular cheeked with narrow eyes, and brown wavy hair combed back at both temples.

"Oh my God!" Marie whispered weakly. "What's he doing *there*?"

Olsen turned his head. "You know him? Who is he?"

"It's him . . . the person it came from. My ex-husband. That's Roland. . . . He must have come with her, to make sure things went okay."

Olsen studied the image thoughtfully. "That means we don't have to listen only to this woman we don't know. We can get his input too. You're sure he's likely to be straight?"

Marie nodded affirmatively. "Oh yes."

"Then let's bring him along." Olsen leaned forward and touched a key. "Watcher?"

"Here."

"The tail is friendly. In fact, we're glad he's here. So include him in the party too."

Rebecca was getting agitated, looking back at Cade and making empty-hands motions. Cade didn't know what was going on. It had seemed that the cab driver had spotted her and pulled over; then he seemed to change his mind at the last moment. Cade signaled back tersely for Rebecca to stop making it so obvious that they were together. She seemed to get the message, calmed down, and directed her attention back toward the motor lobby entrance. An airport shuttle that had been filling with departing hotel guests started up and departed.

Perhaps the business with the cabbie had been genuinely a case of mistaken identity. Cade checked his watch. Seven minutes past the hour. Was it reasonable to expect people in this kind of line to be punctual—especially with all the trouble that was going on? He opened the newspaper that he'd been carrying under his arm and stared at it. He felt like ham in a spy movie. Well, hell, what was he supposed to know about this kind of business? He found he was looking at the sports section. He didn't even understand the rules of baseball. A white limo appeared and disgorged a couple both with long hair and in blue jeans. While the driver came around to begin unloading luggage from the trunk, a bellman appeared from inside the hotel, pulling a cart.

And then a cab appeared in the entrance and slowed. Cade wasn't certain, but it seemed like the same one that had passed through before. This time it drew up directly in front of Rebecca. She stooped to peer inside uncertainly. The nearside window lowered, and the driver leaned across to say something. Rebecca nodded. The cab's trunk lid popped open, and the cabbie got out to take care of the two bags. Finally, everything seemed to be going well. Rebecca opened the rear door, and climbed in, glancing out from the window to nod quickly. Cade watched the cabbie slam the trunk lid shut, then go forward and get back in. Just a few more seconds now, and the whole business would be out of Cade's hands. He exhaled a long sigh of relief.

"Take it easy. Don't turn around. Just get in the cab too." The voice spoke close to his ear. It was low, little more than a murmur, but had a distinct no-nonsense quality.

Cade tensed reflexively, then forced himself to relax again, realizing that anything else was futile. "What is this?" he breathed.

"I don't know either. It seems that the people meeting your friend want to talk to you."

"I'm just a delivery man. I don't know anything about what goes on."

"That's not for me to decide. I've just got orders." There was a pause. Cade hesitated. "Come on," the voice said. "You don't want to mess with us. Let's move."

Cade sighed and walked over to the cab, the stranger following. Somehow, the cabbie seemed to know they would be coming and was waiting. Cade opened the door, shrugged in response to Rebecca's bemused look, and got in next to her. The stranger squeezed in beside Cade and closed the door. He was maybe sixtyish, Cade saw as he sat back. Tanned, wrinkled features; hair going white; dark, indecipherable eyes—the kind that never gave away exactly where they were focused. He was wearing a hip-length coat of brown suede over a tan, crew-neck sweater. The cab pulled back out onto Peachtree, negotiated several blocks, and descended an on ramp to a highway that signs said were Interstates 75 and 85 South, which led back toward the airport. But after a few intersections it exited again onto a road leading among industrial premises, where it entered a parking area and stopped beside a black, windowless van. "Here, we change," the stranger informed them. "Not much of a view from here on, I'm afraid. But I'm sure you understand that these things are necessary."

The three got out. A driver was waiting in the van, wearing a hat over a full head of hair, who could equally well have been male or female from the brief glimpse they were able to get. Before they had even walked around to the rear doors, the cabbie had deposited Rebecca's bags and was on his way. Interestingly, the stranger hadn't paid him anything, Cade noted. The stranger opened one of the van's rear doors, picked up the suitcase, and ushered the other two in. Cade took the travel bag. The interior had seats on both sides and across the front, and was lit by lights in the corners. Cade and Rebecca settled down facing each other across the rear end. The stranger moved past them to sit looking back. He banged his hand a couple of times on the wall behind him, and the van moved off.

Cade quickly lost track of the turns, so that by the time he felt the van accelerating back onto what felt like the Interstate again, he was unable to tell whether they were still going south or had about-turned. As time wore on he made sporadic attempts to start some kind of conversation with the stranger, but the responses were brief and noncommittal, except to say that they could call him "Len" and it was okay for Cade to call Lou Zinner's pilot and say he had been delayed. Cade was mildly surprised that he had been allowed to keep his phone, and concluded that he wasn't some kind of prisoner. Hence, if this dragged on past the pilot's deadline for returning, he didn't think he would have much difficulty getting a regular flight back. Maybe on principle he should ask CounterAction to cover the fare.

A little under two hours passed. Since the people they were going to meet hadn't known how they would be traveling, it made sense that the initial rendezvous should have been set in a regional center like Atlanta. There was no reason why the ultimate destination should be conveniently close, of course. But it puzzled Cade that Len, and presumably those he represented, seemed unconcerned about the possibility of police checks on a journey of this length. The most likely explanation he could think of was that in their own territory they had the highways staked out and were able to pass warnings of roadblocks in time for them to be avoided.

Eventually, the van's motions signaled that they were leaving a highway. A few minutes of intermittent turns and stops followed before it halted, and the engine died. Len got out, turning to retrieve the bags. Cade and Rebecca followed, stretching cramped legs and flexing arms, to find themselves outside the rear of a typical midrange motel.

Len led them to room 127 and rapped on the door. It was opened by a petite woman in a thin, knitted pattern sweater, loose slacks, and lightweight hiking boots. She had wiry hair that wavered between dark blond and burnt auburn, styled short and easy to manage, sharply defined features that couldn't be called "cute," yet were attractive in their own in-depth kind of way, and dark, almost black eyes that in moments gave the impression of never being still, darting over the arrivals and already seeming to have gleaned all the information there was to see. The eyes came to rest on Cade and softened into mischievous liquid pools at the astonishment on his face.

"So hi," she greeted. "I guess, for once, I get a turn with the surprises. It's been a long time."

It was Marie.

◎ CHAPTER SEVENTEEN ◎

It was so sudden and unexpected that Cade found himself at a loss for anything to say that wouldn't have seemed inane. For several seconds, all he could do was stare. While he was still getting over his surprise, Marie brought them all inside. She had doubtless come from a hideout or safe house somewhere in the area to make the initial contact. Cade and Rebecca wouldn't expect to have been taken straight there.

It was a standard motel room with a pair of double beds. A woman's topcoat was thrown on one of them; a couple of magazines lay on the other, which was rumpled, as if Marie had been reading while she waited. Coffee was brewed in the pot provided, and some deli sandwiches, chips, and soft drinks laid out alongside it. Len threw his coat on top of Marie's and handed her a phone that he had been carrying, which Cade saw was a video type. *Now* he realized why Marie hadn't been surprised on seeing him. Len had sent back an image, even before he accosted Cade in Atlanta.

Marie positioned the phone on a corner table to take the room in its viewing angle and attached a speaker extension. Evidently, the proceedings were to be monitored remotely. Cade wondered how normal it was for any face-to-face contact to be permitted at all in a first meeting. It seemed dangerous. Had they relaxed their usual precautions, perhaps because Marie had vouched for him?

"We need you sitting here, Rebecca," Marie said, waving to indicate the nearest of the two beds. "You can munch while we talk." Rebecca moved the coats aside and sat down. "Roland, I'm going to have to ask you to take a walk outside with Len," Marie said. "You'll get to talk later. I'm sure I don't have to explain." Cade nodded, shrugged in a way that said it was okay, selected a sandwich to take with the coffee cup he was holding, and moved to the door. Just before Len opened it, Rebecca got up again, went into the bathroom, and came back out with a towel, which she spread by her on the bed to put her sandwich plate on. "Okay? Let's get started," Cade heard Marie say as Len closed the door behind them, hanging the "Do Not Disturb" sign outside.

He sipped his coffee and stood, looking around. The van was gone—or at least, moved from the slot it had been in. Extending away beyond the fence were the trappings of what could have been the outskirts of virtually any city. In the distance, however, in a direction that Cade judged to be the west or south from the position of the sun, stood a high, flat-topped mountain, forming one side of a valley. He had noticed that the room's call terminal carried the area code 423. Offhand, he didn't know where that was. Two hours driving from Atlanta? . . . But then, he didn't know if all of that had been in the same direction.

"Kestrel suggested we take a walk," Len said. "Let's walk."

"Kestrel?" Cade grinned. "Is that what you call her these days?" Len grunted, seemingly irked at having given away more than necessary. They moved to the end of the block and stood chewing sandwiches and finishing their coffees. Then they crossed to a dumpster standing on a corner of the parking lot to dispose of the cups. Vehicles were parked here and there. It was early yet for the evening arrivals to begin showing up. Cade saw license plates from Georgia, Alabama, Tennessee, one from Florida, another, Indiana. It didn't really tell him much. They strolled back to the room. The sign was still hanging outside the door. They made another circuit of the block. When they came back, the sign had gone. Len knocked, and Marie let them back in.

Now it was Cade's turn to talk to the camera and answer

questions. Len stayed, while Rebecca left with Marie. There were no surprises. Cade told his story as it had happened, omitting details of precisely who had initiated the contact into CounterAction for him, because he wasn't asked. The question that caused him the most difficulty was regarding his motivation: Why had he done it? Why had he gotten involved? He couldn't say it was to help with their cause—truth was, he had never given much thought to it. His own life was pretty comfortable, thanks to no one else, because *he* had made it that way. It was up to others to worry about what he considered to be their problems. He didn't feel that whoever he was talking to would appreciate a discourse on personal philosophies of that nature, however.

"Julia—the person I'm with now. It seemed important to her," he said. "Apparently, they were close friends back in college. . . . I guess I just wanted to do what I could. I didn't have any thought then of getting involved." He gestured to indicate the room he was in. "Not like this." Which was true; but somehow not enough. Cade didn't find it satisfying.

"There was nothing of a more . . . 'personal' nature, maybe?" the voice from the phone speaker queried.

Cade sat back, jolted by the question. "No. . . ." But he wasn't sure. He realized how impossible this would have been had Marie remained present.

There was a pause. Then the voice on the phone said, "Very well." Evidently, Cade had passed muster; the subject was closed. So was that what he had been brought all this way for? It needled him.

"Well, I'm glad that you're satisfied," he said. It was one of those rare times when he was unable to keep an edge of sarcasm out of his voice. "My plane back to LA will have left already. I'm going to have to get some kind of a regular connection instead from here, wherever this is—unless you've got rules that say we have to go on another mystery tour first. You realize that you've cost me my whole evening."

The person who the voice belonged to seemed unimpressed. "There are people out there right now for whom it's costing their homes, their families, their lives," he replied coolly.

The remark hit Cade as disconcertingly as it came unexpectedly.

He sat back on the bed, finding himself too troubled and confused to respond. He had never thought of it that way. Somehow, the thought of putting in an expense claim didn't feel like such a good idea.

Marie and Rebecca came back. Len held a muted conversation over the phone. It seemed that business was concluded for the moment. He would need to go back to confer, he announced. Rebecca would probably be moved to another location later that night and arrangements made to send Cade home. In the meantime they were to remain here. Marie would keep them company. Len collected his coat off the bed. When he opened the door, the van had magically reappeared. As he was leaving, Marie caught Cade's sleeve, and drew close to keep her words private. "We have to take care of business first," she murmured. "Maybe we'll be able to talk a little later. There must be lots. It's been a long time." Cade nodded.

While Marie rinsed out the coffee pot and prepared another brew, Rebecca lay back along the bed they had been using and stared at the ceiling. Cade paced disconsolately to the door and back several times, then settled down on the other and picked up one of the magazines still lying there. An ad at the bottom of the page it was opened at was for a restaurant called the Chattanooga Chew Chew. Its phone number had the area code 423. Well, that answered one question, anyway, he told himself.

The miniature locator that ISS operative "Ruby," currently operating under the field name Rebecca, had attached beneath the collar of Len's jacket while it lay on the bed updated its position from satellite fixes every five seconds and had connected with the national security network via booster relays covering the area. The computers at ISS Regional Command in Atlanta had found voiceprint matches with two samples from previously tapped recordings, both established from interrogation leads as belonging to members of the Scorpion cell. The male was the operative known as "Len"; the female went as "Kestrel."

For ten minutes, the plot from the locator traced a route northwest of Chattanooga to coordinates shown on a large-scale map as pinpointing one of a number of mobile homes situated in a wooded area just over the Tennessee River. Conversation picked up later inside the house identified the Scorpion member, believed to be cell leader, known as "Olsen," and a female voice not on file. Then, after a further fifteen minutes, another male voice was detected. Within seconds, the analyzer monitor in Atlanta started beeping and flashing a box with the caption PRIORITY. An operator transferred spectra samples to an auxiliary screen and ran a full Fourier and time series comparison. He picked up a red phone that connected directly to the section supervisor.

"Bingo!" he reported. "It's him, Reyvek. We've found the defector."

A Status Report, Operations Plan, and Request for Action Approval were flashed to Washington within eighteen minutes. Before a half-hour was up, the response came back: *GO*.

Choppers from a base in the mountains between Chattanooga and Nashville, experimentally fitted with quiet-running Hyadean ducted fans in place of conventional rotors, landed strike teams a mile from the target in opposite directions along the north bank of the river. Their orders were to identify and take out the designated Subject, along with all other opposition on sight. When that objective was confirmed, a second unit would go in to relieve operative Ruby in the motel on the south side of the city, and eliminate the two remaining hostiles there.

◎ CHAPTER EIGHTEEN ◎

Cade lay propped against the headboard and watched as Marie poured two coffees. She added some creamer and a sachet of sugar to his, left hers black, and brought them over. Rebecca was in the bathroom, and from the time that had passed, could conceivably have fallen asleep there. Cade took the cup that Marie offered. She sat down with her own at the foot of the bed and regarded him over the rim as she took a sip. He returned the look evenly for a moment, saw that she was simply being open, inviting things to take any turn from here, and let his face soften.

" 'Mole Woman'! What ever made you remember that? I thought you'd be a million years past any sentimental stuff by now—whatever used to be there, anyway."

"They wanted something personal. You see, you never could get it into your head that I had a side like that. You only saw this cold intellectual . . . and you invented most of that yourself."

"Oh, come on."

"You still can't see it?"

Cade gestured at her. "Look at you, for Christ's sake."

"So there's a side that wants to do something about things I take seriously, too. The two aren't mutually exclusive. It's just as well some people do. . . . Besides, why just talk about me. What's this 'red coal' thing I'm hearing about all of a sudden?" Her eyes flickered over him. "Trying to tell me something, Roland?"

Cade made an exaggerated show of sighing at the ceiling, missing the impish twist of her mouth. "Oh, we're not about to go off into some Freudian excursion are we? The guy I was talking to threw the question across a table, and that was what I came up with. It's not as if there's a huge list of alternatives."

"Oh, I don't know. You could have picked . . ." Marie thought for a few seconds. "Let's see, there's 'red cola,' 'real cod.' Then you've got 'old acre' or 'old care.' Does 'earl doc' work?" She frowned. "Yes, it does, doesn't it?"

"Okay, okay." Cade cocked a complimentary eyebrow. "You're still as quick, I see." Marie showed an empty palm and made a face that said "if you say so." But she wasn't about to drop it. "So why did you come here?" she said.

Cade let his head fall back against the headboard. "Why is everyone around here trying to psychoanalyze me? Look, it wasn't *me* that wanted to come here. I just planned on coming as far as Atlanta to make sure she was collected okay. The rest was your people's idea. I didn't get a lot of say in it. They went through all this while you were out of the room. Why not ask them when you get back, eh?"

Marie stared at him for a moment or two longer, then nodded. She took another sip from her cup. "So is life still being kind to you?" she asked.

Now Cade felt on familiar ground. He answered automatically. "It is, because I let it." Despite the qualms that had assailed him earlier, he couldn't resist being provocative. "You know how I am. I mind my own business. If other people want to make problems for themselves, that's their right, I guess."

"Oh, how can you blame people for what's happening to them? Ordinary, decent people, I mean. They work hard, believe what they're told. They're being sold out."

Cade raised his chin. They were at it again, already. It seemed that the amnesty had been short-lived. "So who are you blaming, the Hyadeans? Well, some of them happen to be friends of mine, and they can be pretty ordinary and decent, too, believe it or not."

"But that's the whole *point*! It's not a simplistic 'them' or 'us' situation. The power on both sides is in collusion. It's like, oh . . . when the Romans used to provide palaces and protection to the local chiefs for keeping the natives in line and the taxes coming in. This whole regime that they've set up in Washington is getting to be just like one of those puppet—" The room's phone units sounded an incoming call. Cade picked up the handset from the bedside stand, pressed the "2" button to select audio only, and offered the phone to Marie. "Dictatorships you used to hear about," she completed as she took it. The latch of the bathroom door clicked barely audibly.

A look of alarm seized Marie's face suddenly. As Cade started to mouth a question, she touched "3" to activate the screen and speaker phone. Sounds poured forth of voices shouting indistinctly, some seeming to be barking commands, others yelling warnings; confused scuffling and banging; then a torrent of what could only be gunfire.

"*What in hell—*" Cade began, swinging his legs down off the bed.

Len's face filled the screen, twisted by fear and desperation. "*Kes, get out! It's a bust! They're already coming in here! We've got—*" Half his head erupted in an explosion of flesh and gore. He vanished to be replaced by a brief image of a black-hooded figure holding a gun in one hand and gesturing to somebody with the other, then disappearing off-screen.

"*Jesus Christ!*" Cade cried.

"*State Security. Freeze right there!*" Cade looked around at where the voice had come from. Rebecca had come out of the bathroom, clasping an automatic in a two-handed grip. He gaped, paralyzed. But she made the mistake of swinging the weapon from him to Marie and back again to cover both of them. As the muzzle moved away, Marie swept her arm up, throwing the contents of her coffee cup into Rebecca's face, then almost in the same movement bunched herself to go in low under it, crashing her shoulder into Rebecca's midriff with her full weight and momentum behind it. The action was instant, reflexive—before Cade had even tuned in to what was happening. The sound of an explosion followed by more shooting came from the phone's speaker.

The bullet went into the wall a foot away from Cade. Rebecca was hurled backward, going down and cracking her head on the drawer unit by the wall, which had the snack leftovers on top. Marie pulled Rebecca's head up by the hair, thudded it back against the floor, then used her knee to pin the arm holding the gun and twisted it from Rebecca's grasp. Rebecca made a V with the fingers of one hand and jabbed upward viciously, aiming at Marie's eyes, but Marie deflected it, then struck sideways at Rebecca's head with the gun, left then right, and then again—pure survival instinct reacting to lethal danger. Cade looked on, horrified, as blood welled from a gash on Rebecca's temple and ran down her face, mingling with the coffee that Marie had thrown. Marie stood up, breathing shakily. But Rebecca was still not out, nor was she finished. She sat up and lunged for the gun, but was too groggy to judge the distance. Marie shot her twice in the center of the forehead.

Cade was still too shocked to have moved. Marie killed the phone and stood looking uncertainly around the room, thinking to herself furiously. "Len must have carried something back. . . ." She went around to the other bed and picked up her coat, still lying where Len's had been, and began searching rapidly through the folds and pockets. Cade rose in a daze, looked disbelievingly at the body crumpled on the floor while he picked his way past it, and moved over to see what Marie was doing. She turned back the collar and held the coat up to reveal a black, rectangular object, about the size of a printed-circuit chip, attached underneath. She pulled it off, and making a sign for Cade not to say anything, went over to the closet beside the bathroom, where Cade had hung his jacket. A quick check found an identical device under one of the lapels. How or when Rebecca had put it there, he had no idea. Marie thrust the jacket at him to put on, handed him the automatic, and then as an afterthought went into the bathroom and added several extra ammunition clips that she found in Rebecca's toilet bag. As Cade pocketed them, Marie put her hand to her ear and made the motions of using a phone. Cade took his unit out and showed it to her questioningly. She shook her head and pointed at the bed. He tossed the phone down, and then after taking a last look back at the body, turned to follow Marie out the door.

Marie had keys to a spare car that had been left around the back of the block—a white Toyota. They got in, Marie driving, and left as quickly as was practical without drawing attention. As they turned at a traffic light to enter a ramp signed as leading to I-75 North, three military trucks painted in dark camouflage shades and moving fast passed them, heading the other way. Still numbed, Cade felt the unfamiliar bulge in his jacket pocket. Why had Marie given the gun to him? Obviously, because she was already carrying one, was the only answer to suggest itself.

⚙ CHAPTER NINETEEN ⚙

Marie drove tensely, moving the wheel in quick, jerky motions to weave through the evening traffic, constantly watching the mirror. She had switched on the radio and tuned it to a local country-music channel where a deejay was playing phone-in requests. It seemed odd to Cade. Maybe it calmed her nerves. A helicopter appeared from the west and went into a wide circle above the highway. Marie slowed down and eased into the traffic stream to be less conspicuous.

"Was it really such a good idea to leave that phone there?" Cade asked. "I mean, it's traceable to me. They'll know I was there."

Marie smiled humorlessly. "You think they didn't know anyway? Rebecca was ISS, or whatever."

Cade shook his head as if clearing it. Of course. His mind still wasn't functioning. "So what do we do?"

"We'll need to get off the Interstate," Marie answered. "They might seal off this whole area, which means everything on the exit routes will get stopped. They'll have voiceprints on both of us—maybe visuals as well. They'll already have yours in any case."

"Great. . . . So where are we heading, right now?"

"Just covering as much distance as we can, while we can. I don't really know this area. I only just arrived here. . . . We have to make contact with local people who are sympathetic."

"How do you propose doing that if you only just arrived in the

564

area?" Cade asked. It didn't exactly sound like the kind of thing someone would advertise.

Marie seemed to be of two minds as to how to answer. "There are ways," was all she said, finally.

The radio deejay prattled on amiably. "Well, that was a good one from way back. And now we have another caller on the line. Hello there? Who are we talking to?"

A man's raspy voice answered. "Hi, Mike. Name's Al. Folks call me Big Al. Been listenin' to that show o' yours for aw . . . must be close to five months now. Moved out here to Cleveland, a little under twenty miles north o' the Big Nooga. Wouldn't go any farther'n that mind you, 'cause I'm kind of a city boy originally. I've always thought that somebody oughta—"

"Well, it's real nice to hear from you, Al. So what kind of a song can we play for you today?"

"Oh yeah, right. Well, what I'd like to hear is one that I used to—"

Marie switched the radio off. Cade glanced at her questioningly, but she kept her eyes ahead. She passed the next exit, and then left the Interstate at the one after that. Cade noticed that it was signposted Cleveland.

They came to a small town center and crossed to the far side, away from the highway. Marie left the main street and found a minimall with a convenience store, several smaller shops, and a Burger King, and pulled in. Outside the convenience store were a couple of public net-access booths. "Stay here," was all Marie said as she got out of the car. Cade watched her go into one of the booths, sit down, feed a bill into the machine, and peer expectantly at the screen. Police sirens were sounding in the direction of the town center, where they had just passed through. Cade eased back in the seat, stretched his head upward, and exhaled shakily. Only now was his mental machinery beginning to operate anywhere near normally again.

Rebecca had been a plant, sent to infiltrate CounterAction. Very probably, an inflammatory piece denouncing President Ellis and the Washington administration had appeared from opposition sources, but she hadn't authored it. That had been part of a cover story exploiting the opportunity. Presumably, the aim had been to uncover a part of CounterAction's routes and methods for moving people out of the country. Cade could think of nothing further. That was all he had asked Udovich to convey in the message—along with the information that would identify Cade as the sender, to Marie.

He looked back at the booth and saw her speaking into the phone handset, at the same time writing hurriedly on a scrap of paper. Whom could she be talking to if she had only recently arrived in the area herself? Maybe they had a way of inserting coded information in local ads and announcements that would give a number to call if you knew what to look for. His mind drifted back to where it had been previously.

Information to identify Cade *to Marie*!

Could finding CounterAction's conduits have been just another part of the cover story too? Had the real objective all along been to track down Marie? Anything was possible for all he knew. How was Cade supposed to have known what she might have been involved in?

And then a more uncomfortable thought hit him. If Rebecca hadn't been what she said, then what kind of a coincidence would just happen to make her an old college friend of somebody living with a man on the ISS watch list whose former wife was a suspected CounterAction operative? A pretty unlikely one, to put it mildly. In fact, the more he thought about it, the more he was forced to conclude that it couldn't happen. So she hadn't been an old college friend of Julia's at all. But if that were true, then Julia had to have been part of the setup as well.

Surely not. After all that time? . . . It had to be impossible.

Then he remembered the strange way in which Julia had suddenly started asking questions about Marie, whom she had never expressed curiosity over before, and insisting that surely there was some way of contacting her again. . . .

He was still grappling with the implications when Marie came back. She got in and sat looking for a minute at the paper she had written on, as if memorizing it, then folded it and slipped it into a side pocket of her coat. "There's a coffee shop we need to find and wait in for a while," she said. "Someone will get back to us there." Cade merely nodded. If she had wanted him to know more, she would have said. He was completely out of his depth by now.

They drove out of the mall parking area and took a backstreet route, slowing occasionally for Marie to check street names and landmarks until they were on a road leading out of town. They followed for about twenty minutes to another township, smaller this time, standing below tree-covered hills looming into the dusk, which was closing in by now. Marie stopped under an intersection lamp to check her directions again, and then stayed on the main street to a traffic light, where she turned right and stopped two blocks farther on outside a diner billed as "Dean's." It was workaday and nondescript, with a few old cars and pickup trucks drawn up facing the building.

Cade had been thinking over events yet again. He looked at Marie as they were about to get out. "That guy who called in on the radio earlier. Was that some kind of code that the station broadcasts? The exit we turned off at was the name of the town that he said. He made it sound like some old fool just chatting, but he said something about not going any farther than that. Were they stopping the traffic farther on up? Was it something like that?"

Marie gave him a look that said he ought to know better than to ask; but there was a hint of a compliment there too. "A lot of people are getting really tired of what's going on," was the most she would admit before opening her door. On the way in, she stopped and took out a lighter to burn the piece of paper she had written on, stirring the ash into a cigarette sand-tray standing outside the door.

Inside was a counter with stools, a row of booths by the window, and tables and a few more booths at the back. The place was moderately busy with people who looked like local farmers and tradesmen, a group of teenagers, and several casual customers, none of whom gave Marie and Cade more than a glance as they entered. Cade found he had no appetite and ordered just a coffee at the counter. Marie took a sweet cold tea. Cade carried them to an empty corner booth, with nobody in immediate proximity.

They sat for a while toying with their mugs and stirring the contents needlessly, looking around with intermittent glances at each other, each adjusting to the situation in their own way. Despite whatever impressions he might have had earlier, Cade got the feeling that this wasn't exactly what Marie did every day. He wanted to talk, but it seemed pointless to start asking about what was supposed to happen next, which would reveal itself in due course.

Taped music was playing from speakers overhead, which would mask conversation. Finally, he brought up the subject of Julia, which was still nagging at him. He summarized the conversations that had led him to attempt contacting Marie, and his sudden suspicion just now, while Marie was making her call, that Julia must have been part of it. "But how could she have been?" he concluded, turning up his palms. "It's been over a year. . . . Yet why else would she pretend to have known Rebecca?"

Marie didn't seem to find it so surprising. "Tell me more about her," she invited. "How did you meet?"

Cade did his best to describe Julia and their relationship in a way that was sensitive to Marie's situation, mentioning her former husband who ran night clubs and how her social life as a consequence had clicked with Cade's own agenda. "I met her at a dinner party somewhere. She had a spare ticket to a show that someone had canceled out of and asked me if I wanted to fill in. It developed from there."

"It sounds ideal." Marie regarded him dubiously, as if not quite sure that what he'd said was adequate grounds for what she was thinking. She ran a fingertip around the rim of her mug, then said, finally, "Doesn't it strike you that it could have been just a little *too* ideal?. . . I mean, a bit over year ago, right? That is, by the time I'd have been marked as a CounterAction active."

Cade shook his head, at the same time smiling as if this had to be some kind of joke. "Surely not. I mean, would they really go so far as to set me up with my own permanent live-in agent?"

This time Marie nodded without hesitation. "Oh sure. It would be routine to put a watch on anyone connected with a marked name like mine. With a person in your position, constantly in touch with influential Hyadeans, they'd want to know everything about your deals and interactions. What better way to do it than that?" Cade could only stare at her aghast. Marie seemed amused. "Are you only starting to notice for the first time, Roland? We're being turned into a Hyadean colony. There might be some friendly ones that you can meet and party with, but the system they work for is ruthless about imposing its own ideas. Their style of security is being introduced into the U.S., and *our own people*—the ones who run the machinery that serves the interests that stand to make big—are collaborating." Cade felt a twinge of discomfort, wondering where that put him. But Marie's phone beeped before he could say anything. She took it out and answered, then produced a pen and another piece of paper and proceeded to jot down more instructions, answering in monosyllables. "Right. . . . Yes. . . . No, I've got it. That'll be okay." She closed the phone and put it away. "Time to go," she said to Cade, rising.

They followed a different road a few miles to a disused gas station, which Marie entered, parking on one side of the forecourt. They waited in the darkness for a little under twenty minutes. Then a car drew up on the roadway outside and flashed its lights once. Marie started the engine, turned on the lights, and exited to pull behind it. The car led them about a mile and then pulled off onto an expanse of open ground that seemed, in the moonless night, to be bordered by trees. Marie's phone beeped again. She answered it, listened for several seconds, and announced that she was to leave Cade here for a while. Meanwhile, the car ahead had moved on a distance and doused its lights. Marie got out, closed the door, and disappeared on foot in the same direction. Cade waited for about another fifteen minutes, feeling as if he had been pitched into the middle of one of those movies that he'd never really managed to connect in his mind with reality; or maybe a country that you read about but never thought about long enough to realize might actually exist. If he got out of this in one piece, that was it, he told himself. No more heroics or dabbling with intrigue and subversives. From now on he would . . . But even as the thought formed, he realized he was no longer so sure. The voice on the phone in the hotel room came back to him. *There are people out there right now for whom it's costing their homes, their families, their lives.* The picture of himself running back to his world of comfort and security didn't sit very well with him either.

Figures materialized from the shadows outside. A flashlight played on him through the glass. Another light showed papers with a picture in somebody's hand, being scrutinized. Finally, the door was opened, and a voice directed, "Come with us, please." Cade got out and found himself between two muffled figures wearing hats. Another was visible on the far side of the car. Cade and the two with him began walking the way Marie had gone, over uneven gravelly ground. When they had covered twenty yards or so, the car started behind them, and its headlights came on. Cade looked back to see it begin moving, turning back toward the roadway. "It's okay. You won't be needing it again," the same voice told him. For a chilling moment Cade wondered how he was supposed to take that. Getting too imaginative, he told himself.

A pickup was waiting along with the car that they had followed, he saw as they got closer. Marie was standing with two more figures. "Okay, it looks as if there's a place where we can stay for a few days at least," she told him. "This isn't the best time to hold a conference. It's been a rough day. We can talk more about options in the morning."

A big man with a bearded face and pulled-down baseball cap ushered them into the pickup and then got in on the other side. As he started up, the car with the three others departed back in the direction of town. They pulled back onto the road, continuing in silence in the same direction as before for a couple of miles, and then turned off onto a dirt track climbing uphill through trees. It led to a camper trailer standing in the corner of a field behind what looked like a farmstead outlined dimly in the darkness. "There's linen inside and some grub. Just help yourselves," the big man said as he dropped them off. "You've got a phone that connects to the house. It would be best if you didn't show yourselves there, at least for a while. . . . Oh, and you can call me John."

The camper had seen better days, but the power and the plumbing worked. From the clothes in the closets and other signs of occupation, it seemed the place had been vacated for Cade and Marie's benefit.

They made themselves a salad and cooked a couple of pork chops. Were it not for the day's events, this might have been a little like old times. The news on TV described a "terrorist hideout" in Chattanooga, which security forces had surrounded following a tipoff; they'd been met by gunfire. Five terrorists had been killed in the ensuing assault, and two had escaped. There was no mention of any incident at a motel. Cade's and Marie's pictures were shown as the two escapees, described as armed and dangerous.

By that time they were both too exhausted to talk more. Cade took a fold-down bunk in the camper's living and dining area. Marie used the bedroom, farther back. As Cade lay thinking back over the day, it occurred to Cade that the photograph of him that they had shown on the TV was one that had been taken around six months previously. How had the authorities gotten it? The only thing he could think of was that it must have come from Julia.

❀ CHAPTER TWENTY ❀

By daylight, the farm revealed itself to be in a dilapidated condition, with little to mark it as a going concern. The fields, for the most part, had been left fallow, and rusting machinery stood among the outbuildings. A few scrawny looking cattle were penned in a muddy patch on the far side of the house.

John called on the phone to ask how things were. Marie took the call, said they were comfortable, and thanked him again for helping out. Right now, they needed a little time to make plans. She listened for a short while longer and then hung up.

"The police are all over the area and still stopping traffic," she told Cade. "They're showing our pictures everywhere." She shook her head. "It was stupid for both of us to have gone into the coffee shop like that. We shouldn't have been seen together. Let's hope there weren't any wrong people there with sharp eyes and good memories." It wasn't something that could be changed now. Cade put on the coffeepot, popped a couple of slices of bread into the toaster, and turned back to the eggs he was about to scramble. Marie set dishes and cutlery on the table, poured two glasses of orange juice, and slid into the narrow bench seat behind.

"Roland. . . . In case we end up going separate ways in all this, or maybe if we both don't come through . . . there's some information that I need to give you. It's important that it doesn't get lost." Cade got the feeling she had been thinking hard about this. He looked over his shoulder to indicate that he was listening. Marie paused, as if searching for the right place to begin.

"Rebecca wasn't being infiltrated so much to find me. It was the particular group I was associated with. It's the group that was blamed for that assassination in Washington a couple of weeks back—when the Hyadean flyer was shot down. What the media are saying is all a lie. We had nothing to do with it. No part of CounterAction did. You have to believe that."

Cade slowed his stirring, and then resumed again just in time to avoid burning the contents of the pan. That was right. . . . The ISS people who came to the house two days after it happened had told him Marie was suspected of being with the cell the Hyadean plasma weapon supposedly found its way to. With all that had been going on, he had forgotten about that connection. "A senator, wasn't it?" he said. "Farden. . . . And some general . . . ?"

"Right. Meakes."

"A couple of Hyadeans too."

"They shouldn't have been there. The targets were Farden and Meakes. The reason the cell I was with got picked was that it had been compromised somehow. Therefore, it could be targeted to be taken out. Get the idea? Nobody who had been implicated would be around to deny it. That was the intention, anyway. But we were warned ahead of time, and disbanded."

Cade turned, frowning, as he scooped the eggs out onto the plates. "So that wasn't what happened yesterday at wherever that call came from—where Len went?"

Marie shook her head. "That was a place in Chattanooga that we were using in transit to wherever next. But there was another man there, who went by the name Otter. He had the information on how those assassinations were really carried out. That's the information I'm going to give you now. The more chance it has to get around, the better. His real name was Captain Wayne Reyvek of the ISS. He'd had enough of what he'd seen and decided to switch sides. They couldn't afford to let somebody like him talk. *That's* who I think Rebecca was sent to track down."

Cade added bacon strips from a plate he had set aside earlier and sat down to pour the coffees while Marie buttered the toast. "But they set me up to lead Rebecca to *you*," he pointed out. "What reason would they have to think that you and Reyvek . . . I guess he's history now?"

"Seems like it."

"What reason would they have to think you and he would be together?"

"I've been wondering that too," Marie said. "All I can think of is that they guessed he'd be asked to compare notes with the people who were being blamed." She shrugged. "The controllers monitoring a trace that Len took back found they had hit lucky, sent in a hit team— and you saw the cavalry heading the other way when we were leaving the motel. Guess who'd have been next."

Cade had already figured that much out. He went over what had been said so far while he began eating his breakfast. It still didn't make sense. "Why go to all that trouble?" he said finally. "If Reyvek knew who really did it, then presumably the ISS knew too. So why not simply go for them in the first place? Why go out of your way to lie about some other group, and then have to take them out in case they get a chance to disprove you?"

Marie sat back and smiled, as if something about the way he still couldn't see it delighted her. "*Because they did it themselves!* It was engineered within the ISS! Reyvek was involved in obtaining the Hyadean plasma cannon. It came from some that disappeared in South America, were recovered but not acknowledged, and found their way into an unofficial stockpile at Fort Benning in Georgia. It was fired by a colonel called Kurt Drisson, who specializes in deniable dirty work for friends in high places. Reyvek wasn't sure, but he believed that a financier called Casper Toddrel was behind it. Toddrel is mixed up in big land deals that are going on in Brazil and Peru. Reyvek had evidence to substantiate his story, which he mailed to a private box in Baltimore. I guess the key's lost, but there are ways around things like that."

Cade was listening, but he couldn't relate any motive to what he was hearing. The story the two ISS agents had given when they came to the house seemed straightforward enough. He shook his head uncomprehendingly. "But why? Farden was pushing bills that would open up big markets for cheap minerals that the Hyadeans are pulling out of Bolivia, right? Now, okay, sure, I can see how that might drop the bottom out of a lot of industries here that have seen their day, and make him unpopular with a lot of people. That would make him a natural target for an outfit like CounterAction, that looks for popular support. But why should somebody like Toddrel care? He's not a titanium miner who got let go last year with no place to go."

"You're buying the standard line that they put out," Marie told him. "Simple. Easy logic. Gives us an instant Enemy of the People to hate."

"Well . . . what other line is there?" Cade invited.

"Farden had enemies within the Terran Globalist elite. He was working with other interests—I suspect British, but I'm not sure—who were being paid by South American land agencies and development investors to expand the Bolivian extraction operations. That earns the Hyadeans the foreign currency they need for their land deals, and in recycling it everyone in the loop gets rich."

Cade still couldn't quite buy it. "But that still doesn't explain why Toddrel should want to get rid of Farden. I mean, isn't he in the loop too?"

"It's a different loop," Marie answered. "Farden's scheme is undercutting a lot of U.S.-capitalized mining, which makes it too radical for some people. Toddrel is part of a more cautious approach to cashing in on the Hyadean economic system by marketing Terran creative skills, which sell at a huge margin on the alien worlds. That means selling out middle-class professionals instead, which doesn't create powerful enemies. Also, you're not giving foreign governments a green light to rush into handing over big chunks of this planet, which not everyone is happy about." She waved her fork by way of conclusion. "Hence, eliminating Farden was convenient for a lot of people you don't find at Washington protest rallies. If you can do it and discredit the opposition at the same time, then so much the better."

Cade nodded reluctantly. It was starting to make sense now. "How come you know so much about all this?" he asked curiously.

"Oh, come on Roland. You know that reading between lines and finding sources that I believe has always been my thing."

"Yes, right. Let's not get into that. . . ." Cade picked up his glass and drank. "So what about General Meakes? The version I heard was that he wanted to beef up our defense capability by introducing more Hyadean weapons and methods, which countries like the AANS didn't want to see happen. So they spread the story that he was going to put our military under alien control, and that made him unpopular enough for CounterAction to target. What's your take on that?"

"From what I've heard, Meakes was sincere," Marie replied. "He genuinely wanted a stronger capability. But that was so the U.S. could run its own security operations independently. But the same people who didn't want Farden bankrupting Western industrial interests *want* an expanded Hyadean military presence here to protect their investments, with our own forces maybe eventually under their command."

Cade was astounded. "You're kidding!"

"I wish I was. The joke is that what they're pushing for is exactly what Meakes was accused of, but which in reality he was obstructing. So they had reason to want to get rid of him too." Marie looked across. Cade had no more questions for the moment, but sat absorbing what he had heard.

"So that's what you need to know," Marie told him. "If I don't come out of this for some reason, get it to the right people in the organization." She finished her toast, thought for a moment longer, and then added, almost as an afterthought, "Unless you still don't want any part of it, of course."

After half an hour of brooding, shuffling restlessly around in the cramped confines of the camper, and saying little, Cade sat down opposite Marie as she sat staring through a window at the tree-covered slopes rising beyond the end of the field. "It's not enough," he declared. "Yes, we need to get this information to the right people in your organization. But it has to go further than that. It has to get to the Hyadeans too—the *right* ones. They need to know what kind of people their government is collaborating with. Because they don't question things, they'd be easy to take advantage of. But that would make them all the more appalled if they knew the truth. Maybe I have spent a lot of the last few years staying out of things that matter, but one thing it's done is put me on more than just speaking terms with a few who would be ideal to start with. One in particular that I'm thinking of is very close to Dee. Do you remember her?"

For a moment, Marie registered too much surprise to be capable of saying anything. She collected her wits quickly and nodded. "Dee? Yes. She's okay."

"We need to use her."

"How? What are you talking about?"

"Well, obviously we can't risk alerting Julia," Cade said. "What are the chances of getting a message to Dee somehow, through this network of yours?

"They could do it, sure," Marie agreed. "But in a situation like this, it's best to assume that anyone who comes to mind as a natural contact will have been marked by the other side too. That means they're likely to be watched and their lines tapped. It could take some time."

"Then the sooner we make a start, the better," Cade said.

⊚ CHAPTER TWENTY-ONE ⊚

They gave John details of how Dee could be contacted, along with an instruction that she was to mention it to *nobody*. After that, there was little else to do but wait. There was no way Cade could use a credit card, write a check, or present ID without being picked up. The confidence of the people sheltering them evidently grew over the next two days, or maybe their story was authenticated somewhere. More of John's friends began showing up at the house, many of them at night. John himself stopped by from time to time to check up on things and drink a coffee or beer with Cade and Marie. Times had grown bad since the coming of the aliens, he told them, and that seemed all that was needed to establish cause and effect. Cade wasn't aware of any activities on the Hyadeans' part that would depress U.S. agriculture, and from what he had heard attributed it more to rising Third World productivity and changes in East-West relations, but there was no arguing with the local wisdom. Cade wondered how typical this might be of thinking across the country. Maybe he had been getting more out of touch than he had realized. Marie borrowed a laptop and encrypted as much as she knew of Reyvek's story in a file that she entrusted to John for consignment to Sovereignty. So at least there was some safeguard now in that respect.

Meanwhile, the news brought reports of more operations by security forces, and an apparent act of retaliation in Minnesota, where a stretch of roadway was blown up while a military convoy was passing over, causing over sixty fatalities. Globalist Coalition fighter-bombers were shown in action against "bandit" forces in South America, long portrayed as organized by drug and other criminal elements to disrupt lawful land transfers and development programs that threatened their business. Cade didn't believe it anymore. Another clip showed Hyadean military advisors training Brazilian counterinsurgency troops in the use of prom guns, which were apparently being introduced into the bush fighting with devastating results, along with other Hyadean innovations and methods. Cade recalled what Marie had said about the real motives behind the assassination of Lieutenant General Meakes. He wondered how long it would take for similar provisions to be introduced in the U.S.

He found he was beginning to see things in a new light. In one of their conversations he asked Marie what was going on behind it all, the big picture. What was it all intended to bring about? She told him he had already half figured it out. It was to serve the elite who controlled the Hyadean power structure. Did she mean by profiting from dumped products that had no value back among the Hyadean worlds, and the resale there of cheap Terran labor? Yes, he could see all that. Hadn't he been involved on the fringes of it himself?

But it went further than that, Marie told him. They were moving in to take over choice parts of Earth as their own private preserves. Huge tracts of places like western Brazil, eastern Peru—and now they were talking about South Africa—were being transformed into estates and palaces for the Hyadean ruling clique to escape to from the drabness and overdevelopment of their own worlds. And the properties came with willing managers and domestics that outperformed Hyadean AIs, and none of the political difficulties associated with hiring subservient labor back home.

A freshly sculpted planet, Cade recalled. Unique in its biological vigor and stunning geology among the planets the Hyadeans had spread to. So finally, he had gotten to the bottom of it. *That* was what was really going on.

"So what happens to the people who live there?" he asked Marie in one of their ongoing debates between games of bézique, rummy, napoleon, and taking in the news and a few movies.

"The old story," she replied. "Obviously, if you want to take over their land, they have to go. So you call them bandits and send in the gunships."

"I never realized."

"Most people don't. It's been a long time since there was any genuinely free reporting."

Cade thought about his conversation with Vrel and Krossig when they were out on the yacht. "I'm not sure it's all that different for the average Hyadean," he said. "They think they're here to protect Earth from itself and introduce it to the benefits of a superior system. This is supposed to be an outpost to protect us from the Querl. It's kind of crazy, isn't it?"

Marie snorted. "I don't recall hearing anything about us ever asking for protection. From what? We don't even know who the Querl are. What have you been able to make of them?"

"Supposedly, they're too unruly and ideologically misguided to make the Hyadean system work," Cade replied. "So one day they'll try and take what they need." He showed his hands and shrugged. "But I've even heard Hyadeans questioning that line."

"You amaze me. I didn't think they were capable of questioning anything."

"I'm beginning to think the Querl are something like their version of our bandits. They want to get away from the glorious Hyadean system."

"Which means they can't really be the big threat that we're told, can they?" Marie said. "So why do the Hyadeans need a military capability?"

Cade could see only one answer. "To keep their system together. They talk about orderliness, but the truth is it has to be held in place by force too. Just the same as ours have always had to be."

"My, you really have been doing some thinking. Is this really the same Roland?"

"Don't be patronizing. Or is it matronizing?"

"But seriously, the aim is to gain control of the U.S. as the focal point of global affairs. That's what the AANS nations are resisting, and why we support them."

"You think that terrorizing people over here is the right way?"

For the first time, Marie's manner became short. "That's pure propaganda. The people's own government has become the terrorists. We're trying to wake the people up!"

"But you'd take it to an open struggle, maybe eventually involving Terrans and Hyadeans directly."

Marie spread her hands. "Look at what's happening. You've got us on the verge of a civil war here, right now."

Cade looked hard at her, as if trying to gauge how serious she really was. "Training programs in the mountains and rhetoric are one thing," he said. "But can you really condone it: firing on American defense forces?"

"Hell, Roland. What kind of defense? They're mounting military assaults on American citizens already!"

The next day, John delivered a reply from Dee. Vrel was anxious to learn whatever it was that Cade wanted to convey. Not knowing where Cade was or his situation, he had arranged in his official capacity as observer to visit a U.S. military base near St. Louis and report on the activities of a Hyadean contingent sent there as technical advisers. That, of course, left the question of how Cade and Marie were to get to St. Louis, since with violent incidents escalating nationwide, all modes of travel were subject to routine checks and searches.

The answer came in the form of two nameless people who arrived the same evening to dye and restyle Cade's hair, stain a distinctive birthmark onto his forehead, and then photograph, fingerprint, and voiceprint him for a false set of ID documents, according to which he was now "Professor Wintner," described as a political scientist. Marie was similarly transformed into a social psychologist called "Dr. Armley." Cade doubted if it was mere coincidence that the professions fitted so well with Vrel's official work. The document forgers obviously knew their business, and came across as being intimately familiar with the official records systems. But those systems were interconnected, which meant that for the false IDs to work, appropriate data profiling the personas would need to be in there. Could it really be that thorough? Cade was intrigued.

"I said you'd be surprised how much support there is out there," Marie told him when he asked. "Sometimes the ones who work for government in the day are secretly our biggest allies. They *know* what goes on."

And they did work. Notification came via John that accommodation had been reserved for Professor Wintner and Dr. Armley at the St. Louis Hilton as guests of the Hyadean Office of Terran Cross-Cultural Exchange, which was the department that employed Vrel. They could book themselves a flight first-class, charged to a Hyadean account. It made a crazy kind of sense, Cade had to admit on reflection—the last place that Terran security would be looking for fugitives. Sometimes Hyadean logic managed to surprise him still. Being Hyadean, Vrel wouldn't be subject to the same scrutiny and restrictions as a Terran trying to make comparable arrangements.

They disposed of the guns and other possibly incriminating articles, and Cade handed over his own ID papers and personal effects for mailing to a collection address where he could pick them up later. A woman from the local network drove him and Marie to downtown Chattanooga, where they got a taxi to the airport. Although, as far as Cade knew, no civilian flights had been affected, much was being made of the dangers of terrorist missile attacks, with signs in the airport warning that passengers flew at their own risk. Cade read it as part of a campaign to promote fear.

With their official credentials and new identity documents, Cade and Marie cleared the airport check-in routine without incident. They departed an hour and fifteen minutes later on an early afternoon flight to St. Louis, changing at Atlanta.

❂ CHAPTER TWENTY-TWO ❂

On arrival at the St. Louis Hilton, Cade and Marie found themselves booked into a twentieth-floor suite consisting of a comfortably furnished and stocked lounge area in addition to two bedrooms—a typically prim Hyadean consideration, although it suited the circumstances. The desk clerk produced a package for collection by Professor Wintner that contained a phone—presumably with "clean" programmed-in identification and serial numbers—a number at which Vrel could be reached, and two thousand dollars in cash. Cade called Vrel as soon as they got to the suite. Vrel was relieved that they had made it, but was tied up in the city on business right now. He would join them at the hotel later.

"I see your lifestyle hasn't changed much, Roland," Marie commented. She had been wandering around, inspecting the contents of the mini-bar and refrigerator while he talked to Vrel. "Always the man with the right friends. It's a change from that camper on the farm." She didn't sound entirely approving.

"Well, suit yourself if you want to stake out a claim on the moral high ground," Cade replied. He picked up the wads of hundreds and fifties and ruffled it at her. "Wearing the same clothes for three days makes me feel kind of grubby. I don't know about you, but I'm going out to do a little shopping, and then freshen up for dinner. Are you coming along, or going to start preaching?" Marie thought about it, sighed, and decided preaching was out for the rest of the day. "So now you're sullying your image by dipping a finger in Hyadean wealth too," Cade said. "What's happening? Are you converting me, or am I corrupting you?"

"I don't know. But you're right. I just want to feel clean clothes again," she said.

By the time they sat down in the hotel restaurant, they were chattering and swapping banalities almost like old times. Despite the public exposure—or maybe as a consequence of surviving it without incident—Cade felt more secure than he had for days. Inwardly, a part of him was waiting for Marie to get around to politics or principles, because she always had—it was usual. Less usual was his realization that the anticipation wasn't bothering him. In fact, he found he wanted to talk more about such things. The irony was that Marie, for her part, seemed to be heeding his preferences for once by avoiding them. It was Cade, finally, who brought the subject up.

"What's happened to the fanatic I remember of old? If this goes on, you'll have me thinking we might actually get through dinner without stepping into quicksands."

"This has been such a change. I didn't want to spoil it." Marie pushed some salad into a wad with her fork and looked up. "Was I always a fanatic?"

"I used to think so," Cade affirmed candidly. "Now, I don't know. Julia asked about it a lot lately—but I guess we know why now." He chewed thoughtfully for a while. "What makes people do a job like that? . . . Live a life of deception. Could you?"

"Some people would say our whole lives are nothing else," Marie said, seemingly not to make any particular point.

"Greed, hatred, and deception," Cade intoned.

"What about them?"

"Those are what the Buddhists say are the root of all of life's evils."

"What's this, a new Roland? How long have you been into stuff like that?"

"I'm not, really."

"Yes, I *had* noticed."

"It was something that Mike Blair was on about once. Do you remember him—Mike Blair, the scientist?"

"I only met him a couple of times, I think. Hair with bits of gray in? Wears glasses?"

Cade nodded. "That's him—except the hair's probably a bit grayer now. He's been getting into Eastern philosophy as well as science. It seems our religions are making a big impression with some of the Hyadeans. They don't have deep philosophical views about things. They just look at what the basic facts are saying and leave it right there. Mike says it has something to do with why they're flying starships and we're not. I didn't really follow it."

Marie stopped eating for a moment to frown dubiously. "In that case, why should they care about deeper philosophies? What do they need one for?"

"Because they live their lives stressed out on treadmills tied to getting better ratings on this 'entitlement' system of theirs, which I don't understand either."

"Right. Like taking a day out fishing in a boat off California."

"I told you, a few like Vrel are different. . . . Well, they're changing. To them, a view of life that values other things beyond just status and material success is a revelation—literally. They've never heard of anything like it. Krossig—he's another Hyadean, who works with Vrel in LA, being moved to Australia—says it's catching on among the kids back home. They talk about Earth as the home of a deeper spirituality: ways of getting in touch with reality that the Hyadeans had once, but lost."

Marie pulled a face. "I guess I'm a little more cynical with regard to human spirituality. I've been too much in touch with conventional reality these last few years." She eyed him for a moment before spearing more of her salad. "Isn't this a bit out of your line, Roland? Are you changing or something, or did I just never see it?"

Cade shrugged in a way that said surprises happen all the time. "I see a lot of aliens."

Marie studied him curiously. "I don't think you realize what an unusual insight it's giving you into alien psychology," she said. "I'll admit, I've tended to see them as all alike—and not all that nice."

"I do an unusual job," Cade replied.

Vrel arrived later in the evening and joined Cade and Marie in their suite. To show off his expanding repertoire of acquired Terran tastes, he started off by refreshing himself after the day with a cool beer, and then settled down to follow it with black, unsweetened coffee. Marie's manner was guarded to begin with, in the presence of possibly the first alien she had spent any time with at close quarters, but she loosened up as time went on.

Vrel was anxious to make it clear that Dee hadn't known Rebecca was a setup. Even with his exposure to Terrans, he didn't seem to grasp that the possibility that she might have had never crossed Cade's mind. His concern seemed to imply that a Hyadean in Dee's position might have sold Cade out knowingly if it gained points somehow in the game-plan calculus that they lived by, and hence by their norms some defense of Dee should be necessary. Cade didn't really follow but accepted it as well meant. It was beyond Marie's experience or comprehension.

Then they got down to the reason why Cade had needed to contact Vrel so urgently. They related the true story of the assassinations of Senator Farden, Lieutenant General Meakes, and the two Hyadeans who had died with them. Vrel listened with growing incredulity, then outrage as Marie explained how the U.S. security services themselves had been responsible, with the implication of possible high-level Hyadean knowledge and collusion. The Hyadeans' nature was not to question what they were told, Cade concluded. It seemed that an unprincipled faction among them were taking advantage of the fact to enrich and empower themselves. Vrel knew the Hyadean system better than they did. There had to be ways of making the truth known in the right places for things to change.

"And you can substantiate it all with evidence?" Vrel said when they were done.

"Not by producing Reyvek anymore," Marie replied. "Although the way he was taken out should be evidence enough. But we have the names and the details, and we know where the documents in Baltimore are."

"Sovereignty will put the story out here," Cade said. "But how much will find its way back to Chryse? That's where any change in policy will have to come from. How can we get a channel back to there?"

Vrel left, promising to contact other Hyadeans that he knew. In the meantime, Cade and Marie could remain in the Hilton at Chryse's expense. Vrel even gave special instructions to the on-site Hyadean security personnel who watched over their official guests to make a particular effort to keep "Professor Wintner" and "Dr. Armley" out of sight and incommunicado. He explained that CounterAction had them listed as Hyadean collaborators, and they were possible targets for retaliation. The hotel's regular security staff were notified and agreed to keep the presence of the two academics highly confidential.

☯ CHAPTER TWENTY-THREE ☯

Casper Toddrel had once fired an assistant who referred to Laura as his "hooker." She could discuss Dostoevsky or Freud, Hegel or Brahms, Dow Jones or the Bolshoi Ballet in four languages, knew how to get a floorside table or instant theater ticket anywhere in New York, and had preferred accounts at Tiffany's, Bendel's, and Saks. The Upper East Side apartment suite that he provided for her had come in at half a million and cost two thousand a month to maintain. He didn't object to how she used it when he wasn't in town, so long as she was discreet. The place had more than paid for itself in the information it yielded from loose-tongued business rivals, whom Laura was an expert at playing. She seemed to get a kick out of it—as if it put her in a role of intimate collusion with Toddrel. Since he never detected any similar ploy being made toward himself, he felt reasonably safe in concluding that she wasn't overextending by trying any double-agent games.

A coalition of churches had staged a demonstration in Dallas to protest the passing of new laws aimed at curbing the dissemination of politically subversive material from pulpits and in parish magazines, and the local police had responded too zealously for prudence. Toddrel sat at the desk in the suite's den, brooding at a picture that had come in over the net, showing a priest holding his arms up protectively against a riot trooper brandishing a baton. This couldn't be allowed to get out. He finished composing a message putting a hold on media release and ordering the removal of the official responsible for security arrangements in Dallas. As he sent it off, Laura's hands began massaging his shoulders through the robe that he was wearing.

"Hey, Big Guy, haven't you had enough of that for one day?" her voice murmured. The scent of perfume touched his nostrils. A lace-covered breast rubbed the side of his head. "Tammy's in the Jacuzzi already. We've got a surprise."

Toddrel slid his hand up to find hers and smiled distantly. "This was urgent. But you're right. . . . There are times when enough is enough." He returned fully to the present and rose from the chair, his manner lightening. "Have you really? This sounds interesting. . . ." And then his phone emitted the tone for his priority-secure channel. "I have to take this."

"Oh, Casper. . . ."

"It probably won't take a minute. Run along and wash Tammy's back." Laura knew better than to argue further and disappeared. Toddrel patched the call through to the desk unit. The screen showed the face of Francis Denham, a British investment banker whom Toddrel had talked to during a recent European visit. The effect on world prices gave Denham his own reasons for wanting to curb the Hyadean mining operations in Bolivia. Before Toddrel departed, they had agreed on the need for a face-to-face meeting with representatives of like-minded Hyadeans. With Senator Farden out of the way, the time was ripe for coordinating further action.

"Good day, Casper—or whatever time it is wherever you are," Denham began. "I trust you had a pleasant trip back?"

"Good enough. What's the news?"

"I've heard back from our friends." He meant Hyadeans who were raising Terran currency by marketing Terran skills back home rather than undercutting Terran industry. "We seem agreed in principle. The official agenda will be on armaments movements." Toddrel had suggested that as the ostensible reason for getting together. Preventing Hyadean and foreign-manufactured Terran weapons from reaching subversive groups was a concern both in the U.S. and

Europe. In the latter case, overland movement from Asia was becoming a major problem, and closing of the Canadian and Mexican borders was being considered on the other side of the Atlantic. Another potentially controversial measure that had been proposed was the stopping and searching of ships bound for U.S. or European waters.

But that would be a smokescreen. Denham went on, "One thing that we have to give due consideration to beforehand, I think, would be the question of, how would we say? . . . extending the principle exemplified by Echelon to more general operations."

Toddrel smiled. Even over a secure line, the Englishman couldn't bring himself to state a delicate matter directly. Echelon was code for the action taken to eliminate Farden and Meakes. What Denham meant was engineering ways of not only concealing but publicly blaming the other side for actions that could not be admitted to. "We'd both like to see the scale of activity in Bolivia cut back," Toddrel supplied. "And there's a guerrilla war going on down there. What I'm hearing is that some destabilization in that part of the world would work to our advantage."

"Er, yes. . . . I think we are on the same wavelength," Denham agreed.

"I'll get proposals from our experts in that department," Toddrel said. "I assume that's what this meeting is for." He bit his lip as he spoke. He still wasn't happy about the security situation concerning Echelon. The ISS's confirmation that Reyvek had been among those killed in the Chattanooga raid had come as some relief; on the other hand, the loss of their undercover operative in the motel meant that nobody knew how much information the two who had escaped might have taken with them. He didn't want to divulge any of that now.

"Yes. . . . Exactly," Denham said.

"Where will this meeting be? Do we know yet?" Toddrel inquired.

"Not for sure. I thought we might go to them this time, and make it somewhere in South America. That sounds like an interesting trip, and to be honest I've never been there. What would you say?"

Peals of laughter accompanied by splashing noises came from along the passageway beyond the door. "Well, New York does have its attractions, but there are times when I could use a change too," Toddrel said. "Sure. Put me down as seconding it."

Vrel reappeared intermittently for two days, during which Cade and Marie remained out of sight in the hotel. Gradually, they opened up, talking more about their lives in the years since they had gone separate ways—he having nothing to conceal; she, more circumspect for obvious reasons. They had drifted apart into different worlds. Now, suddenly and unexpectedly, they were thrown together in the same world. Cade began to remember Marie again as he had known her—living life with an intensity that made each day a unique experience. The difference now was that he was sharing it in a way that he would never have thought possible. Marie, for her part, had to accept that her world hadn't protected them, and their security now stemmed from Cade's world which she had once contemned.

Cade couldn't decide if the erosion of barriers between them was simply a pragmatic reaction to the situation or signified something deeper and more personal. Even in his own case, he wasn't sure. One night, after they had sat up late in the suite talking over a bottle of Grand Marnier and then gone separate ways, he returned and stood outside Marie's door undecidedly. The drink and the closeness had left him mellow, and he found it easy to create scenarios in his mind of reliving lost intimacies. But in the end he turned away and went back to the other room. Something didn't feel right. He marveled at this apparently newfound sensitivity that he was able to muster. Udovich would surely have approved.

The next morning, Vrel appeared and announced that they were going to Bolivia. Marie wasn't used to the Hyadeans' blunt, unceremonious way of going about things once they had set their mind.

"Just like that. Out of the blue. We're going to Bolivia," she repeated lamely.

"Roland, do you remember Corto Tevlak? Wyvex talked about him at that last party of yours," Vrel said.

"The art promoter who was developing Chrysean outlets, right?"

"Yes. He's been worried for some time about the way things are going here in the U.S. and on Earth generally, too. Erya talked to him on her way back. He knows others down there who feel the same way, including some Chrysean media people. The public back on Chryse is being misinformed, but questions are starting to be asked. Earth and its cultures are big news right now. This could be a good moment for getting attention in the right places." Vrel paused to let them absorb that much, then shrugged. "You're not safe here in the U.S. in any case. I'm told that from South America it would be easier to get you somewhere where you can stay out of the way for a while."

Just like that.

"Well, it's a nice thought, Vrel," Cade agreed. "But just how do you imagine you'll get us to Bolivia—when every security agent and surveillance computer in the country will be looking for us?"

"In the same way that we're hosting you now," Vrel replied. "As guests of the Hyadean government. We fly you there ourselves, VIP class." He shook his head. "Sometimes I think that Terrans just look for problems, not solutions."

Cade stared at him strangely. "You do realize what you're doing, Vrel?" he said. "A pure favor, probably at considerable risk, with no immediate payoff. Doesn't it feel just a little bit odd?"

"The idea of being motivated by helping others. Yes, I agree— it's very odd." Vrel paused to consider the question fully. "My honest answer is that I find it . . . strangely uplifting." He grinned apologetically. "I can't explain it either."

The following day, accompanied by two other Hyadeans whom Vrel introduced as Ni Forgar and Barto Thryase, they drove out from the city and were admitted to the fenced compound that the Hyadeans maintained inside the military facility that Vrel had been visiting. A flyer carried them to a Hyadean air base in Maryland, where regular alien traffic connected to other points in the U.S., the Hyadean South American enclave, places in Europe, and elsewhere. They departed several hours later in a suborbital supersonic transport bound for the Hyadean mining center at Uyali, in the southern Altiplano region of Bolivia.

◈ CHAPTER TWENTY-FOUR ◈

Bolivia is a land of color, contrast, and change, which has been nicknamed "the rooftop of the world." The western third of the country is covered by the Andes, extending southward from Peru in two roughly parallel chains a couple of hundred miles apart. The western chain, known as the Cordillera Occidental, marks Bolivia's border with Chile and is the continuation of a high mountain range that begins in northern Peru. Few passes open westward, the lowest being at thirteen thousand feet, and the stretches between are studded with volcanoes, many of them active, with peaks rising above nineteen thousand feet. The eastern chain, or Cordillera Real, consists of a series of great crustal blocks tilted eastward, rising sharply on the western side and descending through a region of rugged, densely forested terrain and mile-deep canyons to the eastern lowlands that make up the remaining two-thirds of Bolivia.

Between the two mountain chains lies a basin of plateau and highlands known as the Altiplano, or high tableland, extending over five hundred miles north-to-south and varying in elevation from twelve to fourteen thousand feet. The northern part of the Altiplano, bordering Lake Titicaca and containing the seat of government, La Paz, is the industrial hub and home to the bulk of the population. Nowhere else does such an industrial area, with cities, railroads, and highways, exist at such an altitude. The southern Altiplano is more arid and barren, consisting of vast salt wastes and rolling plains of steppe vegetation broken by fingerlike remnants of eroded escarpments standing between deep river valleys and basins.

The Spaniards began mining in the sixteenth century, finding large deposits of silver that made Potosí the largest and richest city in the New World at the time. Although later centuries saw developments in the extraction of tin, bismuth, tungsten, antimony, lead, zinc, iron, and copper from accumulations of volcanic ash and ancient sediments, much of the region's mineral potential remained untapped because of political instability and want of capital investment. Then the Hyadeans moved in, and applying such techniques as nuclear-driven particle beam mining, and plasma ionization with magnetic separation, which no Terran operation could rival, began exploiting on a massive scale fabulous deposits along the inner slopes of the Cordillera Occidental in the southernmost reaches of the country. They sold the processed minerals to Terran manufacturing industries in exchange for land-purchase currency on terms highly profitable for the Terran enterprises concerned and also for the national land-management agencies. Development of transportation northward opened up the Amazon route for exporting processed minerals, especially to Europe, and a newer, current project involved blasting a tunnel through the Cordillera Occidental to a new shipping and handling facility being constructed at Iquique in Chile.

The Hyadean residential settlements were farther north in the more picturesque parts of eastern Peru and the highlands in the tip of Brazil, west of Amazon basin. Their main spaceport for connection to the interstellar ships parked in orbit was at Xuchimbo, in western Brazil, near the point where the borders of the three countries meet. The Hyadean presence had brought a prosperity boom to local businesses, and workers and unions were more than happy with the wages. This provided a broad popular base of political support for the Hyadean-backed government operations being conducted against the insurgency forces active throughout the area.

Cade's reality—the accumulation of perceptions and experiences that he lived in—had always reflected the world of the affluent and the comfortable. Having taken twenty-first-century global communications for granted as part of growing up, he had paid a token concession at the intellectual level to the existence of other places ruled by other conditions; but despite the background detail woven into movie presentations and the vividness of travel documentaries, the places he acknowledged at that detached level of awareness had never before, somehow, taken on the deeper, emotional quality that brings on a sense of being *real*.

"Vast," "rugged," "empty" were the words that formed in his mind as he took in the cabin displays while the SST slowed for its vertical descent into the landing zone. It was now late in the day. To the west, broken ramparts of reds, browns, yellows and grays, rising in ranks of fading ridges to a line of snowy peaks barely visible in the distance, were darkening against the background sun. Arid hills and rocky basins extended away north and south, opening out and leveling eastward into barren salt flats. Amid it all stood the installations at Uyali.

Uyali was Hyadean-built to serve as the center of their extraction operations, sprung out of the Altiplano desert south of previously worked Terran mining areas. On the western side was what Ni Forgar, who seemed to be some kind of engineer returning to base, said was the reduction and processing complex. With its metal domes, cylinders, and spherical constructions standing among large, white boxlike structures, it looked more like a refinery than what Cade would have expected, though with less clutter and piping. It seemed ugly and sprawling, but visiting Terran engineers had apparently been amazed at its compactness for the volume of material that it handled. This arrived by way of two gigantic moving-belt conveyors converging in a V across the landscape, carved through hills and spanning canyons until they were lost from sight; farther on, Forgar told them, the root conveyors divided repeatedly to form a branching tree probing its way through to extraction points scattered among the mountains. He described the processing complex with typical Hyadean bluntness, never slow to make a point of what he thought they did better.

"That's where the rock is crushed, vaporized, and separated into its various elements," he told them. "It doesn't have to be high-grade ore. Any shovelful of desert contains traces of just about everything you can name. But low grades aren't economic with your methods. You know how to produce nuclear heat but you don't use it. It reduces all materials to a plasma state of charged particles which can be separated magnetically. All clean and efficient. Tuned radiation fields direct the recombination to whatever compounds, alloys, and other forms you want. Surplus energy is tapped for generating electricity and process heat as byproducts. The refined output is sent up to the rail links and Amazon system." Forgar indicated a wide roadway disappearing to the north, on which processions of robot trucks could be seen moving both ways. "The Pacific coast will become the most important outlet when the tunnel is completed." Forgar looked at Cade and Marie as if expecting questions, but neither of them had any for the moment. He turned toward Vrel.

"Terrans stumbled upon the beginnings of low-energy transmutation years ago, but they didn't read it right. We run reactions at levels far below anything their scientists believed were possible."

"Was that what they called cold fusion?" Vrel queried. This really wasn't his field.

"Bad name. 'Nuclear catalysis' would have been better. They misinterpreted what was going on, then abandoned it because they couldn't explain it."

Vrel looked at Cade. "Is that beginning to sound like someone we know?" he invited.

"Mike Blair?" Cade guessed.

"*Because it didn't fit with the theory,*" they both quoted together.

Forgar looked mystified. "Theories! They'd rather stay with products of their imagination? I don't think I'll ever understand it."

A couple of miles east from the reduction complex was the "town" of Uyali itself—more the advanced-alien equivalent of a mining camp. Stark and utilitarian even for something conceived by Hyadeans, conceding nothing to adornment or elegance, it provided living space, services, and administration for the area. From above it resembled an irregular, colored-tile mosaic. As the SST descended, the tiles took on the form of rectangular boxes and cubes aligned and stacked like creations of children's blocks, making bridges here, adding a level there, the whole giving the impression of being added in haphazard leaps according to need rather than resulting from any unifying design. Beyond, separated by an expanse of fenced open ground, was a sprawl of familiarly styled Terran office units and prefabricated buildings thrown together into streets, blending on the far side into a shantytown of cabins and trailers.

The SST landed and taxied from the touchdown point to a handling area where a mix of Hyadean aircraft was standing amid service buildings, maintenance gantries, and cargo conveyors. A driverless bus took the passengers to a jumble of more Hyadean domino and shoebox constructions that Cade took to be the terminal facility. Along the far side of the landing area, were huge, hangarlike enclosures giving glimpses of sleek shapes surrounded by service platforms and access stairways within, standing in front of clusters of storage tanks, various unidentifiable structures, and tall towers bristling with antenna arrays. To one side, away from the main scene of activity, stood a line of what were unmistakably Terran-built military jets. Armored cars and other camouflage-painted vehicles were parked in a fenced compound nearby. Cade could only speculate as to what they were doing here. They passed a construction area where Terran work crews, some in shirts and jeans, others wearing orange coveralls, using unfamiliar machines, were excavating a new site for something. Evidently, local labor was being employed even inside the air base.

From closer range, the terminal revealed itself as a composition of what appeared to be prefabricated modules and tubelike connecting units stacked and combined in various ways to form office units, living quarters, or work space as desired. The resulting outlandish creations had ends of boxes projecting out into space; blocks straddling gaps and leaving holes through to daylight on the other side; connecting tubes emerging from walls to make right-angled turns in midair, as if changing their minds as to where they wanted to go. It seemed odd that with their obsession for efficiency, Hyadeans should be so incapable of realizing anything that on Earth would be regarded as "pleasing."

The interior was predictably functional. The mission in Lakewood had used a regular building adapted to Hyadean use. This was the first time Cade had been in an environment that was Hyadean in origin. The part of the building they had entered consisted of several large and irregular interconnecting spaces rather than the linear arrangements of rooms and corridors that typified Terran buildings. The predominant color was unfinished metallic gray, with a rigid white mesh in most places serving as ceilings below tangles of cables, pipes, and ducting that were plainly visible. Dividing up the area was an assortment of structures functioning as partitioning, shelving and storage, seating, control consoles aligned and combined in various ways, making it difficult to distinguish furnishings from parts of the architecture. They seemed to be both. One of the Hyadeans working nearby said something to the unit near him and got up to move to another station. The unit reconfigured itself to present a counter and convenience shelf that hadn't been there before, lost a corner, and moved after him to attach itself to a different part of the surroundings. A voice spoke from somewhere in the wall; the Hyadean grunted a reply and carried on. Cade noticed that Marie was staring in surprise. Not being familiar with the ubiquitous Hyadean low-level AIs, she had thought for a moment that the Hyadeans were talking to themselves.

A Bolivian immigration agent processed their papers as well as those of Vrel and his companions. Once again there were no hitches with the system, and Professor Wintner and Dr. Armley were officially admitted to the country. The party came through into what appeared to be the central concourse, where a number of armed Hyadean military were on duty. It was the first time that Cade had seen Hyadean combat troops close-up. They wore dark brown uniforms and black helmets, with lots of gadgets and pouches, and carried short weapons suggestive of assault rifles but stubbier, wider at the muzzle, and studded with controls. They had superb physiques and looked tough, a suggestion enhanced by the blockish, square-faced Hyadean build. Cade decided he could get by without tangling with them.

Forgar left them there to go his own way, along with most of the other passengers from the SST. Several, however, rode with Cade and Marie, Vrel and Thryase, in a transparent-topped car running on a monorail into another modular hodgepodge, only on a larger scale. They learned that this was the Hyadean residential part of Uyali. The area beyond, looking more like a familiar if somewhat ramshackle town, which they had seen during the descent, was the Terran sector. The two areas were segregated because of an ongoing problem of insurgents from the north infiltrating into the work force to spread discontent and conduct sabotage.

The two Hyadeans checked with some kind of office and then conducted Cade and Marie to separate quarters in a hive of cells sprouting off in different directions. They turned out to be quite comfortable accommodation units, plain but serviceable, yet surprisingly spacious. Cade's first problem was with the unfamiliar wall units and gadgets intended for Hyadean voice-direction, which were supposed to have been adapted for English but in reality rapidly became confused. In the end, he settled for the prospect of making do with minimal luxuries and conveniences. He got the shower to work, and in the course of a learning experience that involved a few minor scaldings, freezings, and flow surges, succeeded in taming it. Afterward, he laid out the collection of casual slacks, plaid, check, and plain shirts, lightweight tan jacket, straw hat, reserved sweaters, zippered topcoat, and other items that had seemed an appropriate wardrobe for a visiting academic—all very conservative compared to his customary choices—and considered what might be appropriate for the evening. He really had no way of telling, since he didn't know what the plans were. But before he could give the matter much thought, he felt himself being overcome by a shortness of breath and acute muzzy-headedness. Minutes later, Marie tapped on the door, and when Cade found the right word to open it, tottered in saying that she felt the same way. Then Vrel called to say that he had talked to Corto Tevlak, who was anxious to meet them. Cade groaned that right now neither of them wanted to meet anybody. They'd picked up some kind of South American bug or something already, he was sure.

"Bugs don't work that quickly," Vrel assured him. "It's altitude sickness. Terrans seem to be more affected by it than us. Get some rest. Most people adapt after an initial lousy night. I haven't arranged anything for tonight. We'll be going to see Corto first thing tomorrow."

◉ CHAPTER TWENTY-FIVE ◉

Cade felt better on awakening, able to take on the world again. After showering and shaving, he selected olive pants, the lightweight jacket, and a narrow-check shirt with knitted tie as his attire for the day. When he stopped by Marie's room, it turned out that she had recovered too. Vrel and Thryase arrived soon afterward to collect them. Although there was a communal canteen on the ground floor of the accommodation complex, they ate in a private room nearby, to avoid needless questions as to who the Terrans were. It was gray with metal furnishings and exposed pipes, reminding Cade of the wardroom in a Navy ship that he had visited once. Breakfast was an insipid Hyadean vegetable-based pseudo-sausage covered in a kind of synthetic liquid cheese, accompanied by yellow bread and a warm, fruity drink. Only then, through talking to Thryase, did Cade appreciate fully the audacity that Vrel had displayed in spiriting him and Marie out of the U.S. The normal Hyadean, inured to authority and needing orders from above before acting, would have been incapable of conceiving such a scheme, which was probably why nothing Vrel did had been questioned. Thryase wondered if Vrel's stay on Earth was turning him into a Terran—a remark that Vrel seemed to find pleasing. They departed for Tevlak's in a Hyadean flyer shortly afterward, heading northeast across the southern extremity of the Altiplano.

From the conversation during the flight, it seemed that Thryase was visiting Earth on behalf of a dissident movement of political "doves" who questioned the militant Hyadean policy toward the Querl. The Querl had not been expelled because of their inability to merge into the Hyadean system, Thryase maintained, but had separated because of their refusal to submit to it. He had entertained doubts about the official line for some time, but surrounded on all sides by a majority steeped in the conventional mindset, like many others he had hung back from speaking out strongly. Coming to Earth had opened his eyes to a lot of things and given him more confidence. What the Hyadeans were told represented lawlessness was nothing more than the expression of independent people free to live as they chose. He saw the variety and richness of Earth's cultures as a consequence of the same thing. Marie didn't quite share Thryase's idealistic view of universal freedom on Earth, but she seemed encouraged. It was the first time she had heard the official Hyadean line being questioned by a Hyadean.

They flew low over white salt wastes and reedy marshes where flamingos rose in sunlit flurries of orange and magenta reflecting from the pools like fireworks displays. Ahead, the land became more hilly, rising toward mountains with the snow line of the Cordillera Real visible distantly behind. A valley opened out to reveal a huddled township set astride a meandering creek and giving way at the outskirts to patches of green cultivation crisscrossed by trails. The flyer dipped to pass over red-roofed, Spanish-style houses looking aged and dusty, and singled out one of several residences standing apart among clumps of yucca bush and a scattering of trees along the creek bank on the far side. It was built of adobe with a tile roof, and enclosed by a slatted fence running down to the creek on two sides. Outside the fence, a ramshackle assortment of maybe a dozen cars, trucks, and other vehicles was drawn up haphazardly along the roadside among the boulders and trees. Brown-skinned figures sitting in the open doors or under leanto shelters of blankets or plastic sheeting poles looked up curiously as the flyer descended. It landed inside the enclosure, alongside several automobiles, a newish-looking pickup truck, and a couple of Hyadean personal-model flyers. There was also a larger, more impressive model of flyer, sleek and businesslike, consisting of a dark blue body riding on two yellow nacelles. The Hyadean equivalent of a Learjet, Cade decided. Two men with the high-cheeked, long-nosed features of Andean Indians, neatly groomed and wearing loose white shirts with black pants, but tough-looking nevertheless and carrying sidearms, had already appeared from the house and were standing in front of the door when the arrivals got out.

Before anyone had moved a pace, a rotund figure, chunky-looking even for a Hyadean, swept out of the doorway, arms extended as if greeting long-lost friends. In all Cade's time of dealing with them, this was the most incongruous Cade had seen. His skin hue was dark, varying from blue to purple at the nose and cheeks, and what could be seen of his hair was crimson, protruding at the sides below a native-style, wide-brimmed derby. Along with the hat he wore a poncho embroidered with brightly colored designs, and voluminous trousers tucked into calf-length boots. He recognized Vrel and Thryase, doubtless from video exchanges, and greeted them exuberantly in Hyadean, gripping each in turn in the customary Hyadean fashion, Roman style, hands gripping the other's wrist. Then he switched to Terran handshakes. "You must be Dr. Armley, whom we've heard about. . . . And you are Professor Wintner. . . ."

"This is Corto Tevlak," Vrel managed to squeeze in.

Tevlak waved at the surroundings. "We don't have much in the way of campus life here. But welcome anyway. There are three more waiting inside to meet you." He turned to usher the party back toward the doorway, at the same time speaking in short, simple, but well-formed sentences. "And how are you shaping up this morning? Flew in last night. The altitude sometimes affects Terrans. We don't seem so bothered by it."

"Last night was a bit rough," Cade said. "We're okay now."

"Splendid."

They passed on into the house. In the hallway, Tevlak took off his derby and jammed it on top of one of several gaudily painted Indian devil masks glaring down from the wall above a carved rack bearing coats and cloaks. The interior admitted little sun but was well lit artificially. It was virtually a gallery of art, dress, ornaments, and furnishings, not just local forms but mixing styles from everywhere. Besides Indian blankets and tapestries adorning the walls and covering chair backs, and pottery pieces emblazoned with Inca or in some cases possibly Central American designs, Cade picked out a couple of Benin bronzes, ebony carvings and figurines that looked African, an Arab burnous, and a Cossack astrakhan hat. Crossed Maori throwing spears commanded the rear of an alcove, between an arrangement of Navajo sand paintings. The bureau at the rear of the large room that Tevlak led them to was Victorian European or North American; a hand-cut glass decanter atop an ivory lacework corner table that could have been Turkish held a decorative wax candle (ugh); the Easter Island head set on the sill of the high window was wearing a French kepi. Marie caught Cade's eye and gave a short, bemused shake of her head.

Two of the Hyadeans that Tevlak had mentioned—a youngish-looking man and an older female—were seated together at one end of a large central table, which from the litter of bric-a-brac on the surrounding shelves and side cabinet had been cleared to make room. A shiny cylindrical object with what looked like a lens was set up on a stand at the other end, and a couple of similar devices were to the sides of the room. They looked like cameras. A flat box with a screen lay near the one on the table. There was another box with a screen and controls, along with an opened case of papers, pieces of auxiliary equipment, and other oddments in front of the younger Hyadean. He looked at Cade expectantly and seemed tempted to grin, though uncertain if he should. He had dark green hair blending into black in parts, and had acquired a T-shirt with an animal design and inscription in Spanish, though still worn beneath a regular Hyadean tunic jacket. His features were familiar.

"I know you, don't I?" Cade began. "Where was it . . . ?"

"Veyan Nyarl," the Hyadean supplied. "We met at the mission in Los Angeles a few months ago. I was passing through the West Coast."

"Yes, right! You were the . . . 'investigator'—from some Hyadean reporting outfit that worked with the news media."

"I still am." Nyarl indicated the female with him. "And this is the person in charge of my . . . I suppose you'd say something like 'section': Hetch Luodine."

"Hello, Mr. Cade." Luodine extended a hand. "Hetch," Cade knew, was a Hyadean form of female address, something like "Ms."—not part of the name. It was appropriate for Nyarl to use it when referring to his boss. She had traveled to most parts of Earth, putting together what she described as stories about "more interesting and unusual" sides of Terran life for Hyadean consumption. The blue-and-yellow flyer outside was hers and Nyarl's.

Cade indicated Marie. "This is Marie . . ." He looked at her uncertainly, realizing he didn't know. "Cade?" She nodded. "My, er . . . a very good friend." Marie and they exchanged greetings.

The remaining Hyadean had meanwhile stood up from an armchair—embroidered Queen Anne, fitted with tasseled silk cushions that looked Chinese—where he had been sitting when they entered. He was broad, with curly brown hair, which was unusual, and an exceptionally Hyadean face composed of solid horizontal lines, looking as if it had come out of a press. He wore a loose, dark shirtlike garment tucked into baggy black trousers secured by a belt, which carried a hand-weapon in a gray, holsterlike pouch.

"This is Brezc Hudro," Tevlak informed them. "He is with the—"

"Military," Marie supplied.

Tevlak looked surprised. "How did you know? He is out of uniform."

"I can tell," Marie said.

Cade looked the Hyadean up and down again. He could picture him as one of the Hyadeans they had seen on duty at the air terminal the day before.

"You are from CounterAction," Luodine said to Marie. "Are soldiers so much alike everywhere?"

"Something like that. You develop a radar."

Hudro seemed unperturbed, simply spreading his hands in a gesture that asked what he could add to that.

Tevlak fussed around, finding seats and clearing chairs of trinket boxes and framed prints. An Indian housekeeper appeared, and went away again with orders from Tevlak for refreshments and drinks. Vrel opened the warm-up talk. "You have a genuine native dwelling," he remarked to Tevlak. "Most Hyadeans that I know prefer our own prefabs, even away from the bases. Does it go with the Terran art, somehow?"

"We were just asking the same thing when you arrived," Luodine said.

Tevlak, who hadn't sat down himself but continued moving around the room, made an expansive gesture that could have meant anything. "I like native Terran surroundings. They create a stratosphere that helps me think."

"*Atmosphere*," his veebee corrected from somewhere beneath the poncho, which Tevlak had left on.

"Whatever. You don't have to talk and be prattled back at all the time. We back home have forgotten it."

"Do you feel safe out here, away from the bases?" Thryase asked. "With the trouble that's going on among the Terrans? A lot of them don't like us. I've seen it myself in the U.S. Did you know that we're training their police and military?"

Tevlak guffawed loudly. Cade suspected it was an acquired mannerism. Hyadeans didn't laugh much, tending more just to smile when amused. When they did, it usually signified embarrassment. "It's different here. I am a threat to nobody. Everyone here is aware of it. Do you know what the prices I can get mean to them?" He gestured in the direction of the window. "Did you see those people outside? They travel miles to bring me their work. I am the big father-number."

"*Figure.*"

"Figure." Tevlak laughed again. This time it seemed Hyadean. Hudro seemed to have reservations but chose not to press them at this point.

Vrel, who Cade gathered was the organizer of the meeting, looked at Luodine. "Let's get started. It's your show now. How do you want to do it?"

"I've got a list of things to cover. We go through a dummy run first." Luodine nodded at Roland and Marie. "That'll give you a chance to familiarize and get your lines together. Then we do it again live, a bit more formally. Don't worry about getting it perfect. We do a lot of editing."

"Wait a minute," Cade said. "What are we talking about here, 'live'?" He remembered the direct communications to Chryse that he had seen in the Hyadean offices in LA. "Is this going out over your network back home?"

"Well . . . of course." Luodine looked surprised. "Isn't that why we are here? It's not just to drink coffee."

"You mean it'll be going out right now, as we speak?" Marie queried. She glanced at Cade uneasily.

"Not that directly," Luodine replied. "I said we do preliminary editing here. Then it would be reviewed and cleaned up by the directors back home. But within a few days or so, sure. I'd hope you're going to be big news—the other side to what the people there have been told. Hyadeans involved with Terran leaders who plot assassinations and lie about it. What an exposure! We got the idea from watching how the media works here. Didn't you know? Vrel, didn't you tell them? "

"I was more concerned with getting them out of the country," Vrel said.

Cade shook his head, bewildered. Yes, it was the kind of thing he'd wanted; but it was happening so soon. The thought of talking to aliens at distant stars rendered him momentarily speechless. A week ago he had been just a guy in California making a living and minding his own business. Now he was hours away from possibly becoming an interstellar celebrity.

"What's the problem?" Luodine asked. "I thought you'd be in favor."

Marie began, "It's just that . . ." She faltered, looking to Cade for a moment. "Well, it isn't as if they're not in communication with Earth. In two days the powers back here will have the story, know our faces. Then where do we go?"

"But that's no different from the position you're in anyway," Vrel pointed out. Which of course was true. Cade looked blankly back at Marie. Her expression said she couldn't argue with it either. "You're already wanted by the ISS," Vrel went on. "So I assumed you'd want us to make a version of the take for the U.S. network as well. That's what I told Luodine."

"We're set up to do it," Luodine confirmed.

Cade had a glimpse of how Terrans must look through Hyadean eyes—forever finding reasons why not to. He decided to try being a Hyadean instead. "Okay," he heard himself say. "So let's do it."

Luodine lapsed into Hyadean exchanges with Nyarl, who carried out what sounded like some kind of programming dialogue with the equipment, checking responses on one of the screens. Then they were ready to go. Thryase opened by answering some questions from Luodine, then going off into longer monologues. Since this version was for a Hyadean audience, the language was Hyadean. For Cade and Marie's benefit, Vrel summarized in murmured asides. Essentially, Thryase was repeating the skepticism he had expressed on the way from Uyali regarding the Hyadean depictions of the Querl. He offered the conclusion that the hostility with the Querl was an outcome of the same kind of policy that he saw being enacted on Earth now. What kind of policy was that? Luodine asked. Exploitation, Thryase answered. The Hyadean power elite sought to subdue the Querl in order to establish overlordships for themselves, away from the drabness of their own tired, worn-down planets. But the splendors of Earth went far beyond anything ever seen on the Querl worlds. Now Earth represented the premium pickings for luxury resorts and estates, to be made a quasi-feudal reserve where the privileged could get rich from Terran labor and resources. Financial control was being effected with the collusion of Terran leaders in return for the Hyadeans conferring wealth, power, and protection.

"That's exactly what the AANS is fighting," Marie whispered to Cade. "The West is told it's about Asia wanting to hang on to its economic advantages."

"Now, you will be shown back on Chryse, right?" Cade checked with Thryase when he had finished. "So what kind of risks will that mean? I thought that independent coverage outside the official guidelines was unheard of." He felt strange as the Hyadean cameras, which had been tracking the speakers automatically from different angles in the room, caught his voice and turned toward him.

"I came here as an observer. I described what I observed." Thryase shrugged. "You see, I've been learning a lot since I came to Earth."

That set the background. Next it was Cade and Marie's turn. Luodine briefed them that the object was to get their version of the Farden-Meakes affair, the cover-up and attempt to lay the blame elsewhere, and the bid to silence the witnesses. Luodine had obviously been well versed by Vrel. She put Cade and Marie on-screen together, beginning by asking them questions and then leading them into elaborating in their own words. They spoke in English, naturally, which they were told would be dubbed by a translation for the final version. Vrel explained that the voiceover would describe them as being interviewed after escaping pursuit in the U.S. Exactly where they were and how they had gotten there would, understandably, be left vague. After a few repeats and reruns, Luodine declared that she was satisfied.

Cade still wasn't sure what Hudro's role here was. The "Brezc" turned out to be a designation of military rank, which from his description Marie guessed came closest to "colonel." He had been following the proceedings with a deep, brooding expression. While Nyarl was tidying up notes and details with the equipment, Luodine gave Hudro a questioning look. "So what do you think now?" she asked him.

Hudro took a second to respond. "Even worse than I realize," he said.

"Does that mean you're with us?" Luodine asked. "You'll help?"

Hudro hesitated again, then nodded. "Yes." Cade and Marie were watching, not really comprehending. Hudro turned and explained, "I am like the defector that you talk about. I have been in operations farther north. I see things there that our publics are not told that disturb me." It seemed Hudro was making do without veebee prompting. "For a long time I am not sure if all is bad. Now I hear it is so. I decide that Hyadean way is wrong. Our training deadens minds. Terrans who know love and carings and make fine things are killed, and their beautiful world is taken. I cannot agree with such things. So, as Hetch Luodine tells, I will help."

"What kinds of things are you talking about—that you say you've seen, Brezc?" Vrel asked curiously.

Hudro gestured toward Thryase. "Is as he says. We train and equip Terran government soldiers that news tells are protecting peoples from bandit terrorists who make own laws. Is not that way. They are moved out of lands. Make space for big-money Hyadeans. Clear forest. Make gardens, big palace houses. Is bandits who try to protect them. We send missiles and terrorize. The Asians—they know." Hudro produced a square, flat container, about the size of a box for a finger ring, from a pocket, opened it on the table, and pushed it toward Luodine. It contained what looked like shiny black pellets, held in restraining slots. "Here you have proof. I show you air strikes, and what it looks like from the ground. Did you ever see children burning or shredded by cluster bombs? Or whole village exploded under fuel-air vapors? All this I have. You show it with what Thryase and Mr. Roland and Ms. Marie all tell. Show all is so."

Luodine took the box, handling it almost reverently. "Can we see some of this?" she asked Nyarl. He nodded. Luodine passed it to him but continued looking at Hudro. "This sounds like . . ." She looked uncertain, then asked her veebee. "Dinosaur?"

"*Depends what you mean. What context?*"

"Something stunning. Sensational."

"*Dynamite.*"

Luodine didn't bother repeating it. "We need more than just pictures," she told Hudro. "We need an explanation—by someone who was there, who can interpret them. Will you go on-camera too?"

Hudro shook his head. "I can't be identified. You know that." Luodine seemed unwilling to let it go at that, but finally nodded reluctantly. There was a drawn-out silence.

Then Thryase said, "It doesn't have to be Hudro. Why can't the Terrans do it? Let them go on-screen and say it's as told to them by a senior Hyadean officer. That wouldn't even be lying."

Everyone looked at everyone else, waiting for another to come up with a reason why not. Nobody did.

"It's a thought," Vrel agreed finally.

"It's *brilliant*!" Luodine whispered. "The impact on Chryseans would be even greater. They could present it as what's happening to *their* people." She shifted her gaze back to Cade and Marie. "Will you do it?"

By this time there was nothing to ponder. They were already far enough in that it made no difference. Marie nodded. "In any case, I want to see those clips," she told them.

"Tell us what you want us to do," Cade said.

"First, let's take a break," Luodine suggested. "After that we'll play the videos and hear Hudro's story. Then I'll transpose it into interview format and we'll take you through the same routine as we did before."

"You also wanted some native stories from me," Tevlak reminded her, anxious in case he might be left out. "Don't forget that."

"I know, and we will. In the meantime, I'm getting hungry. How about a snack or something?"

"I'll see what we can do." Tevlak drew in his poncho and bustled out of the room.

Marie picked up a coffee that she still hadn't finished and sat staring distantly at the wall as she sipped. Nyarl rose, stretched, and moved over to do something to one of the cameras. Thryase began dictating in Hyadean to his veebee, which also functioned as portable secretary. Cade went over to join Hudro, who was still in the armchair.

"I'm curious, Colonel," he said. "What turned you around?"

"I haven't moved."

"What changed your mind? Most Hyadeans don't seem to question. And as you said, military training doesn't help. Why were you different?"

Hudro stared at him. He had troubled, introspective eyes, the kind that were never at rest. "Here I discover your Terran teachings of the spirit. Hyadeans know power and violence, but not your God who saves people who cannot help Him. In our way, you kick when the other is down. The ideas of Earth feed the mind. So I question what I do. One day I will save lives too."

Cade looked around the room. Here, in one house, they had Vrel, who was risking all because he had discovered ethical values previously unknown to him; Thryase had found a new politics of individualism and freedom; Tevlak had forsaken security to immerse himself in a culture; and now here was a military officer finding religion. Bombs and guns—the way that Marie had committed herself to—would never break the Hyadean stranglehold taking hold of Earth. But somewhere, Cade sensed, in these things that he was seeing here, was the way to prevail against them. Not to defeat them, for in a straight contest of strength they couldn't be defeated. But where was the need to defeat anyone, when Hyadeans could become even more Terran than Terrans themselves? Somehow, that was the key. It was all just a question of finding the direction of the flow, and then going with it.

Tevlak's name had been on the list that Julia had forwarded to her ISS controller as a matter of routine after its mention at Cade's party. One of the items that subsequently found its way into his house was a slightly damaged—hence unsalable—set of nested Russian dolls now standing in a niche in the hallway, next to a Norwegian carved-horn mermaid. The location was not ideal, but even so the chip concealed in the base of the outermost doll had collected a smattering of conversation from all of the occupants of the house, if not a comprehensive account of what was going on there. The chip responded to its periodic interrogation code sent from a Hyadean satellite as it passed overhead, and uploaded the file of what information it had managed to accumulate.

❀ CHAPTER TWENTY-SIX ❀

The U.S. was in uproar. Sovereignty had made public an account that it claimed was by an ISS defector they named as Reyvek of how the ISS had engineered the Farden-Meakes assassinations, along with documentary evidence. Officials denied it, of course. Nobody of that name had ever been employed by the ISS, they said. The documents were forgeries. Sovereignty retorted that Reyvek was killed in an assault that the security forces had admitted in Tennessee, the expunging of the record was standard cover-up, and they would soon produce proof of that too. Coming on top of the continuing challenges being voiced to the administration's legality, the story was causing a furore. There was open talk about a secession of western states. National Guard units in California, acting on orders from the state governor, had intervened to obstruct ISS operations.

Besides being concerned at the possible effects on his own personal future, Casper Toddrel was also disgruntled. The news detracted from what would otherwise have been a timely escape to an idyllic setting that he had been looking forward to. The Hyadean estate known as Derrar Dorvan had been built in the Andean foothills of southeast Peru for a leading government figure who had come to Earth on his retirement, accompanied by a retinue of family and special friends. It consisted of a thirty-room principal villa constructed Roman-style around a central court, designed by a specially commissioned Terran architect, situated on a clifftop facing a spectacle of foaming waterfalls plunging between forested mountainsides and rocky towers. A hundred acres of landscaped parkland, pools, and gardens on the reverse slope contained domiciles for lesser members of the tribe. With fast, convenient transportation always at hand, they enjoyed a rich and varied social life with other Hyadean immigrant groups scattered around the region's maze of uplands and canyons, revolving to a large degree around parties and sports, sightseeing trips, and elaborate social games played for recognition, prestige, and romantic intrigue.

Toddrel had arrived the day before with several others also attending the unofficial conference that Denham had arranged. The guest accommodation rivaled the best European hotels. After a champagne breakfast on a glazed veranda looking down over cataracts and greenery, he walked with the Englishman and the ISS colonel Kurt Drisson to the Hyadean hoverbus that would take them to the part of the estate where the talks would be held. With them was General Insing, who was Meakes's replacement—hand-picked by Toddrel and his associates, far more cooperative and understanding than Meakes had been. A significant improvement in relationships with the military was expected from now on. Thoughts for the immediate moment, however, were on damage containment following the story that was breaking in the U.S. The biggest threat right now were the Californian influence peddler Cade and the CounterAction woman known as Kestrel, who had gotten away from the motel in Chattanooga minutes ahead of the security forces after killing the ISS undercover agent Ruby. It was virtually certain that Kestrel was the only surviving witness to have heard Reyvek's story firsthand; Cade would be able to testify for her, and had possibly talked to Reyvek also, if only by phone. Producing them when the moment was right had to be what Sovereignty meant when it promised that proof of the Reyvek cover-up would be forthcoming. Hence, finding and getting to them first was imperative. Combing the Chattanooga area, and putting a watch on communications and on Cade's listed contacts in California had turned up nothing. Some of the intelligence people working on the case wondered if the pair were still in the country.

"Cade was friends with a Hyadean political observer called Vrel at their place in Los Angeles," Drisson told the other two. "Three days after the Chattanooga bust, Vrel took a trip to a military base near St. Louis, organized at short notice. Then, yesterday, the Hyadean records show him escorting a couple of academics, who happen to be a man and a woman, to the Hyadean mining center at Uyali in Bolivia."

"You think it's them?" Denham ased.

"I'd bet my next promotion on it. The names are in the system, but so far there's been no independent corroboration that they're real. They were accompanied on the flight by another Hyadean called Thryase, who's a critic of their policy toward Querl and is now questioning what's happening here. It smells from end to end."

"Why Uyali?" Denham asked.

"Who knows? Maybe it seemed out of the way and different—the kind of place nobody would guess. And who would?"

"And she's his ex-wife," Toddrel grumbled. "Does that mean he's been a source for Sovereignty all along? Didn't it occur to anyone?"

"That's exactly the reason Arcadia was put in there more than a year ago," Drisson said defensively. Arcadia was the ISS's live-in agent planted with Cade. "She never found any indication of communication between them."

"A strange way to rekindle an old romance, then," Toddrel commented. "So where are Vrel, this other Hyadean, and the academics now?"

"If they've left Uyali, the vehicle they used isn't registering," Drisson said. "We're giving it maximum effort. The minute anything comes up, I'll be informed."

"So is Arcadia still there—at the house in Los Angeles?" Insing asked.

"For the present, yes."

"Isn't that risky? They must know now about Ruby. If she was supposed to have been an old friend of Arcadia, that implicates Arcadia too."

"Right now, the group in Uyali are the only ones who know," Drisson said.

"All they have to do is get a message back to LA."

"And what would the people there do? Cade's friends are just good at making money. And Hyadean clerks?" Drisson shook his head. "This isn't their line of business. If they're onto her, Arcadia will know in time to get out. In the meantime, with all the uncertainty out there, she's still a valuable resource. She's also the bait if we're wrong about Cade and Kestrel, and they show up there again suddenly."

"It still sounds like a hell of a risk," Insing said heavily. "I read Kestrel's profile. She's good. And she has a big score to settle here."

"Arcadia's a professional. She can take care of herself."

"So was Ruby."

They arrived at the bus and waited while several others ahead of them boarded. Chen, a youthful Hyadean member of the household, was waiting, smiling, to usher them inside. Two of the native house stewards were standing with him. An additional attraction for wealthy Hyadeans acquiring estates on Earth was the availability and willingness of domestic help, which they regarded as a big status symbol. Employing menial labor on Chryse entailed political problems and was generally a privilege enjoyed by only the most prestigious or influential. Screening the flood of native applicants was a full-time job for specialized Hyadean security experts aided by Terran psychologists. Armed native guards supervised by a Hyadean officer watched from a discreet distance in the background.

The interior of the bus was like a luxurious but uninspired waiting room, with Hyadean-size seating and a front-end display screen, at present blank. The doors closed. The bus rose on an invisible cushion and moved away smoothly and silently. The sight of rolling lawns, lakeside walks among trees alive with birds and crossing ornamented bridges, knots of llamas and alpacas staring curiously from grassy glades and rocky stream banks dispelled further thoughts of assassinations and political coverups for the moment. Toddrel lounged back and looked enviously out over the scene and at the mountains beyond. What, he wondered, would be the prospects for somebody who cooperated sufficiently with the Hyadeans one day finding a niche in a place like this too? What a change it would make from the familiar environments he had come to detest, of stultifying boardrooms and choking, congested cities.

Denham's voice brought him back. "One item that the Hyadeans are going to bring up is a proposal to supply remote-detonatable munitions to Earth from now on, and retrofit existing stocks. It's the ideal answer to matériel disappearing. Wherever it's gone to, you can press a button and explode it. How's that for a deterrent?"

Toddrel frowned. "Hmm. . . . It's inviting high collateral. There'd be a lot of outcry, bad press. Do we need more right now?"

"That could actually help us," Denham pointed out. "The scarier the publicity, the better. Nobody would dare touch any of the stuff. Just what we want."

"Let's see what the general reaction at the meeting is when it's proposed," Toddrel suggested.

They came to one of the outlying residences, which had been made ready with conference facilities, a catering and domestic staff, and additional guards. They got out, and Denham and Insing moved ahead as they approached the building. Just as they entered, a high-pitched tone came from the compad in Drisson's jacket. He drew it out and looked at Toddrel meaningfully. "Emergency band. This could be something new." Denham and Insing stopped to look back. Toddrel motioned for them to go on, and that he and Drisson would catch up. They looked around and moved into a more secluded space off the entrance hallway. Toddrel watched the screen as Drisson activated it. The face and shoulders of a Hyadean appeared, in a tunic carrying military insignia. "Borfetz—Hyadean security," Drisson muttered.

The Hyadean peered out at them guardedly. "You are not alone. I need to speak urgently."

"It's okay," Drisson said. "This is Toddrel. He's with us."

Borfetz nodded but didn't look happy about it. "We have located them, both—the man and the woman," he reported. "They are at a house that belongs to an eccentric Hyadean, two hundred miles from Uyali. They don't seem to be planning to depart anytime soon. We can be there within an hour."

"Not another cowboy circus this time," Toddrel murmured in

Drisson's ear. "We need them to talk. I have to find out how much they know and who else they've passed it on to. Everything could depend on this."

"Minimum force, no lethality," Drisson relayed. "They're wanted alive."

"I understand," the Hyadean acknowledged.

◎ CHAPTER TWENTY-SEVEN ◎

The midday news brought reports that two of the freighters used to transport Hyadean-processed minerals out via the Amazon had been sunk by planted bombs. The Brazilian Air Force was conducting retaliatory strikes against suspected guerrilla bases and support centers in the area. In Bolivia, a section of one of the conveyor lines in the extraction region west of Uyali had been blown up. The newscaster expressed fears that this might be the beginnings of a major sabotage campaign against the Hyadean operations. A government commentator attributed it to a sudden increase in external aid to MOPAN—Movimento por la Autonomía Nacional was the name of the general resistance movement formed out of various opposition groups that had grown throughout the region. Asian sources were suspected. Weapons of Asian manufacture in captured guerrilla supplies were presented as evidence, and there was some insinuation of Chinese companies acting as fronts. The commentator feared that more potent Hyadean weapons might find their way through via the same route. He cited the recent assassinations carried out in the U.S. with a Hyadean plasma cannon as a precedent.

Hudro was stationed in Brazil and had taken a few days leave to come down to Bolivia. After hearing the news, he announced that he had to return to his unit immediately. Vrel decided to go with him as far as Uyali. Security would be tightening up, everywhere, and he wanted to make discreet inquiries on his own regarding the options for moving Cade and Marie onward. In the meantime it would be better for them to remain where they were. He would return or send the flyer back for them when he had a firm plan. Vrel and Hudro departed shortly afterward.

The others got back to rehearsing and then recording Cade and Marie's narration of the material they had gone through with Hudro. Luodine then moved on to the take that she had promised for Tevlak. Finally, she settled down with Nyarl to editing the preliminary version for transmission to her organization on Chryse. "This might start another sensation," she said as Nyarl worked with the equipment. "Direct news from the front, bypassing the official system. I don't know if it's ever been done before."

"So why are you doing it?" Cade asked her. "Why are you risking your . . . What do you call it. Career? Entitlement."

Luodine looked at him oddly for several seconds. "Because that's all we've ever lived for. It's the way we were conditioned. But Terrans find meaning in life beyond whatever it is that our entitlements measure. I want to find it too. So I suppose I'm experimenting."

"We all are," Thryase said.

Cade found his curiosity over this strange effect that Earth seemed to have on Hyadeans who spent any time there increasing more and more.

Marie had gone outside. Cade followed and found her standing by the door, taking in the scene of the mountains on one side, the creek running down toward the town on the other. Tevlak was outside the fence with the people who had been waiting there and were now talking excitedly, seemingly all at once, showing him various wares. One of the house guards was standing a few paces behind him.

Marie heard Cade come out and spoke without turning her head. "Why can't the whole world be more like this? People just living their lives, leaving each other alone. Why does anyone have to care what others believe or think?"

"You tell me. Aren't you the one who understands causes?"

"I hate it. But what are you supposed to do about the ones who take everything that other people produce, and give nothing back?

They couldn't build a house or make a shoe or even feed themselves without ordinary people like these. . . . Yet because they can steal from them, they call them inferior. I don't like them getting away with it. It doesn't matter if they're ours or Hyadeans."

The sun was picking out the almost blond parts in Marie's hair, the sharp angles of her jaw and cheek. She still looked slim and lithe, even in the loose sweater and shapeless dun-colored pants. "Anyway, it may not stay so peaceful for long, by the sound of things," Cade said. "I guess that'll slow down all that production we saw yesterday."

"I wonder who benefits," Marie said distantly.

Cade moved closer behind her. He could tell that she sensed his nearness, but she didn't move. "Did you really go to China?"

"Sure. I did the full training routine there: guns and explosives; computers and codes; murder and mayhem. The works. Skiing at Aspen was getting to be so ordinary. You know I have uncommon tastes."

"I thought they were all totalitarians there. Turn you into marching zombies. Doesn't it work like that?"

"Oh, that's all over. They're discovering individualism now, and hurling themselves into it with the same fanaticism they've always shown for everything. They're like the Arabs—with a tradition of resisting outside influence and interference. That's why Asia has become the natural center of opposition to what's going on."

Cade was about to reply, then snorted. "You see: it isn't me. You turn everything into politics."

Marie turned to face him. "But you *asked* me!"

"About China. You could have talked about the Great Wall, or real wonton soup."

"But China *is* politics right now. All of Asia is. Resistance isn't going to come from anywhere else. Not on any organized scale."

"Okay, so I don't care about China. Right now, I—"

At that moment, a commotion broke out among the people outside the fence, where Tevlak was. Marie and Cade turned to see what was going on. Some were gesturing toward the sky. Aircraft of some kind had appeared to the north and were approaching low and fast. They resolved themselves rapidly into three flattened oval shapes, black in color, flared at the tail, spreading out to make a circuit of the town. As Cade wheeled to follow them, a second flight of three came into sight, following the first.

Nyarl appeared from inside the house. "What's happening?" he asked, then followed their gaze.

"Hyadean troop carriers," Marie said tightly. "Their security forces use them. I can only think of one reason that would bring them here."

"There's some kind of problem inside too. Luodine is trying to send the file out to Chryse. The system won't accept. It's been blocked."

"Bad news," Marie muttered.

The first three carriers came out of their turn on a direct course for the house. Two descended toward points a short distance upstream and downstream along the creek bank, while the third passed overhead to the opposite side, presumably to cut off escape in that direction. The second three carriers were heading directly in for the house to complete its encirclement.

"The phone!" Marie said suddenly. "Hyadean communications might be blocked, but ours could still work. We've got to get that file out!"

Nyarl turned and stumbled back into the house, Marie following. Cade stopped to look back the other way. Figures in combat gear were leaping from the carriers that had landed, spreading out and advancing. It looked like a mixed force of Hyadeans and Terrans. The people around Tevlak were drawing back, alarmed, some already running instinctively toward the gate as if the house offered protection. Tevlak was standing, bewildered. The house guard drew his gun and ran forward to stop them. Tevlak waved him aside to let them through. As the second wave of carriers touched down, an amplified voice boomed, "YOU ARE SURROUNDED. DO NOT ATTEMPT TO RESIST, AND NO ONE WILL BE HARMED." Cade turned away and hastened inside after Marie and Nyarl. Marie was handing a phone to Nyarl, who plugged in a data lead, then frantically connected that to an adaptor hooked to a piece of the Hyadean equipment. Luodine was watching one of the screens with an agonized expression. "I have to reformat," she told Cade. "Our codes won't work with the Terran system."

"Where do we send it?" Nyarl asked. Marie seemed at a loss.

Cade thought furiously. "Vrel's got a clean phone. Send it to him. He'll figure out a way to forward it."

"You know the number?" Nyarl asked. Cade nodded. Nyarl passed him the phone. The housekeeper came in, jabbering in Spanish; at the same moment, the other house guard appeared at the opposite end of the room. The guard yelled something. They disappeared toward the rear. Screams punctuated by shouted commands were coming from outside, getting nearer.

"*Done!*" Luodine exclaimed. Cade hammered in the number.

A musical tone sounded. "Acceso inválido. Servicio negado," an impartial voice enunciated.

"*Shit!*" Tevlak's phone was being blocked too.

"What is it?" Marie asked tensely. Cade didn't answer. For several seconds he stood glaring from side to side like a trapped animal. Then he threw the phone down and rushed back out of the house. The yard was filled with milling figures. Tevlak was inside the gate, uniformed Terrans restraining him on both sides, a Hyadean calling orders to others moving forward. More Hyadeans had taken up positions around the perimeter. Some genius ordered a burst of warning shots to be fired. The milling and shouting turned into panic. Cade grabbed a fleeing Indian, wide-eyed with fear, by the shirt front.

"*Do you have a phone?*"

"Eh? No comprendo."

"Jesus. . . . Teléfono. ¿Tiene un teléfono?"

"No."

Cade pushed him aside. A woman in a straw hat and red wrap was screaming and waving her arms aimlessly. Cade saw a phone attached by a loop to her shoulder purse. He pointed at it. "*I need that phone!*" The woman wasn't listening. He tore the phone from the purse and rushed back inside. Nyarl ripped the data lead out of the useless phone and jammed it into the one Cade thrust in front of him. Cade tried the number again.

Ri-ing. Ri-ing.

The front door banged open, and a voice shouted, sounding like the guard who had been outside. The second guard reappeared from the back of the house and ran out toward the front.

"*Christ! Christ! Christ! Come on. . . .*"

Ri— The tone cut, and a voice answered in Hyadean.

"Vrel?"

"Yes."

"It's Roland. No time to talk. I'm downloading the file. You have to get it to Chryse somehow."

"What—"

"*Just do it!*"

An endless pause. Then, "Ready." Cade nodded at Nyarl. Nyarl barked something at the Hyadean electronics. A crash followed by splintering noises came from the rear of the house, and then the terrified yelling of the housekeeper. More thuds from the front door. Indignant shouts, a couple of shots, then more screaming, getting louder as the door was battered in.

"It's going through," Luodine murmured.

Boots hitting the floor at a run; shouts; other doors in the house being thrown open.

An officer in peaked cap and army uniform, brandishing a pistol, appeared from the rear rooms, followed by troopers in helmets and flak jackets. "*Everyone stay where you are! Hands high! Stop that!*" Seconds later, armed Hyadean figures came through from the front, thrusting aside Thryase, who was trying to block the doorway. The leader barked something at Luodine, while another hauled Nyarl away from the table.

"*Sent and deleted!*" Luodine whispered to Cade. He released a sigh of relief. They straightened up to face the intruders.

The Terran officer came forward. "Ms. Marie Cade, otherwise known as Kestrel, I believe. And Mr. Roland Cade. You are under arrest as terrorists wanted for extradition to the United States." More soldiers appeared from the rest of the house, making negative signs. One of the Hyadeans began checking the recording equipment. Luodine and Thryase were protesting in response to questions from another Hyadean, answering in English for Cade and Marie's benefit.

"We're simply doing our jobs. . . . I'm a political observer. She is a media investigator."

"Tevlak doesn't know anything about them. They were introduced as visiting professors."

"No, I don't know anything about a Teera Vrel. . . . Hyadean officer? What Hyadean officer?"

In the end, it was announced that the four Hyadeans would be detained pending a ruling from a higher authority somewhere. Cade and Marie were taken out to one of the craft that had landed, and boarded with a mixed Terran and Hyadean guard detail. The carrier took off immediately, accompanied by a second flying as escort.

☉ CHAPTER TWENTY-EIGHT ☉

Toddrel learned just after the evening banquet at Derrar Dorvan that the two fugitives had been captured. They were being held in a detention facility at a base used jointly by Hyadean and Peruvian military forces near Cuzco, pending further instructions. Hyadeans had been at the house too, but there seemed to be some confusion over their motives and circumstances. In any case, Hyadean security was dealing with it. Toddrel's concern at this stage was purely in establishing how much the two Americans had found out, and whom they might have divulged it to before leaving the country. And then silencing them. He skipped the next morning's session of the meeting and left for Cuzco with Drisson, curious to meet face-to-face this couple who had been the cause of so much trouble. They flew south, with the wall of the Andes standing clear in the early sun, far off to the right.

"I've been thinking about those remote-detonatable munitions that Denham was talking about," Drisson said. "If the Hyadeans are moving troops into the south Altiplano region to protect their action, it means they'll be stashing a lot more hardware around there. If some of the munitions they bring in are of the new type, and someone could get the remote-access codes . . ." He looked at Toddrel meaningfully.

A lot of damage and confusion could be caused, slowing down if not halting operations completely, which Toddrel and associated interests would appreciate. It didn't need spelling out. "And the media have already set up MOPAN with Chinese backing as the obvious culprits," Toddrel completed.

"My thinking, exactly."

"Hm." Toddrel decided that it had possibilities. "It could be tough on a few of our Hyadean . . . allies." He looked at Drisson questioningly.

"Hell, if it's the way to win the war . . ." Drisson left it unfinished.

"Something to bring up with Denham when we convene again tomorrow," Toddrel pronounced.

Cade sat hunched on a coarse mattress covering the single cot, his legs drawn up, arms resting on his knees. The cell was part of a detention facility in the place they had been brought to. It seemed some kind of military base from the glimpses that he'd managed to get. He hadn't seen anything of Marie since they were taken separate ways on their arrival the previous day. Sounds from outside came intermittently through the barred, glass-slatted window, of vehicles, tramping feet, voices calling orders, and aircraft taking off and landing. Besides the cot, he had a chair, a table, a wooden shelf, a washbasin with a faucet that dribbled brown water, and a toilet. Light was from a bulb, hanging by its cord. It all felt very far from Newport Beach.

They had fastened a metal collar around his neck. When he started protesting and demanded legal representation, a jolt that felt as if it were tearing his head apart knocked him off his feet, impressing the message that he wasn't in a position to demand anything. It had been a sobering and effective lesson. In movies, people always breezed through such experiences to perform acrobatic escapes or deliver comeuppances with interest on their aggressors. The reality turned out to be very different. His head still throbbed, and his nerves felt shredded. His body seemed to have gone into a protective shock. Worse was the feeling of humiliation and outrage, the disorientation that came with the realization of his utter helplessness. And he'd had plenty of time to reflect that this could be just the mild beginning.

Perhaps that was an intended part of the process. He tried not to think about Marie.

Footsteps approached outside. Keys jangled in the door. It opened to reveal two of the guards—dark-skinned and hefty, with mean, indifferent faces. One of them said something in Spanish and motioned for Cade to get up. The other was holding a unit resembling a TV remote, which controlled the collar. Cade's body had chilled and stiffened, but he wasn't arguing.

They took him past a row of doors with shuttered grilles, down a flight of metal stairs, and along a corridor of walls painted green up to a brown dividing line and yellow above. Steel lockers stood at intervals along one side, and red fire extinguishers hung on the wall at the end. A soldier in fatigues came out of one of the doors and passed them going the other way. They stopped at a door farther along. The guard who was leading knocked. A voice from inside called, "*Sí.*" The guard opened the door. The other jabbed Cade in the back to propel him through.

It was a bare room of painted brick walls and a concrete floor. A man in a tan jacket and white, open-neck shirt was sitting at a metal desk, empty except for a file folder, some scattered papers, a lamp, and an open laptop. He had a balding head fringed by dark, oily-looking curls, and a rounded face with brooding eyes that followed Cade curiously as he came in. Another man, leaner, with fair, cropped hair and a mustache, wearing ISS uniform with rank designation that Cade wasn't sure of—colonel, maybe—was standing, arms folded, with his back to the corner on one side. An upright wooden chair faced the desk. The guard prodded Cade toward it while the other closed the door. He sat down, and they stationed themselves behind.

The interrogator let his eyes flicker over Cade for a few seconds, as if looking for a visual cue as to how to open. "So, the other half of the duo," he said finally. He was American. "You two have caused a lot of problems." He didn't seem to expect any response at that point. "Okay, let's save us all a lot of time. We know you were at the motel in Chattanooga, how you got there, and that you were brought out through St. Louis by this Hyadean from California, Teera Vrel." He went on to supply some of the salient details. Maybe the idea was to sound as if he knew more than he did, with the implication that telling untruths could be risky. Cade figured that Rebecca and Julia between them would have supplied everything up to the incident in the motel. With surveillance everywhere and taps into all the computers, who knew how they had traced them to St. Louis? Anything relating to the three days between his and Marie's fleeing from Chattanooga and their arrival at the St. Louis Hilton was notably absent from the interrogator's account.

"Did you at any time meet the person who was referred to as Otter? His real name was Reyvek, formerly with the security forces." Cade didn't answer. The man nodded to one of the guards behind. A pain like a three-second migraine headache seared through Cade's skull, then stopped. Just a warning. He realized that the rush of fear had almost caused him to loose bowel control. A sour taste welled in his mouth. His chest was pounding, palms slippery.

"I'm not here to do all the talking," the interrogator told him. "You *will* tell us, so you might as well make it easy on yourself. Again, did you at any time meet Otter?"

Cade licked his lips. Conflicting impulses tore at him. He had never known that the urge of self-preservation could be so strong. In his confusion he couldn't form a coherent answer. The pain began again, rising slowly this time, like a dental drill probing a nerve, only in his head. "*No!*"

"No, what?"

"No, I never met him."

"Did you talk to him at all—by phone, maybe?"

"No."

"You *will* tell us," the interrogator reminded him again.

Cade felt sweat running down his back inside his shirt. "I didn't talk to him! What else can I say?"

"CounterAction arranged his defection. Weren't you involved with that?"

"I don't know anything about CounterAction."

"Don't give us that," the colonel said from the corner. His voice was clipped. "You've been an undercover informer of theirs for years. That's what that whole setup of yours is in California. Isn't it?"

"No. That's not true."

"Isn't it?" the interrogator at the desk echoed. The drill started probing again.

"*It's not true, I told you!*" The drill stopped. Cade gasped for breath. "You've had your spy there for a year. What did she see?"

"Why did you go to Chattanooga?" the interrogator asked.

"You just told me a few minutes ago. I didn't intend going to Chattanooga. Only Atlanta."

"That was the story," the colonel said. "We want the real reason."

"That's all there is."

"Wasn't it to rendezvous with Kestrel, your former wife, whom you'd been in communication with all the time?"

"No. I didn't even know she was there."

"You expect us to believe that?" the interrogator asked.

"Probably not, if you've already made your minds up. . . . But it's true."

The interrogator glanced at the colonel, apparently deciding not to pursue the point for the time being. He jotted something on the papers in front of him and looked back up. "Where were you in the three days after Chattanooga—before you showed up in St. Louis?"

"I don't know." Cade felt a tingle building up. He gulped. "It was dark. We followed a car somewhere."

"So you were still in the general area," the colonel said.

There couldn't be any denying it. "Yes."

"How many hours did you drive from Chattanooga? Which direction?"

"One, maybe two. North . . . I think."

The interrogator made more notes, then consulted something on the laptop. "Vagueness won't get you anywhere in the long run," he murmured, still looking at the screen.

The colonel moved across the room to stand looking down at Cade, giving him no respite. "Where did Vrel go?" he demanded.

"When?"

"Quit stalling, Cade. Vrel wasn't at Corto Tevlak's house. Where is he?"

"He went to check up on some things."

"Back to Uyali?"

"He didn't say exactly where, and I've already been mixed up in this long enough not to ask." Cade looked up. The colonel was watching him distastefully. "Look, whatever you think, I haven't been working with CounterAction. I just make trading deals and mind my own business. If Julia's been any good to you, you know that."

"Who was the other Hyadean who disappeared with him?"

"I'd never met him before."

"I didn't ask that. What was his name?"

Cade couldn't bring himself to answer. He gripped the edges of the chair and stared at the front of the metal desk, feeling himself perspiring in rivers. "It doesn't matter for now," the interrogator's voice said tiredly from above. Cade raised his eyes, half expecting a trick. "We don't want any undue unpleasantness here. This is only a transit facility, you understand. Shortly, you'll be taken to a more permanent location, where they have experts who are more skilled at this kind of thing than I. I'm sure you'll be more cooperative by the time we next meet." He eyed Cade dourly for a moment. "Even if you do discover a reserve of unsuspected heroics, there are usually other avenues of weakness that can be explored. The other person that we're holding, for example, seems to be becoming an object of restored affections, even assuming that your alleged estrangement was genuine. I trust you take the point?"

"*Bastards!*" Cade started to rise and was checked by a jarring sensation in his neck. A hand from behind seized him by the hair, yanking his head back, forced him back down, while another cuffed the side of his face painfully. He glowered across the desk, panting shakily.

The interrogator studied Cade's face pensively. It must have registered abhorrence that a Terran could be capable of selling out his own kind to such a degree. His expression changed to one of amused contempt. "Don't tell me you've fallen for some campus ideology. Our files describe you as a realist. There's only one kind of realism in the universe, and its proponents all understand each other. There aren't any rules to the game. Its sole object is to take care of oneself. You make trading deals, you said? Very well. We can make you an offer to come over to the winning side in return for being sensible. Isn't that what any realist wants?"

Cade didn't hold much stock in any offers. Whichever way things went, he had the distinct feeling that knowing what they knew now, the chances of he and Marie ever getting back to the States were pretty slim. Losing them somewhere would hardly present a problem. After all, they had never officially left.

⚙ CHAPTER TWENTY-NINE ⚙

The Hyadean transport hummed through the air. Cade had no idea in what direction. The view panels were set to opaque, leaving just the stark, metal-ribbed interior and its austere fittings. Marie was next to him, with two Peruvian guards in the row in front, three behind, and their Hyadean officer facing from a bulkhead seat in front. The captives had been issued with baggy gray prison garb, and each wore one of the diabolical Hyadean collars. They had both spent a second uncomfortable night. But at least they were together again—for the time being. Perhaps a chance to renew concern between them was part of the intention—to make things that much tougher later. There had been little opportunity to discuss their experiences. Cade didn't know if she had been exposed to threat along the lines the interrogator had implied. He wouldn't have mentioned it in any case.

"Look. . . ." He kept his voice low, glancing sideways to be sure she was listening. "It's been a long time. A lot's happened. In case we don't get out of this, I just want you to know that a lot of things that seemed smart once don't seem so smart anymore. What I mean is . . . Hell, you know what I'm trying to say."

"Roland groping for words?" she murmured. "I don't believe it."

"Asshole, then. How's that for a choice of word? I was an asshole."

"No talking between the prisoners," the Hyadean officer said.

Cade sensed Marie smiling. Her hand found its way around the metal tubing holding the armrest, to where his was resting. Their little fingers touched and entwined surreptitiously. If only just a little, he felt more at peace.

About fifteen minutes later, the transport dipped suddenly without warning and went into a steep descent. The officer grabbed a handrail on the wall to steady himself and asked something in Spanish to the guard who seemed to be second in command. The second answered negatively. The officer called out in Hyadean to the vessel's control system. There was no response. He called something else, then broke out a manual control panel that hinged down from the bulkhead. The guards began jabbering in alarm as they clung for balance. "¡Silencio!" the officer shouted, tapping frantically at the panel. "¡Espera para órdenes!"

Cade and Marie exchanged ominous looks. "You might just have made that last-words speech in time," Marie whispered. They clutched hands tensely.

The transport leveled out suddenly, causing more disorder; then there was a bump and a swish that sounded as if they had brushed a treetop, followed by sudden deceleration, throwing everyone forward onto the floor and flattening the officer against the forward wall. Cade was pitched fully between the two seats in front and went down in a heap with the guards. Before anyone could begin untangling themselves, there was the *bang* of a hole being blown in the side of the cabin, and then something exploded in a blaze of light that left Cade blinded and helpless except for a bizarre reverse-colored image etched into his retina. He was vaguely aware of shouts, scrambling noises, bodies colliding around him. Fragments of vision began coming together again to reveal the door partly burned away and hanging open, two large, helmeted figures silhouetted against the daylight, coming through, and then others, smaller. A guard tried to rise and was clubbed down. Two of the assailants seized Marie. One threw something like a blanket over her head and held her, while one of the larger figures leveled a device at her throat. "*No!*" Cade screamed. He tried to hurl himself at them, but strong arms gripped him from behind. Then a metallic mesh came down over him, and he felt his head being pushed back.

"Don't resist!" a Hyadean voice shouted near his ear. "It scrambles signals to the collar! They can still blow your head off!" Cade forced himself to relax and felt some kind of shield being forced up between his neck and the band of metal. Moments later there was a *clunk*, and the collar came free. The mesh was removed. He looked over, his eyes still dim with aftershock from the light, and saw that Marie was rid of hers too. He turned back to the Hyadean, who was regarding him in what looked like a jaunty stance, hands on hips, while armed Terrans shepherded the dazed guards and their officer out through the ruin of the door. The details cleared slowly to show him in Hyadean combat garb, belt and shoulder harness loaded with pouches and accoutrements, grinning and waiting while Cade's vision cleared sufficiently to recognize him.

It was Hudro.

"You were going the wrong way," Hudro said. "We figured you needed help." There had to be a response that would go down in history. Cade couldn't think what it was.

Meanwhile, the second Hyadean, who was female, had been locating and smashing key parts of the transport's communications equipment. "That's it," she announced. "Let's go."

"We need to move fast," Hudro told Cade. "The traffic-control system will be flashing alarms already."

The vessel was tilted among a tangle of vines and trees. They climbed out carefully and crossed an open area, where Terrans in forage caps and jungle gear had the officer and two of the five guards sitting on the ground, disarmed, hands on heads, while two others assisted one who seemed to have hurt a leg. There didn't seem to be any more Hyadeans. The female who was with Hudro frisked the captives for personal communicators and took those too.

In a clearing a short distance away was an olive-painted military helicopter, rotor running. The two Hyadeans guided Cade and Marie over to it, where a Terran waiting in the doorway helped them aboard. He shouted to the others, who began backing away from the guards, keeping their weapons trained on them. The guards were looking scared. For a sickening moment Cade thought they were about to be gunned down in cold blood. But the rescuers turned to run the last few yards to the waiting helicopter and threw themselves aboard. Hudro shouted something to the pilot, and it began rising. A couple of weapons were thrown back to the guards as the helicopter cleared the treetops. Minutes later, it was skimming over a green ocean of forest.

"I said that one day I save people," Hudro shouted above the engine noise. "Is good feeling."

"I'm glad you don't waste time once you make your mind up," Cade yelled back.

Hudro gestured to introduce the other Hyadean, crouching next to him on the floor, gripping the side netting—the helicopter's cramped side seats didn't admit to Hyadean proportions. She had taken off her helmet to reveal orange-yellow hair and smooth features for a Hyadean. Cade had the feeling that by their standards she would be young and pretty. "This is Yassem. A long time we know each other. It is she who shows me the Terran God. We decide that Hyadeans who bomb Terrans from homes here are criminals. Terran powers that they act with are criminals. We want no more part." He hesitated, then said something to Yassem in Hyadean. She laughed, which Cade remembered meant embarrassment. "I guess is okay to tell you now," Hudro said to Cade. He gripped Yassem's hand. "Until yesterday, Yassem works with Hyadean intelligence service. Communications technical specialist. Is how we meet. We fall over love. Go away, live together as Terrans now. Who knows where? Away. Maybe Asia someplace."

Marie laid a hand on Yassem's shoulder and smiled. "Good luck," she said.

"Thank you."

The rest of the company in the helicopter comprised a mix of tough-looking characters in parkas, sweaters, flak jackets, combat smocks, decked with equipment belts and bandoliers, nursing an assortment of weapons. One who appeared to be the leader—with a black beret worn forward, sunglasses, and a black mustache—was eyeing Cade and Marie curiously from a jump seat on Hudro's other side.

"Here is Rocco," Hudro supplied, following Cade's gaze. "I know too for long time now. My work with Hyadeans makes me live close with MOPAN bandits, try to spy. But it works backward. I get to know them. Yassem tells me about God, and I learn bandit peoples know God too. So I am on wrong side. Maybe live with bandits for time before go to Asia. Teach defense to Hyadean devil weapons. Many tricks. Makes me the big prize, eh?"

Rocco acknowledged Cade and Marie with a nod. Cade returned it. "We owe you a big thanks. I never realized we were so well known here already."

"If Hudro says you're two important people who could make some difference to this war, that's good enough for me," Rocco said.

"So how did you pull it off?"

Rocco indicated Hudro and Yassem. "You have to ask them. They got into the system that controls the Hyadean robot flyers. Brought it down where it wasn't supposed to go. We were waiting."

"Where are you from, Rocco?" Marie asked.

"It doesn't matter anymore. No family left anywhere. All wiped out in the fighting. Now I just live to fight Globs."

"Globs?" Cade's brow creased.

"Globalists," Marie supplied.

"Forces of governments that work for the criminals," Hudro said. "Is more complicated here than Earth is told."

"And every day getting more complicated," Rocco said. "What do you think is going to happen in the north?" he asked Cade and Marie. "Places in the western states ordering federal troops out. Air bases being taken over."

"We hadn't heard about it," Cade said.

"A lot of people say they're gonna split."

Cade turned his head to Hudro. "After you left Tevlak's, we tried to send a file to Vrel via his phone. Did it come through?"

Hudro nodded. "It comes through. But we cannot send to Chryse. Vrel think he knows somebody in California instead. If they ever get it, I don't know."

"Where's Vrel now?" Cade asked.

"Waiting for us. Is with Luodine and Nyarl. When—" Hudro looked away as a call from the pilot up front interrupted. Rocco got up, ducking his head, and shouldered his way forward between the rows of figures hunched over guns and packs. Hudro straightened up on the floor in readiness to rise. Next to Cade, Marie pulled herself closer.

Rocco came back and shouted down to Hudro. "Segora is under attack. We are being warned off. The pilot wants you up front. We've got incoming radar from somewhere."

"What's Segora?" Cade asked Hudro as he unfolded up from the floor.

"Is where we were supposed to land. Maybe have to change plans now." Hudro followed Rocco forward. The guerrillas had become alert, straightening up in their seats to watch something outside. Cade turned to look out of the open hatch, past the machine gun. Several miles away, perhaps, an aircraft shaped like a black arrowhead was climbing away from the ground, followed by a second a short distance behind and to one side. A boiling cloud of black smoke mixed with flame rose behind them. More planes were visible as dots higher up.

"Air strike," Yassem commented needlessly. Smoke was also coming up from other places among the trees. Whether it was due to air attack, artillery, or conflagrations on the ground was impossible to say. A brilliant pink light flashed past the open gun-hatch; then came the jolting of objects hitting the helicopter's structure. The cold realization came over Cade that they were being shot at. Yassem put her helmet back on and secured it.

At the front, Rocco turned and shouted back instructions. One of those behind clambered up to man the machine gun, while another hooked up the ammunition belt from the feeder box. Everyone else clung tight as the pilot went into a violent evasive maneuver. Cade was thrown outward from his seat, then hard back on the wall. He and Marie braced their arms on the sides and tried to steady themselves against each other. . . .

And then nothing.

❈   ❈   ❈

Fragments of awareness. Blurred smears of sensations coalescing from a vacuum.

Spinning patches of light. . . . Churning noise. . . . Lurching motion.

Thirsty. Sweating. Touch of damp fabric.

Cade was lying down. Every lurch tossed him to the side and back again, causing pain to shoot through his head. His head didn't feel good at all. It felt bloated on one side and numb at the back. The thought came and went hazily. His head was wrapped in something. Stiff. Aching everywhere. . . . None of him felt good at all.

He heard the whirr of an engine revving, then gears being shifted. The lurching resolved itself into the jolting of a truck on a rough road. He tried to open his eyes but they seemed to be stuck. Even the effort made the shooting pains in his head worse. The thirst was unbearable, as if his throat were filled with dry furnace ash. He groaned.

Voices somewhere floated incomprehensibly. A hand lifted his head. He winced, feeling as if his neck would break. Something touched his mouth. *Water!* Not cool, but priceless. He tried to gulp greedily but the hand restrained him, allowing him only to sip. A wet cloth was swabbed over his face and eyes. He tried opening them again and succeeded with an effort. A face was looking down at him. His faculties still hadn't returned sufficiently for him to recognize anything. He sipped more from the water bottle and registered slowly that he was in a truck. Only then did he begin to remember that he had been in a helicopter.

Another face, blue-gray in hue, materialized behind the first. He flexed his lips. "Vrel?" he managed.

"No." The face looked concerned. "This is Hudro."

Oh, right. Vrel hadn't been there. So how come a truck now? "What . . . ? Did we crash?"

"Was more than a day ago now," Hudro said. "Was fighting at Segora. We were hit."

Cade contemplated the statement in a detached kind of way. It didn't take on any immediate great significance. His head had been injured, and it hurt. Pink lights. He remembered the gunfire. Then it all started coming back.

"Marie!" He focused and looked up. "How is Marie?" The Hyadean face stared down at him in what seemed a long silence. "Where is she? What's up?

"I'm sorry, Mr. Cade," Hudro said. "She didn't make it."

◉ CHAPTER THIRTY ◉

The flyer sped low on a southwestward course, a few thousand feet above the barren salt wastes of the southern Altiplano. Ahead and to the right, the line was coming into view of the new roadway with its procession of robot trucks carrying produce from the extraction operations north to the Amazon outlet, and a return flow of vehicles either empty or bringing construction materials and supplies. Vrel and Hudro were over an hour out from leaving Tevlak's house and getting close to Uyali.

"What do you make of it?" Vrel asked Hudro. He meant the news they had heard at Tevlak's that morning of the escalation of sabotage and guerrilla attacks in the Amazon region, and the retaliatory actions by government forces. They were speaking, naturally, in Hyadean.

"Somebody, somewhere gave them a signal. Someone who has been building up backing and support."

"The Asians?"

"They get a lot of the blame publicly, but I'm pretty sure there's more to it. The Asian economy isn't affected that much. A lot of Western finance would like to see a slowdown in the operations here."

"I thought they were supposed to be with us," Vrel said.

"It's all complicated . . . trying to understand what goes on. I don't really understand it."

641

Vrel watched Hudro staring out through the view panels. His face was troubled. "So what are you going to do?" Vrel asked. There was a pause.

"There is a girl that I know up in Brazil—it's best if you don't know her name . . ." Hudro seemed to think better of whatever he had been about to say. "We have plans," he ended simply.

"A Terran girl?"

"No. She is Hyadean."

"I know a Terran girl in Los Angeles," Vrel said. "Very pretty. Blond hair, cut like this at the front." He made a line with his hand to indicate a fringe. "Sometimes I think of going off to live a Terran life—like Tevlak."

"You do?" Hudro seemed more than just casually interested. He was about to say more, when a tone interrupted from the Terran phone that Vrel was carrying. Vrel frowned, took it out, and answered guardedly, "Who is this?"

"Vrel?" A Terran voice.

Vrel switched to English. "Yes."

"It's Roland. No time to talk. I'm downloading the file. You have to get it to Chryse somehow."

File? It could only mean the file they had recorded with Luodine. Vrel was confused. "What—" he began.

"*Just do it!*"

Hudro was looking at him questioningly. Vrel waved a hand to indicate that he couldn't explain. "Some kind of trouble," he muttered, at the same time keying in the code to direct input to the phone's integral storage. "Ready," he said into it. He could make out noise at the other end: voices shouting; distant bangs and crashes. An indicator showed that the file was coming through. In a few seconds, it was done. "Hello? . . . Hello, Roland?" Vrel tried. But the connection was already gone.

"Roland? You mean it was Cade? What did he want?" Hudro demanded. "What kind of trouble?"

"I'm not sure. It sounded as if there was fighting going on there. Roland sent the file. It's here, in the phone. He wants me to get it to Chryse."

Hudro thought for a few seconds. "Security must have traced them there."

"How?"

"I don't know. There are all kinds of ways."

Vrel tried to think what it meant. If they had been traced to Tevlak's, Cade's and Marie's aliases were already blown. Vrel's association with them would be revealed by the Hyadean flight records from St. Louis to the base in Maryland and from there to Uyali. Thryase had used his diplomatic pull to keep the flyer's movements out of the system, but it was a safe bet that a reception party would be waiting at Vrel's room in the Hyadean sector of Uyali. "I can't go back," he told Hudro. "They'll be onto me as well."

"How can you be sure?"

"I came in with the two Americans yesterday. It will be in the flight log." Vrel looked at Hudro dubiously. "How sure can you be about you?"

"Impossible to say."

"You can't just report to the military desk at Uyali," Vrel said. Hudro's intention had been to find transportation back to his unit in Brazil. "They could be just waiting for you to show up. Maybe that's why you haven't had a recall. Why alert you that something's up? We don't want to land back there at all—not until we've found some way of checking the situation."

Hudro frowned, obviously not liking Vrel doing his thinking for him. But he couldn't argue. He interrogated the on-board system about other options and directed it to reroute the flyer to a construction area thirty miles north, where a power generating installation was being built. There, they could try to find some kind of ground transportation, which would be less conspicuous.

Since anything could happen after they landed, the file from Cade needed to be forwarded now. Vrel couldn't use the flyer's system to access the direct net link to Chryse, however. The message protocols would involve his personal ID codes, which were bound to have been watch-listed, and reveal his whereabouts. The only alternative was to use his Terran phone and hope that it was clean. That, of course, couldn't get the file to Chryse. The only way he could think of to do that would be to send it via the mission in Los Angeles. But communications into there were still likely to be subject to surveillance, as would any to his known contacts if he was being sought—which ruled out using Dee or anyone at Cade's house.

"You'd better come up with something soon. We've got less than five minutes," Hudro said.

There was a dealer that Dee used for work on her car. Vrel recalled that he was called Vince something. Something to do with ducks. . . . The service manager's name was Stan. He had wanted to introduce Vrel to golf. Vrel thought, tried to remember. . . . Beak? Drake? Bird? No . . . Walk, waddle? *Web!* That was what they called their funny feet. Vince Web! Vrel called information but didn't know enough Spanish to make himself understood. "Can you connect me to an English-speaking operator?" he pleaded. "Er . . . *Operador. Habla inglés.*"

"Give it to me." Hudro took the phone. "What do you want?"

"United States directory information. California, Los Angeles area. An automobile dealer called Vince Web—somewhere around Venice."

While Hudro was waiting for the information, Vrel copied the file into the flyer's system and encrypted it into Hyadean Code along with a message to Wyvex for it to be forwarded to Chryse. He attached a plaintext note to "Stan, Service Department," asking him to pass it on urgently to "Wyvex, care of Dee Rainier, who drives the white Pontiac." Meanwhile, Hudro had obtained the number. Vrel loaded the package back into the phone and sent it off just as the flyer was touching down.

The first thing Hudro did after they landed was get rid of his military-issue Hyadean communicator, which was traceable. Until he knew whether he was compromised or not, he didn't dare use it. If his name was hot, any message sent from it could trigger a surveillance computer.

They arrived at Uyali late in the afternoon in a Terran truck making a run from the construction area to pick up a piece of equipment that had been ferried from the spaceport at Xuchimbo.

Hudro had found a friendly plant engineer, showed his military pass, and explained with a wink that he and his friend needed a ride back to town after a hot double date in one of the villages farther north. The flyer was "borrowed" and would make its own way back. In recognition, Hudro promised to send back a bottle of Terran "risky"—a Hyadean pun based on the English rhyme with "whisky"—with the truck driver from Uyali. "I'll take two," the engineer had said, which was the Hyadean way of asking who you think you're kidding. Hyadeans saw no point in fulfilling one-time obligations. But he had found them a place in the truck anyway.

Hudro had told Vrel that he had a friend he trusted in Hyadean Military Intelligence back in Brazil, who might be able to find out if Hudro was being watched for and what else was going on. Vrel wondered if it was Hudro's girlfriend, but Hudro didn't say. Whoever it was, Hudro would only be able to talk about such things over a secure link, which would mean going into the sprawling Hyadean military base at Uyali and getting access to the communications there. He was willing to gamble that even if Hyadean military police were checking the air terminal, the alert would not involve every guard and gate sentry in the area, and that his papers would get him in. Vrel couldn't offer any better idea. The only thing for Vrel to do in the meantime would be to lose himself, away from prying Hyadean eyes. The best place to do that promised to be the Terran sector. Accordingly, the truck dropped them off outside a store on the part of the road that ran nearest, and Hudro dutifully purchased a half bottle of pisco brandy for the Hyadean driver to take back for the engineer. The driver accepted it appreciatively and seemed amused. Whether or not it would get where it was supposed to go was beyond Hudro's control.

They had a meal of spicy meat and vegetables on rice in a café on the outskirts and then strolled around to familiarize themselves with the area. It seemed to have grown around three main streets, one crossing the other two like the lines of a Terran English H. The Terrans were happy to see Hyadeans in their sector because Hyadeans drew large paychecks. After further thought, Hudro bought a man's leather wallet—hand-sewn and richly decorated—some pieces of jewelry, and a mechanical, spring-powered Terran watch that had to be wound by hand every day, which Hyadeans found intriguing and prized even on Chryse, where the twelve-hour cycle meant nothing. "You never know. I might need to bribe somebody in there," he explained to Vrel as they came out of the store. "It never hurts to be prepared."

"I'm impressed," Vrel complimented. Coming from a Hyadean, it meant just that.

"Military training," Hudro said.

"Out of curiosity, just what *do* you do in the military?" Vrel asked.

"Counterinsurgency intelligence. Infiltration. The guys you don't hear about, who live on the other side of the lines."

The final item that Hudro bought was a regular Terran pocket phone with clean codes and a prepaid call quota that he could use without opening an account. So at least, he would be able to make calls over the Terran system that wouldn't attract attention. He left after arranging to meet up with Vrel again later. If there were an emergency, now they could call each other.

One thing about being on an alien planet was the guarantee of always getting a lift from one's own kind. Hudro waited no more than a few minutes on one of the approach roads to the base before a Hyadean military vehicle carrying both uniformed figures and others in regular dress pulled up in response to his wave. He would arouse less curiosity that way than if he arrived on foot, he had decided. The crew turned out to be surveyors and construction supervisors who had been out planning a water pipeline, and a detail of Army guards. There were no Terrans, and at the gate they were waved straight through, although the occupants of a bus taking Terran workers inside were being rigorously checked and searched. So obstacle number one was out of the way as easily as that.

Hudro was back in the Hyadean world now. Already, it felt different. The surroundings were functional, businesslike, designed for getting things done. Time seemed to snap along at a Hyadean pace. People moved briskly, with purpose. They wore uniforms and working clothes that he recognized, giving them roles that were familiar—like a picture that had suddenly come into focus. There were weapons emplacements inside the perimeter fence, a transportation depot with a landing area inside the gate, where an officer was supervising a fatigue detail unloading an air-truck, and other figures crossed to and fro on various errands. A Military Police post stood on the other side, with signs indicating directions to such locations as 12TH CLOSE SUPPORT BATTALION; 76TH AIR ASSAULT HQ; TAC COM CMD OPS; QMSUP OFF. 19TH INFTRY REC GRP. Hudro followed a path of fused rock chippings painted white to a multistory configuration of office and service modules designated the Administration Center, which was where Headquarters Command was indicated to be situated. He found it after checking with the desk sergeant inside the door, taking an elevator up two levels from the lobby, and following a corridor into the next riser. Inside the door was a waiting area consisting of seats set around three sides of a low table, with the fourth open to a desk-counter at which sat a female Officer of the Day—a captain. Hudro took a seat, picked up one of the reformattable, universal-book folios from the table, loaded a journal at random, and for maybe fifteen minutes scanned it idly while getting a feel for the place and watching the routine. Then he went back down to the entrance. Just as he was about to leave the building, he turned back as if struck by an afterthought, and went over to desk.

"Excuse me, Sergeant." Although not wearing uniform, he had presented his pass showing his rank when he entered earlier.

"Sir?"

"Can you bring up the Forces Directory for me there?" He indicated the desk terminal. "I need this base's address for somebody to send something to me here."

The sergeant called up the file giving publicly posted information on Hyadean military installations and units, on Earth, Chryse, other worlds, orbiting stations, and elsewhere. He located the entry for Uyali, giving permanent offices, units currently stationed there with addresses, mail codes, commanding officers, and other details. "There. That's us here."

Hudro studied the screen. "So for the HQ Command office upstairs I'd use . . . that one?" He pointed.

"You've got it."

Hudro asked for something to write the details on. The sergeant raised his eyebrows as he passed across a slip of paper. The normal thing would have been to copy it into one's personal communicator. Hudro had thrown his away after landing at the construction site. "In my jacket," Hudro said. The sergeant frowned. Hudro sighed. "I know, I know." He cited the regulation: ". . . to be kept on the person at all times. If it were you I could give you a citation." He noticed that the sergeant was wearing a Terran windup watch. "Nice piece of work," he said.

"You like it? It's got elegance, hasn't it?" The sergeant turned his wrist to show the band.

"It's amazing what these people can do." Hudro produced the watch he had just bought in the Terran sector. "What do you think of that?"

"Wow! Pretty nice."

"I just got it—for someone when I get back home."

The sergeant held it admiringly alongside his own. "Do you know something?" he confessed. "I don't even know how to read what they say."

"Me neither," Hudro whispered as he took it back. There was a rapport. So at least he had a friend here already if the need arose. Infiltration training. Think and prepare.

Outside the building, he found a quiet spot and used his phone to call the Terran number of the Hyadean intelligence unit at the Brazilian police facility in Acre province that Yassem worked with. A clerk located her and transferred the call.

"Who is this?" her voice asked.

"The guy who questions."

"Yes?" Since he hadn't used his name, she knew the subject was sensitive.

"We need to talk privately. Here's where I'll be to take it." He read out the code he had copied for Uyali Headquarters Command. "Make it thirty minutes. There's something slightly wrong that'll need straightening out. That's important. Okay?"

"Okay. . . ." There was anxiety in her tone. "Is there—"

"Later."

Yassem would know what to do. The remark about something being slightly wrong was a code they had agreed previously for emergencies.

Hudro went back into the Administration Center, sent a cheerful nod to the desk sergeant, and made his way up to the Headquarters Command office. The female captain was still at the desk. Hudro approached her.

"Yes?" she inquired.

"My name is Hudro." He showed his identification.

"Sir!"

"I was here earlier. I'm expecting a call on a secure channel. Did it come through yet?"

"I haven't heard anything." The captain called a log onto a screen and consulted it. "I'm sorry, there's no sign yet."

"Thanks."

Hudro took a seat, browsed through some journals again, and made a show of looking irritable and restless. "Are you sure there isn't anything through for a Colonel Hudro?" he called over to her ten minutes later.

She checked again. "I'm sorry, sir."

Two soldiers appeared, conducted a brief conversation, and were taken by a clerk to one of the rooms. "Who's your commanding officer?" Hudro demanded after another ten minutes or so.

"That would be Major Sloorn, sir." She was getting rattled. Just what he wanted. He sat glaring at the folio, flipping the pages and moving his head in short, jerky movements. Finally, her voice almost cracking with relief, the captain called, "Colonel Hudro, sir!"

"Yes!" He got up and strode over.

But already she was looking uncertain. "A secure-channel call just came in. . . . But it's specifying a Colonel Mudro. I don't know if . . ."

"*Well, of course it's the one!*" Hudro snapped. "Some native clerk somewhere."

"Well, I really should call them back and . . ."

"Look, this is an important matter, and I need privacy. I've waited long enough. Where can I take it? Just connect it through, please."

"Room 1304. It's just along the corridor."

"Thank you." Hudro strode away in the direction she indicated. Being a communications specialist with an intelligence unit, Yassem would be able to make the call without its being logged as official procedure required. In the past, some of the things she had managed to extract from official files had been astounding. Misspelling his name by one letter—the "something slightly wrong"—would be a fairly elementary error—to any *person*. But it meant that the surveillance computers wouldn't have found a match.

A minute later, he was looking at the features of Yassem. "Are you all right?" she asked. "Where are you? Still in Bolivia? That was the longest half hour I've ever spent. I've been so worried!"

"I'm not hurt or anything. But I might have been compromised. If so, then we might have to move our plans forward and get out right away. Is that still what you want to do?"

Yassem swallowed and nodded her head. "If we must."

God, how he loved this girl, Hudro thought. Had he just appealed in his mind to the Terran deity? Yes, he had. "Look, this is what I want you to do," he said. First, he needed to know if his name was on any surveillance lists. That would be fairly straightforward. The next thing was trickier. He summarized what had happened at Tevlak's and named the persons, Hyadean and Terran, who had been there when he and Vrel left. Could Yassem find out if the house had been raided by security forces—maybe from operations lists? If so, what had happened to those who were there? Yassem promised to see what she could do. Some of the things she had extracted from official files in the past had amazed him. Hopefully, she could turn up something within three or four hours, she said. Hudro thought he could lose himself in the officers' club or somewhere during that time.

✺ CHAPTER THIRTY-ONE ✺

Luodine had engineered her posting to Earth to escape from the banality of life among the professional and social elite on Chryse that her work immersed her in. She had to find something different, far away, she had decided—before she either destroyed her career by reporting what she really thought, or became one of them. As an executive investigator with one of the major media organizations, she had specialized in exploring success stories, which was an approved and well rewarded choice because it put her among the molders of the role images that it was felt healthy for average Chryseans to emulate. It kept them busy, distracted them from thinking too much about what it all meant, and the economy as a whole remained prosperous.

The only problem was, just about everything she saw brought out the side of her that was decidedly not average for a Chrysean. She met officials in charge of government bureaucracies that dreamed up forests of regulations and employed thousands who buzzed around importantly day after day, intent on their mission, no end result of which, as far as Luodine could see, added up to anything of actual *use* to anybody. All that the elaborate machinery did was get in the way of the few left who *were* trying to do something useful. A long, red curvy fruit called an *iliacen* grew on parts of Chryse, not unlike a Terran banana, but larger. There were specifications giving the limits of size, weight, color, water content—even curviness as determined by a procedure spelled out in detail—that defined what was a permissible *iliacen*. Any commercial transaction involving one that didn't conform was illegal. They couldn't even be given away by producers. Huge numbers of perfectly good, edible fruits had to be thrown away because they were a little bit too straight or a little bit too curvy. This was considered "efficient." Efficiency, Luodine discovered, had little to do with what was obtained for the cost. It had to do with the extent and effectiveness of *control*. When she pressed for an explanation of why it mattered, and how the enormous effort expended on preventing people deciding for themselves what kind of *iliacen* they liked could be justified, nobody could give her one. It seemed that the regulators were simply unable to function without books of rules and numbers telling them what to do. They had become extensions of their own machines.

She had once talked with the head of a large contractor involved in developing and supplying advanced space weaponry deemed essential for meeting the threat posed by the Querl. Said to be among the richest thousand on Chryse, he worked in his office from early morning until after the staff had left, and hadn't taken private time off for two years. When Luodine asked why he didn't do something else now, he had looked at her blankly and asked in seriousness what else there was. "Build a house with your own hands. Learn to sail a boat," Luodine had said. "When you were a young man, weren't there things you dreamed of? Things you told yourself you wanted to do some day, when you had the time, and circumstances permitted?" The executive had become angry and terminated the interview.

She had listened, smiling, to wives whose lives revolved around hosting ever-more bizarre parties, the principal aim of which was to achieve prominent mention in the socialite gossip columns—one had been set on an island park stocked with over two thousand animals from one of the Querl worlds; another was held orbiting in freefall. She dutifully recorded the wisdoms of generals who measured the cost-effectiveness of a battle with a formula that mixed money, fatalities, and five categories of casualty; of media chiefs who sold rights to dictate what slant should be put on news stories; and of "image consultants" who had built a respectable profession out of presenting things to the world as other than they were, and coaching influential people in the art of lying convincingly from a screen.

Somewhere, she had told herself, there had to be a place where words meant what they said and not the opposite, and reality was what it seemed. And then she heard of the amazing planet that had been discovered in the course of exploring more distant star systems following development of a new, range drive—a planet whose inhabitants wove dreams into worlds of thought, created forms for no other purpose than to delight the senses, and described realms of vision and being that confounded all of the professors and scientists. Fads and fashions extolling Terran art and creativity appeared all over the Chrysean worlds. The ingenuity and imaginativeness of Terran minds stimulated great demand among Chrysean industries. And Luodine talked her way into an assignment there.

At first she had found herself bewildered by this world of chaotic, colorful craziness. But then, as she traveled and learned to reorient her thinking, she began to discover ways of looking at life, its values, that Hyadeans could never have conceived—unless, as some maintained, they had once known such things in a distant past age and forgotten them. There was the advertising executive in Sweden who gave up a secure, lucrative career and mortgaged his house to raise capital because he had always wanted to make a movie. She met a couple in Iran who for two years had been bicycling around the world—utterly pointless to the average Hyadean; captivating to Luodine. There were the religious missionaries in Africa who taught and treated the children of strangers with no prospect of gain other than the following of their convictions. There were dozens of stories from every continent.

And then Luodine found that the real policy being enacted was to turn them all into Hyadeans. Not only that; they were expected to be grateful. Sometimes, apparently, a little help was needed to make them see the benefits.

"Look, I've already told you, one of them had come from the United States; I don't know who the other one was." Luodine turned in front of the table in the room at Tevlak's house and regarded the officer in charge of the Hyadean security unit, who was dictating notes to a communicator pad. Cade and Marie had already been taken away in two of the six personnel carriers that had arrived. Since the officer had disclosed that Vrel had been identified, she wasn't giving anything away by repeating it. "We refused even to consider recording the kind of story they wanted. They realized they were wasting their time, and they left."

"Heading where?" the officer asked.

"I don't know. It's not the kind of thing people in their situation would shout to everyone."

The officer looked at her uncertainly. He was young and seemed not very experienced. Luodine was taking the only line that held any promise of getting her and Nyarl out. "You're saying that none of this was actually used?" He gestured at the equipment set up in the room, which the technicians had examined and pronounced clean of any recent recordings.

"They were talking about *subversive* material!" Luodine looked and sounded shocked. "Claims directed at undermining our Terran policy! Would you believe that?" She shook her head. "We'd simply been told there would be an interview involving some important, undisclosed people. After all, that's our job. That's what we're here for. We didn't know anything about fugitives from the U.S. We set up and prepared, sure. When they arrived, and we found out what it was all about, we said no." Luodine shrugged, turned away, and then back again. "And the rest I've already told you."

The officer seemed perplexed. He went outside the door to consult with a colleague for several minutes, and then retired to another room for privacy while he sought instructions from a remote higher authority.

The remaining Terran security soldiers—those who had not gone with Cade and Marie—had dispersed to other parts of the house or were carrying out routine searches of the people and vehicles outside while the Hyadeans settled their own affairs. Thryase was in the next room, where he could be heard protesting vehemently to officials at the Hyadean General Embassy at Xuchimbo, the principal diplomatic presence on Earth. He was here as a political observer, he insisted. When he was approached in St. Louis to accompany two Terrans introduced to him as social-science academics to South America for what he was told would be a major political news event, of *course* he had accepted. What did they think he was—some kind of parasite who came to Earth to enjoy the scenery and avoid the work he was paid to do?

Tevlak had taken the line of simply knowing nothing. Sure, he had agreed when somebody from the U.S. contacted him to ask if they could use his house—he was Terran in his ways now: hospitable to everybody. Had he known who they were? No, he didn't care. How had they known of him? As far as he could make out, Tevlak said, his name had been mentioned at a party in California.

The officer came back in. Luodine confronted him, hands on hips. "Well? Are we supposed to have committed some kind of offense?"

"Ah, no. It appears not. . . ."

"Then I take it we are free to go." Without waiting for confirmation, Luodine began disconnecting pieces of equipment and motioned at Nyarl to start packing up.

"It would be considered cooperative if you remained while the rest of our business is being concluded," the officer said.

"Are you making some specific charge or charges?" Luodine asked him.

"No. All the same—"

"Well, we have our business to think of too, and we've lost too much time already. If your people in the U.S. had been doing their job, we wouldn't have their renegades coming down here in the first place. Now, I suggest you follow after them, wherever they've been taken, and make sure they don't get away again, instead of wasting more of everyone's time here."

The officer capitulated. Luodine and Nyarl stopped to say a brief farewell to Tevlak and Thryase on the way out to their blue-and-yellow flyer. "We'll come back when the atmosphere and the company are more conducive to something constructive," she told Tevlak. "I *must* do a piece on these art collections of yours! Absolutely fascinating! The viewers back home will love it." She left, giving them a brief glance that conveyed there had been nothing else she could do. Their looks in turn said that they understood.

Ten minutes later, Luodine and Nyarl were airborne, heading north along the eastern edge of the Altiplano. Evening was approaching. The first thing they needed to do was warn Vrel and Hudro against going back to Tevlak's.

Luodine still had the phone that Cade had used to send the file. Vrel's number would still be in its log. After the way Vrel and the others had been traced to Tevlak's, however, Nyarl was leery about using it. "I wouldn't risk calling direct," he said. "It would be safer to go through an intermediary."

Luodine thought for a moment. "You're right," she agreed. "But who? We don't even know where they are."

"Hudro was going back to his unit in Brazil, which means they were heading for Uyali. Who have we talked to there, that we know can be trusted?"

Luodine thought back to a documentary they had made about Hyadeans who worked at Uyali and the lives they lived there, and slowly, a smile came into her face. "I think I know just the person," she said.

❂ CHAPTER THIRTY-TWO ❂

It was getting dark in the Terran sector of Uyali. The streets of the shanty city that had grown in months from a jumble of prefabs and mobile units were filling as workers back from the mining operations and construction projects headed for the restaurants, the bars, and the clubs. Vrel still hadn't heard anything from Hudro. A few other Hyadeans out shopping or curious just to visit the Terran sector had stopped to talk and in a couple of cases invited him to join them, but it had seemed prudent to keep his own company. He sat nursing a fruit juice and nibbling on a roll of flat, crispy bread filled with some kind of cooked vegetable paste in a dingy coffee shop that he had found near one of the three main thoroughfares. It was quiet but not empty, out of the way but not isolated in a way that would make him conspicuous—good for losing himself in for another half hour, say, before moving on to somewhere else.

The more respectable Hyadeans were drifting back to their own sector, which was fenced, orderly, and felt safer after sunset. Those who remained prowled around in ones and twos or groups, acting too self-assuredly: off-duty troops; engineers with billfolds full of Terran money; lonely clerks light-years from home—all curious to sample the forbidden fruits they'd heard about. Mind-altering drinks that it was illegal to possess on Chryse; the atmosphere of a place where Terrans sang, danced, and for a while let their feelings take over—some Hyadean doctors said it could be beneficial; an experience with a Terran woman, perhaps? Hyadean and Terran military police patrolled the district in pairs of either one race or the other. Vrel felt himself tensing when any of them came too close or treated him to anything more than a cursory glance. But so far he hadn't been troubled. If anyone was looking for him, he could only presume they were concentrating on the air terminal, where he would be expected to appear.

Six years ago, Vrel would have looked at a scene like that around him now with a sense of incomprehension at the purposelessness of the ways Terrans chose to spend so much of their lives, and contempt for their inability or refusal to do anything to improve themselves—especially with the Hyadean example before them. So much time and energy wasted on things that weren't needed. No plan. Contrived evasion of what should have been duty. The incredible *inefficiency* of it all. And underneath, there would have been a feeling that didn't need to be expressed, since the facts were so obvious, of the innate superiority of the Hyadean—the kind of smugness that he had detected in so many Hyadeans since, and now found mildly sickening. It was only in the latter part of his time here that he had finally come to grasp one of the most profound insights that the whole Terran worldview and way of life expressed, which most Hyadeans weren't within a lifetime of understanding: The purpose of existing, what mattered, was simply to *experience* it. Just that. Nothing more. If one chose to seek additional satisfaction from achieving or striving, then that was fine too. But it didn't *matter*. Dee had told him once that she thought they put statues up to the wrong people: usually those who had lasted the longest in contests of wiping each other out, or invented the most ingenious ways for legalizing thievery.

"Who should they put them up to, then?" Vrel had asked her.

"The people who do the important things. Except, there wouldn't be enough room."

"Why? What are the important things?"

Dee had shrugged. "Raising kids. Fixing roofs. Clearing drains. I think the others are really Hyadeans with unblue skin. Why don't you take them back?"

A musical tone sounded from the phone in Vrel's pocket. He snatched it out and said "Yes?" in Hyadean, just checking himself from blurting Hudro's name. But the voice that answered was that of a Terran female.

"Is this Mr. V.?"

"Er . . . yes." Instant befuddlement.

"I am Ramona. I get a message from Luodine asking me to call you."

Vrel faltered, then managed finally, "Where is she?"—probably irrelevant, but nothing else suggested itself.

"The person who called me didn't say. But it's important that you don't go back to the house. I guess you know what that means, eh?"

"Yes. . . . I had already figured it out."

"And there is more. Luodine needs . . ." Ramona's voice trailed off, as if something had just occurred to her. "She said you would most likely be in Uyali. Is that right?" Her English was simple—not her natural language, Vrel guessed. Probably, she had been told he was not a Spanish speaker.

"Yes," he replied.

"I am here too. Maybe it is easier if we meet somewhere. Do you know the Terran sector?"

"Yes."

"How long it would take you to get there?"

"That's where I am now," Vrel said.

"No kidding?! Where in the Terran sector?"

"I'm not sure."

"Okay, then I tell you where I will be. There is a bar called the Gold City. You find Central, which is the street in the center—it makes sense, eh?—and the bar is halfway along. Or ask anyone."

"I think I know where that is," Vrel said. "It'll just take a few minutes. How will I know you?"

Ramona laughed. "I think is better if I look for you, no?"

Vrel found the Gold City without difficulty. It had a window with orange lights inside looking out over the street, a flashing neon sign overhead, and a bright red door. It was only when Vrel was halfway through the door that it occurred to him that he might just have walked into the most elementary trap imaginable. But if so, the place would be staked and he was already spotted. Hudro would never have done this. He swore inwardly at his own naïveté, braced himself, and went in.

Inside was a long bar with mirrors behind running the length of one wall, a dance floor taking up one corner of the room, the rest being filled with tables and chairs. The place was busy and crowded. The throng included several Hyadeans, all male, in a knot clustered at one end of the bar, clearly military although out of uniform. A few others were scattered around at the tables, and two somewhat clumsily and self-consciously working hard at mastering the mystique of dancing. While Vrel was still looking around, a petite dark-skinned girl with wavy, shoulder-length hair and wearing a bright red, tight-fitting dress materialized in front of him. "You are Mr. V.?" she said.

"Yes. How did you know?"

"I learn to tell these things." Without further preliminaries, Ramona took Vrel's elbow and steered him toward some tables by a wall forming the side of some stairs going up. None of the tables was empty, but Ramona said something in Spanish to two girls seated at one of them, and they got up and left after a brief exchange. Ramona sat down and waved for Vrel to take the other chair. She had a lot of the artificial coloring that many Terran women wore around the mouth and eyes, he saw. Makeup was unknown among Hyadeans—although he had heard recently that some youngsters were causing all kinds of reactions by introducing the practice back home. A waiter came to take their order. Ramona asked for simply "a beer." Vrel decided he had better stick with fruit juice.

"So Luodine didn't talk to you directly," Vrel said.

"No. A friend that she has called me. I guess maybe she thinks someone might be checking her calls, eh? Sounds like some kind of trouble." Ramona shrugged in a way that said whatever it was, it didn't worry her. "Luodine has many friends everywhere. She travels around, makes movies of people. People like her. She listens to what they say. Too many of the aliens, they don't listen." She gave Vrel an approving nod. "See, you are listening. You're okay too."

"Have you met Luodine yourself?" Vrel asked.

"Oh sure. A couple of months ago, when everything here is like a camp. She is making a movie about the Terrans that Hyadeans meet when they come here to work—and then when they are not at work. She is very interested in the working girls who come to the mining town. It sounds like a lot of people where you come from are not too happy about it, eh?" Ramona eyed Vrel saucily and smiled. Vrel realized with a start that she was one of the Terran women who hired themselves out for sexual pleasure. Such a thing was highly illegal on Chryse, even its depiction in fictional settings being banned. There had been calls from home to have the Terran authorities close such practices down on parts of Earth where young Hyadean soldiers were posted. The Americans that Vrel had met in California called them "fishers" . . . or something like that. His first impulse was to express some kind of disapproval. But he controlled it and forced himself to see things the way he had learned to since coming to Earth.

"The girls, they all like her too, when they get to know her better," Ramona completed.

Vrel pulled himself back to matters of the moment. "On the phone, you started to talk about Luodine needing something," he said.

"Yes. The person who talks to me for her says that she thinks her . . . what do you call those things like little airplanes without wings?"

"Flyer?" That was what most Terrans seemed to call them.

"Right. Luodine thinks hers is being tracked somehow. Anywhere she goes, the computers will know. Maybe is normal for you guys, I don't know. But it sounds like she doesn't want this."

The drinks arrived. Vrel paid. "Okay," he said slowly after the waiter left. It meant that Luodine was mobile. So, assuming that Tevlak's house had been raided after his and Hudro's departure, it sounded as if she—and probably Nyarl too—had been released. But she thought it likely their blue-and-yellow flyer was being monitored, which was probably true. That all made sense.

"She says you have a 'clean' flyer," Ramona said. "I guess that means one they're not watching, eh?" That could only mean the flyer that had brought Vrel, Thryase, Cade, and Marie to Tevlak's from Uyali, and which was now at the construction site thirty miles away where Hudro and Vrel had left it. Thryase had somehow arranged for its movements not to be recorded by the traffic system (which eliminated that as an explanation of how they had been traced to Tevlak's).

"Go on," Vrel said.

"Well, it sounds to me like she wants to go someplace without them knowing all the time. She needs to use yours."

Vrel leaned back on the chair, sipped from his glass, and thought about what he should do. In the end, he decided it would probably be best not to do anything until he heard from Hudro. He glanced at his wrist unit unconsciously. Still nothing. Where *was* Hudro? They had agreed to call only in an emergency. Vrel wondered much longer he ought to give it before deciding that this was becoming one.

Ramona had shifted her attention to another presence that had appeared by the table. Vrel looked up to find a Terran glowering at him. He was tall and lean bodied, with a short beard and hair tied by a band at the back, wearing a black shirt under a leather vest, and pants held up by a wide, ornate-buckled belt. Two more were behind him, looking equally mean and ugly. He shot something in Spanish at Ramona, causing an abrupt change in her manner. She gripped her glass tightly, as if to throw it; her eyes flashed. She retorted just as sharply, and an angry exchange in rapidly rising voices followed, accompanied by gestures and challenging looks from the man, at Vrel. Conversation around them died. The Hyadean military by the bar looked questioningly at each other and started to move closer. Somebody ran out the door, and his voice could be heard calling along the street. A man across the room called out in English, "Leave them be. You are assholes. Why don't you mind your own business?"

"When they come here taking our women, it *is* our business," the leader of the three shouted back. "Who the hell are you, pig shit? *You* mind your—"

"I am not anybody's woman!" Ramona spat.

Two Terran military police appeared in the doorway—peaked

caps with red bands, white gaiters, drawn batons. Fingers pointed across to the table. They came over. One of them asked what was going on. Several onlookers began telling the story all at once. The Hyadeans by the bar drew back but remained alert. Ramona dropped her aggressiveness, shrugged and shook her head, and answered the MPs' questions meekly. Their attention turned to the three men, still standing their ground, and an argument broke out between onlookers supportive of both sides. The MPs began shouting and waving their batons to try and calm things down.

Ramona looked at Vrel resignedly. "Should I call this friend of Luodine's and give some answer?" she asked him.

"No. There is a colleague of mine here somewhere that I need to hear from first."

"What you want to do now?"

Vrel shook his head. "I don't know. Just wait."

"You don't need this trouble. My place is near here. We can go there and wait to hear from your friend. Will be easier, no?" Ramona looked at him as if there was nothing more to say. Vrel hesitated. She laughed. "If you worry about I might be losing business, you don't need to. Is good for everyone to have a break sometimes. Besides, if it helps get Luodine out of some kind of trouble, then there is nothing to think about. Okay? So, we go." It seemed a good idea. All Vrel needed was for this to turn into an incident that would result in his being identified. They left unnoticed while the argument was still proceeding furiously.

They walked along Central to one of the two major intersections and crossed it to enter a maze of narrower dirt streets and alleys twisting among trailers and instant buildings, dark except for isolated lights outside doors or occasional glows from some of the interiors. Ramona led the way to a small, flat-roofed cabin set on blocks. It had a split-height door behind a screen, and an outside lamp showing a green cross on an orange background. Vrel waited while she went ahead up several wooden steps to unlock the door, and then followed.

The interior, when she turned on the light, was what he supposed a Terran would describe as feminine and homey—but to Hyadean eyes a riot of decorative ingenuity. "You drink coffee?" Ramona asked.

"After a day like today? Sure, why not?"

Colorful woven tapestries and prints of animal and plant themes filled the walls; a carpet of rich designs covered the floor. All the pictures and curios that Vrel had come to expect of a Terran dwelling were there, with the added touch that females seemed to show for softening the effect with cushions and flowers, and frilly edgings to covers and drapes. It brought to mind Dee's apartment in Los Angeles, though with a distinctly different "style."

"You like it?" Ramona said, seeing him looking around while she filled a pot and took cans and mugs from a closet. "Is not like your Hyadean places, eh? Like army barracks or factories. How can anyone live in those? I buy it from a Chilean girl who is singer with a band, but has big gambling problems. Owes maybe ten thousand dollars to the clubs. You don't mess those guys around. So she comes here to work in Uyali temporarily. Tells husband the band is on foreign tour. Is funny, eh?" Vrel wasn't sure why, but grinned obligingly. "Do Hyadeans gamble?" Ramona asked him.

"No. The statistical demotivations are too obvious."

"Oh? I guess I'm not too smart. What does that mean?"

"I'm beginning to doubt that. It means that nothing is more mathematically certain than that the class of gamblers as a whole loses. So why would anyone pay to belong to that class?"

Ramona put the coffeepot on and stared at it as if for advice. "Really so, eh? But what if you win?"

"It's possible, of course," Vrel agreed. "But the chance you buy isn't worth what you pay for it."

"Okay. . . . If you say so." She didn't seem convinced but wasn't about to make an issue of it. They tossed the matter back and forth while the coffee was making, then sat down with their drinks in a couple of easy chairs in the living area adjoining the kitchenette.

"So what's your story?" Vrel asked her curiously. "How did you come here? Any plans for the future?"

Ramona leaned back and sighed. "I am from Rio a long time ago, you know—over on east?" Vrel nodded. "Is big difference, who is rich and who is poor. I come from wrong part." She laughed suddenly. "Maybe you are right after all: Luck doesn't pay off, eh? The only way you're gonna get rich is maybe be big soccer star if you're a boy, or a girl, do this. Or maybe else you can sell drugs, either one. But is not for me. Too much nasty people—all the time killing, violence. And after? . . . I don't know." She winked. "Big savings already. Maybe buy my own bar someday. Lots of music, dance. I like to see people having fun. Maybe a Hyadean bar. They need teaching how to have fun, no?"

Vrel grinned tiredly. "Maybe." He looked at his wrist unit again.

"Where you go tonight if your friend don't show up?" Ramona asked him.

"I hadn't thought about it. I didn't think it would get this late."

"You think he is okay?"

Vrel shrugged. "I don't know."

Ramona looked him up and down over the rim of her mug. "You can stay here if you want." The color-enhanced eyes widened suggestively. "Maybe relax and make the best of it a little if you stuck anyway. Is okay, on me. I'm not working tonight."

Vrel found himself flummoxed, even after years on Earth. "Really, no. . . . It's a nice thought, but I'm okay. Aren't there any hotels, places that'll do a bed for the night?"

"I thought you say they look for you. Maybe is not so good idea out there. Better off here." Ramona emitted a sigh that said she really didn't understand but if he insisted, and waved a hand to indicate the part of the cabin beyond the living area. "Is okay, anyway. I have two bedrooms. One is for work, the other where I sleep. Just one would be like living in the office, eh? You take one of them. Either is okay."

At that moment, a call came in on Vrel's phone. He pulled it from his pocket. It was Hudro. "Can you talk?" Hudro asked.

"Sure."

"Okay, we have news. Where can I find you?"

Vrel paused, momentarily perplexed. "You're not going to believe it," he answered.

"Why? What's happened?"

Vrel couldn't think how to begin. "Look, I'll pass you over to someone else. She'll give you directions," he said finally.

❊   ❊   ❊

Hudro recovered quickly from his astonishment. It seemed he had found more tolerant grounds for his religious convictions than some that Vrel had encountered on occasions. Vrel updated him on the message he had received from Luodine via Ramona, and offered his conclusion that Tevlak's had been raided as they had suspected, and that Luodine was now free but her movements were being tracked.

Hudro was able to confirm it. Since his business in the military base was not Ramona's affair, he spoke in Hyadean. Tevlak's house had been visited by a combined force of Terran and Hyadean security following a surveillance alert that Cade and Marie had been identified there despite their aliases. How surveillance had found them, Hudro's contact didn't know. Proof of criminal activity sufficient to justify detaining the Hyadeans who had been there— Tevlak, Thryase, Luodine, and Nyarl—had not been established, and they had been released but would no doubt be subject to continued surveillance— as Vrel had surmised. Cade and Marie, however, who were wanted by U.S. federal authorities, had been arrested. Finding out what happened to them had taken the contact a lot longer. The essence was that they were at a detention facility in Peru, awaiting some VIP with an interest in their case who wanted to conduct a preliminary interrogation personally. After that, they would probably be moved to a military prison farther east, in Brazil.

Hudro continued: "If that happens, it won't be good news, Vrel. What they know could be too damaging to some powerful individuals, both Terran and Hyadean. They'd never get out alive. If we're to do anything at all to help them, it will have to be before they get there. That may not give us very long. So this is the plan.

"Do you remember when we were on our way here, I told you about a girl that I have here? I said that one day we intended disappearing to Asia or somewhere and living as Terrans? Well, she is the contact I've been talking to today. We have decided that the time must be now. My work here has brought me into contact with some of the Terran so-called terrorists that we are sent to fight, and I have found that more often than not they uphold Terran ideals more faithfully than the governments do. So I can no longer fight on the side of Terran governments—you heard me say all this at Tevlak's. I know some resistance fighters up in Brazil who I think can be persuaded to help."

"To rescue them?" Vrel checked. "Roland and Marie. You can get Terrans to work with you?"

Hudro smiled faintly. "I said I wanted to save somebody one day, didn't I? My name is clean so far—not on any watch lists. Tonight I will get regular transportation back north to Brazil as I originally intended. My partner and I will make our arrangements to meet a Terran guerrilla leader there whom I have known for some time—we have both helped each other in the past. We can only hope there will be enough time to come up with something. It would have to be while Roland and Marie are being moved."

Vrel was couldn't help feeling apprehensive. "You really think you can rely on Terrans that you're supposed to be fighting?" he said. "Is it wise to trust in them that much?"

"What other choice do we have?" Hudro answered. After a second or two more he added, "Anyway, I trust in their god."

Having established that much, they got Ramona to call Luodine's intermediary and pass on instructions for her and Nyarl to fly to Uyali the next morning, setting the regular air terminal as their destination. When they were on final approach but not before, they were to change the landing point to a pad area in the Terran sector, which Ramona said would be busy and crowded all day. Vrel would meet them and take care of things from there. With that, Hudro left for the terminal to find a ride back to Brazil. Vrel stayed the night in Ramona's "office."

The next morning, after preparing them a breakfast, Ramona took Vrel to the part of the Terran sector that she had told them about, which turned out to be a nonstop commotion of people, activity, and vehicles coming and going as she'd promised. Vrel used his phone to summon the flyer that he and Hudro had left at the construction site to the north. It arrived ten minutes later. A little under an hour after that, Luodine and Nyarl's blue-and-yellow craft appeared overhead, descending steeply. Vrel greeted them as they emerged and indicated his own waiting flyer. While Ramona and Luodine embraced and laughed like long-lost sisters, Vrel helped Nyarl transfer recording and other equipment across. In order not to be lose touch with other events that might develop, Nyarl set a link in the blue-and-yellow flyer's communications system to forward any incoming messages to a code that he set up in Vrel's flyer. Even if it were seized and the link code found, it wouldn't mean anything to anyone else. Finally, Vrel thanked Ramona and conceded a hug.

And then they were airborne, heading north to get clear of the area before anyone following the movements of Luodine and Nyarl's flyer would have time to react to what had happened. To add further confusion, Nyarl had set it instructions to take off again, empty, and head off in a different direction as a decoy. After a hundred miles or so it would land near a village picked at random off the map, and anyone monitoring it could make of it what they would.

They continued northward to be nearer to where anything involving Cade and Marie was expected to happen, and put down around midday in a remote spot past Lake Titicaca. They waited there through the middle part of the day, eking out the fruit juices and snacks that were all the flyer had to offer, talking over the events of the past days, trying to guess possible outcomes, and speculating about future plans. Vrel talked vaguely about making for Asia or Australia, maybe trying to join Krossig. Luodine wasn't sure she wanted to leave just yet. She was an investigative journalist, after all, and the things that seemed to matter were happening here.

Hudro called around the middle of the afternoon and informed them that the operation would take place tomorrow. He gave no details apart from the map reference of the place where he and the Terran guerrillas would meet them afterward, which was farther north, inside Brazil. Vrel and the others were to head there tonight and were expected. The name of the place was Segora.

◎ CHAPTER THIRTY-THREE ◎

At last, Luodine could breathe easily again, not feeling that their every movement was probably being tracked by surveillance computers.

From maps retrieved via the flyer's communications system, Nyarl had determined that Segora was in a low-lying forested and swampy area around one of the southern headwater tributaries of the Amazon. Luodine had expected it to be something like a village, in the sense of dwellings clustered in some kind of clearing, but it turned out to be more a general name for an extended area of huts, houses, and other constructions loosely strung together beneath the forest canopy with little attempt at forming any identifiable center. It could be an unconventional type of living arrangement that put seclusion before neighborliness, she supposed as the flyer descended out of gray overcast; equally well, it could have been contrived for harboring an illicit militia in a way that afforded anonymity, concealment, and dispersal.

The flyer landed in a slot cut between high trees, at the bottom of which nothing more could be seen than a strip of bare earth and a couple of tin-roofed shacks. On touching down, they found that the strip was just the edge of a larger, undercut space concealing an assortment of trucks, cars, and other vehicles that had been invisible from above. A group of figures in shirts and jungle smocks, some with weapons slung on their shoulders, watched the flyer roll in. Two of them directed it to park by several helicopters standing to one side. A reception committee came forward as the occupants emerged. Vrel was not conversant with the local languages and left the talking to Luodine. Her experience was more with Spanish whereas the prevalent speech here was Portuguese, but with help from her veebee and a smattering that Nyarl had picked up, they were able to manage.

The spokesman was small and wiry with a beard, wore a soft-peaked forage cap, flak jacket, and string vest, and carried a basic Terran automatic firearm. He didn't give a name but described the three Hyadean arrivals to the others as "the alien news team who are here to tell our story"—which, discounting Vrel, was close enough. The others seemed suspicious all the same, and regarded the Hyadeans warily.

They boarded an open-topped Terran military truck, along with the guide in the peaked cap, another, and the driver, while the rest of the party piled into a second vehicle behind. Whether they were guards or an escort, Luodine wasn't sure. As the vehicles moved away, she saw sandbagged positions under the trees commanding the landing strip and its approaches, with bunkers and entrenchments concealed among the vegetation behind. Farther on, they passed cabins and houses, what looked like a storage dump, some kind of a water landing, and a workshop for vehicles. The road became a leafy tunnel, in places crossing stretches of swamp on wooden causeways. There were tent cities mingled with the undergrowth; squads training with weapons; at one point, a pit with earth protecting walls under camouflage nets, that looked like a missile emplacement.

"This might go on for miles," Luodine said to Nyarl. "They could have the equivalent of a whole town hidden down here."

"Or an army," he replied.

Luodine became more certain in her own mind, and more excited. "*This* is the story we should be working on!" she told him. "Right here, not in Asia. I want to see for myself those things that Hudro showed us. What do you think? Would you stay if we could?"

"Yes, I'd stay," Nyarl said.

A spur off the roadway brought them to several low wooden buildings standing together beneath the trees. The vehicles pulled up in front of one, and everyone dismounted. While the guards or escorts—whichever—dispersed themselves around the outside, the leader in the forage cap and his second conducted the three Hyadeans in and through to a large room, bare except for several closets, a central table with chairs, and kitchen facilities at one end. An adjoining room contained six double-tier bunks arranged around the walls, and there were several more rooms with stacks of boxes, items of kit, and further oddments of furniture. Evidently these were to be their quarters for the night. In the meantime, apparently, they were to wait.

A window looked out toward the way they had come in off the road. As dusk was closing in, two trucks appeared, embarked armed figures from one of the other nearby buildings, and drove away again. The roadway itself seemed to be busy with an irregular but continuing flow of vehicles and porters on foot carrying loads. "Something's going on. There's a buzz in the air. Don't you feel it?" Luodine said to the other two. She asked the squad leader in the forage cap. He seemed uneasy but would divulge nothing.

After about half an hour, headlights appeared, and a Terran open-topped military car sped up and screeched to a stop outside. Two figures jumped out and marched up to the door, while two more began lifting out cartons and boxes, helped by a couple of the guards who had been posted outside. The man in the forage cap went out, and there was an exchange in lowered voices outside the door. Then two of the arrivals came in. The first was tall, swarthy skinned with a thick mustache, and wore a belt with sidearm over a bush jacket, jungle camouflage pants, canvas boots, and a black beret. He identified Luodine as the spokesperson and introduced himself as Rocco. The man with him, black, shorter, stockily built, wearing an olive shirt and bandolier of cartridges slung across his body from one shoulder, was called Dan.

As the Hyadeans had already inferred, they would be staying here until tomorrow. In the morning, Rocco would leave with a guerrilla force to meet up with Hudro and Hudro's unnamed companion, and attempt to rescue Cade and Marie. Where and how this was to happen Rocco didn't disclose, but from the things that had been said before,

Luodine presumed it would be while the two captives were in transit somewhere. Afterward, assuming the operation was successful, they would all return to Segora. What the plan was after that, Rocco didn't say. Dan would remain to take care of the Hyadeans and deal with any needs or problems if he could.

The other two who had arrived with Rocco and Dan were women. While Rocco was talking, they brought in the cartons that had been unloaded, put them on the counter at the kitchen end of the room, and began taking out bread, vegetables, cans, and other provisions. Rocco left shortly afterward, explaining that he had preparations to attend to. If all went well, he would see them again tomorrow.

When the meal was ready, the two cooks took portions out for the guard detail around the building. Dan and the man in the forage cap, now revealed to be "Zak," joined the Hyadeans at the table in the large room. Dan told them they were the first Hyadeans he had seen brought here as guests, although it appeared he had met Hudro previously somewhere. The rest of the men had seen the aliens only from a distance, and then on the other side. They were not clear what was going on, which made them understandably wary.

"Could they learn to accept us, do you think?" Luodine asked him.

Dan seemed puzzled. "Why should they have to? What do you mean?"

She indicated herself and Nyarl. "We are journalists from Chryse who are a little different. We've been reporting what *is*, not what's supposed to be—even if it has been causing us problems. We think our work is here. Suppose we wanted to stay. Could something like that be arranged, do you think?"

"I don't know. Maybe. . . . You'd need to talk to Rocco and Hudro tomorrow, when they get back."

Luodine noted the same edginess in Dan's manner that she had detected in Zak earlier. "Something is making everyone nervous tonight, isn't it?" she said. "I saw it in Rocco too. What's happening?"

Dan glanced uneasily at Zak, as if acknowledging that he wasn't sure this was the right way to be talking. "There's a lot of Glob activity everywhere. Air strikes, troop drops. This area has to be targeted.

Rocco's got bad feelings about staging this mission tomorrow, but it seems like it can't be any other time. I'm not sure why."

"I think we already know," Luodine said.

Dan shrugged in a way that said he didn't need to hear. "My job is just to make sure you're all here, ready and waiting, when they get back."

It had been an eventful and arduous day, and the three Hyadeans turned in early. Just as she was drifting off into sleep that promised to engulf her in seconds, Luodine was brought back to reality by the sound of what could have been distant thunder coming in through the screen of the open widow, but with a sharper, more percussive bark. "What was that?" she asked into the darkness.

"It could be artillery fire. Or maybe an air attack somewhere," Vrel's voice replied.

The sound continued for maybe fifteen minutes, sometimes seemingly a little closer, then farther away. In the next room, Dan and Zak were engaged on a radiotelephone with others elsewhere. They sounded tense and agitated. Dan poked his head in around the door a few minutes later. "Sleep in your clothes and keep your boots near at hand," he told the Hyadeans. "We may have to move out in a hurry."

It was daylight when sounds of loud explosions accompanied by a shrieking roar tore Luodine out of a deep sleep. She sat up, struggling to integrate the impressions into some kind of coherence. Aircraft, passing low overhead. Bombs! Vrel and Nyarl were already tumbling out of nearby bunks, finding shoes and grabbing coats. The door was thrown open, and Dan entered. "We're under attack!" he shouted. "Glob forces moving in on the area. We're taking you back to the strip now."

They tumbled through into the large room where the table was. One of the two women was waving her hands at Zak and wailing something. The other was nowhere in sight. A guard stuck his head in from outside. "The truck's coming now," he called. Dan ushered the Hyadeans across to the door and outside. Smoke clouds were billowing skywards from somewhere not far away, where flames could be seen among the trees. A truck was turning off the approach lane from the road. As several of the guards moved out from the building to meet it, the sounds of approaching aircraft came again, followed by staccato chattering of gunfire. The guards threw themselves down into the undergrowth or beside the wall of the building, a couple under the truck.

"*Down!*" Dan yelled. Luodine stood outside the doorway, confused. "*Get down!*" She came to her senses, ran a few paces, and hunched herself awkwardly by Nyarl against the base of a tree. The roars grew to a screaming din overhead. Luodine covered her head with her arms. A series of jarring concussions came, numbing the ears, and then a sharper *crack,* followed by what sounded like a tremendous blast of hail slicing through the trees, shredding leaves and cutting branches. Fragments of metal *pinged* off the truck and embedded themselves in the wall of the building. Somebody screamed.

"Come! Now! We have to go!" Dan's voice shouted.

Luodine straightened up, dazed, her ears still ringing. Somebody grabbed her elbow and steered her toward the truck. Figures were already clambering aboard. Vrel was there. Nyarl appeared from behind her. Someone was reeling drunkenly, gushing blood from a partly severed shoulder. It was the second cook. Hands pulled Luodine up over the tailboard. The truck began moving.

The attack had hit on the far side of the roadway. Smoke was pouring from the remains of several demolished buildings among the trees, which nearer the center of the blast area had been stripped practically bare. A vehicle was hanging upended in the branches; another lay on its side, surrounded by bodies, some moving. As the truck turned right onto the road and headed back in the direction of the landing strip, Luodine made out more figures crawling and staggering amid the smoke. The sound of the attacking planes faded, and the steadier, deeper drone of higher-flying aircraft became noticeable behind the engine noise and rattles of the truck, and the voice of Dan shouting into a hand radio. A series of muffled crumps sounded somewhere off to the left. "ATG," Zak said tightly. Luodine looked questioningly at Nyarl as they clutched the sides of the wildly bouncing vehicle.

"Air-to-ground," he supplied. "Missiles. Incoming."

"Troops are landing to the south and east," Dan announced. "They've already taken the main river crossing. Gonna sweep the whole area."

"Will Rocco's group have to call off the mission?" Vrel called from the other side of the truck.

"Too late for that. They left hours ago."

They drove past armed guerrillas hastily forming up, squads with packs running at the double along the roadside; vehicles being loaded, others racing in both directions. The background of explosions and gunfire was now continuous. At one point they had to drive off the road on a bypass flattened through the undergrowth around a truck and a car that had collided. Just past them was a blackened area, still smoking, everything flattened, where Luodine was sure she had seen a mobile missile launcher the day before. Exactly as she had wanted, she was right there in the middle of everything, and far sooner then she had ever expected. Yet she and Nyarl could capture none of it. They had left all their equipment in the flyer.

They arrived back to find the landing area in pandemonium. One entire side—fortunately, not where Vrel's flyer was parked—was a mass of blazing vehicles and storage sheds, while across the remainder of the area figures ran frantically to load what could be salvaged onto departing trucks and carry over the wounded. Two helicopters were wrecked, but another out on the open strip took off as the truck bringing the Hyadeans pulled up. Dan waved toward the flyer and shouted at Vrel, "Make it ready, whatever you have to do."

Vrel spread his hands. "What about Cade and the others? We were supposed to wait for them."

"I'm going to try and find out what I can now," Dan threw back, already running toward a frond-covered bunker protected by sandbags and logs, partly dug into the ground nearby. Vrel turned toward the flyer. Luodine followed after Dan, Nyarl close behind her. Inside the bunker was a map table and cabinets of electronics, weapons and kit slung along one wall, and a half dozen or so people, two talking into phones, two more following something on screens, one marking a map, a girl in a camouflage smock watching the scene outside through a firing embrasure in the bunker wall. Dan was talking tensely with a man in a peaked cap who seemed to be in charge. He waved for Luodine and Nyarl to wait a moment as they entered. One of the operators was calling into a microphone. "Emergency! Repeat, emergency! Divert! Do you read me, Yellow Fish? You must divert. The LZ is under attack."

"It's them," Dan told Luodine and Nyarl. "They're on their way here now. They've got Cade and the woman. But they can't land in this."

"Where will they go?" Luodine asked, daze at trying to take it all in.

"I don't know. They'll . . ." Dan's voice trailed off as the operator became alarmed.

"Hello? . . . Hello, Yellow Fish. . . . Yellow Fish, come in. . . ." He waited, looked across, and shook his head. "We have lost contact. They were taking fire."

"Jesus! What's this?" Eyes turned to the girl watching the outside. A peculiar violet light was coming in through the embrasure. Dan and the officer in the peaked cap stared uncomprehendingly for a moment, then moved toward the entrance, practically pushing the two Hyadeans out ahead of them. They emerged to find the surroundings bathed in a strange radiance of an eerie, electrical quality.

"What is it?" the officer asked, bewildered.

Dan shook his head. "I don't know. I've never seen anything likes it."

Then, abruptly, it was gone. Their eyes took several seconds to readjust to normal illumination. Then Dan touched the officer's arm and pointed across the open stretch of landing strip. The violet had shifted to an area beyond the far tree line and was now revealed as a pencil of light coming down from the sky. Even as they watched it shifted again, as if probing. Then the column flickered briefly in several pulses that turned it brilliant orange, and the entire area surrounding the base of the beam erupted into a fireball expanding above the trees. Moments later, a concussion wave swept across the landing area, followed by a blast of wind that bent the treetops, sent a storm of leaves, sand, and pieces of wreckage swishing across the open ground, and toppled Luodine over a wall of logs fronting the entrance to the bunker. A rain of torn branches and debris began falling over the entire area.

The flyer, already moving from its parking spot, lurched visibly and then steadied. Dan pulled Luodine to her feet. Nyarl was holding onto the top of the log wall. "What about the others?" Vrel called from the doorway of the flyer as it neared, at the same time turning.

"They're down somewhere!" Nyarl yelled. "We have to go! Now!"

"Go where? We have no plans."

"*It doesn't matter! Just GO!*" Dan shouted, pushing Luodine toward the flyer. Vrel heaved her in, Nyarl followed with the door closing, and the flyer began accelerating toward the open ground. Then it was under the strip of sky, airborne, climbing. It rose to skim the treetops. Smoke and fires were everywhere, with aircraft dotting the sky in all directions.

"That light. What was it?" Luodine gasped as she buckled into one of the seats.

"Orbital bombardment maser," Nyarl said. His voice sounded strained. "Ours. Area obliteration weapon. I didn't know we were using anything like that here."

For a while they flew north toward the main basin of the Amazon, away from the combat zone, debating what to do. Returning to Tevlak's seemed risky, with no idea of the situation there. Vrel had lost his Terran phone somewhere in the confusion. Nyarl was reluctant to use the flyer's system, since incoming calls to Tevlak's would probably be monitored and could be traced back. In the end, Luodine remembered an Indian tribe that she had spent some time with as part of putting together a program on Terran cultural diversity. They lived in a remote area north of the main river and had no interest in worldly affairs. And they were friendly—not to each other, especially, but they were to the blue-giant aliens, to whom they apparently attached a religious and mystical significance. Nyarl found the location in his records, and in less than two hours the craft was descending toward a forest clearing showing leaf-thatched huts scattered around a stream, watched by an awed crowd of brown-skinned figures and children, most of them barely clothed. They remembered Luodine well, and greeted her and her companions with laughter, much excited chatter. A spicy meal was arranged for the evening, attended by the whole village and accompanied by dancing apparently put on for the aliens' benefit, despite their exhaustion, and the presentation of gifts ranging from a sweet fruit preparation to a necklace made from flowers, beads, and the dyed shells of nuts. The arrivals fell asleep in the hut provided for them, still too numbed by events of the day to be capable of discussing any further options objectively.

When morning came, the whole situation had changed. News via the flyer's system brought the staggering announcement that the Western part of the U.S. had seceded and declared itself a sovereign federation governed from Sacramento. As fugitives on an alien planet, by no means sure where they stood with their own authorities, none of the Hyadeans was sure of the implications or what they should do. The easiest and perhaps safest choice seemed to be simply to stay on in the village, making the best of the peace and seclusion it offered, get the rest that they all needed, and give things a couple of days to see what happened. The villagers and their headman had no objections, and the children found the blue aliens fascinating, following them everywhere.

But before they had finalized any plans, an even stranger thing happened. A call came in over the flyer's system, forwarded by Luodine's blue-and-yellow flyer, still landed far to the south in Bolivia. It was routed via Chryse, but had been sent by the Hyadean girl that Hudro had returned to Brazil to collect before joining Rocco's force for the attempt to free Cade and Marie. Her name was Yassem. The operation had succeeded, but the helicopter bringing them all back to Segora had been shot down. As far as Yassem knew, she and Marie were the only survivors. She was relieved to learn that all three Hyadeans had got away safely from Segora. Right now, Yassem and Marie were at a Brazilian military base on the southern side of the Amazon basin. For the moment, they were managing to pass themselves off as affiliated with the security forces under a story that Yassem had dreamed up, but that cover could only last so long. Using codes obtained from registration records on Chryse, Yassem had located the blue-and-yellow flyer down in Bolivia. She wanted to use it to get them away. Now that they knew where Luodine and the others were, she and Marie could fly there and join them. Nyarl was worried about surveillance risks. That was okay, Yassem assured him. Military communications was her job. She would take care of that.

⚙ CHAPTER THIRTY-FOUR ⚙

Pink lights flashed past the open gun-hatch; then came the jolting of objects hitting the helicopter's structure. Yassem, crouched on the floor in front of where Marie was sitting, put her helmet on and secured it. Rocco shouted back instructions from the front, and one of the men clambered up to man the machine gun, while another hooked up the ammunition belt. Marie and Cade braced their arms on the sides and tried to steady themselves against each other as the pilot went into evasive maneuvers. And then a giant fist seemed to slam the helicopter, bursting the wall behind them inward and tearing Cade away from her grasp.

Impressions kaleidoscoped together of bodies tumbling and hurtling about the interior, cries of pain and fear, a blast of wind. The figure that had been at the hatch was gone. Everything was turning. A force pinned Marie with her face and chest to the wall, unable to move. Yassem rose from somewhere and then fell against her, entangling them. Past Yassem's shoulder, Marie saw Cade caught in the side webbing, blood pouring from his head and down the back of his jacket, and Rocco nearby, clinging to the edge of the hatch. The helicopter hit the ground to a cacophony of screams, objects crashing against the sides, and the shriek of metal rending and buckling. Marie heard herself cry out as Cade and Rocco collided and disappeared. The helicopter carried on sliding downhill, slewing, and coming apart, spilling bodies, equipment, and debris. A limb of a tree reared up through pieces of disintegrating cabin and floor, and Marie was pitched forward onto a headless body that gushed blood over her face and chest. There was a wrench that felt as if she were being pulled apart; sudden light; leaves and branches rushing and tearing at her. . . .

She was underneath a section of what had been the fuselage, ensnared in foliage among pieces of wreckage. Her face felt on fire. Her whole body ached. She became aware of guns firing, sounds of aircraft, explosions. They had come down in the middle of a battle. She tried to move, and winced as every muscle and joint protested. But there was no other way out of this. Testing herself warily, she concluded nothing was broken. Then, gathering her breath, she bit her lip against the pain and forced herself to move, first freeing the thorns and vines from her clothing. The activity seemed to help. She extricated herself gradually, straightened up, and took stock. The headless corpse was doubled grotesquely over a seat attached to part of the cabin wall. The only other figure in sight was in Hyadean military garb, lying facedown and motionless on a section of buckled flooring. Marie hauled herself across and turned the helmet to reveal a flash of yellow-orange hair against the blue skin. It was Yassem. She was breathing. There was no sign of Hudro. Marie could smell smoke and burning. Forcing herself onto her feet, she turned the Hyadean's body over and secured a grip under the arms. Yassem was spattered with blood too, but there was no way of telling if it was hers. There were no obvious gashes in her clothing. Gritting her teeth and straining, Marie dragged her inch by inch clear from the wreckage.

They were on one side of a sloping, rocky-sided ravine filled with dead trees. The rest of the helicopter was in parts farther down, with seats, pieces of rotor, parts of the tail assembly, and more bodies strewn in between. Flames were licking around the largest section. Somehow, Marie pulled Yassem's inert form through the thickets of dead branches and thorn bush to the rocks higher up the ravine side, where she collapsed with her burden into a hollow. A dull *whoosh* sounded as the wreckage ignited, and black smoke curled upward from below. The crackle of small-arms fire was coming from very close, interspersed with bursts from a heavy machine gun. At one point, Marie heard voices shouting. She lay still, too numbed with delayed shock to know what she should do. Time passed. She nudged and tried to shake Yassem. The Hyadean groaned but wouldn't stir. Marie located the water bottle on Yassem's belt, unscrewed the cap, and pressed it to her lips. "Yassem, can you hear me . . . ?" This time Yassem reacted, feeling for the water bottle and holding it to her mouth. "How bad does it feel?" Marie asked. "Does it hurt anywhere?"

Yassem gulped and took in a series of long breaths. "Hudro?" she whispered. "We were hit. Is he here?"

"Don't worry about that now. We have to move."

Like Marie, Yassem was torn and bruised but seemed otherwise uninjured. After waiting perhaps a half hour for her to orient herself and collect her strength, they began moving, stopping frequently for rests. Marie had no clear plan. Her vague thought was to find a river or creek and follow it downstream. Water led to habitation. Yassem seemed too dazed or perhaps overcome by grief to object or offer anything more constructive. The sounds of fighting drew farther away. They carried on, movement still painful, making slow progress over the rough, forested, hilly terrain.

Nightfall brought them to a deserted collection of huts and trailer cabins by a dirt road, several demolished, and the rest riddled with bullets—clearly the scene of recent fighting. A number of bodies lay scattered around, including some charred black in a burned-out gun pit. Despite the macabre surroundings, Marie and Yassem could go no further. Finding some packs and cases with unused rations, they scraped together a meal of sorts—even a dash of brandy—and lay down with makeshift blankets in the corner of a relatively unscathed house, away from what appeared to have been the center of the action, to spend the night.

They were found and awakened next morning by Brazilian soldiers sent to clear up the scene and bury the corpses. Seeing Yassem and her military garb, they fetched the Hyadean officers accompanying their unit. The Hyadeans were tough-looking, confident, reminding Marie of the ones she had seen in the air terminal at Uyali. Yassem had regained much of her strength by now, and answered their questions in Hyadean. From their general manner, Marie got the impression that she and Yassem were considered to be on the same side—certainly not prisoners.

A medic was summoned to check both of them. He pronounced no major injuries but used up a lot of adhesive dressings and gauze on minor things, including a lot of superficial lacerations to Marie's face, which he said would heal. Shortly afterward, a Hyadean military flyer landed, and they were put aboard. One of the Hyadeans and two Terrans would be apparently coming too. Just before entering, they turned to exchange a few final words with others outside. It was Marie and Yassem's first moment of privacy since their awakening that morning.

"What's happening?" Marie asked in a whisper as they sat down.

"I told them I'm one of our communications liaison officers, and you're a Terran aide who works with me," Yassem replied. "We were attached to a Terran unit mixed up in the fighting here, and we were separated. They're taking us back to their base."

Marie couldn't feel totally happy about it. "Won't they check?" she queried.

"Eventually. But it will give us some time."

Marie looked down at the drab gray tunic that she was still wearing, which she had been given at Cuzco. "I'm surprised nobody noticed this prison garb."

Yassem looked Marie up and down. "With all that blood, I'm not sure anyone could tell what it is," she said.

They arrived at a camp of wooden and corrugated steel huts, depot facilities, an airstrip, and defensive positions, set inside a perimeter of double wire fences. Beyond were grassy hills cloaked by scatterings of trees. The camp was bustling with Terran and Hyadean aircraft arriving and departing, presumably in support of the operations still in progress elsewhere. Yassem declined a suggestion of the base medical officer to put her and Marie in the sick bay for a couple of days, which would straightaway have required information on who they were and from what unit. Staying on their feet would leave them more in control of their own affairs. So instead, they were shown to quarters where they were given clean clothes and left to freshen up.

Later, when they came out, and tottered over to the officers' mess for breakfast with more effort than they let show, it turned out that their story was not anyone's special concern just for the moment, anyway. The big news was that in the north, the governor of California, William Jeye, had declared the secession of the Federation of Western America. The talk among the Brazilian officers was about whether an all-out North American war was imminent, and if so, where they would stand in it. But the most astounding thing was when the newscaster replayed notable incidents from the days leading up to the declaration. One event cited as having had a profound effect on the American people was a documentary released from unofficial Hyadean sources to the Western news media. It was none other than the one featuring Cade and Marie that Luodine had made. *It had gotten through!* At least, it had as far as California. Marie stared disbelievingly. Yassem watched her in puzzlement before making a connection between the face on the screen and the swollen, discolored one next to her swathed in dressings—and even then, probably only because Hudro had told her about it. Marie excused herself to go back to their quarters. It wasn't only to recover from the shock and absorb the implications. Even with the dressings, she couldn't rid herself of the conviction that it would only have taken minutes for somebody in the room to recognize her. Some time passed by before Yassem joined her.

"I've been getting a picture of the situation," she told Marie. "It doesn't sound good. Segora was heavily attacked yesterday. It's in government hands now. Vrel and the others would have been right in the middle of it all if they got there the night before. We have to try to contact them. Obviously we're on borrowed time here. Do you know the number of Vrel's phone—the one Roland sent the file to?"

Marie shook her head. "There was never any reason to think I'd need it."

Yassem looked vexed. "Communications is my specialty. We talk routinely to people on Chryse. There *must* be some way. . . ."

It took Yassem ten minutes of pacing about the room and frowning out the window to realize what she had said. "Chryse!" she exclaimed suddenly. "Luodine and Nyarl's flyer—the one that's still in Bolivia, somewhere. It carries Hyadean communications that can be reached from there. The registration record to Luodine's agency on Chryse will have its call code, and it's accessible via the Hyadean equipment here at the base. We can get through to them that way!"

"You're going to connect via some other star system, to talk to somebody maybe a couple of hundred miles from here?" Marie was incredulous.

"Probably safest," Yassem said, smiling. "With the situation, all the local systems are likely to be watched. But Hyadeans make calls home all the time. Let me go see if I can find a friendly operator."

For once, things went as straightforwardly as hoped. Yassem got through, and it turned out that Vrel, Luodine, and Nyarl, after narrowly escaping the day before, were still shaken but all right. Currently, they were at a remote Indian village to the north that Luodine had known, and hadn't formulated any plans yet. Of course they would wait there if there were some way Yassem and Marie could join them. Once again Yassem was determined that it had to be possible. Marie could only marvel at Hyadean tenacity, once they had set their minds to something.

And again, there was a solution. The flyer sitting in southern Bolivia, where Nyarl had sent it as a decoy, was no doubt being kept under observation and its log monitored. Using access codes to its control system that she retrieved from the vehicle registry on Chryse, Yassem was able to delete its connections to the Hyadean South American traffic control network, thereby rendering it invisible to the tracking computers. Then she obtained the coordinates of its present location from the on-board local control and fed it instructions to fly to the base in Brazil where she and Marie had been brought. Thus, when the Hyadean adjutant asked about scheduling their return, Yassem could tell him that it was okay, they had made their own arrangements. Transportation was arranged for them. So little curiosity was aroused two hours later, when the blue-and-yellow flyer landed itself on the airstrip. Yassem and Marie bade thanks and farewell to the two Hyadeans who walked out with them to see them aboard. Minutes later, they were climbing and turning north on a course that would cross the Amazon basin. Yassem made sure that the flyer would return a "friendly" identification code if interrogated by a Hyadean or Brazilian antiaircraft fire-control system.

Marie gazed out at mile after mile of rain-forest canopy sliding by below like a sea of frozen green waves. Finally, she could feel some respite from the chaos assailing her life for the last . . . was it nine days? Ever since Roland walked back into it. She laid her head back into the roomy, Hyadean-size seat and put a hand to her brow wearily. It met bandages. Roland. . . . Years ago she had tried, despaired, and given up. Then he had come back, starting to become what she had always known he could be. . . . And now this. She replayed scenes of the crash in her mind, trying to tell herself there might be a way he could have survived. It had been only a moment before impact when he and Rocco disappeared. They couldn't have been more than a few feet from the ground by then. But there had been blood pouring from Roland's head. It was no good. She was trying to create wishful fantasies. Eventually, whatever the reality was would have to be faced. She looked across at Yassem and found the Hyadean watching her with an expression that seemed to read her thoughts. But then, Yassem was having the same problem.

"Hudro's pretty tough," Yassem said. "Sometimes I think he is, what did you say once, 'charmed'? Like Roland."

Marie took in the crisp, clean Hyadean military fatigue garb that Yassem had been issued. Everything was so mixed up. Marie was used to thinking in terms close to black and white. There were "us" and "them," good guys and bad; you knew who was on which side. Hyadeans had always been "them." In the last week she had found herself trusting them as much as she had ever trusted anyone—which was ironic, for it seemed that the concept of "trust" itself was something that they themselves were learning from Terrans. Now one of them might have died helping to save her and Roland. And the person to whom that one had meant the most was now Marie's confidante and companion, whose life Marie had recently saved, yet wore the uniform of those who were hunting them. Marie could no longer make any sense of the world.

"How does this happen?" she said. Yassem raised her eyebrows but said nothing. "Hudro was with your counterinsurgency forces. You were with communications, attached to Terran intelligence." Marie shook her head uncomprehendingly. "I *know* how people are selected for jobs like that. They look for a particular kind of personality, the kind that identifies with the system it serves and takes pride in loyalty. People like that don't change their minds and go over to the other side. The one from the federal ISS, Reyvek, that you saw Roland and me talking about on that recording this morning, was an exception. He was very disturbed in some ways that went deep, and the system must have missed it. But normally that doesn't happen."

Yassem had to think for a while, as if the subject were something new. "On Earth, you mean," she said finally. "That's the way it is here."

"Well, yes. . . ." Marie was surprised. "Wouldn't it be the same anywhere?"

Yassem paused again, searching for words. "Here you have these 'religions' and ideologies—big schemes that try to explain everything."

"Are you saying they're bad? I thought you and Hudro wanted to understand religion. That was why you left."

"No, they're not especially bad. They can be wonderfully inventive. But sometimes they program your thinking. Who is right and who is wrong becomes accepted as part of the indoctrination. Then life is simple, and killing who you're told to becomes easy."

"So how is it different with Hyadeans?" Marie asked.

"We just accept what we see. We don't try to make it something else because of ideas of what it should be. So who is right and who is wrong depends not on who people are, but on what they *do*."

Marie still didn't follow. "So why is your planet supporting a government that's working with the powers here who are exploiting Earth's peoples? Isn't that supposed to be wrong? Why won't they accept that when they see it?"

"*Because they never have seen it!*" Yassem replied. "Don't you understand? It works both ways. Because Hyadeans don't question, they accept what they're told. And what has happened on Chryse is that for longer than I know, a powerful ruling caste has controlled what Chryseans are given to believe. But when they come here and see for themselves that what they have been told is not true, it's easier for them to decide that what they are doing is wrong and change sides. It happened to Vrel, to Hudro and me, and to others I have known. And it sounds as if it happened to some of the ones you know. *That* was why Luodine was so anxious to make the recording and get it to Chryse. She knew the effect it would have there. Terrans assume they will be lied to and regard it as normal. But to Hyadean minds that have never questioned, the realization would be devastating. You should have seen the effects in the Hyadean officers' mess this morning after you left. For the first time, some of them are questioning what they are doing. You see—until now they have been told they were helping the people defend themselves against terrorists. It never occurred to them that there might be another story. That was just from watching a news item here, put out by the new Western federation. Can you imagine the effect if it were broadcast all over Chryse?"

Marie stared at Yassem fixedly. Finally, she could see what Roland had glimpsed but not had time to understand. The scientist in Los Angeles that he'd talked about had credited the Hyadeans' ability to see things as they were as the reason why they had built ships that could bring them to Earth, while Earth's scientists were still trying to divine from abstruse mathematics whether or not it was possible, and arguing over whether they had evolved from molecules or been created by a god—neither of which the Hyadeans saw any point in caring about. That same faculty could determine whether or not they would tolerate what was happening on Earth. The Hyadean ruling element and the force they controlled could never be defeated in a straight, stand-up firefight—despite her commitment to CounterAction, deep down Marie knew that. But they would topple if the people back home ever learned the truth. And they knew it too. No wonder they fought with all the fear and repression that came from insecurity. Marie snorted to herself at the offbeat humor: "Security" forces described them pretty well.

They arrived to a warm but sad welcome from the others, and expressions of added delight from the villagers. Vrel in particular was devastated by the news that both Cade and Hudro were lost. There was concern at Marie's appearance, but she assured them the damage was not as bad as all the bandages and tape suggested. The villagers provided a meal, but even before she was halfway though it, Marie, her body stiff and protesting everywhere by now, felt her eyes closing and exhaustion sweeping over her. Yassem seemed to be in about the same condition. The Indian medicine man, assisted by two of the women, applied medications and poultices of pastes and leaves that worked wonders, and the two new arrivals were asleep before there was a chance to discuss anything further.

It was late in the morning when Marie awoke. Yassem was already up, but as yet nobody had agreed on any firm plans. Luodine had wanted to stay to cover the South American situation, and Vrel's thought had been to head across the Pacific, but now they were wondering about trying for the newly formed Federation territory in what had been the U.S.A. Both the flyers were personal short-haul vehicles and didn't have the range for such a journey. However, Nyarl ascertained from the web that commercial flights into western North America were still operating from Quito in Ecuador, which was reachable. To check on the American situation, Vrel tried calling his colleagues at the Hyadean mission in Los Angeles, which he seemed surprised to find was still functioning. He asked to speak to a Hyadean called Wyvex.

✺ CHAPTER THIRTY-FIVE ✺

The physical similarities between Terrans and Hyadeans, not just in general appearance but in terms of chemistry and genetic codes as well, had been devastating to Earth's prevalent theory of life and its origins, but had come as no particular surprise to the aliens. They had listened skeptically but with interest to the idea of how ooze could turn itself into a jellyfish and a jellyfish into a horse by selectively accumulating random mutations, and when the evidence claimed to support it proved not to, they dismissed it as another of Earth's secular religions, invented to displace an earlier one.

In a way that fitted well with the Hyadeans' catastrophic account of the origins and development of planetary systems, Darwin's original notebooks were filled with observations of evidence written worldwide of epochs of sudden, cataclysmic change. But twenty years later when he published, he had come around to adapting to biology Lyell's principle of gradualism, by then established as the guiding paradigm of geology. Under the new scheme of things, no catastrophic upheavals needed to be invoked to explain the past. Everything could be accounted for by the processes seen to be taking place in the present, provided they were allowed operate for a sufficiently long time. Hence, from an ideology were constructed the immense spans of time that the Hyadeans found it astonishing anyone from Earth could look at the surface of their own planet and believe in.

Earth's history fascinated the Hyadeans. Revolution in the

American colonies and then France had terrified the ruling houses of Europe. Napoleon's armies had carried notions of rising up against traditional authority from Catholic Spain to Tsarist Russia, and by the middle of the nineteenth century the continent was seething with militant political movements advocating socialism. All it needed now was for science to declare that violent upheaval was the natural way of change. The new scheme, however, depicted change as a slow, gradual accumulation of tiny advantages—so slow that little significant difference should be evident even in the course of a lifetime. And on the other hand, an explanation for life that did away with the supernatural served the new, technocratic wealth, based on commerce and industry, by completing the undermining of the authority on which the old power structure rested. Expedient and intellectually satisfying, it was embraced from all sides and rapidly enthroned as science. When the evidence that had been predicted failed to materialize, and contradictions continued to accumulate, ingenious and imaginative possibilities were devised to explain the facts away. No serious con- sideration was given to the possibility that the reason so little proof could be found of life's having evolved from simple molecules on Earth might be simply that it hadn't; it had arrived *there.*

Yet it had long been known that bacteria and other microorganisms exhibited an extraordinary tolerance to extremes of such quantities as radiation, temperature, and pressure, that was difficult to account for by any selection process on the surface of the Earth, where such conditions had never existed. But it made them ideally preadapted for space. Carbonized structures uncannily suggestive of familiar forms of microbe had been discovered inside meteorites—and yes, with the possibility of contamination excluded beyond reasonable doubt. Refractive indexes in part of the interstellar clouds matched those of biological objects more closely than any of the alternatives put forward to explain them. Some scientists over the years had pointed to these findings as a case for supposing that the genes that directed life had originated from somewhere else. The mainstream scientific community saw warnings of the theological can of worms opening up again, and their general reaction was to ridicule the suggestion or leave it alone.

The Hyadeans had made the same observations. Having neither supernatural nor secular fundamentalism to defend, they accepted the evidence as meaning what it said and concluded that living organisms were constructed on planetary surfaces from local materials under the direction of genetic information with which space was seeded. These incoming code units were combined into complex genetic programs that built organisms suited to local conditions. Infection was the principal mechanism for spreading new genetic combinations around and establishing initially compatible breeding populations—much faster and more efficient than sexual transmission, the slowness of which was another problem with Terran theory—especially given that the enormous time spans contrived to make it seem plausible were wrong anyway. The programs were ruggedly constructed in possessing a degree of adaptability to cope with environmental fluctuations, and this had been extrapolated into an explanation of everything.

The upshot was that similar kinds of places would originate similar kinds of life. Life did indeed evolve on planets, but not in the way Terran scientists had thought. Chryse was roughly like Earth, even if worn down and not reworked as recently, and that was why Hyadeans were roughly like humans.

Since they had never observed genetic information originating either through a mechanistic or an intelligently guided process, the Hyadeans hadn't asked how it came together in the first place. About the only possibility they seemed to have considered was that it could be an advanced culture's way of propagating itself through the galaxy using a radically different form of starship. Where that culture might have come from wasn't the kind of thing that Hyadeans were going to spend a lifetime worrying about.

Hence, the Hyadeans rejected Terran evolutionary theory as a construct having more to do with Earth's political religions than scientific reality. What captivated them, however, and came as a totally new revelation to their thinking, even if the Terrans who had first dreamed it up were now rejecting it, was the concept that life itself might have a purpose. So while Terrans were contriving mechanisms to deny all the meaning in, and reasons for, existence that they had once believed, the Hyadeans were discovering questions that it had never occurred to them to ask.

◎ CHAPTER THIRTY-SIX ◎

In the room that he had just about taken over as his permanent office in the Hyadean West Coast Trade and Cultural Mission in Los Angeles, Michael Blair hung up after taking a call from Krossig, now established in Australia, and pushed his chair back from the desk to stretch. The Hyadean scientific station was on the outskirts of Cairns, in the northeastern coastal highlands of Queensland, which over the last twenty years had grown into a sprawling, medium-size township of cosmopolitan flavor following "discovery" of the region by wealthy escapees from Asia, the U.S., and elsewhere, attracted by the region's combination of independence, rugged informality, and the chance of a quiet life. His previous experiences having been limited to the U.S., Krossig was rapturing about the racial variety and contrasts of lifestyle that he was finding here. Blair had assured him there was a lot more of Earth to be sampled yet.

The latest home news was that Texas had declared for the Federation. The Eastern part of the country was staking claim to legitimacy by resurrecting the Civil War term "Union" and threatening the use of armed force to suppress what it insisted was rebellion. Federation spokespersons, by contrast, referred to it as the "Globalist puppet regime" to emphasize its non-American underpinnings and backing. Already, the Union was challenging the Federation's hegemony by sending armored units forward between the Mississippi and Dallas, and flying provocative military demonstrations over the seceded territory. There were rumors that Mexico was already under Globalist diplomatic pressure to allow supporting operations from the south. To the north, Federation forces, for their part, were advancing eastward to secure a flank along Lake Superior. What Canada would do, nobody knew.

Although it had been threatened for some time, the secession when it finally happened had come with a suddenness that took everyone by surprise. And the Hyadean mission in Los Angeles, due to its being in unusual circumstances at the time, had played a big part in bringing it about.

Following disagreements with the Hyadean Office in Washington that Blair neither understood nor wanted to, the Hyadean head of the legation had been recalled east along with key members of his staff for "policy discussions." Orzin, the political official who was still visiting, had taken it upon himself to manage the day-to-day operation of things in Los Angeles until whatever was going on got sorted out. And while this was the state of things at the mission, an event occurred which some said was a key factor in bringing about the secession. The story was so bizarre that Blair hadn't, even yet, been able to construct in his mind the beginnings of an explanation.

Dee had appeared at the mission, asking to see Wyvex, and handed him a storage cartridge containing a file encrypted in Hyadean code. The file was from Vrel, who had last been heard of five days previously, when he left saying something vague about visiting a place near St. Louis. Somehow, he had ended up in South America. Dee had known no more than that. The cartridge had been given to her by the service manager of the dealership that took care of her car, who said the contents had come in over the phone. He'd suggested that next time she wanted her car checked, she should take it to the phone company. Why Vrel couldn't have used the regular communications to contact Wyvex was a good question. Presumably, he was in some kind of trouble and his access was blocked; or he didn't want to broadcast his whereabouts by using a system that would need his ID codes; or he was worried about general surveillance on mission traffic.

The reason became clear when Wyvex decoded the file and ran it. To his astonishment, it featured none other than Roland Cade and his former wife, Marie, giving an account of the truth behind the Farden-Meakes affair and the measures taken to suppress it. Along with their allegations was a portrayal, by other Hyadeans, that nobody at the mission knew what was happening in South America, including harrowing clips of the aftermath of air strikes, Hyadean-equipped ground units in action, with Cade and Marie again, relaying the narrative of a disillusioned Hyadean officer. Coming at a time when emotions were high everywhere following Sovereignty's release of the Reyvek documents, it was enough to finally demolish official denials and the entire government position. Vrel, in his message to Wyvex, asked for the recording to be sent to Chryse.

Blair didn't know what Wyvex would have done if the mission's official head were still in charge there. He doubted if Wyvex would have had the nerve to forward the recording on his own initiative as Vrel had requested, and had he sought higher approval, the legation head would surely have quashed it. Orzin, however, standing in temporarily, was more flexible. He had become a familiar face in Cade's social circle and mellowed to Terran ways, learning to enjoy the entertainments, turning a blind eye to staff dealings in illicit exotics, and some said not being beyond having a hand in a few himself. The important thing was that he had developed an affection for Earth that many Hyadeans seemed eventually to come to share. When Wyvex showed him the documentary, Orzin had been very disturbed. After much talk and deliberation that Blair had not been a party to, he had decided it *should* be forwarded to Chryse—which meant straight from the mission, since it would never get through Washington. Not only that: Orzin had authorized a version in Terran format to be released to the Western news media. Whether it had constituted a prime cause or not, the Federation had declared its secession within forty-eight hours of the broadcast's going out.

What Cade, who hadn't been heard of for days either, was doing in South America was anyone's guess. Nobody that Blair had talked to at the house had a clue. Even Julia had professed being at a loss, saying he'd gone to Atlanta on personal business and that was all she knew. Equally mystifying was what Marie was doing with him, since as far as they were all aware she had long been history in Cade's personal life. But it would all presumably be revealed in time, and until then there was nothing they could do, since Vrel had given no means of contacting him. They were in no position to devote a lot of thought to such matters, in any case. Right now, there was an impending war situation to contend with.

Blair propped his heels on the desk and clasped his hands behind his neck. He hoped that all this was not about to disrupt the progress he was making toward a better understanding of the way Hyadeans thought, and how those who spent any period of time on Earth began to be affected by it.

Earth had been dogmatizing itself into a virtual Dark Age for the best part of a century, discovering little that was fundamentally new, concentrating on technological improvements that it persuaded itself constituted science. The cause was a system of social dynamics that encouraged the pursuit of rewards in the form of accolades and funding, and then conferred them in recognition of what was "right" rather than what was true. The result was an Establishment that repeated the history of the medieval European Church by selling out to the political system as purveyors of the approved Truth in return for patronage, prestige, and protection. The irony, Blair was beginning to suspect, was that the solution might well lie in what all the great religions of the world, in essence, had been teaching all along: controlling passions and cultivating the ability honestly not to care what the answers to supposedly objective questions turn out to be. An even greater irony was that the Hyadeans, who seemed to possess this quality innately, seemed bent on imparting to their discoveries the significance and deeper meaning that generations of Terran scientists had been working diligently to expunge from theirs.

The Hyadean account of subatomic phenomena was close to what had become known on Earth as the Many Worlds Interpretation of Quantum Mechanics, and described a vast, fantastic, virtually infinite superposition of everything that had happened, would happen, or could happen. In making the decisions to follow one path rather than another through this ever-branching labyrinth of possibilities, the individual assembled together the sequence of perceptions and experiences that were interpreted as the universe and its flow of time. In fact, there were uncountably many universes, but isolated in such a way that at their normal, day-to-day level the inhabitants of any one had no knowledge of the others, or awareness that they even existed. Other "nearby" realities did, however, interfere at the quantum level, which was another way of saying that information could travel between them.

People had been insisting for centuries on the reality of things that science was unable to explain. Now, instead of dismissing such possibilities out of hand, it had become fashionable for scientists to grant that there might be something to some of the claims and to cite quantum "leakage" as the answer. Hence, there was still no case for invoking any "supernatural" phenomena beyond what science could account for. It was just that "science" covered more now, the world was a bigger place, and "natural" meant more than it used to.

The Hyadeans saw things the other way around. Whereas the Terran physicists found an ultimate mechanistic explanation that removed the illusion of purpose from all equations, the Hyadeans were beginning to see the whole, immense totality as a framework ideally suited to making morally meaningful choices possible. From there, having no preconceived notions to get in the way, they had followed their propensity to simply accept what the facts said and seemed to be arriving at the—to them, utterly new and revelational—conclusion that it had been designed that way, by an intelligence, for a reason.

At first, Blair had been taken aback. Since graduating, he had generally accepted uncritically the materialist doctrines that underlay his training, and their assumptions had become habit. But now, since meeting the Hyadeans—and particularly after having to forget so much of what he had believed before—he wasn't so sure. Even before the Hyadeans came, increasing numbers of Terran biologists had been astounded by the complexity that they were finding even in allegedly primitive organisms, and saying that such organization couldn't have come together of itself. Blair tried to fit this in with the Hyadean picture of the cosmos as initially hot, high-density entities spinning off progressively lower-energy objects from quasars down to stars and eventually planets. What else were planets but assembly stations for constructing living organisms and providing an environment for them to develop in? If it was purposeful, then the purpose of life was to evolve consciousness; and what other purpose could consciousness serve than to provide the means of undergoing experience? It was all so uncannily close to what Krossig was getting so excited about. What did Blair make of it? He really didn't know. Maybe he was becoming a lapsed atheist.

All the same, even if the Age of Materialism should turn out to have been overhasty and based on misplaced confidence, it would be wrong to conclude that no good had come of it. Blair had never understood what the horrors of the Inquisition, wars of extermination, and witch burnings had to do with a creed supposedly based on tolerance, kindness, and compassion. Perhaps a pause in social evolution to forget the old vengeful, spiteful god hadn't been such a bad idea.

Earth had invented religion, even to the extent of turning its science into one. The Hyadeans had produced a science free of unsupported beliefs and irrational convictions, and now they wanted to project religion into it. Maybe the future would see a merging of the two: the Hyadean form of science, restrained by the notions of modesty and humility that stemmed from an awareness of powers greater than oneself—what earlier ages had idealized but never been able to make a reality. There was so much that they could be working toward together, instead of the conflict that seemed to be relentlessly approaching.

An incoming call sounded. Blair swung his feet down and sat forward to take it. It was Wyvex, in the communications room on the floor above. "We've just heard from Vrel again," he announced. "A direct call this time."

"Okay! Are they still in South America?"

"Yes, but he wasn't specific about where. He said something about being in a village and trying to get a flight from Ecuador."

"You mean they're on their way back?"

"It sounds like it—soon, anyway. They've added more to the party.

The journalist who made that documentary is there. Her name is Luodine. Her associate, Nyarl, was here a while ago."

"I remember him. Striking hair—kind of green and black."

"Yes. And there's another Hyadean woman, called Yassem. None of us knows her. Some kind of communications specialist."

"So when should they be here? Any idea?"

"As soon as they're sure there's no problem entering Federation territory. We can't think of any reason why there should be, but we don't really know. Orzin is checking with Sacramento now."

"Of course there won't be a problem. They're heroes. Roland and his ex are celebrities."

There was an unnaturally long pause. Then Wyvex said heavily, "She's there, but Roland isn't. Apparently, he was in a helicopter that got shot down over a combat zone. Yassem and Marie were there too. As far as they know, they were the only survivors."

Blair exhaled shakily, and then nodded. "I see." He had to swallow a lump in his throat

"I'm not sure how Terran social conventions work with regard to Julia," Wyvex said. "What's the way to handle her situation?"

"I'll take care of it," Blair told him.

✺ CHAPTER THIRTY-SEVEN ✺

Cade's gray prison garb was gone, and in its place he had acquired a pair of baggy white peasant-style trousers, a colorfully embroidered shirt something like a vest with sleeves, and a coarse woolen cloak that also doubled as a blanket at night. He even had a floppy, flat-topped hat with a brim. As his faculties slowly returned sufficiently for him to be able to follow, Hudro told him the story.

The helicopter had been downed by a proximity burst and crashed in a rocky ravine full of fallen trees, spilling bodies as it tumbled down the side. Rocco had found himself thrown out near Cade and dragged him clear. Hudro joined them, hauling another of the occupants, also unconscious. They found another stumbling around, dazed, and another impaled on a shattered tree limb—he died later that day. And that was it. There had not been time to search for any more. They had come down under fire in an area where MOPAN guerrillas were retreating before part of the government force that was endeavoring to encircle Segora, where the helicopter had been heading. A group of MOPAN had gotten to them before the regular soldiers and rushed them away.

Faced by regular troops deploying Hyadean weapons that they had not encountered before, and for the first time in some places by Hyadean ground troops who turned out to be not especially adept at using the terrain but commanded fearsomely effective firepower, the guerrillas had been routed. What remained of them were straggling southward, still hunted and harassed, to regroup. Besides Hudro, Rocco, and the two other survivors from the crash, one of whom was immobilized with leg injuries, a local MOPAN leader called Miguel was riding in the same truck, along with five of his troops—three youths and two girls. The truck was also laden with a miscellany of weapons, equipment, and supplies lashed to the sides and the cab roof, or piled in the rear with the passengers underneath netting woven with leaves that were changed twice a day. The local population had long been in the habit of aiding in concealment by lighting plenty of fires to clear undergrowth and burn trash, and scattering incendiary devices about to confuse infrared imagers. The high-resolution satellites had to be told where to look, so that with experience it was possible to remain invisible to a surprising degree. Even so, Miguel was wary of moving when the skies were clear of cloud cover.

What of the others? Cade wanted to know. Had Hudro or anyone heard from Vrel, Luodine, and Nyarl since the attack at Segora? No. It had all been too sudden and confusing. Cade borrowed a phone and tried calling Vrel's Terran number. It rang somewhere, but nobody answered. Was there any news of Tevlak? No, nothing.

Cade listened dully to a summary of events elsewhere. The sensation was that in what had been the U.S., the mountain states—Montana, Wyoming, Colorado, New Mexico—along with Texas and those toward the Pacific, had formally denounced the Washington regime as illegal and seceded as the Federation of Western America, its capital Sacramento, with the former governor of California, William Jeye, as president. Already there were reports of clashes with federal and security forces in the region who refused to come over or be disarmed, and military overflights being shot down after ignoring warnings to turn back. The South, essentially, had declared neutrality and been occupied at key strategic points within hours by Hyadean-assisted Eastern forces.

Hounded in the jungle, wary of using communications, the guerrillas hadn't pieced together the full story. Hudro thought the recording they had made at Tevlak's house could have been a factor.

He confirmed that Vrel had received it and sent it on. But Cade no longer cared; or maybe a defense mechanism in his mind was protecting it from something that it wasn't yet ready to deal with. He had already been coming to terms with the realization that his life was going to change in some fundamental ways from what it had been. Now, the alternative that he had glimpsed had been snatched away before he'd even begun to understand fully what it meant.

"You're sure nobody else could have made it out of the crash?" he asked Rocco.

"What was left of the helicopter went up in flames while we were dragging you away. If anybody did, the Globs have them now. So we'll never know."

Cade had gashes in the side and back of his head, and a mild depressed fracture that had been treated during the two days he was unconscious, and which with luck would now heal; also, a strained neck and a collection of body cuts and bruises. Events passed for him as a series of incoherent impressions, like disconnected fragments of a movie that was no longer of interest. Whether this was due to his condition or the drugs that the medic who checked him periodically and changed the bandages on his head gave him to dull the pain, Cade didn't know.

The truck was bumping past people who look strained and exhausted, trudging along the roadside leading pack animals, pushing loaded carts and bicycles, or carrying bundles on their backs. A woman sat looking blankly, her belongings strewn around her, heedless of her crying child. The man propped against the tree beside her didn't move. . . .

It was night. Houses were in flames, with explosions sounding distantly. There were cries and wailing all around. People crowded around the truck, pleading to ride. The truck had already picked up as many as it could. There was no more room. . . .

The noise came of aircraft flying low overhead. The figures under the netting strung between the parked truck and the trees fingered their weapons nervously. An Indian woman tried to quiet her restless baby, as if the pilots might hear. . . .

They had pulled off the trail. Gunfire was sounding somewhere ahead. Two men came back from another truck to report that the Globs were holding the bridge over a river. They had to go back and try another way. . . .

Never had Cade seen such human misery and suffering. What was it all for? Who benefited?

✺ CHAPTER THIRTY-EIGHT ✺

The commander-in-chief of the Hyadean military forces on Earth was called Gazaghin. Normally, he was based in his headquarters near the General Embassy in Xuchimbo. When he stopped by Casper Toddrel's Washington club to meet for lunch the day after Toddrel's return from Brazil, however, it was from the liaison office that the Hyadeans had established in the Pentagon just across the river. He had flown up on an emergency visit to discuss strategy and coordination with the Eastern regime's forces following the secession of the FWA two days previously.

Toddrel didn't like him and never had. Besides having an extreme case of innate Hyadean bluntness and an inability to grasp even the rudiments of finesse or subtlety, he held a disdain for anyone outside the military caste, which he made no attempt to conceal. His basic attitude seemed to be that the task of the military was essentially to clean up the messes that others—and in particular, financiers and politicians—had created yet again and learned nothing from, and it was just as well the soldiers had a better grasp of reality.

"I want to talk because I want to warn you," Gazaghin said, tearing into a quiche salad, to which he had allowed some grilled salmon to be added. His hair varied from black to dark blue; his features were purple-gray, compressed and fleshy. He wore a dark green tunic with designations of rank on the shoulders, breast pockets, and cuffs, and a cap which he continued wearing at the table. "We have ships sunk in the Amazon areas. Now, I hear sabotage begins in our operations at Uyali. Four Hyadeans killed in explosions there this morning." He pointed menacingly with his fork. "I hear sayings that all is not straight with you, Toddrel. Too much Hyadean production from Uyali means your friends lose big money. So maybe your left hand is holding up what your right hand plays at knocking down. You see what I say? These terrorist rebels get money from somewhere."

"That's the most outrageous suggestion I've ever heard," Toddrel said tightly, his color rising. "We know their backing comes from Asia."

"North America has more interest for Asia, now maybe even more after the secession." Gazaghin waved a hand. "They don't care about Uyali. You care about Uyali."

Toddrel felt himself gripped by a mix of guilt and fury. He couldn't afford to be put on the defensive. "I'd have imagined you'd have business enough looking into the ineptness of your own people than questioning my motives," he retorted curtly.

"What you mean by this?"

"How were the Hyadeans who were with Cade and his woman at that art dealer's house permitted to leave? How was it possible for them to be snatched out of one of your transports and vanish without trace? Today I've just learned that the Hyadean journalist's aircar that's been sitting in Bolivia, which you've been waiting for to lead you somewhere, has vanished from the surveillance log. When an observation team went to check, the vehicle had vanished too. So it's obviously gone to pick them up somewhere, and not one of your experts with all their satellites and gadgetry can tell us where. And *you* are the ones who will instruct *our* military services?" The strata of Gazaghin's features seemed to puff up, like a saggy beach ball being inflated. Toddrel saw that his words had hit home and pressed on with a quiet inner satisfaction. "These two people have become a personal issue with me now. I *want* them found. It may be just a job to you, General, but because of the inability of the security forces to stop them in time, what they've done has cost me an immense personal fortune. How much has it cost you?"

Gazaghin waved it aside impatiently. "Pah! Still all you can think of is your money and fortune. You don't understand what this secession by west states means. If new Federation and Asia unite with Querl powers, it would make big troubles on home world. Could be end of everythings for you and for me. This Federation must be crushed quickly. But who is there that will do it? Too many U.S. weapons in California, Nevada. Your forces not reliable. So it must be with Hyadean forces. Little get-rich power games don't matter now." Gazaghin's face darkened, even from its normal hue. He wagged a threatening finger. "I know story about assassinations in Washington is true. Now I don't have time to worry if you are behind sabotage of Amazon ships and Uyali also. From here on we have serious war business. If we find you interfering to make different plans, is all finish for you, Toddrel. You go back tell your friends too. If Hyadeans direct this war, we do it Hyadean way." Gazaghin flipped an olive off his plate and ground it into the tablecloth with his thumb. "That means anyone who gets in path is crushed. Like little vegetable. You understand what I tell you, Toddrel, yes?"

Toddrel seethed but had to contain it. Every adversity that had befallen him, including his humiliation at the hands of this barbarian now, were due to that infernal couple. Whatever other priorities might intrude, he would have them hounded down. That much he vowed.

The caller who appeared on the screen in Laura's apartment suite on New York's Upper East Side had lean, firm features with dark hair, cropped short, and a cleanly trimmed mustache. Although she was unable to register a detailed impression because of the dark glasses he was wearing and the low level of lighting—no doubt deliberate—at wherever he was speaking from, her instincts and experience at once tagged him tentatively as "military."

"Hello, Laura," he opened. "Who I am doesn't matter for now. Let's just say that we're both acquaintances of Casper. I know quite a lot about you—knowing things about people is my business. In particular, I know you're an astute and discreet business lady. We have certain interests in common that we should discuss."

Laura smiled in a way that was part professional but at the same time genuinely curious. She assumed already that end-objective would be for her to take on another client. Some men thought the mystery image added appeal. Others overaffected assertiveness as a cover for awkwardness. She had seen all the lines: candid, humorous, businesslike, nice-guy. . . . Or this could be someone Casper needed to know more about, being set up. "Do I take it you just happen to be in town at the moment?" Laura asked, treating him to a knowing look. "People should get to know each other a little before they commit to things. Suppose we meet up for cocktails someplace?"

"No, I think you misunderstand. Recent political events could have bearing on the personal safety of both of us. I'm talking about mutual protection."

Laura's expression at once became serious. "I don't understand," she said guardedly.

"Of course not. That's why we should talk. I expect to be in New York within the next week or so. I'd like to meet sometime then. Unobtrusively would be best. Is that agreeable?"

"Well . . . of course." If this was just another line, Laura told herself, it was the weirdest one yet.

"I'll contact you again before then."

"Do I get a name to recognize you by?"

"For now, call me . . . Timothy."

In a public net-access booth a few blocks from Internal Security Services headquarters in Washington, D.C., Colonel Kurt Drisson cut off the screen and turned up the interior lighting. Blonde, tanned, shapely, and sophisticated. Toddrel knew how to pick them, he was forced to compliment inwardly. There was no reason why adding a more personal dimension when the time was right should interfere with business.

Toddrel's position was shaky. And when people like Toddrel felt insecure, those closest and with the most inside information had cause to worry. Not that Drisson feared any imminent danger for as long as he continued to be useful. But he believed in taking out early insurance.

◉ CHAPTER THIRTY-NINE ◉

They were back in Bolivia, at the north end of the country, east of the frontier with Peru. The truck, accompanied by an escort riding in a captured military Hummer, had continued south and crossed the border at night. Hudro showed how to put patterns of absorptive paint on the vehicles that would minimize the profile on image enhancers. Also, it turned out that playing static out of the speakers at full volume to disrupt acoustic patterns transmitted by sensors scattered from the air was more effective than coasting silently on the downhill stretches. The computers looked for engine frequencies and harmonics, and didn't know what to make of white noise.

Cade was slowly becoming himself again. "Are you getting over Yassem yet?" he asked Hudro as they stared back at the dusty trail winding away behind. They were out of the denser forest now, entering mor open, hilly country.

"No. Maybe never. Why you think it?"

"You get on with your job. You don't seem to let it bother you."

"Inside it bothers. Must get on with job and get done. Is Hyadean way."

Cade decided there was something to be learned, and tried to find useful things to do. It seemed to help his head.

The altitude became higher, the surroundings more rugged. They came to a settlement of adobe houses, farm buildings, and sheds, tucked in a fold of the hills. Miguel had sent word ahead of their coming. Food and accommodation would be provided for the night. Also, a white-haired leader of the local arm of MOPAN, called Inguinca, was waiting to meet them with some of his followers. Ahead lay the most populous region, around Lake Titicaca and La Paz. From here on, Rocco and his escorts would merely attract attention. Their job was done, and they would turn back. Miguel volunteered to continue with Cade and Hudro to act as interpreter and general lookout.

A special evening meal was prepared for the occasion, consisting of a bean soup followed by meat, sweet potatoes, and a vegetable dish, with a plentiful supply of dryish red wine. It was held in a large, smoky room spanned by wooden beams and lit by oil lamps in one of the larger houses. There was nothing secretive or furtive. Just about the whole settlement, it seemed, from wide-eyed children and dark-braided women—several of them puffing pipes—to old men, squeezed themselves in around the walls and by the stove to take part, or at least be an audience. Maybe this was one of the things that passed for entertainment in these parts. It was clear that most if not all of them had never seen a Hyadean in the flesh before. Apart from curiosity that none tried to conceal, reactions were varied. Some, encouraged and not a little surprised by the alien's familiarity with Spanish, did their best to be polite to the guest in the ways they had been taught. Others seemed hostile, showing their feelings by glowering or staring sullenly from far parts of the room. Cade was unsure of the risk they might represent, but nobody else seemed unduly bothered. Maybe the closeness of these communities was such that betrayal was unthinkable. Hudro seemed to accept such variations without surprise.

Inguinca told of the intensive search going on everywhere for the two Americans who had been snatched from a military transport intercepted between Peru and Brazil. All the Andes passes were under close surveillance; air connections out of the region were being watched. Although it might have seemed at first glance that the Amazon system would offer a choice of routes impossible to police effectively, they all converged in a gigantic funnel through a few checkpoints that it would be risky to try passing through, especially with all the military activity in the region following the outbreak of sabotage attacks. Inguinca denied that MOPAN guerrillas were responsible for these. Their fight, he said, was against the operations to clear populations farther west. Other groups were being funded from somewhere, and MOPAN being made the scapegoat.

Inguinca's recommendation, therefore, was that Cade and Hudro should press on southward, even though their ultimate aim had not yet been agreed. Clearly, they had to get out of the South American continent. Poring over a map that Inguinca produced, Cade thought of getting past the Andes into Chile, somehow, and then south to Santiago. The Hyadeans were boring an outlet from the Uyali region through the Andes to the Pacific. If it was too risky to go over the mountains, with the kinds of friends he was collecting there might be a way to get himself and Hudro smuggled under them, through the tunnel workings. The idea became less crazy as he recalled the highway with its procession of robot trucks as a possible way of getting there. From Santiago it might be easier to get a commercial flight over the Pacific, perhaps to New Zealand, where Neville Baxter was, and then return on a regular flight into the Western Federation, avoiding the politically doubtful areas on the direct line between. Hudro could perhaps go on from New Zealand to join the Hyadeans with Krossig in Australia, and work out a new life from there.

That still left the question of how to get them through the populous area around Lake Titicaca and La Paz. Someone made a suggestion that brought laughter from some quarters and ridicule from others. Cade couldn't follow, although Hudro seemed to be able to. As the noise fell, an old man near the stove began speaking. Miguel moved closer and translated in a low voice for Cade's benefit. "He says the two of you can't travel together. The American is no problem. It's easy to make you invisible among the people, even if we have to darken your skin a little. But how do you hide a blue giant with a face like a rock statue?"

At that point, a man in a dark shirt, with straight hair combed forward and a thick mustache, rose and began talking loudly, pointing a denouncing finger at Hudro and making appealing gestures to the room. He was angry and had maybe taken a bit too much wine. The gist was that he wanted to know why they were talking about helping an alien at all. The aliens were behind the people who sent planes to destroy their villages, and soldiers who took their land. He had lost his farm and his son. Why was this alien here, eating their food and expecting them to save him? Heated words and admonishments followed, with Miguel getting involved and hence failing to keep Cade informed. It ended with the man in the dark shirt stalking from the room.

A clear-skinned boy with deep, dark eyes, probably around fifteen, brought them back to the subject by reminding everyone that next week would be a time of festivals and parades, with devil dancers in costumes designed to exaggerate their height, and masks that covered their heads completely. What better way could there be to disguise the blue giant?

Hudro said something that brought laughs from all around. "What was that?" Cade asked Miguel.

"He says does that mean he has to learn to dance too?"

A woman pointed out that seeing devil dancers in a parade was one thing, but how would you explain one out on the highway or halfway across the Altiplano? Eventually it was conceded that ingenious though the idea was, it had too many difficulties.

As Cade watched and listened, he contrasted the company to the kind he was used to at his own parties. These were just simple, self-sufficient people, asking no more than to live as they chose and be left alone. Nobody was coerced or robbed to provide their needs. Dee had said something to him once about the people who did the really important things, but he hadn't understood what she'd meant. Now, he did. The people he had known were as incapable of turning wilderness into food, rocks into a home, plants into a coat, or a dead tree into a table as they were of levitating. They depended for their very survival on the knowledge and skills of others. Told that their comfort and affluence arose from their innate excellence and the free interplay of market forces, they were happy to accept it. But Cade had seen what really went on.

As the debate continued, Cade remembered how Vrel had

concealed him and Marie in St. Louis. Seizing a moment, and using Miguel again as translator, he told everybody, "If somebody is that conspicuous, then instead of trying to hide him, the thing to do might be to put him out in the open as something everyone would be expecting to see."

"Such as what?" Miguel asked.

"Would it be possible to get hold of a Hyadean military uniform somehow? Miguel and I dress as Bolivian army. We ride through openly in a jeep or something—a Hyadean officer and two Terran troopers." Cade looked around. The idea seemed to have merit.

"The uniforms might take some time. . . ." Inguinca said finally. He sounded dubious. "And then a suitable vehicle? . . . I don't know. That might be more difficult still. You would need papers to get gas. . . ."

More debate followed. Then a girl that Inguinca had introduced earlier as Evita, wearing jeans and a red shirt, her hair woven in braids, said, "Let me be the guide who will take them through. There is no problem with the vehicle. I drive a van for the telephone company, which passes everywhere. Hyadeans work with the telephone people sometimes when they put in special equipment. So he can wear his own clothes." Evita nodded toward Cade. "The American's idea is good. Let the Hyadean ride up front with me where everyone can see him. Hiding him in the back would look suspicious if there was a check. Miguel and the American come as workmen. When a pretty girl drives, the soldiers want to be nice guys. It is the best plan."

Nobody came up with any objection.

"Is this van of yours here?" Cade asked Evita.

She hesitated for a moment. "Yes. . . ."

"And I assume it would have a phone in it too?"

"Sure. All the regular phone company equipment."

It was the first prospect of being able to use trustworthy communications since Cade and Hudro were shot down. "Maybe we could call Baxter ahead and see how it looks," Cade suggested. "Get him started on making arrangements at his end."

"I guess. . . ."

At that point Rocco raised his hands. "This, I will leave to you. It is no longer our concern. It is time for us to be leaving now. So, we will say farewell and good luck, my friends."

A gaggle from inside came out to get some of the night air and watch as Cade and Hudro walked with Rocco to where the truck was waiting behind the Hummer, which was already filled with figures, engine running, ready to go.

"Remember to piss on body-scent detectors that they drop from the air when you find them," Hudro said. "And wear fresh flowers in hat. Works pretty good too."

Rocco's smile showed against the black of his mustache in the feeble light. "I'll remember. And the other thing I'll remember is that who are the good guys and who are the bad guys is more complicated than people think. But they have to learn it if this kind of thing is ever going to stop. That's the most important thing to learn."

He shook hands with Cade, then Hudro, and turned to heave himself up onto the tailboard. Somebody banged on the roof of the cab, and the truck started up. It flashed its lights for the Hummer ahead to move, and then followed twenty yards behind. Cade and Hudro stood watching, their arms raised, until the tail lamps disappeared, and then turned to go back to the houses.

Afterward, Evita took Cade to the van, where he used its phone to call Neville Baxter in New Zealand. Baxter was surprised and delighted. "What the hell gives?" he demanded, ever indomitably jovial.

"A long story that I'm not even going to try to get into, Neville. Look, I need help. I might be taking you up on that offer to visit you there sooner than you thought."

"You sound like you're in some kind of trouble."

"You could say that."

"Something to do with that documentary you did with your ex? We saw it here. It was dynamite." There was a pause, as if Baxter were putting the pieces together. "You were in South America when you made that. Is that where you still are now?"

"Right. And we need to get out."

"Who's we? You mean the ex? What was her name . . . ?"

"No, I told you it's a long story. I'm with a Hyadean—not one that you know. Heading directly north might have problems. The easiest way might be to come out your way. We're trying to get to Chile, and then down to Santiago."

"Where are you now, exactly?" Baxter asked. "We've got associates in a number of places down there. Maybe they can help."

For a second, Cade was unsure whether to answer. But then it was he, a moment ago, who had said he needed help. "Bolivia," he said. "Should be arriving in La Paz sometime tomorrow."

"Leave it to me. We might be able to come up with something."

Next, Cade called Luke at the house in California. To his surprise he learned that Julia was still there—acting about as normally as could be expected after a secession, and with war breaking out. Cade cautioned Luke to be careful of her. There was reason to believe she wasn't what she said. Until he got back, Luke shouldn't trust Julia with anything confidential. That, of course, included any mention of the fact that Cade had been in touch.

◎ CHAPTER FORTY ◎

The city of Nuestra Señora de la Paz, Our Lady of Peace, had seldom lived up to its name since its founding in 1548 by the envoy to whom the King of Spain had entrusted the rule of the empire seized from the Incas. It was supposed to mark the peace after the original Conquistadors, their companions at arms, sons, brothers, and heirs finally wiped themselves out after sixteen years of senseless civil war. Then, revolts plagued the nearly three centuries of Spanish rule. Aymará Indians besieged La Paz for six months in 1781, when latter-day Inca uprisings extended from Peru to Argentina. In 1825, Simón Bolívar, the liberator after whom the country was named, became the first national leader, only to resign the next year and be succeeded by six presidents in the next three years. Over the following two hundred years, sixty-odd men held the top spot, many lasting only days or weeks, tumbled by one another in more than 150 uprisings during the period. Twelve were assassinated.

Cade's first view of the world's highest capital city came as he, Hudro, Evita, and Miguel drove down off the Altiplano along a concrete boulevard of wide, sweeping curves overlooking an immense, tightly packed labyrinth of streets and terraces sprawling across the slopes of a river-gouged canyon cutting into the edge of the tableland. In front of them as they descended, dwellings, business premises, and office buildings clung to the steep, red, slide-prone slopes, while beyond the plateau line above, the snow-capped triple peaks of Illimani rose to 21,000 feet. Cade was taking a stint up front in the cab with Evita and Hudro. Miguel was in the rear. The drive southward had passed without incident, although news of sabotage attacks in the Uyali area and consequent tightening of security made the prospect of journeying farther in that direction worrisome.

The chief inspector in the city's police headquarters had received instructions to contact military security immediately if anything was heard concerning the American man and woman who were being hunted, and the two missing Hyadeans, again a male and a female, believed to have been involved. Hence, the oaf responsible for sifting intelligence reports had been looking for *couples*, and a whole day had slipped by before it occurred to someone else that the tipoff from a disaffected rebel in a remote village to the north might refer to the two males in question. If so, then what had happened to the females was anyone's guess. But it appeared that half their quarry might be on its way to the city right now.

"My information is that they are traveling in one of your vans," the chief inspector said over the phone to the general manager of the telephone company. "The driver is known as Evita. I don't know if that is her correct name, but I have a description. . . ."

"You can never get lost in La Paz," Evita said as she swung the wheel first one way, then the other to negotiate the series of downward bends. "Just keep going downhill. The whole city is a funnel that comes together onto one big main street that runs out the bottom." She lifted a hand momentarily to indicate two boys doing something to the wheels of an upturned coaster wagon. "They can go twelve miles without a break in that. Twenty-three hundred feet drop vertically. Good sport for boys, yes?"

Inguinca had given them instructions for contacting a highway construction foreman who could make arrangements to hide them in one of the robot trucks returning southward. However, as they came onto the main thoroughfare that Evita had mentioned—a tree-lined mall of shops, offices, and restaurants, called El Prado—the phone in a receptacle on the dash panel rang. Evita took it as she drove, listened for a moment, then passed the handset to Cade. "It's for you," she told him. "Neville Baxter again, from New Zealand."

"Hi, Neville."

"Roland. Is it all right to talk?"

"Sure. What's up?"

"Are you anywhere near the city yet?"

"Just coming into it now."

"Good. Look, this might be short notice, but I think we can do better than that schedule you talked about. I'm going to give you a number for somebody there—a business associate of my company. His name's Don. Call him right away. He'll tell you what it's all about. If you move fast, we might be able to swing something your time tonight."

They pulled off and stopped in a side street. Cade called the number. Don was with a shipping office at El Alto Airport, a few miles from the city, that handled local dealings for Baxter's business. He arranged to meet Cade and Hudro in town within the hour.

The general manager of the telephone company called the chief inspector back. "Okay, I have it. Her name is Carla Mayangua. She is one of our area service technicians." He gave a description of the van and its license number.

The chief inspector wrote down the details and passed the slip to his assistant. "Get a call put out to all units to look out for this vehicle. It is believed to be in the possession of a woman and man who go as Evita and Miguel, harboring two fugitives who are wanted for questioning: Roland Cade, alias Professor Arthur Wintner, an American, and Gessar Hudro, a Hyadean military officer who has gone missing. The occupants are to be apprehended immediately. Have any units sighting them call for full backup."

Evita and Miguel dropped the two off at a sidewalk cafe along El Prado, where Don had arranged to meet them—he said that Hyadeans were becoming a familiar enough sight in the capital. Don was already waiting at a corner table inside, sipping a Cinzano. He was small and dapper in a dark business suit, with a white handkerchief folded in the breast pocket, and a pencil-line mustache. Cade ordered coffee; Hudro, a Coke. Don's manner was nervous and fastidious. After preliminaries, he began, "Baxter's company imports agricultural machinery."

"I know," Cade said. "We met at a party I held about a month ago—"

Don held up a hand. "Please, it is best if I don't know your backgrounds." Cade nodded for him to continue. "Currently, he is experimenting with fitting his machines with Hyadean low-level Artificial Intelligence control units so they will be able to operate semiautonomously. The units come in at Xuchimbo, and we ship them out from here. Briefly, we have a consignment going out tonight to Auckland via Papeete, in Tahiti. I can get you listed as a Hyadean technical adviser traveling out there to instruct on the equipment, and Mr. Cade as a member of the flight crew. The controls are not strict for people leaving Bolivia. It's the contents of the shipments that they check. They're worried about Hyadean weapons and munitions getting out of the country."

"What about entry to New Zealand?" Cade queried.

"Neville knows people at the Immigration Department. You'll be brought in as political refugees. Low-key, no questions."

Cade recalled what Marie had said about AANS support being widespread, and how they had obtained false papers before traveling to St. Louis. He turned his head toward Hudro in an unspoken question, but there was really nothing to deliberate. At that moment, the wail came of approaching sirens. Traffic on El Prado pulled sluggishly aside as two police cars sped past with lights flashing and turned the block. More sounded distantly, coming from the other direction. Evidently, whatever was going on was quite close.

Don turned his head back and licked his lips. "Something's happening. Maybe it would be better if you lie low in the city for the afternoon. I know somebody who has an apartment you can use. When it gets dark, we'll send a car to bring you to the airport."

Cade looked at Hudro again. This wasn't something for them to judge. "How do we get there?" Cade asked Don.

"I'll take you now. It's not very far, but uphill. Everywhere from here in La Paz is uphill."

"Yes, we heard." Cade looked around. "First, we need to say goodbye to the people who brought us. Can we call them?" Don signaled a waiter and asked for a table phone.

"Maybe see Australia after all very soon now," Hudro said.

"One day at a time," Cade told him. Just one agonizing afternoon to get through. Then they might be finally out of it.

The phone arrived. Cade called the van, while Don sat back to sip his drink. The phone seemed to ring for an unnaturally long time. Then Evita's voice said, "Hello?"

"It's us," Cade said. "Okay, we're done. I guess we can—"

"Hello?" Evita said again.

"Can you hear me?"

"Yes, I hear."

Only then did Cade register the fear in her voice. "Is everything okay? You—"

"*No! Not okay. You must—*" There was what sounded like a slap, followed by a cry of pain. Cade stared at the phone in his hand, for an instant mystified, and then horrified.

"What's up?" Don demanded.

Cade turned the phone off and stood up suddenly. "Move!" he snapped. "We have to get out of here!"

Don fished a key from a niche above the door, let them in and then left, saying he would be back later. The apartment was small, plain, modestly furnished, but clean. A man's coats hung on hooks inside the front door, and a couple of soccer posters brightened the kitchen, along with a corkboard showing postcards, local business cards, and family snaps. A corner of the bedroom had been made into a religious shrine with a Sacred Heart statue, flowers, and a candle in a red glass. Cade and Hudro ate a lunch of tortillas and rice that they had picked up on the way, and settled down to wait.

"So how might it affect things for tonight?" Cade asked. They had agreed that what he heard over the phone could only mean that Evita and Miguel had been picked up. Cade still hadn't recovered from the shock of realizing that they themselves must have escaped by mere minutes.

"Is likely they are watching everything at airport," Hudro replied.

"How would they know anything about the airport?"

"Don't have to. They suspect everywhere. Is way police mind works. We just have to wait if plans changed now. Is not our thing to control anymore."

They turned on the news. In the former U.S., the provocations and responses by both sides had escalated to open belligerency. Twenty years ago it wouldn't have been possible. Incredulous, Cade watched Union fighter-bombers attacking bases, rail centers, and highway interchanges in Texas, Colorado, and Utah, apparently to slow communications to what looked like becoming a war front. The situation was confused, and the commentator couldn't make much sense of it. No city areas had been targeted as yet, but tensions and frustrations that had built up over years were suddenly being released, and things could heat up rapidly. Hudro was apprehensive of the effects if Hyadean weaponry were introduced on any significant scale. "So far we only use people-control tactics here," he told Cade. "Police action. You haven't seen what Hyadean war weapons do."

"What if Asia comes in and backs the Federation?" Cade asked.

"Then Asia is finished too."

"That would be practically an all-out planetary war."

"Is not first time. Hyadeans call it imposing the peace. Their way of peace. So you learn order and civilization, and everyone is happy and grateful."

"Unless Earth turns into another Querl," Cade mused. He found he didn't particularly like the image of passive submission.

"Not happen, Mr. Cade. Earth doesn't have Querl army and weapons."

They watched the lights going on across the canyon slopes as day darkened into evening. The phone rang, persisted for a while, but they left it alone. Don returned about thirty minutes later.

"We have to change the plan," he said. "Every Hyadean inside the airport is being checked. But we're going to try something that maybe nobody expects." That was all he would tell them.

He led them back downstairs, where they found a small Fiat waiting with a figure in the driver's seat. Cade and Don got in the back, and Hudro squeezed his bulk into the passenger side in front. The driver had a floppy hat, hooded zipper jacket over a sweater, and features impossible to make out in the darkness. He pulled away in silence and drove up from the city. When they came out onto the plateau he doused the headlights, and for the next half hour they picked their way carefully along roads and tracks, sometimes at little more than walking pace, with Don getting out twice to guide them through a difficult spot with a flashlamp. This brought them onto a dirt track following a chain-link fence with orange and blue runway lights beyond on one side, and knee-high grass on the other. The airport terminal facilities, outlined dimly in a halo of glows, were visible maybe a mile away to the right. After a few hundred yards, they came to a tube-frame gate. Don got out and stood scanning the area for several seconds. Then he walked up to the gate, tried it, then turned and waved his arm. Hudro and Cade got out with muttered thanks to the driver and hurried forward, while the car backed away among some rocks and scrub. The gate had been left unlocked. Don ushered them through, closed the gate carefully behind, and motioned them forward through the grass, checking from side to side at intervals to keep track of their bearings. Finally, he whispered, "Here," and motioned them down. They settled into the grass to wait.

Lights appeared in the distance above, grew brighter with the sound of approaching engines, and a plane landed. Several minutes later, another moved out from the terminal, taxied up along the perimeter-way, turned onto the main runway, and took off. Soon after, another followed. Both of them halted within fifty yards of where the three figures were crouching before making their turn prior to the takeoff run. Don checked his watch in the light from his flashlamp, shielding it with a flap of his jacket. "Should be the next one now," he whispered.

The night air was clear and getting cold. There seemed to be activity at the far end of the airfield, where vehicles were moving and searchlights probing, but nothing came closer. Then the sound carried across of another jet starting up, and a low, sleek shape moved out from the terminal area. It rolled toward the perimeter about a mile away and swung around, causing its landing lights to brighten suddenly. Cade tensed as the plane moved toward them. It had four engines slung beneath the wings, he saw as it enlarged, and the tailplane carried atop the fin. Several hundred yards away, it slowed. Cade thought he saw what looked like a light flash several times from a window of the flight deck. Don stood up, raised his flashlamp, and pressed the switch several times. The aircraft moved in front of them—a windowless cargo transport with low-slung body and tail loading doors. As it came to a halt in the gloom, Cade made out the side door already opening and its internal stairs hinging down. Cade and Hudro rose from the grass.

"Now, go!" Don brushed aside their attempts to shake hands and waved them on. At the top of the steps Cade turned to send back a salutation from the doorway, but he had already disappeared.

The convulsions had caused Miguel to bite through his tongue. Congealing blood covered the front of his bruised, naked body. Evita, her own faced swollen, lips split from the softening-up process, watched with dull horror creeping over her as he was dragged unconscious from the room.

The interrogator turned toward her. "Now, I ask you. Where did you leave the American and the Hyadean?" Evita felt dryness in her mouth. She was unable to swallow. She had heard that the best thing was to say nothing. Once you began to give a little away, there was no stopping it. The voice barked. "Where were they heading for? What was the plan to get them out of the country?" She felt herself shaking, tears running uncontrollably down her face. The interrogator's hand moved toward the box connected to the electrodes. Evita closed her eyes and began to pray.

The jet lifted into a clear sky filled with stars. Minutes later, the ghostly shapes of Andes peaks were drifting by in the night below. Then they were high over Chile. The Moon appeared slowly over the horizon, and in its cold, expanding light, the dark mass of the Pacific opened out before them, extending endlessly toward the west.

❄ CHAPTER FORTY-ONE ❄

Dee had always been of that independent turn of mind that led her to be her own person. She didn't like others trying to program her thinking, and when it suited her, took an inner delight in shocking them by daring to be different. That was probably why, when Vrel had contacted the office not really knowing what a travel agent was but needing a guide to show some Hyadeans from the mission around the area, she had elected to take charge of the party personally; and then, when Vrel turned out to be an intriguingly different alien also, in his own kind of way, probably been a little forward in propelling things toward a more personal relationship. The simple Hyadean readiness to accept words for what they meant and people for what they said had come as a welcome relief after the minefield of California dating politics that she was accustomed to, and from then on whatever friends and neighbors thought hadn't figured into it. Vrel had introduced her to Cade and his seemingly limitless list of friends who supplied, arranged, or were looking for just about anything one could name. And life had taken on a progressively more interesting slant ever since.

Then Rebecca had appeared, trying to trace Julia after being referred by a friend of Julia's former husband, and disappeared with Cade about two weeks later. Three days after that, Vrel left for St. Louis suddenly and hadn't been heard of since. There had to be some connection, but without Cade around there were few leads she could follow. Julia had professed to know nothing—and seemed curiously impersonal about it for someone in her situation, for what Dee's opinion was worth. Then, less than a week after Vrel's departure, when the whole country was in uproar over allegations of political assassination by the government, Cade and his former wife, long supposed to have become part of the past, appeared in a Hyadean news documentary, filmed in South America of all places, that exploded the official denials. In something approaching a dream state, Dee had listened to the announcement two days later that she was living in a new country. . . .

And now this.

The Residents' Committee of the condominiums where she lived on the edge of Marina Del Rey had sent maintenance staff around to tape all the widows in case of air attack, and check fire extinguishers. Other measures were spelled out in an instruction sheet that Dee had just retrieved from her mailbox: a list of first-aid and emergency supplies that everyone should acquire; the ground floor of the community block would be made into a casualty clearing station and bomb shelter; part of the parking lot was to be kept clear for emergency vehicles. Gasoline restrictions were already in effect, and coupon books were being printed to ration essential foods. A Labor Directorate had been established in Sacramento, empowered to shut down nonessential businesses and transfer labor to war-related work. She didn't know yet how her own job at the travel agent's would be affected. Guesses yesterday had been that a percentage of those in the business could expect to be assigned to other work. Vehicles and weapons assembly and munitions production were being expanded with emergency priority and already taking in drafted trainee labor. Males over eighteen were registering for the draft. There had been missile attacks on West Coast military bases and two aircraft assembly plants near Los Angeles.

Dee sat in her kitchen area drinking a coffee and blinked disbelievingly as she checked through the rest of the mail after skimming the morning's paper. These things didn't happen in the U.S.A. They happened to other people in other places that had never been quite real anyway. . . . Then she remembered that there no longer was a U.S.A. No, even though she had heard the air-raid warning sirens tested yesterday and seen the damage on last night's news, she couldn't believe it. Older folk talked about the erosion of freedoms her generation had never known, such as being able to drive coast-to-coast without having to give a reason, or not being profiled in the federal records system, and said that things had been heading this way for a long time. But all the same, Dee had grown up feeling a fond familiarity for the country she'd learned about at school with its flag and list of presidents, Fourth of July tradition, and national institutions that ranged from the Football League to the Postal Service. It *couldn't* be over. When her father died, she had taken weeks to accept it and continued seeing figures on the street that for a moment she would believe were him, telling herself there had been some huge mistake. She felt something similar now, as if suddenly she would wake up and everything would be back again the way it was supposed to be.

The door chime sounded from the hall. Dee got up, went out, and peered through the spy hole in the door. It was Mike Blair from the Hyadean mission.

"Hi," he greeted as she let him in and led the way back to the kitchen. "I probably should have called first. Have you got a minute?"

"Sure." Dee gestured toward the newspaper and mail scattered over the table. "I can't believe all this, Mike. Tell me it isn't real."

"I know. I've got the same problem. *We* don't do this to each other because someone tells us to. That's what people in other countries do." He spread his hands. "But what else do you do when the other guys are coming over here with bombs? And the crazy part about it all is that they probably think exactly the same about us."

"Can I fix you a coffee or something?"

"Thanks, no. I'm in a rush."

"So what gives?"

"I talked to Wyvex earlier today. And guess what. He got a call from Vrel. Vrel's okay!"

"*What?!*" Dee stared disbelievingly. "*Really?!*"

Blair grinned and nodded. "I just told you—really."

Dee threw her arms around Blair's neck, and kissed him on the side of his face. "So what happened? Where is he? What's going on? Did Wyvex say when he's coming back?"

"South America someplace. It sounds as if he's with some kind of Hyadean news outfit. They're making sure they've got clearance into the Federation. It could be in the next day or two."

"*Terrific!*" Dee sat down and looked around ecstatically. She was still having trouble absorbing it. "News team? You mean the ones who made that documentary? So are Roland and his ex coming too?" Blair became solemn and shook his head. "What's up?" Dee asked.

"Marie's there, but Roland isn't. It seems they were in a chopper that got shot down. It's . . . bad news, I'm afraid."

"Oh." Dee's jubilation died abruptly.

"Someone needs to break it to Julia before they get here. I told Wyvex I'd take care of it. I'm on my way over to the house now."

"I'll come with you," Dee said.

Blair arrived with Dee at Newport Beach a little under an hour later. En route he had received a further call from Wyvex, saying that Vrel and the others hoped to arrive the following day. Julia and Luke were both at home, and Blair broke the news to both of them together. Julia received it stoically. "I see," was her rejoinder. "How certain are they of this?"

Blair could only shake his head. "I don't know if Wyvex knew any more than he said. I didn't press him for details. As far as he knew, Marie and the Hyadean girl were the only two survivors."

"So there weren't any actual witnesses."

"Not as far as I could gather, no."

"I'm so sorry," was all Dee could say, again.

Luke had been watching Julia's face long and thoughtfully throughout. He said nothing.

A half hour after Blair and Dee left, Julia told Luke that she had some errands to run and left in her cream-colored Cadillac. Two miles from the house, she pulled into a parking area and used the phone that she carried in her purse to call the ISS unit that she reported to under the field name Arcadia. The phone was a special-issue model and connected directly on an encrypted channel. The duty controller took down the details and advised Arcadia to expect further instructions later. He then relayed the information immediately to Kurt Drisson, as per standing orders. Within minutes, Drisson was through to Casper Toddrel, still in Washington, at that moment in an office of the Senate Building, sorting through notes he had made during meetings that morning. Toddrel found a more private room, and Drisson related what he had just learned. For once, it seemed that the intelligence services had better information than Cade's friends did.

"Obviously, these people in Los Angeles don't know about Cade and the Hyadean defector," Toddrel said.

"Check."

They had been tracked to La Paz following a lead from an informer, and then missed by a matter of minutes. An agent at El Alto Airport had picked up something about two illegals being smuggled out somewhere but hadn't been able to fix the destination. Now it seemed clear.

"What's your assessment?" Toddrel asked.

"If the bunch who skipped in Brazil are heading for Quito, that's where Cade and the Hyadean were heading," Drisson replied. "They're all going to meet up there, then fly up to LA together."

"That's the way I'd be inclined to see it too," Toddrel agreed. "But why wouldn't they mention Cade and the Hyadean to the people in Los Angeles?"

"If they're not all in Quito yet, it would be premature to presume it. . . . Or maybe they just didn't want to talk too much about their movements."

It sounded probable. "And then we'll have all our problems together—in one place," Toddrel said. The implication was clear.

"Mmm . . . It would be difficult to arrange an incident there, in Quito, with the time scale we've got," Drisson said. "We don't have readily available operatives there."

"I'm not sure I'd want that in any case," Toddrel told him. "Ecuador is trying to stay out of things politically. We don't want to risk any embarrassments there. Wait until they get to California. With the current situation, anyone could be suspected. You could use Arcadia. She's right there, on the spot. Then pull her out immediately afterward." Toddrel quite liked that idea. It seemed poetic. Keeping her there had been a risky decision. Maybe it could pay a dividend now.

"I'll get on it right away," Drisson promised.

Late that night, a message appeared in Julia's phone via its special channel, giving a number and instructions to ask for "Laredo." She called the number, and shortly afterward drove out through roads busy with military traffic to a rendezvous not far from LAX, Los Angeles International Airport. Laredo gave her a heavy black suitcase, which she stowed in the trunk of the Cadillac.

Next morning, in the residential quarters of the Hyadean mission in Lakewood, Wyvex took a call from Julia on his personal number. "Mike Blair and Dee gave me the news," she told him.

"I'm sorry it couldn't have been better about Roland," Wyvex replied.

"It's one of these things we have to learn to live with. They're due in today, right?"

"Yes. At five this afternoon."

"What's the plan? Were you planning on collecting them?"

"Yes." Wyvex hesitated, unsure of the correct Terran etiquette in view of Marie's presence. "Why? Did you want to be there?"

"I'd rather see them later. But look, I know that with the way things are, Hyadeans are trying to keep a low profile and stay out of sight. I could arrange for Luke to pick them up instead."

"Well . . . that would probably be a good idea. You're sure it's no trouble?" Wyvex said.

"Of course not," Julia told him. "No trouble at all."

◉ CHAPTER FORTY-TWO ◉

Between quitting the Navy and running into Cade, Luke had been a professional bodyguard and security consultant. That meant he was suspicious of anything that didn't quite feel right. The seeming matter-of-factness with which Julia had accepted Cade's disappearance, and the little inclination she had shown to try locating or contacting him since had seemed unusual even before Cade's call warning that Julia might not be what she appeared to be.

What did it mean?

Because she'd been installed into Cade's life around a year ago after a romance that had bloomed too smoothly and easily, a clear possibility was that she had been planted. With Cade commanding a growing social circle of influential Hyadeans and Terrans who did business with them, and then having a former wife connected with CounterAction, it was the kind of thing they should have expected. And then the broadcast had told of his almost being killed after going off with Rebecca, who had been introduced by Julia. It reeked of "setup."

Midway through the day that the flight bringing Vrel and the others from Quito was due to arrive, Julia asked Luke to have the limo ready to collect Wyvex and Dee from the mission and then go on to LAX to meet them. She explained that it would avoid the Hyadeans having to venture out in public at a time when hostility was being shown from some quarters.

Luke would normally not have thought twice about it, but the present circumstances caused him to question everything. Why was Julia showing such concern, when nobody from the household would be among the expected arrivals? It felt odd. Had the Hyadeans asked her to arrange for the party to be collected? Luke called Wyvex to check. No, Wyvex said. Julia had called him to suggest it. Even odder. If it were merely to keep the Hyadeans out of the way, why not use any of the commercial limo or shuttle companies at the airport? Why did it have to be *this* limo? His suspicions fully aroused, Luke went out to the garage and checked over it from end to end. And concealed in a cardboard carton in the trunk, he found a heavy black suitcase that shouldn't have been there. He took it out and stood it out of view between the wall and the rear of Julia's Cadillac. By now it was almost three in the afternoon. Luke went out the back of the garage, across the rear yard to the dock, and boarded the yacht. Warren Edmonds, the *Sassy Lady's* skipper, was in the main cabin, taking in a movie with Charles, the boat's cook. "Warren, I need to talk to you," Luke said. They went out onto the foredeck, Luke closing the door behind them.

"What's up?" Warren asked.

"I'll explain it all later—I have to leave for the airport in a few minutes. But there's a black suitcase by the wall in the garage. I think it might be a bomb."

"*Jesus*, you're joking! Where—"

"I said, later. What I want you to do is pick it up after I'm gone, take it out over the water in one of the dinghies, and drop it down on the end of a line. It's just a precaution." Luke looked around and lowered his voice. "Look, I haven't told anyone this, but Roland is okay."

"*What?!*"

"He called me a couple of days ago. I'm not sure, but I think he might be arriving this afternoon with the others. If so, then we'll be able to straighten everything out after he gets here. You mustn't mention anything to Julia about this. But in the meantime, just to be safe, I want that thing out of the way."

Warren nodded. "Okay, Luke. If you say so."

✖ ✖ ✖

Julia finished packing the black leather pilot bag and set it alongside the garment bag, red suitcase, cosmetic bag, and shoulder purse on the bed. She made a final check through the drawers of the vanity and added a few final items to the blue carryall containing her jewelry boxes, personal papers, and some casual clothes and shoes. Then she moved to the window, which overlooked the rear of the house, and peered past the drapes. Luke was just coming down the steps from the yacht. He crossed the rear yard and disappeared from sight into the door at the back of the garage. Julia went from the bedroom to the far side of the suite, where the window commanded a view of the front. A minute or two later, the limo backed out of the garage, turned in the circle at the top of the driveway, and left. Julia went back to the bedroom, picked up two of the bags, and carried them down through the house. "Henry," she called out as she approached the door into the garage. "Are you anywhere around, Henry?" He appeared as Julia put the bags down behind the Cadillac.

"Yes, ma'am?" His face registered surprise.

"Something has come up suddenly. I have to make a trip. There are some more bags on the bed upstairs. Fetch them for me and load them, would you, while I collect some other things?"

"Er . . ." Henry waved a hand undecidedly and looked perplexed. He seemed far from happy, as if some explanation were called for, yet at the same time conscious of his station.

"It doesn't *matter* why, Henry," Julia said sharply. "I do not have to justify myself to you. Just kindly do as I ask, please."

"Yes. . . . Yes, of course." Henry turned and went back into the house.

Julia followed, going to the den, where she retrieved the briefcase and book bag that she had previously filled with documents and files from her own drawers. She took them through to the garage along with her laptop, placing them by the bags that she had left previously just as Henry came back with three from upstairs. He was agitated and unsure, depositing the bags with the others and departing, as if to spend as little time around her as possible. As Henry was about to leave, Warren Edmonds came in through the door from the rear yard. He stopped, seemingly confused.

"Ah . . . has anyone seen Luke?" he asked. It sounded like an excuse. Evidently, he hadn't expected to find Julia and Henry here.

"He's just gone," Henry said from the doorway. "Picking up Vrel and the rest at the airport, remember?"

"Oh . . . right." Warren gazed around the garage as if reluctant to leave.

"He'll be back in a few hours. Was there something else?" Julia said impatiently.

"Er, no. . . . No, I guess not. Okay." Warren turned and went back the way he had come. Henry exited into the house. Julia went through to the front hall to sort coats and jackets from the closet. By the time she returned to the garage, Henry was back and had just lifted the last of the bags into the trunk. Julia opened the driver's door, threw the coats onto the back seat, prepared to get in, then saw that Henry was watching her strangely. Something needed to be said. It didn't matter what. Five minutes more and she would be out of this place permanently. "I told you, something unexpected has come up," Julia told him. "I'll be back in a day or two." Henry nodded but didn't look as if he believed her. She climbed in, started the motor, and backed the car out.

As she came onto the freeway, Julia called her ISS control unit and left a message that said, "Arcadia checking in. Rooster is on schedule. Gamecock. Surfing." The code words meant that Luke had left on time, the device was planted, and she was on her way out.

A couple of miles farther south, she pulled into a service area to fill up with gas. She decided it would be a good time to eat too, rather than stop again later. On her way into the coffee shop by the gas station, she threw her regular domestic phone into the trash bin by the door. That part of her life was over now.

Warren found Henry in the kitchen, doing something with the program of the autochef. Henry was looking worried, but Warren was too flustered to notice. "Henry, drop that and come this way. I've got a problem." Warren led the way back through to the garage, then waved a hand around. "There's supposed to be a black suitcase here somewhere. I've looked all over. You were in here a few minutes ago. Have you seen it?"

"I loaded all the bags into the Cadillac," Henry said. "Julia's orders."

Warren looked around, as if noticing for the first time that it was gone. "Where'd she go?"

"I don't know. She didn't say. But she was acting strange. Packed. Gone. I don't know what it's all about."

Impossible thoughts raced through Warren's mind. "*All* the bags?" he repeated.

"That's what she said. The mood she was in, I wasn't asking questions. Why? Is something wrong?"

Warren thought frantically, then went out into the yard and called Luke's number from his pocket phone. "Hello?" Luke's voice answered.

"Luke, it's Warren. We may have trouble. There isn't any black suitcase in the garage. Henry says he put it in the Cadillac with a bunch of other stuff of Julia's that he just loaded. She's gone."

"Gone? Where to?"

"We don't know. She's blown. Taken off. She was set to go right after you left. Henry says she was acting strange." Warren paused, but there was no immediate response. "What does it mean?" he asked finally. The silence persisted for a long time, as if Luke were wrestling with all manner of imponderables. "Luke?" Warren prompted.

"Don't worry about it," Luke's voice said at last. "Just leave everything to me."

❀ CHAPTER FORTY-THREE ❀

It was different from the last time he had looked down over Los Angeles from an incoming flight, Vrel reflected. Then, he had been traveling on official business for the Hyadean authorities, returning to their West Coast office of the United States. This time he was a renegade seeking asylum at an unofficial enterprise in a new, rebellious Federation gearing up for war. He really had no comprehension of the political and economic tangles that had led up to it, he realized. Perhaps he was still only at the beginnings of understanding anything about Earth and its squabbling, disorganized, variously colored natives.

In the window seat next to Vrel in the First Class section, Luodine stared out, looking for signs of the war. After her experiences in Brazil, she hadn't been sure what to expect, but Los Angeles still looked very much the way it had when she last visited. They had been fortunate in getting a flight into the Federation at all. Many airlines had suspended operations because of the military risks. The morning had seen a major attack by air-launched missiles on the naval installations in San Diego, farther south, which the Federation had taken over. Also, Union aircraft had been allowed across Mexican air space to lay mines and other underwater devices at points along the West Coast. The Federation was reinforcing its southern border. Luodine looked to the future with a mixture of excitement that the big story she had been working toward was about to break here, and trepidation as to what it might entail.

In the row in front, Nyarl was despondent that at the end of it all, nothing they did would have any measurable impact on Chryse. The control over what Hyadeans were told was too effective. What had Luodine and he been thinking to imagine they could change it? They had become too distracted by what they had seen on Earth, and then in their minds projected it into Chryse. But Chryse was not Earth. The flyer had given them a direct connection to Chryse before they had to leave it at Quito. The documentary that they made at Tevlak's had not been aired there. The director of the agency that Luodine and Nyarl represented had balked when he saw it and requested guidance from the authorities. That meant it never would get aired. Oh yes, Luodine would get her story here. And nobody would ever get to see it.

Across the aisle, Yassem and Marie sat together, saying little. Each, in her own way and for her own reasons, had imagined that if this journey ever took place it would mark the beginnings of a new life. Hopes for that were now gone, and both of them faced a life that opened up to a long prospect of uncertainty leading nowhere.

The plane landed and taxied to the terminal. Military vehicles and personnel were scattered along the airport perimeter, where work crews were constructing antiaircraft defenses and dispersal bays, and digging slit trenches. There were fewer civil aircraft than had been normal for LAX, although many painted olive drab or camouflage. An official from the newly inaugurated Federation immigration office met them as they deplaned and took them through arrival formalities in a secluded area, away from the public facilities. Wyvex and Dee were already waiting beyond. Police escorted the group out through one end of the regular Baggage Claim level to the pickup zone, where Luke was waiting with Cade's maroon limo. They climbed aboard amid an arriving military unit jostling to sort out packs and kit bags on the sidewalk.

Inside, Vrel and Dee hugged warmly, but then Dee put a restraining hand on his arm and eased him away. Vrel frowned at her, puzzled. She moved her eyes in Marie and Yassem's direction.

Vrel returned a faint nod that he understood, at the same time reproaching himself for needing reminding.

Introductions were completed as the limo pulled out into the traffic. Wyvex and Dee already knew Marie's face from the documentary she had made with Cade. Vrel indicated the front, where Luke had left the limo's privacy screen down. "And that's Luke, who was Roland's right-hand man, I think you say." Luke's eyes left the road for a moment to glance into the mirror showing the rear compartment.

"Luke, hello," Yassem said. The eyes found the mirror again, and Luke nodded in acknowledgment.

"Hi, Luke," Marie said. "It's been a long time."

"You're right about that. So how was China?"

"Oh, I didn't know you already knew each other," Vrel said.

"Maybe we never really did," Marie told him. She looked toward the back of Luke's head again. "It feels as if it's all my fault, Luke. I'm sorry I didn't bring him back. . . . Things could have been so different. One day I'll tell you the whole story."

Luke didn't reply. Marie was hoping to begin building a bridge between them to close a gap that had existed in the past. His failure to respond struck her as strangely insensitive, even for Luke.

The gray Dodge following several cars behind had pulled out from the sidewalk parking strip opposite as the limo left the baggage claim pickup area. With the intervening traffic and melee of soldiers, Laredo hadn't been able to positively identify all of the expected arrivals. But the importance of carrying through the mission there—before any of them had an opportunity to meet people from the media or Federation government—had been stressed, and in his judgment that didn't constitute sufficient grounds to reconsider. He slid the detonator control out from the map receptacle under the armrest and flipped the primer switch to the ARMED position. An amber light came on to confirm.

Luke put the phone back in the holder on the limo's dash panel. Still no answer. He wasn't sure why, since there was hardly any reason to feel sentimental, but he had been trying to raise Julia ever since Warren's call. It hadn't required an effort of genius to fit the pieces together. If Julia had played her hand and gone, then nothing Luke said could make any difference now. He chewed on his lip as he drove, trying to decide if he should tell them.

" . . . the Midwest states might be about to come over," Wyvex was saying behind. "But the East is pushing solidly into Texas. Everything's confused."

"Might Hyadeans be getting ready to play a bigger part?" Luodine asked in a worried voice.

"Nobody knows."

"We heard there's been a lot of air fighting," Nyarl said.

"Especially in the center, yes," Wyvex confirmed. "We've had raids here too. NATO is mobilizing in Europe."

Marie was being very quiet. Luke glanced in the mirror again. She was still watching him, her face showing hurt and confusion, on the verge of fighting back tears. Drawing a long breath, he turned his head to call over his shoulder. "Hey, everyone back there . . ." His tone brought immediate quiet. "There's something you all ought to know." They waited. "Roland and Hudro are both okay. They made it through the crash. The MOPAN got them to Bolivia. Roland called me from there a couple of days ago. There were reasons to keep it quiet. He was talking about trying to get back via New Zealand. I thought he might have changed his plans and met up with you people somehow."

The traffic on I-405 south was noticeably thinner due to the gasoline restrictions. Laredo moved out a lane and accelerated gently past the limo. He watched in his mirror as it fell back a comfortable distance behind, then released the safety latch over the FIRE button. A red warning light confirmed that the circuit was active. He kept the Dodge well ahead and waited for a clear stretch in the traffic pattern.

Marie and Yassem were hugging each other in delight, Yassem smiling and trying to suppress a compulsion to laugh at the same time, Marie openly weeping. Vrel was speechless; Dee flung her arms around his neck. Luodine and Nyarl were grinning and smacking palms together in the way they had picked up from Terrans.

"You mean we can call them?" Marie said, finally managing to speak coherently.

"I don't have the number here," Luke answered from the front. "But sure, as soon as we get back to the house."

"But . . . why couldn't you have told us?" Wyvex stammered.

"I said, there were reasons," Luke replied. "But they don't matter anymore."

Laredo pressed the FIRE button. A green light indicated positive function. Yet nothing had happened. The limo was still there in his mirror, a couple of hundred yards back in a gap behind a truck and a Chevrolet sitting close together. He shook his head bemusedly and pressed the button again.

Nothing happened.

Thirty miles farther south, traffic braked and swerved wildly to avoid the remains and falling debris of what, a few seconds before, had been a cream Cadillac moving fast in the direction of San Diego and the border.

In the trash bin outside the coffee shop by the gas station, the phone rang again for a while, then fell silent.

Back in the limo, Luke replaced the phone for what he decided was the last time. He had done all anybody could do, he told himself.

◉ CHAPTER FORTY-FOUR ◉

After a scheduled stop in Tahiti, Cade and Hudro arrived in Auckland without further incident. Neville Baxter, jovial as ever, met them personally with several other people from his company to make sure there was no hitch with the arrangement for them to enter the country as political refugees. They were granted temporary visas, and then Baxter took them to an apartment in Auckland that he had procured and placed at their disposal, recommending that they rest, relax for a few days, and adjust to the world as seen from the other side. After that, they could consider their options.

The first thing Cade did was call Luke in California to let him know that he and Hudro were safe. It turned out that Luke had some news for him too. "Vrel and those two Hyadeans that made the movie, they're here. They arrived yesterday on a regular flight from Ecuador."

"Hey, that's great!" Cade exclaimed. He looked up. Hudro was staring at him from the far side of the room. "Vrel and Luodine and Nyarl are okay. They're in California."

"Yes, I heard." Hudro got up and came across.

"That's not all," Luke said from the screen. "Are you ready for this? You guys weren't the only ones to make it out of that chopper crash. Marie's here too—a bit thinner than when I last knew her, but looking pretty good." Hudro gripped Cade's shoulder as he looked past him, squeezing hard enough to make him wince.

"I'm happy for you, Roland," he murmured.

Luke went on, "And the Hyadean girl is with her, Yassem. She's the one who got out with that other guy there, yes?"

"*Yeaaah!*" Cade exulted. He held out a palm. Hudro gripped it. They squeezed and shook deliriously, both unable to find words. Eventually, Cade looked back at the phone and managed, "But they don't know about us yet, right? You're still having to clam up because of Julia."

"Oh, they know," Luke replied. "The Julia problem kind of solved itself. It's complicated. She's history. Mind if I wait on that till you get back?"

Cade had suddenly decided that Julia's story could wait anyway. "They know?" he repeated. "So is Marie there at the house? Can I talk to her?"

"Sure." Luke's head turned away as he called offscreen. "Hey, Henry. You wanna go tell Marie she won't believe who's on the line here? And you'd better check around and see if you can find Yassem while you're at it."

The next day, Cade contacted Krossig at the Hyadean scientific center for fieldwork that he had gone to in northeast Australia. Naturally, Krossig had also seen the documentary that Cade, Marie, and the others had made in South America. "So where are you calling from now?" he asked.

"You won't believe it."

"Mr. Cade, if you told me it was from the far side of the Moon, I would believe it."

"I'm a lot closer to you now, as a matter of fact—in New Zealand."

"Ah, that means you must be with that man, what was his name . . . ?" Krossig probably asked his veebee, "Neville Baxter."

"Fast, Krossig," Cade complimented. "But there's more. Look, I have another Hyadean with me. You probably won't know him. His name's Hudro. To cut a long story short, he needs a new start in another part of the planet. I thought that Hyadean group that you're with there might be able to take him in—at least for a while."

They talked for a little longer, Cade giving the gist of how they had ended up in New Zealand.

"I'll make inquiries," Krossig promised.

Two days went by, during which the news brought reports of growing turmoil in America. Hyadean ground forces, apparently from several ships of reinforcements that had recently arrived in orbit, were occupying the Panama Canal Zone, which was generally interpreted as presaging operations in the Pacific. Already, there was talk of Asians "defending" Hawaii, which everyone understood meant securing trans-Pacific supply routes. The Hyadean move also prepared for the possible arrival of Globalist forces from South America in Mexico. The Mexican response was an outbreak of insurrection by a movement that had obviously been organizing for some time, no doubt linked to MOPAN, opposing the government's Globalist supportive policy.

The Dakotas, Minnesota, and Wisconsin joined the Federation, anchoring its northern frontier solidly along the Great Lakes. Washington was making accusations of Canadian railroads moving Federation supplies inland from Vancouver and through the Rockies. Significantly, perhaps, Canada had refused overflight permission to the Union. In the southern sector, the Unionist drive into Texas was continuing, with ground forces now coming into contact, maneuvering for positions, and with actual outbreaks of skirmishing in places. Cade watched shots of tanks with familiar white star markings firing on positions a few miles west of Fort Worth. If he hadn't seen it with his own eyes, he would have said it was impossible.

Then Krossig called back. Yes, indeed, his superiors at the Hyadean field center would be extremely interested in meeting Cade and Hudro. Arrangements would be made to receive them as soon as they wished.

And so, just five days after their arrival in New Zealand, Cade and Hudro bade Neville Baxter farewell before boarding a New Zealand Air Force jet transport bound directly for Cairns, on the Queensland coast.

✳   ✳   ✳

While Cade and Hudro were looking out over the sunlit blue of the Tasman Sea, it was a close, muggy evening in New York. There had been air-raid alerts, fire drills in offices and schools, and a lot of merchandise moved to safes and basements, but nothing had come of it.

Drisson met Laura for dinner in an out-of-the way but highly rated Greek restaurant frequented by gourmet aficionados on the East Side above 70th Street between Second Avenue and the river. He had decided that some investment in up-market taste could be justified in this instance. They got around to business after the appetizers and salad, and a second choice of wines to suit the entrées.

"People in my line of work don't trade social niceties," he said. "That way, we save time and avoid misunderstandings. You and I are both in situations where we know things about Toddrel that he wouldn't have wanted his mother to know. You keep him happy at playtime and know how he really does business. I know what happens to people who get in his way. It isn't pretty." He paused for a reaction. Laura continued watching him silently over her glass as she sipped. Drisson went on, "His South American operation has backfired, which put him right next to the big fan when the secession hit. When people like Casper are in trouble, life for everyone around them tends to get insecure."

Laura looked mildly reproaching. "You're not trying to tell me I could be in some kind of danger, surely?"

"I think you should be certain you know the person you're dealing with." Drisson studied her for a second or two, as if weighing whether to elaborate. "He had a wife once. I assume you know that."

"She drowned in a boating accident seven years ago."

"Right. They were heading for a divorce that was going to be bloody. She knew a lot about him that he wouldn't have wanted to see in the papers, and she meant to use all of it." Drisson shook his head. "It wasn't an accident."

"How do you know this?"

"I told you, my job is to know things."

Laura's expression registered the more serious dimension that this was taking on. "What are you asking me to do?" she asked warily.

"I'm suggesting that you change your insurance. Or at least, take out extra cover."

"Which your company, of course, happens to deal in."

"Very professional and experienced. Long established in the business."

"Why? What's in it for you? It sounds as if you can take care of yourself."

"Information. Access. If it ever comes time to claim on the policy, it can work a lot smoother with help on the inside." Drisson indicated her with an extended hand. "Like I said before, separate, we're both vulnerable. Working together, we could look out for each other pretty good."

Laura's gaze flickered over him, reading the face and the eyes, comparing their message with that of the words. If things really could get that ugly, it was beginning to sound as if she might need this person around. But then she would end up in an even stronger position of knowing enough to compromise him if events took such a direction, and she felt so inclined. And he had already shown how much he believed in taking precautions. She was going to have to play this carefully, she decided. Very carefully.

◎ CHAPTER FORTY-FIVE ◎

The group waiting to greet Cade and Hudro at Cairns, which boasted a modestly sized airport in spite of its billing as "international," consisted of Krossig; his Hyadean boss, Freem; and an Australian biologist by the name of Susan Gray, who worked with them. With them, local officialdom was represented in the form of a grinning Aborigine in the full regalia of khaki shorts and a white shirt worn shirttails out, and an equally affable Asian in a casual jacket and slacks. They were called Tolly and Hueng. Both were nominally based at the local authority's offices in Townsville, two hundred miles south, which served as an outpost of the state government in Brisbane. They maintained a loose contact with the Hyadean presence in Cairns and had flown up to "coordinate" with Cade and Hudro, and make their stay comfortable.

Accommodation had been arranged in a hotel called the Babinda farther in toward the city—although Susan was from Melbourne originally, and said that nobody in Queensland knew what a real city was. They drove there in a bright orange minibus through grassy, hilly farmland and spread-out suburbs of broad streets and modern frame buildings tucked among palm trees and stands of tropical greenery. On the way, Freem talked among other things about the inefficiency of internal combustion engines. The hydrogen atom, he explained, could be catalytically induced to assume lower energy states than the "ground" state held by Terran science to be the lowermost possible, and in the process released energies hundreds of times greater than conventional combustion. It was inherently clean, using water as a fuel and producing degenerate hydrogen as exhaust, which was totally inert and diffused up out of the atmosphere. Cade had heard this from Vrel, but he didn't want to spoil Freem's line by saying so.

"But here's an angle that these guys never thought of," Tolly said.

"I suspect we did, but it got suppressed," Krossig interjected.

Tolly continued, "Cars powered that way could run all the time without choking up the planet. So how about this: Instead of owning a big chunk of capital investment that spends most of its time depreciating in driveways and parking lots, you use a turbine driving an electric generator-motor system to make it a mobile power plant as well as a vehicle. When it isn't going anywhere, you plug it into the grid and get credited for what you deliver. Millions of people take care of their own power requirements. We reckon an average car could net the owner around ten thousand dollars per year."

Cade was intrigued. "You think something like that could happen?"

"We're working on it."

"So who would own it?"

"I don't know. Scientists from all over are working here with Hyadeans."

"Mike Blair's due to be joining us anytime," Krossig said.

Hueng, who it turned out was on some kind of loan from the Chinese government, chimed in. "The Western Federation has the right idea. This side of the world is the way of the future. The interests that the Globalists are trying to hang on to are finished. When a system has to resort to force and deception to preserve itself, you know it's only a matter of time before it collapses. I am Chinese, Mr. Cade. I know. The military empires of earlier times have passed away. The fascist and socialist political empires of the last century are gone. Now we're seeing the end of the Western- and Hyadean-style financial empires. Everybody will manage their own affairs." He grinned broadly. "So we still call it the People's Republic. It fits the reality rather well."

"Maybe Hyadeans are discovering their own version too," Krossig said. "Away from the restrictions of the system we've known."

"The same kinds of restrictions that Americans and Europeans have come to regard as normal," Susan Gray put in. She was in her thirties, Cade guessed, with neck-length blond hair, sun-bronzed and frighteningly fit looking, dressed in a tan shirt and light green jeans. "We do things kind of casually and informally around here. The region has a strong independent tradition of minding its own business and not trusting the central government. Somehow it seems to provide the right atmosphere for everyone to get along. That was a big reason why the Hyadeans stayed."

"I feel I have begun to awaken," Krossig said. "Many Hyadeans that I've met here say the same thing."

Cade stared out as they drove into the outskirts of the city. All it took was to experience what free thinking could be like. Then there was no going back. If this was what the Hyadeans who came here were finding, could exposure to Earth eventually cause their whole population to wake up?

The hotel was in the tradition of the architectural cloning which for decades had been creating airport environs and urban peripheries that were in danger of becoming indistinguishable the world over. But it was cool, clean, and comfortable. Cade and Hudro were given separate suites and then left to freshen up, change, and spend the remainder of the afternoon relaxing with beers by the pool among palm-tree-enclosed gardens at the rear.

That evening, there was a dinner in town for the occasion, hosted by Tolly and Hueng on behalf of the state and attended by Krossig, Freem, Susan, and others from the scientific center, several more Hyadeans connected with other enterprises, and a mix of a few business figures and other local notables that it seemed fitting to invite or who had otherwise wangled their way in. It was all very colorful and cheerful, especially as the drink continued to flow generously, and at midnight they called Cade's house in California, got Marie and Yassem, and toasted them over the phone. Cade promised he would be back before much longer. Hudro hadn't decided yet what his intentions were.

The late stayers then retired to a private bar. Krossig, by then well stimulated and loquacious, told Cade, Hudro, and Susan about his discovery of Asian philosophies from his dealings among some of the area's varied populace. He was particularly enthralled by the notion of reincarnation, according to which individual personalities were created for the purpose of assisting a soul on its path of development. The circumstances of each incarnation were chosen to provide the experiences and lessons that the soul needed in order to heal itself and grow. This seemed to follow so naturally from the many-worlds view of quantum reality that Krossig and Mike Blair back in California saw as a purposefully contrived learning environment in which the choices that a consciousness made created its path of experiences. Their latest thought was that despite all the things that were heard about Eastern mysticism and Western science converging toward saying the same thing, perhaps both were missing the whole point of it all equally. Krossig explained:

"Physics exposes the backstage machinery. Eastern insight says that what the machinery supports is illusion. But surely the whole purpose of it is to *experience* the illusion." The company was listening intently. "It's a bit like a physicist finally figuring out that the movie is a product of electrical patterns and photons, and the mystic observing that what they depict isn't real. But all the time, neither of them sees that the purpose of the movie was to . . ." He waved a hand about. "Whatever the movie is made for."

"Tell a story. Teach a lesson," Susan supplied. She was now transformed in a close-fitting black cocktail dress and looking devastating.

"Exactly."

Susan looked at the others. "Interesting. I've always thought of myself as a hard-boiled science type too. But you know, fellas, I like it."

"You see, it needs Hyadean and Terran brains combined," Freem said.

Hudro was enraptured. "So, is all designed for consciousnesses to make choices and learn," he said to Krossig. "What is it does the designing?"

Krossig spread his hands. "I don't know. Not my department."

Hudro turned to Cade. "Here is what I seek. Is as you say, like fresh air. We bring Yassem here. Already I think we stay in this country."

Cade looked inquiringly at Susan and Freem.

"I don't think that would be too much of a problem," Susan said. "There's a good community of Hyadeans here—all learning to be individuals. Sounds like they'd fit right in."

For the next couple of days, Cade and Hudro were given a tour of the area, particularly to see some of the ways in which Hyadeans and Terrans were working together without organizing directives from above or centralized policies favoring corporate economics. The scientific station was larger and more diverse in its activities than Cade had imagined. He toured the labs and workshops, saw prototype rigs of the catalyzed hydrogen turboelectric system that Tolly had talked about in the bus on the way from the airport, and didn't really understand a lot else. Like the mission in Los Angeles, the station had gravitic communications equipment in touch with Chryse via the orbiting Hyadean relay system, and Cade watched Terran scientists still spellbound at the thought of interacting with counterparts light-years away.

"This makes the web look like Pony Express," one of them told him.

They were from a surprisingly wide range of places and backgrounds, brought in one way or another through influences of the cosmopolitan influx of the individualist-minded from Asia, Europe, and the Americas to what had already been a mixed region. There were also a lot more Hyadeans than Cade would have expected. Freem said that most had paid their own way privately to come to Earth in search of the independent way of living they had heard of that was new to them. Krossig felt there was more going on here than just a collaborative scientific center. It could be a microcosm of how an alternative might evolve to the imposed, top-down form of organized dealings between the two races that had taken root in the West.

But there was another side that was disconcerting. "China's policy," Susan said when she and Cade were with Freem in Freem's office, next to the gravcom room. "What we think is their real aim in leading the AANS—and we've talked to Hueng about it, and he agrees. They see the lineup of Hyadean and America-Europe as an attempt to preserve a Western-dominated economic order that should have died after the twentieth century and two world wars. They made the Hyadeans a symbol for the rest of the world to rally against. Beijing seems to think that now the U.S. has broken up, it's as good as over. All it has to do is deliver a knockout blow. They're underestimating what they could be up against. We could never beat Hyadeans by taking them on in a straight fight—if it ever came to that. Hudro understands that. But there's no need to. From the things we're hearing here, they're ripe for their own form of revolution. Why confront when you can undermine? With the right strategy, we can win enough of them over that their system caves in."

Cade was both intrigued and gratified. In effect, this was stating in other words what he himself, Vrel, Luodine, and others had also concluded. At the same time, he was mildly perplexed. "I agree with what you're saying," he told them. "But why are we going through all this? You sound as if you expect me to do something about it."

"I talked to Hueng," Freem replied. "His connections in Beijing go higher than you perhaps imagine. I'm sure he provides an efficient direct conduit back of anything of interest that goes on here." Freem held up a hand before Cade could respond, as if to say that was of no consequence. "But he also shares our concern. Naturally, he has made his superiors fully aware of the presence here of the American featured in the South American documentary, and the Hyadean officer whose story he helped narrate. Hueng put out some feelers, and it seems they would be interested in inviting you there. You have a chance to present our case maybe where it stands the most chance of having some effect."

Cade blinked. "You mean go to Beijing? Me?"

"While there's still a chance," Susan said. "You understand Hyadeans as well as anyone."

Cade didn't have to think too much about it. He was prepared for just about anything by now. "It would need Hudro there too," he told them. "The documentary wasn't only me. He'd carry a lot of weight there too."

"Then let's talk to Hudro," Freem suggested.

Hudro returned that evening from visiting an experimental school the Hyadeans had set up for teaching their way of science, which was proving to be a big hit with the local children. Cade and the other two put Hueng's proposition to him over beer and burgers in the station's canteen. "There are people in Beijing who have the power to make decisions that will affect many people, but I'm not sure they understand what a full-scale conflict might bring," Freem told him. "You are a former Hyadean military officer. Also, your experiences in South America give you insights that they do not share. If you really want to prevent what could happen, there would be your place to try."

Cade and Susan stared at each other somberly. Hudro gave Freem a long, searching look. Finally, he nodded. "Very well. I will go to Beijing with Roland and say what I know and what I think. Then I come back to you here. Yassem comes across from over ocean. Then we live here in Australia as Terrans. Is what we dream."

"That would be understood," Freem said.

◈ CHAPTER FORTY-SIX ◈

They stayed in Cairns a little over a week. Everything Cade saw reinforced his impression that it modeled on a small scale the way things could have been: Australian whites and blacks, Europeans, Asians, Americans, Hyadeans, working out their own ways of getting along.

Meanwhile, three Eastern Union nuclear supercarrier groups had put to sea in the Atlantic and were heading south, presumably to enter the Pacific via Cape Horn. The confrontation in Texas was heating up, with both sides using air support. Oil installations along the banks of the Houston ship canal were ablaze under artillery fire. A suburb of St. Louis had been hard hit by overshoots from an attack on an air base.

Then the formal invitation that Hueng had set up came through from Beijing. A farewell party that included Krossig, Freem, Susan, Hueng, and Tolly but which had grown significantly from the one that had greeted them accompanied Cade and Hudro to the airport, where they boarded a Chinese government executive jet sent with two officials from the Department of Foreign Affairs to collect them. The flight north lasted six hours and brought them to Beijing's International Airport, ten miles south of the city center. A white limousine flying the new pennant of the Democratic Republic of China from its hood, preceded by a police escort that seemed to delight in using its siren and lights to clear regular traffic grudgingly out of the way, conveyed them to the seventeen-story Beijing Hotel on Wangfujing Avenue, the busiest of Beijing's shopping streets, marking the eastern edge of the old Imperial City.

The atmosphere was very different from the colorful, provincial informality of Cairns. Even with the time together through the plane trip, the two officials who accompanied them seemed stiff and formal after the easygoing smiles of Tolly and Hueng. The talk was of things hypothetical and impersonal, grandiose schemes for the future, and how people would need to adapt and be educated to play their part—not of people simply allowing life itself to determine whatever kind of scheme took shape.

The same mood set the tone of the obligatory dinner that was given later in one of the hotel's private rooms. Cade had the feeling that in addition to paying the requisite courtesies, it was designed to send a political message. The ranks and numbers of the guests seemed calculated to convey that Cade and Hudro's presence, while acknowledged to be of interest, shouldn't be seen as carrying cosmic significance.

The speeches dwelt on political theory and abstract ideals. China might have made heroic efforts to change the form, but the old habits of thinking were still there, Cade thought as he nodded, smiled, and applauded. It was still the thinking of Earth, which created vast, imaginative symphonies of fantasy setting out what ought to be, and then tried forcing reality to fit. The community that had grown at Cairns embodied, even if it probably didn't understand, what Hyadean thinking had been before opportunism took advantage of it, and conformity stifled it—the thinking that had accepted reality as it is, and pointed the way to building starships; understood it the only way it could be understood: spontaneously, by living and expressing it.

It would have been an oversimplification to say even that Asia stood for one side or the other of the tussle that was dividing Earth. Should that be resolved, then Asia itself would break up into factions, as would other alignments that seemed stable for as long as the greater common threat persisted. Cade was beginning to see Terrans from something like the perspective that he imagined Hyadeans saw them. Whether one agreed with and liked what one saw depended on where in the Hyadean social order the viewing was from. The true dividing lines were complex. There were bulky, blue-to-gray "Terrans," and there were slender pink-to-black "Hyadeans." What better words might have more accurately described which of both groups stood for what was far from obvious.

The next day, they were taken on a tour of the city by four intense young people, two men and two women, polite, impeccably groomed, dressed, and mannered, all speaking English, and two, to Hudro's surprise and commendation, ably versed in Hyadean. One couple was from the public relations office of the Department of Foreign Affairs, the other from the Central Military Directorate. Beijing had been China's capital city since its founding in the Yuan Dynasty during the thirteenth century, and the layout was still dominated by its imperial past. The city proper, as opposed to the greater metropolitan area of modern times, consisted of two distinct sections: the square Inner, or Tartar City to the north, and adjoining it to the south, the more cosmopolitan and commercial, oblong Outer, or Chinese City. The Tartar City, dating from the earliest period, had originally been enclosed by walls forty feet high, removed only during the 1950s, in the Communist period. Within its fifteen-mile perimeter, it enclosed two other nested walled cities erected during the fifteenth-century Ming Dynasty: the Imperial City, with parks, temples, secondary palaces, and residences and offices of the nation's leaders; and within that the moated Forbidden City, containing the Imperial Palace with its 9,000 chambers, as well as audience halls and terraced courtyards extending over 250 acres, now maintained as a museum. Cade and Hudro stood in reverence at the shrines and temples of wooden beams, red clay walls, and massive, yellow tiled roofs with upturned eaves; admired the broad marble steps, carved stone lions, and ceremonial gates; and walked among the gardens with their ornamental lakes. But it was all an enclosed wonderland, a preserved relic of a past that had gone. When they came back outside, the humorless office blocks of glass and concrete, and imposing government buildings with brooding stone frontages pushing their way in and joining up like a rising tide around the shrinking islands of times gone by, reminded them that the serious business of the world at large and its future set the tone and the rhythm now.

The four young guides talked eagerly about plans for the future and a new society to be built. Yes, mistakes had been made in the past, but they had brought their lessons. In essence, the global conformity that the Hyadeans would impose on Earth if they were allowed threatened the same kind of exploitation that the West's imperialism had the century before. Eastern Asia had resisted successfully then, and it was natural and inevitable that it should form the nucleus of the resistance growing across the world today. Cade heard the total self-assurance that can come only from minds incapable of conceiving the possibility that they could be wrong. The belief that the future could be molded as desired determined planning, and guidance remained unquestioned. Only the plan had changed.

"You're still inventing the perfect society in your minds, then trying to figure out how to shape people to fit in with it," Cade commented to one of the young women.

"Yes. It gives purpose and requires dedication." She looked at him bright-eyed, as if waiting for a revelation. "Is there a better way?"

"Leave people the way they are, and accept whatever society comes out of it," Cade said. "Like the Hyadeans do with facts. You're making your society a theory. Just let facts and people be what they are, and lead to whatever becomes. That's the way to build starships."

But she couldn't make the connection. Her programming didn't include such a concept.

Cade and Hudro were subdued by the time they returned to the hotel. This was going to be tougher than they had thought. That evening, they dined less ostentatiously with a half dozen people from foreign affairs and military departments. Conversation focused on plying Cade and Hudro with questions about Hyadean-Terran relations in the former U.S.A., their impressions of the guerrillas in South America, and Hudro's experiences in counterinsurgency operations. The undisguised object was to gather advance material for the more senior representatives whom they would be meeting in the morning.

The meeting was held in a large, somber room of paneled walls with portraits of mostly forgotten military and political leaders in one of the government buildings off Tiananmen Square, a couple of blocks from the hotel. There were shelves of ornately bound books that Cade could never imagine anyone opening, brown leather armchairs arranged with side tables along the sides and in the corners, and a bench seat below the end window. Cade and Hudro sat at one end of a polished table forming the centerpiece. The chairman, who had been introduced as Brigadier General Zhao Yaotung of the Army, faced them from the far end. Arranged along the two longer sides were five other principal participants and their several secretaries and translators. Two microphones on the table and a video camera commanding the table from a corner indicated that the proceedings would be recorded.

The other five were: Madame Deng Qing, an undersecretary of the Directorate; Liu Enulai, military scientific adviser; Colonel Huia Xianem, of the Air Force; Abel Imarak, an Iranian liaison officer from the Muslim side of the AANS; and Major Charles Clewes, from a Canadian military mission that was apparently visiting. The Muslim and Canadian presence was revealing. It seemed that coordination within the AANS was farther advanced than Cade had realized.

Zhao began by working through a list of questions compiled from the things the deputies had raised the previous evening. He was heavily built with a saggy face, and spoke with a tired detachment, as if used to commanding an authority that was never questioned. His points covered tactics and logistics of the ground operations in South America, the morale of the guerrilla fighters there, their training, equipment, and attitudes toward receiving support from Asia. When the questions zeroed in on specifics of Hyadean weaponry and ways of countering it, Hudro reiterated what he had already told Cade: Although he had come to the conclusion that the Hyadean military intervention on behalf of the Globalist Coalition was wrong, he could not justify saying anything that might contribute to causing casualties or deaths among his own kind. He had left all that now, to begin a new life. Mme. Deng, sharp of face and manner, her hair tied in a bun, wearing a black skirt and jacket over a high-necked, lilac floral-pattern blouse, wanted to know, with a hint of disapproval, if that was the case, why had he come to Beijing? Because he had been asked to, Hudro said. He had accepted in the hope of finding some way to avoid escalation, not to promote it.

That seemed to open up the latent course that the meeting had been predisposed to follow. Zhao launched into a recitation that flowed smoothly and monotonously as if he had been through it many times, of why the time to strike hard and fast was precisely now. In North America, the Washington regime was still taken by surprise, its forces divided among themselves and disorganized, with reports of defections. The day before, at Amarillo, an entire Union armored brigade had come over to the Western Federation. Their drive into Texas was running down. Mexico was heading toward open civil war against cooperating, which blocked the threat of a Globalist outflanking move from the south for the time being.

Meanwhile, the Federation was solidly established across the north all the way to Lake Michigan. The underground front and irregulars that the AANS had been cultivating for years were emerging as an effective auxiliary arm of the regular forces. Alaska was pro-Federation, although formally maintaining a neutral stance, and Canada, for a long time seeking ways of easing itself from domination by Washington, was supportive. Zhao gestured across the table toward Clewes, as if by way of vindication. And on the European front, Russia had declined to follow the NATO Globalist alignment, securing Asia's position from the west. It was a time for decisiveness and vigorous action. Nothing worthwhile in history had ever been attained by half measures.

Imarak, the Iranian, took up the torch. "At this moment, China and the other Asian AANS nations have over five million men under arms. Our air forces started equipping for something like this a long time ago. Hawaii has agreed to cooperate in staging operations and is being reinforced." He looked at Zhao for a moment as if for approval to divulge further detail. The general returned a curt nod. Imarak continued, "With the transportation at our disposal right now, we can airlift five divisions with supporting armor and artillery into Mexico in ten days, followed within a month by landings to intercede in South America. With such a demonstration of support, the South American states will arise." Imarak waved a hand. "From the things you have said yourselves, the *people* are with us already! What's left? A few tottering governments that are rotten on the inside anyway. With the South gone, Canada denied, and the western two-thirds of the U.S.A. effectively part of the AANS already, the Washington-based Union reduces to an extension of the decaying remains of Europe. We can swing practically the rest of Earth behind us now. How could a few nonrepresentative states—states that do not have the support of their people—backing an alien power stand against that?"

Cade had a foreboding that they were not going to penetrate this kind of euphoria and overconfidence. "You're not allowing for the aliens," he said, nevertheless.

Liu Enulai, the scientific adviser chimed in, taking up the party line. "That is the reason why it is so important to move fast," He was lean and hollow cheeked, with close-cropped white hair and skin stretched tight over his skull, looking as if it were about to crack. "We are here *now*, already mobilizing, our weapons deployed. The Hyadeans won't have fully worked-out plans for intervention, nor any presence here, as yet, in numbers. They have large problems of logistics to deal with and vast distances to cross. But once they set a goal, they pursue it relentlessly and effectively. Therefore, delay is to our detriment and their benefit."

Cade shook his head, alarmed now at what he was hearing. "You can't take those guys on in a straight slugging match. It isn't a question of numbers. You've all been around for the last twelve years. You can figure out what they're capable of."

Hudro, beside him, was equally disturbed. "I think you underestimate," he told the company. "These weapons you see in South America are just the small-scales. Experiments, yes? Nothing crosses ocean under orbiting bombs and beam platforms to land in

South America. Saturation field turns air into fire, burns whole forest. Same forces that drive Hyadean starship bend space, pile desert into mountain, collapse city block like egg shell. I have seen in Querl wars. But Querl have defenses and understand."

Clewes, the Canadian, was looking worried—understandably: His country was next door to the developing battle zone, not six thousand miles away. Huia Xianem, the Chinese Air Force colonel, who had asked Hudro a lot of questions earlier, was nodding agreement solemnly. So not everyone was being carried away.

But the cautious were evidently not the ones calling the tune. "Indeed, that's the whole point," Mme. Deng answered. "To avoid such a direct conflict. Moving quickly now will eliminate the remnant of Terran power that depends on Hyadean support. By the time the Hyadeans are in a position to deploy significant force here, any reason to use it will have gone away."

"Is reinforcements arriving already from Chryse," Hudro started to point out, but Zhao brushed it aside.

"They still think in terms of the local-scale conflicts in South America to protect their elite in their palaces there," he said. "In taking things to a planetary scale, speed and surprise will be with us."

"Do you see Hyadeans intervening actively in your country, Mr. Cade?" Imarak asked, as if that made the point.

Maybe for the same reason that there weren't any Asians either, Cade thought to himself. Yet, anyway. Surely, the spectacle of Chinese troops landing in California to fight alongside Americans against other Americans was unthinkable. But similar enough things were written all through history.

"Is fine, maybe, while East Union army is in Texas and they still hope for help through Mexico," Hudro said. "But if Union gets in trouble, yes, you likely see Hyadeans fighting there then."

Zhao seemed unmoved. "You were in California how long ago, a few weeks?" he said to Cade. "CounterAction has been operating for two years there. Did you ever see any direct involvement of Hyadeans with the federal security forces?"

"They supplied equipment, advised on training . . ."

"But were they ever involved in *action*?"

Cade could only shake his head. "No." Zhao nodded, satisfied.

"And before they have time to get involved, Washington will have fallen," Mme. Deng said. "The Hyadeans' base of political collaboration will have ceased to exist. The only option open to them then will be to renegotiate their position here on new terms." She looked from Hudro to Cade. "Our terms."

Cade looked around at their faces. Clewes, and to a lesser degree Colonel Huia, were uneasy, but they weren't in control here. The rest were committed to their course and intractable. He'd thought that he and Hudro had been brought here for the benefit of their insight and experience. But it was clear that nothing they had to contribute was going to change anything. "What do you want from us?" he asked.

"Your face is known as the American in the movie," Zhao replied. "You and your former wife . . . What happened to her, by the way?"

"She's safe—back in California," Cade said.

"Oh, really? I'm glad." Zhao gestured at Hudro. "And here is the Hyadean whose story you told. We want to use you both in the same capacity here—at this crucial moment when we are about to launch our maximum effort. Talk to the people. Endorse our cause. Tell them that we are taking back our world from the aliens . . ." His gaze shifted to Hudro. "The human aliens as well as the ones who are propping up the Globalists."

So that was it. A public-relations campaign to promote the war. Cade sat back heavily in his chair. "You seem to disapprove, Mr. Cade," Mme. Deng commented. "Do you have some alternative strategy to suggest?"

Until the day before, Cade had thought he had. Especially after Cairns, he had entertained visions of sharing his new understanding of how both races were victims of exploitive minorities who together constituted the real common enemy; how the way to defeat them was not by taking on the Hyadean army but by winning over the mass of the Hyadean people. Why confront when they could undermine? Susan Gray had said.

Although dispirited by what he had heard, now that they were here, he had to try. He spoke with as much force as he could muster about the way Earth affected Hyadeans and how it awakened them to what they believed they could have been, and perhaps once had been. The way to defeat their economic imperialism lay in that direction, Cade said. Missiles and bombs could only bring disaster. Hudro followed, citing his own and Yassem's experience. Hyadeans didn't question, he pointed out. On the one hand that made their society easier to control; but it also meant that when they finally found out that they had been lied to, the effect would be incomparably more devastating than to any population on Earth—who pretty much took it for granted anyway. What had just happened to the U.S.A. could happen a hundred times more intensely across the whole of Chryse. "As Roland says, is the way you win here," he concluded. "Is not with bombs. That way, you, your cities—all goes is destroyed."

But it fell flat. Cade had told himself that surely the Chinese, if anybody, would respond to such a philosophy. Hadn't they themselves practically invented it? Or was the notion of fomenting a "people's" rebellion now part of a past that they considered themselves to have progressed beyond? But it was clear, even while Cade and Hudro were speaking, that the listeners who mattered were impervious. The leaders they served were already committed and were not going to be budged from their course. It was equally plain that Cade and Hudro would have no heart for the role that had been planned for them, and the matter was not pursued further. Thus, the meeting ended on a note of tacit withdrawal by both sides, each acknowledging that there was nothing further of mutual interest to be discussed.

Cade spoke briefly with Clewes in a corridor downstairs as they were leaving the building. "They're taking an awful gamble. I know you know it too. If Hudro's right, it's going to be a mess. Is there nothing that can be done?"

"Believe me, I've tried," Clewes told him. "But the high command back home are as bad. They've never had war in their country. It's something that happens in other places and in movies, or in exercises where nobody gets hurt. They're still academy kids playing a game. What they're letting themselves in for is beyond their comprehension.

✳ ✳ ✳

What was really going on came to him only later that evening, when he was sitting morosely with Hudro in the hotel bar. China was using the Hyadean presence as a justification for uniting a power bloc to end to the West's domination of the world's affairs. The Beijing leadership was set on a path that seemed to guarantee the destruction of America as a world leader and the probable demise of Europe, which would lose the Hyadeans their economic leverage. And then what, if a stable measure of autonomy from the Hyadeans was achieved? The AANS breaking up into rivalries—China and the Arab world, maybe; perhaps a fragmented China; a revitalized Russia—all emerging to take on each other? Would there ever be an end to it? Cade watched the other bar patrons and sipped his drink. He was starting to think like Marie.

The thought of her turned his mind back to the prospect of going home—he presumed there would be little further to detain him this side of the Pacific. "Tomorrow, it will be time to start making plans again," he said to Hudro. "I guess I go back to LA from here. Then I can make arrangements for Yassem to come over. What do you think you'll do? Go back to Cairns and wait there?"

Hudro seemed to have been thinking along the same lines. He answered without needing much time to consider. "Now, I am not sure what I do. Is not right that Yassem is there and I decide here where we go. Maybe I come back with you. Then Yassem and I make plans together about what we do."

"You're serious?"

"Yes, why not? Is better idea, yes?"

Cade reached over and gripped Hudro's arm. "I think it's a lot better," he said. "Things wouldn't be the same anymore without you around, Big Guy. I'll make arrangements with the office in the morning."

❁ CHAPTER FORTY-SEVEN ❁

Two days later, Cade and Hudro departed China on a Federation transport flight heading for California and carrying on its wings and fuselage the new, color-reversed insignia of a dark blue, five-pointed star on a white-circle ground. Due to uncertainties resulting from Union interceptors ranging out over the Pacific from bases in northwest Mexico, the flight was routed via Fairbanks, Alaska, and then down the coast of Canada. Washington had declared a war zone extending five hundred miles off the Federation's west coast, in which all aircraft and vessels were declared to be at risk of attack. This was drawn far enough north to affect the approaches to Vancouver, exacerbating the already volatile situation with Canada, already threatening to fire on further intruders into its air space. Airborne units from several South American states had landed in southern Mexico to aid government troops embroiled in the developing civil war, and an amphibious force was being embarked at Caracas in Venezuela. With its southern front stabilized, the Federation had gone over to the offensive with air attacks on Union bases and crossing points over the Mississippi.

The airfield at Fairbanks was busy with traffic landing and showed recently added antiaircraft defenses and dugouts, still being worked on in places. A tense but purposeful atmosphere prevailed in the terminal building during the four-hour stopover. There were a lot of evacuees from the fighting areas in the continental states to the south, some dispersing in Alaska, others en route to more distant destinations in Asia. One family that Cade talked to were from Chicago, which had become a scene of street-to-street fighting, with the Sears Tower and other high-rise observation points heavily damaged.

Communications were restricted, with military and official use getting priority. Apparently, there had been much attrition of Federation-controlled satellites. The Asians were rumored to be providing additional capacity, but so far it wasn't making up the difference. Cade was unable to put a call through to Marie at the house, although he did leave a message with Wyvex at the Hyadean mission saying they were on their way. The mission seemed to be functioning in some kind of autonomous role, independent of the official Hyadean presence in Washington. It seemed that Orzin was in charge, but Cade couldn't quite figure out where he stood amid the shifting politics.

The flight down the Canadian coast passed without incident. One of the crew told Cade that the plane was fitted with "special" equipment to confuse the Hyadean surveillance satellites. It implied a degree of cooperation from at least some faction of the aliens. Interesting, he and Hudro agreed between themselves. Hudro wasn't sure what to make of it.

They landed at March Air Force Base, thirty miles east of Los Angeles, at around the middle of the day following their departure from Beijing. It presented the same scene of recently initiated defenses and protective works that Cade had seen in Bolivia and Alaska. This time, however, he was startled to see evidence of actual attacks. The hulks of about a dozen burned-out aircraft had been bulldozed off the cratered apron area, which was still being cleared and repaired. Parts of the base facilities and hangars had been destroyed, with damage extending to surrounding buildings and houses. The regular control tower was demolished, and a temporary structure erected alongside the remains, while a dispersed annex of army tents and trailers kept other essential services functioning.

A bus painted Air Force gray took the arrivals to a section of the terminal buildings that had survived, where they went through the routine of presenting papers and answering questions for a clerk completing forms at a folding table. When it came to Cade and Hudro's turn, a tall woman with black hair piled high and tied in a band detached herself from the knot of people waiting in the background and came forward. It took Cade a moment to recognize her, in the slacks and unadorned zipper jacket that she was wearing over a military-style shirt, as Clara Norburn, once the fashion-conscious, upwardly mobile star of the former state governor's office. The last time Cade saw her, she had been talking about ways of marketing California's high-tech skills profitably on Chryse for the state's benefit. She nodded to an inquiring look from the clerk processing the papers and murmured, "Yes, these are the ones. It's been taken care of," then looked at Cade while the clerk initialed boxes and appended stamps. "Welcome back, Roland. You've been getting around. Into some trouble too, I see." Cade still had marks on his face, a remaining light dressing, and patches of regrowing stubble from the injuries he'd received in Brazil. "How is it looking?"

Cade grinned. "It's rumored that I'll live. You people haven't been exactly idle here yourselves. I leave you alone for a few weeks and look at the trouble you've gotten yourselves into already." One of the men in the group at the back was with Clara. Cade introduced Hudro. "What happened to the socialite?" He waved at Clara's appearance. "You look as if you've taken up driving a truck."

"I guess personal aggrandizement got put on the back burner. We've all got a common cause now." They began walking toward a double door at the end of the room.

"So what are you doing, specifically?" Cade asked.

"Coordinating with the mission in Lakewood. They're still operating, but not tied to the Washington office anymore—obviously."

"I know—I talked to Wyvex."

The first person Cade saw among the groups waiting on the far side of the doors was Marie, looking something like the way she had when he first saw her in Chattanooga; a lightweight patterned sweater, loose slacks, and suede hook-lace boots. He approached warily. They stared at each other. Even now, after everything, each seemed unsure of exactly what reaction would be appropriate. Her face was blotchy, still carrying angry black and red marks from the crash. None looked as if they would scar permanently. She was looking at him, seemingly equally unsure. . . .

And then she was pressed against him clinging, and his arms enveloped her, pulling her close. He smelled her hair, felt the slenderness of her body through the sweater. It was the first intimate contact they had experienced since their reunion. To his surprise, she was trembling. "I thought it was all over . . . before anything began," she whispered, raising her face. "And then Luke told us. It was days after you called him."

"He had reasons," Cade murmured.

"Yes, I know."

Luke was there too, Cade saw—waiting patiently, a faint and rare smile on his lips. And Yassem—whom Cade had barely met during the ill-fated helicopter flight. And Vrel and Dee were there too, clustering around Yassem and Hudro, who were hugging ecstatically, Yassem weeping. Just for a brief moment, the war was far away and forgotten.

They went out to one of the mission's Hyadean flyers, parked at the rear of the building among an assortment of cars, trucks, and military vehicles, and within minutes were airborne over Riverside. The freeway traffic was thin compared to what used to be normal. Clara said the gasoline restrictions were having a big effect. Southern Californian oil installations had been hit, and a tanker from Asia had been sunk off Santa Rosa Island the previous day. Cade saw damage to some of the freeway intersections, in one case amounting to total demolition and causing a crush of diverted traffic in the surrounding streets. Aircraft flying sorties up the coast from Mexico had been trying to take out key nodes of the road system with offshore-launched missiles, but so far with limited success. Links through the Rockies were under constant attack, the southern I-10 route to Phoenix and El Paso being completely cut. It would get a lot worse if the carrier groups now moving north in the Pacific got within striking range. There had been a lot of air combat over the Gulf.

For Cade, only just returned, it was all a new experience. Even with the tensions that had been mounting for years and the more recent instances of open domestic violence, he was unable to conceive jets carrying the insignia that had always meant USAF swooping in from the Pacific to attack targets in places like Anaheim or Pasadena, Bakersfield or San Diego. He looked down at the wreckage of an interchange that they were passing over. A swath of devastation extended through the nearby houses. "How can this be happening?" he asked Clara. "Isn't it obvious that there's been a corrupt administration on the other side for years? How can anyone there support it?"

"They're building a stronger America by allying with a superior power," she said. "We've been duped into becoming tools of the Asians. If we're not stopped, Chinese armies will be landing within a month and pouring through to make us a colony again."

Cade stared at her. "They believe that?"

"It's what they're being told. I'll run you some New York news clips and propaganda spiels when we get back."

"This *is* Roland I'm listening to?" Marie checked, still holding on to his arm.

From Luke and Vrel, Cade learned the story of Julia's untimely end. Marie had the grace not to say anything that might have sounded vengeful. Cade was dumbfounded. If he hadn't warned Luke, every one of those around him, Clara excepted, wouldn't have been there now.

Dee had moved out of travel agenting and was helping with school reorganization following separation from the federal system. It was only a small part, she told him, but everything counted. A contrast to the good-time-girl that he'd known, Cade reflected. The new feeling of dedication to something that mattered was affecting everybody.

Vrel asked about Krossig. Cade said he was fine and described his situation. "And what about the mission?" he asked. "Orzin's running things, right? So what's the status of the place now? I couldn't quite figure it out."

"I'm not exactly sure either," Vrel confessed.

"Do you still have the link to Chryse?"

"Not after Luodine tried to get her agency to put out that documentary there. They ran straight to the authorities. Xuchimbo cut us off in retaliation—and to avoid any further risk." Cade remembered that the gravity-wave converters in Earth orbit and the outer-Solar-System relays were controlled from the Hyadean General Embassy in Xuchimbo. Vrel shrugged. "Orzin is with us, trying to find a way around the censorship. If the real story got out on Chryse, it would create havoc. That's what we should be doing."

"Hudro and I tried to tell them in Beijing, but the hawks are in control there," Cade said. "What's the line here? What will Jeye do?" He meant William Jeye, who had become the FWA's president.

"He's under pressure to go along with the Chinese," Clara Norburn said. "You can see the argument: Washington has the backing of technically superior aliens. We're going to need as much of the world with us as we can get." Cade listened gravely. Clara sounded as if she almost bought it herself. She went on: "And so far things are looking good. I can't see the people in Sacramento throwing away the initiative here and expecting Chryse to cave in. Tanks and bombs, they understand. But the psychology and social dynamics of Hyadeans they've never met, light-years away?" She shook her head. "You might as well ask them to put their trust in voodoo."

The flyer landed at the house first to drop off Cade, Marie, and Luke, and also to introduce Hudro to the rest of the household. Then Hudro departed with the remainder for the mission, where he would be staying. Cade would join them tomorrow after resting from the journey. He showered and changed while Henry put away the bags, clothes, and other things Cade had acquired in New Zealand, Australia, and China. Marie had been using one of the guest rooms, and without Julia's effects the master suite was strangely empty and bare. But the atmosphere was a lot lighter.

He joined Marie downstairs and took a stroll with her around the house and the outside to see if much had changed during his absence.

Not a lot had. Henry had acted quickly before the rationing began to bite, so stocks of most things were good for the time being, apart from gas, which had been the first of the restrictions—although they wouldn't have to worry about running the Cadillac anymore. The neighborhood now had a siren to warn of incoming air attacks—in Newport Beach! External walls of sandbags had been put up around the garage and adjoining gym to make them into something of a blast shelter. Warren was worried about the vulnerability of the yacht, moored at the rear.

Despite the way they seemed to have found each other again, Cade was conscious of a vague uneasiness between himself and Marie when they sat down together for the evening meal. He had obtained this house since their splitting up, and he could tell that she was uncomfortable in the ostentatious surroundings. But there was more, also. It was as if there were something unseemly, almost, in the rapidity with which it had happened. Marie had been there at one time, and then gone; then there was Julia; and now Julia was gone and Marie back, it seemed virtually instantly. Thousands of miles away in South America, everything had been too different to matter. But here the change was too immediate. He would have felt more comfortable to have been alone for a while before Marie moved back into his life again. He sensed that Marie felt it too. But the mood didn't have time to take root. A string of old acquaintances began dropping by to say hi, having heard that Cade was back.

Anita Lloyd, from Norm Schnyder's law firm, had previously been an expert on reinvesting currency earned from cheap Hyadean imports in high-profit land deals. Now she was involved in rebuilding money, credit, and the trading system in conjunction with Asian markets, following the severance of ties to traditional East-Coast-based financial institutions and the issuing of its own currency by the Bank of California. Norman himself was away in Sacramento, working on emergency labor and housing allocation—to conserve fuel, thousands of people were being relocated closer to work. Anita joked that the firm was learning to do things that needed to be done, without worrying about billing. Her own personal million had been wiped out in the currency transition. To Cade's surprise, she didn't seem to care all that much. On reflection, she told him, she didn't really like that person that she used to be.

Damien Philps, the art dealer, had suspended business and volunteered his labor services. George Jansing, who used to sell rare Terran skills for high Hyadean profits, was involved in dispersing aircraft production. Homeowners were taking in refugees from the war zones. Whole new attitudes were being shaped. Despite the dangers and inconveniences, a lot of people said it gave life a purpose that had been lacking before. "Obsessive money grubbing and alienation," was how Jansing put it.

"Let's see how they sound when things start getting really tough," Luke commented to Cade dourly.

Later, the sirens wailed, and they all moved into the gym to be on the safe side; but nothing happened.

After the all-clear sounded and the visitors had gone, Cade helped Marie move her things out of the guest room. There was an interval of unspoken awkwardness, of fussing too long to arrange hangers in the closet, or dwelling pointlessly on snippets of the evening's talk and trivia dredged from the past. But closeness dissolved their misgivings. As Cade lay falling asleep, holding her, for the first time in all the turbulent years he could remember, he knew peace. Marie burrowed into the sheets and nuzzled her face against his chest.

"Cold nose," he mumbled drowsily.

"It's Mole Woman."

In rediscovering Marie, Cade had finally discovered himself.

❀ CHAPTER FORTY-EIGHT ❀

News the next morning was that Washington was threatening action against the Canadian supply routes. The rebellion in Mexico was spreading southward into the Central American states. Little was said of events on the Midwest and Southwest fronts. Wyvex sent one of the mission's flyers to collect Cade and Marie from the house. Again, damage was visible at several of the freeway interchanges and around LAX. Clara had said the previous evening that commercial flights over the Pacific had ceased for the time being. The Canada-Alaska route was being used for Asia.

On arriving, they found that a cordon of barriers and soldiers backed by military vehicles had been placed outside the mission's perimeter fence. Facing them were groups of demonstrators numbering maybe several hundred, displaying banners and placards. They were orderly as of the moment but seemed surly and restless. Cade couldn't pretend to be totally surprised.

Inside, they were greeted by Wyvex, still wearing his Navajo patch. He was pleased and intrigued to meet Marie at last. Vrel was out at UCLA with Mike Blair. They would be back later. "What's going on outside?" Cade asked as they walked through into the building.

"Some anti-Hyadean feeling is surfacing. The documentary you two sent from South America didn't help. Some Eastern units have been using Hyadean weapons in Arkansas. It makes us all the enemy to some people." Cade nodded. It was pretty much as he had guessed.

The elaborate security procedures at reception were gone—a sign of independence from the Hyadean Washington office, Cade presumed—and Wyvex conducted them straight through to the open-plan work areas with their cream-painted walls and dull metal furnishings. On the way, they talked about events that had taken place with both of them since Cade's departure for Atlanta, including another account of Julia's demise. Cade saw that many of the screens were shut down, and none of those that were functioning showed the kinds of scenes that he remembered from direct connections to Chryse and the other Hyadean worlds.

There were more people about than had been usual before—Hyadean and Terran. Seemingly, the mission had become a collecting center for stray Hyadeans left in the western half of the country after the secession. Also, to ease travel problems, a number of Terrans who worked here had moved in. They took an elevator to the top floor. Wyvex showed Cade and Marie into Orzin's office, and then left.

Orzin greeted them with smiles that made his unusually rounded Hyadean features look rubbery. He had shed his tunic top for a tan, casual jacket which he wore open over a shirt with a low-tone colored design. But it was colored—the Hyadean equivalent of a Wall Street banker showing up at the office in a beach shirt. Of course, Orzin was delighted to meet Marie. They went over a summary of the same salient events that Wyvex had gone through.

"So what exactly is going on here, Orzin?" Cade asked when they had settled down. "It seems like you've taken over the mission. Where does it stand? Are you some kind of independent, one-building, Hyadean nation state now, or what?"

"We are Chryse," Orzin replied.

Cade shot Marie a puzzled look. She shook her head. "What do you mean?" he asked Orzin.

"We shall find again what Chryse once was. It will begin here." Orzin spread a pair of pudgy, blue, oversize hands. "Here in this mission. Not, as you say, a one-building nation-state. A one-building planet! When I first came here from Chryse, I saw only the things that confirmed what we had been told. Earth was disintegrating in chaos and disorder. We had come to save it by introducing our system of organization and discipline. Of course, there were stubborn elements of the old structure that would not give up their traditional powers so easily. But, with the cooperation of the more enlightened interests that you have termed the Globalist Coalition, they could be induced to come around." He held up a hand before either Cade or Marie could say anything.

"However, that wasn't the way things were. This system that Hyadeans have been conditioned to serve is a lie by which a layer of social parasites drains them of everything they produce. They do it by convincing them of the need to subjugate themselves to a higher authority that knows and represents the greater good of all. In doing so, they rob them not only of the right to think as individuals, but even of awareness of their ability to. And so they are made into expendables: sacrificial objects to enrich the lives of others.

"What I began to see on Earth after I had been here some time was not what I had been told to see. I saw a world of *individuals*, with different ideas and choices about how they wanted to live their lives. And yes, at times those differences caused disagreement and strife. But it was not a pathological world destroying itself in chaos; it was world of variety and vigor asserting its nature: the right to be *free*." Orzin showed his hands in a despairing gesture. "Yet in spite of all that, the same forces that enslaved Chryse are operating here. And *those* are the forces that we have been allying with. Other Hyadeans see it too. That is why Luodine and Nyarl are here. And Hudro and Yassem . . . and many others."

Cade frowned at the top of the desk with its several displays, rewritable paper pads with strings of Hyadean characters, and assortment of other objects, the function of all of which was not obvious. He feared that Orzin was oversimplifying. Earth's history showed a far less consistent and universal dedication to such values than the picture he was painting. . . . But if that was what he was seeing, Cade wasn't about to muddy the issue now.

Marie was all attention, looking as if she wanted to believe what she was hearing but just couldn't see it. "But you just told us, you're a one-building operation. Do you really think you can change anything?" she said.

"Us, no. But the people of Chryse can. The people of all the Hyadeans worlds . . ." Orzin waved a hand high, as if inviting them to visualize it.

"We were talking about that yesterday," Cade said. "It's what Hudro and I tried to get across in Beijing."

Orzin nodded. "I know. Hudro told me. Hyadeans don't question what they see and what they are told. That was what made them exploitable on such a scale. But that same fact means they won't tolerate deception. Luodine saw the same thing."

"But what can just a few of you *do*?" Marie asked again.

Orzin gestured as if it should have been obvious. "Show them the deception. Tell the real story to Chryse. That's her business."

"But Xuchimbo controls all the channels," Cade said.

"The official channels, yes," Orzin agreed. "But who said we have to use those?" He turned one of the flatscreen pads around on the desk and pushed it across, at the same time uttering commands. An image appeared that Cade and Marie had seen before in New Zealand and China: themselves, narrating the documentary recorded at Tevlak's house in Bolivia. It took Cade a moment to register that there was something different. The sound had been dubbed. The voices he heard were speaking in Hyadean. He looked up, nonplussed. "I don't understand. What's going on?"

"That's you two," Orzin said needlessly. "You know the item. This is a recording of a version of it that went out *across Chryse* last night!" He looked from one to the other, noted their incredulous looks with evident satisfaction, and went on before they could ask, "Luodine tried to get her agency to put it out, but the people in charge there wouldn't do it. Too obedient to the system. So Yassem decided that if there was no way through the official net, she'd go around it. She used our facilities here to access the Xuchimbo system, and piggybacked a coded message on their outgoing trunk beam that the Querl intercepted. *They're* doing the broadcasting for us!"

Marie stared. "Querl? You mean the rebel worlds?"

"Yes! Amazing, isn't it! That was several days ago now. The Querl have positioned an arc of their own relays somewhere outside of Earth—they can't come as far in as orbit, since the Chryseans control near space. So we have our own link now. We lose contact for a little under ten hours each day."

Cade was having trouble taking it in. "Querl?" he repeated. "You mean they've showed up *here* . . . in our Solar System?"

"Well, they're out there somewhere, anyhow," Orzin replied, waving a hand vaguely. "And you can bet the Chryseans are out there looking for them too. But it's a lot of space to get lost in. And they have sophisticated ways of deploying decoys and switching the incoming return signals around to make it impossible to get a sure fix on where the relays are."

Cade and Marie looked at each other, stupefied. *They* were being broadcast around alien star systems light-years away . . . ?

"And you two aren't the only news that's going out. Luodine and Nyarl have been collecting material from all over." Orzin voiced more commands in Hyadean. The image on the screen changed to show Luodine speaking to the camera, and then soldiers and rescue workers pulling dazed and bleeding figures from wrecked vehicles scattered and upended all ways in front of a background of burning buildings. "A refugee column hit by an air strike near Minneapolis," Orzin commented. It was followed by an aircraft's gun-camera view of missiles flaming away and bursting among trucks halted on the approach to a pontoon bridge. Figures were jumping out, fleeing, falling. . . . "FWA fighter-bombers attacking one of the Mississippi crossing points." Then there was Luodine again, superposed on a desert scene littered with knocked-out armor. "Aftermath of a tank duel south of Odessa, Texas. There's lots more." Orzin looked across at Cade and Marie pointedly—as if this could have significance out of all proportion to appearances. "According to the first reports we're getting back from Querl sources, it's creating a sensation back home. This is the first time anyone has reported anything direct from the other side of what's been happening on Earth. We must be doing something right. Reactions from the Chrysean government are furious. Naturally, they're denouncing it all as Querl propaganda and fakery. But people on Chryse are taking notice. Luodine's face is familiar there. They know she talks straight." Orzin wagged a finger. "But that's not all. She doesn't want to just sit here passing on news that comes in. Her style has always been to go out herself and find it. She's persuaded the Air Force to provide her and Nyarl with a jet to turn into a mobile studio. You'd have to hear her enthusiasm to believe it. I think she has finally discovered what she really wants to do."

In an NBC news studio at the Rockefeller Center in New York, Casper Toddrel gazed somberly at the camera showing "live" and completed the address that he had prepared as part of a public relations effort being coordinated from the White House. "It will be a painful duty. It will not be a pleasant duty. But it is a necessary duty. For as long as it takes, we cannot speak of these places as belonging to America anymore. They have become an extension of foreign power into this continent. The next step will be a bridgehead for invasion. We, in the East at this hour, stand as the last bastion of defense for the values that America has always stood for. The people in California and Oregon, New Mexico and Montana are not our enemy. The enemy is the corrupt gang of traitors and opportunists who have turned Sacramento into a provincial capital of China. I ask you all to stand by us and our Hyadean allies to reverse this tragic aberration that had befallen us. We can, and we will, not only bring all of America back into the fold, but build out of it a stronger and more united America than has ever existed. A new United States, purged, reformed, revitalized, fit not only to assume again its rightful place as leader among the nations of this world, but to establish this world as a full and equal partner, enjoying all due rights and dignity, in the wider community of our newfound interstellar cousins." Toddrel paused to let his audience contemplate the vision, then nodded solemnly. "Thank you."

The red camera light went out. "Thanks, Mr. Toddrel," the set manager called from behind the lights. "That's was good. That's it. You're done."

Toddrel collected together the notes he had laid on the desk, got up, and headed for the door. Ibsan, his bodyguard, saw him through the glass wall of an adjacent monitor room and came out.

"Mr. Toddrel. You'd better see this." Ibsan nodded back over his shoulder.

"What is it?"

"Flash just coming in from Bolivia. That Hyadean mining center at Uyali. Half their military base down there blew up. It's like it got nuked."

"*Jesus. . . .*"

Toddrel followed Ibsan into the room, which was lined on one side with consoles and screens. Three of the operators were grouped in front of one showing a scene panning across the wreckage and carnage of whole blocks of peculiar Hyadean building-block architecture shattered and twisted into grotesque shapes, with a pall of smoke hanging over the background. Crews from emergency vehicles had started bringing out survivors, while more flyers and Terran-built helicopters descended into view from above. A voiceover was talking excitedly and breathlessly.

"About fifteen minutes ago," one of the operators commented, seeing that Toddrel had joined them. "The whole back end of the place just went up. From the accounts, it sounds as if it was the armory. It was loaded. A shipment of Hyadean ammo and stuff just arrived from orbit. They're counting the death toll in hundreds already." Toddrel watched grimly for a few minutes, but there was nothing of further significance to be learned. He caught Ibsan's eye and jerked his head curtly in the direction of the door as a sign for them to leave. They stopped by a door at the end of a corridor of offices.

"It had to be those new remote-detonatable munitions," Ibsan murmured. "Somehow the wrong people got access to the codes. I don't know what kind of a can of worms it opens up, but I figured you ought to know right away."

Toddrel nodded, still thinking frantically. "You did right, Earl."

He should never have agreed to letting Drisson look into it, he told himself. There were too many factions at large, too many conflicting interests. The opportunities for betrayal should have made the risks unthinkable. In normal circumstances he would never have condoned it. He had no idea who the perpetrators might have been. The Asians or one of their breakaway groups? Part of the guerrilla front? Some other lunatic sect? Drisson himself for some reason? Somebody Drisson was mixed up with, who had an agenda of their own? . . . But whatever, there was one person who was sure to be high on everybody's suspect list.

Roger Achim, the program's producer, came through from the set, accompanied by a couple of assistants. "Everything all right, Mr. Toddrel?"

"Yes, just fine," Toddrel responded mechanically.

"Good, good."

"Oh, one thing."

"Yes?"

"Is there somewhere private that I could use? I have to make a confidential call urgently."

"Sure. Susie, find Mr. Toddrel an empty office along there somewhere, would you?"

Minutes later, Toddrel was confronting the blue-purple features of Gazaghin, the Hyadean military commander in Washington. He had heard the news, and his mood was murderous.

"I just wanted to assure you personally that I had absolutely no knowledge of this appalling—"

Gazaghin interrupted. "Don't waste the breath, Toddrel. I don't believe for long time anything you say. It makes no difference now who does this, in any place. I warned you. Now it's not your war now."

"What do you mean?"

"Is too much. We trust to let Terrans in charge. Look what happens. Now there is protest risings and angry questions all over Chryse. We have orders from our government to put the stop. We control now."

"But it's not within their jurisdiction to," Toddrel objected. "You are still aliens within a sovereign territory. . . ."

Gazaghin slammed a hand down on the surface where he was speaking. "When Hyadean dead are hundreds, it *is* our jurisdiction!" he bellowed. "When illegal propaganda pictures are flooding our world, it's our jurisdiction. Your President Ellis has just signed the order. This country's armed forces are now under my command."

◈ CHAPTER FORTY-NINE ◈

Cade decided that the luxurious Newport Beach mansion offended him. He instructed Henry to have the valuables and personal effects packed and put into storage, and the house made available to the authorities for housing evacuees. The influx would improve the tone of the neighborhood, he told Marie. As for the yacht, Warren was to place it at the disposal of the military for the coastal transportation fleet being hurriedly expanded. He and Marie would move into quarters at the mission. Luke elected to come too, retaining his position as Cade's right-hand man for the duration. Besides putting them close at hand for the work there, it would ease traveling. Marie preferred this arrangement.

Luodine planned to tour the front-line areas, rear bases, refugee centers, hard-hit zones, collecting original material that the mission would send back to Chryse along with whatever could be got from other sources—the fruition of the idea that had begun forming in her mind during her experiences in Segora. The plane that the Air Force provided turned out to be a C22-E twin turbofan military airlift VIP transport, normally carrying sixteen passengers, but in this instance fitted out as a flying communications post. It arrived with a pilot, copilot, and technical sergeant for support at Edwards Air Force Base in the high desert above Palmdale. The base had been hit by intermediate-range conventional missiles launched from over the Rockies but was still flying operations. Yassem flew out there with Hudro and Nyarl in one of the mission's flyers to meet the crew, brief them on the mission, and check over the equipment before tomorrow, when the team was due to depart. Since Hyadean flyers were few and in demand, after being dropped off at Edwards, they sent it on to Newport Beach to collect Cade, Marie, and Luke, and take them to the mission with the belongings they were bringing from the house.

Meanwhile, Luodine was organizing the mission's communications room as a clearing center for forwarding despatches to Chryse. A Colonel Nacey from FWA military intelligence, along with a small staff, was attached to the operation to ensure that sensitive information was not released prematurely. The main item that she had not mentioned in her outgoing reports—although the Union commanders who needed to know would be aware of it from their own sources in any case—was that a mixed AANS force under a Chinese flagship had sailed from Hawaii to intercept the carrier groups moving north, now approaching the equator west of the Galápagos Islands. The officers on Nacey's staff called the situation "Midway in reverse."

But it was becoming clear that the move from Hawaii was just part of a far larger and more audacious plan only now beginning reveal itself. Luodine sat, stunned, alongside Nacey, while on a screen in front of them a spokeswoman from Beijing summarized the action that had been taking place since early that morning. Confused reports had been coming in from various sources about air drops in Mexico and fighting along the Panama Canal Zone, but this was the first coherent account linking it all together. President Jeye himself had been notified officially only within the previous hour—although Nacey thought it likely that he and his military commanders had known privately before then.

"Scattered resistance only is being encountered at Acapulco. We have already commenced air operations farther to the south, supporting the landings north and south of the canal. The main Hyadean defenses were neutralized before they could come into effective operation. . . ."

"Wyv, you'd better get Orzin here," Nacey told Wyvex, who was hovering behind. "This is unbelievable." Wyvex tried calling Orzin on his communicator, failed to get a response, and left. Luodine thought of calling Nyarl at Edwards with the news, but then decided to let it ride. He would find out soon enough.

The Chinese had intervened in Central America with a series of long-range airborne landings and support strikes to secure air bases. So far, they were down at six locations in Mexico and two in Costa Rica, with planes refueling and flying missions from one of them already. In addition, forces had been dropped on both sides of the Panama Canal, clearly with the object of cutting the reinforcement and supply connection from the Caribbean to the Union carrier groups in the Pacific. In what sounded like an incredible series of blunders on the part of the defending Hyadeans, the attackers, moving fast and with sound jungle training, had achieved almost total surprise, in some instances overrunning opposition still flailing around, trying to get dressed. In others, the cumbersome and complicated Hyadean heavy weapons had been seized before they could be brought to bear, and spearheads had reached the shores of Gatun Lake, separating the two sections of the canal, in at least four places. With the defending airfields taken out preemptively by undetected sea-skimming cruise missiles, an entire Union supply squadron and battle group trapped between Colón and Balboa were shooting it out against shore-based missiles and guns that were becoming more effective by the hour, and which would soon be augmented by local air support.

Michael Blair hurried in, looking flustered, and came through between the Terrans and Hyadeans who were watching. "What's happening? I heard there was something big," he said. Luodine turned from the console and summarized. "Oh my God!" Blair breathed.

"Whoever dreamed this up isn't someone I'd want to play poker with," Nacey said. "They're stretched out to the limit—hanging on until the fleet from Hawaii gets within support range." He pointed at a situation display map on one of the walls. "Obviously, the aim is to get viable land-based air flying from Mexico to pincer those carriers that are coming up. If they pull it off . . ." He drew a breath, shook his head, and left it at that.

Wyvex reappeared with Orzin in tow. Luodine and Nacey repeated the story. By this time, the Chinese spokeswoman was reporting Mexican government troops protecting Union air bases changing sides and opening them to the rebels.

Luodine was excited. The entire Union position in the south seemed to be collapsing. Reports since yesterday had described them as all but halted in Texas, with armor and other units standing down or coming over to the Federation en masse. She stared at the wall screen showing the map and saw the Pacific Coast secure, Alaska a part of the Federation in all but declaration, Canada on the verge of allying formally. All that was propping the Union up now was their Hyadean backing. And she and the others at the mission were revealing its true nature to the people of Chryse already. Surely it couldn't last much longer now.

Only then did she become aware of a shrill tone emanating from one of the consoles across the room. Orzin turned his head sharply in alarm; at the same instant, an eerie wail started somewhere outside the building, rising in pitch and volume. A screen illuminated, showing a map of the Los Angeles coast with an inset of Hyadean symbols. On it was a line beginning from a point twenty miles or so out in the ocean and passing right over the mission's location on Carson Street. The line bore a red dot moving steadily inland. A Hyadean voice in public-address mode filled the room. "Alert! Alert! Submarine missile launch detected thirty-one kilometers, bearing two-twenty degrees. Three of them, heading directly at us. Estimated impact forty-two seconds. Evacuate immediately!" Wyvex translated for the Terrans, his voice cracking.

Luodine felt her mouth turn dry. Orzin turned a dazed face to the room. "Get out of the building as fast as you can. Keep it orderly. Use the stairs at both ends. . . ."

Even as he spoke, figures were sliding up out of chairs and converging toward the door, some forcing to get ahead, others refusing to yield as survival instincts took over; a few remained unmoving, transfixed in disbelief. Luodine found herself being drawn forward into the crush pressing to get through the door, conscious of a raw smell of fear all around, somehow being contained just short of panic. Somebody behind her was whimpering, shoving her in the back. Luodine jabbed back savagely with a elbow. There was an eternity of jostling, pushing, frightened voices, some blows. Then she was out in the corridor, running with the bodies around her, colliding with others coming out of doorways, running again, through onto crowded stairs . . . even though she knew already that they were never going to make it.

Luodine was still on the stairs between the third and second floors when the three missiles hit their target precisely at five-second intervals. Sending three had been insurance against possible defenses that had failed to materialize. Each of them carried a Hyadean catalyzed hydrogen warhead of power intermediate between high explosive and nuclear, and was capable of taking out a city block.

The flyer was over Seal Beach, when the synthetic voice of the vehicle's supervisory AI issued from the forward panel. "*Attention, please. Situation irregularity. We have lost our destination beacon and ground coordination transmission. Request instructions.*" Cade, startled, looked at Marie, then across at Luke. Luke shook his head to say he didn't know what they were supposed to do, either.

"Er . . . you'd better give us more detail," Cade said.

"Sys on," Luke hissed.

"Oh, right." Dialogues with the system needed to be prefixed. "System on. More detail," Cade said.

"*We were in contact with Hyadean traffic control located at the mission. Contact has been lost. Attempts to recontact the mission on other channels have failed. What do you want me to do?*"

Cade looked at Luke and Marie again, as if for inspiration. "What options do we have?"

"*Continue under manual guidance to the same destination. Alternatively, go somewhere else.*"

"We don't know how to fly this," Cade said.

"*I can fly and land it. You just supply voice directions.*"

"Okay, let's do that. . . . Continue to the mission."

"*Acknowledged.*"

Marie was staring ahead through a view section of the nose. "Roland," she whispered, clutching his arm.

"What is it?'

"*What is what?*" the AI queried, still toggled to dialogue.

"System off," Cade said. There was no need to ask Marie again. Following her horrified gaze, he could already see the pall of smoke hanging over the skyline ahead. Although still five miles away, it had to be the mission.

"Oh, Jesus Christ," Luke breathed.

They stared, numbed and speechless, as the flyer closed over the houses and boulevards. In places below them, lines of cars could be seen pulling over, making way for police and emergency vehicles already speeding in the direction of whatever had happened. The phone in Cade's pocket emitted a call tone. He drew it out, still staring ahead woodenly. "Cade."

"Roland, you're okay!" It was Dee. "Thank heavens! We thought you might have been there already."

"It's Dee," Cade murmured to the others. Then, louder, "Almost. We're on our way, just a couple of miles south. What's happened?"

"I don't know. I'm at Anaheim, at work. Vrel's here too. He stopped by for lunch. There were these huge explosions toward the coast. We heard them from here. Nobody at the mission is contactable. Something terrible has happened there. . . ."

"Vrel's with her. Nobody's answering from the mission." There was no longer any wondering about why. The belt of demolished houses, shattered office towers, and streets choked with overturned cars, rubble, and debris was coming into view. Beyond, where the mission building had been, was just a crater partly visible through hanging dust and smoke. "Look, Dee, we're just coming in on our approach now."

"What can you see? Is it the mission?"

Cade had to swallow to prevent his voice from choking. "Bad news, Dee. Real bad. It's been taken out. I mean right out. There can't be any hope for anyone who was in there. Tell Vrel I'm sorry."

"*Terrain doesn't match records,*" the flyer's AI reported. "*Unable to execute stored landing profile. Request instructions.*"

"Dee, I have to go. We'll call you right back as soon as we know any more. You might want to call Hudro and the others out at Edwards. At least we know they're okay."

"Vrel's talking to them now. . . . Okay, Roland, we'll be waiting to hear from you."

Cade directed the flyer to a section of street where several police cars were parked haphazardly in a cluster, another visible from above, approaching a block away. Several uniformed figures were in a group, trying to take in the situation, while others ran to check a partly collapsed house alongside, and another directed an ambulance that was just drawing up. The surroundings looked as if they had been combed by a giant lawn rake. There had been a grotesque rain of bodies—probably the protestors who had been picketing the mission. The police in front of the cars looked up as the flyer descended; two of them waved it toward a clear area on one side. "Forward slow, two o'clock," Cade instructed. "Lower. . . . Hold it here. Take it straight down, vertically."

"*Confirm landing vicinity free of personnel and obstructions?*" the AI requested.

"You're clear."

"*Landing and terminating.*"

"System off."

It was worse outside the insulating confines of the flyer's cabin. Stinging dust and fumes assailed Cade's eyes and nostrils. Sirens whooped and howled from the surrounding streets; police radios cackled. In the lulls between, he could hear screams and terrified shouting not far away.

There was little more to be learned at this juncture. The officers had been among the first to arrive. None of them knew what had happened. One speculated that something had come down from orbit. They took details of the Hyadeans at Edwards and Anaheim and how they could be contacted, of Cade's involvement with the mission, and relayed the information to headquarters. One reported to Cade that Clara Norburn had just heard the news and was on her way. Meanwhile, a helicopter had appeared and was circling overhead; more ambulances, a string of fire engines, and a truck filled with soldiers arrived. A police mobile command post began setting up to coordinate rescue and casualty-clearing operations among the surrounding city blocks. But it was already plain that nobody within the mission building itself or its close vicinity could have survived.

Cade called for Hudro and Dee to get over and gave the location. By the time they arrived in Dee's car, the scene resembled a small war. Clara Norburn appeared with staff and military liaison people in a flotilla of cars and escorts; shortly afterward, a National Guard helicopter touched down, bringing Hudro, Yassem, and Nyarl from Edwards.

What they should do next was not obvious. Going back to the house wouldn't address the immediate issue of four Hyadeans who no longer belonged anywhere. Clara arranged for them all, including Cade, Marie, and Luke, to be taken to her department at the municipal offices near the Civic Center. Vrel was still in shock and unable to communicate much that was coherent. So far, just he and five others who had been elsewhere for various reasons were all that was left of the Hyadean West Coast Trade and Cultural Mission.

◉ CHAPTER FIFTY ◉

They sat despondently around a staff room that had been put at their disposal until something could be worked out. Luke had gone to call Henry and tell him to put a hold on clearing the house in case they were about to receive some unexpected house guests. A meal had been brought in but nobody had touched very much of it. Only now were the Hyadeans recovering their faculties to a degree anywhere within sight of normality.

"Just when we had achieved what Luodine was working for," Nyarl said, staring at the carpet. "It was done to shut down the channel to Chryse. So we must have been having effect there. Now she will never know."

"She should have lived long enough to have known," Yassem agreed.

"Is Chryse that has problem, but missiles are from Terran submarine," Hudro said. "So who commands this? These politics are all double faces."

Vrel just sat, holding Dee's hand. He had remarked several times that if he hadn't decided to stop at her office on the spur of the moment on his way back to the mission, he would have been there too.

Cade sat to one side, saying little. Marie was with Clara in Clara's office, following the reports coming in via Sacramento. For once, he didn't know what to say. Despite the time he had spent with Hyadeans, he didn't have any privileged insight into the inner workings of their the minds. And just at the moment, he was having enough trouble with the conflicting thoughts welling up from the deeper recesses of his own mind.

News that afternoon had been that the tide in Texas had turned, with Federation and turned-around Union tank columns reoccupying Forth Worth and Austin. The lines in front of Houston were declared open. Units defected from the Union cause were moving back toward the Mississippi, while growing agitation among the Southern states was rumored to be destabilizing the rear of the crumbling Union. Cade wondered if the Chinese in Beijing might have had it right all along when they insisted that the Union would cave in before the Hyadeans could intervene effectively. They had the professional military staffs, after all, and should know. Cade didn't. In that case, his fears based on the things he had seen had been wrong. Okay, he could live with that. And Hudro's convictions, based on his own direct experiences, were wrong too. With a slightly bigger push, Cade could accept that. But something still didn't feel right about it.

If the Washington regime's situation was really that precarious, then they would surely know it too. What didn't feel right was that they should choose such a moment for the strike against the mission, which didn't affect the military situation but could easily have the result of outraging the Hyadeans and dividing them to the degree that effective intervention became impossible, just when the East appeared to be in most need of it. It didn't make sense.

Or was he simply refusing to face that everything the Hyadeans he had come to know as friends had striven for, and finally achieved at the cost of today's tragedy, had been for nothing? For if the collapse of the Union was imminent with or without any action on the part of the population of Chryse, then all that Luodine, Orzin, Wyvex, and the others had hoped to bring about was happening anyway.

Cade's phone beeped. It was Marie. Her voice was low but tense. "Roland. I'm still with Clara. Something's come in that you ought to hear about. Can you get up here?"

"Sure." He cut the connection, hesitated, and then stood up. "They want me for something," he said to the Hyadeans. As he walked to the door, he was conscious of their stares following him. He had the strange feeling of abandoning them, as if they were his charges. It was ridiculous.

Clara's office was on the floor above. With the two women were Chester Di Milestro, a Los Angeles-based aide to President Jeye, and Major Gerofsky from the military liaison, both of whom Cade had met earlier. One of the screens on the wall next to Clara's desk showed the east central Pacific with colored lines plotting courses of naval units. Another held a frozen head-and-shoulders picture of an officer with lots of braid on his cap, addressing the camera. "It's big, Roland," Clara said without preamble. "Admiral Varney—commander of the lead carrier force. He's defected."

Cade looked from one to the other. "What do you mean?"

Di Milestro answered. "He issued a proclamation two hours ago, saying he took an oath to defend Americans, not attack them. If the other carrier groups continue on their present course, he will consider it his duty to oppose them with all the force at his disposal. It means he's with us."

Gerofsky waved a hand at the map. "Look—the red there. Varney has turned his force ninety degrees. He's steaming east, converging with the Asian fleet from Hawaii to head them off. With land-based air from Mexico, that sews it all up."

Marie came across and gripped Cade's arm. Her face was ecstatic. "Isn't it incredible news, Roland! You heard about Texas. Now they're expecting Canada to come in at any moment—close the northern edge all the way to the Atlantic. It would *have* to be all over then! We've won!"

"It's a bandwagon," Clara said. "And it's rolling."

Cade searched their faces. They were all intoxicated with the news. And they could be right, too. . . . But still he couldn't quite bring himself to share it. He sensed again the same relentless certainty and refusal to be deflected that he had seen in Beijing. Yet something kept telling him it felt wrong.

"What's the matter, Roland? I'd have expected to see a little more excitement," Marie said. Of course she was being swept along with it too. She was still the revolutionary. Everything which, for years, she had endured dangers and hardship for, seen her friends die for, was happening.

Cade wasn't sure what to say. He pictured again the four faces that he had just left in the room on the floor below. "I don't know. . . . I guess maybe because it's *our* bandwagon," he answered.

"I'm not sure I follow," Gerofsky said.

"Us. . . . Terrans." Cade made a motion with his head to indicate the direction he had come from. "What about those four downstairs? They put everything on the line too, and today they lost everything. It seems as if they're about to be left behind in the dust and forgotten, while we all go on a binge of self-congratulations." But even as he spoke, he knew it was just words to fill the space. It wasn't the reason.

Clara nodded, trying to be diplomatic. "I hear what you're saying, Roland. They did a heroic job—for us, because they decided it was right. And that won't be forgotten. But the part they wrote isn't in the final script. Nobody was to know it would work out this way."

"And it's cleaner," Di Milestro put in. "Fast. Surgical. Without depending on some other planet that nobody understands."

"They're in a nutcracker on both fronts," Gerofsky said. "In the Pacific, and on the mainland. They have to know it's over too. I'd bet even money we could get a peace offer from Washington before the end of today."

Which made it all the more incomprehensible that they should take out the Hyadean mission, Cade told himself. What was there for Washington to gain? Downstairs, the Hyadeans had been just as mystified. "These politics are all double faces," Hudro had said. Then his other words repeated again in Cade's mind: "So who commands this?"

Who commands?!

It hit Cade then what was wrong. Of *course* it made no sense for Washington to have ordered the mission strike. The only explanation, then, was that *Washington* hadn't ordered it. At least, not of their own initiation. *They were no longer in charge!*

"Oh, my God," Cade breathed. He licked his lips and looked quickly around the three faces watching him. "You're wrong," he told them. "All of you—Sacramento, Beijing. You're all wrong. It isn't over. It hasn't even started."

Clara gave the others a puzzled look. Marie alone seemed to have registered the graveness of Cade's expression. "What are you talking about, Roland?" Clara asked him.

He wiped a hand across his brow, still struggling to come to terms with the enormity of it. "The mission . . . that thing today. The Hyadean high command ordered it. It wasn't anybody in the Washington government. Don't you see what that means? They've taken over. And they've just cut the only independent link back to Chryse that could tell anyone there what happens next. What do you think *that* means?"

Gerofsky fingered his mustache and turned away to confront the shelves on the far wall. "No. . . . No, it can't be," he muttered.

"That's merely a speculation," Di Milestro said. "It's obviously something that's just occurred to you. You don't *know*." His tone accused Cade for even being capable of conceiving it.

"Then get the Hyadeans up here and see what they think," Cade said. "Hudro as good as said it already. Only he's still too shaken up to put together what it means." He looked around at them again. Di Milestro and Gerofsky were unsure, not wanting to believe him, yet unable to fault what he had said. Marie was persuaded but needed a moment to absorb it. Clara had been around long enough to know that Cade didn't let many things become serious enough to weigh down his life, and when he did, they were serious. But for now she had to consider her official position too.

"Suppose you're right, Roland," she said, standing behind her desk, her knuckles resting on the surface. "How can we change it? What are you suggesting we do? Just capitulate? Are you saying we should try to get Jeye to prevail on the Chinese to call it all off, then back down and accept whatever the Hyadeans choose to dictate?"

"Never!" Gerofsky wheeled back to face them. "And hand the world over as a colony state? I'd see it in flames from end to end first."

Just what they needed, Cade groaned inwardly. Yet this was would probably be the kind of reaction at every level. He realized that he wasn't sure himself exactly what he wanted them to do. Di Milestro talked direct to Jeye, but Cade didn't know him, and right at this moment he was acutely conscious of not commanding Di Milestro's confidence. Di Milestro confirmed it a moment later. "I think you're overreacting, Mr. Cade," he said. "Which is understandable. You've lost a lot of friends. But the way I see it, this attempt to set up a back-door PR link into Chryse was only a supplement to the military effort, anyway—in case we needed extra leverage." He shrugged. "It seems to me we're doing just fine without."

"Just fine? I'd say we're doing pretty damn great," Gerofsky said. "It looks like the Chinese are about to walk right over them in Panama. They don't need any link to Chryse."

Cade sighed and looked away. No, there wasn't a link from China to Chryse because the Hyadean Washington office controlled the channels, and right now they were permitting only approved traffic. That was why Yassem and Luodine had set up their illicit connection to the Querl. Cade blinked as the obvious finally struck him. He thought back to the things he had seen at Cairns: the scientific base and its easygoing independence; the local spirit of cooperation with the aliens and getting to know them. No, there wasn't another independent link. But there *could be*!

"We can still do it!" he said, turning back. "Luodine set the mission up as a collection center for items to go back to Chryse. But they've got the same kind of gear at Cairns, where we were with Krossig. We can set up another link to Chryse from *there*—from Australia!"

Gerofsky shook his head. "Throw away the initiative and get involved in alien psychology that we don't understand, when the things we do understand are working fine? What's the point? It goes against every rule in the book."

"How would these people in Australia know how to set their end up?" Di Milestro asked.

"I don't know," Cade retorted. "But the experts who set up the one at the mission are downstairs. We can still talk to Australia, can't we?"

"We don't need it," Gerofsky said again.

Cade stared from one to the other. Why were they hesitating, looking for reasons why not? "There's nothing to lose," he insisted. "If you're right and we take the board anyway, then it'll be a piece of insurance that costs nothing. If things turn sour, it could be the most important insurance we ever took." He pointed a finger in the direction of the floor. "And either way, it gives those four Hyadeans down there a chance to play a part. Are you going to deny them that, after what happened today?"

A deadlocked silence fell over the office. It was clear that neither Gerofsky nor Di Milestro wanted to be the person who was going to take this thing further; at the same time, they could find no refutation to what Cade had said. They looked as if they wished the whole thing would just go away. Before any resolution suggested itself, the terminal by Clara's desk sounded a priority tone. She answered at once, having blocked lower-level channels for privacy. Cade didn't recognize the face that appeared—a man in his fifties, white haired, professional looking, showing a jacket collar and necktie. "Clara, is Chester there?" he asked.

Clara moved aside as Di Milestro stepped forward. "It's Ed Flomer, from Sacramento," she said.

"Chester, the VP wants you on a conference call that he's setting up right away," Flomer said. His voice and expression were strained. "Can you get to a private line?"

"Sure. . . ." Di Milestro frowned inquiringly at the screen. "What's happening, Ed?"

Flomer shook his head. "I can't tell you. This is for a secure line only."

Di Milestro looked at Clara. "This way," she said, and led him out of the office. Cade and Gerofsky remained facing each other. After an awkward silence, Gerofsky moved over to the bookshelves to scan idly over the titles. Cade shook his head despairingly at Marie and began flipping mentally through his catalog of acquaintances for names that he might have to start recruiting to bring more weight to bear. Then Clara returned.

"Can't we have it referred to someone else?" she said, looking at Gerofsky. "Couldn't the commander at Edwards handle it? All you'd need to do is arrange an order from the top to authorize full cooperation, and then get on with your job. As Roland said, the cost is nothing. The payoff could be incalculable. There's no penalty clause. We can't lose."

"It would depend on what Sacramento has to say," Gerofsky replied. His manner was stiff, uncompromising. Clara studied him for a moment, then looked at Cade and Marie. "Why don't you go back down and update the others on what's been said?" she suggested to them. "I'll call you." Clearly, she wanted words with Gerofsky alone. Cade indicated the door with a nod, and he and Marie left.

Back in the staff room, Cade told the others the latest news, and then went on to relate his conclusion that the strike on the mission hadn't been ordered by Washington. It shook Hudro out of the stupor that had been gripping him. "Of course it wasn't Terrans who give order!" Hudro exclaimed. "How do I not see it? Hyadeans in charge now—maybe Gazaghin. Is not good."

Nyarl shook his head. "We had a channel working. . . ."

"And we can again—" Cade began. But before he could continue, the door opened and Clara came in with Di Milestro and Gerofsky. Di Milestro was pale. He faced the room while Clara closed the door. A hush fell. Something had changed very drastically in the last few minutes.

Di Milestro looked around. He had to take a long, shaky breath before speaking. "I'm breaking security on my own decision and telling you people what I've just learned because you might represent the only chance for averting a world-scale calamity." Cade caught Clara's eye with an incredulous, questioning look. But whatever this was about had apparently left her too numbed to respond. Di Milestro shifted his gaze to Cade. "Do you really think this thing you were telling us about could work?" he asked.

Cade nodded. "I believe it could work." What else was there to say?

"Run it by me again."

"Hyadeans see a different world here from what we see. Convince them that their government is about to destroy it and turn it into what they've got, and they'll pull out the rug." Cade flashed the

Hyadeans a glance that let them know he was as mystified as they, then looked back. "What's happened?"

Di Milestro swallowed. "Admiral Varney's carrier group has been wiped out. A plane coming back off patrol shot the whole thing. I've just seen it upstairs. His flagship lit up like the Sun. There was nothing incoming on radar. The scientists are baffled."

"But Sacramento isn't budging," Gerofsky told the room. "Jeye says he would rather go out fighting than submit to a tyranny. If this other way of yours has a chance, we're going to have to do it ourselves."

❊ CHAPTER FIFTY-ONE ❊

The wall screen in the staff room showed a replay, wired from Sacramento at Di Milestro's request, of the carrier and its closer escorts disappearing in a gigantic ball of fire and vaporized ocean. The wall of foam surging outward capsized the more distant ships or scattered them like toys caught beneath a waterfall.

"Neutron beam from orbiting warship," Hudro pronounced. He explained that the flux would send critical any fission explosive not suitably shielded or designed to be resistant. Hence, it had detonated the carrier's nuclear weapons inventory. Since neutrons were uncharged, Hyadean gravitic technology was necessary to create and focus the beams.

A watered-down press release issued from Sacramento an hour later stated merely that Varney's task group had been "engaged" by hostile forces, implied to be the other two groups still with the Eastern Union. It was also announced that President Jeye would make a public address later that night. Di Milestro predicted it would be a rallying call for maximum effort and endurance side-by-side with the Asian allies now they were on the brink of success. Making the most of Gerofsky and his military credentials, Clara found working space in the communications section of the city administration's emergency headquarters, located beneath the Corry Building, containing more offices and a meeting center, situated along the next block. It was a dismal setting of concrete walls, fluorescent lights, fireproof doors guarding vaults of generators and the air-conditioning plant, and a disaster relief shelter. The people in the building above had long ago christened it "the Catacombs." Normally, nobody worked there, but since the Federation's secession, a caretaker staff had been installed to maintain a state of standby readiness.

The first thing was to open a connection to Krossig's group in Cairns. Yassem had kept a backup of the codes for linking to the Querl relays in a portable laptop-like device that she had taken with her to Edwards, so they were not lost. However, satellite communications were disrupted, and Gerofsky had to demand military priority before technicians established a land-line and cable connection through a Navy facility in San Francisco to Hawaii to Sydney, and from there to Cairns via the regular telecommunications system. Meanwhile, Di Milestro used his security clearances to get a line through to the Catacombs from an assistant in Sacramento who would keep him updated on developments. Cade and Luke got busy organizing contacts with wire services, news studios, military press officers, and other likely sources from Cade's numerous acquaintances, in order to recreate as far as possible the collection center that Luodine had set up at the mission. Australia would need to move into Earth's dark side before the link through Cairns, beaming outward toward the Querl relays, could be tested. This wouldn't happen until the early hours of the morning, California time. The crew of the C22-E waiting out at Edwards were notified that departure was on hold for the time being.

Nyarl was the obvious one to go in Luodine's place. Besides having the experience, he was resolved as a tribute to finish the work she had begun, in the way she would have finished it. He was already assembling further material to send. In addition to the sensational clips showing the annihilation of Varney's carrier group, he now had—obtained via Di Milestro's connection from Sacramento—a shot that a Marine flight had caught of the missiles actually going in at the Hyadean mission. Nyarl asked if Cade and Marie would go too—he seemed to think Cade possessed a proclivity for drawing the right people together to deal with any crisis. Yassem needed to remain in LA to guide the people setting up the link from Cairns. Who else would be flying, and who would form the rest of the base team at the Catacombs, was still to be decided.

President Jeye's message went out at nine o'clock and was along the lines that Di Milestro had anticipated. Jeye admitted that Varney's losses had been "more severe than we were initially led to believe" and included the admiral along with his flagship, but the full extent of the disaster remained undisclosed. But this was not a time to let one setback, however grievous, deter us from pressing home the victory that was already within grasp. The armies in Texas were moving up to leap across the Mississippi to where our Southern brothers and sisters were waiting to greet their liberators. Canada was opening a vast superhighway for supplies and reinforcements. Jeye concluded: "I don't pretend that this will be a pleasant task. The people of New York and Boston, Atlanta and Pittsburgh are not enemies. But the regime that they have been duped and coerced into serving has become an alien power standing for alien interests. We, in the Western Federation, must defend and preserve the values that have always been America. I call on each one of you to play your part and stand firm until our AANS allies sweep through in their millions to bring this sad episode in our history to a just and honorable close. Out of it will emerge a restored United States, prouder and stronger, ready to take its place alongside the other free nations of this world as a full partner in the planetary community that we are all now, irrevocably, a part of."

Forty minutes later, the AANS fleet steaming east-southeast from Hawaii suffered the same fate as Varney's force. It was deployed in several squadrons spread over a greater area, however, and a number of the capital ships presumably not carrying nuclear devices escaped destruction by the induced fission explosions. They were taken out during the next half hour by bombs sent down from orbit. Some of the lesser vessels survived to scatter away across the Pacific. In retaliation, the Chinese used tactical nuclear missiles against the naval force immobilized in the Panama Canal and Gatun Lake, including

Hyadean defensive positions. By midnight, Union forces in Mexico were responding in kind against bases that the Chinese airborne units had seized earlier. Meanwhile, the two remaining carrier groups in the Pacific were continuing northward, now unopposed. Guesses were that their commanders had been threatened with similar treatment to the others if they failed to carry out their missions as ordered.

An exchange of nuclear weapons, even if relatively small ones, in Central America was hardly something that could be concealed from a world wrapped in communications networks. The early hours of the morning brought fear that the escalation would spread to the Midwest and Southern battle areas, and then engulf the whole continent. Emergency plans were set in motion to evacuate local populations from the vicinities of military installations and other likely targets. Indiscriminate destruction of cities was considered improbable, however, for the same reason that nobody in Sacramento felt any great urge to wipe out populaces wholesale in Pennsylvania or New Jersey—but with an imponderable alien element, who could be too sure? As a precaution, key government and military personnel began occupying their long-prepared emergency bunkers, while public announcements called for everyone else to keep calm, stay tuned, and heed the authorities. Even so, the night saw mass exoduses from major metropolitan areas from San Francisco to Minneapolis, burning up gasoline and precipitating clashes with police bent on imposing order before general panic could set in. No doubt similar scenes were occurring between the Mississippi and the East Coast too.

Staff called in on emergency shifts began arriving in the offices of the Corry Building, many of them bringing their families through fear of being separated in the event of sudden evacuation. The Catacombs below became a scene of increasing noise and activity as more functions were staffed and brought on-line, and personnel from above came down seeking space to move into, now at a premium.

A 2:00 A.M. news bulletin brought the surprise announcement that Louisiana, Arkansas, Oklahoma, and Kansas, no doubt following secret negotiations, had come over to the Federation, opening the way to the Mississippi. Virtually simultaneously, Federation aircraft and ground-based missiles opened a wave of attacks against Union positions on the far side. Gerofsky guessed that secretly prepared assault units for the crossing were already moving into position, while the armies in Texas raced forward in support. It all followed the policy that Jeye had committed to: going all-out now, before the odds against success got any less. And it seemed he was getting others to go along.

Then, at 3:35, Di Milestro's private channel from Sacramento brought the terse statement that McConnell Air Force Base near Wichita, one of the Federation's primary bases flying combat and support operations for the central sector of the front, and the air logistics center at Tinker, southeast of Oklahoma City, had been obliterated. Not simply "attacked," but "obliterated." Nine minutes later, it was the turn of the bomber and missile-support base at Grand Forks, North Dakota. They were being picked by something in polar orbit. The next sweep could be north-south through California. If so, Edwards would surely be a prime target.

Cade came around from the cubicle that Di Milestro and Gerofsky were using and into the cubbyhole where Hudro and Yassem were talking to a technician in Cairns. "Hudro, get onto the plane crew out at Edwards!" Cade exclaimed. "Tell them the hold's off. We're on our way *now!*"

Hudro looked startled. "What's happened?"

Vrel was nearby, looking across in alarm. Cade turned to him. "Vrel, bring the flyer here from the other building. We're loading up." On Vrel's other side, Nyarl was juggling data on one of the screens. "Time to wrap up," Cade told him. "That's Yassem's job now. Get the stuff sorted out now that you need to take." And then, finally answering Hudro's question, "We just got an answer to the air strikes. They're wiping out our main bases." Vrel nodded. There was no need to say anything. He hurried away. Luke finished a call he had been making. "Can you organize getting everything to be loaded up to the lobby?" Cade said to him, at the same time pulling out his phone. "See if you can get a cart from somewhere." He tried Clara's regular number. A voice told him calls were being switched to the answering system. He punched in Clara's priority code. "Where are Marie and Dee?"

"I'm here," Marie said from behind him. She had come over from the far side of the room to investigate the commotion. "Dee's upstairs talking supplies."

"Go find her. We're moving now."

"Why? What's happening?"

Clara's voice answered sleepily. "Tell you later. . . . Hi, Clara? It's Roland." Marie turned and disappeared toward the door.

"What time is it? I had to take a break."

"Sorry, but things have changed. We're leaving right away. Chester will give you the whole story. Briefly, they've started zapping air bases, and I don't want to wait for Edwards to be next. I guess you'll be the one keeping an eye on things at this end. We need to agreee who else you need to stay on here."

"Well, Luke, I guess. . . ." Clara and Luke had known each other for years. She was still having trouble surfacing.

"Yassem, we already decided," Cade said.

"Does that mean Hudro will be staying too?"

"I don't think we can let him. Neither of them knows anything about LA or anyone here. I'd rather it be Vrel. Besides, we'll need an on-board expert in Hyadean technical and military matters. That can only be Hudro. Dee can stay with Vrel."

"Fine." Clara sounded more herself now. "Do you want me to come over there? It would take me about thirty minutes."

"No, get some rest. We'll be in touch."

"Then . . . good luck. You take care, Roland. Of yourself and those others. Bring them all back in one piece."

"You too. 'Bye."

As Cade repocketed his phone, he realized that Gerofsky had joined him and had been listening. For a moment, the major seemed to have difficulty finding words. "Look, Cade . . . You were right, and we were wrong. I'd like to do more to help. Chester has to stay here as the contact man with Sacramento. But you don't know what you'll run into out there. You're going to need someone along who can deal with military people and situations. . . . Well, what I'm saying is . . ."

Cade managed a tired grin. "It's okay. You don't have to spell it out. And the answer's 'sure.' Welcome to the team."

It was a little after 4:15 A.M. when the flyer finally rose from the city and headed east of north for Palmdale. The night was clear with no moon. From above Pasadena, trains of lights showed on the darkened roads below, all heading northward to the desert. En route, Nyarl checked with the Catacombs. Yassem reported that the link from Cairns was sending, but so far there had been no response from the Querl. President Jeye wasn't backing down. The Federation had just launched IRBMs at Union air bases in Alabama and Ohio. Nobody aboard the flyer had much else to say.

Radio traffic indicated that flight operations were busy at Edwards. Ignoring ground control procedures, Hudro brought the flyer skimming in low over the perimeter fence to land at the hangars at the north end where the C22-E was waiting. The transfer of bodies, equipment, and bags still in the flyer from Cade's house that morning took place swiftly against a background of engine roars and black shapes lifting off into the night. The captain, Bob Powell, told them that operational aircraft were being dispersed to other fields and landing strips, with supply transports loading to follow later. He obviously didn't know about recent events and assumed it was a standard precaution. While they were stowing gear, Powell introduced Cade, Marie, and Gerofsky to his copilot, Lieutenant Koyne, and Technical Sergeant Davis, an aircraft engines and systems specialist. Nyarl and Hudro had met them previously.

"C22 Six Five Zero to Edwards control, we're ready to move out now and request immediate clearance," Powell said into his mike. As they ran up the engines, Koyne spotted lights approaching along the perimeter road and pointed. "Probably someone coming to check what came in over the fence," Powell grunted.

"We don't want to get bogged down now. Just pretend we haven't seen them," Cade said from behind.

Powell's face creased in the glow from the instrument panel. "Ground Control is gonna be sticky with all this traffic going out. I wouldn't want to upset them right now." He listened to something for a few seconds, then spoke into the mike again. "When? . . . We didn't see anything. . . . No, nothing to do with us. . . . Roger."

Meanwhile Nyarl, using headphones, was keeping contact with the Catacombs. He interrupted suddenly, "I'm talking to Chester. What's Travis?"

"I read you," Powell sang in the captain's seat. "Moving out now. How long is this queue gonna last?"

Koyne answered Nyarl, "Big air base up near San Francisco. Main transportation center for Pacific supply routes. Why?"

"It just got taken out."

"Never mind the queue! Get us out of here!" Cade snapped at Powell.

"You're talking court-martial offense here."

"Right now, that's the least of your worries."

"You'd better be sure about this." Powell sucked in a long breath, gunned the engines, and jerked the control column to take the plane around the shapes outlined ahead in the starlight, and across a connecting ramp to a shorter, auxiliary runway. Even from where he was sitting, Cade could hear indignant squawking in Powell's phones. Ahead, what looked like a bomber was turning to join the line lumbering toward the run-up point on the main runway. Another was waiting to mover forward. At the end of the base, several miles away in the other direction, a slim finger of peculiar violet radiance appeared suddenly, seemingly coming down from among the stars. Nyarl stared at it, speechless with sudden terror.

"*Captain, go! Go now!*" Hudro shouted.

His fear communicated itself. Powell opened the throttle, and the plane surged forward, even as the bomber began rolling onto the runway ahead. They squeezed through the gap accelerating flat-out. The runway seemed to flow by endlessly. Cade looked back and saw the beam of violet shift, as if registering. Nyarl seemed mesmerized by it. Finally, the plane lifted, banked, and turned away.

There was a lull, followed by several pulses of yellow light behind. A moment later, the desert lit up for miles around.

❀ CHAPTER FIFTY-TWO ❀

In the research center at Cairns, Krossig still hadn't recovered from the shock of learning that the Los Angeles mission, where he himself had been based until just recently, was no more. Orzin, Wyvex, Krossig's Terran colleague and friend, Mike Blair . . . all of them gone. What was happening to this world that had once been so wondrous?

The situation seemed to be deteriorating by the hour. Chinese news sources were revealing only parts of the story that he was getting from Yassem in Los Angeles—and not always accurately, at that. Further, it was only now becoming clear how much of the Terran satellite network—especially that operated by American and European concerns—the Hyadeans, by offering better technology for lower cost, had quietly replaced or come to assume control of over the years. With the remainder suddenly being subjected to jamming and neutralization following the widening hostilities, communications throughout the AANS states were drastically restricted. That meant that the connection through the precarious, politically sensitive patchwork of cables and submarine links between Cairns and Los Angeles could be broken at any time.

He sat with Ominzek, the resident Hyadean communications technician, in the gravcom room next to Freem's office in one of the timber-framed lab blocks, in front of several Terran conventional terminals and the array of gravitics gear. The center still had access to the official Chryse channel, although now subject to monitoring by the General Embassy in Xuchimbo. One of the Terran screens showed the room in Los Angeles, where Yassem reappeared intermittently to send further code patches or news input for the collection that Ominzek had ready, waiting to transmit. The Hyadean equipment showed readings from the outgoing beam control, probing regions of near-space to make contact with the Querl relays.

It was now night in Cairns. Communications with the LA mission had ceased abruptly in the early hours of the previous morning. Nobody at Cairns had been aware then of Orzin's plan to initiate an independent, uncensored channel to Chryse. The first reports that the mission had been hit by missiles came second-hand from Federation news sources. It had seemed so incongruous and devoid of rational motive that Freem had been skeptical, advising the staff not to accepting anything as final until reliable confirmation was received. The confirmation had come with the direct communication from Yassem later. Yassem was also able to confide information somehow extracted from privileged Federation sources, which so far neither side was telling the world at large.

Networks worldwide were blaring hysterically about the nuclear exchanges in Central America, which couldn't be concealed or played down. But Beijing was maintaining a blackout on the annihilation of the AANS fleet in the Pacific, and instead putting out strident appeals for solidarity and stressing the Federation's opening air offensive in the south. The retaliation against Federation air bases, carried out with direct Hyadean intervention, had not been publicized by Washington, Sacramento, or Beijing. The last thing heard from Yassem was that Cade had left in haste with Nyarl, Hudro, Marie, and a Terran officer to get their aircraft away from a base that Cade feared might be a target for further such strikes.

Freem and Susan Gray, the Terran biologist, came back in. "Anything yet?" Freem inquired.

Ominzek looked over the displays showing tables of beam-setting parameters and trial transmissions, and a graphical summary of the results so far. "Still scanning coordinates and spectra. The night's early yet."

Farther along, Krossig was watching a devastated Terran township, buildings flattened and in flames, with rescuers digging bodies and injured survivors from the ruins. The background was lost in an eerie glow, clearly radiating intense heat. "What these it show now time?" Susan asked, staring. She was one of the Terrans who attempted to learn Hyadean. The results were sometimes amusing, but Krossig and the others respected her effort.

"The latest from Yassem," Krossig replied. "Shots from McConnell. Just in over their wire from Sacramento."

"Who there provides them like this? Why?" Susan asked.

"Yassem didn't say."

An image of Nyarl appeared to one side, supplying a commentary. "The aftermath of a defenseless American habitat caught in the kill zone of one of our orbital bombardment masers." Nyarl was not actually present in LA when Yassem put the sequence together, of course; he had spoken from the flyer. "Its crime? Aircraft from the nearby McConnell base flew in defense of the newly proclaimed nation against armies sent by the Chryse-supported Washington regime. . . ."

Just then, a shrill tone sounded from the Hyadean equipment. Another display lit up with lines of data and code, while the system voice announced, *"Probe attempt Sector five six, scan three-nine, four-zero-three, five-five, Mode 7A-3, successful. Connection is to Querl deep-space monitor station, location undisclosed."*

Ominzek turned sharply and stabbed at control keys. "Gravcom Sys, Supervisor. Report link quality status."

"Resolution high at seven-two-zero. Submodal encoding. Recipient active and acknowledges."

"We're through!" Krossig whispered to Susan. "It's found one of the relays."

"Identify," Ominzek instructed.

"Nebula Two"—obviously a code name—*"Deputy commander, Querl long-range task group, nature of mission, undisclosed. Range and location coordinates suppressed. Identified as former contact established by Hetch Luodine from West Coast Trade and Cultural Mission."*

"Connect."

A relief display opened to show the figurine likeness of a lean, red-haired Hyadean in an officer-style tunic, seated against a background tableau of panels and bulkheads in what was evidently some kind of control room. Nebula Two stared for a second or two, looking at first uncertain, then suspicious. Finally, he said, "I don't know you. We've been awaiting further contact for over fifteen hours. What's happening? I wish to speak with Luodine or Nyarl."

"There is unfortunate news here," Omnizek replied. "The place Luodine was in has been destroyed. There were no survivors. Nyarl was elsewhere and escaped. I cannot specify our whereabouts, but we have established an alternate connection. I am a communications technician. You can refer to me as *K*. The person who has taken over Luodine's function is with me. His name is *G*." Krossig moved closer to come within the viewing angle of the unit that Omnizek was addressing.

"I must ask you to submit the agreed security verification sequence," Nebula Two said.

"I can't. It was held in equipment that was also destroyed," Ominzek said. "Everything was destroyed." Codes of that kind would have been too sensitive for Yassem to carry around as a copy. That was apparently how the technical information needed to reconstruct the link had been preserved.

"Then how can I be sure you are who you say you are?" Nebula Two asked.

The question had been expected. "Does it really matter?" Krossig replied. "If we're sending you reports that the Chrysean authorities would suppress if they could, you can do nothing but help your own cause by rebroadcasting them. Would impostors who were working for the Chryseans do that?"

Nebula Two frowned as he considered the unexpected logic, but evidently couldn't fault it. He killed the audio and disappeared from view, presumably to consult with others.

"It isn't the time to count fishes," Susan said, attempting a Hyadean saying. It was the right sentiment but the wrong phrase. Krossig smiled tolerantly.

"How long it will take Xuchimbo to track down this equipment and silence it?" Freem muttered.

"I was wondering the same thing," Krossig said moodily. A movement caught his eye on the Terran screen connected to Los Angeles. He moved back to it. Yassem had reappeared. "We're through," he said before she had a chance to ask. "There's an authenticating problem, as we thought. I told them our answer. They're debating it now. . . ." He paused, seeing that the news wasn't having the effect he had anticipated. Yassem was looking dazed. Then Krossig realized she was in tears. "What is it?" he asked.

"They've just wiped out Edwards," she said, her voice choking. "Ten minutes after Hudro and the others arrived there." Krossig stared, horrified.

"Oh, no," Susan groaned behind him.

Nebula Two returned on the Hyadean display. "Very well," he said. "Send us what you have." Krossig nodded mutely to Ominzek.

"Gravcom Sys, Supervisor. Proceed with transfer of prepared file as previously specified," Ominzek instructed.

"*Executing.*"

Phones and terminals were beeping throughout the offices and work spaces in the vaults beneath the Corry Building. People tumbled in and out of doorways and scurried along the corridors. Everyone wanted details; city services everywhere were requesting updates and instructions. All that was known for sure was that Edwards Air Force Base had gone up in a fireball seen from Barstow to Bakersfield. There were no clear accounts of the extent of the damage, and anything could happen next.

Yassem was weeping freely, still looking at the image of Krossig in Cairns. Her tears were of relief. An adjacent screen showed Nyarl and Hudro, cramped together in the cabin of the Terran aircraft, now heading east. They had come through minutes after the news from Sacramento about Edwards. "You've got Roland to thank for it," Nyarl was saying. "If it hadn't been for him, we would never have gotten out in time."

"People seem to have a habit of surviving whenever he's around,"

Hudro commented, still seemingly having difficulty believing it himself.

"Marie always told me he lived a charmed life," Yassem said.

While the C22-E was setting course toward Arizona, it was early morning in New York State. It had been a night of panic in the city and continuous hysteria from the news. Drisson and Laura had moved for a couple of days to a lodge that he had rented some weeks previously away from town, up in the Catskills—as a precaution. Laura, wearing the short housecoat that she had slipped on, came back in from the kitchen, carrying two coffee cups. Drisson was sitting propped against the end of the bed. He accepted one and tasted the contents, all the time watching her contemplatively.

"Why the long, silent look?" she asked. "Don't tell me you're not satisfied. I'd never live it down."

"Oh, I'd say that's close to the last thing you have to worry about," he complimented.

"So what's such deep thought about at this time of the morning?"

Drisson took a moment to compose himself into a more serious vein. "Things are a bit more complicated than I thought. Everybody's building walls. Somebody like me can't go near Toddrel without being logged and taped. If we end up having to do this, it'll need to be from the inside. That means you being point."

"You mean the one who actually does it? I thought you were supposed to take care of that. I was only an inside source. Information and access, remember?"

Drisson sighed in a way that conveyed both an apology and weariness from considering alternatives. "I know. But like I said, things have changed. Believe me, I've been through all the angles. There isn't any other way." Laura said nothing but didn't look happy about it. He set his cup down and reached out to grip her shoulder reassuringly. "If it comes to it, it'll be worth it. Trust me. Then . . . it's whatever you want. Choose a life. This outfit doesn't just deal in insurance, you know. With me you get the whole package." He eyed her for a moment. His voice took on a coaxing tone. "Don't let me down on this, Laura. We've both got too much at stake. He's dangerous. You'd need it for yourself in any case, with or without me. . . . What do you say, eh? Are you made of what I thought?"

"I'll need to think about it."

Drisson got up and went into the bathroom as if that already decided the issue. His voice came back through the open door. "What makes it different with you is that you can get close and be invisible. I can't. I figured the way would be to make it look like a hooker or something—we all know about Casper's kinky predilections. Totally anonymous. Nothing anyone would want to be bothered putting any time into—especially at times like this, with everything else that's going on." The sound came of the shower being turned on. Drisson's voice rose to carry above it. "So it just gets written off. We collect our retirement. Then it's away from the war to some sunny place in the world. Get the big picture, baby?"

"Oh yes." Laura murmured. "I get the picture."

❂ CHAPTER FIFTY-THREE ❂

Dawn greeted the C22-E, winging low over the mesas and canyons of Arizona. Cade pulled his blanket around his shoulders as he lay in the reclined seat, trying to force some sleep in the few hours that the flight would last. But he was apprehensive. The most recent news to be passed on by Yassem was of Asian missiles launched against Globalist satellites, along with orbiting Hyadean ships and other targets. Little seemed to have penetrated the Hyadean defenses, but it brought things to a new dimension of direct conflict between the AANS and the Hyadeans. Surely, there had already been clear warning of what further escalation could be expected to bring. Yet news of the setbacks was being withheld, and the Federation-AANS leaders still seemed committed to exhorting maximum effort for a swift victory, even though, as far as Cade could see, the gamble had already failed.

Marie was in the seat next to him—whether asleep or not, he couldn't tell. Copilot Koyne was flying the plane while Powell rested farther back, along with Hudro and Davis. Nyarl and Gerofsky were at consoles, editing and adding commentaries to items coming in from various sources and tagging them for transmission back to LA. The sequences included armor and supply columns moving forward to consolidate the Federation's positions between the Red River and the Mississippi, air cargo lifters delivering tanks to forward jump-off areas, and dramatic shots of the air attacks delivered during the night.

The current plan was to land and refuel near Russellville, Arkansas, in the southern Ozarks, at one of the secondary fields that the Federation's air strength was being dispersed to. There, they were to meet headquarters staff of an engineer brigade that Major Gerofsky had contacted via the military network, who would fill them in on the situation and look into further options for them to explore. In getting a connection to LA when the entire communications system was inundated, and finding contacts among the military commands in the area they were heading to, Gerofsky's contribution was already invaluable. Nyarl seemed possessed by fierce determination to carry through the task that Luodine had begun, which precluded rest and all other considerations.

As for the crew, in the little time he'd had to form any impression at all, Cade saw Powell as capable, easygoing, and sufficiently amenable to the unorthodox for an undertaking like this. Davis was taciturn, methodical, and, Cade guessed, solidly competent. Although Koyne hadn't said anything openly, Cade detected rancor at why they should be working with aliens when aliens were wiping out warships and bases, and a lot of people along with them. Cade had explained that Hudro and Nyarl were here to inform their home world of what was going on, not entertain it, and a lot of their colleagues had died, too, as a result of pursuing the same goal. Koyne seemed to accept it intellectually, but beneath, the resentment was still there. Cade hoped he would be able to just stick to his job and not let feelings become a problem.

Marie stirred, sighed drowsily, and pulled closer to his shoulder. He opened an eye momentarily. "Hi."

"Mmm. . . ."

"I thought you were asleep."

"Not really." A pause. "How do you sleep when you think the world might be about to be blown up?" A short silence passed while Marie blinked, yawned, then laid her head back, looking at him. Up front, Koyne was talking into his mike, identifying the flight in response to an interrogation from somewhere. Finally, Marie said, "Roland . . ."

"Hmm?"

"In case this whole thing doesn't . . . Well, if it all comes to the worst. I just want you to know that it could have worked again with us. There's a different side to you that I never saw until recent times."

"Maybe it didn't exist until recent times."

"It was always there. People are what they always were. It just sometimes takes new situations to bring other sides of them out."

It was meant as a genuine compliment. But Cade couldn't get lyrical at a time like this. "Well, you've sure got yourself a new situation," he said dryly.

Did Hyadeans really have a different side to them too, the way Cade thought, and Vrel, Luodine, Hudro, and others had said? If so, could it be brought out in time? Marie had told him why Luodine had believed things would happen quickly on Chryse. Cade hoped Luodine was right. From what he could tell, everything hinged on it now.

By the time they cleared the Rockies, they were getting reports of the Union opening interdiction attacks on supply routes through Calgary, Saskatoon, Regina, and Winnipeg in answer to Canada's coming out openly for the AANS. The reason for the sudden activity in the northern theater quickly became clear. In keeping with the policy of going all-out for a quick win, the Federation was opening a second offensive, thrusting eastward between Chicago and Indianapolis, presumably to cut off the Michigan peninsula. Maybe taken by surprise, somebody in the Union command authorized the use of pocket nukes against armored spearheads that had broken through south of Indianapolis to secure a flank along the Ohio River. Sacramento ordered retaliation in kind, and a panic reaction set in on both sides to take out the other's launch sites before they could fire first, which spread rapidly. The Hyadeans in Washington decided that they weren't prepared to sit there, waiting to be nuked by squabbling Terrans, and before the C22-E reached Russellville, they were intervening everywhere.

Powell was back in the skipper's seat. Everyone was awake. The airwaves were swamped with confusion on all bands as the plane descended above scrubby flats scarred by a winding creek bed, with dry hills rising on one side. There had been no response on the tower or emergency frequencies. Powell was making a visual approach based on map reading and using landmarks given by the on-board database. Ten miles out, they flew over the remains of a ground-attack intruder bearing Union markings, formerly USAF, still burning. Black smoke rose into the sky where the airfield lay ahead.

Little of it was left. The airfield buildings and hangars were blown to pieces, the fuel storage area at one end ablaze, and the two major runways cratered and strewn with wrecked aircraft. Passing low, they could see figures moving about among scattered vehicles, many overturned or burning, more strung along the road serving the base. Some of the figures waved frantically, but it was impossible to make out what was meant. It didn't much matter, since landing was out of the question. Koyne managed to raise somebody local on radio, but what they were saying was incoherent. Nyarl got some telephoto shots.

They turned eastward to follow the Arkansas river downstream toward Little Rock. Koyne scanned frequencies for an alternative landing ground, finally making contact with the ground controller at a small airport for private planes that a Marine Corps unit had taken over in the mountainous country to the north. "C22 Six, Five Zero. We read you, Control, and are on our way in. What's the gas situation there? We're running on less than a quarter full."

"*I'll be watching for you. Every situation's a mess here. Right now we have stocks, but everyone and his brother is showing up. You may have to fight it out at the trough.*"

"Roger."

They were stacked in a pattern waiting to come in, which took them out over the flatter country around Conway and Greenbrier. Twisting plumes of smoke from downed planes and recently hit targets hung over the landscape like gigantic mutant trees. There was a lot of military activity below, with tanks and other vehicles deploying, artillery and missile positions being dug among the overlooking hills. The whole pattern of movement seemed to have reversed. In place of the confident pushes forward that had been reported all day, everything spoke of a sudden falling back on the defensive. Things were going wrong.

They had to make a slow circuit at the last moment while a crippled fighter limped in on one engine. Then, finally, they landed amid a confusion of aircraft loading and taking off, trucks and service vehicles jostling for space, and Marines digging in on the facing hillside. While Powell and Davis went to investigate the fuel situation, Cade, Gerofsky, and Hudro sought out a harassed adjutant officer who seemed to be the nearest there was to anyone knowing what was going on. It didn't amount to a lot. Orders were to get operable combat aircraft out to reserve strips farther back and clear the field for evacuation flights. Nobody was going anywhere across the Mississippi. The big buildup had been shattered by a storm of counterattacks unleashed from the other side, and what was left of it was in retreat all the way from St. Louis to the Gulf, apparently to try and form a line along the edge of the Ozark Plateau. Frantic efforts were being made to issue Nuclear, Biological and Chemical contamination suits, but preparations for such eventualities had been inadequate.

"Is wrong way," Hudro said, shaking his head. "Static lines no good against Hyadeans."

"What's the right way? Gerofsky asked.

"Move fast, all way back to Rockies, deploy new strategies, strike back unexpected. Need more air, orbit support than exists. There is no way. Terrans don't have mobility to fight Hyadean armies."

Reports coming in from elsewhere were garbled and contradictory. Even with Gerofsky's credentials linking him to the presidential staff, it proved impossible to get a connection to Yassem for the rest of the day. Amid the turmoil, Cade found a lieutenant in charge of a supply unit sending ammunition to positions being prepared farther forward. Cade explained their mission, and the lieutenant offered a ride out the next morning to see for themselves what was going on there. Cade put it to the others. They decided that Nyarl should go, naturally. Marie volunteered to assist. Since it would be a venture into a military operations area, they agreed that Gerofsky should go too. They spent the night with a Marine antiaircraft company on the edge of the airfield, sleeping in foxholes and listening to the distant drumming of artillery fire. Aircraft continued arriving and departing through the night.

After they had shared a dawn breakfast with the troops of sausage, beans, hash brown potatoes, and coffee, Hudro went to the tower with Davis to continue trying to contact Yassem. Cade remained with Powell and Koyne in the plane, preparing the new material for immediate transmission if a link was found. Marie, Nyarl, and Gerofsky hitched a ride to the supply unit, and an hour later drove out aboard an ammunition carrier going to a battery command post seven miles ahead. Nyarl carried the portable recording equipment. Gerofsky got himself and Marie issued with infantry submachine guns. She looked back in her element.

❋ CHAPTER FIFTY-FOUR ❋

Clara Norburn had told Major Gerofsky that Cade possessed an infectious charisma that turned people who started out as opponents into willing collaborators. That was how he had prospered in his unique business of trading commercial and political contacts. The South American TV documentary that had helped propel the Federation to secession had been the work of a mix of Terrans and Hyadeans that he, more than anyone, had brought together. And then Gerofsky had experienced it himself in the space of a few hours, when he found himself reversing his initial position to first endorse, and then join, the enterprise they were committed to now. Admittedly, Cade had failed to win any converts among the high command he had met in Beijing, but the fact that he had even gotten a hearing was in itself an accomplishment not to be belittled.

After hearing Hudro voicing his doubts, Gerofsky was even more mindful now of Cade's warning that a head-on clash with the aliens could only lead to disaster. If the news they were getting of the Federation's offensive being hurled back all the way down the southern Mississippi front was correct—never mind what was happening farther north between St. Louis and Indianapolis—the war was not going to be won in a rapid pincers movement through Pittsburgh and up the east side of the Appalachians as had been intended. But the mood permeating from Sacramento was still to defy and fight, not look for ways of winding down. What disturbed Gerofsky most after hearing Hudro's pronouncement on mobility was the speed with which counter-thrusts seemed to have materialized out of nowhere, already this side of the river—in less than a day! It went against all the accepted norms and doctrines of what should have been possible. Conceivably for that very reason, the commanders were failing to grasp the implications and still preparing for defense against the kind of war they knew.

They drove past pits and emplacements being prepared among the low hills overlooking the plains extending away toward Stuttgart and the Mississippi valley: 125 mm howitzer batteries; 155 mm self-propelled howitzers being dug in hull-down; medium-range ground-to-ground missile launchers; mobile AA missile carriers and multibarrel antiaircraft cannon. Heavy-lift helicopters *whup-whupp*ed their way overhead, hauling dangling artillery pieces and crates of missiles to forward positions. Finally, the carrier bearing him and the others came to a false crest ahead of a ridge line, behind which the battery they were delivering to had been situated. The view over the lowlands ahead showed tanks spreading out and deploying behind cover; weapons emplaced along a creek bed; a command post undergoing camouflage and concealment. . . . All according to the book. But this was over a hundred miles from the Mississippi. If they were already facing a credible threat as far advanced as this, then what they were facing was from a totally different book.

Nyarl kept busy throughout, capturing anything that caught his interest. Since there was no quality connection back to the plane, he was storing the clips offline for delivery later. Some of the troops they passed reacted sourly to seeing a Hyadean, once or twice with open hostility, and Gerofsky had to defend Nyarl's presence repeatedly. He himself was having to work at accepting Marie—until so recently one of the enemy in the form of CounterAction. He studied her as she sat perched on one of the carrier's box sides, cradling her weapon, clearly awed by the extreme to which those efforts had finally contributed, yet also deeply apprehensive. She saw him from the corner of her eye and turned her head.

"It feels strange, us being on the same side." Gerofsky looked around. "A bit overwhelmed? Not what you expected?"

"We wanted to awaken the people," Marie answered. "Not all-out war. Somehow it all went out of control. Do you understand it?"

"I'm not sure anyone understands it. These things take on lives of their own."

The whoosh came of an outgoing missile launching distantly, followed by another. Marie gazed after them as they cleared the skyline. "And now we're trying to do the same thing again, only this time on Chryse."

"Is it possible to make it work there, when it didn't seem to here, do you think?" Gerofsky asked.

"Nyarl thinks so. He says minds work differently on Chryse."

Gerofsky stared across at him on the far side, panning the camera at a field radar being set up. "Let's hope he's right. It might be the only chance we've got."

As a precaution, Powell had moved the C22-E out to a corner of the field, away from the airport buildings and the crush of aircraft loading or maneuvering into a takeoff line to evacuate the field. That was probably what saved it when the attack came in.

Cade was in the cabin, keeping an open radio channel to Hudro and Davis in the tower; Powell was standing outside, taking in the general scene. Suddenly a shriek of warning sirens went up, and within moments, all over the airfield amid shouted orders and calls to stations, figures were jumping into slit trenches, running for cover, manning antiaircraft weapons. Short-range ground-to-air missiles were already flaming away all around like birds lifting in response to a spreading alarm call. Cade grabbed the helmet he had been given and tumbled out of the plane to join Powell in the ditch by the perimeter taxiway. The thudding of gunfire, felt as continuous jolting to the ears rather than heard, was already coming from the north. Then the harsher barking of fast-firing, smaller-caliber weapons joined in, getting nearer.

They came in low over the hilltops with a roar rising to a scream, a loose formation of maybe ten or twelve. Cade didn't know the type—they were just glimpses of bodies and wings outlined against the sky. One disintegrated as it cleared the ridge and fell on the slopes below in a cascade of flame. The lead group blanketed the ground defenses with rockets and fragmentation cluster. The rest went down into strafing runs to pour cannon fire and scatter low-yield bomblets across the field. One aircraft failed to lift with the others, hitting the ground and exploding somewhere beyond the far end of the field. Cade pushed himself up slowly from the ground, dazed by the suddenness and the violence of it. Slowly, he registered planes sagging and broken amid the smoke; figures picking themselves up, staggering among the wreckage, pulling others out; the cacophony impressing itself from all sides as his numbed ears recovered, of exploding ammunition, screams for help, voices shouting. Beside him, Powell straightened up, looking about. A transport on the main runway, one of its wings torn at the root and draped back over the fuselage, erupted into a fireball. Smoke billowed outward over the ground in a churning curtain, and then several figures ran out covered in blazing fuel. Somebody from a rescue tender doused them with foam while others grabbed them and tried to roll them on the ground. Another was trying to unfold a tarp. Cade could only stare, numbed by the horror of it. Then the sharp *crack* of something detonating overhead made him look up. It was like a Fourth of July star burst, except that the objects being ejected from the center were not incendiary submunitions but self-powered devices like birds that seemed to be dispersing. Another exploded above the far end of the field. Then another, off to one side. Still bewildered, Cade turned his head toward Powell. "What the hell are those?"

Powell shook his head. "It beats me. All I know is, I've never heard of anything like 'em before."

The side of the tower facing the field had been raked by cannon fire. In what was left of the day room on the ground floor, Hudro groped his way through the smoke and dust, lifting aside a steel locker that had been thrown at an angle against the wall. A body that had been pinned behind it slid down into a heap. Somebody was groaning and calling for aid in the direction of the stairs. A corpsman in a helmet bearing a red cross appeared from outside and went on through. Hudro came to the daylight but kept back within the frame of the doorway while he took in the situation. Sergeant Davis, his face bloody and covered in dust, stumbled up beside him.

Flocks of what looked like gliding, stubby-winged birds were spiraling down to settle all over the airfield. A plane that seemed to have escaped serious damage lurched its way out from behind a transport that was starting to burn and turned toward the main runway. A swarm of maybe a dozen small shapes, some rising from the surrounding ground, others not yet landed, converged upon it like dogs around a bear, each exploding on contact to leave the aircraft crippled and immobile. Two more homed on a staff car racing along the nearby verge, causing it to swerve and overturn. One came down off a hangar roof to explode among a group of figures running toward the fire shed. Another rose up from the sand to pursue a soldier who jumped up from a foxhole, getting close enough before detonating to blow off his upper body.

"What in the name of Christ are they?" Davis asked fearfully.

Hudro scanned the surrounding. Similar things were happening in every direction as panic took over. The sounds of intensifying battle were coming distantly but insistently from the east. "Smart drones," he replied. "Is way to deny use of base but not destroy. Means they plan to take over soon. Next attack will be with fragmentation—like rain of razors."

Davis gulped. "You mean we're supposed to just sit here, waiting to get blended?"

"Terrans don't have defenses."

"So what are we supposed to do?"

"Must first stop fear and movement. Need radio." Hudro led the way back inside, where they picked up a dazed tower crew operator in a blood-streaked shirt. "Find working radio," Hudro told him. "Local channels, all commanders you can talk with outside. Tell nobody to move. Stay still, is okay. Tell them pass message on."

A Marine private who had come down from the upper level overheard. "There was a Hummer out back. Its radio should be okay. It may have a loud hailer too." He thought about it. "Would that be safe?"

"Is good," Hudro said. "Drones don't use sound sensor. We go see."

While the tower officer started checking the equipment, Hudro, Davis, and the Marine made their way through to the rear of the building and looked out. A Hummer command car was parked along with several other vehicles, all looking unscathed. Hudro raised a warning hand as they were about to emerge. "Now must move very slow. Good chances. You see." They approached the Hummer like slow-motion mimes. Hudro indicated the driver's seat to Davis. "I never learn to drive Terran machines. Is yours."

Davis looked nervous. "With those things everywhere?"

"Must drive very careful. Move no more than one foot in two seconds. Can do, yes?"

They climbed in. Davis started the motor, and with his knuckles white on the wheel, negotiated the Hummer foot by foot around the building until they could see out over the field again, then stopped. The Marine located the loud hailer and began addressing the general area. "HEAR THIS. HEAR THIS. GENERAL ALERT. BE AWARE OF MOTION DETECTION. MAKE NO RAPID MOVEMENT. REPEAT, DO NOT MAKE RAPID MOVEMENTS. . . ."

Hudro, meanwhile, toyed with the vehicle's radio and raised the operator they had left inside the tower. "We've managed to contact some of the units out there," the operator reported. "Still trying more." Sure enough, the panic seemed to be abating, giving way to a strained, nervous paralysis spreading across the field.

"Maybe there is way to get out," Hudro said finally.

"What?" Davis asked.

Hudro squinted, peering through the intervening smoke in the direction of a large, four-turbofan freighter that he had spotted earlier, stopped at the far end of the runway. It had been about to turn for its takeoff run when the attack came in. Its tail was in tatters, but it seemed otherwise intact. "What kind of aircraft is this?" he asked Davis.

"Which?"

Hudro pointed. "Far away distance. Other end of runway. Tail in pieces."

"Looks like a C-17."

Hudro talked to the operator in the tower. "This airfield. It has electronics for take-off blind, yes?"

"Yes sir. The Marines set up mobile ILS system that would do that. Don't know if it's still functioning, though."

"So we have to risk. Is C-17 plane at other end runway. Can speak with captain?"

"Let me try." The operator did, and got a connection.

"Tell him this," Hudro instructed. "Turn plane very, very slow so that engine fans blow down along field, yes. Contact officer who commands unit that end. Must get together tires, spare wheels from trucks . . . whatever. Cover with gasoline and set fire. C-17 must blow across field. Thick rubber smoke confuses drone sensors. Is even better if they add magnesium flare or white phosphorus from smoke rounds. Set plenty fire to grass."

"You think it could really work?" Davis asked dubiously.

"You want wait for blender instead?"

While the instructions were being relayed to the far end of the field, Hudro told Davis to begin heading back to where the C22-E was parked. The Marine private opted to stay with them. They inched their way agonizingly toward the edge of the field, Hudro remaining outwardly impassive, the Marine white-faced and rigid. Davis had to stop three times to calm his nerves. They had about fifty yards to go, when a desperate voice called out to them. Davis stopped. They looked around. "There," the Marine said, pointing.

It was Koyne, lying in the grass behind a mound of sand where he had taken cover—presumably on his way back from the workshops, where he had gone to check for some parts. "Are you hurt?" Davis called over. Koyne shook his head in a short, jerky motion, then inclined it to indicate a spot to the side of him. A drone was lying there, just a yard or two away. It was yellow with black markings, about the size of a crow, but at close range looking more like a malevolent giant insect.

"Oh shit. . . ." Davis hissed.

"Is okay if you move slow," Hudro called over, striving to keep his voice calm. "But careful." In a lowered tone he muttered to the other two, "More close, gets riskier."

But Koyne just shook his head again. "I can't." Clearly, he was petrified. He must have been pinned there for over thirty minutes.

Hudro looked around. There was a fire extinguisher behind the seat on the Hummer's passenger side. "Give that," he said to the Marine, motioning with his head. The Marine moved warily, as if he were picking up Koyne's terror, unclamped the extinguisher and passed it forward. Hudro took it, removed the pin, and clasped the activating lever in readiness. Then, moving in carefully controlled slow motion, he straightened up from the passenger seat to place one foot outside the vehicle, following it slowly with the other.

Davis, the Marine, and Koyne watched barely daring to breath as the alien took what must have been five seconds to complete one step, then did the same again with the other foot as if approaching a coiled cobra. Koyne looked up, rivers of perspiration running down his face, while Hudro drew nearer until he was standing immediately over the drone. Keeping his movement just as slow, he raised the nozzle of the extinguisher and covered the drone in foam.

"Is safe now," he told Koyne.

It took Koyne a few seconds more to move. He rose slowly and backed away toward the Hummer, unable to take his eyes off the drone. Hudro gave it another blast of foam and then followed.

"You okay?" Davis asked Koyne as he climbed shakily into the seat behind.

Koyne licked his lips and nodded. He looked disbelievingly at Hudro as Hudro got back in up front. "I guess those people were right. . . . Some of you guys are okay. That took a lot of guts. Thanks."

"Is we Hyadeans who make drone and bring here. What else I can do?" Hudro replied.

They were in the form of immense, flattened pyramids, five times as wide across the base as they were tall, glinting a peculiar bronzelike luster between black ribbing and casement structures in the light of the late afternoon sun. Armor-piercing shells skidded harmlessly off their angled faces. Proximity-bursting missiles seemed to have no effect. They advanced in a line several hundred feet above the ground, generating a zone of boiling light and fire beneath that progressed like a wall. Nothing stood up to it. Gerofsky had watched tanks, armored personnel carriers, gun emplacements, consumed like paper balls thrown into a furnace. A wing of the newest supersonic F-19s that went in against them had been picked off like ducks by beams of some kind directed from unseen sources above.

In the positions among the crests of the overlooking slopes, order was starting to break down, with troops getting jumpy, some already falling back, commanders frantically talking into field radios and pleading for orders. Gerofsky could feel himself verging on panic. Yet Nyarl was actually standing, his face expressionless, training his camera, catching everything. The task had become an obsession with him. Suddenly, he looked at Marie, crouched behind the edge of the trench they were occupying ahead of the battery, clutching her useless submachine gun. "Come out and stand up," he called to her. "I want you in the foreground. A Terran woman facing Chrysean war engines that are destroying her world." Marie stared at him, as if checking that his sanity hadn't snapped. He gestured and smiled humorlessly. "I know the psychology of Hyadeans. . . . No, don't put the gun down. Keep it in your hand. Defiant to the last, eh? They'll love it." Gerofsky watched as Marie climbed out from the trench and complied. "The world that invented painting and music, philosophy and dreams," Nyarl went on as he lined up the camera. "Einstein and Mozart. Both crafters of realities that captivate the imagination but could never be."

Surely, Gerofsky thought, if Nyarl could get this one shot back to Chryse, it would be enough to stop this. It was obscenity, not war. For the first time in his career, he found himself wondering if there had ever been a difference.

Bolts of plasma began coming down from the sky and exploding among weapons positions, defense lines, supply dumps. There was nothing for the targeting radars to register on, nothing to be done if they could. The troops entrenched along the crests began falling back; then the support units. Soon, everything became a scramble to get away to the rear. Gerofsky halted the ammunition carrier that they had ridden out on, now jammed with troops, just as it was pulling out and bundled Marie and Nyarl aboard. A half mile down the road it became bogged down in a jam tailing back from some kind of obstruction ahead. It would be a death trap when the next attack came in. Gerofsky ordered the other two out. Hauling a radio after him, he stumbled with them across the slopes toward a dirt track rising to follow a ridge. It was bumpy and not all that wide; but it ran straight. Before very much longer there wouldn't be any other chance.

The smoke swirled by outside as an opaque fog. From behind Powell, Cade watched the lights of the transport ahead vanish as if they had been switched off. Powell counted off fifteen seconds and then gunned the C22-E's engines. The plane headed into a black wall hurtling by at increasing speed. Cade felt his hands and back going clammy, wishing he could share the faith in technology of the two seated in front of him. Powell concentrated on the ILS readouts, while Koyne read off the instruments. Cade didn't want to think about the consequences if something had screwed up invisibly ahead of them. There could be no ground control. Visibility from the tower was zero. Finally, they were at liftoff speed. Powell hauled back the stick, and moments later they emerged into evening. Leveling out low, he banked into a broad right turn that would take them over the hills toward the east, where ominous black clouds towered over the skyline.

They had waited while the evacuation proceeded, following Hudro's crazy plan. With an attack expected at any time, Powell had set a time limit, after which the safety of the aircraft would have to come first. They would leave and endeavor to make contact with the others again later, somehow. Despite his sickening visions of being parted from Marie yet again, Cade had been unable to argue. Gerofsky reached them on radio minutes before the deadline was up. Now, all they had to do was find him.

"Okay, we're airborne, turning your way," Powell said into his mike. "Keeping it down, just above stalling. Let us know when you have visual."

"Jesus, it's a mess down there," Koyne said, craning on the other side of the cockpit. "Whatever happened up front? They're streaming back everywhere." Cade stared down. How could the confidence that had been everywhere this morning have degenerated to this in one day? Hudro looked out sadly, shook his head, and said nothing.

They took a slow, winding course, banking to sweep left and right. Suddenly, Powell announced, "They've got us!" Then, into his mike, "Roger, Major. I read you. Turning as directed. . . . Yes, I see a ridge with a track. Okay, got it. . . . I'm going to have to go around again and line up. . . ."

It was a bone-shaking landing, but they made it. Nyarl climbed in first, still with his camera. Marie followed, and then Gerofsky. With them were three young, frightened soldiers they had run into on the way. Powell took them aboard.

Marie collapsed into Cade's arms before the plane had even commenced its run. She was pale and gaunt, with a look in her eyes that Cade had never seen before—the kind of look that might never completely go away. He looked at her and shook his head uncomprehendingly, not sure what to say. She leaned her head against his shoulder for what seemed a long time. "Oh God, Roland," she managed finally. "It was horrible. I thought I was tougher than this by now. . . . This has become insane."

"Was always insane," Hudro said neutrally from his seat farther back.

Cade pulled her close and pressed her head against him. "We don't split up again," he told her. "Through whatever happens, wherever it leads. We're together until the end now."

◎ CHAPTER FIFTY-FIVE ◎

They flew west into the night, heading north of Tulsa toward what had seemed to be a major staging area. Koyne reported air activity in the vicinity and registered numerous radar contacts. There were many fires along the route: some isolated and confined, suggesting burning vehicles or downed planes; others covering whole areas. In one place a sizable town looked to be ablaze from end to end. With the navigation aids disrupted, it was difficult to say exactly where it was.

The snippets coming in over the radio were garbled and panicky. A Union spearhead was already halfway between St. Louis and Kansas City, with another thrusting north along the Mississippi valley and threatening a massive left hook at Chicago, which would cut off the Federation armies that had advanced into Indiana and Illinois—assuming they hadn't been annihilated already. To the south they were reported to be near Shreveport, and the Dallas area was under attack. Gerofsky shook his head in bewilderment as Nyarl read off the details. "How is it possible? Under combat conditions? Nothing could move that fast."

"I tell you, you don't have mobility," Hudro said. "They don't move like you think. Hyadeans unroll carpet from sky." Twenty minutes later, Nyarl proved it with a shot he had received from somewhere along the Missouri valley, of Union armor emerging from huge, lumpy, gray vessels, looking like wedge-shaped landing craft, that had descended from the sky. "They're the size of battleships!" a commentator's terrified voice jabbered. "The defense is just coming apart! We've got a total rout on our hands here."

There were some heroics to record. West of St. Louis, a Federation Ranger force drew a detachment of Hyadean ground troops that had been landed on a flank into a classic ambush with pre-targeted mortars and prepared mines, and wiped them out. A pair of aging F-15s destroyed one of the flying pyramid-fortresses at Texarkana—and Nyarl got a clip of it. But the overall picture was grim. But still there seemed to be no word from Sacramento to call it off. Gerofsky's guess was that events had happened so quickly, and communications were in such chaos, that nobody there had grasped the enormity of what was going on.

"Darn it, look at that!" Powell exclaimed suddenly, at the same time banking the plane sharply to port.

"What is it?" Gerofsky called from behind Cade.

Koyne half turned his head, keeping his eyes on the outside. "Tracer coming up. Friendly fire."

"I guess there must be a lot of trigger-happy people down there tonight," Powell growled.

"Let's hope they're nervous enough not to shoot straight," Marie said. Even as she spoke, a series of flak bursts lit up ahead.

Powell throttled up and went into a tight, diving, starboard turn. "This is getting serious," he muttered. Moments later, there was an explosion outside close enough to light up the inside of the cabin, and the plane shuddered under a hail of impacting fragments. Wind whipped through the cabin from a rent in the skin somewhere. Powell straightened out but held the dive, shedding altitude for ground cover. Something was beeping up front. From where he was sitting, Cade could see alarm indicators flashing and lighting up all over the instrument panel. Powell and Koyne went into an emergency check routine. "Losing fuel on one engine," Powell called. "We're going down. Be ready for fire." Behind him, Davis broke out an extinguisher from a bulkhead rack. Marie found another at the rear of the cabin. Powell switched to emergency band and began sending out Mayday messages for a landing ground.

They found haven at a airstrip that was being used for night operations. A young Officer of the Watch who met them informed them they were twenty miles southeast of Wichita. The strip's combat aircraft were being evacuated before dawn; then it would be handling ambulance flights for as long as possible. Apart from that, he didn't know too much except that things seemed to be a mess everywhere. He sounded as if he was from New York.

The three soldiers that the C22-E had picked up left to find a unit to attach themselves to. While Powell and Davis began checking over the damage to the airplane, the others shared a beef stew supper with a maintenance crew in an Air Force trailer. Afterward, Gerofsky and Hudro borrowed a jeep and drove off in the direction of Wichita to seek news at the headquarters of an armored corps stationed in the area. A little over an hour later, a corporal from the signals unit serving the airstrip telephoned the trailer to report that he had Gerofsky on another channel with a data connection open, and could Nyarl get over with the material to be transmitted? Cade and Marie went with Nyarl to the sandbagged dugout that the CO's staff and signals unit were occupying, close to the airstrip's few buildings. Gerofsky had a landline connection to the Southern California Military Command in Los Angeles, and from there had succeeded in getting through to the Catacombs. So, finally, they were able to send through the recordings that had been accumulating. Yassem and Vrel were at the other end. Having spoken with Hudro and Gerofsky already, they had recovered by now from their anxiety at hearing nothing for two days.

They still had the link to Cairns, but it would be six or seven hours before Cairns would be able to link with the Querl. The unpublicized news from Beijing, obtained via Di Milestro's line from Sacramento, was even more alarming than what had happened in the previous forty-eight hours in the Midwest. A Chinese nuclear antisatellite missile had knocked out a major Hyadean vessel in orbit, and the Hyadeans were retaliating against military targets on the Asian mainland. Nothing of the kind had been heard in Australia. The entire global situation was unstable. Collapse into universal catastrophe seemed only a matter of time.

"I don't understand it," Cade said to Yassem and Vrel. "Why isn't Jeye doing anything to restrain them—after what's happened here? He must know it's all over."

"But that's the problem," Yassem said. "I don't think they *do* know. It's as Major Gerofsky feared. They're still talking about a decisive struggle going on along the Mississippi valley—as if they still think they really can be in Washington in days. None of the advisers there understands how fast Hyadeans can move. They've lost touch with the real world."

"Get Chester to find someone up there that he can talk sense into," Cade pleaded. "We may have to be out of here by morning. I'm not even sure the plane will be able to fly."

They slept, exhausted, in an adjacent trailer serving as a billet. As Cade was dropping off, he heard the first of the helicopters coming in, bringing wounded to the ambulance planes. Nyarl was still over in the signals dugout, sorting through clips that Gerofsky and Hudro had sent via the data line and adding his own histories and commentaries for the benefit of the Chryseans. Sounds of gunfire and explosions came continuously from the direction of Wichita like dull, intermittent thunder.

Cade regained consciousness sluggishly to the feeling that something was strange. A reflex inside him didn't want to know what. It wanted to retreat back into sleep and not face any more of reality. But a more responsible part of himself still in control forced him back to wakefulness.

The distant booming was still going on, but he had already learned to tune that out. Nearer, everything was too quiet. There were no sounds of helicopter rotors or the roars of planes taking off. He sat up in the bunk and looked around the trailer. Marie was still fast asleep. So was Nyarl—for once—and Hudro, who must have returned with Gerofsky sometime in the middle of the night. Voices sounded nearby outside, followed by a truck motor starting up. Cade felt a mind-deadening weariness. It was as if the adrenaline charge that had kept him going through the previous few days had finally worn off, letting him sink to rock bottom. He had no recollection of the names of the officer who had received them or the signals corporal. They were just faces in a daily pageant that unrolled, and beyond the immediate object of staying alive, was ceasing to mean anything. And right now, he admitted to himself, he was scared. He didn't care that much about the Federation, what happened on Chryse, or great plans for how things would be a hundred years from now. What mattered was getting through until next week.

He swung his legs down to the floor and pulled on his boots. His face, when he rubbed it, felt stubbly and greasy. He went through to the washroom at the end of the trailer and ran water into the metal basin. The water was cold. The only towel was wet. He dried himself with tissue, came back to put on his shirt and jacket, and went outside.

The scene in daylight was the kind of litter that only the military in wartime can produce. Cartons, cases, drums, and debris were everywhere, with scatterings of dead cartridge cases, oddments of ammunition, tangles of wire, emptied food cans and rations packs, remnants of clothing. All that was left of the air traffic were several disabled planes and a helicopter, which a demolition crew was wiring with charges. A huge pall of smoke hung in the sky to the northwest. The remainder of the detachment that hadn't already left was congregating around a mix of cars, trucks, a couple of tankers, and other vehicles in the final stages of loading. Some civilians had appeared in a gaggle of heavily loaded cars and pickup trucks standing along the road at the end of the strip. Evidently, they were pulling out but had decided it would be safer to stay with the soldiers. Several men were rummaging among the piles of discarded supplies. Gerofsky and the C22-E's crew were conferring by the aircraft, parked fifty yards or so away. They saw Cade emerge. Gerofsky and Powell came over.

"We've got a problem with one of the pumps," Powell informed him. "Davis has rigged a temporary fix, but it needs a part we don't have. If it fails, I wouldn't trust the other engine alone to keep us up. We can risk it, but we might not be so lucky finding a place to get down next time. The alternative is to go with these guys in one of the trucks."

Cade didn't like the thought of leaving all that equipment while it might still have some use. He looked at Gerofsky. "What do you think, Major?"

"I say we risk it. Look at the jam we ran into yesterday—and that was up among hills. Everything's going to be squeezing through Wichita." A series of cracking sounds rippled from the north. They looked and saw the smoke of air bursts a mile or two off, that had come in several seconds previously. "And that's going to get worse," Gerofsky added.

"Where do we head for?" Cade asked.

"Anywhere. Union troops are already in Kansas City. Let's just get out of here."

"That's good enough for me," Cade said. He nodded to Powell. "Okay, let's have her loaded and ready. I'll get the others up."

Wichita had become a bottleneck of retreating infantry, armor, and support columns, and streams of refugees converging northward from Oklahoma City and Tulsa, and west from the region south of Kansas City toward routes west through Dodge City and Pueblo. The area had been under attack through the night, and by the time the C22-E skirted low over the city on the southern side, presented a virtually unbroken spectacle of burning and devastation.

Connecting the camera directly to one of the cabin displays, Nyarl brought telescopic views of knocked-out tanks, cratered malls and highways, streets ablaze, strewn with bodies and overturned vehicles. In one place, an overpass had fallen on a line of army trucks and yellow schoolbuses. A suburban airfield was covered with the wreckage of dozens of planes caught on the ground. Stranded vehicles were everywhere, their occupants sitting outside waiting for direction, besieging dressing stations and aid posts, or simply taking what they could and joining a tide of stragglers heading onward toward the west on foot, or at least just getting clear of the city.

Radio traffic was primarily local and concerned with emergencies: a hospital somewhere was on fire and being evacuated; a supply battalion was out of reserves of gasoline; a plane was in trouble and needed a directional fix. From an armchair up in the sky, it was easy to let it all feel unreal and detached. But just looking at Marie's face as they listened to the snatches of people in fear, people dying, calling for help, others just trying to do their jobs, forced Cade to be mindful that every one was a tragedy happening to somebody right now, each representative of a hundred others that they didn't know about, and very probably no one ever would know about. The pointlessness and the waste of it all came to him then in a way as never before. The inexhaustible potential of human creativity, and what it could produce, the limitless resource of young, educated minds to turn worlds into gardens, tame the power that drove stars, bring life and consciousness to the cosmos. And instead of what could have been, how much of it was squandered on death-dealing and destruction? The Hyadeans had created a whole legend out of what Earth could have been—what they described as the world of dreams. Was it to end as a nightmare?

As they came around onto a course heading for Denver, the skyline behind erupted in a series of black fountains from another salvo of missiles descending on the stricken city.

Nyarl made contact with an airborne command post flying somewhere above Colorado. The latest they had heard was that the attacks on China were now public news and intensifying. Houston was in Union hands, San Antonio was threatened, and Chicago encircled. Ellis in Washington was demanding unconditional surrender, but Jeye, following Beijing, had vowed to fight on and was escalating the use of battlefield nuclear devices. Nyarl sent off his latest package.

They covered a further four hundred miles, most of it over a flat, checkerboard Kansas landscape of straight roads and rectangular fields before the pump that Davis had jury-rigged failed. Soon afterward, the other engine began misbehaving under the added load, and Powell decided it would be better to land now, while they still had power at all. They were past the Colorado border, above dry prairie grasslands beginning to give way to desert. Powell found a road carrying military traffic widely spaced against air attack, mixed with clusters of civilian vehicles, all heading west, and put down on a stretch of sandy flat close by. The nose wheel collapsed, probably from a combination of plowing into the soft ground and the rough landing on the ridge the previous day, and they came to a spectacular skidding, grinding halt, shaken but otherwise unharmed.

Nyarl selected a minimum of equipment to be carried, while the others sorted out personal kit, tools, maps and documents, and supplies from the plane's galley. Davis broke out a cache of weapons that he had acquired and distributed them in addition to the ones that Marie and Gerofsky were already carrying, giving Cade an automatic rifle. Cade had never fired a gun. Marie promised him an improvised lesson.

Hudro refused. "No," he said. "I see too much. I no longer carry weapons."

◉ CHAPTER FIFTY-SIX ◉

A staff car stopped in response to Gerofsky's flagging. It was carrying the acting commanding officer of a motorized infantry regiment pulling back to a redoubt that was being formed south of Denver. Apparently, the armies of the central front were attempting to consolidate a line along the eastern edge of the Rockies. The vehicles were already crammed with wounded and stragglers picked up along the way, and the group from the downed plane had to be spread out among several to find room. Gerofsky squeezed into the staff car with the officers. Koyne insisted on accompanying Hudro in an armored personnel carrier to make it clear to any objectors that "this guy is okay." Nyarl went with Powell and Davis in a supply truck. Cade and Marie found space in an open truck carrying a field-gun crew with their artillery piece hauled behind. Cade felt as if he were back in Brazil after the helicopter crash. But this wasn't happening in Brazil; it was the middle of what used to be the U.S.A. At least, whatever lay ahead this time, he and Marie would face it together.

The air attacks came in at intervals ranging from twenty or thirty minutes to an hour or more. Sometimes they took the form of jets screaming in low to strafe and walk bombs and rockets along the column; at others, air-bursting missiles launched from several miles away. These were Terran weapons systems, not Hyadean, and Cade saw a number of the attacking aircraft brought down. Existence degenerated into a dull, stomach-churning, constant awareness of vulnerability and feeling helpless. The shouts of *"Cover! Air incoming!"*; the sour taste of fear, face pressed to the sand while the ground shuddered and white-hot metal hissed overhead; climbing wearily back into the truck, blurred into a routine that he found himself acting out mechanically with deadened senses. A few images remained etched in his memory: a soldier staggering from a truck that had been hit, one arm and one side of his face a blackened mass; a limbless torso in a ditch; a civilian bus with corpses hanging out of the shattered windows. And he began to understand how it was possible for people to see others killed, maimed, burned, blown apart, and no longer be capable of feeling anything. When survival became the driving consideration, something primitive and protective took over, shrinking one's focus to a narrow world of self and the few who qualified for the time being as one's "own."

Changing drivers in shifts, the depleted column carried on through the night through Pueblo, the terrain becoming more broken and craggy. Flashes and lights continued to light up the horizon all around, but the immediate attacks slackened to a few intermittent missiles coming in just often enough to make rest impossible when physical and nervous exhaustion craved relief into sleep. Cade sat hunched by Marie, his body aching and protesting more as with every mile the truck's metal-and-fabric seats seemed to get harder and grow new sharp corners. If life ever returned to normal, and if they survived to enjoy it, he would never complain about airlines again, he told himself.

Daybreak brought a scene of dry gulches, mesas, and rocky bluffs rising among broken, dusty mountains of brown and gray ahead. This seemed to be the outer edge of the defensive line, with forward positions being prepared and activity visible away into the distance on both sides. The commander called a halt to regroup the regiment's scattered vehicles, give the stragglers time to catch up, and assess losses. Two trucks were missing, which was not as bad as the attrition that some units had suffered. One of them, however, was the one that Nyarl, Powell, and Davis had been riding in. Radio calls for it to report in brought no response. Hudro and Koyne were the most shaken by the news—understandably.

Heroic and desperate, maybe, but it all seemed an invitation for a repeat of the carnage that had happened yesterday. Cade and the others made themselves as useful as they could, all the time waiting apprehensively; but as the morning drew on, the skies remained strangely quiet. Subtly but significantly, something had changed. Everyone could sense it, but nobody was quite able to say what.

Cade watched a tank crew carrying out repairs under camouflage netting to something in the engine compartment of their machine, which they had opened up. None of them could have been more than in their early twenties, except maybe the captain, who could have been brushing twenty-five. They worked calmly and competently, despite the stress and fatigue they had to have suffered over the past few days. Cade had never had much of a head for machinery or technicalities—his talents lay more with human foibles—but he had always respected and marveled at the mentalities that could conceive and construct generating plants, jet planes, automobiles, and telephone networks, and generally bring into being the world of material productivity that enabled his world to exist comfortably and prosperously. He marveled at it now, seeing the exposed, precisely machined gears, tangles of piping, bundles of color-coded cables snaking like vines to reach mysterious cylinders and inscrutable metal boxes. What had it taken in human worth and ingenuity, education, training, dedication to make possible the display of skill that he was witnessing now? And by how much more would that need to be multiplied to take into account everything else that was going on across the continent right now? And then add the factories that had produced it all, and behind them all the mining, drilling, rolling, forging, refining, processing that sustained them. For what? The price in expended human value was incalculable.

Though awesome in its image of menace and power, the tank was ugly and utilitarian. Cade took in the squat lines of the turret carrying its long-barreled cannon; the impersonal lethality of the grenade throwers and machine guns protruding from invisible stations within; the hatch lids open, revealing the armor thickness that its crew would depend on when they became the stakes in a duel pitting the abilities of rival teams of designers. Two armorers were loading ammunition from a field tractor: different shapes and casings, some with dull black bodies, others yellow, another kind white. Gerofsky had described a standard type of armor-piercing round which punched a hole through the hull and blasted a jet of white-hot molten metal into the interior.

He looked at the crew again: each life potentially priceless by the measures of the economy of Chryse, dedicated to the sole purpose of killing and maiming indistinguishable others who had played the same games, had the same kinds of kid brothers and older sisters, parents, lovers, guys on the street in the same kinds of neighborhoods of the same kinds of homes. In Australia, Krossig had described the new insight that he and Mike Blair had found, which made all of physical reality an environment contrived—implicitly by some as-yet incomprehensible intelligence?—for the purpose of enabling consciousnesses to make choices. If so, then surely the choices being made by the consciousnesses dominating this particular part of that reality qualified it as the lunatic asylum of the cosmos. Or was it as bad everywhere? Cade wondered.

"*Guys! Look!*" A shout from Marie pulled his attention away. He turned to where she had been managing a stove and dispensing hot water for washing, shaving, and coffee to the troops, and found her standing, pointing toward the road. Hudro and Koyne climbed up from a slit trench that they had been digging. A dust-covered flatbed carrying two large-caliber howitzers, and with disheveled passengers taking up every spare foot of space, had stopped to let several figures dismount. Most were in regular combat dress, carrying packs and weapons, but two stood out immediately. One was of pinkish countenance beneath streaks of dirt and a field dressing on one cheek, with a wide brow, and wearing a bedraggled Air Force flying suit; the other was big and wide although youthful in looks—and blue-skinned. It was Nyarl and Davis. They both managed tired grins as they traipsed across the rocky shoulder of the road to where the regiment's vehicles were clustered. Gerofsky appeared as the others went forward to greet them.

"We'd given you up," Koyne told Davis, clapping him on the back. "What happened to the truck? They've been trying to raise you on radio."

Hudro clasped both Nyarl's hands and said something in Hyadean that sounded very emotional and happy. Cade took the camera and shoulder bag of ancillary equipment, which Nyarl still had with him.

"A stick of bombs went through us while we were taking cover," Davis said. "The truck was totaled, and some of the guys didn't make it. We thought we might end up walking all the way, but that transporter picked us up."

The news was not all happy, however. Powell was among those who hadn't made it. Something like that had been expected eventually, of course. Nevertheless, it dulled what spirit they had been managing to summon back together that morning.

Shortly afterward, Gerofsky revealed what perhaps was the reason for the absence of hostile activity all morning. The Hyadean conveyor had unrolled around and behind them. Denver to the north and Albuquerque to the south were already occupied. A blocking force had landed in the pass this side of Grand Junction. There was no way open to the west.

Presumably, the lull was an invitation to give it up in the face of a hopeless situation. But no surrender appeared to be forthcoming. Jeye—assuming orders were still coming from Sacramento—was sticking to his word. The brigade that the regiment belonged to received orders to move on deeper into the mountains to a position in what was evidently being prepared as a last stronghold for the Federation forces fleeing westward along the central front. Cade and the others stayed with them. What else was there to do?

That night, they found themselves preparing to bed down with one of the sections dug in on a forward slope ahead of brigade headquarters. The air was calm, bringing the creaking of tanks moving among the light of arc lamps in the darkness below. Still, the respite was continuing. It was generally interpreted as a last lull before the storm that would unleash with the morning: a final chance to reconsider. Apparently, there had been heavy air attacks in California, but once again, it proved impossible to get a communications link to the group in Los Angeles to find out more.

It was going to be a chilly night, spent in holes scraped in the ground, huddling in blankets or whatever else could be improvised. Cade and Marie sat sharing a mess tin of soup in the pit that they occupied with Nyarl, separated by a parapet from Hudro, Koyne, and Davis. Gerofsky was away, conferring with the brigade staff in the tents and trailers farther back below the ridge line. Soldiers were talking, brewing coffee, and sharing cigarettes in sandbagged positions dimly visible on the far side.

"I don't like it," Marie said, dunking a piece of biscuit and nibbling on it. "It feels too much like where we were in Oklahoma—before the big attack came in. Everything's going to hit in the morning. I can feel it."

Cade stared at the rocky hillside, formless in the starlight, while he searched for an encouraging response. There wasn't one. "Well, if you're right, at least we go out together," he offered finally. "We made it in time to do that."

Nyarl shook his head. "Fighting to the end when there is no hope. Again this is part of the Terran mystery. Hyadeans would never understand it."

"So how would it affect them on Chryse . . . if they knew?" Marie asked.

"It's part of the mystery," Nyarl said again. "Or is it mystique? They wouldn't let you do it."

"Then maybe Jeye's doing the right thing without realizing it," Marie said. She turned her head toward Cade. "I thought I was a born fighter. You know—one of those deluded self-images that you carry around in your head. And in the games I got mixed up in these last five years. Because that's what they were, games. . . . But all this in the last few days—the real thing. I never knew the insanity of it. Whatever problem this is supposed to solve, it could have been solved for a fraction of what it all costs. And it doesn't even solve anything. It only makes it worse for next time."

"I was thinking the same earlier," Cade said. He shifted to ease a cramped foot. "I used to think that what made people worth getting to know was who they networked with, what favors they could do—what you could get out of them. Now I've seen the qualities that make people truly valuable. And often it's in the same people . . . like Clara, maybe, or George, or Anita, Neville Baxter . . . even Dee."

"Dee was always okay."

"Yeah, well. . . . But you know what I'm saying. Why does it have to take something like this to bring that side of people out? Why couldn't they be what they're capable of from the beginning?"

"I hope they're okay back there," Marie mused. "Dee and Vrel, Luke, Henry . . . all of them."

"It's the same with us too," Cade went on. "Don't you get the feeling it's a bit late to find out now who you really are? Especially since it seems there's not going to be a lot we'll be able to do with the knowledge."

Marie could only shrug. "Maybe better late than never, all the same."

"Unless those things that Krossig and Michael Blair used to get excited about turn out to be close after all," Nyarl suggested.

"What things?" Cade asked.

"Personalities in this reality being incarnations of souls to help them develop. The things Hudro wants to discover. As do many Hyadeans."

"If it's true, then I must be working some enormous piece of karma off the debit side," Cade said resignedly.

"If?" Nyarl repeated. "Now you're sounding as if you don't believe it yourself."

Cade looked at him, the dark-hued face all but invisible against the jacket hood pulled around in the darkness. "It was a legend that you wanted to hear, and we played at being. It was how I got rich, and my friends got rich."

"You're making you and them sound responsible," Nyarl objected. "But you just used the situation that you found. You didn't create it. It resulted from the worst elements of both our worlds working in collusion."

"That's my point," Cade said. "If Earth had really been the legend that you thought, none if this could have happened. The best elements of both worlds would have . . ." He sighed and shook his head. "I don't know what." The strange thing was, he found himself almost believing that it could have been different. But even those who he'd thought might bring about something better had ended up going for the throat when they thought everything was in their favor. He leaned back and looked up at the stars. "Maybe one day it will all be told differently as stories change," he said to the others. "Another legend of an Earth that never happened."

⚛ CHAPTER FIFTY-SEVEN ⚛

Cade awoke chilled and stiff. He freed his arms from the blanket and stretched sluggishly. Marie was gone; Nyarl, still asleep, was wrapped in blankets and a greatcoat. He stood up, brushing frost from the predawn cold of the mountains off his jacket and beating his arms across his chest, while his breath steamed in white clouds. A thin film clung to the tops of the sandbagged parapets and the boulders, adding extra bleakness to the scene of daybreak creeping into the landscape like the light being slowly turned up on a stage setting. He saw Marie now, with Hudro, Koyne, and some soldiers, huddled around a stove under the awning covering the field kitchen a hundred yards or so back in a gully.

The scarp they were on faced east, overlooking an expanse of sand and broken rock that lay flat for a mile or two before rising to a line of craggy uplands. They were about twenty miles behind the forward positions that they had seen being prepared yesterday, looking down over rearward missile and gun emplacements, antitank defenses, and staging areas for reserve armor. Over the ridge behind them would be the long-range artillery, antiaircraft positions, command bunkers. Cade was getting to know the pattern already.

Footsteps crunched on the gravel behind. Cade turned to find Gerofsky in a combat jacket and helmet, accompanied by a couple of troopers, coming down from the ridge, where he had gone to learn the latest at brigade HQ. The troopers went off toward their own unit.

Gerofsky came to the edge of the parapet and stepped down to join Cade. He looked grim.

"Forget any ideas of a breakout west from the Rockies. They've as good as closed the ring. This is the last act, right here. Or something has to change pretty drastically somewhere."

"Nothing from Sacramento?" Cade asked.

Gerofsky shook his head. "Not much from the West Coast at all. I'm not sure what it's supposed to mean. Orders are to hold out with maximum effort. I don't know what with, though. Our air support is practically nonexistent. They still have satellite cover. We're like ducks in a barrel."

Cade didn't reply. Nyarl, stirred by the talking, sat up, rubbed his eyes, mumbled something incomprehensible, and began removing frosty wrappings from his equipment. Behind him, Marie was coming across from the kitchen, carrying a metal lid as a tray for steaming coffee mugs. Slowly, the scene around them was coming to life. Troops began appearing out of the ground to congregate around spots dispensing heat and breakfast. Some tanks away to the right were moving out from their parking area. A jeep scuttled by busily below, raising a train of dust. But beneath the appearances of calm ran an undercurrent of tension everywhere, waiting for the first shocks and rolls of thunder that would signal the opening assault at the front. Or would it begin as a sudden saturation from the sky by some unknown form of destruction?

Marie arrived and passed the coffees around, setting one down by Nyarl. Davis joined them from the far side of the dividing parapet. Gerofsky repeated for their benefit what little news there was.

"Nothing on what's happening in China?" Davis inquired.

"I'm not even sure there still is a China," Gerofsky said.

Davis watched Nyarl laying out components and checking them into pockets in his various carrying cases. "What's the point, Nyarl?" he asked. "Whatever you get, who's ever going to see it? LA might not be there."

"I'll see it through to the end. It's what Luodine would have wished." Nyarl thought, then added, "Terran sentiment. I thought you'd understand."

The sound of jets flying low came from far away to the left. Heads turned, but the aircraft were out of sight. A lot of birds were aloft and making agitated noises, disturbed by all the unfamiliar activity. A loud hailer somewhere back over the hill was reciting something in a monotone unintelligible at the distance. As Cade watched, a field radar sited near the top of the rise to command the forward approaches tilted to maximum elevation, probing directly above.

Marie moved closer to Cade as he stood, warming his hands around the mug. "You finally look the part—a soldier," she told him. "There was a time when I'd never have believed it."

Cade glanced at the automatic rifle he'd been given, standing propped against the parapet next to where he had slept. Marie and Gerofsky had shown him what the various knobs and catches were for, but he had never gotten around to actually firing it. Some soldier!

He gazed back out over the terrain. "You know, now and again you find yourself wondering how it will be in the end . . . when it's checkout time. You hope that when it happens it won't be too drawn-out and messy. I never imagined anything like this: stuck on some mountainside in Colorado, in a place I've never heard of." He shrugged. "You'd have thought that after the life I've lived, I could have managed something with a bit more style, wouldn't you? You know, lots of friends at the funeral, big speeches. . . ."

"I thought all that really mattered was that we were together," Marie reminded him.

He turned, and looked at her, checking himself. Then he put an arm around her and drew her close. "Yes. A pity we won't be able to do a hell of a lot with it. . . . But I'm glad it worked out in the end. Do you always do things in such roundabout ways?"

"Why just me? You got here via China too, as I recall."

Cade pulled a face, couldn't argue, nodded, and conceded the point. "And Australia," he said, as if that somehow made a difference. He stared moodily for a while, content with the feel of Marie pressing against him. "It was a shame about Mike Blair. He shouldn't have put off going over there to work with Krossig. They were getting into such great ideas on what life ought to be about trying to understand. . . ." Cade motioned briefly with the hand holding the coffee mug, indicating nothing in particular. "Instead of whatever it is we're blowing each other up over. As if any of it mattered . . ."

Cade's voice trailed off as he registered alarmed voices around them. Faces were turning skyward. He looked up, and at the same instant felt Marie tense. An object that looked like a blunt, black arrowhead had appeared overhead, silhouetted against the brightening sky. It appeared about the size of a dime held at arm's length, hanging practically stationary but getting perceptibly larger—evidently descending. A second became visible behind and to the side, smaller but also enlarging. Then a third. More . . . They were unlike anything that had ever emerged from assembly shops on Earth. Cade felt his mouth turning dry, a knot tightening in his stomach as the realization came that the rest of his life might be measured in minutes or less.

Klaxons and alarm sirens were sounding in all directions. Across the slopes below, figures scattered to take cover in foxholes and trenches. In the gun pits and antiaircraft emplacements, barrels and missile racks were swinging to near vertical. Nyarl was already unslinging his camera, resolved to see it through to the last, whatever the futility. "Looks like they've decided to save Washington's ground forces the trouble," Davis commented dryly. Beside him, Gerofsky just stood staring upward incredulously, at a loss for coherent words.

Still the shapes were enlarging, now taking on a sinister aspect, with rows of bulges, nacelles, studs and rodlike protuberances becoming discernible along the dull black of their undersides. As finer levels of detail continued to resolve themselves, awareness came over Cade slowly that these structures were *huge*. He had thought of them as aircraft and unconsciously assigned them a comparable scale. But although just covered by the palm of his hand now, they were still high up. "Large warship" might have been a better comparison; or even small town. A dull pulsing, hinting of immense power being contained and ready to unleash, throbbed in his ears and seemed to permeate his body through his legs from the ground, as if the entire basin to the far wall of mountains were resonating. A second formation was becoming visible above and beyond the first, diamond-shaped this time.

A series of *whoosh*es sounded from somewhere along the ridge to the left. Cade jerked his head away to see a salvo of missiles streaking upward from some hidden battery. Then more came from immediately behind. They were antimissile types, with fearsome acceleration; even so, seconds passed by with the flaming tails dwindling as they climbed toward the shapes looming above, telling of the distance that still intervened. The first salvo exploded in a string of crimson bursts like a fireworks display. Cade watched, looking for some sign of damage inflicted; then he realized that they had never gotten close but been destroyed by some kind of shield or defensive beam. The second salvo fared no better, nor the others that followed. The shapes were impregnable: self-contained battle units built for combat of a different kind, on a scale that was incomprehensible.

A flight of aircraft appeared from the rear. Nyarl turned to catch them releasing their missiles and breaking away, and then followed the missiles toward their targets until they exploded harmlessly like the rest. He moved his face away from the eyepiece of the camera to look up at the craft directly for a few seconds. He seemed puzzled. Then he peered through the sighting lens again. Finally, he looked away toward Hudro, still at the field kitchen, and shouted something in Hyadean. Cade saw then that Hudro had been looking up with the same bemused expression. Nyarl called again. Hudro looked toward him, seeming to hear for the first time, and called something back. There was a brief exchange in Hyadean. Nyarl saw Cade looking at him. "The markings on those craft. They're not of any Chrysean military units, Roland. They're Querl!"

Only then did what should have been obvious become clear: The ships weren't engaging in any acts that were hostile. Everything they had done was defensive. Gerofsky was the first to snap out of the trance that had gripped all of them. Not saying anything, as if unwilling to come to any premature conclusion as to what it might mean, he climbed the parapet out of the entrenchment and set off almost at a run back up the ridge toward the brigade headquarters. Hudro and Koyne were already heading across the slope to meet him higher up. Cade and Marie followed Gerofsky. Davis grabbed Nyarl's carrying case as they brought up the rear.

They arrived at the brigade communications post, sandbaggged under a camouflage net awning. Radios were chattering, operators calling reports from consoles and battlefield displays, figures rushing excitedly among the tents and trailers. On one of the screens, Cade saw a flotilla of daughter vessels descending from one of the mother ships toward the basin that they had just been overlooking. Another screen showed the head and shoulders of a Hyadean in a military-style tunic. Gerofsky, breathless, was with two staff officers. He turned toward Cade and Marie as they approached.

"Word from the front is that all Union forces are standing down! Washington has called a truce!" he told them. The look in his eyes was still disbelieving. "The government on Chryse has collapsed. Their military here have disengaged. It's over!"

❀ CHAPTER FIFTY-EIGHT ❀

A QUERL LANDING CRAFT, looking something like the personal flyers but larger and sleeker, brought a deputation of officers from the command ship down to brigade headquarters after preliminary landings had ascertained its location. Since Querl were not accustomed to dealing with Terrans and had little experience of English, Nyarl acted as interpreter. It turned out that the news clips sent by the brigade's communications unit to Los Angeles the previous evening had made it through Cairns and been received by the Querl relays. Querl intelligence located the military unit that the two Hyadeans shown in the recordings—Nyarl and Hudro—said they were attached to, and the Querl leaders directed the initial landing to the area where it was operating.

There was something more dynamic about the Querl compared to what Cade had come to accept as typical of Hyadeans. Their manner was more expressive; they walked with more bounce; their uniforms had more style. These were the bad guys? It dawned on him how much he and probably just about all Terrans had been influenced by the Chrysean propaganda image—practically as much as any unquestioning, xenophobic Chrysean. The commanding general of the Federation forces in the central area was being rushed by helicopter from divisional headquarters some miles to the rear. In the meantime, Nyarl summarized events to Cade and the others, along with a mix of weary, red-eyed staff officers, many still struggling to grasp that a last-minute reprieve had been granted them. Behind them, the Querl war craft hung like geometrically fashioned islands in the sky, while life began showing itself again across the hills and the plain below as news spread that the war was over.

"After the AANS attacks on Chrysean craft in orbit, the Chryseans began launching punitive strikes against China and elsewhere. It was a panic, overreaction, and ill-judged in the light of the other things that had been going on back at Chryse." Nyarl paused to check something in Hyadean with a couple of the Querl officers. "We don't have all the details yet, since these people have been here in your Solar System for the last week, but unrest has been sweeping over Chryse since the Querl started broadcasting what has been taking place on Earth." He looked across to Cade and the rest of the group to address them specifically. His voice caught. "She did it! It worked the way Luodine planned—the way we carried on. It bypassed the controls that had always operated in the past. The Chrysean population learned the truth." Nyarl indicated the Querl deputation. "Until just now, even these people didn't know where the reports were originating from. But they caused an upheaval on Chryse that was unprecedented. The whole Chrysean system has fallen. The people are calling for the Querl to take over. Their ships are moving in there now, even while I'm speaking. A standoff between Querl and Chrysean military forces has been going on around Earth, the Moon, and as far out as the orbit of Mars, for several days now. But without political legitimization from Chryse, the Chrysean military here has ceased operations." Nyarl finished with a helpless gesture that said he was having trouble enough absorbing so much in so little time, too. "And the same seems to be happening here. Deprived of its Chrysean backing, the Globalist Coalition is in disarray everywhere. Washington is on stand-down, waiting for terms from Sacramento. Europe is in chaos. Nobody has any idea where it might all lead."

And for the time being—probably for a while to come after that too—that was about as much as could be said. The general arrived shortly afterward and went into conference with the Querl deputation. All around, as the morning wore on, the winding down and disbanding commenced of the elaborate orchestration of men and machines that had come together to make a last stand. The group found transport to an air supply base in the rear, where Koyne and Davis bade their farewells and departed to report to Air Force administration. Two hours later, Cade and his remaining companions boarded an airlift flight bound for the Los Angeles area. On the way, they restored contact with the Catacombs via one of the temporary satellite links that the Querl were setting up. Yassem, Vrel, Dee, Luke, and Di Milestro had stories of their own to tell, but they were all fine. Los Angeles was going to need some rebuilding in places. But perhaps that wasn't such a bad thing, either.

◈ CHAPTER FIFTY-NINE ◈

Cars by the thousands, along with trucks, buses, and planes were pouring back into Washington, D.C., reversing the exodus that had cleared the city of eighty percent of its population. Compared to what had gone on in other places, however, damage in the east was light. Hyadean orbital weapons had dealt effectively with the long-range missiles lobbed from submarines and the easternmost parts of Asia, while conventional interceptors and antiaircraft ground systems had stopped most of the bombers and cruise missiles on their way from Federation territory or from Canada. The ones that got through had not brought the all-out nuclear annihilation of cities that the panic had been about. Now, Ellis's administration had been toppled by rebellious military chiefs, following the Chrysean pull-out, and what might happen next was anybody's guess. One sure thing was that the shakeup would be worldwide.

The news going around the Hill didn't exactly speak of loyal camaraderie and trusty friends staying true to the end. With protectors and patrons tumbling by the hour, and the power holders of yesterday rushing to denounce each other while displaying their own clean hands, distinct risks could attend knowing too much about those with dangerous rivals. Acting as Toddrel's dirty-work specialist had paid off and brought its benefits; but that same history also meant that Toddrel had much on Drisson that could be bargained or turned around to sanitize his own image. In short, it was time to claim on the insurance.

Drisson pushed a package wrapped in a plastic bag across the table to Laura as they sat in a secluded corner of a cocktail lounge called the Fairway, on the west side of the city toward Georgetown. "Untraceable. All identifying marks removed," he murmured. He had established long ago that she could use a gun. Making sure of detail was another part of his business. Toddrel was in town, staying at a hotel called the Grantham that he often used, a couple of blocks off Rhode Island Avenue.

Laura took the package and put it in her purse on the chair beside her, zipping the top closed. "You're really sure you want to trust an amateur with this?" She made it sound mildly playful, as if complimenting his own professionalism.

Drisson smiled. "We both know it has to be this way. You're sure you have the routine? You call him to say you're in town and need to talk to him. Turn on the charm once you're over there. Then do the job after you've serviced him. Throw a few things around the room, fingernail scratches on the body.... Use your creativity. So when they find him, it's a simple, open-shut case of Casper getting some relaxation after all the tension, ending up in a fight, and things went too far. Anonymous hooker. No political implications. Clean."

Laura swirled her drink while she considered, then took a sip. "Isn't it being a bit overfinicky?" she queried. "From what I hear, political cleanups are likely to be the fashion around here. Is anybody going to be caring about one more, one less?"

"Why risk anything needlessly?" Drisson watched as she thought it through, still looking for the flaws, her gaze darting now across the items on the table, then to the far side of the room. His hand gripped her wrist reassuringly. "Just this one thing, and we'll be in the clear," he told her. "Then we break out the stash, make a big transfer to Australia, south of France, Argentina—wherever you want. A year or two of yachts, classy people, sunshine, and beaches while the heat here dies down."

Laura stared for several seconds at the almost-emptied glass of bourbon in front of him, then raised her eyes to meet his. For a moment, Drisson thought she was about to decline or start debating the issue. But she nodded finally and said, simply, "Okay."

Drisson smiled, relieved. "I knew you had it in you. Call me immediately to confirm, before you leave. That's important. I need the timing right to make sure Ibsan isn't around when you leave. Afterward, I'll meet you back here at say . . . eleven, unless we agree something different. Any more questions?" Laura shook her head. Drisson raised his glass, emptied it, and brushed his mustache with a knuckle. "Okay. Then we probably shouldn't walk out together. I'll see you here later." He rose and squeezed her shoulder. "Don't let me down, eh, baby?"

Actually, Drisson had arranged a quiet meeting between Ibsan and a confidential informant from the Pentagon concerning private matters that evening, so Ibsan wouldn't be anywhere around. But the timing was still important. Drisson had other plans.

"No, no! I don't want to talk to them. Just say you couldn't find me. . . . I *said* I'd take care of it." In his room at the Grantham, Toddrel cut off the phone. Everything was closing in. The Hyadeans were looking for blood over what had gone wrong in South America. Police detectives were already rounding up victims for the war-crimes show-trial circus that would be staged eventually to allay the public's already emerging thirst for revenge and justice. His name would surely be on a dozen lists. He wiped his brow. The clean shirt he had put on after getting back was already sodden. Had to control his nerves. He reached for the printout he had taken of the progress being made in restoring travel services. As he did so, his eye caught the shot being presented on the room's view screen of Cade, Cade's former wife, and the two Hyadeans talking to a news reporter on their arrival in California. *Cade!* . . . Toddrel's fingers crumpled the paper involuntarily. Ever since their interference in Chattanooga, vanishing and subsequent reappearance in South America, and then the screening of that disastrous TV documentary, it seemed they had been at the center of everything connected with the reversal of Toddrel's fortune's. Arcadia, the agent in California, was supposed to settle the score; only, Arcadia turned out to be the one who was blown up instead. Toddrel still hadn't heard a satisfactory explanation of how that could have happened. Cade hadn't even been there, in any case. So Cade had to be dead—killed in South America somewhere, Toddrel had been told—until intelligence reported him turning up again, alive and well in Beijing with the Hyadean. And finally bringing the whole house down, Cade and his woman were there in the broadcasts coming back from Chryse itself!—which had resulted in a whole planet erupting in turmoil there and the final ruin of everything here. Now all Toddrel had left was his neck, and that was on the line.

The phone beeped again before his anger boiled over. Even though it was his private channel tone, he kept it on audio. "Yes?"

"Casper, it's Laura. I was in town. With everything that's going on I thought you might be here."

Toddrel keyed the screen on to reveal Laura. "I . . . I am rather busy just now." He didn't sound especially pleased.

"Staying low? I hear it's a witch hunt out there. The long knives are coming out everywhere."

"That's friends for you. It's what you get to expect."

"Can I come over there?"

"I'm hardly in a mood for romantic distractions right now."

"Nothing like that. I'm scared, Casper. I need to talk to you. A lot's going on that I don't understand." Her gaze from the screen was insistent.

Toddrel gazed at her sourly, seemed about to refuse, then thought better of it. "Very well," he said curtly. "I'll order dinner in the room at, say, eight. We can talk then. Would that suit you?"

"That would suit fine. I'll be there shortly just. Which room is it? The desk wouldn't tell me."

"Six fifty-one. I'll tell them to give you a key."

Laura called Drisson immediately afterward. "It's arranged," she said. "He's having dinner in the room. I'll be arriving there at seven."

"Don't forget to call me as soon as it's done," Drisson said.

She entered the main door of the Grantham Hotel shortly before seven, walked to the desk, and collected a magnetically coded key to room 651. Then she paused, looking in her purse, until there was a knot of people waiting at the elevators before crossing the lobby to join them. As she did so, she had the strange, prickly sensation of being certain that unseen eyes were watching her. A car arrived. She got in with several others, made sure that the sixth floor button was pressed, but went all the way up to the penthouse bar and found a booth far from the door, where she ordered a coffee. She stayed there almost an hour. Ten minutes before eight, she took the elevator back down to the mezzanine terrace, from where she was able to observe the lobby floor below from behind a screen of ornamental ferns and a rubber-tree plant. She had stopped by earlier, after leaving the Fairway lounge, to check over the hotel layout. Laura believed in getting the details right too.

She called Drisson's number from there, making her voice shaky and a little breathless. "Okay . . . it's done. I'm on my way out."

Drisson appeared from a corner of the lobby below, talking into his phone. "No, don't. We've got an unexpected problem. Ibsan is around in the building. Stay where you are. I'm coming there to get you out a safe way."

"How long will you be?"

"On my way now. Just a couple of minutes."

Laura watched him cross to the elevators and push the call button. One of the sets of doors opened. He disappeared inside. She nodded faintly to herself. It was the way she had guessed. She raised the phone again and called Toddrel's private number. He answered almost at once. "I'm on my way up now," she told him. "There was a crowd around the desk. I'll get the key later." Unzipping the top of her purse, she made her way back across the terrace to the mezzanine-level elevator doors and pressed the "up" button.

Drisson would arrive at the room any moment now. He would knock, thinking Laura was there, waiting. Toddrel would open the door, expecting Laura; or even if he checked through the spyglass first, seeing it was Drisson, he would let him in. Finding Toddrel alone and unharmed, Drisson, being Drisson, would immediately conclude a double cross and have seconds to decide his move. Laura thought she knew what the outcome would be.

She came out of the elevator and followed the corridor to 651, holding the key in one gloved hand, the other resting lightly inside the top of her purse. She looked quickly left, then right. The corridor was empty. Producing the gun, she slid the key softly into the slot until she heard the lock disengage, then pushed the door open and stepped quickly inside. Toddrel's body was crumpled on the floor, crimson spreading across his shirt and oozing onto the carpet. Drisson was between it and the door, already turning at the sound of its opening, the gun still in his hand. Laura shot him before his mouth had framed the first word. Then she eased the door shut and stood motionless with her back pressed against it, feeling her chest pounding while she listened for any reaction to the shot. Everything outside seemed quiet. She looked apprehensively at Drisson, dreading that he might make some sound or move, and if so, wondering if she would be able to bring herself to finish the thing. But he remained inert. Laura could detect no sign of breathing. She forced herself to be calm.

The line about making it look like a hooker had been for Laura's benefit. She was supposed to have been next. Drisson's real intent had been to set up a scene that would look like a fatal quarrel between Toddrel and his high-class mistress. Being the only other person who would have known about Drisson's insurance to protect himself hadn't seemed like the surest way of getting to see much sunshine or many beaches.

Laura walked past Drisson to where Toddrel was lying, stooped to press his hand around the gun that she had used, and then tossed it on the floor in the middle of the room. Then she dug deeper into her purse, took out a plastic bag stuffed with napkins, and from them carefully extracted the glass Drisson had been drinking from in the Fairway lounge earlier. She looked around, and after a moment set it on the countertop above the room's mini refrigerator, along with a half bottle of bourbon which she had partly emptied. She had no idea, really, what the police would make of it; but she had every confidence in their ability to come up with something ingenious and satisfying.

The final thing that caught her eye as she checked over the room was a picture frozen on the viewscreen of two people facing the camera in front of a background of planes releasing missiles at targets on what looked like the outskirts of a city. It was the man called Cade, from California, who seemed to have been involved wherever trouble broke out during the past few weeks. The woman with him was his former wife, who had been with the CounterAction terrorists. Casper had developed some kind of an obsession about them.

As Laura walked away along the corridor, she reflected that curiously it was those same two who, in a way, had been instrumental in bringing about the events that had just transpired in Room 651. Ever since the first documentary they had appeared in, which a few renegade Hyadeans made in South America, Laura had found herself seized by a growing feeling of revulsion at the pictures of burning villages, maimed children, pain, suffering, terror on the faces of defenseless people—the real price that had been paid to make possible the life she had enjoyed. Now, somehow, she felt cleansed of it, as if, to some degree at least, she had atoned.

Had Toddrel had some kind of premonition that they would be a cause of this? she wondered as she waited for the elevator. She had never really had much time for things like that. By some accounts that she'd read, Hyadeans found such possibilities intriguing. And they seemed pretty smart. Maybe it would be something to look into.

A feeling of relief enveloped her as she came out into the night air without incident. Getting away from Washington and the East Coast in general for a while seemed like a wise move in any case, she decided. As she walked away along the street, the thought occurred to her that maybe the kind of work she heard was going on in California could use some help: putting the U.S.A. back together again along the lines that had been intended—or maybe along new lines that were even better; learning to work with the Hyadeans in ways that would benefit everybody; discovering the other sides to life there were besides just making money. Maybe she would even get a chance there to meet this mysterious Mr. Cade and his ex—Marie, was it?—in person there. Now *that* sounded interesting and different.

She came to an intersection, managed to stop one of the few cabs that were back on the streets, and gave the address of the hotel across town that Drisson had checked her into.

Something challenging, creative, and useful to people. A way, maybe, to make up to some degree for a life that so far hadn't had a lot going for it that she felt particularly good about or proud of. Yes, Laura decided as she settled herself back in the rear seat of the cab. That was the kind of change she wanted.

◎ EPILOGUE ◎

Cade had seen pictures of the Hyadean launch complex at Xuchimbo in western Brazil, which gave him a general idea of what to expect. But none of them had quite prepared him for the scale of the engineering—even "grandeur" would not have been an inappropriate word, despite the characteristically dull and utilitarian flavor of all things Hyadean. The optimists and visionaries on both worlds were saying that would all change very quickly now in the years ahead.

He stared out at it from a medium-size Hyadean passenger transport completing its flight from Denver. The pointed gray, white, and silver spires of the landers stood amid immense service gantries towering above the pad and associated constructions like a metallic castle from some giants' fairyland dominating the surrounding landscape of forested hills and steep-sided valleys. On the near side, several miles from the launch complex, was the landing area for conventional craft toward which they were descending, attended by a conglomeration of base facilities, roadways, bridges, pipe systems, and conveyor lines. One of the Querl officers in the party picked out a tall shape of pale gray, flaring at the tail into cruciform deltas set between a booster cluster. Cade studied it, intrigued. That was the ferry that would carry them up tomorrow morning to join the orbiting Querl mother ship due to depart for Chryse.

Marie was with Cade, looking for once the part of a presentable, urbane Western woman instead of a desperado, in a cream jacket-skirt set with chocolate blouse and trim. Vrel was there too, insistent on being their self-appointed tour guide and general attendant on Chryse. And Dee was with Vrel too, of course. And finally, making up their group, was Nyarl, going home by popular demand to meet millions for whom his face had become a phenomenon on display screens, and receive a public honor decreed by the provisional administration that the Querl had installed to take stock of the Chrysean condition.

A month had gone by since the people of Earth—bewildered and frightened; resolute and defiant—had emerged from foxholes, come out onto streets, listened to announcements in refugee centers, turned on radios and TV screens, to learn that the war which yesterday had seemed about to explode into ever greater levels of ferocity and consume the whole planet, was over. It didn't mean that the world's problems or the future of Terran-Hyadean dealings was solved, or that anyone had clear ideas as yet of how to solve them. Nobody knew what form the reconstruction of what had been the United States was to assume, based on what formulation Constitution. It was not even agreed where the capital would be, which was why negotiations were taking place in Denver: as effectively neutral as anywhere, and the nearest principal city to the Querl's first landing. But what it did signify was something akin to a collective version of the shaking up experienced after an automobile accident that could have killed everyone. If all the pain, grief, and loss of those three weeks of mass insanity—and it had been substantial—had been for anything, it was the imperative now acknowledged across both worlds that the fundamental values that life should be seeking were in drastic need of reexamination. And the people who needed to make the judgment were not the ones who so far had been allowed to be in charge.

Representatives from various Terran nations, organizations, institutions, other interests, had been invited to Chryse to begin a joint exploring of which way to go next. The other passengers on the flight from Denver were some of them. More had arrived the day before. And to Cade and Marie's amazement, they had been invited too. Nyarl, it seemed, wasn't the only one to have become an instant celebrity among the Chrysean worlds. The Terran couple who had appeared with him and symbolized their world's defiance and determination to fight through in the face of impossible odds, facing Hyadean war engines, speaking against backgrounds of burning cities, were equally famous. The Chryseans wanted to meet them too.

The transport landed among rows of cavernous cargo-carrying hulls looking vaguely like monstrous, flattened guppy fish; single-stage space-planes that could make orbit, maneuver for hours, and return; assorted special-purpose craft whose nature could only be guessed. From ground level, the peculiar alien structures rising in the background were as imposing as the launch complex had appeared from the air. Cade had the feeling of practically being on a small piece of Chryse already. The transport's cabin section detached from the airframe as a unit and slid onto a conveyor rail alongside. Moments later, it was being carried toward an opening into the terminal complex.

Hudro and Yassem were installed in Cade's place at Newport Beach, which was where Vrel would be returning. The area had escaped damage, although the house itself had shown the wear and tear of being used as a shelter for displaced children from the war areas by the time Cade came back to it. Cade wasn't quite sure what he wanted to do with the house. It struck him as gaudy and extravagant now, somehow. Luke had suggested making it an open house for visiting Hyadeans. Whatever the outcome, Cade couldn't see the kind of life being resurrected that he had come to know over the years. It wasn't so much that the rewards seemed shallow now in comparison to the cost—which was true enough—so much as life having so much more to offer that was too intriguing to ignore. Trying to understand some of the questions that Krossig and Blair had raised, for example; or seeing people in terms of more than just gains to be assessed and realized. And in any case, the prospects, contacts, hangers-on, around whom that life had revolved and depended weren't going to be around anymore—at least, not in those roles. They all seemed to have changed too in some fundamental ways, just as he had.

As, indeed, had the world. For what else did all the fumbling and reexamination to find a new direction mean than the dawning, finally, of a new perception that sought more than could be captured by Terran monetarist bookkeeping or the Hyadean calculus of efficiency as the sole measure of the worth of a life or the purpose of existence? Maybe now, together, the two races could build the legend the Hyadeans had created of what Earth could have been. If so, then perhaps the war had not been in vain.

The cabin came to a halt beside a platform in a roomy concourse of service desks and seating areas laid out beneath bright panel lights set amid a typically functional configuration of tie beams and roof supports. The arrivals disembarked to a throng of Hyadean officials and agents waiting to receive them. The Hyadean who had accompanied Cade and his companions from Denver conducted them to the two Hyadeans, a male and a female, who had been assigned to look after them. Waiting with them was a familiar purple-and-crimson-haired figure, dressed glaringly in an embroidered Bolivian shawl, straw hat with a band of wildy colored design, and bright green gaucho pants. It was Tevlak, going back on the same ship to spread Terran art on Chryse.

"So how things have changed since we were together," he said, shaking hands vigorously with Vrel, Cade, and Marie. "Then, the security people invaded us. Now they no longer exist." He put a hand on Nyarl's shoulder. "So sorry about Luodine. She should have been here today to see this."

"It was still as much her doing as anyone's," Nyarl told him. The guide from Denver performed the remaining introductions.

"You know, this routine at airports is getting to be kind of old," Cade said to Marie as they began walking toward a ramp leading though to another space.

"I guess we're just going to have to get used to being famous for a while," Marie replied.

"Without the gun, I could get used to it," Cade said. He snorted. "I never even got to shoot it. I told you I was never cut out for that kind of stuff."

"So we complement each other. That's supposed to be a good thing."

Dee was looking around and up at the utilitarian drabness of what passed for decor, and raw engineering of the architecture. "Is it all going to be like this?" she asked Vrel. "If they're catching on to our ways there, there has to be a whole load of openings for interior designers."

"I think there are going to be some big changes very soon," Vrel said. "We can't import the Andes valleys or the Amazon forest. So what we lack naturally, we'll make up with through ingenuity."

"Ten years from now, Terran tourists will be flocking to sample the exotica of Chryse," Tevlak assured them.

"That soon, eh?" Dee sounded skeptical.

"It isn't going to be just enthusiasts like me—just one person on his own," Tevlak said. "Bringing Earth to Chryse will involve everybody. Lots to do for lots of people."

Cade glanced at them and thought for a few seconds. "You reckon so, eh? I think I know a few people who could be a big help. Maybe we could sound out a few leads for them as part of the agenda while we're there."

Marie nudged him pointedly. "I thought we said that all that's over. You were going to find a new meaning in life."

"But hey, people still need to talk to each other. A lot of them are still going to be too busy to know all the options. . . . And besides, I *like* meeting people."

"What happened to the celebrity?"

"Oh, by next month they'll have found another one to put on the screens everywhere. That's the way it works. But with real friends you don't get forgotten." His voice warmed to the thought as a lot of aspects he really hadn't considered before started clicking into place. "In fact, it could even be a lot *better* now, considering what we know. Take those people in Australia that I told you about, for instance. They're already doing it right, but only in a small way that suits their own needs. You know what scientists are like. Now if a few more of the right people on Chryse knew more about that . . ."

They came out into a glass annex with a walkway leading down to an outside door. Through the wall they could see the landing area with its assembly of Hyadean aircraft, and across a stretch of terrain beyond, the distant silhouettes and towering shapes of the launch complex. Cade stopped to stare again at the Querl vessel that would ferry them up to the mother ship tomorrow. Even after all that had happened, he still found it unreal to think that in the morning they would be leaving Earth itself, and in a matter of days be at a different star system. What changes the rest of his life might have in store beyond that, he was unable to imagine. But he would make certain that it was all for worthwhile things. He thought of people like Rocco and Miguel and the things he had learned from them; Mike Blair and Bob Powell, who wouldn't be seeing Chryse, ever; Wyvex and Luodine, who wouldn't be going back there. All so that something better might come out of it. He resolved to himself that he wouldn't let them down.

He felt a tug at his sleeve. It was Marie. "Come on. We'll be there soon enough." The rest of the party were disappearing through the door at the bottom of the walkway.

Cade grinned and took her arm. They followed down after the others, through a ramp to a Hyadean ground vehicle that would take them to the accommodation arranged for the night.

✪ ABOUT THE AUTHOR ✪

James P. Hogan (1941-2010) was a science fiction writer in the grand tradition, combining informed and accurate speculation from the cutting edge of science and technology with suspenseful story-telling and living, breathing characters.

Born in London, he worked as a digital system engineer and sales executive for several major computer firms before turning to writing full-time. His first novel, *Inherit the Stars*, beginning his celebrated "Giants" series, was greeted by Isaac Asimov with the rave, "Pure science fiction . . . Arthur Clarke, move over!" and his subsequent work quickly consolidated his reputation as a major SF author.

He wrote over thirty novels, nonfiction works and mixed collections, including *Echoes of an Alien Sky* and *Moon Flower* (both Baen). His earlier works include the Giants series (Baen) the *New York Times* best sellers *The Proteus Operation* and *Endgame Enigma*, and the Prometheus Award winners *Voyage from Yesteryear* and *The Multiplex Man*.